Fallen Angels

and the

Psychology of Control

Ascended Master Teachings, Volume 2

Kim Michaels

More to Life Publishing

Fallen Angels

and the

Psychology of Control

Ascended Master Teachings, Volume 2

Kim Michaels

More to Life Publishing

Fallen Angels and the Psychology of Control
Ascended Master Teachings, Volume 2
by Kim Michaels.
Copyright © 2012 by Kim Michaels

Published by More to Life Publishing, owned by More to Life OÜ, Estonia. To contact the publisher, use the contact information on *www.morepublish.com*.

ISBN 978-9949-9251-8-6 (paperback)

ISBN 978-9949-9251-9-3 (hardcover)

ISBN 978-9949-9251-5-5 (series)

Cover design by Helen Michaels.

Contents

Chapter 6:
Teachings about fallen angels, 2007   269

Chapter 7:
Teachings about fallen angels, 2008   **389**

Chapter 10:
Teachings about fallen angels, 2011   597

Epilogue   643

Glossary   668

About the author   694

Introduction:
About This Book

The teachings in this book were all given by the ascended masters in dictations. They were given between 2004 and 2011. The masters have given a huge amount of teachings through me, but in this book I have selected only teachings that talk about the fallen angels, the power elite and how certain people seek to control humanity.

In most cases, what you see here is an excerpt from a longer dictation. I have taken only the teachings relating to the topic of this book. However, a dictation is always a spherical work of art, so if you find that a particular excerpt speaks to you, it is a good idea to read the full dictation. It will be available for free on our website *www.ascendedmasterlight.com*. You can easily find it by using the name of the master and the date.

The first chapter of this book will give you a brief introduction, that will help you understand who the ascended masters are and how they seek to help us human beings. The chapter will also explain how the teachings in this book were brought forth. Finally, you will find a brief introduction to the masters' teachings about the creation of the universe as a series of successive spheres. In some of the later spheres, some beings fell as the sphere ascended, and this explains the existence of fallen beings who think they are superior to all other beings on earth.

Chapter 1:
Introducing the Ascended Masters

This is a brief description of what an ascended master is and how they give us their teachings. We will approach this from two vantage points:

Beings who took embodiment and ascended:
Let us first explain this from our point of view as human beings in embodiment on earth. The material universe is truly a sophisticated feedback "device" that is designed to facilitate our growth in self-awareness.

Many people don't really like the word school, but there is one aspect of the concept of a school that applies here. Most schools have a final exam, and when we pass it, we are free to move on with our lives without looking back. So if we keep raising our consciousness and transcending our self-awareness, what happens?

Well, at some point we reach the final "exam," meaning we enter a process that leads to our "graduation" from the schoolroom of the material universe. This is a profound and complex process, that involves us dis-identifying from the ego, the separate self, and embracing a new self-awareness as one with the spiritual realm above and one with all life in this world. It also involves letting go of all desires or attachments related to this world.

This process is often called the spiritual path, but the final stages of it are called the ascension spiral, leading to the ascension. After we ascend, we are permanently free from earth and the material universe. And given that the only way to complete the ascension process is to gain mastery over our own minds, we have now earned the title: "Ascended Master."

Throughout the long history of planet earth (far longer than recorded in official history), many lifestreams have ascended. A newly ascended master faces a choice: Will it move on in the almost infinite rungs of the spiritual realm, or will it remain with earth and seek to help other beings ascend?

Many ascended masters have made the vow to stay with earth in order to help those of us who have not yet ascended. So technically, these are what we call ascended masters, because they have experienced what it is like to be in embodiment on earth (or other planetary systems) and then ascend from this very dense realm. Given that they have experienced what we are going through, they have a unique ability to help us pass the same initiations that they have passed.

Beings who did not take embodiment:

The universe is created as a hierarchical structure. The realm, or sphere, in which we live was created by beings in the sphere immediately above ours. Yet their realm was created by beings in a higher realm, and so forth, forming a hierarchical structure that leads back to our Creator.

The important point to grasp is that the beings who are able to create a new – unascended – realm have earned this power by coming into oneness with the beings that created them and the entire hierarchical structure above them. In other words, the essential difference between the material realm and the spiritual realm is that in the material world, we tend to see ourselves as separate beings living in a separate world. In order to ascend to the spiritual realm, you must overcome this illusion and truly merge into oneness with all life.

So when beings in a higher realm create a new – unascended – realm, they do so out of their own beings. In other words, they don't see the new sphere as being separated from themselves. However, the new sphere is created with a lower or denser vibration than the spiritual realm. The purpose is that the beings who create the new sphere will now send extensions of themselves down into the new sphere to take embodiment in bodies made from the energies of the sphere.

This has a two-fold purpose. One is to raise the vibration of the new sphere until it ascends and becomes part of the spiritual realm. Yet the real purpose for this process is that the beings in the spiritual realm create individualized extensions of themselves, who then grow in self-awareness by helping their sphere ascend.

So in one sense, we can say that the beings who created our sphere have not taken embodiment in their fullness. Yet in a sense they have taken embodiment through the individualized extensions they have sent down. These individualized extensions are not some mysterious or perfect beings that are fundamentally different from the rest of us. They are us!

Even though we have been programmed to look at ourselves as human beings, who are limited, perhaps even sinners, we are extensions of the very beings who created our sphere. In fact, the very purpose of the spiritual path and the ascension is for us to truly accept our identity as individualized extensions of the entire spiritual hierarchy above us.

The important point to grasp here is that even though there are many beings among the Ascended Host who have not taken embodiment in their fullness, they have indeed taken embodiment through us—the extensions of themselves. Thus, ascended beings simply do not fit into the traditional image of the remote – and often angry – God in the sky. They are not seeking to judge or condemn us; they are ONLY seeking to raise us up.

For even though we have forgotten that we are extensions of ascended beings, they have not forgotten. And obviously, you only want to raise up what you know is part of your own being. Yet being raised up does not mean we lose our individuality. On the contrary, it means we merge with our spiritual individuality and transcend the limitations of our human "individuality," the separate self. This is not a loss but a gain

The hierarchy of ascended beings

Let us begin with our vantage point here on earth. The material universe is made from energies that vibrate within a certain spectrum. Right above this spectrum is the lowest level of the spiritual realm. There are other realms above this, stretching through 6 spheres (ours being the seventh) to the Creator. In each of these spheres, there is a hierarchy of spiritual beings.

The material realm was created by beings in the realm right above us in vibration. Thus, these beings are what we normally call ascended masters. The masters also use the name "Ascended Host," and this refers to all beings in all spheres above us. However, many of these beings do interact with us here on earth.

So from our vantage point, we can talk about several levels of the hierarchy that exists in the sphere right above ours. Let us look at the most well-known:

Newly ascended masters

When a being ascends from the material world, it usually takes some time to explore its new self-awareness and the spiritual realm to which it now has conscious access. Yet some masters have already been involved with teaching human beings before they ascended, so they may indeed immediately begin to fill a teaching position.

The Chohans

There are seven spiritual rays, which are the basic energy spectra from which the material universe is made. In order to walk the spiritual path and qualify for the ascension, we must attain mastery on all seven rays. Thus, we can see the spiritual path as a structured process, where we learn from each of the seven rays.

To facilitate this learning, each ray has several ascended masters who are seeking to help us pass the initiations represented by their ray. The leaders of this group of teachers is called the "Chohan." Thus, each ray has a Chohan, who is kind of like the headmaster of a particular school.

The Chohans normally present themselves as masculine or feminine. Not all chohans have a counterpart of the compimentary polarity. For example, a masculine chohan may not have a feminine counterpart, either because the feminine counterpart has not yet ascended or because it has moved on to other realms and is not directly working with earth.

The Archangels

Some ascended beings are not created to take embodiment, namely the angels. Angels have many different assignments, but from our vantage point, the most helpful are the angels assigned to helping us grow. These angels are also organized according to the seven rays.

Groups of angels are often referred to as "bands," and each band has a leader, with the title of "Archangel." Thus, there is an archangel for each of the seven rays. The archangels are always masculine, but they also have feminine polarities, called the "Archeia." For example, the feminine polarity of Archangel Michael is Archeia Faith.

The Elohim

The material universe is created from the energies of the seven rays, and this is done by reducing the vibration of the rays by a certain factor. A mental blueprint is then superimposed upon this energy in order to form the basic structures that make up the material universe.

The beings who initiated and oversee this process are often called the "Elohim," but they can also be called "God and Goddesses." Again, there is a masculine/feminine polarity at this level. For example, the Elohim Hercules has a feminine polarity named Amazonia.

The Central Sun

The highest level of ascended beings known to us is represented by two beings, called Alpha and Omega. It is sometimes said that they reside in the "Central Sun," but this is not a physical sun in the material universe. It is a "place" in the spiritual realm.

As explained, there are six spheres above our level. Each of these spheres forms a hierarchical structure, somewhat comparable to a pyramid. In each sphere, there is a central sun in which resides two beings, named Alpha and Omega. In the very first sphere, there is the ultimate level of Alpha and Omega, namely the beings who are direct expressions of the Creator.

However, it is important to understand that what is given here is a linear representation, and the linear mind is not capable of grasping the non-linear reality of the spiritual realm. Thus, it is important not to place too great importance on the words or their interpretation. To truly grasp the non-linear reality of the spiritual realm, one must experience it directly.

Gods and Goddesses

Although the Elohim are sometimes called Gods and Goddesses, there are other ascended beings who have attained to the level represented by a God. For example, there is a Goddess of Liberty, a Goddess of Justice (Portia) and a Goddess of Mercy (Kuan Yin).

Solar Logoi

Each planetary system has a sun and each physical sun has a polarity of two solar hierarchs, who are actually making it possible for the sun to be the open door between the material and the spiritual realm. If energy was not constantly streaming into a planetary system from the spiritual ream, no life would be possible in that system. The hierachs of our physical sun are named Helios and Vesta.

Lord of the World

For each planet, there is a being who holds the office of Lord of the World. This is a being with Buddhic attainment, meaning it has mastered space. Thus, this being literally holds the spiritual balance for the earth to exist in space. The Lord of the World for earth is Gautama Buddha.

Planetary or Individual Christ

For each planet there is a being who holds the office of Christ. Regardless of the sectarian nature of the Christian religion "Christ" is a universal word that signifies oneness between the Creator and its creation. Thus, you can ascend only by attaining the Christ consciousness and overcoming the illusion of separation. When Jesus said, "I am the way, the truth and the life, no one comes to the father save by me," he was not talking about his outer person but the Christ consciousness. Currently, Jesus is holding the office of Planetary Christ for earth.

Cosmic Christ

For each planet, a master holds the office that represents the universal Christ consciousness for that planet. Lord Maitreya holds this office for earth. He was also the master depicted (in distorted and primitive form) as the "God" in the Garden of Eden. The reality behind the myth is that Lord Maitreya was and is the overseer of the spiritual schoolroom (sometimes called a Mystery School) in which lifestreams are prepared to take embodiment on earth and deal with the initiations represented by the density of this realm.

For profound teachings from Lord Maitreya, especially concerning the fall in the Garden of Eden, see the book *Master Keys to Spiritual Freedom*.

World Teachers

These are beings who oversee the general progression of humankind's consciousness and determine how to best teach people the universal lessons. They also determine which new teachings to release, based on the progress (or lack of it) in the collective consciousness. This office is currently held by Jesus and Kuthumi.

The Karmic Board, Lords of Karma

The ascended masters seek to teach us at two levels. One is that they give us spiritual teachings and encourage us to use them for self-observation, leading to self-transcendence. The other is what is called the "School of Hard Knocks," where they allow us to experience the physical consequences of our state of consciousness. This is what is popularly called "bad karma."

Overseeing the karmic aspects of teaching is a board consisting of 8 ascended masters. It is important to realize that despite the popular concept of "bad karma," karma never has the purpose of punishing anyone. The purpose is only to teach those who have made themselves unreachable for a spiritual teaching.

As a result, the Karmic Board can withhold the descent of a person's karma, if they estimate the person has learned or is close to learning the associated lesson. On the other hand, they can also accelerate the descent of karma for a person who is in a negative spiral and is abusing other people.

The Karmic Board performs a very complex task of not only looking at each individual lifestream embodied on earth but also looking at groups and humanity as a whole. They determine who is allowed to take embodiment on earth, and they sometimes decide that a certain lifestream has misused its opportunity and will no longer be allowed to embody here.

The Karmic Board also teaches in a more direct way when we are in between embodiments. Along with other spiritual teachers, members of the Karmic Board help each lifestream determine the specifics of its next embodiment, based on an evaluation of which circumstances best help that lifestream learn its lessons and express its divine plan (the gift we came to bring).

The current members of the Karmic Board are: The Great Divine Director, The Goddess of Liberty, Pallas Athena, Nada, Portia (Goddess of Justice), Kuan Yin (Goddess of Mercy), Elohim Cyclopea and Vajrasattva.

Dhyani Buddhas
In traditional Buddhism, these are considered "primordial" Buddhas, meaning they have never taken embodiment as did Gautama. There are six of these in the ascended realm, and they each represent the anti-dote to a specific spiritual poison. By invoking the Presence of the Dhyani Buddha, you receive help in transcending the anti-dote.

NOTE: In terms of all of the above positions in hierarchy, it is important to keep in mind, that these are offices. As it is on earth, an office is held by a specific person, but that person can be replaced by another person over time. Thus, the Archangel of the First Ray is an office and has throughout time been held by various beings. The same is true for all other offices. In fact, as we ascend, we have the potential to fill some of these offices. This might explain why various spiritual teachings associate different names with these offices.

How are the teachings in this book brought forth?

If you want to understand how the ascended masters communicate with those of us who are still in embodiment, you need to understand the Law of Free Will. The purpose of our existence is to grow in self-awareness, and this can happen only when we make choices and experience the consequences of them. Thus, we might say that planet earth is like a cosmic classroom in which we – the students – have the potential to learn certain lessons.

There are many such classrooms throughout the material universe, and each has certain characteristics. Planet earth still belongs to a category in which it is possible to have a very specific experience, namely that one is a separate being – separated from God and separated from other humans – and then awakening from that experience.

This experience is made possible by the density of the energies that make up planet earth. There are planets in the universe that have risen to a higher level, in which "matter" is not as dense, meaning one can directly perceive that it is made from a finer substance, namely spiritual light. On such planets it is no longer possible to have the illusion that one is a separate being, but on earth this is still a possibility.

Why plausible deniability must be maintained

According to the Law of Free Will, the density of the energies that make up a planet is a product of the consciousness of the inhabitants of the planet. It is quite possible that the earth will be raised in vibration, so that it one day becomes impossible to believe that matter is separated from Spirit. In fact, the ascended masters – along with many of us in embodiment – are working towards that point. Yet until a critical mass of people voluntarily raise their consciousness to the level where this shift can occur, the masters will respect the Law of Free Will.

This means (among other things) that the masters cannot simply appear in the sky or through some undeniable manifestation. Instead, they can communicate with humankind only in such a way that the basic illusion of separation can be maintained by those who still want to see themselves as separate beings. In other words, the basic principle that the masters must follow is that plausible deniability must be maintained. It must be possible to deny God's existence, to deny that there is a spiritual reality beyond the material world, to deny that ascended masters exist and to deny that they can communicate with us.

This goal is attained by the masters communicating with humans in very specific ways, so that it is easy to overlook or deny this communication. Up until the mid 1800s the masters were not actually allowed to make their existence know through any public means of communication, such as books that could be found by anyone. Instead, they worked exclusively with so-called secret societies in which the existence of the masters was revealed only to people who had passed certain initiations.

Yet in the second half of the 19th century, the masters were allowed to make their existence known through public forms of communication, such as books and organizations that openly proclaimed to be receiving communication from the masters. Since then, there has been a string of books and tools published by single authors or organizations. Yet in each case, there was no undeniable proof that this was coming from beings beyond the material realm.

How the masters communicate with us

The ascended masters can communicate with human beings in various ways. Truly, it is important not to be too intellectual in wanting to confine the ascended masters to categories that can be grasped by the human intellect (the reason being that the masters can help us only if we are willing to rise above the linear mind). Yet it can be helpful to talk about two different types of communication: direct and indirect.

Indirect communication can be compared to what a radio or television station is doing. The ascended masters are constantly broadcasting certain energies and messages from the ascended realm. Yet it is important to realize that these signals cannot be received by people in what is currently the "normal" or common state of consciousness. The minds of all of us do have the ability to tune in to these signals, but it can only be done by raising one's consciousness beyond what is currently normal. However, anyone willing to raise his or her consciousness can indeed tune in to what is being broadcast by the masters.

Throughout history, many people have made use of this ability. In many cases, people were not even consciously aware of where the ideas came from, which has given rise to the classical idea of muses or inspiration. Some people have been able to receive an idea only once in a lifetime, whereas others have had a higher degree of attunement. Nevertheless, through such general broadcasts, the masters have been able to bring into the physical realm many ideas that had a positive impact on the evolution of humankind.

Yet beyond this indirect or non-specific communication, the masters can also communicate in a more direct manner. This happens only to people who acknowledge that ascended masters exist. In some cases people receive direct communication and put it into books without exposing the source. Yet in other cases, people do expose that the messages they receive come from ascended masters. And for such people it is possible to receive communication, where an ascended master can speak directly through a person in embodiment. This has traditionally been called "a dictation" or a message. Some people write such messages, while others speak them aloud, even in front of a group of people.

The teachings and tools on this website are brought forth as a link in this tradition of the ascended masters giving more direct forms of communication. Since 2002 I, Kim Michaels, have been receiving both dictations and tools from the ascended masters. My wife, Helen, has been doing this since 2009. Yet despite the fact that I have been doing this for some time, I feel I am still in training. I think it is wise to recognize that earth is a schoolroom, and as long as we are here, we have more to learn.

In some organizations, the person receiving dictations has been called a "messenger." Personally, I feel that this should be seen as a very humble position. Unfortunately, some organizations have idolized the position of being a messenger, making the person more important than the members, almost as if the messenger was the only link between people and the masters. Therefore, I prefer to refer to myself as simply an "open door." And I recognize that all people have the ability to tune in to the ascended masters. In fact, if the teachings in this book are successful, they will empower many people to attain such attunement.

What is a dictation?

For many spiritual people, the process of communicating with the masters will be what they know as channeling. However, "channeling" is a word that has been used to describe a wide range of phenomena. So I will describe how I receive my material from the masters. This is not to in any way put down what others are doing; it is simply to clarify what I am doing.

A dictation is where I attune my mind to the Presence of a specific ascended master. I do not go into a trance, because it is my understanding that the ascended masters do not work with trance channels. The reason is that this is a violation of free will, as the channeler is not aware of what the channeling entity will do or say during the trance. So I am fully conscious during the process, but I have been trained to go into a neutral or pure state of mind, where my personal thoughts or feelings are not engaged.

In most cases, I have no advance conscious awareness of what a master will say during a dictation. In some cases I have an awareness of the topic, and I often have a beginning thought that has been given to me ahead of time—just to get me started. Yet once the dictation starts, it is my task to stay attuned to the master without being distracted by external noise or my own internal noise (I have taken dictations in front of groups up to 100 people and also in public places). I have often started a dictation without having any idea of what the master will say, and the dictation has lasted for over an hour, giving a perfectly consistent message—something my outer mind simply would not be capable of doing.

What the master releases to me is not words that I hear in my mind and repeat. Nor do I see them in flaming letters and repeat them. What I tune in to is a stream of consciousness that is beyond the linear vehicle of words. This stream of consciousness is then "translated" into words in my mind. I literally hear the words as they are being spoken, but I could, of course, choose to interrupt the process at any time.

However, the most important element of a dictation is not the audible words, but the stream of spiritual light that is carried by the words. A dictation always has a message that can be grasped by the linear, intellectual mind. Yet if you read or hear a dictation only with the mind, you will miss the most important part, namely the light. Because I have taken dictations for so long, I am used to the process, but I recently had an interesting experience. I took a dictation during a conference. In the audience was a person who was new to the concept and somewhat skeptical. After the dictation, he made the remark that it simply wasn't possible for a human being to speak for nearly an hour with such power in his voice, and even to increase that power towards the end of the dictation. I realized this is true, and it brings up an important point.

My dictations often last an hour or more, and in most cases I am standing up the entire time. Yet I never feel physically, mentally or emotionally tired afterwards. Instead, I feel energized and feel my consciousness has been raised to a new level of clarity. I would be concerned if I felt depleted afterwards, because that would mean the being dictating had taken energy from me. Instead, the ascended masters give me light during a dictation, and at the same time they release light to the audience. If you want the full benefit from a dictation, tune in to the light (which is best done by listening to the recording).

Chapter 2:
Basic facts about the creation of the universe

Where did God come from?

You live in the material universe, which is made from energies that vibrate within a certain spectrum. Your physical senses can detect only the lowest range of this spectrum, namely the matter, or physical, universe. Your conscious mind, conscious self, has the capacity to tune in to and experience higher levels than what can be detected by the senses. Above this physical spectrum is the emotional energies, above that the mental and above that the identity level.

As you go beyond the four levels of the material universe, you reach the lowest level of the spiritual realm. In this realm there is a large number of spiritual Beings. Some of these are the Beings who created the material universe, including planet Earth. A common name for these is Elohim, a plural name for God used in the Old Testament. Some of the spiritual Beings have descended into physical embodiment but have now ascended back to the spiritual realm. When you balance all karma, resolve all false beliefs by putting on the mind of Christ and fulfill your original reason for coming to Earth, you too can become an ascended Being or ascended master.

After you ascend, you become a spiritual, or an immortal Being, meaning that you do not have to come back into embodiment on Earth. You then have two options. You can choose to continue your personal growth and rise up through the various levels of the spiritual realm until you reach the very highest level of consciousness, normally called God consciousness. Jesus said, "Ye are Gods" (John 10:34) because you have the potential to reach the full God consciousness. Your second option is to temporarily set aside your own growth and serve to help those on Earth who have not yet ascended. You then become a spiritual teacher for unascended beings. Jesus, Krishna and the Buddha are the most well-known examples of such teachers.

As you go up through the levels of the spiritual realm, you eventually reach the highest level of the world of form. Here you find the highest possible vibration of the Ma-ter Light. If you go beyond that level, you reach the Being who created the world of form. This is what most religions call the supreme God or the Creator.

Most religions teach that there is nothing beyond the Creator. However, if that is true then where did the Creator come from? In reality, there is a level beyond the Creator, namely what is called the Allness. The reason this level is unknown to most people is that there are no words, images or even concepts in the material realm that can describe the Allness. In fact, while you are still on Earth, it is not possible for you to fully understand the state of consciousness that exists in the Allness. The reason for this will become clear shortly.

In the Allness there are self-conscious, intelligent Beings, but they do not see themselves as separated from each other or from God. They know they are God, are expressions of God, for in the Allness everything is clearly seen as an expression of God. In the Allness there is still only one God, but there are many expressions of that One. The illusion that something or someone could be separated from God is impossible in the Allness. The Beings in the Allness cannot build a sense of identity as separate Beings and have not experienced anything separated from the Allness—for nothing can truly be outside of all there is.

The Beings in the Allness determined that there was value in creating a world in which separation was possible. Thus, an individual being could start out with a very limited sense of identity as a separate being. It could then grow in self-awareness until it reached the consciousness of the Allness. This Being could then enter the Allness with an awareness of what it was like to feel separated from the Allness, thereby having a greater appreciation for the Allness.

The Being who created the world of form in which you live was once one of the Beings in the Allness. This Being volunteered to temporarily set itself aside from the Allness and create – out of its own Being and consciousness – a world that seems to be separate from the Allness.

In this world can exist separate forms, forms that do not seem to be expressions of the One God. Also, there can exist separate beings, beings who are not consciously aware that they are expressions of the one God.

These beings can then start out with a limited sense of identity and self-awareness in which they think they are separated from their source, from each other and from the world in which they live. By gradually rising to higher levels of consciousness, they will eventually come to see the oneness of all life. They can then either enter the Allness with full God consciousness or they can become Creators of other worlds of form. Yet until such a being reaches the level of God consciousness, it simply cannot fathom the Allness. Obviously, you are one of the beings who was created with a limited self-awareness but with an infinite potential to expand that self-awareness. That expansion of self-awareness is the essential purpose behind the creation of the world of form. Thus, it is the overall purpose of life.

How did the Creator create the universe?

Because the Allness has no separate forms, the easiest way to conceive of it is to compare it to an empty space or a blank page. The Allness is not nothing; it is no thing. Thus, an illustration of it is a white space illustrating that it has no forms that can be conceived of or pictured in this world.

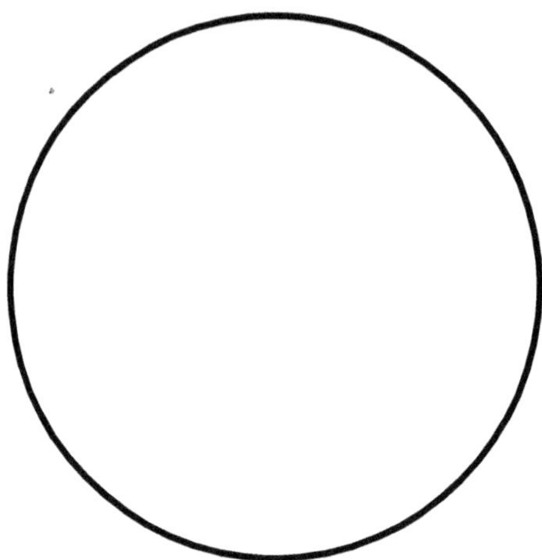

The Creator made the decision to create a world with separate forms, and as the first act of creation the Creator drew a spherical boundary around itself. This boundary set the Creator apart from the Allness and created a space within the Allness that was filled with the Creator's consciousness and Being.

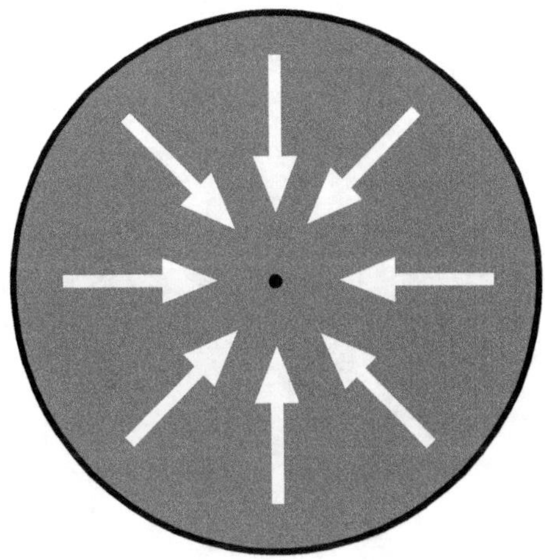

The Creator then contracted its Being into the center of the sphere, pulling itself into a singularity. This emptied the rest of the sphere so that it became a void that was set apart from the Allness but still had no manifest forms within it. Yet because the void is less than the fullness of the Creator's Being, separate forms can be created in the void.

From the singularity, the Creator then projected part of its own Being outward, yet this did not happen in the uncontrolled explosion envisioned by the Big Bang theory. Instead, the Creator projected itself as a sphere around the singularity, a sphere that was set apart from the void because it contained the basic substance out of which everything would be created. This is what the Bible calls light, as in "Let there be Light." Science calls it energy and this book has called it the Ma-ter Light.

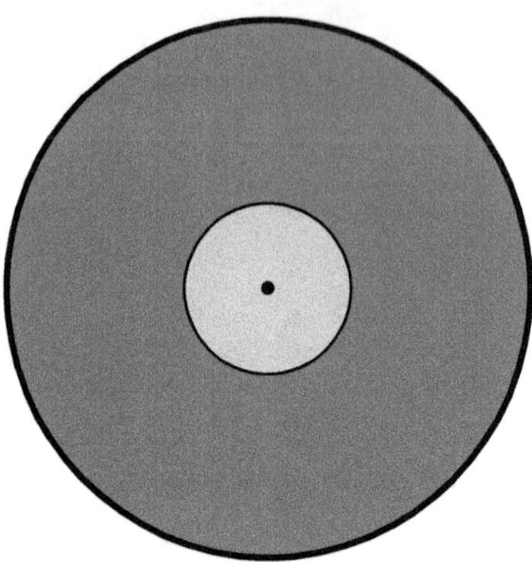

This first sphere was not filled with light. In fact, it still contained a lot of darkness, which does not mean something evil but simply an absence of light. Within this first sphere, the Creator now created certain forms, certain structures that could serve as the basis for life. The Creator then projected self-conscious extensions of itself into this first sphere, this first level of the world of form. These beings were designed to be co-creators, but they started out with a very limited sense of identity and self-awareness. This sense of being separate entities was possible only because the first sphere was not filled with light. Thus, the sense of separation can exist only under the cover of darkness.

In the beginning, the first co-creators were tutored by the Creator itself. As they grew, they began to become self-sufficient and attain mastery over their creative faculties. They attained the mastery of mind over matter, which meant that they became increasingly adept at co-creating within their sphere. This had a two-fold effect. One is that the co-creators created additional structures by building on the foundation set by the Creator. The other is that the co-creators brought more light – from the Creator's infinite supply – into their sphere.

Thus, the first sphere eventually attained such an intensity of light that it was no longer possible for any being in that sphere to maintain the illusion that it was separated from its source, from other co-creators or even from the structures within the sphere. When the total light in the sphere reached a critical intensity, it became obvious for all to see that everything was created from the Creator's light and consciousness.

Thus, all co-creators reached a state of enlightenment in which they directly experienced themselves as extensions of, as individualizations of, the Creator.

The Creator now projected itself into the void and created another sphere that was set apart from the void. This sphere once again contained only a limited amount of light. The co-creators who had reached a level of mastery in the first sphere now used that mastery to create structures in the second sphere that could serve as a platform for life. When this was done, the masters from the first sphere now projected self-conscious extensions of themselves into the second sphere.

These second-generation co-creators again started out with a limited self-awareness and an identity as separate beings. Yet they were tutored by the masters from the first sphere, their spiritual parents. Thus, they again grew until they reached mastery of the first sphere, and that sphere also reached the critical intensity of light. At that point, the Creator created the third sphere. Some of the masters from the second sphere chose to continue to raise their consciousness so they could enter the first sphere. Others became the masters who created structures and then co-creators in the third sphere.

Thus, the process of life begetting life continued and a number of levels or spheres were created inside the void. A new sphere was created as a twilight zone. It was set apart from the void but did not have as much light as the higher spheres. When a sphere had ascended to the critical level, it too would become part of the spiritual realm. Thus, the material universe is simply the latest extension of this process. It was created with a limited intensity of light, which makes it possible for the co-creators in this sphere – meaning yourself and everyone else – to start life with an identity as separate beings. The low intensity of the light also makes matter appear more solid and sets it apart from the more fluid forms in the spiritual realm. Thus, a new co-creator can believe that there is nothing beyond the material universe or that this world is separated from the spiritual world by an impenetrable barrier.

The material universe is created out of the same stuff as every other part of the world of form, namely the Ma-ter Light. The material universe is created out of light of a lower vibration, but this light has the built-in potential to be raised to the vibration of the spiritual realm, whereby the entire universe will ascend to a higher level. This ascension process is the outer purpose behind the creation of the material realm.

Yet the inner purpose, the real purpose, is that the material universe serves as a science laboratory for the co-creators who were sent into this world. It is only as they raise their own consciousness that they will become the open doors for bringing more spiritual light into the material realm. And only such light will raise the vibration of the matter universe. By serving in this capacity and by seeing their world being raised as a result of their creative efforts, the co-creators will expand their self-awareness until they too can ascend to the spiritual realm. And this, of course, is the real purpose behind the creation of the material universe. Everything revolves around the growth in self-awareness. And the end result is that you can grow to the same self-awareness as the Being who created the world of form. You are a God in the making, and realizing this is not blasphemy but supreme realism.

God's law is not punishment

If human beings are Gods in the making, how come they can descend into a state of consciousness in which they express qualities that are far from God-like? The reason is that the Creator did not create you as a robot who is forced to follow his will and obey his laws. You have free will, and your free will would not be complete if you did not have the option to disobey God's laws.

However, having free will does not mean that you have to go against God's laws or that you are only truly free when you do so. To illustrate this, compare your options in life to the road net. Roads are built to help you quickly go from place to place, and traffic laws are designed to help you travel safely. You can go just about anywhere on the roads, and if you decided to drive outside the roads, you would damage the environment and possibly get yourself stuck in a mud hole. Deciding to disregard traffic rules would potentially get you in an accident and hurt yourself and others. Thus, it does not make sense to say that roads and traffic rules limit your ability to travel. Likewise, it does not make sense to say that God's laws limit your free will and your ability to express your creative faculties.

God's laws are not a straightjacket. Following God's laws does not mean that you have only one way to act or that you lose your free will. Unfortunately, some religions have presented God as an angry and judgmental being in the sky who will condemn you to hell for violating his laws. And this has made some people prone to rebel against God's law or at least against religion. In reality, there are infinite possibilities for expressing your creativity within God's laws. The laws are actually set up to help you express your creativity in such a way that you do not destroy yourself, other people or the planet upon which you live.

Consider the situation from the Creator's perspective. By giving co-creators free will, God takes a calculated risk. It becomes possible that one co-creator can self-destruct or that co-creators can assemble into factions that seek to destroy each other. Thus, humankind could potentially self-destruct or destroy planet Earth. Obviously, this would defeat the purpose of co-creators growing in self-awareness, so God has to find ways to minimize the risk.

One way is to define a set of laws that guide how co-creators can use their creative powers. Another is to make sure co-creators start their journey under loving supervision, so they can easily learn from their experiments.

One of the basic spiritual laws states that everything is made from one substance, namely the Ma-ter Light. In order to create anything in the material world, you must have a quantity of Ma-ter Light that vibrates within the spectrum of the material realm. The natural way to get this light is to receive it directly from your I AM Presence. When you first descended into the material realm, you were given a certain amount of light as your starting capital. If you used it wisely, you would be given more, which would increase your creative powers. Thus, the stream of light from your I AM Presence would be increased and your life would become an upward spiral, leading to greater and greater self-awareness and material abundance.

As mentioned before, Jesus illustrated this law in his parable about the three servants who were given a number of talents by their master (Matthew 25:14). The master then went away for a time, but when he came back, he took stock of how the servants had used their talents. Two of the servants had multiplied their talents and they were both rewarded. However, one servant had buried the talents in the ground, and he lost what he was given. Although this sounds harsh, it actually illustrates an impersonal law.

The goal of life is growth, meaning that everything is multiplied. So if you multiply the light and your creative powers, you are lifting up yourself and all life. If you do not multiply what you were given, meaning that you act selfishly, you will degrade yourself and all life. Thus, the stream of light from your I AM Presence will be decreased, and your life will become a downward spiral. Your ability to create material abundance will be reduced and your self-awareness will become self-centered awareness, leading you to feel that life is suffering and that you are a victim who is being unfairly punished by an angry God.

In reality, God never punishes anyone. God has simply set up certain impersonal laws that affect all human beings. If you jump out of an airplane without a parachute, the impersonal law of gravity will drag you to the ground and kill you. Yet this is not God's punishment but a mechanical consequence of your own – ignorant – choice.

The law of balance

When the material universe was created, the light in this sphere had a certain level of intensity and a certain level of vibration. This represented the starting level, the "cosmic background radiation," and co-creators are meant to use their creative abilities to raise both the intensity and vibration of the light, until the material universe can become part of the spiritual realm. If co-creators had multiplied their talents, there would have been no suffering on planet Earth. Yet because of free will, it is possible that a co-creator can misuse its creative abilities and generate light of a lower vibration than the original level. This will then create an imbalance in the universe, and for you to grow, the imbalance you have created must first be restored to balance.

As you descend into the material universe, you are given a certain portion of light and the free will to do with it whatever you want. If you use the light in a loving manner, you will raise its vibration and intensity, thus being in harmony with the purpose of creation. If you use the light in a selfish or even self-destructive manner, you will lower the vibration of the light and create an imbalance in the universe.

You do have free will to do whatever you want, but the law of free will does not work alone. It is inseparably linked to the law of consequences. This is what science calls the law of action and reaction and what many spiritual teachings call the law of karma. It basically states that you are responsible for what you do with the Ma-ter Light. If you use it lovingly, you will raise up yourself and all life and your powers will be expanded. If you use it selfishly, you will create a debt to life and you cannot move on until you have paid back the debt, balanced the karma, purified the misqualified energy or however you prefer to describe it. In other words, you have complete freedom to do whatever you want, but every action has consequences and you cannot escape experiencing those consequences. You do not have freedom to do what you want without experiencing any consequences.

The purpose of the universe is your growth in self-awareness, meaning that you are here to learn. You learn by conducting an experiment and then learning from the consequences of your actions. If your actions did not have consequences, how could you possibly learn? And if you did not learn from your actions, how could you grow in self-awareness and fulfill your reason for being? In other words, you were not created for the purpose of enjoying – forever – what this planet has to offer. Nor does your own higher self want you to remain stuck forever in a limited sense of identity as a miserable sinner or a sophisticated animal. You descended here in order to grow in self-awareness and eventually ascend to higher levels of learning. The question now becomes how you chose to learn from the consequences of your actions.

The Fall of man

When a new co-creator first descends into the material realm, it is not simply sent into the jungle without a compass. Instead, it descends into a protected sphere, where it is under the supervision of a teacher from the spiritual realm right above the material universe. The teacher will guide the new co-creator and lovingly explain the consequences of its actions. The teacher will also take responsibility for the student's karma, meaning that when the student has learned its lesson, the teacher will actually balance the karma so the student can continue to learn without being held back by its mistakes.

Many of the world's religions contain stories and images of such an ideal state. The most well-known example in Western society is the story of the Garden of Eden. This story illustrates in a mythological form what has happened to every human being on Earth, meaning that Adam and Eve were not literally the only beings in Paradise. Every human being started out in such an Edenic state and had the direct supervision of a spiritual teacher. Yet as the Garden of Eden story illustrates, people then started doubting the teacher and they had to leave the garden. In reality, they were not forcefully cast out, but by lowering the vibration of their consciousness, they simply lost the conscious awareness of the garden and lost contact with the teacher.

After co-creators lost contact with the teacher, the spiritual law mandates that the teacher can no longer carry the karma made by the students. The teacher cannot be responsible for the student's karma when the student is no longer under his supervision. Before this separation, co-creators learned from the consequences of their actions through the loving guidance of the teacher. After the Fall, co-creators learned from the consequences of their actions by experiencing how the cosmic mirror reflected back to them what they had sent out. Genesis describes it this way, "In the sweat of thy face shalt thou eat bread" (Genesis 3:19).

In other words, Plan A was for co-creators never to experience human suffering but always have the guidance of the teacher as a buffer between them and their karma. Yet after co-creators lost contact with the teacher, Plan B took effect. And since co-creators were no longer open to guidance, they had to learn by experiencing the consequences of their actions. This is, so to speak, the school of hard knocks, as opposed to the school of Divine Direction.

Those co-creators who separated themselves from their teacher lost his direction and consequently made more karma, which they had to carry themselves. The law of balance states that if you make karma in the material realm, you cannot ascend back to the spiritual realm until the karma is balanced. In the spiritual schoolroom, co-creators lived in purer bodies that did not age or get sick. Yet because of their karma, the physical bodies started to age and manifest diseases that shortened the life span further. Thus, it became impossible for many co-creators to balance their karma before their physical bodies died. As a way for such co-creators to receive additional opportunities to redeem themselves, reincarnation became Plan C. Thus, you will continue to reincarnate on Earth until you have learned your lessons and balanced sufficient karma.

Reconnecting to your spiritual teacher

You have two options for learning your lessons in life. You can continue in the school of hard knocks, whereby you must figure it out by yourself and balance all the karma on your own. Or you can make an effort to reconcile yourself with your spiritual teacher, so that you can receive the guidance and grace of the teacher. This reconciliation with the spiritual teacher is one of the major purposes of the spiritual path. You can begin by studying outer spiritual teachings and practice techniques that purify your four lower bodies. As you remove the false beliefs and misqualified energies, you will naturally and gradually regain your direct inner contact with your Christ self, your I AM Presence and your spiritual teacher(s).

There is a large number of spiritual teachers serving to raise the consciousness of humankind, and every human being has one such teacher that serves as his or her personal master. These teachers have inspired many of the world's major and minor religions (in their original forms) and have also released many scientific discoveries. The teachers have been called many names, such as the Ascended Host, the Heavenly Host, the Great White Brotherhood ("white" referring to the color of their light, not race) or the ascended masters. They work according to certain cycles or time periods, some of which last approximately 2,000 years.

Jesus came to Earth 2,000 years ago to set the stage for the spiritual cycle known as the Age of Pisces. During this age, humankind was meant to learn from his example so they could follow the path he demonstrated and thus attain the same state of consciousness as the one demonstrated by Jesus. That is why Paul said, "Let this mind be in you, which was also in Christ Jesus" (Philippians 2:5) and why Jesus said, "He that believeth on me, the works that I do shall he do also" (John 14:12).

The Earth is now moving into the next spiritual cycle, called the Age of Aquarius. In this cycle humankind is meant to build upon the consciousness attained in the Age of Pisces and reach a higher level of spiritual freedom. Unfortunately, the inner teachings of Jesus have been largely misunderstood, and thus most people are not aware that they are meant to attain the Christ consciousness. Yet a large number of more spiritually sensitive and aware people do sense that they have an important mission and a contribution to make in this age.

The reason being that these people came into their present embodiment with the desire to help facilitate the transition from the Piscean to the Aquarian consciousness. If you have read this book up until this point, you are most likely one of these people. You will never feel completely fulfilled until you reconnect to your spiritual mission and your personal divine plan. To fully understand what this mission is about, you need to understand the difference between the mind of Christ and the mind of anti-christ.

Christ and anti-christ — to BE or not to be

When the Creator decided to give co-creators free will, he knew that it became possible that they could misuse their creative powers. This could result in the creation of a veil – made of misqualified energies and incorrect beliefs – that would separate co-creators (in their own minds, not in reality) from their spiritual teachers, their spiritual selves and their Creator. They could then forget their spiritual origin and identity and come to believe they were nothing more than highly evolved animals and the products of hereditary and environmental factors. How could the risk of this be minimized and how could the Creator make sure a co-creator would always have the option to come back to its true identity, no matter how far it had descended below it? The Creator came up with an ingenious solution, a cosmic safety mechanism.

As described earlier, the Creator started the creative process by contracting its Being into a singularity, thus creating the void. Since then, the Creator has gradually been expanding itself in a move to eventually fill up the void. Thus, there are two basic forces involved in creation, namely an expanding force (God the Father) and a contracting force (God the Mother). If the expanding force was dominant, the Creator's energy would expand in an uncontrolled explosion and instantly fill up the void. If the contracting force was dominant, everything would contract into a black hole and no organized structure could survive. Since the purpose of creation is to provide a gradual expansion that allows co-creators to grow in self-awareness, there must be a force that balances the expanding and contracting forces, thus ensuring a balanced growth that gradually leads toward the end goal.

The force that is designed to balance the expanding force of the Father and the contracting force of the Mother is the only begotten Son of God, namely the universal Christ mind, which the Bible calls the Word. This is a mind that transcends any single human being, but it is possible that a human being can attain a sense of unity with this universal mind and thereby become the Christ in embodiment, become the Word incarnate. In fact, the highest potential for all human beings is to let the mind that was in Christ Jesus be in them and thus fulfill their role of being fully enlightened co-creators who have the dominion of mind over matter demonstrated by Jesus and other enlightened Beings.

The Christ mind is designed to be the unifying element behind all of the myriad manifestations in the world of form. The Christ mind contains the blueprint for creation, including the Creator's purpose and all of God's spiritual and natural laws. And as the Bible says, "Without him was not any thing made that was made" (John 1:3), meaning that behind all outer appearances is the one reality of the Christ mind. The consequence of this is that you can never lose your potential to reclaim your true identity. No matter how far you might have descended into a lower state of consciousness (compared to the consciousness with which you were created), you can never be completely lost. You ALWAYS have the option of reaching for the Christ mind, which is the true savior of humankind. Jesus himself talked about the Christ mind but since he was allowed only to give his teachings in parables, he used a symbol for it, namely "the kingdom of God." That is why he said that the kingdom of God is within you (Luke 17:21), meaning that the kingdom of God is a state of consciousness.

The Christ mind is the unifying factor that is meant to assure oneness between the Creator and its creation, specifically the self-conscious co-creators with free will. It follows that because of free will, co-creators must be given the option to go against God's laws. Yet they cannot go against God's laws by using the mind of Christ, which means that the mind of Christ must have an opposite, namely the mind of anti-christ. The mind of anti-christ is what makes it possible for co-creators to separate themselves from God and their spiritual teachers, creating a veil that makes it seem as if they are separated from their Creator, separated from other co-creators and separated from the planet upon which they live. This makes it possible for co-creators to forget God's purpose for creation or deliberately rebel against that purpose, refusing to play their intended roles.

When you have some measure of the Christ mind, you see the underlying oneness of all life, which makes it impossible to hurt others. Jesus told you to do unto others what you want them to do to you because he saw the oneness of all life. Thus, he knew that what you do to others, you are doing to yourself, your greater self. Yet when you are trapped in the mind of anti-christ, you think you are separated from this self or that it doesn't even exist. This gives rise to the illusion that you can hurt other people without harming yourself. It even creates the illusion that your actions do not have consequences or that you can somehow cheat the universe and escape those consequences.

You have no doubt heard the question raised in Shakespeare's play, Hamlet, "To be or not to be, that is the question." The higher meaning is, "To be the Christ, or not to be the Christ, that is the real question." You have the potential to be the Christ in embodiment, but only you can answer the question of whether you will choose to be the Christ or choose not to be the Christ.

Understanding the fruit of the knowledge of good and evil

The choice between the mind of Christ and the mind of anti-christ is actually found behind the symbols in the story of the Garden of Eden. The God in the garden was a spiritual teacher who had become one with the universal Christ mind and thus represented the cosmic Christ. He was tutoring Adam and Eve (as symbols for a large group of co-creators) on the path to personal Christhood. This path leads co-creators (who start out with a limited self-awareness and an identity as separate beings) to become one with their source and reclaim their true identity as sons and daughters of God. That is why the Bible says about the Christ, "But as many as received him, to them gave he power to become the sons of God" (John 1:12). Thus, the path to Christhood is the Path of Oneness.

As part of that path, students had to face and overcome the temptation to use the mind of anti-christ to separate themselves from their teacher and their source instead of seeking oneness with their source. This is symbolized by the "fruit of the knowledge of good and evil." The key to understanding the true meaning behind the symbol is to realize a subtle but all-important distinction. When you see the world through the mind of Christ, you clearly see that the Creator is the source of everything, and thus there is an underlying oneness behind all appearances. You see the Creator's purpose and you see that following his laws is to your own benefit. You also see that your own higher Being made the choice to create the Conscious You because it wanted to be part of God's creation. Thus, there is no conflict between God's purpose and your own higher desires. In the mind of Christ, there is an absolute standard for separating good and evil, meaning what is real and unreal. The Christ mind knows that what is one with God's purpose and laws is real and what is separated from God's purpose and laws is unreal.

When you see the world through the mind of anti-christ, you cannot see the underlying oneness of all life, God's purpose and God's laws. Thus, the mind of anti-christ does not see reality; it sees an image of reality that it has created and projected upon reality. This is described in the first two of the ten commandments, "3 Thou shalt have no other gods before me. 4 Thou shalt not make unto thee any graven image" (Exodus,

Chapter 20). The meaning is that when you see the world through the mind of anti-christ, you create a mental image of how you want God to be, and you project that image upon God, thus worshiping an idol before the real Creator who is beyond form.

To the mind of anti-christ there is no absolute standard for separating good and evil. Good and evil have become relative terms, and they exist only in relation to each other. Good is the opposite of evil which is the opposite of good. Yet the mind of anti-christ defines both good and evil, and both of them are separated from reality, meaning that what is humanly good is not in harmony with God's absolute good. This is what makes it possible for people to create a veil of illusions that separates them from their source and makes them forget their origin. This is why people can believe they are sophisticated animals instead of spiritual beings or that they are miserable sinners instead of sons and daughters of God. It can even make people believe they are very religious and guaranteed to be saved, whereas they are still trapped in the mind of separation and thus cannot enter the kingdom of God that is within them. That is why Jesus talked about a true and a false path:

> 13 Enter ye in at the strait gate: for wide is the gate, and broad is the way, that leadeth to destruction, and many there be which go in thereat:

> 14 Because strait is the gate, and narrow is the way, which leadeth unto life, and few there be that find it. (Matthew, Chapter 7)

This is a concept that will require serious contemplation before you fully internalize it. The reason being that you have grown up in a society that is influenced by the mind of anti-christ in many subtle ways. This has caused various institutions to define their own "truth" which they claim to be infallible. It is precisely because so many groups of people each claim to have their own infallible "truth" – instead of reaching for a clear vision of God's truth – that there are so many conflicts on this planet that seemingly cannot be resolved. It is such man-made "truths" that make it possible for two groups of people to kill each other in the name of the same God. However, this is not because of a flaw in religion itself but a flaw in humankind's approach to religion.

The fact is that all problems seen on this planet were created because people had become blinded by the mind of anti-christ. And the reason so many problems and conflicts seem to have no resolution is because people continue to look at the situation through the relative, dualistic logic of the mind of anti-christ. It is an eternal law that you cannot solve a problem with the same state of consciousness that created the problem. There is a solution to every problem seen on Earth, but in order to find the ultimate solution, you must first raise your consciousness above the consciousness that created the problem. And since all problems spring from the mind of anti-christ, you must first reach for the mind of Christ. That is why Jesus said, "First cast out the beam out of thine own eye; and then shalt thou see clearly to cast out the mote out of thy brother's eye" (Matthew 7:5).

There are millions of people who volunteered to come into embodiment at this precise time in history because they wanted to help solve the many problems on Earth and help bring society into a new and better age, even a Golden Age of peace and prosperity. Yet in order for this to happen, humankind must fully learn the lesson people were meant to learn from Jesus and his mission. The main lesson is that there is an alternative to the relativistic, dualistic "truth" of the mind of anti-christ. The mind of anti-christ always thinks in terms of two opposites, and one must be right and the other wrong. Jesus was saying that as long as your vision is divided, both opposites are wrong, "The light of the body is the eye: therefore when thine eye is single, thy whole body also is full of light; but when thine eye is evil, thy body also is full of darkness" (Luke 11:34).

The evil eye is a vision divided by the relative opposites of the mind of anti-christ. Thus, in order for you to fulfill your personal mission and Divine plan, you must first raise your consciousness so you can begin to see beyond the veil created by the dualistic vision of the mind of anti-christ. And only when your eye is single, meaning your vision undivided by the relative opposites, will you see clearly how to solve your personal problems and larger problems. Only when a critical mass of people attain this one vision of the Christ mind, will they be able to raise society into a better age. Thus, the starting point is to purify your mind of the illusions of anti-christ and reach for the vision of Christ— and then you will find the solutions to the problems you are here to solve. As Jesus said, "But seek ye first the kingdom of God, and his righteousness; and all these things shall be added unto you" (Matthew 6:33). The kingdom of God is the Christ consciousness, and when you have it, the solution to all problems will be added unto you. Again, Jesus said, "With men this is impossible; but with God all things are possible" (Matthew 19:26). Only through the mind of Christ can you be with God.

Why is there evil in the world?

The psychologist M. Scott Peck said that during decades of practice, many people had asked him, "Why is there evil in the world?" but no one had ever asked the equally logical question, "Why is there good in the world?" It is as if people know that the world is fundamentally good and that evil is an abnormality, something that isn't supposed to be here.

Based on the previous discussion, it becomes clear that evil is the result of the consciousness of anti-christ, which makes it possible for people to separate themselves from God's purpose and laws. This traps people behind a veil of illusions that gives rise to many forms of selfish behavior. People don't see the underlying oneness of life and think they can harm others without hurting themselves. People create their own definitions of good and evil, making it possible for them to believe – for example – that God will reward them for killing members of other religions. People simply do not know better, and thus they cannot do better.

The mind of anti-christ is the option that accompanies free will, and it remains a temptation until you attain the highest sense of identity as a son or daughter of God, as the Christ in embodiment. Even Jesus was tempted by the devil before he started his mission. Thus, evil is not created by God, it is not the opposite of God and it is not necessary for God's plan to unfold. Evil is the result of a choice, but it is an uninformed choice. Evil springs from ignorance, but it is not the innocent form of ignorance. It is a willful form of ignorance, whereby people create an illusion that makes them think what they are doing is not really evil.

This explains another question, namely why God allowed the serpent to be in the Garden of Eden. The broadest definition of the serpent is that it is a symbol for the mind of anti-christ, and before co-creators attain full Christhood, they must face this temptation, as Jesus did. Yet there is a more specific meaning, namely that the serpent is a symbol for co-creators who deliberately rebelled against God's laws and are trying to prevent God's purpose from coming to fruition.

It was earlier explained that God created a number of spheres in the void. A new sphere has only a limited amount of light, which makes it possible for the mind of anti-christ to exist in that sphere. There is still so much darkness that the illusions of the mind of anti-christ are not exposed for what they are. When a specific sphere reaches a critical intensity of light, it ascends to a higher vibration, and the light becomes so intense that there is no darkness left. Thus, there is no room for the mind of anti-christ to exist in that sphere, there is no darkness left in which it can hide.

The ascension of a sphere is brought about by a majority of the lifestreams in that sphere, but because of free will, there is no guarantee that all inhabitants of a sphere are part of or in agreement with this process. Thus, there can still be some lifestreams who hold on to the illusions created by the mind of anti-christ. The law of free will allows them to do this for a time, but when their sphere ascends, they cannot hold on to their illusions and remain in that sphere. Thus, they must go somewhere else, namely a place where there is still sufficient darkness to allow their illusion of separation to remain. In practical terms, this means that these lifestreams descend to the newly created sphere, the sphere created after the previous sphere ascended. This process is actually described in the Bible:

> 10 And I heard a loud voice saying in heaven, Now is come salvation, and strength, and the kingdom of our God, and the power of his Christ: for the accuser of our brethren is cast down, which accused them before our God day and night.

> 11 And they overcame him by the blood of the Lamb, and by the word of their testimony; and they loved not their lives unto the death.

> 12 Therefore rejoice, ye heavens, and ye that dwell in them. Woe to the inhabiters of the earth and of the sea! for the

devil is come down unto you, having great wrath, because he knoweth that he hath but a short time." (Revelation, Chapter 12).

This somewhat obscure quote describes what happened when the sphere above the material universe ascended and became part of the spiritual realm. The co-creators who were still attached to the mind of anti-christ, and who refused to ascend, had to descend into the material universe. These co-creators have embodied on Earth, which can explain that some people seem absolutely committed to evil. Yet they also form a "force" of evil that can hide behind the veil of misqualified energy created by humankind, seeking to influence people in embodiment. These disembodied beings exist in the energy field around planet Earth, and they can influence people through their egos. Thus, the dualistic beliefs and misqualified energies that support your ego give these rebellious beings an inroad into your consciousness, which explains why people can sometimes lose control of their lives.

The most important fact to understand about such beings is that they have been cut off from the flow of energy from their own spiritual selves. Thus, they cannot receive energy directly from above, and they can survive only by stealing energy from people who still have the connection. That is why some people and some disembodied spirits are seeking to manipulate people into committing acts that misqualify energy. Only when energy is lowered in vibration can these lower beings absorb it.

This explains many of the worst atrocities seen on this planet, such as meaningless wars, child molestation, rape, serial killing and other violent crimes. When you look at such actions, you ask, "Why do people do this, what could possibly be the purpose?" In reality, the people who perform such acts have no purpose. Their minds are temporarily – perhaps permanently – taken over by a force that is manipulating them for the sole purpose of generating misqualified energy that these beings can use to survive. Thus, much of the conflict between human beings is truly a battle over spiritual energy. Those who cannot get it from within themselves have to steal from those who can, the have-nots must take from the haves.

Chapter 3:
Teachings about fallen angels, 2004

Turning back the tides of war

Mother Mary, February 28, 2004

A new definition of war

I have told you that the Earth Mother herself is under such great strain that she can hardly hold the balance for the negative emotional energy being produced by humankind. I am sure you can see that one of the greatest causes of such negative energy is, and has been for thousands of years, war itself.

Is there any single cause that is responsible for more killing, bloodshed, anger, hatred and acts of revenge than war? I am sure you can see that no other activity causes such wholesale inhumanity as when nations go to war and seek to destroy each other, thereby destroying their own people in the process. Therefore, I come to enlist your help in giving my Miracle Peace Rosary that I am releasing this day. [Available on www. transcendencetoolbox.com]

I come also to explain to you what is the true cause of war on this planet, but first I desire you to understand what war is. The simplest explanation of war is that it is an extreme state of imbalance. It is a state in which all normal considerations have been blown aside by what seems to be an all-consuming necessity to fight an enemy that is considered to be the ultimate threat. Therefore, higher principles have been cast aside, and people now feel justified in doing whatever is necessary to defeat the enemy and preserve their lives and their way of life.

Oh my beloved, the very essence of life itself is balance. What keeps this planet spinning on its axis is balance. Yet as you well know, the axis of the Earth is tilting, and this shows you that there is a state of imbalance on this planet. This imbalance is caused by the negative energies produced through man's inhumanity to man, and the greatest cause of such energy is, naturally, war itself. War then is the ultimate form of imbalance known to man.

I am not saying it is the only form of imbalance, but it is truly the ultimate form of imbalance. The reason being that the checks and balances that normally keep people from going to the extremes have been set aside, and now people are trapped in the ultimate illusion, namely that anything goes, that the ends can justify the means, that it is necessary to do evil that good may come and that it is necessary to kill more people in order to bring peace.

So what then is the cause of war? What causes people to become unbalanced? You see, my beloved, contrary to surface appearances, human beings are not inherently evil and they are not inherently unbalanced. Human beings naturally strive to attain balance, so when they are unbalanced, it shows you that they are being manipulated by forces outside themselves.

You see my beloved, your scientists talk about the balance of nature, and nature, and all of the creatures of nature, are the children of the Earth Mother. The Earth Mother herself always strives for the perfect balance, and all of her children have a natural tendency to strive for balance. Human beings are also children of the Earth Mother and have a desire for balance. Yet human beings are more than animals because human beings have souls that descended from the spiritual realm. The soul is a child of the divine Father, and he too strives for balance. So you see that when human beings display imbalances, it is because some outside force has manipulated them into losing the natural balance of body and soul. So let us now understand that outside force.

As my son Jesus has explained on his website, [www.askrealjesus. com] the Father-Mother God created the entire world of form. The characteristics of the Father-Mother God have never been more beautifully illustrated than in the Taoist symbol of the Tai-Chi. This symbol depicts the two basic forces of the universe, and those two forces are an expanding force, which represents God the Father, and a contracting force, which represents God the Mother.

The nature of God the Father is to expand, to grow and to self-transcend. The nature of God the Mother is to contract but not in a way that restricts the Father's growth. The nature of the Mother is to provide a counterbalance to the expansive force of the Father so that there can be balanced growth.

What I am telling you here is that the nature of the world of form is to expand. This growth is attained through the harmonious interaction of the expansive force of the Father and the contracting force of the Mother. What you will see from this image is that the expansive and the contracting forces are not opposite, but complementary. They do not cancel each other out; they merely balance each other. Both forces are necessary, and they must have the right relationship. In other words, the interaction of the two forces produces offspring, and the form of that offspring is determined by the balance between the Father and Mother forces.

You also see that the force of the Father is meant to be a little bit stronger than the force of the Mother. This ensures that the offspring will be alive, meaning that it is growing and self-transcending. This self-transcendence, this growth, is the very purpose, the reason for being, of the entire world of form. This is indeed why the Bible says that the father is the head of the household. This does not mean that there should be inequality among the sexes, because truly the Father and Mother God are equals in every way. They simply have different functions, different roles to play in the drama of creation.

In a family, the husband and wife should be equals, but the role of the father is to make sure that the family (and the entire universe) serves as a platform for growth and constant self-transcendence. It is the role of the mother to make sure that the growth remains balanced and that all participants are nurtured in the process. When the two forces are in the right polarity, the expanding force of the Father is always a little bit stronger than the contracting force of the Mother. If it was not, there could be no growth, and the entire universe, or a part of it, would remain stagnant.

So you now see that if one force becomes too strong, it will have the effect of creating an unbalanced state. If the force of the Father was allowed to expand without any restrictions, it would expand so forcefully that it could not sustain itself and its creation would be blown apart. In other words, if the universe was expanding in an unrestricted manner, all of the galaxies, suns and planets would be blown apart and there would be no basis for life. On the other hand, if the contracting force of the Mother becomes too strong, it will stop the growth of the Father and therefore the universe will stagnate. As your scientists have discovered, that which stagnates will begin to contract and will eventually collapse under its own weight. So you now see that the harmonious growth of the universe depends on the right polarity, the right balance, between the expansive and the contracting forces of the Father-Mother God.

The creation of angels

My beloved, you now understand the two basic forces of the universe. We now need to understand that God created two distinct evolutions. God first created a number of spiritual beings that were created to serve in the heaven world, or what we might call the spiritual realm. These spiritual beings are what many human beings call angels, so for clarity let me use that terminology.

The Father-Mother God, created a world with many different layers, or realms. The lowest of these realms is the universe in which you live, namely the material universe. God then created an evolution that was separate from the angelic evolution. These beings were meant to descend into the material realm, start at the bottom and work their way up through the different levels of God's creation. It was these beings that were the first human beings to descend to Earth. As the Bible says, human beings were made a little lower than the angels, meaning that the angels were created with a higher level of God-awareness. Human beings have the opportunity to gradually acquire this God-awareness, yet they have to work to attain it by ascending through the different levels of the world of form.

Some of the angels were given the task of serving human beings and helping them in their evolution. This is a principle that you see explained by Jesus to his disciples, when he said that he who would be greatest among them should be the servant of all. You see, the highest being of all is God. Yet, contrary to the man-made image of God as an all-powerful ruler, God is also the most humble being of all. God truly is the servant of all because God has allowed its own substance, its own Being, to be imprisoned in the world form. God has allowed the conscious beings who have free will to do whatever they want with its Being. God has done this to give its sons and daughters the opportunity for growth, and therefore one might say that God truly is the greatest servant of all.

By embedding its own Being in everything, God has given all beings created in its image the potential to reach the full stature of a God, which allows them to create their own universes. However, to attain that Godhood, a being needs to prove that it is willing to be the servant of those below it. So indeed, it was natural that the highest angels should be given the task of serving man who was lower than the angels. Yet some of the angels did not understand the law that I have just explained. They did not understand why they had to serve man and they were not willing to serve man.

As the Bible explains, one being in particular rebelled against God's decree that the angels serve man. His name was Lucifer, and he created a rebellion in Heaven. [NOTE: A later teaching by Maitreya on the spheres gives a deeper understanding of where Lucifer's rebellion took place.] This rebellion was a protest against the call to serve man, and it eventually caused a great number of angels to side with Lucifer and rebel with him.

My beloved, even though angels have free will, the free will of angels is slightly different from the free will of humans. You see, in the heaven world beings have full awareness of the laws of God. With this awareness comes responsibility, which means that a being in Heaven can exercise its free will within the framework of the laws of God, but that being cannot deliberately violate the laws of God. If an angel chooses to go against the laws of God, it cannot remain in Heaven, and it must therefore descend into the material universe. Humans, however, are already in the material universe and they can violate the laws of God (within certain limits) without descending any further. Obviously, humans will be fully responsible for the misuse of their free will, yet it will not have the effect that they have to leave the material universe.

To fully understand Lucifer's rebellion, you need to realize that, contrary to popular myth, Lucifer was not an evil being. He was created by God as a being of great light. Lucifer's problem was pride, and this caused him to feel that he knew better than God. He believed that the plan to allow humans to have free will, and the call to let angels serve them as they exercised their free will, would be a disaster. Lucifer thought it would cause human souls and angels to become lost and that it could cause the destruction of the material universe.

In his pride, Lucifer thought he had to save God from himself. He thought God did not understand the ramifications of his decision, and therefore Lucifer had to take it upon himself to correct God's mistake. Lucifer began to believe that even though he clearly saw that his actions were in violation of God's law, it was necessary to violate God's law in order to prevent a greater calamity. Lucifer therefore became the father of the mindset that the ends can justify the means and that it is necessary to do evil that good may come.

Lucifer fell prey to the illusion that it is necessary to violate God's law in order to preserve God's creation. In reality, the only way to preserve God's creation is to uphold God's law, because God's law ensures balanced growth. For all his light and mental sophistication, Lucifer did not understand this truth, and he never saw through his own illusion.

The war in Heaven

The Bible tells you that there was a war in Heaven, that Lucifer and his angels fought and that they were cast out. In reality, the war in Heaven was not fought as a war is fought on Earth. On Earth both sides are fighting, but in Heaven there was fighting on only one side. You see, God was not mocked by Lucifer's rebellion. The angels that did not rebel maintained their peace, and therefore they did not engage Lucifer and his energies. They simply remained balanced in the harmony of the Father-Mother God so that Lucifer had nothing in them whereby he could cause them to fight him.

Therefore, Lucifer was not actually cast out of Heaven as explained in the Bible. Lucifer cast himself out of Heaven through his rebellion against the laws of God. Lucifer cast himself out because through his rebellion he lowered the vibration of his consciousness, and when his consciousness fell below a certain level, he could no longer perceive the higher vibrations. Therefore, he could see only the lower vibrations of the material universe.

You now see that Lucifer was the only one who created the war. He saw himself in opposition to God, and he deliberately rebelled against God's laws and the basic intent of creation itself, namely the need for self-transcendence. Lucifer attempted to draw all of the angels of Heaven into his war against God. This was a prideful act that made him think that if all of the angels took his side, then God would have to bend to his demands and his logic. Lucifer truly was consumed by pride and thought he knew better than God how the universe should be run and how souls should be "saved."

What had happened to Lucifer was that he had become afraid of growth and unwilling to transcend himself. You see, Lucifer was truly the highest of the angels [in that sphere]. He had risen as high as he could rise in the angelic realm and he felt very powerful and in control. Yet the law of God is self-transcendence, and when you have reached the highest level, how can you transcend yourself? You can do so only by making yourself the servant of all, and this is what Lucifer was not willing to do. Therefore, he became unbalanced, and he wanted the universe to remain the same so that he could feel he was in control.

To maintain the sense of being in control, Lucifer attempted to take the contracting force of the feminine aspect of God into an unbalanced state and stop growth. Because of this imbalance, Lucifer caused his own consciousness to become so dense that he could no longer perceive the higher vibrations of the spiritual realm. So one might say that Lucifer fell into the material realm because of an imbalance in the feminine aspect of his being, which gave him an insatiable desire for control. In order to attain this control, he sought to use the feminine force itself to restrict and contract everything so that there was no possibility of growth and self-transcendence.

One might say that Lucifer is a prime example of a being who has perverted the Mother aspect of God. Please make an effort to understand the logic of what happens when you pervert the Mother aspect of God. When you pervert the contracting force, you can go into one of two extremes. You can refuse to grow and self-transcend, or you can demand freedom from the laws of God. You can refuse to grow or seek to grow without restrictions. Either way leads to a state of imbalance, and as a result, your consciousness becomes denser until you can no longer remain in the Father's kingdom. You will then descend into planes in which the contracting force of the Mother becomes gradually stronger.

In the higher spiritual realms, the expanding force of the Father is stronger, and that is why the vibrations of that realm are very high. As you go towards lower levels of the world of form, you eventually descend into the material universe. The energies are gradually lowered, and that is why the material universe is denser than the spiritual realm.

This does not mean that the material realm is inherently unbalanced, but it does mean that the balance between the expanding and contracting forces is slightly different than the balance in the spiritual realm.

The devil has come down to you

Lucifer perverted the contracting force of the Mother, and he inevitably descended into the denser realm of the material universe. For an angel, who was used to living in a higher realm, this was a very big change. Because of Lucifer's pride, he saw it as a degradation of his rank, which in one sense one might say is true. Because of his anger against God, Lucifer greatly resented having descended to a lower realm, and even though he was the one who misused the light of the Mother, he now blamed it on the Mother of God.

You see, Lucifer descended because he refused to stop his rebellion against God. He refused to admit that he had made a mistake, and he refused to undo that mistake by making the choice to bring himself back into alignment with the laws of God. So Lucifer refused to take responsibility for his actions, and therefore he needed a scapegoat. And so he blamed it on the Mother and developed intense hatred of the Mother. He also blamed it on human beings because, after all, it was his refusal to serve human beings that caused him to fall. Since he would not take responsibility for his own choice, he blamed it on human beings. That is why the Bible says that the devil has come down to you having great wrath because he knows that he has but a short time.

You see, when an angel descends into the material universe it has the potential to work its way back up to the spiritual realm, just as a human being. Yet neither of the two types of beings have forever to do this. They have a certain time to prove their worth and ascend to a higher level. If they do not ascend within the allotted time, the soul will be extinguished in the second death. Lucifer, and all those who followed him, knew that he had only a certain time in the material realm.

Lucifer was so blinded by his anger that he decided not to change his decision and seek to come back to God. Instead, he decided that he would carry on his self-created, one-sided war against God here in the material realm. He would use the forces of this realm, and he would try to make all humans rebel against God's will in an attempt to avenge himself. He would attempt to destroy God's plan for having human beings work their way up to becoming gods themselves.

My beloved, please understand this crucial point. Lucifer's original rebellion was based on his belief that free will would cause souls to be lost and the universe to self-destruct. Everything Lucifer did after his fall, and everything his followers are doing today, centers around proving this original point. Lucifer wanted his words to become a self-fulfilling prophecy. He wanted all souls to be lost and he wanted the universe to self-destruct. If that had happened, he would have felt that he was right and that God was wrong.

My beloved, please understand the extent of Lucifer's arrogance. He was literally ready to destroy all souls and the entire matter universe in order to prove that he was right and God was wrong. This is the ultimate perversion of the call to be the servant of all. Instead of serving all, Lucifer was willing to turn all into slaves of his desire to prove himself right. Do you see that there is no reasoning with this state of consciousness? Do you see that there is no way to turn such beings around and make them see the light?

Those in a Luciferian state of mind will wage war indefinitely against those who spring from the Mother's substance, the ma-ter of the material universe. Therefore, the only way to remove their darkness from the Earth is to bring the Light of God, the light that comes from the perfect balance between the expanding and contracting forces of God. Only this Light can replace the darkness resulting from an imbalance between the two basic forces of the universe. Imbalance is simply an absence of balance, as darkness is an absence of light.

Lucifer's war against God

You now see that the plan of Lucifer is to carry on his war against God by manipulating human beings into rebelling against God's law and thereby destroying themselves. And so, what is the ultimate form of rebellion against God in the material universe? Well, the ultimate gift of God to human beings, to human souls, is life itself. So the ultimate rebellion against God is to take life away, either through suicide or through killing another human being.

You now see that in his war against God, Lucifer decided to attempt to manipulate human beings into waging war against each other. One aspect of this strategy is Lucifer's attempt to prove his original point that human beings cannot use their free will responsibly. Another aspect is that war is a way for the dark forces to maintain their existence. As Jesus has explained, dark forces are cut off from the light of God, so they can absorb only light of a lower vibration. Therefore, they must manipulate people into misqualifying the light of God, so that the dark forces can steal that energy.

You now see that war serves two Luciferian purposes. One is to get people to kill each other and thereby make the ultimate karma (create the ultimate imbalance) that prevents them from ascending to the spiritual realm. The other is to cause people to misqualify huge amounts of energy, that the dark forces can use to sustain themselves and expand their power over human beings.

How dark forces manipulate human beings

What are the means whereby the dark forces seek to manipulate human beings into waging war against one another? Well, they will use any means available to them because their main goal is to cause people to become unbalanced. When people lose their balance and centeredness, they take things to the extremes, and then it is only a short step for them to fall into the same trap that Lucifer fell into and begin to believe that the ends can justify the means.

You see, when people lose their state of balance, they fall from grace, meaning the perfect balance between the two basic forces of God. People then begin to feel agitated, to lose their sense of peace, and they begin to feel that it is necessary to do whatever it takes to restore peace. As they become increasingly agitated, they often label another group of people as the cause of their agitation. They believe these people are a threat because they are different from themselves. They feel that the imbalance is so threatening to them that the immediate need to remove the imbalance can neutralize any long-term concerns or higher principles. Therefore, they often reason that the ultimate way to restore peace is to kill the people whom they think caused the imbalance.

The main weapon used by the dark forces is to manipulate the creative process itself, a process that has four elements. The world was created from four basic elements, namely the Father, the Son, the Mother and the Holy Spirit. When these four forces exist in perfect balance, the universe will grow in a harmonious manner. If one or more of the forces is taken to the extreme, imbalance will be the result. The dark forces can use either element to manipulate people into killing each other and feeling that the killing is necessary, even justified by God. Let us look at the four elements:

• The Father element is the expansive force, which gives souls the drive to grow and the free will to self-transcend. However, the Father also defines a set of laws designed to maintain the balance of the universe, so that souls can grow without destroying themselves. The Father wants to see self-transcendence, not self-destruction. He wants to see a constant and balanced growth.

• The Mother element is the contracting force. The Mother is also the element that adapts to the creative force of the Father. The role of the Mother is to allow the expression of free will so that souls can experiment and learn. However, the Mother is also a counterbalance to unrestricted growth, so that souls do not expand so quickly that they lose their sense of identity. The role of the Mother is to provide a safe environment and to secure balanced growth. The Mother does not stop growth, she keeps it balanced and she nurtures the souls as they grow. One might say that the Father provides the drive for growth and that the Mother keeps the growth balanced. To experience balanced growth, a soul must maintain a certain state of balance between the expanding and contracting forces of its being. How can a soul maintain this balance? It does so through the consciousness of the Son.

• The Son is the offspring of the Father and Mother, and the role of the Son is to balance the expanding and the contracting forces by holding the vision for a balanced creation. To do this, the Son must discern what is truly the balanced growth of God and what is either too expansive or too contracting. Through the Christ consciousness, a soul can exercise its free will within the framework of God's laws, and thereby it can maintain a constant and balanced growth. However, a soul is not created to grow simply for its own sake. As Jesus has explained many times, a soul is created to be a co-creator with God and express God's perfection in the matter universe. A soul is created to bring God's kingdom to Earth. It can do so only through the power of the Holy Spirit.

• The Holy Spirit is the life force itself, and without a continual flow of the Holy Spirit, nothing could survive. The role of the Holy Spirit is to express God's perfection in the material universe. It does so by maintaining a constant state of growth, a growth that is balanced because it expresses the perfect vision of the Son, a vision that incorporates the perfect polarity between the expanding and contracting forces of the Father-Mother God. The Holy Spirit is committed to expressing itself in perfect alignment with the laws of God.

The false polarity

My beloved, I hope you can see that the key to survival is balance, a balanced expression of the basic forces of the universe. What the dark forces seek to do is to disturb this balance, and they do so by seeking to make souls misuse either the expanding or the contracting force. They seek to manipulate souls into taking one force to the extreme, thereby creating a false polarity.

The universe is created from the polarity of the Father-Mother God. The forces of the Father and Mother are not opposite or mutually exclusive. They complement each other, so when they meet, they do not cancel out each other. Instead, their interaction gives rise to a balanced creation. When a human being is balanced, it is able to create something that is sustainable, and it will continue to grow. When a society is balanced, it will not destroy itself but continue to prosper.

The plot of Lucifer was to destroy this polarity, and he did so by creating the illusion of a false polarity, that is based on a perversion of the expanding and contracting forces. When the two forces become unbalanced, you create two extremes:

• One extreme is the anti-father. This force is created by taking the absolute authority of the Father and combining it with the contracting tendency of the Mother. This creates a totalitarian form of authority that seeks to restrict people's expression of their free will. It seeks to restrict growth through control. It sees freedom as dangerous, and therefore it seeks to eliminate the danger by removing freedom. This leads to the lie that people don't need to follow God's law to grow and self-transcend, but that everything can stay the same.

• The other extreme is the anti-mother. This force takes the expanding drive of the Father and combines it with the adaptability of the Mother. This creates a drive for freedom without any restrictions, leading to rebellion against the laws of God that are defined to sustain a balanced growth. This leads to a philosophy of government that seeks to remove all laws or restrictions. It claims to work for freedom, but fails to see that freedom can exist only within the safe framework of God's laws. This leads to the lie that people don't need to follow God's laws about balanced growth, but that they can do whatever feels good at the moment without worrying about long-term consequences or higher principles.

These two forces form a false polarity because they are opposite and mutually exclusive. The desire for control cancels out the desire for no restrictions, and thus the interaction of the two forces can never produce sustainable offspring. They can only produce a continued tension and imbalance. My beloved, it is the tension between these two false polarities that has been the source of all conflicts you have seen in human society since the beginning of time.

Since their fall, the dark forces have attempted to manipulate people into pledging their loyalty to one of these extremes. Their first step is to pervert the consciousness of the Son. They do this by making people subscribe to the idea that there is no absolute or ultimate truth because everything is relative. This is the consciousness that the serpent used to tempt Eve in the Garden Of Eden. When people eat of the fruit of the knowledge of relative good and evil, they can no longer discern what is the right balance between the expanding and contracting forces of God. They can no longer discern the laws of God. Therefore, they begin to create a false image of reality. They then begin to believe that this image is true and that they have a right to define their own "reality."

Once people believe in a false image, it becomes easy for the dark forces to manipulate them into fighting for one of the two extremes of totalitarian control or excessive freedom. These then are the two basic forces you see working in human society, one seeking to restrict freedom through excessive rules, one seeking to give a false freedom with no rules. My beloved, I hope you can see that neither of these forces can restore the proper balance to society. This can be done only by following the laws of God and not the laws, or lack of laws, defined by man.

After people have lost the Christ consciousness, the gift of the Son, they become vulnerable to a perversion of the Holy Spirit. This makes them feel that the extreme to which they belong is the ultimate truth and the only key to survival. They feel there is an absolute need to either restrict freedom or to remove all rules. They might feel their authority comes from God through a particular religion, or they might feel that there is no God and therefore people have a natural right to be free from all restrictions. Either way, once people pervert the flame of the Holy Spirit, they feel absolutely justified in doing whatever is necessary to promote their "just" cause. They now easily fall prey to the Luciferian lie that the ends can justify the means and that it is necessary to do evil that good may come. They are easily manipulated into a crisis in which it seems absolutely necessary to wage war to prevent some greater calamity or overthrow a tyrant.

My beloved, can you see that countless wars have been fought as a result of the perpetual tension between these two false polarities of the anti-father and the anti-mother? Can you see that regardless of what people believe, such wars can never serve to restore the balance of the true polarities of the Father-Mother God? Such wars merely generate negative energies that cut off the flow of the Holy Spirit, and this inevitably leads to a breakdown in society.

Even your physical bodies stay alive only because there is a flow of the Holy Spirit through all matter. This is truly what your scientists have described as the second law of thermodynamics, which states that in a closed system disorder will increase until the system self-destructs. The true meaning of a closed system is a system that has no flow of the Holy Spirit. Therefore, it inevitably becomes unbalanced and eventually self-destructs.

Spiritual blindness

The process of imbalance that leads to self-destruction will be driven by one or even both of the forces of excessive control or excessive demand for no rules. Yet the people cannot see that they are taking things too far into the extremes because they have refused to use the discernment of the Son. This will eventually cut off the flow of the Holy Spirit, and society falls into the ultimate imbalance of believing that it has a right to do whatever it takes to fulfill its goals. Those goals might be to prevent anarchy and chaos by imposing control, or they might be to remove a tyrant by setting people free from restrictions. Yet if people are willing to go to war, or violate the Law of Love, to secure their goals, it is proof that they have become unbalanced.

What often happens is that certain powerful people begin to believe that the ends can justify the means, and they seek to manipulate the population into supporting a war against their proclaimed enemy. The people in this elite really believe that this is a just cause, and their justification can even be expressed through a particular religion. People in that society now begin to believe that killing is justified by the laws of God, and they might even feel they have a holy duty to kill others in the name of God.

Oh my beloved, I hope you can now see that the belief that you should kill your fellow humans in the name of God is the ultimate triumph for Lucifer and the Luciferian mindset. It is the ultimate justification for war among human beings, but it is truly an extension of the mindset that Lucifer used to justify his self-declared war against God. The statements, "Let us do evil that good may come" and "Let us kill people to bring peace," were never spoken by God or a representative of God. They were spoken by beings who are trapped in the ultimate illusion that they are against God and that they are waging a war against God.

This leads to the ultimate form of ignorance in which people are completely out of alignment with the reality and the laws of God, yet they are completely convinced that their man-made or devil-made beliefs are absolutely true. Therefore, they feel the ultimate justification for using all means to impose these beliefs upon others.

War is the ultimate burden for the Earth Mother

My purpose for giving you this long explanation is to show you that war is the ultimate cause of the imbalances that burden the Earth Mother herself. Over the course of history, wars have generated a huge amount of misqualified energy that has been added to the energy field of the planet. At certain times, this energy reaches a critical mass of intensity, and it becomes too much for the Earth Mother to bear. The energy is then released in an outburst that manifests as natural disasters.

In my previous discourse, I explained the five spiritual poisons and their link to natural disasters. I hope you can now see that the spiritual poisons spring from the state of ultimate ignorance that I have just described. When people are out of alignment with the reality of God, when people are ignorant and unbalanced, they start producing the spiritual poisons of anger, pride, greed and jealousy. They lose their will to be co-creators with God in this world.

Human beings are the highest link in the evolutionary chain on Earth. Therefore, they have the responsibility for keeping the Earth balanced. As Jesus explains throughout this website, people create through the power of their minds. The human mind has four levels, and each of them corresponds to one of the basic forces of the universe.

- The highest level of the human mind is the etheric "body." It is the seat of people's sense of identity and the memory of their spiritual origin. This corresponds to the Father element. The task of the etheric body is to keep people in alignment with the laws of God and their highest potential—which is the potential for self-transcendence.

- The next level is the mental body, the logical, rational mind. It corresponds to the Son, and its task is to maintain the vision of balance between the expansive and contracting forces.

- The feeling body corresponds to the Mother. It function is to nourish the soul and all forms of life by maintaining a balanced and nurturing environment, in the home and on the planetary home.

- The physical mind or brain corresponds to the Holy Spirit, and its function is to make sure that the material realm stays in alignment with the laws and the vision of God so that it does not become unbalanced and self-destructs.

The dark forces seek to create imbalance in one or all of these levels of the mind in order to cause people to become so agitated that they lose their state of inner peace. When people lose their inner peace, it is only a matter of time before an outer conflict or war is the result. All outer wars start as a warring in the members, a war in the psyche, of individuals. When a critical mass of people in a society reach this state of inner war, outer war will soon follow.

You now have a deeper understanding of how people are manipulated into producing the spiritual poisons by thinking that their state of agitation is unavoidable, is caused by an outer enemy or is justified by the laws of a religion. I hope you see that the true cause of war is an unbalanced state, and therefore wars are never justified in the eyes of God. God is always in a state of perfect balance, so imbalance is never in alignment with God. The ultimate form of human imbalance is war itself, so how could war ever be necessary in the eyes of God?

The greatest need of the Ascended Host

My beloved hearts, I hope you can see that the greatest danger to life on this planet is war. Therefore, the greatest need of the Ascended Host is to have the balanced people on Earth make a never-before-seen effort to put an end to war on this planet. Obviously, stopping war will require many activities, including enlightening human beings to the teachings I have given in this discourse. They can then make informed choices about war instead of allowing themselves to be manipulated into conflict time and time again. Yet I must also tell you that war has been going on for so long on this planet, that it has indeed become a self-destructive downward spiral. It is in the process of becoming a self-fulfilled prophecy.

As Jesus has explained, when energy is allowed to accumulate, it forms a vortex that becomes like a black hole and sucks everything into it. Because war has been going on for so long, there are a number of such energy vortexes, and they are so strong that they can blind or overpower people. Therefore, the people who are caught in such a vortex are completely unable to grasp the teachings that I have given you in this discourse. They are unable to see that they are being manipulated into waging war against others. Even if they could see it, their hatred for one another is so strong that they are unable to see that they are actually destroying themselves in the process.

So my beloved, my purpose for this long discourse is to show you that there is indeed a great need at this time for those who are willing to be the shock troops of the Ascended Host. I need those who will make an effort to consume the energy vortexes and the momentums of war on this planet. I am in need of those who will be like the firemen who go into the burning city to pour water upon the fires of war and quench the flames and smoke, until people can see clearly and are not overpowered by the energies of war. I am come to give those who are willing to take on this task a powerful tool for consuming the energies of war. That tool is my Miracle Peace Rosary that is a special gift from my heart. [There are now several rosaries and invocations suited for helping to consume the energies of war. You can find them on *www.transcendencetoolbox. com*.]

Do not feel overwhelmed

My beloved hearts, I hope you will not feel overwhelmed by my requests to give more rosaries, and I especially hope that you will not feel overwhelmed about the burdens upon the Earth Mother. It truly is not my desire to overwhelm you, and I hope you will not feel so burdened that you become paralyzed, as so many people have become in this day and age. They are so overwhelmed by the many challenges facing society that they do nothing, because they reason, "What can one person do, what difference could I possibly make?"

My beloved, I will be very honest with you and tell you that you alone cannot turn this planet around and start to turn back the tide of war that has been rising now for many years. Yet I will also tell you that if no one does anything to stop the tide, then surely the floodgates will one day be opened, and you will see a war that will be more devastating than anything seen in recorded history. You are all aware that the weapons scientists have created are more powerful than ever, and therefore the potential for destruction and loss of life has never been greater. So you see my beloved, I cannot promise you that if you give my rosaries, we will avoid war.

However, I can give you one certainty and that is that if everyone does nothing, there will surely be a third World War, and it will be more devastating than the two first World Wars taken together. So you see my beloved, you can make a tremendous difference. Even one person giving these rosaries will make a positive difference, and even though one person cannot turn the tide, the effort of a number of people can gradually build a critical mass, that eventually consumes so much negative energy that a major war will not come to pass.

You see my beloved, it is like throwing buckets of water upon a fire. One bucket seems to make no difference but many buckets will make a difference. Yet if just one bucket is missing, the fire might not be quenched. Your personal contribution could be the one that brings the power of the rosaries to the critical level and therefore makes all the difference in the world. So please do not feel that you cannot make a difference, and do not allow yourself to be paralyzed by the forces of this world.

You have heard the saying that, "For evil to triumph, it only takes that good men - and women - do nothing." The truth behind that statement is that there are many unbalanced people on this planet who are prone to war and conflict. These are the ones who are easy prey for the dark forces that are using the tools I have described to manipulate people into war. These people are trapped in such a low state of consciousness that they cannot stop a war. Therefore, the only people who can stop war are the people in a higher state of consciousness, namely those who are so balanced that they can hold on to higher principles. The devil knows this, so he has a two-pronged attack.

One part of his strategy is to agitate the people who are in a lower state of consciousness until their anger breaks out as open conflict and war. The other part of his strategy is to get the people in a higher state of consciousness to feel so overwhelmed that they feel like they could not possibly make a difference, and therefore they end up doing nothing. Discouragement is the sharpest tool in the devil's toolkit, and he uses it very efficiently against those who are the balanced people on Earth.

Do you realize why this tool works so efficiently against the balanced people? It is because when such people look at the forces and the people who are creating conflict upon conflict, they cannot understand why these people will not stop the conflict. You see my beloved, you know in your hearts that you could never kill another human being, no matter how necessary it might seem. You know that you could never create the conflicts that you see all around you, and therefore you cannot understand why these people are doing it. Because you cannot understand how these people think, you feel powerless to do anything about it. That is why you feel overwhelmed and discouraged, and you end up thinking, "What could I possibly do to make a difference? Why even bother trying?"

Well, my beloved I have now giving you a deeper understanding of the spiritual cause behind war, and I hope you can see that there is indeed something you can do, on the spiritual level, to stop war. You cannot change people's minds, but you now see that many people are simply overwhelmed by a vortex of negative energy. They have little chance of making the choice to stop their conflicts as long as they are burdened by this negative energy that turns their emotional bodies into raging volcanoes. So you see that by giving the rosaries and other spiritual exercises, you consume this energy and free these people so that they can maintain some degree of emotional peace and mental clarity. This gives them the opportunity to make the choice to abandon conflict, and this can indeed be the key factor that prevents the forces of war from being unleashed on this planet.

Finally, let me say that my rosaries always have a planetary and a personal effect. My Miracle Peace Rosary will not only consume the forces that create conflict in the world, it will also consume the forces in your own mind and being that cause you to feel that you are not at peace. I think that at some level of your being, you realize that one of the greatest needs and desires for human beings, one of the keys to happiness, is to have peace of mind. By consuming the forces that cause the imbalances that lead to a warring in your members, you will make great personal strides towards the ultimate goal of all spiritual seekers, namely the inner peace of mind, the peace that passes understanding.

Gratitude is the key to the abundant life

Mother Mary, March 28, 2004

The spiritual cause of terrorism

I come today to address a problem that you have seen manifest in this past month, namely the problem of terrorism. While terrorism might seem like a manifestation of the imbalance that causes war, there is more to it than meets the eye. Terrorism has its roots in the very state of consciousness that caused Cain to slay Abel. It is the consciousness of one son of God being jealous of another son of God, and therefore deciding to destroy or kill the brother that seems to stand in the way of him being the favorite son.

As you will know from my previous discourses, there is always more to the stories in the Bible than meets the eye. As my beloved Jesus explains throughout his website, there are many layers of meanings hidden behind the stories and statements found in the Bible. And of course, there are also layers and meanings that are not found in the Bible.

So my beloved, let me now give you a deeper understanding of the story of Cain and Abel. In reality, this story symbolizes the relationship between those who allow the light of God to work through them and those who have separated themselves from God. Abel is a symbol of a being with great spiritual light, meaning that the expanding force of God the Father is stronger than the contracting force of the Mother, as mandated by God's law of perpetual growth. Therefore, Abel has more light than his brother Cain, and he is more able than Cain. Those who have spiritual light can accomplish what seems like miracles to most people, as demonstrated by Jesus himself.

Nevertheless, this does not mean that God loves Abel more than Cain. It simply means that both were created as individualizations of God, as the expressions of God's perfection; they were simply created with different roles in the drama of life. So how can it be that Cain, or rather the conscious beings living in the material universe, ever came to envy their brothers and sisters who have more spiritual light, making them feel that they were being unjustly treated by God? Well my beloved, the answer to that question was given in my last discourse, in which I explained the fall of Lucifer.

I explained to you that Lucifer rebelled against God's unyielding law of constant self-transcendence, of constant growth. I explained how Lucifer descended to the matter universe and how he waged war against God and the sons and daughters of God in this universe. I explained how he attempted to pull every human being into his own state of consciousness. He attempted to create the mindset that no one in this world is allowed to have great light or to rise above the crowd. He attempted to make all people accept the lowest common denominator, so that no one could manifest Christ consciousness. He even spread the lie that striving to become the Christ is blasphemy.

The story I told you is true. There was truly a being named Lucifer, who rebelled against God's purpose and who then attempted to draw all beings on Earth into that rebellion against God. Nevertheless, there is more to the story. And it is that Lucifer was not the only being to ever rebel against God. You see my beloved, Lucifer rebelled because he decided to embody a state of consciousness. That state of consciousness was in existence long before Lucifer, because it came into existence when God decided to create beings that have free will.

My beloved, this is a very subtle topic that can be difficult for people to understand while they are in a physical body, and therefore tend to think in the linear way that is programmed into the physical brain. However, there is great value in stretching the mind, trying to understand that which is incomprehensible to the physical brain and to the carnal mind. It is in so doing that you reach for the higher perspective of the Christ mind, and even if you only attain a faint glimmer of that perspective, it has still lifted you much higher. So I ask you to stretch your mind.

The consciousness of death

In my last discourse I explained that the entire universe sprang from the creative tension between the expanding force of the Father and the contracting force of the Mother. I also explained that the universe is meant to constantly expand but that the expansion is meant to happen in a balanced manner that creates sustainable growth. What is the key to maintaining this balance between the expanding and contracting forces? It is the perfect vision that is held in the universal Christ mind, and in the individual Christ minds of God's sons and daughters.

When creation expands according to this perfect vision, there will be balance between the expanding and contracting forces. Yet when God gave his sons and daughters free will, it became possible for them to move away from this perfect vision of the Christ mind. It became possible for them to take on a state of consciousness that is out of alignment with the balanced vision of the Christ mind. This state of consciousness is based on an imbalance between the expanding and the contracting forces of the Father/Mother God.

I told you that the forces of the Father and the Mother are not opposites; they are complementary. And when they are in balance, they form a harmonious whole that creates offspring in accordance with the vision of the Christ mind. Yet when the two forces are out of balance, out of harmony, they no longer form a whole. Instead, they become opposites, and as opposites they begin to cancel out each other. They begin to counteract each other, and therefore their offspring will not be in harmony with the vision of the Christ mind. As a result, the offspring is not sustainable. It cannot survive in the long run because it becomes subject to imbalance.

This imbalance is described by your scientists in the second law of thermodynamics. Scientists have discovered that when a system becomes closed, it will begin to break down and deteriorate. What this really means is that when anything in the material universe becomes cut off from the flow of energy originating in the spiritual realm, it becomes a closed system. When that happens, the structures and forms that are created in the material universe can no longer transcend themselves, can no longer grow. Therefore, they now become subject to the contracting force of the Mother, which will cause everything to enter a spiral of contraction and decay, that eventually ends up returning everything to a state in which there are no forms or structures. In other words, when creation no longer follows the vision of the Christ mind and the drive to continually self-transcend, it will simply contract until the force of gravity causes matter itself to collapse into a black hole from which nothing can escape.

So you see, my beloved, the key to maintaining a sustainable and balanced creation is the vision and the truth of the Christ mind. This vision creates constant and balanced growth. It is a law of God that in exchange for the gift of life, you must constantly grow and self-transcend. Life itself is growth and self-transcendence, so if you choose not to grow, you are choosing death. God allows you to make that choice, yet the inevitable consequence is that you will enter a spiral of decay, leading to death.

When you choose to partake of the consciousness of death, you can no longer see the expanding and contracting forces as true polarities that complement and enhance each other. You can no longer see that the expanding force of God the Father must always be a little bit stronger, so that creation can continue to self-transcend. Instead, you begin to see the expanding and contracting forces as opposites, and you begin to fear self-transcendence. You begin to fear that if you change, if you transcend yourself, you could lose what you have.

The acceptable offering

You see my beloved, in order to grow to a higher state, you must be willing to surrender yourself completely unto God. You must be willing to lay your attainment upon the altar as the acceptable offering, whereby you literally give everything back to God. When you do this, God's law will multiply your offering manifold, as Jesus explained in the parable of the talents. Yet before the multiplication can occur, you must be willing to truly give up your attainment as if it was gone forever. In so doing, you demonstrate that you are not emotionally attached to anything in this world of form, and this demonstrates your undying love for the

Father who is beyond all form. This then allows you to take another step toward union with God.

The act of surrendering everything you have to God is the key to spiritual growth. The act of giving up your limited sense of identity is the key to becoming all that you are as an individualization of God. As Jesus explained in the parable of the talents, there is a state of consciousness which makes people fear that, by giving up what they have, they could suffer loss. People become attached to what they have and therefore refuse to give it up for multiplication. This causes people to bury their talents in the ground (in the carnal mind) and it prevents their multiplication. People become prone to holding on to what they have, refusing to let it go in order to transcend and become more of God.

As I described in my last discourse, this is what happened to Lucifer. He had reached a very high level of spiritual attainment, yet he faced the same test that is faced by everyone, namely to let go of everything you have in order to take the next step on the path of growth. Yet the more you feel you have, the more difficult this test becomes, as Jesus explained in the parable about the rich man. Lucifer had the opportunity to descend into the material universe to bring the balance and the light of the Christ mind to all beings in this world. Yes my beloved, it is true that Lucifer means light bearer or light bringer. Lucifer was indeed meant to bring light, the light of Christ and the truth of Christ, to the beings evolving in the matter universe.

Yet because he became afraid of losing his light, he refused to be the servant of all. He refused to lay everything upon the altar and truly give it up to God. He began to hold on to what he had, and as a result of that, his consciousness became subject to the contracting force of the Mother. His consciousness began to contract, and his entire vibration became lowered, until he could no longer see the higher vibrations of the spiritual realm.

So my beloved, the important point to understand here is that although Lucifer is truly an example of what can happen to every being with free will, you should not focus undue attention on Lucifer or turn him into some kind of scapegoat. You should not fall into the trap of thinking that Lucifer is to blame for all of the problems on Earth. In reality, Lucifer simply partook of a state of consciousness that is apart from the perfect vision of the Christ mind. We might therefore call it a consciousness of anti-christ.

This consciousness is based on a lie, and the original lie is the lie that the expanding force of the Father is in opposition to the contracting force of the Mother. Yet from that original lie springs an almost infinite variety of other lies that make up an entire conglomerate, an entire state of consciousness, which I would like to call the serpentine mind.

This is the state of consciousness that is symbolized by the serpent in the Garden Of Eden. It was the state of consciousness that was there to tempt Adam and Eve because they were given free will by God. You see, you cannot have free will without having the opportunity to go against God's law and his purpose for creation. God wants you to follow his law and purpose, but he wants you to do so as the result of a completely free choice. You cannot make that choice without knowing that you have the option of going against God's will. Ideally, God wants you to know this and then choose to follow his will out of love.

The lie of good and evil

When souls decided to partake of the forbidden fruit, they fell into that state of consciousness and now began to see the contracting and expanding forces as opposites, namely the opposites of good and evil. They actually began to think that God the Father is good and that God the Mother is evil. Therefore, they began to think that everything they did in this matter universe was evil and this has led to the concept of original sin. It has also caused people to blame women for the Fall.

In reality, there is nothing evil about the contracting force of the Mother. it is simply there to act as a counterbalance for the expanding force of the Father. It is the contracting force that keeps the entire universe together and gives form to the world of form. Evil only enters the picture when the contradicting force becomes so unbalanced that it overrides the expanding force and therefore stops growth. This can happen only when conscious beings refuse to grow, so they cut themselves off from their spiritual selves. Thereby, they become closed systems that are outside of the spiritual laws of God and therefore subject to the material laws that contract everything and return it to the lowest possible energy state.

So my beloved, I hope you can now see that the problems on planet Earth are not caused by one being. Even though Lucifer's followers are filled with pride and think he was very powerful, he was simply not powerful enough to create all of the problems and imbalances found even on this small planet. It takes two to tangle, and it takes an entire humanity to create the problems and the suffering you currently see on Earth. Therefore, most people on Earth share in the responsibility for the current problems seen on this planet. They share this responsibility because they have descended into the lower state of consciousness, the anti-christ mind, the serpentine mind.

They have done this by accepting some of the serpentine lies that make up this state of consciousness. What are those serpentine lies? Well my beloved, there are a number of God qualities, and those qualities can be envisioned as spiritual flames of a certain color and a certain crystalline structure. There are many such qualities, such as love, power, truth, wisdom, mercy and many others. My point here is that for each of the positive qualities of God, each of the facets that make up the world of form, there are perversions, a set of lies, that counteract the God quality and the God flame.

Each soul springs from one of the flames of God, and it came into this universe to express its individualized version of that particular God flame. Yet when the soul fell into a lower state of consciousness, it did so because it began to believe some of the lies that are perversions of its particular God flame. For example, some souls sprang from the flame of God power. They failed by believing some of the lies that are perversions of God power. One example of such a lie is that a small elite must attain power over the majority of the population and exercise totalitarian control to prevent people from destroying themselves.

My beloved, the point of this explanation is to show you that each soul descended to planet Earth for the purpose of expressing its particular God flame. As I explained in my last discourse, human beings were not created in the fullness of God consciousness. They were meant to descend to this realm and experiment with their free will and with their God flame, so that they could gradually build their God consciousness. Therefore, they were given a safe environment in which they could experiment and make mistakes without destroying themselves and others.

God does not require perfection

What I am telling you here is that God did not require instant perfection of his sons and daughters. God knew that when a new soul descends to Earth, it does not have the full Christ consciousness. Therefore, it cannot always find the proper balance between the expanding and contracting forces of its particular God flame. You see my beloved, within each of the God flames you find the eternal polarity of the expanding and contracting forces.

For example, within the flame of God power, there is an expanding tendency and a contracting tendency. When these two tendencies are balanced, you will express God power in a harmonious way. When they become unbalanced, you express God power in and unbalanced way that often causes you to ignore the free will of others and seek to attain unlimited power over other people, including unlimited control.

My point here is that when the first souls descended to Earth, they made many mistakes but none of the mistakes were so serious that they created a downward spiral. You see, these souls were in constant contact with their spiritual teachers. Such teachers are symbolized in Genesis as the God in the Garden Of Eden. This being was truly a representative of God, a being from the spiritual realm who served as a teacher for souls.

So the souls were allowed to experiment with their God flame, and when they made a mistake and expressed their flame in an unbalanced manner, their spiritual teacher would lovingly make them aware of their mistake and help them correct it. Thereby, souls could continue to grow and become better and better at expressing their God flame in a balanced manner.

You see, these souls would lay everything they did on the altar of God with complete love, meaning complete non-attachment. Through this surrender, all of their mistakes were instantaneously forgiven and the misqualified energy purified. All of their right actions were multiplied and the energy stored as their treasure laid up in Heaven. In other words, both their right and not so right choices were used as stepping stones for the continuous growth of their souls. They were truly living in a positive, uplifting spiral in which every decision brought them closer to God.

Unfortunately, certain souls decided to partake of the forbidden fruit, namely the consciousness of death that opens you up to the fear of irretrievable loss. My beloved, the first waves of souls that descended to Earth experimented with their God flames without ever considering that they could go against God's purpose for life. They continued to learn and transcend themselves, and they became better and better at expressing their God flames. They refused to let the consciousness of death enter their beings.

Yet there came a point, when the souls on Earth decided to partake of the forbidden fruit of the serpentine consciousness. They fell prey to the serpentine lies, and as a result they became afraid of making mistakes. They suddenly saw themselves as "naked," meaning imperfect, and they became ashamed of their mistakes. Instead of simply learning from their mistakes, accepting God's forgiveness and moving on, they now became afraid of experimenting and wanted to hold on to the attainment they already had.

They fell prey to the serpentine lies that God would love them less or judge them harshly because they were imperfect, and they felt like they could never be as worthy as their brothers and sisters in the spiritual realm. This is the birth of the Cain consciousness in which people begin to believe that if they have less than others, they are less worthy of God's love. So instead of surrendering everything they have on the altar, they want to hide their imperfections from God, they want to hide their mistakes from their teacher. And in their attempts to do this, they are willing to "kill" those of their brothers and sisters who seem to have more light, who seem to stand above the crowd. They do this out of the mistaken belief that if no one is above them, they must be the favorite son.

My beloved, Abel was able because he was willing to surrender his all to God, and it was God's multiplication of Abel's offering that made him worthy. As Jesus said, "I of my own self can do nothing, it is the Father within me who is doing the work." Cain could have become equally worthy by surrendering his all to God. Yet because he was not willing to make the acceptable offering, God had nothing to multiply, and therefore Cain was always second to Abel. Instead of surrendering himself and letting God make him worthy, Cain sought to become worthy by removing what he thought was the obstacle to him being loved by God. He sought to remove his brother who served as a constant reminder of his own imperfection.

This mindset is, of course, an illusion, for God loves all his sons and daughters with an unconditional and infinite love. Because God's love is infinite, how can there be favorite sons? How can there be inequality in infinity? As Jesus' parable of the talents demonstrates, it does not matter to God that one son has more attainment or more light than another. All who are willing to lay their attainment upon the altar will have their gifts multiplied and will enter into the joy of the Lord.

Breaking the circle of life

My beloved, the real problem with the Cain consciousness is that it causes people to hide from their teacher. When you make the decision to hide from your teacher, you break the flow of energy between the spiritual realm and the matter universe. You break the flow between your spiritual self and your soul. This then breaks the circle of life, and you now become cut off from God, cut off from your spiritual self, and your soul becomes a closed system.

Now my beloved, when you are cut off from the flow of life, you gradually begin to realize that you have lack, that you are incomplete, that you are imperfect. And this can give rise to the sense that God has treated you unfairly, that God has not given you what you deserve and that God has made it too hard for you to grow.

Even though your soul is in the material universe, it has the potential to manifest God's perfection in this world, as your ascended brothers and sisters are manifesting that perfection in Heaven. Yet to manifest that perfection, you must attain the Christ consciousness that gives you the balanced vision of how to express your God flame in the perfect polarity of the expanding and contracting forces.

This is within the reach of everyone, but as I explained in my last discourse, human souls were meant to gradually attain this Christ consciousness, and therefore they were not given all of it at once. Yet one of the lies found in the serpentine consciousness is the lie that human souls should have been given the Christ consciousness without earning it through their own experimentation and effort.

Now my beloved, human souls were given life. They were given a beautiful and harmonious planet on which to experiment with their free will, on which to express their individuality and their God flames. My beloved, what more could a soul possibly want?

What a beautiful and wonderful gift from God to have the opportunity to self-transcend and gradually become all that God is. Yet in becoming all that God is, you also have the opportunity to become a unique individualization of God. You have the opportunity to become more than you were created to be, because you can build your own individuality through your experiences in the world of form.

You see my beloved, human souls were truly given the highest gift that anyone could want. Yet through the lies of the serpentine consciousness, some souls began to believe that they had been shortchanged by

God, that they had been treated unfairly, that God had made unreasonable demands of them by making it possible for them to make mistakes. This then is the consciousness that I described in my discourse, in which Lucifer attempts to make everyone feel that God made a mistake by giving them free will.

My beloved, please understand that when God gave you free will, he gave you the possibility of making a mistake. Yet God also gave you a spiritual teacher who could instantly correct your mistake. And I can assure you that there was no blame associated with making a mistake. Contrary to the serpentine image of God as an angry and judgmental God, God is a God of unconditional love. God never blamed you for making a mistake. As soon as you recognized your mistake and decided to correct it, God's forgiveness was instantaneous and unconditional.

You now see that human souls were given a safe and loving environment in which to experiment. They were given free will and the right to experiment with that free will, even the right to make mistakes and have those mistakes corrected by a loving teacher. And they were given instantaneous forgiveness for any mistake they made. My beloved, what is the one ingredient that can break this edenic state, what is the one thing that can break the flow of energy between Spirit and matter, what is the one factor that can take people out of paradise?

Well my beloved, remember that God's forgiveness is instantaneous. However, because you have free will, you must accept that forgiveness. Otherwise, you would not be free of your mistakes! So the one aspect of the serpentine mind that prevents you from accepting God's forgiveness is that you begin to feel ingratitude toward God.

When you allow the serpentine lie of ingratitude to enter your consciousness, you cannot accept God's forgiveness for your mistakes. Therefore, you can no longer see life as a gift, and you begin to see it as a risk. And by not accepting life as a gift, you will inevitably break the thread of contact, break the flow of energy between spirit and matter and thereby break the circle of life. This then is the very thing that prevents people from returning to the Garden Of Eden, which is truly a state of consciousness. In that state of mind, that state of Grace, every human being is connected to his or her Christ self and through that to the I AM Presence and the spiritual teachers in Heaven.

The master key to Paradise

So my beloved, I hope you can now see that the master key to restoring Heaven on Earth is to restore the sense of gratitude, the sense of infinite gratitude for God and for the opportunity that life truly is.

My beloved hearts, take a look at this planet and see how few people feel gratitude for the gift of life and the opportunity to make of life what their souls desire. See how many people feel ungrateful toward their parents and blame them for their misfortune in life. See how many people feel ungrateful toward their spouses and blame them for their problems. See how many people feel ungrateful toward their societies and blame them for not giving them everything they need. See how many people feel ungrateful toward God, blaming God for everything under the sun, including blaming God for the very fact that they exist. See how many people blame God for having created the misery and suffering that you currently see on Earth, instead of acknowledging the truth that human beings have created the imperfect conditions that are found on this planet.

Oh my beloved, by blaming others for your problems, you solidify those problems because you make yourself powerless to change them. Yet by acknowledging that to have free will and therefore have the opportunity to align yourself with the Christ truth in your heart, you empower yourself to bring the power of God into your life to change the conditions that lead to suffering and a sense of lack. And by doing so, you can escape the Cain consciousness and rise to the consciousness of Abel, whereby you will become able to manifest God's abundance in all aspects of your life.

My beloved hearts, it is truly the Father's good pleasure to give you the kingdom of the abundant life. God wants you to have abundance of every good and perfect gift. Yet you have free will, and God must respect that free will. And therefore, he cannot force his abundance upon you. If you decide to break the circle of life, your life will become subject to the unbalanced pull of the contracting force of the Mother. This will cause your life to contract, until there will be lack and suffering. And if you insist on continuing on this path, because you will not accept God's forgiveness, then you will create a downward spiral that will eventually lead to your personal destruction. When a critical mass of people take this path, it can lead to the destruction of entire civilizations, as it has indeed done in the distant past that is not recorded in your current history books.

So my beloved, the choice is yours. God has given you this planet, and he has given you the right to experiment with your free will. You can choose to remain in the serpentine state of consciousness that causes you to build mistake upon mistake, until you are caught in a maelstrom of karma and imperfect energies that inevitably takes you down into a black hole, from which there seems to be no escape. Or you can choose to reach for the Christ mind, which is always available as the still small voice in your heart, and break the downward spiral. Hereby, you can begin the upward climb back to the abundant life.

And the key, the master key, to breaking the downward spiral of self-destruction is to reestablish your soul's sense of gratitude for God. By truly feeling this gratitude, by filling your soul with an infinite and unconditional gratitude for God and for God's perfect gifts, you will reestablish the flow of energy between spirit and matter, between your spiritual self and your soul. Thereby, you will once again close the circle of life that was broken when you ate the forbidden fruit of the serpentine consciousness.

The Miracle Gratitude Rosary

My beloved hearts, it is precisely to help you reestablish the circle of life that I today release one of the most powerful spiritual tools you have ever seen on this planet, namely my rosary of the Miracle Gratitude. [Available on www.transcendencetoolbox.com] This rosary is the antidote to every human lack and every aspect of human suffering.

I am not hereby saying that my other rosaries are no longer needed. They are truly needed for their specific purpose. Yet I must tell you that there is hardly any problem on Earth that could not be solved and removed through gratitude. And the reason is simple, namely that gratitude brings God (back) into your life. And with God all things are possible. Therefore, when God is in your life, all problems can be solved and suddenly the abundant life is manifest.

My beloved hearts, I now turn back to the topic of terrorism. The terrorists who have been attacking the Western nations have truly descended into the Cain consciousness, and they feel jealous of their Western brothers and sisters who seem to have more abundance than themselves. They feel this is unjust, so they are now out to destroy Western civilization by the faulty logic of the Cain consciousness, which makes them feel that if they slay their brother, then God must love them all the more. Oh my beloved, what an illusion this is because God already loves them with an infinite and unconditional love. It is simply their own state of consciousness which prevents them from accepting God's love.

I am sure you can see that it is impossible to reason with terrorists. It is impossible to reason with those who are trapped in the Cain consciousness. Yet what you can do is to consume that Cain consciousness, and the key to doing this is to send waves of infinite gratitude into the collective consciousness of humankind. This then is precisely what my Miracle Gratitude Rosary will accomplish—if it is given by a critical mass of people.

My beloved hearts, you who are my enlightened ones, my best hopes for the turning around of this planet, my shock troops, I say to you once again that I count on you to embrace this rosary and give it with all the fervor of your hearts. I count on you to spread the word of all of my rosaries and to give them in every situation possible.

Total forgiveness leads to total freedom

Mother Mary, April 29, 2004

Over this past month you have seen several examples of another force, namely the force of non-forgiveness. While this force is not the cause of terrorism and war, it is indeed the force that keeps terrorism and war going strong on this planet. You have especially seen this in the Middle East, where even the state of Israel has engaged in state-sponsored assassinations, which truly are acts of non-forgiveness that only breed more non-forgiveness from the other side. Thereby, these acts contribute to the downward spiral of violence in revenge for violence that has engulfed the Middle East for thousands upon thousands of years.

I tell you that even the Ascended Host wonder if the people living in that region will ever have enough of this punch-counterpunch of revenge and revenge for revenge, until it truly becomes revenge for the sake of revenge itself. Truly, there can no longer be any real meaning to these acts of revenge because the spiral of violence started so long ago that no one can remember why it started. They only remember that they must perpetuate it by getting even, by getting revenge.

So my beloved, I come to you today to release a gift from my heart, a gift that can help those of you who are my awakened ones break this downward spiral of revenge and non-forgiveness, found not only in the Middle East but in many places throughout this planet. That gift is my rosary of Miracle Forgiveness.

My beloved, I desire to give you a teaching, so that you may understand why forgiveness is so important. To truly understand the importance of forgiveness, you need to realize the profound truth that my son Jesus has explained so many times, namely that the basic law of this universe is the Law of Free Will. You also need to understand, as I explained in my previous discourses, that the very purpose of life, the very essence of life, is to grow, to move on, to self-transcend.

So what is it that prevents you from growing, from moving on, from transcending your current state of consciousness, your current sense of identity? Well, it is the point of non-forgiveness. You see, when there is something you have not forgiven, there is something you are holding on to, there is something you cannot let go of, and in that point of emotional attachment to the things of this world, you are holding yourself back. You are holding yourself tied to a limited and imperfect sense of identity, and you are essentially worshipping an idol of your own making, or at least the making of your culture.

By not forgiving, you are taking away your own freedom to move on. And as I tried to explain in my previous discourses, when you do not move on, you will stagnate. And if you stay too long in one place, you will become subject to the second law of thermodynamics, which means that a downward spiral, a negative vortex, of energy will begin forming around you. When that vortex becomes too strong, it will begin to overpower your feelings and your thoughts, until you begin to believe either that there is nothing outside the vortex or that you cannot escape the downward pull of the vortex.

This is what causes so many people, especially in the Middle East, to believe that there is no other way to live than to be in opposition to the Jews or in opposition to the Arabs. It causes them to believe that there is no way to escape the cycle of violence, the cycle of revenge. They feel they simply must continue the cycle because they must have revenge, they must set things right by committing another act of violence to supposedly neutralize or make up for previous acts of violence.

Unfortunately, the intense energies of this negative vortex prevent people from asking the very logical question of when and how this could possibly end. Think about this, my beloved. Can there ever be an ultimate act of revenge? Can there ever be an ultimate act of revenge that will settle the score permanently and thereby bring about an end to violence?

My beloved hearts, those of you who are not trapped by the relativity of the carnal mind and by a downward vortex of non-forgiveness will be able to see the pure and simple logic behind these remarks. There can be no peace through revenge. It simply is not possible. There can be no act of revenge which stops the cycle of violence, because if you avenge what has been done to you by doing something to another, you will inevitably create the desire for revenge in your opponent.

This should be obvious to anyone who knows elementary school physics and has learned about the law of action and reaction. For every action, there is an opposite reaction of equal strength. That is simply a law of the material universe. So when you take revenge, you are reacting to what was done to you but your reaction becomes a new action, and it inevitably creates a reaction from your opponent, even from the universe itself. And this cycle can literally go on forever—or at least it seems like forever.

Now my beloved hearts, there is indeed a very small minority of the people on this planet who do not want peace, who do not want resolution, who do not want an end to violence or an end to this spiral of revenge. These are the people who are completely trapped in the Luciferian state of consciousness that I described in my previous discourses. Yet those people are few, and the vast majority of the people who are caught in the spiral of revenge actually do want peace. And this then gives rise to the paradox that they say they want peace, but that they are not willing to stop the cycle of revenge.

My beloved hearts, while this can be almost impossible to understand for a person who is not caught in a negative spiral, your new understanding of energy and energy vortexes allows you to see the explanation. When people are caught in such a vortex of anger and revenge, they simply cannot see the fallacy of their thinking. They cannot think logically and rationally because they are so overpowered by the emotional energies that they do not even stop to think. This then is why there is a need for something to break the spiral, to break the downward pull. And that something is that someone must consume the energies created through revenge and non-forgiveness, the very energies that form a magnetic pull on people's emotions and overpowers them, so that they lose all logic and rationality. Those someone must be the balanced people who are not caught up in these negative momentums and vortexes. My beloved hearths, those someone are you.

The serpentine lies behind non-forgiveness

Before you can truly become an effective force in consuming the vortexes of non-forgiveness on this planet, you must free yourself from the point of non-forgiveness. You might say, "But Mother Mary, you just told us that we are not caught up in a vortex of non-forgiveness." And that is perfectly true. You are not caught in a vortex that is so intense that it overpowers your feelings and prevents you from thinking.

Yet many of you do not realize what is the true cause of non-forgiveness. And you do not realize this because you were not brought up with a proper understanding. And you were not brought up with a proper understanding, because the beautiful teachings on forgiveness that my son gave 2,000 years ago have been obscured and distorted by the orthodox Christian churches.

The problem we have is that most people on Earth simply do not see that non-forgiveness is based on a set of lies. They do not understand these lies, and therefore they cannot see the mindset behind those lies. And if you cannot see through the lies of the devil, if you are not wise as a serpent, then you cannot completely free yourself from those lies that permeate every aspect of life on this planet. If you do not become wise as a serpent, how can you be harmless as a dove?

So let me now give you a teaching in an attempt to help you free yourself from the lies about non-forgiveness. As I said earlier, the basic law of this universe is the Law of Free Will. You have the right to experiment with your creative abilities. In fact, your lifestream and your soul were created with a drive, a desire to experiment with God's laws and God's energies. Unfortunately, what has happened to most people on this planet is that they have lost their contact with their spiritual selves, and thereby they have become enveloped in a lower state of consciousness that causes them to see themselves as being separated from their spiritual selves, even separated from God. Because of this sense of separation, you no longer realize the basic reality that God has never hurt you whatsoever.

God has not created the conditions on this planet that have caused your soul to be hurt and wounded. Those conditions were created by human beings trapped in the lower state of consciousness, in which they are easily controlled by dark forces, as I explained in my previous discourses. So you see my beloved, God has not created the conditions that caused you to be hurt, and God never wanted you to be wounded. Yet most people on this planet cannot fully understand and accept that the misery on Earth was created by human beings and not created by God. Somewhere deep within their beings, they have a sense that either God must have created their misery or God must have allowed it to be created. And therefore, most people blame God for certain conditions in their lives.

Many people blame God for various negative experiences they have had in this lifetime. But when you go deep within the subconscious mind, you see that many people actually blame God for what happened to them in the Garden Of Eden. They blame God for the fact that they fell into a lower state of consciousness. After all, where did the serpent come from if it was not created by God? And where did the tree of the knowledge of good and evil come from if God did not put it in the Garden Of Eden? So if God had not put the tree in the garden and allowed the serpent to be in the garden, then their souls would not have fallen, and therefore it must be God's fault.

My beloved, these beliefs are not your own. They have been carefully manufactured by Lucifer and his followers to trap you in a state of consciousness that makes it almost impossible for you to come back to God, to come back to a full realization and acceptance of who you are as a son or daughter of God. The dark forces have created such a web of interwoven lies that it is almost impossible for me to help you see through them, and it is certainly impossible for me to do it in one single discourse.

As I said in my last discourse, Lucifer fell because he truly believed that God made a mistake by giving people free will. So he has created a lie, namely the lie that free will was a mistake because, after all, if people had not had free will, how could they have been tempted by the serpent and eaten of the forbidden fruit? So this causes many people to blame God, not only for the fact that he gave them free will but even for the fact that he created them.

In reality, the serpent is a symbol for a state of consciousness, namely that of rebelling against God's laws. It is an inevitable result of giving you free will, because if you could not rebel, you would not have free will. Nevertheless, you do not need to rebel to exercise your freedom of choice—that is simply a subtle lie promoted by those who chose to embody the serpentine consciousness. Do you see that the serpentine consciousness simply follows free will, as the shadow follows your body? Nevertheless, God never wanted you to identify with your shadow or to be afraid of your own shadow. He wanted you to always face the light of your I AM Presence and keep the shadow behind you.

My beloved, what is the result of blaming God? Well, the result is that you paralyze yourself, and you do this because deep within you, you have accepted the belief that you are not responsible for your situation. You have accepted the belief that you did not create your current situation, and because you did not create it, there is nothing you can do to uncreate it.

I hope you can see the very simple logic here. If you go outside without an umbrella, and it suddenly starts raining, then obviously you did not create that rain, and so there is nothing you can do to make the rain stop. This then is the experience that causes many people to say that they have not created their current situation and they have not created the current misery on planet Earth. They have not created the conditions that caused them to fall into a lower state of consciousness because they did not give themselves free will, they did not choose to be created, they did not choose to be born, they did not choose to come to this planet, they did not even choose to exist.

And therefore, they can push aside all personal responsibility and accountability and feel that there is nothing they could do to change the situation for the better. Oh my beloved, I must tell you that this is the most insidious of all lies. The most insidiously of all lies is the idea that you could possibly be in a situation in which there is nothing you could do to transcend that situation and come up higher. The most insidious of all lies is the idea that there could possibly be a prison, a prison in the matter universe, from which there is no escape. It is the idea that you could possibly make one mistake that would make you doomed forever.

Oh my beloved hearts, I wish you could see through my eyes as an ascended being and see how ridiculous this lie truly is. My beloved, I chuckle as I say this because once you have ascended, you realize that everything in the matter universe is created from God's energy. God's energy is simply vibration, and no matter how low that vibration is, no matter how dense the energy or the physical matter might seem, it is always possible to raise the vibration and bring it back into alignment with the purity and the perfection of God. My beloved hearts, please make an effort to understand this truth, this fundamental truth about the universe in which you live. There is nothing that you could do, or that any force could possibly do to you, which cannot be undone and purified by the light and the love of God.

The very idea that you could possibly do something that could not be undone is the most insidious lie created by the serpent and his seed. It is the most insidious misuse of the contracting force of the Mother, the very Mother of God. It is such a misuse because it is the contracting force of the Mother which gives you life, which gives you form, whether it be a physical body or a soul. Were it not for the contracting force of the Mother, you would have no individual consciousness, no individual sense of identity.

Yet as I have tried to explain with great care in my latest discourses, it has never been the intention of the Mother of God to trap you in a particular form. So the very idea that the form created by the energies of the Mother of God could become a prison from which there is no escape is such an abomination, such an injustice against the Mother of God whose unconditional love is what gives you life and form.

How can you overcome this lie? Well my beloved, there is only one way to overcome the lie of the serpent. And that is to take full and complete responsibility for your current situation.

My beloved hearts, I am well aware that this will be a very provocative statement to many people, and they will find it extremely difficult to take responsibility for their situation. However, the reason for this difficulty is that many people have lost the true recognition of who they are. They have lost their true sense of identity, and they have been trapped, not only by the lie of a false identity, they have also been trapped in a negative vortex of energy that overpowers their feelings and their ability to think rationally. This vortex is not a vortex of revenge, but it is a vortex of energy that reinforces the false sense of identity, the idea that you are separated from God. Therefore, you think you are a victim of what God has created, and you have no responsibility for your situation because God set you up to fail.

My beloved son has given many teachings on his website in an attempt to help you overcome your false sense of identity and realize that you were created as a spiritual being. While I do not in any way claim that I can do this better than Jesus, I would like to add the perspective of the Mother of God.

Nothing can hurt the real you

The problem we see on Earth is that people think that because they have fallen into a lower state of consciousness, because they have made mistakes and because they have sinned, they have somehow been permanently stained. My beloved hearts, you need to see through this illusion and this lie, and you need to do so by realizing the reality of energy.

What I would like you to do to overcome this illusion is very simple. You can do this physically if you like, but I am sure that for most of you it will be enough just to imagine this exercise. Imagine that you go outside at night with a flashlight. You hang the flashlight in a tree so that the light beam is shining on the ground. Now imagine that you have a bucket of mud and you start throwing the mud at the light beam. Can you make that mud cling to the beam of light?

My beloved hearts, I am sure you can see that this is impossible but why is it impossible? Well, as your scientists have told you, everything is created from energy. So the mud is simply another form of energy than the energy of the light beam. Both are forms of energy but the difference is that the mud has a much lower vibration than the light. And because it has a lower vibration, it cannot cling to and pollute the light beam.

So you see my beloved, your true identity is not your soul, the soul that abides in a physical body in the material universe. Your true identity is the spiritual self, and that spiritual self resides in a higher realm, in a higher world that is made entirely of higher vibrations. So the very idea that the soul that descends into the material world could commit a sin that could permanently stain the spiritual self, residing in the spiritual world, is as ridiculous as the idea that mud can cling to a beam of light. Do you see my point?

Your true identity is a spiritual being, your I AM Presence. That spiritual self is, at this very moment, residing in the spiritual realm, and it is as perfect and as beautiful as when it was first created by God. Nothing you have ever done, and nothing you could possibly do, could pollute or destroy your spiritual self. Therefore, you are as pure and you are as worthy of God's love as the day you were first created. Nothing you have done in this world has made you unworthy of God's love. Yet the forces of darkness want to make you think that because you have done this or that terrible thing, you are no longer worthy of God's love. And when you subscribe to this lie, you begin to believe that you need to hide from God and that there is no point in trying to come home to God or even ask for his forgiveness. You accept the lie that God is such an angry and judgmental God that he would not forgive you after all you have done. So you do not even try to come back to God, you keep seeking to hide from God.

My point here is that what keeps you trapped in your current state of consciousness, in your current set of limitations and even in your outer circumstances, is that you cannot accept God's forgiveness. And why can you not accept God's forgiveness? Well my beloved, the answer to that question lies in the Law of Free Will.

According to the Law of Free Will, you have a right to create anything you want. Yet if you create a false image of yourself, you can become trapped in that image, in that sense of identity. And the only way you can overcome that limitation, the only way you can escape that prison, which is truly created by your mind and exists only in your mind, is that you must decide that you no longer want to be that way. You do not want to be the limited person that you see yourself as being. You want to let go of those limitations and move on.

How can you let go of limitations? You can do so only by forgiving yourself for creating those limitations in the first place. And how can you forgive yourself? Well my beloved, you can do so only when you fully recognize and accept that it was you who created the limitations and not God, and not even Lucifer or all of his henchmen.

You see my beloved, this is what has put so many people in a Catch-22 from which there seems to be no escape. They cannot improve their lives because they do not take responsibility for their situation and realize that they have created it. Yet the reason they cannot take responsibility for the situation is because they believe that there is no forgiveness. There is no escape from the limitations, so if they were to admit that they have created the limitations, they would condemn themselves for doing so. They would be permanently locked in experiencing suffering and limitation, and on top of that they would be blaming themselves for the situation. To the soul, this feels like adding insult to injury, so to avoid condemning themselves, they avoid taking responsibility. And so what could possibly break this stalemate?

The only way out is to recognize that you have created the situation but that God does not condemn you for doing so. Therefore, there is no reason for condemning yourself. What you have done is simply to experiment with your free will and with the energy of God.

I am not trying to say here that everything you have created is what God wanted to see for you or that it is in alignment with God's laws. God never wanted you to create limitations that cause you suffering and pain. What I am saying is that when God made the decision to give you free will, he gave you the right to experiment. And in so doing, he also set you free from all blame.

What God has done in creating you and giving you free will is that he has given you the opportunity to grow in awareness and identity, until you can fully accept yourself as a son or daughter of God. Thereby, you become a co-creator with God who eventually becomes so powerful that you can create your own world. God has literally given you the opportunity to become all that God is and more. And in creating you and giving you free will, God has no desire to blame you for doing what you were created to do in experimenting with your free will, or even for creating circumstances that cause you suffering.

God does not blame you

Do you see my point here? God does not want you to blame yourself and God does not want to blame you. God wants you to approach life as a scientist conducting experiments. Imagine that you were Thomas Edison trying to find the material that would make it possible to create the electric light bulb. As you might know, Edison tried dozens and dozens of different materials before he found one that worked. Yet imagine that Edison had blamed himself for being a failure or a sinner every time he tried a material that didn't work. He would soon have become so burdened and traumatized that he would have given up before he found the material that gave birth to the electric age. Instead, Thomas Edison simply discarded the material that didn't work and immediately went on to try another one. This is how God wants you to participate in the experiment of life.

When you become a spiritually aware person, you can begin to think rationally and logically about life. When you experience conditions that cause you suffering, the rational way of thinking is to say, "I do not want to experience these conditions any more. I have had enough of that experience, so what can I do to change my experience? The first step I must take is to overcome the belief that I am the victim of circumstances beyond my control. Because as long as I feel like a victim, there is nothing I can do to change the circumstances that cause me suffering. So I must take responsibility for my situation and recognize that I have either created these circumstances or I have attracted these circumstances to me because I have allowed myself to be in a lower state of consciousness than what is by highest potential. And so the very key to changing my circumstances is to change my state of consciousness. When I do change my state of consciousness, the first thing that will happen is that my experience of my circumstances will change, and I will begin to suffer less, even if the outer circumstances do not change instantly. Yet if I keep raising my state of consciousness, I will eventually experience a change in the outer circumstances."

You see my beloved, the material universe is created from energies that are quite dense. As Jesus and I have attempted to explain, there are levels in the material world. So everything that is created in the matter universe started as an idea in the etheric realm. It was then solidified as a thought in the mental realm. It received energy and motion in the emotional realm, before it finally broke through in the material realm. That is why a spiritually aware person cannot expect that outer circumstances, material circumstances, will change overnight.

It will take some time to change the circumstances, and the reason for that is simple. To change the circumstances in the material universe, you need to go to the source. So you need to begin by changing the images in the etheric realm, which will then change the thoughts and change the feelings, and finally cycle through to the material realm. However, because the energies in the material realm are the densest, it will take some time before you will see a change in the visible world. That is one reason Jesus told you that in your patience you will posses your souls.

Jesus has used the image that the material world is like a movie projected upon a screen. The driving force behind the movie is the white light coming from the light bulb in the film projector, and that light receives form as it passes through the filmstrip. Yet what I am telling you here is that there are three film strips in your subconscious mind. One is your sense of identity, which abides in the etheric realm. The other is your mental image of yourself and the world, which abides in the mental realm. And the third is your feelings about yourself and the world, which abides in the emotional realm. Your outer circumstances are simply projections upon the screen of life, as the light of God passes through your consciousness and is colored and given shape by the images you hold in your etheric, mental and emotional bodies.

Change yourself!

That is why in order to to change your outer circumstances you must begin by changing your inner circumstances, your state of consciousness. And that is why you need to realize that your outer circumstances are created by your consciousness, they are a reflection of the images in your consciousness. And those images were created by you.

I am aware that these images are the products of a complicated process that has been going on for many lifetimes. This process has been affected by your culture and by the lies promoted by dark forces. Nevertheless, the images were created by you, and this then brings me to the central truth that all spiritual people need to understand.

To explain that truth, let us begin with the spiritual self. Your lifestream was created by your spiritual parents and it is a spiritual being. It is as pure and perfect as when it was first created. I can assure you that your lifestream, your I AM Presence, is in constant, conscious contact with God. It constantly feels the infinite and unconditional love of God, and therefore there is absolutely no point in your I AM Presence that has any negative feelings about being created or about having free will. Your I AM Presence feels only infinite joy and gratitude for the opportunity to exist and to be part of God's magnificent and wonderful creation. In other words, none of the negative feelings that affect so many souls on Earth exist at the level of your I AM Presence.

My point for telling you this is to help you realize that the very idea that you are created by God is a truth with modifications. Your I AM Presence was created by God but your soul was not created by God.

Your soul was created by your I AM Presence as a vehicle for experiencing the material universe and for expressing its creativity in the material universe. [NOTE: A later teaching gives a deeper understanding by explaining the existence of a Conscious You that created the soul.] My point here is that it simply is not logical and rational, nor is it true, to blame God for the fact that your soul exists. God did not create the soul that descended into the material universe and fell into a lower state of consciousness. Your I AM Presence created that soul, but your I AM Presence is you. You created your soul because you made the choice to create that soul, and you made that choice because you wanted to experience the material universe and you wanted to help co-create this universe as the kingdom of God.

So you now see that even though you presently might experience yourself as a victim of circumstances beyond your control, your soul is not a victim. Your soul is the result of a choice that you, meaning your true identity as a spiritual being, made. You made that choice because you wanted to descend into the material realm and have a positive experience that would lead to your growth, to a growth in your sense of identity as a co-creator with God. When you realize this truth, you can see that there is no point in blaming God and there is no point in blaming yourself.

Stop the blaming game!

If you are currently experiencing circumstances that cause you suffering, then instead of blaming God, blaming other people, blaming dark forces or even blaming yourself, you simply need to stop the blaming game. You need to forgive yourself and say, "I conducted an experiment that did not work out as I intended. So I am going to leave that experiment behind and come up higher in consciousness." You need to decide that if your current situation does not give you the positive experience that your soul desires, then you will take the necessary steps to change your experience and use your present circumstances as a springboard for creating a positive experience for your soul.

To fully make the decision to simply leave behind that which is imperfect, you need to recognize the profound truth that no matter what the outer appearances might be in this world, nobody ever did anything to you. Let me say that again, "Nobody ever did anything to you. No human being ever did anything to you and God never did anything to you."

The only force that ever did anything to you was yourself. The meaning behind that statement is that even though your soul is in the material universe, it is not made from the energies of the material universe. Therefore, your soul is truly a light beam that is shining from your I AM Presence. And therefore, the energies of the material universe cannot cling to your soul, they cannot damage your soul. However, what is your soul?

Your soul is a state of consciousness, a sense of being, a sense of identity. It is a being that has imagination and free will. And therefore your soul creates its own sense of identity, and it recreates that sense of identity every moment. The point here is this. If someone comes to you and slaps you on one cheek, that person has done something to your body but that person has done nothing to your soul. Yet you have the ability, through your imagination and free will, to let the action performed by the other person affect your sense of identity. And in so doing, you are doing something to yourself, to your soul.

Do you see my point here? Another person cannot change your sense of identity—only you can do that. And in order to change your sense of identity, you must make a choice.

I clearly realize that there are forces in this world who use very aggressive means in order to manipulate people into accepting an imperfect and false sense of identity. Those forces are very insidious, and they are very persuasive in the lies they use to make you believe that you are a sinner and a mortal human being who has done something so bad that you can never be free of it. I am not saying that it is easy for you to escape the clutches of these liars and their lies. What I am saying is that it is possible for you to escape all the lies in this world. To do so, you must come to a full acceptance of the fact that they cannot harm you, that none of the forces of this world can harm your soul.

What can harm your soul is that you allow the forces of this world to cause you to change your sense of identity. That is what will harm you, but that harm can come about only through the decisions you make. And the wonderful thing about this realization is that anything that has been done to your soul through a choice that you made can be undone by you making a better choice. So the key to being free of all imperfections of the past is that you must make a choice to let those imperfections go, to leave them behind, and you do so by forgiving yourself for making those choices.

Once again, we are back to the paradox that if you recognize that anything that ever happened to you was the result of decisions you made, you have been programmed by the forces of this world, and you have accepted their lies, that you need to blame yourself for making wrong choices. Well my beloved, as I have tried to explain to you, there is no need to blame yourself for making wrong choices. If you blame yourself for making the wrong choice, you will bind yourself to that choice because in blaming yourself, you are reinforcing that choice. You are reinforcing it by the energy that streams through your mind and attention. You are feeding the wrong choice, and as you keep feeding energy into it, you will build a vortex that will overpower your thoughts and feelings, until you can no longer see beyond it.

Think back to my thought experiment about the light beam from your flashlight. You cannot throw mud at the light beam and make it stick to the light. However, you can make bricks out of mud and build a wall around the light until it is no longer visible. That is what most people have done to their souls. They have made wrong choices, and instead of simply forgiving themselves and moving on, they have reinforced those wrong choices. By feeding energy into these imperfect images, they have built a wall around their souls so that they no longer realize that they are beings of light. They think they are sinners and imperfect human beings who have all kinds of problems and errors that make them unworthy of God's forgiveness, unworthy to forgive themselves.

Ultimately, those walls are not real because the imperfect energies have no permanent reality in God. Yet as long as your soul is in this world, the wall will affect your sense of identity, and that is why you need to break it down systematically. You need to break down one brick at a time and throw them into the spiritual fire to be consumed. Thereby, you gradually uncover the original beauty and perfection of your soul.

The only thing that can break the negative spiral is that you make the decision that you will no longer feed the vortex, that you will no longer feed the wrong decision and that you will no longer blame yourself for making the wrong choice. You will accept the fact that God gave you the right to experiment, and that in so doing God gave you the right to learn from a failed experiment and decide to simply leave it behind.

When Thomas Edison tried copper as the filament of a light bulb and it didn't work, he simply threw the copper away never to use it again.

He left behind the idea that copper would ever produce light. He did not insist on keeping the materials from his failed experiments cluttering up his laboratory until he could barely move around. He simply threw away what didn't work and moved on, trying something new until he found something that worked.

Unmasking the serpentine lie that God caused you to fall

My beloved hearts, we now come to one of the most insidious lies promoted by dark forces. As I have explained in a previous discourse, the very essence of life is that the world of form is created by the expanding force of the Father acting upon the contracting force of the Mother. The very nature of the expanding force of the Father is to experiment. It is the force of the Father that causes your soul to have the desire to experiment, the curiosity to experience something new.

Here comes the subtle point. It is very true that it was the desire to experiment that made it possible for you to fall into a lower state of consciousness. You conducted certain experiments that gradually caused your consciousness to fall in vibration, until you forgot your spiritual origin. Now my beloved, I have tried to explain to you that many people on this Earth were misled and manipulated by dark forces into falling, into making the wrong decisions that caused them to fall. This should not be difficult to understand. Obviously, you made the choice to accept the lies of the serpent but nevertheless those lies were there and they were directed at you.

Here comes the important point. After you had fallen into a lower state of consciousness, the serpents now kicked in phase two of their plot. They now told you that it was precisely your desire to experiment, it was precisely the fact that you have free will, that caused you to fall. And therefore, the only way to salvation is that you stop experimenting, that you stop exercising your free will and that you allow Lucifer, or some of the other serpents, to control you so that they can save you. They want to make you believe that God's way of doing things, meaning the gift of free will and imagination, has put your soul in danger because there is no guarantee that you will be saved. They also want you to believe that if you follow them and allow them to control you, your salvation will be guaranteed.

My beloved hearts, this is precisely the lie that permeates this world and has given rise to numerous claims that an outer organization or institution, be it a church, a dictator or a political ideology can save people or can save the world. You should not try to experiment, you should not think that you can know truth on your own. You should simply follow the leaders who know best.

This is the lie that has trapped more people than any other lie. Yes, it was your drive to experiment that made it possible for you to fall, but at the same time it is only your drive to experiment that can help you rise back to the Christ consciousness. Do you see what is actually happening here? It is true that you could fall only because you have free will and a desire to experiment. Yet it was not the desire to experiment that caused you to fall; it was the serpentine lies that caused you to fall. It was perfectly possible to experiment with your free will without falling. The fall was caused by the fact that you made the choice to accept some of the lies produced by the serpents. So in reality, it was not God but the serpents who caused you to fall.

Here is the essential truth. The serpents used their lies to manipulate people into creating the current misery on this planet, and they have also attempted to set themselves up as the true saviors, as the only saviors, who can save you from the problem that they created. Their plot is to create so much suffering that you are willing to follow them blindly in order to escape the suffering. They create a problem and then try to sell you the "only" solution to the problem.

In reality, the serpents will never save you and the reason is simple. Salvation means that you reestablish your true identity as a son or daughter of God, as being one with God. The serpents have chosen to leave that sense of identity behind, and they identify themselves as being in opposition to God. As long as you see yourself in opposition to God, you cannot possibly obtain union with God, and therefore you cannot possibly be saved.

Please take note that the true Savior, my beloved son Jesus, always affirmed his oneness with God. He came to show all people that they have the potential to attain oneness with God, yet the serpents have perverted the original teachings of Jesus so that no one dare follow in his footsteps, lest they be accused of blasphemy by those who embody the serpentine consciousness.

So what is it that gives you the opportunity to reestablish your union with God? It is your free will and your desire to experiment. Do you see the essential point? It was your ability to experiment that led to your fall but it is this very ability that can lead you back to the Christ consciousness. And it is precisely the plot of the serpents to use every subtle lie they can think of to prevent you from using your drive to experiment to come back to union with God. They want to stop you from experimenting so that you don't even dare to attempt reestablishing your union with God.

Do you see the very simple truth I am trying to explain? Your soul is a vehicle for experiencing the world. It experiences the world through imagination and free will. And through those faculties it can add on to its sense of identity. What causes the soul to become trapped in the material world is a limited sense of identity. And that limited sense of identity is the result of an experiment with undesirable consequences. Yet the only thing that can help the soul escape the prison of the material world, the only thing that can save the soul, is to continue experimenting until you find the higher identity of the Christ mind. The soul must come back to a state of grace in which it accepts that it is worthy in the eyes of God, because it identifies itself as a son or daughter of God.

The only way to get back to that true sense of identity is that the soul must recreate its sense of identity as a Christed being; it must experiment with a higher state of consciousness. The soul must dare to look for a higher understanding of truth than what it has found in the serpentine lies that permeate the world.

My beloved hearts, Jesus gave a very profound discourse on the fact that human beings can create their own god. I must tell you that there is indeed an angry and judgmental god, as envisioned by many people on this planet. Yet it is an absolute truth that the angry god is a false god created by human beings and dark forces. The true God is a God of unconditional love. In fact, God's love is so unconditional that you have no need to even ask for his forgiveness. The moment you forsake the state of consciousness that caused you to accept an imperfect sense of identity, at that very moment you are forgiven by God.

Why the key to your freedom is to turn the other cheek

My beloved, I have given you many thoughts to ponder, and I know these are difficult concepts. I know that when a soul has been programmed for many lifetimes to accept the very subtle lies of the serpents, then the soul cannot in an instance, cannot as the result of reading one discourse, overcome those lies and leave them behind. There are those who claim to be spiritual teachers who tell people that they could change their minds in an instant, but it is not true.

A soul is a being of energy, of spiritual energy. Over many lifetimes, the soul can clothe itself in many layers of lower vibrations. And it is those layers that give the soul a mortal sense of identity. So the soul cannot simply in an instant throw off the false sense of identity because it would be left with no sense of identity. The soul must gradually replace the false sense of identity with a true sense of identity. It must, as Paul said, die daily. It must put off the old man and put on the new man. And this will take time.

However, you can greatly reduce the time it takes to build a new sense of identity by contemplating the fact that the key to true spiritual freedom is to forgive yourself, to forgive every part of life and to forgive God for anything that you think has ever been done to you, both in this lifetime and in other lifetimes, going all the way back to when your soul first descended into the material universe, and even beyond to the Garden Of Eden.

The key to freedom from your current limitations is to forgive all who played a role in creating those limitations. My beloved hearts, those who seek revenge against other people, even those who engage in a battle against dark forces, are simply reinforcing the prison walls around their souls. You might recall that the Bible says, "Vengeance is mine; I will repay, saith the Lord." The truth behind that statement is that God has created an impersonal law, the law of karma, which makes sure that no soul will ever escape the consequences of its uses and misuses of God's energy. Therefore, you do not need to become angry at those who harm you. You do not need to seek revenge because in so doing you misqualify God's energy and thereby you reinforce the prison around your own soul, your own mind.

My beloved hearts, that is why my son Jesus gave the wonderful teachings to forgive your enemies, to forgive those who harm you and to always turn the other cheek. When someone harms you and you turn the other cheek, you set yourself free from any negative influence of their actions. You avoid creating or reinforcing a negative sense of identity. You reaffirm that you are a spiritual being who is above and beyond any influence from the lower vibrations in the material world. Therefore, you will not let anything done to you in this world limit your sense of identity.

This is choosing God over mammon, and it is precisely what Jesus came to show all human beings. He came to show them that when you reunite with your Christ self and become a Christed being, the forces of this world might harm your body and do all kinds of things to you, including nailing you to a cross. But no matter what they do to you, they cannot harm your soul, they cannot harm your true identity because you will rise above it all. You will rise above all of the limitations, all of the chains, that they use to bind you. You rise above it because you realize that they are simply throwing mud at the light beam of your soul. And that mud has no power to cling to the true light that you are.

So my beloved, I give to you the tool of my Miracle Forgiveness Rosary as a way, an extremely efficient and powerful way, for you to consume the layers of negative energy and the imperfect sense of identity that surround your soul and keep you believing in the image that you are a mortal human being trapped in a prison from which there is no escape. There is indeed an escape, and it is to simply leave the imperfections behind and come up higher in consciousness.

My beloved hearts, this has been a very long discourse, and I commend those of you who have endured to the end. There is so much more to say, but your cup is full and runneth over. Therefore, I seal you now in the infinite and unconditional love of God, and I charge those who are willing with the infinite power of Forgiveness Flame, the spiritual flame of forgiveness that conquers and consumes all sin, all mistakes, all imperfections and all limitations. And therefore I say, "Be free in the infinite forgiveness of God. Follow your highest love and come up higher. Be free of the shackles of mortality and sin and accept God's forgiveness of all imperfections that your soul has encountered during its journey in the lower vibrations of the material world."

My beloved hearts, you will be free of these imperfections only when you fully accept that you are free, only when you fully forgive yourself and accept your true identity as a spiritual being who has never been touched by anything in this world.

In reality, you are who you are, namely a spiritual being. However, at the level of your soul, you are who you think you are. So stop thinking that you are an imperfect being and accept your true identity as a spiritual being. Be ye therefore perfect, even as your Father in Heaven is perfect.

Accept the kingdom of God on your planet

Mother Mary, May 29, 2004

The pattern of how religion is used to control people

I am sure you remember that my son Jesus told you that one of his main goals for coming to Earth was to bring the kingdom of God to this planet. Yet I must tell you that not even a being as powerful as Jesus can single-handedly bring God's kingdom to Earth. Even Jesus faces an obstacle that he cannot overcome. In fact, no power in Heaven can overcome this obstacle. That obstacle is your ability and willingness to accept the kingdom of God manifest in your personal life, in your society and on the planet as a whole. Let me now explain to you why this non-acceptance is an insurmountable obstacle for the powers of Heaven.

I have told you already that the Law or Free Will is an absolute law. There is no being in Heaven who is allowed to violate the free will of a human being. I am sure you can see that the dark forces, who are rebelling against God's law and God's purpose, have no such limitations. They have already turned their backs on God's law, and therefore they have absolutely no respect for the free will of human beings. They will violate and manipulate your free will for as long as you allow them to do so. They have indeed manipulated most people on Earth into a state of consciousness that makes it all but impossible for them to accept the perfection of God's kingdom manifest in their lives and on the planet.

How you co-create the Earth

In my previous discourses I have explained to you how the universe was created. I explained that there is a stream of light that flows from your I AM Presence through the levels of your subconscious mind and into your conscious mind. As it flows through the levels of your mind, this light, this energy, takes on the images that you hold in your consciousness, and those images are then projected unto the screen of life. The images you hold in your consciousness will affect your personal life, your circle of influence. Yet they will also contribute to the images that are held in the collective consciousness of humankind. And the images held in this mass mind will affect human society and even the physical planet.

My beloved hearts, I hope you can now see the simple fact that if the kingdom of God is to become manifest on Earth, a critical mass of human beings must be able to envision what the kingdom of God is like, and they must be able to accept that the kingdom of God could manifest in this world. If a majority of the people on this planet either cannot envision the kingdom of God or cannot accept that kingdom as a real possibility, then it simply is not possible to bring God's kingdom into manifestation on Earth.

If the Ascended Host attempted to bring God's kingdom anyway, we would be violating the Law of Free Will. If we were to do that, we could not remain in Heaven but would instantly descend into a lower state of consciousness. Therefore, we would join the ranks of the forces who have attempted to manipulate the free will of human beings for millennia. Some of these forces do indeed think they have the best intentions, and they believe they are seeking to manipulate people into being saved. Yet these forces do not understand the basic intent of God, namely that human beings must consciously choose to accept his kingdom before it can become a manifest reality on Earth.

Do you see the simple equation? The material universe is literally a mirror that reflects back whatever is projected upon it through the minds of self-conscious beings. Planet Earth is currently reflecting back the imperfect images that human beings have held in their minds for much longer than both orthodox Christians and orthodox scientists would be willing to accept.

What you don't know can hurt you

My beloved hearts, when you understand the existence of dark forces, and when you understand that these forces have no respect whatsoever for the free will of human beings, it should not be difficult to see that these forces have no desire whatsoever to see God's kingdom manifest on Earth. If God's kingdom became manifest tomorrow, the dark forces would no longer be able to steal the energy, the lifeblood, of the people on this Earth. They would be forced to descend into lower realms, where they might eventually run out of energy or out of time and opportunity. As I explained in a previous discourse, these forces are absolutely determined to prove that God made a mistake by giving human beings free will. They will therefore do anything possible in order to maintain the current imperfect conditions on this planet.

When you put this fact together with what I have explained above, you will see that in order to prevent God's kingdom from being manifest on Earth, the dark forces only have to do one thing. They have to prevent a critical mass of human beings from accepting that the perfection of God could become manifest on Earth. If people do not know what the kingdom of God is like, how can they possibly imagine that it could be manifest on Earth? If they cannot accept that the kingdom of God is a possibility, or if they cannot accept that they are worthy of that kingdom, how can the kingdom of God manifest on this planet? My beloved, this is indeed what the dark forces have been attempting to do for a very long time. For thousands of years, the dark forces attempted to accomplish their goals by withholding information from the people. They attempted to control the flow of information so that people simply would not be given a clear or an accurate vision of what it would be like if the kingdom of God was manifest on Earth.

One consequence of this attempt to control information is that the dark forces have sought to manipulate every religion on this planet. That is why you see so many religions follow a very specific pattern. The original founder of a true religion always has a direct connection to the Ascended Host, and through that he or she can receive at least a partial vision of the kingdom of God. After the original founder of the religion is no longer on this Earth, the direct connection to the Ascended Host is often lost. Therefore, the religion gradually becomes perverted and distorted until the original teachings have been lost or replaced by a set of false teachings. As both Jesus and I have attempted to explain many times, this is indeed what they did to the beautiful teachings that my son brought 2,000 years ago.

This also explains why the Ascended Host have brought forth many religions and why we continue to bring forth new religions or new movements within existing religions. This also explains why there is an absolute need for ongoing progressive revelation to counteract the manipulation and distortion of existing religions.

Information overload

If you think back to times past, you will see that the task of controlling information was relatively simple. The reason was that there was no technology that allowed for the preservation and the widespread dissemination of information. Just imagine how difficult it was to preserve and distribute a spiritual teaching when all books had to be copied by hand. My beloved, do you understand that Gutenberg's invention of the printing press was one of the major blows to the dark forces on this planet? It was precisely this seemingly simple invention that turned the tide on the dark forces and their control of information.

I am sure you can see that the continued growth in technology has accelerated this trend and made it even more difficulty to withhold information from people. Virtually all of the communications and information technology that has been brought forth over the past 500 years has been directly inspired upon the minds of the inventors by the Ascended Host. We have done this because we know very well that it is the truth that will make people free, and therefore we want there to be a free distribution of information, so that all people on this planet can have access to any information they need or want. I can assure you that it is only dark forces who are trying to prevent the free flow of information, and I can assure you that the religions who still attempt to limit what their members can or are allowed to know about God are doing so precisely because they are being manipulated by dark forces.

Even though modern communications technology, especially the internet, is a major blow to the dark forces on this planet, these forces are by no means giving up. They have indeed used modern technology to further their goals of preventing people from finding and accepting a higher truth. If you cannot prevent the availability of truth, what can you do to prevent people from finding it? You can do precisely what you see on the Internet and in the media today. When you can no longer withhold information, you can flood the market with so much information that people either cannot find the truth, they cannot find the needle in the haystack, or they find so much information that they are overwhelmed, they literally experience information overload and close their minds to new information.

So my beloved, even though information is now more easily available than ever, we still see the problem that the majority of the people on this planet do not have a clear vision of what the kingdom of God is like and what the Earth would be like if that kingdom was manifest. And even those who have found true spiritual teachings about the kingdom of God still find it difficult to fully accept that such a perfect kingdom could actually be manifest on Earth.

How the concept of sin is used to prevent progress

In reality, most people have at least a sketchy idea of what the kingdom of God is like. They know that in the kingdom of God there is no war, there is no famine, no poverty, no exploitation, no natural disasters and no disease. Most people realize deep within their souls that many of the activities that they see all around them, either in their personal lives or in the media, are clearly out of alignment with God's laws. Therefore, it should not be difficult for people to accept the fact that such activities simply could not take place in the kingdom of God. Such activities could not continue if the Earth was to outpicture the perfection of the kingdom. These unbalanced activities would simply have to go.

Yet one of the most insidious plots of the dark forces, the serpentine liars, is to create the impression that things are so bad on planet Earth that the perfection found in the kingdom of God could never be brought to this planet. These forces have made the many ungodly activities that take place on this planet seem almost inevitable, and as a result many people believe such activities are simply the expressions of human nature. My beloved hearts, this is the most insidious plot, and it has achieved a very strong hold over the minds of most people on this planet. The influence of this plot goes back into the mist of history and one of the main ideas used to promote this plot is the concept of sin, especially the idea of original sin.

As I explained in an earlier discourse, human beings were indeed given a safe environment in which to experiment with their creative powers. There is absolutely nothing on this planet that is not made from the energy of God. Therefore, all of the imperfect conditions that are currently appearing on this planet have no permanent reality. These conditions are created by the misqualification of the pure energy of God. They are simply mirages projected upon the screen of life through the imperfect images that people hold in their minds.

Both Jesus and myself have compared this process to a movie projector, and you know very well that the images that appear on a movie screen have no permanent reality. They will continue to appear only as long as there is a film strip in the projector. If you are watching a horror movie, you know that what you see on the screen is not real. You also know that if someone changed the film strip in the projector, the movie screen would instantly reflect the images of the new movie. Therefore, even the worst horror movie could instantly be replaced by an inspirational movie about love and courage.

So my point here is simply this. Over thousands of years, the dark forces have attempted to program all human beings on this planet to accept the permanency and the inevitability of imperfect conditions. My beloved hearts, the miracles performed by Jesus were attempts to shock people out of this belief in the inevitability of disease or other imperfections. Jesus even attempted to shock people out of the belief in the inevitability of death. Yet so few people have truly understood, internalized and accepted the magnificent example given by Jesus. And the reason is that they cannot shake off the programming of the dark forces. One of the most insidious offsprings of this programming is the idea that all people are by nature sinners and that once you have committed a certain sin, there is no turning back, there is no way to raise yourself out of sin.

A most insidious lie

My beloved hearts, will you please make an effort to see through this lie, this insidious serpentine lie that has been projected into your minds? This lie is indeed being projected into your minds by mechanical devices created by the dark forces in lower realms, and these energy guns are constantly beaming their death rays into your subconscious minds. It is almost as if you had a loudspeaker in your mind that was constantly broadcasting the message that you are a miserable sinner who can never become one with your God. My beloved hearts, this is indeed the lie that I have come to dispel. Jesus and myself have come to help you see through this lie and rise above it.

We have taken great care to explain to you that because everything is created from the energy of God and because energy is vibration, any mistake, any limitation, any imperfect condition can be erased by changing the vibration of the energy back to its original purity. Oh my beloved hearts, please, please make an effort to contemplate this in your heart and reach for the inner confirmation from your Christ self that will demonstrate to you the truth of what I am saying. Your Christ self will show you that there is indeed no imperfect condition which cannot be changed and replaced by the perfection of the kingdom of God.

There is only one thing that can prevent imperfect conditions from being changed, and that is your inability or unwillingness to accept the possibility that your current limitations could be transformed into perfect conditions. Because you have free will, you must make a conscious choice to replace the imperfect images in your mind with a higher image, the true image, of the perfection of God.

My beloved hearts, how do you think Jesus healed the sick and raised the dead? He healed because his mind was so disciplined that he did not for an instant allow it to see the diseased body. Jesus focused all of his attention on seeing only a perfect body, and because he had achieved full Christhood, his mind was so strong that the images he held in his mind would instantly be manifest in the matter world.

Both Jesus and myself have attempted to explain that all human beings are co-creators with God. You are always co-creating because there is a constant stream of energy flowing through your mind from your spiritual self. That stream of energy, like the light in the movie projector, will take on whatever images exist in your subconscious mind. So if you truly want to change your life, and if you truly want to see conditions improve on the planet as a whole, here are the three things you need to accomplish:

- You need to cleanse your mind of all imperfect images and imperfect beliefs. You need to reach for the higher vision of the Christ mind that allows you to see the perfection of the kingdom of God.

- You need to reach for the Christ consciousness, which allows you to take dominion over the Earth by taking command over the forces of your own mind. By taking this dominion, you can discipline the mind so that it no longer sees and gives power to the imperfect images but is constantly focused only on the perfect images of the kingdom of God.

- You need to remain constant in focusing on the perfect images. You need to be vigilant in not allowing the forces of this world to manipulate you into once again accepting imperfections as inevitable. Because Jesus had reached such a high degree of

Christhood, he could instantly manifest changes in the material world. When you reach that level of Christhood, when this mind is in you, which was also in Christ Jesus, you can do the works that Jesus did. Yet until then you need to be patient, because you need to realize that it will take some time to change conditions in the material world.

The alchemy of the spirit

In a previous discourse Jesus has explained that there are four levels of the material world, namely the etheric realm, the thought realm, the feeling realm and the material realm. In order to produce a change in the material realm, you need to start in the etheric realm and then allow the energies to filter through the thought and feeling realms until they reach the material realm.

To successfully manifest the kingdom of God in your personal life, you need to start by changing your sense of identity. You need to stop seeing yourself as a mortal human being, as a miserable sinner or as a person who has made such mistakes that you could never be redeemed. You need to accept that you are a son or daughter of God, that you are a co-creator and that your mind has the power to replace all imperfect images, or an imperfect sense of identity, with the higher images of the Christ mind.

Once your sense of identity begins to change, your thoughts will inevitably follow suit and begin to change also. They will become purer, and you will no longer think in terms of limitations and what cannot be done. You will not think that imperfection is permanent. You will begin to realize and fully accept the truth in the statement made by Jesus that with God all things are possible. This will change your approach to life from being focused on what cannot happen to having a can-do spirit that empowers you to see new possibilities around every corner.

As your thoughts begin to change, it is inevitable that your emotions will also take on a new direction. Your emotional body will be less influenced by negative emotions, such as fear or blame. Instead, you will feel the flow, the natural flow, of energy through your emotional body, and you will begin to feel the joy and the love that is the true driving force behind all life.

As your sense of identity, your thoughts and your feelings are purified, it is inevitable that your outer actions will change also. Yet beyond that, you will see that after a time your outer circumstances will also change. This change would have seemed impossible with your old state of consciousness, but with your new frame of mind it seems so natural and effortless.

My beloved hearts, this is the true alchemy of the spirit. It is indeed regrettable that so many people in today's world ridicule the ancient alchemists. There were many charlatans in the field, but certainly no more charlatans that you currently find in the field of science and religion. Yet there were also many true alchemists for whom changing base metals into gold was not the real goal. Their goal was the alchemy of changing the human consciousness, the lead of the carnal mind, into the gold of the Christ consciousness. The reason being that the true alchemists realized that the Christ consciousness has the power to change the composition of matter itself, as Jesus clearly demonstrated when he turned the water into wine.

The philosopher's stone so eagerly sought by the alchemists is indeed the Christ consciousness. It is the Christ consciousness that will bring God's kingdom to Earth, and only the Christ consciousness has the power to do this. Yet as both Jesus and I have explained in great detail, it is not enough that one Christed being walks the Earth. For God's kingdom to be fully physically manifest on this planet, there must be a critical mass of people who have manifested their individual Christhood. The number of Christed beings needed to fully bring in the kingdom of God is, as Jesus has already explained, 10,000. As Jesus has also explained, there are currently 10,000 people in embodiment who have the potential to manifest that Christhood very quickly.

Yet once again we face the obstacle that those people need to be awakened to their potential for Christhood, and they need to accept their Christhood. Jesus has also explained that there are millions of other people who have the potential to manifest a high degree of Christhood. If all of these people were awakened and started to accept a higher vision of God's kingdom, and started to accept the real possibility of manifesting that kingdom on Earth, then things would begin to change very quickly and very dramatically—for the better.

Choose to BE!

Mother Mary, June 1, 2004.

Abandon the false religions

If you will take time to ponder the teachings I have given you in the previous discourses, you will see that the true goal of the Ascended Host is to bring God's kingdom to Earth. You will also see that in reality God's kingdom is a state of consciousness. Therefore, for God's kingdom to be manifest on Earth, a critical mass of human beings in embodiment must change their state of consciousness and embrace a new sense of identity, a sense of identity that is not based on separation and division but on indivisible oneness with their God. My beloved hearts, this has been the goal of the Ascended Host for eons. This is the only message that has been given through all of the true religions found on this planet, and there are indeed many true religions. There is only one message behind all religion, and it is the message of oneness, the message that you are one with your God and that the sense of separation is an illusion.

I am aware that there are many people on this Earth who will not be able to understand or accept this message of oneness. They will reject it, and through the relative faculties of the carnal mind and the human intellect they will come up with innumerable clever and sophisticated arguments for doubting the message of oneness. You can find these arguments broadcast through the institutions of society, such as governments and educational institutions. You can find them broadcast through the media. And you can even find them broadcast through many religions that have departed from their original Gospel of Oneness and are now preaching a Gospel of Separation.

If you care to look at the historical record, you will see that the early followers of my son Jesus were not called Christians. They were called "Followers of the Way" because Jesus truly came to teach all people the true way to oneness with their God. When Jesus said, "I am the way, the truth, and the life: no man cometh unto the Father, but by me" (John 14:6), he was not referring to his outer person or to an outer Christian church. He was saying that the way to salvation is the way to oneness with your God, and without establishing oneness with your God, you cannot come to your Father and enter the kingdom of your God. And of course, the key to oneness with your God is the Christ consciousness that Jesus embodied and to this day represents to humankind. Therefore, to come into that oneness you do go through the Sacred Heart of Jesus.

If you will make the effort to stretch your mind and heart and ponder this message, you will see the underlying logic, the underlying truth. God created everything that was created and without him was not anything made that was made (John 1:3). You need to be saved because you have departed from your God, meaning that you have departed from oneness with your God. So how could you possibly be saved and return to your Father's kingdom, except by reclaiming your true sense of identity, your sense of oneness with your God? My beloved, there is no other way to God but to reclaim your sense of oneness with your God by allowing the Presence of Oneness to be in you.

This then is the message of oneness, the Gospel of Oneness, the religion of oneness that is the one true religion. Throughout the ages, this message and gospel has been preached through many different religions, and it is still being preached through several religions. Yet throughout the ages, we have seen the same pattern, namely that a new religion was started by a person who had dared to reclaim his or her oneness with God. Therefore, that person became the open door for preaching the Gospel of Oneness to a specific group of people.

Yet when the original founder was no longer in the material realm, the religion slowly started disintegrating, and after a period of time the Gospel of Oneness was lost. In many cases, as is certainly the case with my son Jesus, the original founder was elevated to the status of an idol and seen as the only one who could reclaim his or her oneness with God. Therefore, what started out as a true religion, preaching the Gospel of Oneness, was gradually turned into a false religion, preaching the Gospel of Separation. This then is the false gospel that has been present on this planet since Lucifer and his followers first descended to the material realm.

My beloved hearts, it is time to see through the false message and abandon the false gospel, the gospel that is often disguised as the "only true religion" yet is truly a wolf in sheep's clothing. It is time to stop following the blind leaders, the false prophets, who are posturing as true leaders but are inwardly like ravening wolves (Matthew 7:15). It is time to stop following those who are like unto whited sepulchers, which indeed appear beautiful outward, but are within full of dead men's bones (Matthew 23:27).

It is time to rise above the lies and the manipulations of the forces who have chosen to separate themselves from their God and who have become trapped in that consciousness of separation. It is time for you to stop worshiping the false gods who are clamoring for your attention by every means conceivable. It is time for you to stop playing around in the sandbox, building your elaborate castles that will crumble when the Living Waters of the Holy Spirit come to wash them away. It is time to climb the rock of Christ and anchor yourself firmly on the true way that leads to Christ consciousness, the consciousness that empowers you to see and to claim your oneness with your God, as Jesus did indeed claim that oneness.

It is time to realize that life on planet earth is currently a contest, a game, and that the prize is your soul. The prince of this world is constantly trying to tempt you, in numerous subtle and clever ways, to deny your oneness with your God. And we of the Ascended Host are constantly seeking to help you reclaim that oneness. My beloved, as long as you continue to deny your oneness with your God – no matter how important your reasoning might seem to your outer mind – the Devil holds your soul captive in the consciousness of Hell. You are worshiping a false god who is not the One God behind all appearances but is simply one of the appearances. Yet the moment you fully abandon that denial and accept your oneness with the One God, your soul will be in the consciousness of the kingdom of Heaven.

The True Community of the Holy Spirit

Jesus, July 26, 2004.

Oneness versus sameness

When you get in the consciousness of thinking that you are the doer, that you of your own self can do something and that it is up to you to combat these people that you think are doing evil, then you set yourselves up in opposition to them. And that is how you see the divisions among brothers and among nations that lead to conflicts that can't be resolved, to revenge, to anger, to terrorism, to war, and the pattern of human power plays that have plagued this planet now for as long as anyone on Earth can remember, but for far longer because we of the Ascended Host remember all that has gone before on Earth.

This is what I came, 2,000 years ago, to call people to come apart from, that consciousness of duality, that consciousness of carnality. But you see, there is only one way to achieve union and oneness on Earth. It cannot be done as a horizontal oneness, as a forced oneness. Do you not see that so many regimes and systems in this world have attempted to force people into oneness by destroying their differences, by setting up a mold for how a human being should be?

And as in the fairy tale of the princess who could not fit the glass slipper, and one cut a heal and one cut a toe to fit the slipper, and so the ideology of communism, and for that matter capitalism and many other cultures, is that you should deny your God-given individuality in order to fit within the system. This cannot be, because God has created you in his image and likeness, and he has endowed you with the unique individuality that is God's desiring, in you, to be more of himself.

And therefore when you try to suppress your individuality, it will only create tension and anger. And eventually, you will explode, as you see so many people, both in Christianity, in other religions and in the New Age Movement, who crash and burn. They suddenly become converted, they have a reawakening or a re-birthing experience, and for a while they are so enthusiastic. But because they are not balanced, they come to a point, where they crash and burn.

An acceleration in Christhood

Mother Mary, September 29, 2004

All imperfect appearances are unreal

I encourage you to study my previous discourses on the expanding and contracting forces of God. You see, as long as the Ma-ter light is unconscious, it will blindly contract and thereby break down all organized structures. This is simply the natural expression of the unconscious Ma-ter light that is designed to balance the expanding force of the Father light. The Ma-ter light naturally contracts, unless it is counterbalanced by the expanding force of the Father focused through the Christ mind.

As I explained in previous discourses, after the fall of Lucifer, the dark forces have misused the contracting force of the Mother in their attempts to control human beings and neutralize their free will through physical and spiritual slavery. This has led to the creation of a counterfeit and unnatural force on this planet, and it is a perversion of the Mother. This force actually breaks down organized structures faster and with greater intensity than mandated in the mechanical laws of God. In other words, there is a gravitational force, a magnetic force of darkness, that is currently stronger than the contracting force of the Mother as designed by God.

Because most people fail to understand the existence of this counterfeit force, and because they do not realize that by falling into a lower state of consciousness they have actually contributed to the strength of this force, many of them have come to resent the Earth Mother and the resistance they feel to their creative efforts. This has generated a worldwide force of hatred of the mother, and among many expressions are the hatred of women and the belief that man has to subdue and control the natural environment instead of working with it.

The forces of darkness that work on this planet are seeking to gain absolute control over human beings, and they can do this only by controlling the minds, especially the power of vision, of human beings. They seek to do this by causing people to worship a false image of God and by causing them to accept false images of what this planet should be like. They then cause people to accept that these graven images are real and permanent. That is why you see so many people on this planet who accept certain limitations for how life can or should be, and they think life could not possibly be any other way than what they have been brought up to think is real and permanent. It is precisely this mass illusion that has formed a veil of energy [energy veil = evil] that separates human beings from their true God and from their spiritual teachers of the Ascended Host.

Therefore, an essential part of taking back planet Earth and raising it to its original purity is that you must consciously free your mind from the false visions, the false God and the graven images, that have been programmed into your minds since birth, and indeed for many lifetimes. You must make an effort to clear the faculty of your vision, and you must do this by understanding that all of the appearances currently found on Earth, all of the imperfections and imbalances, are nothing more than images projected unto the screen of life. The movie screen itself is made of the unconscious Ma-ter light that takes on any form projected upon it through a conscious mind. The light that drives the film projector is your attention, and the film strip is the images you hold in your conscious and subconscious minds. Therefore, when you change the images held in your mind, and look beyond all imperfect manifestations and appearances, you will change the images projected upon the screen of the unconscious Ma-ter light.

When a critical mass of human beings take back the power of their vision, you will see such dramatic changes for the better on this planet that most of you simply could not envision or accept them today. If I were to tell you what can happen within a matter of decades, you would refuse to believe me, and you would call me a hopeless idealist and a utopian. Yet I am not trapped inside the energy veil of imperfect images and beliefs. I know the reality of God, and I know the reality that the unconscious Ma-ter light will simply take upon itself any appearance superimposed upon it through the minds of human beings.

There is only one way to change the world, and that is to change the way human beings look at themselves and the world. However, for that to happen, we must also change the way human beings look at God and their relationship to God.

Take back the power of vision

I therefore encourage you to consciously use your power of vision to see that behind all imperfect appearances is the Ma-ter light. You might envision this light as tiny particles or strings that vibrate at very high speed. This is like the subatomic particles or the superstrings that your scientists are currently using to describe the process whereby the unconscious Ma-ter light takes on visible form.

So when you are confronted with an imperfect appearance, whether in your own life, in your physical body, in your society or on the planet as a whole, I encourage you to make a firm decision that you do not accept it as permanent or real. You make a conscious effort to see it as a temporary projection upon the screen of life, and then you see beyond it to the white screen itself, namely the vibrating particles of the Ma-ter light. You then use your attention to see beyond the outer appearance and to see the perfect vision of Christ instead of the outer appearance.

Do you understand what I am saying here? You are alive because you are constantly receiving a stream of spiritual light that flows from your I AM Presence through your soul and is directed by the power of your attention. Whatever you focus your attention upon, you will magnify through the power of the light within you. So if you focus your attention on an imperfect appearance, especially if you accept it as real and permanent, you will actually reinforce that condition.

I encourage you to consciously take back the power of your attention and vision. When you are confronted with an imperfect appearance, I am not asking you to ignore it or even to deny it. I am asking you to acknowledge that it does exist, but you also acknowledge that it is not ultimately real and it is not permanent. Therefore, you do not accept it as permanent, and instead you look beyond it and see the vibrating Ma-ter light behind the outer appearance. You then fix your attention upon a more perfect vision, the most perfect vision you can imagine, and you affirm that vision as real and permanent.

What is the perfect vision of Christ? Because so many of you have been brought up with imperfect images, I encourage you to ask your Christ self to hold the perfect vision for a particular situation or condition. For many of you it is currently impossible to imagine the perfect vision of Christ in some of the situations you encounter on a daily basis. Yet your Christ self can hold that vision for you, if you will but ask. And if you keep asking with an open mind, your Christ self will gradually lower that perfect vision into your conscious mind.

I am asking you to be wise as a serpent and acknowledge that there are currently many imperfect appearances on planet Earth. Yet I am also asking you to be harmless as a dove by consciously acknowledging that they are not real or permanent. You therefore see beyond them and allow the light of God to stream through your attention and superimpose the perfect vision of Christ upon the imperfect condition.

Do you see that this is how Jesus healed the withered hand and performed his other so-called miracles? When people saw the man with the withered hand, they immediately accepted the condition as real and they thought it was permanent. Jesus did not accept this illusion. He saw beyond the outer appearance and focused his attention of the vibrating particles of the Ma-ter light. He then fixed his inner sight on the vision of a perfect hand, and he consciously, and with the full power of his Christ mind, superimposed that vision upon the particles of the Ma-ter light. He took dominion over these Ma-ter particles and commanded them to outpicture his vision. By letting the light of the Father stream through his mind, Jesus changed the vibration of the Ma-ter particles, and they now immediately outpictured the perfect vision held in the mind of the embodied Christ.

If you believe on Jesus, you shall indeed do the works that he did. Yet if you believe on the prince of this world and his lie that imperfect appearances are real or permanent, then the prince will have something in you that will prevent you from being the open door for the light of God to stream through your mind and spiritualize your life and world.

So I encourage you to see your life as a game in which you are constantly confronted with imperfect appearances and tempted by the prince of this world to accept them as real or permanent. And instead of falling for the temptation, you can attune to your Christ self and ask him to give you the perfect vision of Christ to replace the imperfect appearance. Then hold on to that vision – be faithful over a few things – and see how your life and your world will change.

I know that some will think this is a fruitless exercise, and you may use all manner of science to ridicule my suggestion. Yet I can tell you that the imperfect appearances you see all around you were created by the very same process. It was the energy streaming through the souls of human beings, misqualified by the imperfect images held in their minds, that created the imperfections you see on this planet today.

The true and the false path to salvation

There are two ways to remove the imperfections on planet Earth. One is to allow them to intensify until the imbalance becomes so great that the contracting force of the Mother, that has now become an unnatural force, breaks down all structures and even causes the physical planet itself to implode. This is the process of a "guaranteed salvation" started and reinforced by Lucifer and all of the dark forces who are seeking to destroy this planet in their prideful attempt to prove that God was wrong by giving human beings free will. If you want to align yourself with them, then keep reaffirming that the current imperfections are real and permanent.

Yet if you want to reverse the process of self-implosion and turn it into a process of self-transcendence, then follow my suggestion and use the power of your vision to affirm that the kingdom of God is manifest on Earth. Walk the path of personal Christhood, until you are person-ally transfigured and become the son or daughter of God on earth that you have the potential to be. Then radiate God's light, until the entire planet is transfigured and the kingdom of God is superimposed upon the unconscious matter substance. The Ma-ter light will then become self-aware and consciously and lovingly materialize the kingdom of God on Earth.

I can assure you that the Ma-ter light has no greater joy than to outpicture the kingdom of God, and it has no desire to remain trapped in the imperfect temporary appearances you see on Earth. The Ma-ter light has no greater joy than to obediently follow the perfect vision of God. It is through this process of conscious and loving obedience that the Ma-ter light can grow in self-awareness and become spiritualized, so that the entire material universe becomes a permanent sphere in the body of God.

Yet for the Ma-ter light to consciously outpicture the perfection of God, it must be awakened, it must be spiritualized. And this can happen only when the Ma-ter light is infused with the spiritual light from the Presence of Infinite Light. That spiritual light can enter this universe only through a self-conscious being who has become awakened to his or her Christ potential. Therefore, one might say that matter is simply waiting for you to set it free from all imperfect images and awaken it to its inherent divinity.

The year of willpower

Mother Mary, December 31, 2004

Why the American government has not learned its lesson in Iraq

As a note of caution, may I draw your attention to the situation in Iraq and the upcoming elections. Let me please convey to you that the key to resolving this situation without an escalation of bloodshed that leads to civil war is truly not found in Iraq but is found in Washington DC, in the White House, the Congress and the Pentagon.

As my beloved Jesus has explained, the American government and military have created a force, and the universe has generated a counter-force, which you see manifest as the insurgency in Iraq. And when you sow the wind, you will reap the whirlwind by being opposed by people who are more prone to violence than yourself. Thus, you might note that while the rest of the world was moved to compassion by the tsunami disaster, the insurgents in Iraq continued their bloodshed as if nothing of importance had happened. So the American government, by pursuing a selfish political agenda in Iraq, is now faced with opposition from people who are far more selfish. These insurgents are indeed consumed by their self-hatred, projected unto the outer enemy.

The American government has so far taken the completely wrong approach to this crisis. They are so trapped in the same consciousness that caused them to go to war in Iraq that they cannot see that the more they push to destroy the insurgency with violence, the more the universe will push back in an attempt to awaken them to the folly of their ways, so that they can learn their lessons.

As we recently said, humankind must be awakened before the year 2012, and if they cannot be awakened through spiritual understanding, they will be awakened by an increase in the intensity of man-made and natural disasters. Likewise, for there to be a peaceful resolution to the situation in Iraq, the American government and military must be awakened to the folly of their ways. And if they cannot be awakened through spiritual understanding, they must be awakened through greater resistance to their policies.

I can assure you that the killing you have seen in these last months, the senseless killing, will continue to escalate until the American government and military finally learn their lesson. You might note that the American government has been very generous in giving aid to the victims of the recent disaster in Asia. Yet you might compare the amount of aid given by the Bush administration to the amount of money spent on the war in Iraq. And this will give you an idea of the priorities of these people and the fact that furthering their worldwide political agenda is far more important to them than serving God within all people.

My beloved Jesus said that he who would be greatest among you should be the servant of all. So far the leaders of the American government have completely refused to learn that lesson. They have enveloped themselves in the illusion that they are serving the cause of freedom and democracy by furthering their political agenda and forcing democracy and freedom upon people who are not ready for it.

Yet I can assure you that they have not learned the lesson of humility and of servant leadership. And therefore, America currently does not live up to its potential to be the greatest nation on Earth. It is indeed sad to see people who use the religion that claims the name of my son to justify such actions. It is indeed sad to see some Christian leaders in the United States who backed this war before it started and who continue to back it out of pride, because they will not admit that they were wrong. It is sad to see an administration who will not admit their mistakes, and who will not admit that every single reason they gave for going to war has been proven to be invalid or flawed.

How shall this nation learn its lesson, when the leaders in both church and state cling to their pride and out of unwillingness to lose face, will not admit their mistakes, learn from them and take this nation in the direction of national Christhood that will make it the greatest nation on Earth? So we now see that in the year 2005 there is a great need that the people in both Mother Russia and in America are awakened to their responsibility to put their leaders in their rightful places as the servants of the people, instead of the servants of the agenda of the power elite who are seeking to control the spiritual people on this planet, turning them into slaves of their agenda of darkness.

Chapter 4:
Teachings about fallen angels, 2005

Help me consume the conflict in the Middle East

Mother Mary, January, 23, 2005

Understanding why the Middle East is such a focus for conflict

How can it be that this particular region of the Earth has been the source of so much conflict? How can it be that this particular region has been allowed by God to play such an important role in terms of having control over so much of the world's oil reserves? How could God allow this to happen?

Well, as always, God did not allow it to happen. Humankind has allowed it to happen because despite the fact that three major religions have been started in that region, the vast majority of the inhabitants of that region have refused to embody the true inner teachings of any of these religions. Truly, any person who embodies the mystical teachings of Islam, the mystical teachings of Judaism or the mystical teachings of Christianity will not be cattle for the fodder of those who want nothing but bloodshed and warfare. Truly, such a person would refuse to participate in these ceaseless conflicts and quests for revenge, fueled by the insane belief that human beings must meter out justice because God is not doing so. Or the belief that God has commanded human being to administer justice by killing their fellow humans.

So because of the widespread refusal to embody either of these three religions, we now have a situation in the Middle East, where a group of souls, who are almost completely dedicated to warfare and revenge, can control a large part of the world's oil reserves and can thereby intimidate the rest of the world. We might say that the general population in the area have refused the means given to them by God to raise themselves above the warring in their own members, and because of this refusal they have fallen prey to the warmongers in their midst. You see my beloved, when you do not defeat the enemy within, you become easy prey for the enemy without.

Laggard souls

We might call these souls the laggard souls because they came to Earth after the fall of man, and they came because they had been engaged in warfare on other planets. And ever since they came, they have continued this ceaseless and – seen with the eyes of mature souls – groundless warfare. And this is what you see in the Middle East today, namely those, even some in leadership positions, who talk about peace, but they never talk honestly about peace. They only talk about peace on their terms and they simply pay lip service to world opinion as a means to get their way. These souls are so consumed by their pride, that getting their way is more important to them than anything else. Thus, they are ready to kill their own people, even die themselves and blow up the planet upon which they live, in order to get their way. And in this they truly stand apart from most of the people on this Earth.

Precisely because these souls refuse to let go of their pride, their egos and their never-ending demands for human justice and revenge, they are today lagging far behind the spiritual development of humankind in general. And thus it is indeed time to call forth the judgment of Heaven upon such laggard souls and the dark spirits that support and imprison them. It is high time for these souls to be removed from the Earth and taken to other systems of worlds, where they might be given another opportunity to grow, or where they can self-destruct without pulling down so many of the good souls that are currently embodied on Earth.

Yet for these souls to be taken, a critical mass of people must come apart from the laggard souls and their laggard philosophy of revenge and of the necessity to wash clean the sins of the past through the spilling of human blood. And despite the fact that these laggard leaders have shown their colors any number of times, the world has yet to rise up and denounce them and their philosophy. In fact, the world keeps tiptoeing around these Middle Eastern leaders, refusing to call out as the little child, "But the emperor has got nothing on!" And likewise the world has yet to make itself independent of the oil reserves controlled by these people.

You will see clearly that the world was warned in 1973, when these laggard souls brought the world to the brink of nuclear war and then plunged the world into an economic crisis. Yet since then the rich nations have forgotten the warning, and they have done very little to remove themselves from the dependency upon Middle Eastern oil. Yet this has happened because both the leaders and the populations of Western countries have allowed themselves to be fooled by a small number of multinational companies that are also controlled by such laggard souls. And thus you once again have a situation where oil can become the trigger for starting another large-scale war.

Thus, the karmic return of people's neglect has been building a tension, and this is allowed according to the Law of Karma. Such tension must be allowed to rise until it can no longer be ignored and finally wakes up the people. Will the rest of the world allow these souls in the Middle East to continue their warfare and their conflict? Will they allow those in the Middle East who claim to be working for peace, to go on committing their atrocities without challenging them?

Will the world allow itself to remain dependent upon Middle Eastern oil when surely the Ascended Host have already released new technology and new knowledge that could make the world independent on Middle Eastern oil or any kind of oil by replacing oil as a fuel?

New technology for energy independence

Yes, this new technology exists but it has been hidden by both private organizations and certain governments and thereby withheld from the people. And this has been done because those in big business will not release their monopoly and control over the energy sector. And thus we see again that the people in the West have not stood up to their leaders. They have allowed themselves to be herded as cattle into the fold, where they are forced to consume oil to heat their houses or drive their cars or run their societies, so that they are being controlled by their governments through the threat of skyrocketing oil prices or a cutoff in the oil supply.

This then becomes the collective karma of a people who ignore their responsibility to know what is going on in their countries and who ignore their duty to demand accountability of their leaders. There should be a widespread outcry in the West, demanding that all appropriate technologies immediately be released, even to the point of boycotting certain companies that are possessing such technology or the patents. There should be the peaceful overthrow of governments who will not allow technology to be released or used, because they have been bought or pressured by monopolistic companies that want to create artificial scarcities to drive up their profits.

This technology is truly the property of no human individual, organization or government. It is given by the Ascended Host for the express purpose of removing the dependency upon oil or other fossil fuels. This is a gift from the Ascended Host that is meant to take the world to an entirely new level, where the growth of society will not be limited by these big monopolies controlling the fossil fuel reserves.

Through the release of this new technology, it will be possible for the world to eradicate poverty and starvation on the entire planet. This then will be a new era that is truly meant to have as great an impact on the world as the industrial revolution had upon the Western world. It is meant to eradicate poverty and starvation, so that all of the children of the world can grow up in a society, where they have enough to eat and where they have economic opportunity to improve their lives according to their willingness to make an effort to improve themselves.

This then will be a technological revolution that will grow into an economic and social revolution that will overthrow the untenable situation that a small group of nations are extremely rich and waste incredible resources, while a large group of nations are living in abject poverty, where the people can barely feed their children.

Truly, the Western industrialized nations have become like the noble class of the Middle Ages, who are consuming and controlling the vast majority of the planet's resources. And truly, the Western nations are as blinded by their own power as were the noble class. Thus, they refuse to see or honor the call to be their brother's keepers. And as happened with the noble class, this power will blind them until the counterforce they have created reaches the critical mass and overthrows their power, as surely as happened to the feudal lords of medieval Europe.

This is inevitable, but it can be accelerated greatly by a few people making enlightened calls. Yet it is not the time to make the calls for energy independence, and thus this will be the subject of a future rosary. However, I desired to give you a vision of the coming changes, so that you can have this vision in mind as you call for the removal of those laggard souls who create conflict upon conflict in the Middle East and elsewhere—and who do this by playing on the world's dependency on fossil fuels.

It is time you realize that every aspect of human society is being manipulated by a small power elite of laggard souls, as explained by Jesus [See the following discourse.] And although these souls parade themselves as the high and the mighty, they are truly underdeveloped in a spiritual sense. And thus they are no match for the spiritually mature souls—as long as those souls are enlightened and willing to unleash the power of God within them. So I ask you to take a stand against the laggard souls and their lies, and as a tool for doing so, I give you a new rosary [The Rosary for Consuming Conflict].

Understanding the dynamic between the creative elite, the power elite and the general population

Jesus, 2005

All nations go through a process of moving from a dictatorial form of government to greater freedom and democracy. Along the way, there will be tensions in society, and they can manifest in a variety of ways, but there is always a tension between an elite – that is often divided into factions – and the general population.

If you take a look at Europe, you will see that during the Middle Ages, most nations were monarchies. Almost every aspect of a nation was controlled by a small elite who had total control over the general population. Yet there was often a small part of the population who was able to bring forth new ideas. The ruling elite always resisted any change that could threaten their power, but eventually they were not able to maintain total control and they had to give the people greater freedom.

This process of moving away from a society controlled by a power elite and moving toward a society with greater freedom and equal opportunity for all is inevitable. It is a product of the fact that humankind is progressing toward a higher state of consciousness. Yet the process does not happen with equal speed in all nations. And even in Western democracies, the process can be temporarily slowed down or reversed when an elite attains power behind the scenes.

The speed with which this transition occurs depends more than anything on the consciousness of the people. To fully understand this process, it is necessary to consider that people have different levels of consciousness. To simplify things, let us divide the population of a country into three categories depending on their level of spiritual awareness and Christ consciousness:

- The people who are the lowest 10 percent in terms of Christ consciousness make up the power elite. I know this will be difficult to believe for many people, because this actually includes many of the people who are the leaders of society, in politics, business, the media and entertainment. These people might seem to be very intelligent, powerful and sophisticated, but I am not here talking about worldly abilities and appearances. I am talking about Christ consciousness. And the bottom line for measuring Christ consciousness when it comes to leadership is described in my statement: "And whosoever of you will be the chiefest, shall be servant of all. (Mark 10:44)" This describes how a person with Christ consciousness acts in a leadership position. This person is not out to get power, money or fame because the person has transcended the desire for personal gain. So the person seeks a leadership position with the pure motive of serving the people. My point being that most leaders are not truly selfless, and this demonstrates that they belong to the ten percent of the population with the lowest level of Christ consciousness.

- Next we have the top ten percent of the population, and they form what we might call the creative elite—although they ideally should not see themselves as an elite but as part of the population. These are the people who have some awareness of what is going on. They have some degree of creativity that allows them to be the open door for new ideas, and they have some degree of courage to fight for higher principles. Yet they often have no desire for power, so they are easily pushed out of decision-making positions by the lowest ten percent who have an insatiable desire for power.

• The third group are the 80 percent that make up the general population. Although they have various levels of awareness, they all fall into the category of being followers. They do not have a sufficient level of Christ consciousness to be true leaders, and they do not have a sufficient level of anti-christ consciousness to belong to the power elite. Consequently, they have no desire to lead and they want someone else to lead so they can focus on their daily lives.

What determines the fate of a nation

The fate of a nation depends largely on whether the general population follow the power elite or the creative elite. Now, one might think that the power elite has an unfair advantage in that they are good at getting power and they are ruthless in terms of crushing opposition to their control. In a sense this is true, and it explains why so many nations have taken a long time to establish true freedom and democracy. In fact, it explains why no nations have truly established a free and democratic society that is not dominated by a power elite.

Nevertheless, the reality of the situation is that the people who are truly deciding the fate of a nation are the top ten percent, the creative elite. If these people do not have a sufficient level of Christ consciousness to pull the population up, the population will either follow the power elite or they will be so controlled by the power elite that they cannot challenge the power and control of this elite.

Yet if the top ten percent have a sufficient level of Christ consciousness, they can pull the population up. And when the population rises above a certain level of awareness, the control of the power elite begins to slip. The more the consciousness of the people rises, the more the power elite will lose their stranglehold on the nation. The reason being that the power elite can maintain their control only by keeping the population ignorant. So when the population's awareness is raised, the power elite can no longer hide, and thus they must give up some of their power.

Yet the population simply cannot be the driving force behind positive change. They can only follow the strongest current in the nation's consciousness. So it really is up to the creative elite to manifest a high enough degree of Christ consciousness to awaken the population to the need for change, the awareness of how change can come about, the acceptance that change is possible and the determination to take a stand for change.

Take note that it doesn't take the entire top ten percent to bring about change. Even one person who attains Christ consciousness can shift the equation of consciousness for an entire nation. In some cases a Christed person becomes the catalyst for change without ever being known to the public. This is the case for many spiritual people who can hold the balance for a nation behind the scenes.

In some cases a number of people have reached a high enough degree of Christ consciousness to be the catalysts for change. One example is the American revolution in which a group of people had some degree of Christ consciousness. Out of such a group often emerges one person who becomes the focal point for national change, such as George Washington, who is today an ascended master.

I am not hereby saying that the American revolutionaries were perfect people or had full Christ consciousness. If they had had a higher degree of Christ consciousness, the revolution could have happened without bloodshed, although it would have taken longer to achieve independence. I am saying that there was enough Christ consciousness to bring the first democratic nation into existence, which was a major victory over the forces seeking to suppress the population. The fact that the birth of the American nation involved bloodshed shows that neither the creative elite nor the population had a high enough level of consciousness to achieve progress without violence. In several European nations, the transition to democracy did happen without violence and this can indeed happen in many other nations today. Yet this can only happen when the consciousness is raised above a certain level.

How to change the equation in a nation

So what can be done to change the equation in a nation? Well, besides striving for Christ consciousness, it can be helpful to be aware of the spiritual poisons that Mother Mary describes in a previous discourse. The basic poison is ignorance, and although this poison affects all people, it has the greatest effect on the general population. Many people are simply so overwhelmed by the poison of ignorance that they cannot lift their awareness to find out what is really going on behind the scenes. Many of them don't want to know because they don't want the responsibility that comes with knowledge. Yet the extreme effect of the poison of ignorance is an unwillingness to know the truth.

Members of the power elite often have a sophisticated knowledge of the material world but they are ignorant about the spiritual world. Yet they are primarily controlled by the four poisons that are derivatives of ignorance, namely anger, pride, greed and envy. These people are often angry at God and seek to spread this anger to the people. They take great pride in their skills and position in the earthly hierarchy, and their pride prevents them from changing their ways or admitting they have made a mistake. They simply will not see that they are being hypocritical in claiming to work for good causes while suppressing and exploiting the population. Their greed gives them an all-consuming drive to gain money and power, and their envy often splits them into rivaling factions.

For example, before the French revolution, a small power elite controlled society through the monarchy and the Church. Yet this elite was too small to include all those who were in the lowest ten percent of the population. So a rival faction formed, and it was made up of people who were lusting after the power held by the king and aristocracy, a power they could not get because it was inherited. They then formed the revolutionaries who overthrew the king and the aristocracy.

Take note that although these people claimed to be fighting for the freedom and equality of the people, many of them were driven by a quest for power. They did not want to free the people; they simply wanted to steal power from the king. The proof is the grizzly bloodbath of the Guillotine that would never have been perpetrated by the creative elite. These people set themselves up as a privileged elite by using the government, at the same time as they claimed to be working for the people. This pattern can be seen in many other nations, such as the Bolshevik revolution in Russia that created a totalitarian regime far more abusive than the Tzar.

The final poison is non-will and non-being. Again, it affects everyone, but it has the greatest effect on the top ten percent. These are the people who have acquired some level of Christ consciousness, so they have the potential to be the catalysts for bringing positive change. Yet to bring that change, they need to avoid the trap of pride that makes them feel better than the population. And they have to be willing to step into the limelight, which will expose them to attack by the power elite.

This is the story you see outpictured in my life. You will notice that at the wedding in Cana I hesitated to turn the water into wine, even to the point that my mother had to remind me that I could no longer procrastinate my mission. What I was dealing with at that moment was the poison of non-will that prevents so many people from actually expressing their Christhood.

So one might say that the fate of a nation depends on whether the top ten percent will summon the awareness, determination and courage to overcome the poison of non-will and non-being. Will the creative elite dare to step into the limelight and challenge the power elite? Will they dare to give the population an example of true leadership, so the people have someone to follow and are not tricked into a lynch-mob consciousness, where they blindly scream "Crucify him, crucify him!" and reject the living Christ in favor of a murderer from the power elite.

The power elite controlled by dark forces

On top of the poisons, you also have the influence of dark forces who can use the poisons to take over people's minds. These forces often have complete control over the power elite, and they use them as their henchmen to subdue the population. Once the majority of the people are pacified or controlled, the dark forces can easily milk them of their energy, almost as you milk cows. Once the dark forces control the lowest 90 percent of a population, you cannot expect positive change to come from these people. The reason being that these people are now getting what their carnal mind's want. The power elite are getting position, fame, privilege, money and power. And the people are getting a somewhat secure and comfortable life, especially in the industrialized nations. So the only way change can come about is if the top ten percent refuse to be controlled through the poisons of pride and non-will, and thereby are able to see through the serpentine lies that seem to solidify status quo.

How can you begin to produce a noticeable change? You can make the greatest possible effort to manifest your own Christhood, because this will not only raise the entire top ten percent but also the population. You can also seek to consume the poisons that keep the people in ignorance or imprisoned by anger, pride, greed or envy. And finally you can educate the people as much as possible.

For those open to the teachings in this book, I strongly recommend seeking your Christhood first. There is an essential truth in my statement: "But seek ye first the kingdom of God, and his righteousness; and all these things shall be added unto you." (Matthew 6:33)

The kingdom of God is the Christ consciousness. As one of the means to attain Christhood and consume the poisons and dark forces burdening your nation, use Archangel Michaels Rosary to bind the dark forces and the power elite. Then use Mother Mary's rosaries to consume the spiritual poisons burdening the people. As you begin to manifest your Christhood and lift the heavy cloud of poisons that are weighing down your nation, you will get a clear vision of what else you can do. Yet you will also make it easier for other people from the creative elite to receive new ideas and new courage. [For teaching son how to manifest Christhood, see the book Master Keys to Personal Christhood.]

Obviously, I am not saying that using the spiritual tools is all that you can or should do. The spiritual tools only provide the driving force behind change, but people must still take action to manifest that change. They must take a stand for truth. Nevertheless, take note that the deciding factor in any nation is the level of Christ consciousness manifested by the top ten percent and by the general population. So the first step toward positive change is to raise the consciousness of the people. If the consciousness is not raised, there will not be real change. Instead, you will see fighting between rivaling groups of the power elite. This can never improve the lot of the people, and in many cases it makes things worse.

My point being that when a nation seems stuck in a conflict or has problems that seem impossible to solve, the underlying cause is that the creative elite has not manifested a high enough degree of Christ consciousness. The only thing that can break the stalemate is that someone must manifest a higher degree of Christ consciousness. Even one person can make a tremendous difference and a group of determined people can turn around an entire nation. So if you want to improve a kingdom on Earth, begin by reaching for the kingdom of heaven. Yet don't forget that the kingdom of God is not above you but within you.

Will you accept or reject my love?

Mother Mary, March 12, 2005

No need to blame women for the fall

Oh how that Mother Flame has been put down over the centuries, and even the millennia. What a curse has been put on the Mother of God and the feminine aspect of every soul. What a curse has been put on women, blaming them for the Fall Of Man. My beloved, it was called the "Fall Of Man," not the "Fall of Woman," because it was the fall of the feminine aspect of every soul—both men and women.

All chose, all chose to adapt to the ways of the world. All chose to accept the temptations of those who had already separated themselves from God and who desired to pull others with them. These tempters wanted to steal people's love, their light, that they could no longer receive from Above because they were not willing to receive it in love.

There is no reason to blame women; there is no reason to blame anyone. God does not want to blame any human soul because blame is a fear-based emotion, and fear breeds fear and it traps you in a downward spiral, whereby you become more and more separated from your spiritual self, from who you really are. God has no desire to see you separate yourself from who you are, from your highest potential. God desires every human being to be all that they are, all that he created them to be, and even to be more, because he gave them free will.

When you use your free will in love, you will grow and become more than God created you to be. And thereby God becomes more through you, and the entire creation is magnified. This is true love; not human love that is conditional and shuts off the flow of love. Human love wants to own and gather to itself. And once it has gathered what it thinks is enough, it wants to keep it by controlling it. And so when you love another person in a human way, you are afraid you could lose them. So you want to control them and bind them to you.

Life is pure joy

Presence of Wisdom, March 27, 2005.

This is another aspect of wisdom that the human mind finds it difficult to understand. You see, the Creator of this universe is not the ultimate God, the ultimate Presence of God. There is a level beyond your Creator. And that level has set down certain rules and laws for how creators can create universes. And one of the cardinal rules for all creation is that anything that is created must be alive. And in order for it to be alive, it must continually transcend itself and grow and expand, because that is the definition of life. Self-transcendence is the definition of life.

And therefore, when the Lord Christ talked about those who were dead, he talked about those who were not transcending themselves any more, because they had stepped outside of the flow of the Presence of Wisdom, the flow of the principle, the creative principle itself. And they had set themselves apart, and therefore they had died to that principle.

The serpentine logic

And thus, when the serpent tempted Eve and said, "Thou shalt not surely die if you disobey the rules of God, the will of God," then he was right in the sense that the soul does not instantly die but it does die spiritually, when it is no longer transcending itself and continually coming up higher and expanding. And thus, wisdom is that which is in alignment with the creative intent and with the laws of your particular Creator, so that you are continually growing, you are continually becoming more of who you are, more than you were created to be. And in that becoming more, you find the joy, the love, the freedom, the enthusiasm that simply keeps you going and going, never stopping. And you are continually experiencing more and more joy, more and more love, more and more perfection. And it becomes a self-reinforcing spiral that takes you up, up, up and up—almost indefinitely.

Laugh at the devil—and yourself!

El Morya, March 28, 2005.

Don't take the devil seriously

And for all of the prayer work and all of the serious work that can be done – and indeed it must be done and we commend you for putting forth the effort – I can tell you that in a few minutes of laughter of coming together, you can transmute so much that it would literally take hours and hours of prayers or decrees or rosaries to obtain that same effect. Because it was said, by Thomas More, who was one of my previous lifetimes, "The devil, the proud spirit, cannot endure to be mocked."

And so true it is. The devil takes himself so seriously. He believes he is the most important being in the universe, and everybody should take him seriously. So, when someone shows that they are not willing to take the devil seriously and they are not willing to go into the doom and gloom consciousness, thinking that the Earth is going to hell in a hand basket, then they show the ultimate disrespect for the devil by simply laughing at him and his illusions that he is trying to put upon you. And so the devil will withdraw, and if you keep laughing all the way to the bank, he will withdraw from this planet.

...

And it is easy to say, "Well, what does it matter in the world? The world is so big. The world's problems are so serious that they seem insurmountable." But truly, that feeling, that the world is such a serious place, is all an illusion created by the devil himself and all those who support him. And once in awhile it is very healthy to have a good laugh at the devil's expense, and to refuse to be pulled into the net of seriousness that hangs as a black cloud over this planet.

Truly, life is joy. Life is the flowing joy that always finds a way around every obstacle. And if there is no way around the obstacle, it goes through it and dissolves the obstacle in the process.

Transcend time and space!

Mother Mary, May 2, 2005

The illusion of time and space

You see, in order to inherit the kingdom of Heaven, you have to transcend the illusion that you are separated from the kingdom, and that illusion is based on the two coordinates that human beings call time and space. The illusion that if you are here, you cannot be everywhere and that if you are in this particular moment, you cannot be in the eternal now. This is the illusion created by the consciousness of separation from the source of all life. This is the illusion created by Lucifer and all those who followed him. It is the illusion they have done everything in their power to force upon the people of Earth, and they will do everything in their power to prevent you from escaping that illusion.

But my beloved hearts, they will not be able to maintain the stranglehold which that illusion has had over the minds of humankind. Because the chains have already been broken. And as more and more people, yourselves included, shatter the illusion and throw off the shackles that you are limited by time and space, that time and space separates you from God's kingdom and prevents you from inheriting that kingdom, well then, the trail in the collective consciousness will be expanded and more and more people will be able to discover and follow it.

And thus, we who are above time and space have created a plan to help those of you who still think you are trapped in time and space to transcend that final illusion, which is truly the illusion of death. Not so much the illusion that death is the end, but the illusion that eternal life and the kingdom of God does not begin until after death, until after you exit this world.

And so my beloved, the illusion that we have come to shatter is the illusion that you cannot inherit your Father's kingdom while you are in a physical body on planet Earth. The illusion that although it is the Father's good pleasure to give you the kingdom, you cannot have that kingdom on Earth because Earth cannot express the perfection of God. Oh, what a lie this is. What a lie it is. What a ridiculous lie it is. And one day you will truly see how ridiculous it is and you will laugh with me. You will laugh at the devil until he runs away and gives up planet Earth, seeking some other place to play his tricks on those of weaker minds.

...

Why the power elite want to uphold the illusion of lack

And so my beloved, you need to reach deeper than the outer desires, the false desires, programmed into your mind by a consumer culture that makes you think that you are incomplete unless you have this or that trinket that they offer you for a price. And what is behind this culture? It is the very consciousness of anti-christ, which makes you think that you are incomplete in and of yourself, that you need something from somewhere outside of yourself in order to be complete. And thus, the kingdom of God is outside of you, and you must go through some door outside yourself to enter that kingdom. This is the entire strategy of the prince of this world; to make you believe that the kingdom of God is outside of you, and that you must go through a door, through this or that religion, through this or that belief system or through this or that pleasure or possession. My beloved, can you not see that his scheme is set up for only one purpose, namely to control you!

In making you believe in this lie, you automatically come to believe in the lie of lack, that there is not enough of God's abundance in this world for everyone. And thus, some people are the haves and some are the have-nots. And the difference is that the haves have been willing to take it by force, to control it, to hold on to it, to hoard it, whatever they want to possess. They have taken their reward here on Earth instead of laying up treasures in Heaven. And in thinking that you need to possess one aspect, one thing, then you set yourself apart from the flow of God's abundance that flows as a giant river through all of God's creation.

And yet, because of free will, that river has been diverted so that it currently by-passes planet Earth and so many people live in lack, suffering and poverty. And this is not the will of the Father, for it is his pleasure to give all of his children his kingdom. Yet you have the free will to reject that kingdom, if you so choose. And many souls on Earth have done that because they have somehow come to accept the illusion that they want or need to experience lack, that they are not worthy to have the fullness of God's kingdom or that it is not possible for all people to have the abundant life.

And my beloved, much of this lie springs from the fact that Lucifer and certain other beings in Heaven wanted to be recognized as being above and beyond other beings created by God. And so anyone caught in the mindset of anti-christ wants to uphold the culture of lack on Earth, so that they can have more than the general population and therefore feel that they are above and beyond that population, that they are more and more important. And this is a perversion of the expanding force of the Father, the drive to become more.

You see, they are not trying to become more, they are trying to trick you into becoming less so that it seems like they have more, they are more. But in reality, they are less for they have no love, no light, in them. And they can only maintain their illusion of being more by forcing you to live in poverty. And that is why the power elite on this Earth does not want the abundant life to be manifest on Earth. They want to stand out as an elite that has more than the rest of the population.

And my beloved, this is in complete opposition to the will of God, the vision of God, the original desire of God for this planet and this universe. And so, before you can inherit your Father's kingdom, you must overcome the temptations, the temptations that Jesus experienced when he came out of the wilderness and was tempted by the devil. And take note that in one of those temptations, the devil promised him that he could have all the kingdoms of this world if he would fall down and worship the devil.

And there are people on Earth, those in the elite, who are pursuing that dream, thinking that they can somehow come to own and control and possess all of the kingdoms of this world by following the devil— even though they do not see it as following the devil and would never admit that they are devil worshippers. They think they are either doing what God has appointed them to do or even doing God's work because they are his favorite sons.

Forming the Circle of Oneness

Presence of Oneness, July 3, 2005.

The Chalice of Oneness

Your oneness here below forms a chalice, and that chalice is the Holy Grail. Ah, so many people have sought the Holy Grail. Throughout the centuries they have pursued this dream, and some have seen it. But I tell you, it is not an individual quest, for the Holy Grail is the cup of Christ and Christ did not come to this Earth for his own gratification. He came to unite all life with their Father, with their Source.

And yet that union can only happen when people come together in oneness. And that is why Jesus did not walk around alone, but called his disciples, hoping to establish that oneness among them that would eventually become the catalyst for the Oneness of Christ to spread through the entire Body of God on Earth.

And thus you saw that the disciples, 2,000 years ago, could not hold that vision and that balance. And that especially Peter and Judas could not remain in the oneness but did their respective things that broke the Circle of Oneness. And thus the challenge in this age is to reach beyond, to reach higher than the disciples did 2,000 years ago, and to establish that oneness here below that becomes the Holy Grail, whereby Christ can pour in the water of life that will give the abundant life to all people.

And that can be done only when you are fully aware that you must overcome both the enemy within and the enemy without. So many spiritual organizations have gone the way of the power struggles of the human ego and the forces of this world. Your challenge in the Age of Freedom, is to remain true to that oneness, that oneness that is greater than any differences you can have.

And rest assured that we do not want you to become carbon copies, to fit into a mold. We do not want you to set aside or lose your individuality. That is not the oneness we talk about. That is indeed the oneness of the fallen angels and their mechanization concept, who want to turn everyone into robots who are blindly following the blind leaders. We want you all to be individuals, to be the individuals you are. And when you know that your individuality is an individualization of God, then you know that the individuality of your brothers and sisters is also an individualization of that God. And that is when you can have a greater oneness, the oneness that is not Satanic, but the oneness whereby all transcend and become more, because when you come together you become so much more than any of you could be alone.

And thereby you share and you magnify and multiply, you multiply your talents by putting them together and that is the true abundant life on Earth—that all freely receive from Above, freely give here below and thus the abundant life spreads like rings in the water, spreads out from the nucleus, from the Sun Center that you form here today. And thereby it becomes the light that shines in the darkness. But I tell you, in this age, the darkness will begin to comprehend the light (John 1:5) and therefore more people will be awakened than ever before in Earth's history.

I call the Guardians of the Mother Light!

Saint Germain, July 4, 2005.

This is the beginning of the Age of Aquarius

This is my message on this Fourth of July, 2005, which marks the beginning of what I consider the real Age of Aquarius. And if you would time it, then time it from 12 o'clock Noon, Eastern Standard Time, 2005. [NOTE: This is the BEGINNING of the Aquarian age, and the official Aquarian age was inaugurated by Saint Germain on March 22, 2010.]

Yet, be careful that you do not pay so much attention to the outer things, and the precise time and the alignment of the stars that you become lost in the outer and forget that the real key to the Age of Aquarius is freedom from the ego, freedom from pride, freedom from the consciousness of anti-christ, the serpentine mind of pride, saying that one individualization of God is more important than other individualizations of God. This has been the bane of the Earth now for thousands upon thousands of years, since those lifestreams that fell from Above were allowed to enter this realm. And it is time to get them off, those who will not bend the knee in humility to the Lord Christ within themselves and within others. It is time that they leave.

But in order for them to leave, the law requires that someone must be raised up to the level of Christhood that the fallen being had before they fell. And only then can they be taken. And thus it is up to you who are on the Christ path, who understand the true inner teachings of Christ, to raise up your own Christ attainment to that level, where you can be the counterbalance in the Earth that allows Michael, Archangel Michael, to come in and take those fallen angels who will not bend the knee to the second death, to the court of the sacred fire, where they face the ultimate choice—will you bend the knee or will you dissolve yourself into your own evil.

Form a nucleus for world change

El Morya, July 4, 2005.

Therefore, the most important concept you can take with you about the spiritual path is that you will not be given a clear vision of where you are going. If you knew the destination before you started the journey, what would you possibly learn from the journey? The important point in life is not the destination but what you learn as you walk the path, making decisions to the best of your ability, learning from all of your decisions. Whether they be considered right or wrong from an outer human perspective matters not. What matters is that you learn and that you use that decision, no matter how it turned out, to say, "Ah, but now I know how to take the next step, now I can come up higher."

And thus, no decision is truly wasted, no decision is truly a mistake—as long as you are willing to take that next step on the path. And of course, the essence of the human ego is that it will try to manipulate you, so that you do not take that next step. The essence of the false hierarchy of the fallen angels is that they will try to prevent you from taking that next step closer to God, so that you are stopped in your tracks where you are. And they have devised many cleaver schemes to create this illusion that you cannot or that you are not allowed to, or that you do not need to, take that next step and come closer to God.

...

For truly, it is only the ego that has perverted the Mother Light. You may say that it is the fallen angels who have been instrumental in perverting the Mother Light on Earth. And this is partially true, but only partially, for remember the statement in Genesis, "God created man in his own image and likeness" (Genesis 1:26). And then he said, "Multiply and take dominion over the Earth" (Genesis 1:28).

Take dominion over the Earth

You see, my beloved, God did not give dominion over the Earth to the fallen angels; he gave dominion over the Earth to the sons and daughters of God. And thus, the fallen angels cannot come down here and corrupt Mother Earth and the Mother Light. They can do so only indirectly through the sons and daughters of God, whom they manage to trick into creating an ego, which then takes the Mother Light into an imperfect matrix. You see, my beloved, if the fallen angels had had the power to pervert this planet, then this planet would long ago have self-destructed and disintegrated in the fires of hell.

They must work indirectly through the sons and daughters, as we Above in the Ascended Host, must work indirectly by inspiring you to come up higher and realign yourself with the Will of God. This is the key equation that you need to understand on Earth.

The dark forces do not have the amount of power that some people ascribe to them. They have no more power than what you give to them. And therefore, when you uncover the ego and dismiss that ego, you will stop giving them power. And as their power quickly burns out and diminishes, they will be removed from the Earth. Because she will start spinning faster on her axis, and she will spin them off, for they no longer have the power to hold on.

That is the day that is not as far away as you might think. And from that moment on, you will hear almost the sound of water splashing on hot rocks and being consumed, being turned into steam and sizzling away. And that is indeed the fallen ones being spun off this planet so fast that you will not believe the changes that can happen when it finally breaks and they are starting to spin off at a faster and faster pace. Because you are raising your vibration and thereby raising the Mother Light up, until she finally reunites with the Father, with the Buddha in the crown, and outpictures that perfect lotus blossom, that perfect balance of Alpha and Omega, as Above, so below, that cannot be corrupted. And therefore, the Earth is sealed in the immaculate concept.

Visualize a better future by understanding the problems of today

Saint Germain, August 31, 2005

Americans worshiping a false god

My beloved, since you are a spiritually inclined, a spiritually aware, person, I am asking you to take a step back and look at the United States of America today. I am especially asking you to look at the state of consciousness of most people in this nation. We have a nation that has been gifted with unparalleled prosperity and unparalleled freedom, not only economic freedom and political freedom but also freedom to be who you are, freedom to live life according to your highest vision. Yet what have most American's done with that freedom? They have become as spoiled children who are used to getting everything they want. They have developed the attitude that they are entitled to get everything they want, that it is a basic human right to get everything they want, and that they can whine and complain when they don't get everything they want.

If you look at the state of consciousness that affects most Americans today, you will see that they have developed a new religion. Most Americans will claim that they are religious people, and most of them will claim that they are Christians. Yet their true religion is the religion of worshipping what Jesus called "mammon." This is not simply money, but also comfortability, material goods, material pleasures, material security. Most Americans worship comfortability, a comfortable way of life, beyond everything—including beyond the freedom that is the original purpose for establishing this nation and allowing it to become both prosperous and powerful.

I am one of the primary ascended masters who have sponsored the United States of America. I did so because I saw the need for a nation who could provide a bastion of freedom against the rising red tide and a rising tide of totalitarian forces seen around the world. Yet instead of using their prosperity and power to promote true freedom, the American people have allowed themselves to be lulled asleep by a comfortable lifestyle. Instead of using the freedom they have been given to raise their vision for a better society, they have accepted a limited vision based on creature comforts. They have refused to acknowledge that freedom comes with a responsibility and an obligation to use their freedom and prosperity to help other people, both the poor in their own nation and the poor and disadvantaged around the world.

Instead of using this freedom to set others free, too many Americans have started worshipping the god of mammon. And thus they sit in their churches every Sunday, feeling holier than thou, because they have declared Jesus Christ to be their Lord and Savior. Yet they do not realize that they are not worshipping or following the true Jesus Christ, the real Jesus. They are indeed following an idolatrous image of Christ. They are dancing around a golden calf created by the false pastors that control most of the so-called Christian churches in the United States.

The power elite lulling the people to sleep

These false pastors do not want the people to be awakened, they do not want them to think for themselves, and thus they are carrying on a tradition of lulling people to sleep, a tradition that was started 1,700 years ago with the founding of the Roman Catholic Church by the Emperor Constantine. He was indeed trying to lull his people to sleep in order to maintain his power.

This pattern of putting the people to sleep, so that a small elite can control a majority the population, has been continued and reinforced ever since, not only by the Catholic Church but by most of the mainstream Christian churches. This is indeed a pattern that is in such opposition to the mission of Jesus that it is nothing less than blasphemy. Jesus came to awaken people so that they could choose the immortal life of Christ, the immortal life of the Christ consciousness, rather than the death of the human consciousness, the duality consciousness, the consciousness of anti-christ.

So the problem we see in the United States today is that too many people worship the god of comfortability, and they want their lives to continue as they are today. They do not want to seriously change their lifestyles, change themselves, change their attitude to life. They do not want to reach for a higher understanding of life. They do not want to take responsibility for their own lives, for their own salvation or for their nation. So they are allowing a small elite, a power elite, to run almost every aspect of life in the United States, from the churches to the government to the media and the educational establishments—and of course the business world.

The spiritual cause of hurricane Katrina

What has happened here is that instead of using their freedom to educate themselves and become Guardians of the Mother Light, the American people have allowed themselves to be bought off by a small elite who gives them a comfortable lifestyle in exchange for allowing the elite to have unlimited power over this nation. And it is precisely this refusal to take responsibility for your life and your nation that made the United States vulnerable to this hurricane.

How can this be so? How can there be a connection between a natural disaster and a refusal of the American people to take responsibility for their nation? My beloved, do you think it was a coincidence that this hurricane went up through the Gulf of Mexico, hitting the oil facilities in that part of the country? It was indeed no coincidence because one of the main areas in which the American people have been asleep is in terms of energy policy.

It is an undeniable fact that for many decades oil has been one of the major causes of tension on a planetary scale. Oil was one of the hidden reasons behind the second World War. The American people, and many other people around the world, have been given a false image of the real causes of this war. They have never been told about the hidden power plays of the rivaling power elites that brought about this war in an attempt to establish greater planetary control. And ever since then oil has been one of the major causes of tension on this planet.

What does it take to awaken people?

My beloved, what does it take to awaken a people to the fact that they need to drastically change the course of their nation and demand that their leaders put in place a responsible policy for making their nation self-sufficient and thereby less vulnerable to being dragged into armed conflicts that do not serve the cause of freedom? This nation is one of the primary consumers of oil on the planet. Yet it has enough oil resources and technology to be virtually self-sufficient. Nevertheless, the United States is not self-sufficient when it comes to energy, and this is a result of a behind-the-scenes manipulation by the powers who want the United States to be vulnerable to being dragged into military conflicts that do not serve the cause of freedom but serve the cause of global control.

What does it take to awaken the American nation to the fact that people need to make it a national priority to establish self-sufficiency in terms of energy? What does it take to make people realize that they cannot allow their leaders to keep them dependent on receiving oil from the most unstable and volatile region on the globe, namely the Middle East?

My beloved, you have heard the saying that history repeats itself. But why does history repeat itself? It repeats itself for one reason only, namely that people have not learned the lesson from the first event and therefore they draw to themselves another disaster as another opportunity to learn their lesson and change course.

How many people in America today remember the oil crises of 1973? Yet this was a crises so powerful that it should have been a wake-up call to the United States, as it was a wake-up call to many nations in Europe—although those nations have since lost their determination to become independent of Middle Eastern oil.

My point here is that the United States had a very powerful wake-up call in 1973. Yet because the American press and the American leaders did not expose the truth to the people, most Americans do not realize that the entire world was on the brink of a third world war over oil. Only an absolutely extraordinary effort on the part of the Ascended Host prevented this war, which would most certainly have been very devastating and most likely would have led to at least a limited nuclear exchange.

Yet the American people remained largely asleep. Then there was another oil crises in the early 1980's. And although prices went up, the American people remained asleep. They did not demand that their leaders make this nation self-sufficient. Then there came another situation with the first Gulf War, where once again the vulnerability of relying on Middle Eastern oil was exposed for all to see. Yet after the war the American government simply made behind-the-scenes deals with the Arab nations, so that the United States could continue to rely on Middle Eastern oil and therefore continue to be vulnerable to being drawn into a future crisis.

Once again, there came a wake-up call on September 11, 2001. Should it not have been obvious that the terrorists coming out of the Middle East was a clear demonstration of the instability of that region and therefore a possible disruption of the oil supply? Yet did the American president make it a priority to lessen or remove the dependency on Middle Eastern oil? Not so. He continued the decades-long tradition of having virtually no energy policy. Instead, he allowed this nation to be drawn into an armed conflict that has done nothing to promote the cause of freedom and democracy, despite his claims to the contrary. It has only further destabilized a region that was already on the brink of violent conflict. And thus you see the clear sign of rising oil prices that could precipitate a global recession. And need I remind you that recession often leads to war.

...

Why is America vulnerable?

Those of you who are familiar with karma might have the impression that you make bad karma for yourself when you do something that is wrong. In other words, if you hurt other people, you make personal karma and if a nation hurts other nations, it makes national karma. And based on this, you can look at history and you can see that the United States is a young nation and that it has not been a tyrannical nation like certain other nations. On the contrary, the United States has been willing to sacrifice much in two world wars and in terms of helping other nations around the world in many ways.

Yet, although the United States has not made a huge national karma by doing wrong acts, there is another way to make karma. This is what we might call the sin of omission. It is not that you do something wrong; it is that you do not do something right, something that you could have done and that you were indeed in a unique position to do. This is precisely where the United States has created a very substantial national karma that makes it vulnerable to many forms of disasters and calamities.

Take note that the very cause of this karma is that the American people have allowed themselves to be lulled asleep. Thus, when this karma returns, it will take the form of events that will seek to awaken the American people, that will shock them out of their coma. Was not the terrorists attacks on 9-11-2001 such an event? And while it did have the effect of awakening the American people in the short term, they were not truly awakened to the need to ask the very difficult long-term questions that could have put this nation in a positive spiral of self-examination and self-transcendence.

Instead, the American nation, led by the President, the power elite and the media, took the easy way out by appointing a scapegoat and going after that scapegoat. The American nation looked at the mote in the eyes of other nations instead of looking for the beam in the eye of this nation.

The American people simply wanted terrorism to go away, so that they did not have to make any profound and long-term changes to their lifestyle. They wanted to continue the materially comfortable lifestyle and they wanted their government to make the threat to that lifestyle go away, rather than examining that lifestyle and seriously considering whether it needed to change.

The need for an energy policy

Once again, we now see a natural disaster that has hit the nation's oil supply and production capacity, with the result that oil prices have gone up nationwide to the point that it might put the economy into a recession. What precipitated this disaster was, as I have said, that the nation has been asleep and has not developed a determined energy policy. Instead, this nation has allowed its energy policy to be dominated not only by a hidden power elite who has global geopolitical goals, but also by large multinational oil companies who think only about short term profits for their companies and shareholders and do not care about the long-term perspectives for a nation. Therefore, allowing the oil companies to make the biggest possible profit has been a more important driving factor behind United States' energy policy than has the actual goal of providing long-term stability and prosperity for this nation.

Likewise, you see that both the republicans and the democrats are more concerned about scoring cheap political points than about working together to make the fundamental changes that are needed in order to put this nation on a positive track. And although the American people witness this political wrangling on a daily basis, they have not stood up to their elected representatives and demanded that they do the job for which they were elected. Why have not the people demanded that the politicians in Washington start taking care of the long-term interests of this nation, instead of catering to the short-term interests of their own political party and the special interests of lobbying groups that should have no influence whatsoever on the democratic process?

Well, the people have not demanded this because they are so busy living their comfortable lives that they have no vision of the long-term potential of this nation, nor do they care enough to educate themselves about this potential. They want to continue living the comfortable life they are living, and they want their politicians to secure this life, so that they do not have to make personal or national sacrifices in order to promote the true cause of freedom.

My beloved, be aware that although I talk about a power elite with a hidden agenda, I am not implying that all politicians are aware of or involved with such a conspiracy. Most politicians have no desire to support the agenda of such an elite, but neither will they do anything to acknowledge the existence of a power elite until their constituents demand it. Thus, we see that as long as the people remain asleep, they cannot elect the kind of politicians who can change the course of this nation. And thus, we see a political apparatus that is impotent when it comes to asking long-term questions and making decisions that require sacrifice. Instead, they are focused on giving the people what they want, namely a continuation of a comfortable lifestyle.

...

The brutal fact is that there are many people in the United States, including in the area affected by this hurricane, who are truly good and well-meaning people. They simply want to live a normal life and take care of their families. They have no ill intentions toward anyone, and thus we might say that they have never done anything bad to bring upon themselves a disaster like this. Yet when the good people on this Earth allow themselves to be lulled asleep, they will inevitably support the evil people who are attempting to gain absolute power and control. It has been said by one of my disciples that, "For evil to triumph, it only takes that good men do nothing." And it is an eternal truth.

The good people of the United States have not done enough to take command, to take dominion, over their nation and make sure that their government is of the people, by the people and for the people. And therefore, the people who want power and control have taken over the government and other institutions of society. Thus, the good people have become mixed in with the bad people, as Jesus explained in his parable about the tares among the wheat. And thus, when a karmic return comes back, that return will affect both the good people who did not create the karma directly and the bad people who did create the karma through their actions or lack of actions.

And so what is the solution? Well the solution is that the good people come apart and become a separate and chosen people, who are elect unto their God because they have elected to reach beyond the consciousness of anti-christ and know the truth of Christ that will make them free from the manipulation of the power elite. There is literally no other solution that will prevent a precipitation of future disasters in the United States, disasters, I might add, that could be even worse than this hurricane.

...

Be the creative elite in action

The problem today is that the lowest ten percent of the population, the power elite, have been very successful in imposing their vision for a new world order upon the United States of America. And the eighty percent of the general population are asleep and are not realizing that they are being manipulated into accepting a lifestyle that might have certain creature comforts but is a very far cry from the highest potential for this nation. And so as Jesus has eloquently explained, the only possible solution is that the top ten percent of the population raise their vision, so that they can counteract the vision of the lowest ten percent. It is absolutely necessary that the spiritually aware people focus their vision on manifesting a Golden Age. But to do this, you must have an awareness of the factors that are preventing the manifestation of a Golden Age, so that you can visualize the solution that will consume those factors.

Share my vision of the Golden Age America

Saint Germain, Columbus Day, October 10, 2005

I AM Freedom, Freedom I AM!

Beloved friends of Freedom, I AM your Saint Germain and I AM come to call those who are the true Friends of Freedom – in America and around the world – to rise up and take a stand for Freedom. And to give you a most powerful tool for beginning the process of taking a stand for Freedom, I release to you Archangel Michael's Golden Age Rosary for America.

Truly, this rosary incorporates the four pillars that must and will carry America into the Golden Age. Those pillars are God the Father, and his representatives El Morya and Archangel Michael, God the Mother, and her representatives of Mother Mary and the Goddess of Liberty, God the Son and his representative Jesus and God the Holy Spirit and his representative that I AM, as the Master of the seventh ray of the Holy Spirit. This is the seventh ray of the Holy Spirit that bloweth where it listeth.

And so, this rosary is a chalice that is capable of holding the energies of the Holy Spirit so that they will not be spilled upon the ground of the human consciousness, the duality consciousness that is the main problem that keeps America and the rest of the world from manifesting the Golden Age. What is the essence of this duality consciousness? Well, it is, as Mother Mary explains so eloquently in her new book, [Master Keys to Spiritual Freedom] the sense of separation from God, the illusion that anything could be separated from its source, that any part of God could be apart from God.

This is indeed the original cause of the fall of Lucifer and all beings who fell from Above. These are the ones who were cast out of the spiritual realm [a previous sphere] by Archangel Michael. Or rather, they cast themselves out because they set themselves up in opposition to the Will of God, for which Archangel Michael serves as the supreme guardian. Therefore, through the sense of separation and the sense that they were opposed to the Will of God, they descended to the realm of duality and thus created the very opposition that cast them out of the spiritual realm—where all is oneness and therefore no opposition is possible.

Ever since then they have been in the realm of duality, creating their own opposition, thereby creating the dualistic struggle between the two extremes, whether you call them good or evil, capitalism or communism or anything else that human beings can think up—and that the fallen ones can think up in their attempts to drag those who did not fall from Above into this never-ending dualistic struggle. This is the struggle that will prevent them from coming home and prevent them from fulfilling their destiny and divine plan.

The birth of elitism

My beloved, the original problem on this planet is truly the sense of separation and the fact that the sense of separation opens up for the possibility that humankind can be divided into those who have and those who have not. And thus, from the consciousness of separation itself springs the consciousness of elitism. This consciousness causes some people to believe that – due to this or that outer characteristic – they belong to the elite. They are better than other people and they are entitled to certain privileges and certain powers over the general population.

Ah my beloved, can you see that this entire consciousness is based on the sense of separation from God? For truly, when you see yourself as one with God, you realize that without him was not anything made that was made. Thus, God's Being is within everything that was created and so, comparisons and value judgments have no meaning. How could one aspect of God be more valuable than any other aspect of God, when all aspects of God are of infinite value? How could any expression of infinity be worth more than any other expression of infinity? This simply cannot be when you are in the consciousness of oneness, the Christ consciousness, meaning that your eye is single because you see no duality but see only oneness with your source.

But when your eye becomes evil, meaning that your vision is divided by the dualistic extremes that spring from the consciousness of antichrist, then it becomes possible to divide humankind into the "haves" and the "have-nots" and this then is the main problem on planet Earth. And my beloved, America was indeed conceived as an ideal for a nation that would become the forerunner for the banishment of this elitist consciousness from the Earth. Therefore, America is the key to ushering in the Golden Age, which can only come when humankind recognizes its oneness with its source.

The perception of America

My beloved, I am quite aware that most people who live in America – and take note that I am deliberately not saying "most Americans," I am talking about those who live in America – are unaware of how America is perceived outside her own borders. I am also aware that many of you, who have grown up in other countries, have been conditioned to look at America with somewhat mixed or even negative feelings. This is indeed understandable given the track record of American foreign policy over many decades.

Most people in America fail to understand this because the American press has kept the people in America woefully ignorant of what goes on in the rest of the world. And thus, instead of serving the cause of freedom by holding up a mirror to the people in America, the press has instead created a smokescreen that prevents people from seeing the beam – the power elite and its abuse of power – in the eye of their own nation.

I am aware that many of you who do not live in America might have to process your feelings toward America before you can wholeheartedly give this rosary for America. So I will take you on a little journey and tell you about the original vision behind the founding of this nation.

Beloved friends of freedom, before I made my ascension, and even for some time after, I was serving on the European continent, and it was my clear vision and desire to create a united states of Europe. Yet this proved to be an impossible task, even for a Being of my considerable diplomatic skill. The reason this was impossible was that Europe was completely imprisoned by the consciousness of elitism that goes all the way back to the fallen angels.

It is a sad fact that many of the kings and noble men of Europe were indeed embodied fallen angels who had an absolute commitment to maintaining the elitist "paradise on Earth" that they believed they had created for themselves. They were completely blind to the fact that the raising of humankind's consciousness and the release of new knowledge and technology had already pulled the foundation from under their castles. They refused to accept change, wanting – as the power elite always does – to maintain status quo.

They rejected all my attempts to create greater unity among European nations, they resisted change, and you saw the ensuing blood bath in the French Revolution. This blood bath was completely unnecessary and did not actually bring true freedom and democracy, but simply replaced one power elite with a rivaling power elite. Thus, the lesson is that true change can often be brought about without bloodshed. And in today's age, true change MUST be brought about without bloodshed.

So there I was in the midst of these death throes of one class of fallen angels, many of whom have indeed been taken from this planet. I saw clearly the impossibility of having the European nations shed the snakeskin of elitism and come together in a true spirit of unity. So I conceived – in counsel with a number of other ascended beings – the plan for establishing a new nation, where we could start on a clean slate and therefore have a greater opportunity of establishing a nation that was "one nation under God" and that gave "liberty and justice" to all.

The divine dispensation to create America

However, in order to establish America, I had to receive a dispensation from a Cosmic Council that is called the Great Karmic Board. This is a council of Ascended Beings who oversee the overall karmic conditions for planet Earth and who are assigned to plot the course that can best allow humankind to balance its karma and thereby restore this planet to its original purity.

The Karmic Board had some justifiable concerns about establishing a new nation. One of these concerns was the native peoples living on the American continent and the purity of the natural environment. Another concern was that by creating one very powerful nation, it was indeed possible to create a Frankenstein's monster that could become so drunk with its power that it would ignore or reject its spiritual origins and use the light to take power, material possessions and pleasure. This is indeed a pattern that has been seen in many past civilizations, most notably the civilization of Rome, which self-destructed due to an abuse of power, an abuse of the light that had been given to the Roman people in an attempt to raise civilization to a higher level.

And precisely because many of the people who would come to America would be reincarnated from the Roman Empire, the Karmic Board was extremely concerned that they might simply repeat their old ways, aiming to gain power, riches and pleasure, rather than being willing to sacrifice for a higher vision, a higher spiritual goal. The danger was that they could start acting as spoiled children, thereby demonstrating that they had not really progressed spiritually since their embodiment in Roman times.

There was also a very legitimate concern for the fact that creating a new nation would not necessarily keep the power elite out of that nation, and thus elitism could indeed sail as a stowaway on the ships that brought the settlers from the old world to the new.

Beloved friends of freedom, I must tell you that although I was fully aware of these concerns, I was so enthusiastic about my vision for a Golden Age in America that I swept aside the concerns of the members of the Karmic Board, being – quite frankly – almost too eager in my determination to secure the grant for the creation of a new nation. And so, due to my contagious enthusiasm – and I might add that the Flame of Freedom truly has great persuasive powers – I did indeed receive the grant for the founding of the United States of America.

Yet this grant was bought with a price, for I did indeed have to put up a substantial part of my personal spiritual attainment as collateral for this nation. And thus, I can assure you that I have much invested in the United States of America. And my ability to take this planet into the Golden Age of Aquarius is indeed very tightly linked to the future of the United States.

Feel the Spirit of Freedom

My beloved hearts, I wish to impart to you a portion of the immense enthusiasm I felt in those early days. What a joy it was to watch the people who left the European continent with the greatest hopes of escaping the poverty, the oppression, and the heavy weight of hopelessness which they had experienced growing up in Europe. What an intense joy it was for me to see how their spirits lightened as they crossed that big blue ocean, and how their hearts swelled when they caught the first glimpse of the American coastline and realized that they were entering a land of opportunity.

Ah, my beloved, is not freedom the opportunity to become more, to break free of limitations and to rise to your highest dreams? In today's world, few of you have experienced the oppression and the shear sense of hopelessness that the "common" people had in those days in Europe. You can scarcely understand how these people's spirits were so weighted down by the heavy weight put upon them by the fact that they were so boxed in by limitations from above and limitations from below and limitations from every corner of the globe.

Thus, it is hard for you in today's world to understand the sense of freedom, the sense of hope, with which they first set eyes on the American coastline. Yet I can tell you that it was an immense joy to my heart to see so many people embrace the opportunity they were given on this continent. And what a joy it was for me to watch a small band of people come together and become the open doors for bringing forth the vision of not simply another British province but of an independent nation that had a new – and never before seen – vision of being free of a power elite that dominated the population, turning them into literal slaves.

Ah, my beloved, the vision shared by America's founding fathers was indeed inspired by me, for I worked with many of them at inner levels. And I was able to inspire them, at critical moments, so they grasped the vision that it was possible to create, not only an independent nation, but a nation with an entirely new form of government that gave every person the opportunity to influence the destiny of the entire nation.

In today's world you take democracy for granted and you can scarcely understand what a groundbreaking, what an earth-shattering, idea it was in those early days. But consider that throughout known history most people on this Earth had lived in a highly elitist system, often having their entire destiny in the hands and mind of just one person. Consider how many people throughout history have spent their entire lives catering to the needs of one human being and how many people have had their lives destroyed or lost because of the blindness – or the outright madness – of this one leader.

So consider the joy of the Ascended Host over the fact that the founding fathers of America were able to grasp a higher vision and bring it into the physical—and indeed write it into the Declaration of

Independence and the Constitution. Consider our joy when we saw their willingness to put aside their own safety, their own comfortability – and indeed their own lives – in order to bring this vision to the level of reality and, therefore, fight against all odds to forge a new nation.

Ah, if you could only feel the joy that wells up in my heart even today when I consider how it was to see a point of light starting to form in those early American colonies. This point of light grew in strength until it began to shine through the dark cloud of misqualified energy that had been hanging over this nation like a shroud of death for a millennia. Truly it was like a sun parting the dark clouds, and suddenly there was indeed a silver lining through the dark clouds shining. There was hope that the power elite that had been oppressing the people of Earth for eons could finally be dethroned and the Earth could give birth to a Golden Age and eventually turn into the Freedom's Star that is her ultimate destiny.

Catch the vision of a free planet

Beloved friends of freedom, I strongly encourage you – no matter where you live in this world – to study the birth of the American nation. Watch whatever documentaries are available to you. Read whatever books are available to you. But first of all make an effort to tune in to the Spirit of Freedom that was behind the creation of this nation. For truly it is that same Spirit of Freedom that can spread to every nation on Earth and therefore set your own nation free from an elitist system that oppresses the people.

Look at how the idea of democracy spread from America to Europe and from there to almost every continent. This is indeed the potential, the greatest potential for America, that she will spread freedom throughout this planet. And my beloved, what is true freedom? Well it is that the people are free from the power elite, that they are free from the spiritual slavery and oppression imposed upon them by those lifestreams that have set themselves up in opposition to the will of God and therefore actively oppose the manifestation of God's kingdom on this planet.

These are indeed the lifestreams, as Mother Mary has already explained, who are seeking to enslave humankind in their senseless, mindless attempt to prove that God was wrong by giving human beings free will. And my beloved, can you see that the very essence of a free, democratic nation is that the people have an opportunity to exercise their free will and thus learn by reaping the consequences of their own choices—instead of spending their lives reaping the consequences of the choices of a small elite, thus insulating the elite from the consequences of their dualistic, egotistic, self-centered choices.

My beloved, Jesus has explained that the universe is a mirror. Whatever you send out will be reflected back to you by the cosmic mirror. And while this is ultimately true and while it is also true that every man will reap what he has sown, it is indeed possible that a power elite can postpone the return of their own karma by forcing the people under them to form a buffer between the elite and their karma. This is a practice that has been going on ever since the first fallen angels embodied on this planet, which was indeed a very long time ago.

And thus, you who are the true friends of freedom, you who are the spiritually mature people, you who belong to the top ten percent of the people on Earth, as Jesus has explained, must indeed become wise to this practice that is called "karma dodging." You must become wise to the ways in which the power elite is always trying to set itself up so that the people are the ones who suffer the consequences of the choices made by the elite. You must therefore come apart from this power elite. You must separate yourself from the tares so that God can pull up the tares without pulling up the wheat. This means, first of all, that you must come apart in consciousness by separating yourself from the consciousness of the elite. Ultimately this means that you must separate yourself from the duality consciousness which Jesus explains throughout this website.

Come apart from the consciousness of elitism

Yet you must also become aware of one aspect of this duality consciousness, which is the very consciousness of elitism itself. My beloved, those souls who make up the current power elite on planet Earth are absolutely convinced that they belong to a separate class that is above and beyond the rest of the population. There are many different factions in this power elite and each group has its own reasons for claiming superiority.

And thus, when you survey the planet, you see rivaling power elites, for truly how could those who are trapped in the consciousness of duality ever come together in unison? Had they been able to achieve this union, they would long ago have taken over the entire planet—and the creation of free democratic nations would have been impossible. Yet the very nature of the duality consciousness makes such a union impossible. And that is indeed why you see many wars between two elitists groups, elitist factions, that fight each other because each has an insatiable desire for ultimate power, for ultimate control. And contrary to the claims made by the winning elite, these wars did not bring true freedom. They either brought a new power elite to replace the old one or they cemented the power of the existing elite. Yet each dualistic war cemented the hold that the consciousness of duality has over humankind.

Behind the rivaling power elites on Earth, you do see the nonmaterial power elite made up of the prince of this world and the forces of darkness. They are simply using the elitist people on Earth as pawns in their greater game of proving God wrong. Yet even they are divided amongst themselves and within themselves, and this will ultimately be their downfall. They must use the divide-and-conquer strategy against the spiritual people because they themselves are so divided. And thus, they can maintain their power only as long as they can divide the spiritual people more than they themselves are divided.

I ask you to consider this elitist consciousness because I must tell you that there are many people in today's world, even many people in the free democratic nations – even many spiritual people – who have come to believe in various aspects of the many elitists philosophies that have been promoted by different factions of the power elite. I must tell you that most people in America do indeed have many elitists beliefs that they hold to be completely true or which they simply have never considered questioning because they were brought up to accept them without even thinking about how they originated.

And so, my beloved, I must tell you that even the founding fathers themselves were not completely free from such elitist beliefs. This can be seen by some of their actions, such as the fact that Thomas Jefferson used slave labor to give himself a comfortable lifestyle on his beloved farm. Even George Washington was not completely free from elitist beliefs, but to his great credit, it stands forever that he refused to be America's first king and instead settled for the Presidency. Thereby, he did indeed set a magnificent example of a person who has the power but who does not become drunk with that power because he maintains a greater vision. George Washington clearly saw that the potential of creating a free democratic nation was far more important than his personal power, his personal fortune, his personal pleasure, and even his life.

Rekindle the Spirit of Self-transcendence

My beloved, this then is the spirit that needs to be rekindled among the spiritual people of the world—if America is to fulfill her destiny to become the forerunner for the Golden Age of Aquarius. Ah, my beloved, when you look at the history of America, you will see that she was born out of conflict. She was born from a conflict between the colonies and the English King, who represented the power elite. And even after she won her freedom from the English Crown, she was still mired in the dualistic struggle that led to the Civil War. This shows you that the forces of duality had now entered the American nation and were seeking to destroy her from within. Then came the struggle against Nazism that culminated with the end of the second World War. And even after that, the dualistic struggle was not over and for decades America was engulfed in the Cold War with Communism.

All of this should show you that forces of duality have been working in America from her very inception. Yet I can tell you that America now stands at a crossroad, where the spiritually mature people in this nation – and indeed around the world – have a unique opportunity to raise America beyond the dualistic struggle.

My beloved, with the fall of Communism, many people felt that America's struggle was over. In fact many of the truly dedicated freedom fighters in the American government and armed forces, have felt like they have been in a vacuum since the Berlin Wall fell, now many years ago. They have felt like they have had no clearly defined enemy, and even the rise of the specter of terrorism has not removed the sense of being in a vacuum. Yet my beloved, what this truly signifies is the opportunity to take the fight for freedom to a higher level that is beyond military might and the fight against a physical enemy with material weapons.

It is the opportunity to rise to the understanding that the true fight for freedom is a spiritual battle—and it is not a battle between the two dualistic extremes defined by the consciousness of anti-christ. Nay, it is a battle between the Christ consciousness and the consciousness of anti-christ. And truly, when your eye is single, when you see beyond the consciousness of duality, you realize that – in reality – there is no battle, for it is completely one-sided. Those who are trapped in the consciousness of anti-christ see themselves in opposition to the forces of Christ, they see themselves as enemies of Christ and enemies of God. Thus, they are always fighting a battle, but the battle exists only in their minds.

Those who are anchored in the eternal bliss of the Christ consciousness realize that the forces of anti-christ are ultimately unreal. They have no permanency and therefore, they are not truly enemies. They are simply temporary mirages projected unto the screen of life. And when you realize this truth, you realize how wise Jesus was when he told people not to resist evil, but to turn the other cheek.

My beloved, the greatest potential for this age is indeed the awakening of the American freedom fighters worldwide, to the realization that the fight for freedom is a fight between the consciousness of Christ and the consciousness of anti-christ. And the real key to winning this battle is to rise above the dualistic extremes of the consciousness of anti-christ. For thereby, the battle will be won without a shot being fired.

Who are the real Americans?

Who are the true freedom fighters, who are the true Americans? They are the people who recognize God and God's law as the ultimate authority because they realize that God's will is indeed the will of the higher parts of their own beings. The true Americans are those who recognize the I AM Presence as God individualized within them, thus knowing that the kingdom of God is within them and therefore above any divisions found on Earth. Thus, living within the borders of the United States does not automatically make you a true American, and living outside her borders does not mean you have no responsibility for America.

The true Americans are the I AM people, the spiritual people on this Earth, and they have been strategically positioned all around the globe. You have volunteered to be part of the forerunners for Saint Germain's Golden Age, and I know that many of you have grown up with a negative view of America. Yet no matter how justified that view might be, I am asking you to look beyond outer appearances and catch the true vision of America's spiritual potential.

If the spiritual people are to have a decisive impact in this age, they must overcome the dualistic divisions that have been programmed into their minds by the power elites of this world. They must rise above those divisions and forge a greater unity that makes them the one Body of God on Earth. And one of the artificial divisions that must be overcome is the sense of division concerning the vision of America's potential. As I have explained to you, America was not a nation created for a few hundred million people. America was created as a gift to the entire world, and her highest potential is that she will become the catalyst for the manifestation of the Golden Age of Aquarius, a victory that will spread like a chain-reaction around the globe.

Thus, I tell you bluntly that no matter what you might feel about America, it is a fact that the Golden Age of Aquarius cannot be brought to this planet unless America is raised to her highest spiritual potential. And I tell you also that this can happen only when the I AM people worldwide unite in holding the spiritual vision for America, resolving all negative feelings and truly visualizing that America rises above all dualism and elitism, becoming a truly free nation. It is not a coincidence that America has people who have come from virtually every nation on Earth. This fact alone should demonstrate that America has ties to every other nation and thus has the potential to spread spiritual freedom to the entire planet.

I am fully aware that America deserves much of the reputation she has around the world. Yet as a spiritually mature person, you should be able to see beyond outer appearances. Is this not the entire reason for being of the Guardians of the Mother Light, namely that you see beyond outer appearances and impose the vision of Christ upon the Ma-ter light? So is it too much to ask that you see beyond outer appearances, seeing that America's behavior is heavily influenced by the consciousness of dualism and elitism, the consciousness of anti-christ? And when you realize this, you can then see these manifestations as unreal and impose the vision of Christ upon this nation, thus holding the immaculate concept that America sheds the snakeskin of the serpentine consciousness.

Therefore, I am now calling to all true freedom fighters worldwide, to arise. I am calling you to capture the spirit of freedom that led to the creation of the American nation.

Be the third great generation

I am also calling to all true freedom fighters within America to be inspired by the great generations of the past. Truly we have seen two great generations in America. There was the generation of the American revolutionaries who gave birth to this nation. And then there was the generation who won the second World War and defeated the forces of fascism, for which they have been called the "greatest generation." If you will study these generations, you will see that even though they had grown up as seemingly ordinary people, they were able to grasp a higher vision that went far beyond their daily lives. They were willing to set aside those daily lives and fight for a cause that was greater than themselves. And they were even willing to give their lives for that cause. And truly, greater love has no man or woman than to give their lives for the cause of Christ that goes beyond the dualistic struggle of anti-christ.

And thus, what I ask you today is to look at your lives and see that you have two options. You have been brought up to see yourselves as ordinary human beings, and you can indeed continue to live your lives as ordinary beings. But the alternative is that you grasp the higher vision for the Golden Age and that you realize that this cause is far greater than your ordinary daily lives. And thus, you are willing to set aside some time, some energy, and some of your daily comforts in order to strike a blow for freedom and make an effort to bring about the Golden Age that is today's highest potential.

And my beloved, contrary to the people who fought in the second World War and the Revolutionary War, I am not asking you to risk your physical lives. For truly, the battle we face today is more than anything a spiritual battle that does not require you to lose your physical life. But if the battle is to be won, it does require that you are willing to set aside some of your daily comforts and give some time and energy to waging this battle, the battle for the minds of humanity.

Truly, there is much you can do. And as you strive to attain your inner attunement and clarify the vision of your divine plan, you will begin to see what you can personally do. But right now what you can do is to give this rosary, the Golden Age Rosary for America, and the other rosaries released by Mother Mary, as well as the other rosaries that are forthcoming.

Truly, this should be a sacrifice that any spiritual seeker should be able to make in order to serve as the shock troops that are softening the enemy's defenses and thereby paving the way for the main army, namely the rest of humanity that has not yet been awakened. My beloved, is it too much to ask that you give a rosary a day and that you talk to your friends, who are also spiritually aware people, and explain to them the potential of a Golden Age and how they too can make an invaluable contribution to that Golden Age by setting aside a half an hour every day to give a rosary?

My beloved, there is much more to say about the Golden Age, about America and about the cause of freedom. And I shall surely return and give you further teachings on these and other topics, but for now I ask you to contemplate the Spirit of Freedom that drove the American patriots to fight overwhelming odds and self doubts in order to give birth to a nation that truly ushered in a new age of freedom and self-determination for the people on this planet.

You are closer than you think

I ask you to see that you have the potential to become the generation that will usher in a new age of spiritual freedom. And truly, as the forerunners of a new age, you should not expect that the general population will understand why you do what you do. Many people are not yet ready to share the spiritual vision that you have grasped – or at least glimpsed – so do not expect them to thank you. And be prepared for the fact that they might indeed ridicule your efforts and your beliefs. But my beloved, even the early American patriots were subjected to ridicule. And they often had their doubts about the validity of their cause or the point of fighting what seemed to be impossible odds.

Yet my beloved, you are much closer than you think to bringing about a breakthrough in the collective consciousness, a breakthrough that will open the door to the spiritual awakening that surely will come to pass. It is not a matter of if but only a matter of when. As I said in my last discourse, I and many other members of the Ascended Host are absolutely determined that humankind must be awakened to the spiritual reality.

And we are absolutely determined that the American nation will be the first nation to be awakened to its true spiritual potential. This awakening will take place, but the more time that passes, the more it becomes necessary to bring about upheavals in society and upheavals in nature that the people cannot ignore. This is what I explained in my last discourse, and it is a reality. America will indeed be tested severely in the coming years—unless the American people awaken to their spiritual potential.

And truly those who are already awakened can do much to shorten the time it takes before the general population opens its eyes. And therefore, the future truly is in your hands, your hearts and your voices. It is up to you to shorten the time for the elect, so that the awakening can take place with a minimum of calamities.

Is it not worth it to set aside some time every day to fulfill the promise you made before you came into embodiment? I can assure you that most of the people who will ever read this teaching will belong to a band of volunteers who chose to take embodiment at this time because they have a tie to my heart and they wanted to help bring in my Golden Age.

My beloved hearts, many of you stood before me in the spiritual realm before you came into this embodiment, and you promised me that you would strike a blow for freedom. I am in no way trying to make you feel bad for what you have done or have not done. I am simply lovingly reminding you of the promise you made. And I am reminding you that by fulfilling that promise you will regain your sense of purpose and mission. You will overcome all sense of emptiness in your life, and your life will be filled with the infinite joy that comes from feeling the energies of the Holy Spirit, the very Spirit of Freedom, flowing through all levels of your Being.

So join me, join Jesus, Mother Mary and Archangel Michael, as we flow with the River of Life that is carrying this planet into the Golden Age. I bid you farewell until we meet again, and I seal you in the heart of Freedom.

The gratitude and the judgment of the Divine Mother

Mother Mary, October 21, 2005.

You are more than animals

What is true freedom? It is spiritual freedom from the false sense of identity that you are a human being, that you are nothing more than an animal, that there is nothing after death, that you will disappear when your body dies. Freedom from the belief that you are a miserable sinner who can only sin and who can never do anything right in the eyes of God. This is such a denial of the God within you that it is the worst form of blasphemy that you could possibly imagine. And yet it has run rampant on this planet, to the point where scarcely anyone is unaffected by it.

I am here because I have heard the cries of those who have realized that they are suffering, they have been put in a small box by the false preachers in Church and State. They feel their spirits have been dampened, they have no room to move, but they have cried out to me for deliverance even though they are not consciously aware of it. So I have responded, and I am here to set them free.

And my rosaries is only the first level of tools that I will give you to set free those who need to be cut free, those who are already mature at inner levels but who have not yet freed themselves from the outer programming that has been put upon them for so many years through the Christian churches and then through the scientific establishment, always, always, always controlled by that power elite who wants to deny the spark of Christ in the true sons and daughters of God in order to maintain their control over this planet.

Truly, I say to you, the key to the Golden Age is to hold the immaculate concept that behind all outer manifestations is the pure Mother Light. Presently, that Mother Light has taken on innumerable imperfect manifestations on Earth. But I tell you that that Mother Light would rather be set free to manifest the kingdom of God. And the kingdom of

God can be manifest almost instantly if enough people will hold the immaculate concept for this planet.

And thus, in my new book [Master Keys to the Abundant Life] I explain the immaculate concept, I explain the importance of freeing yourself from the duality consciousness. Because until you free yourself from that consciousness, you cannot fully hold the immaculate concept, you cannot fully understand and embrace that immaculate concept and understand what it truly means. And truly, I shall give other teachings on this, as shall other masters. And for now I simply come to say, "Thank you for giving my rosaries! You are making a difference!" And thus, I seal you in the love of my heart until I shall speak again.

Enough is enough!

Omega, October 22, 2005

I am Alpha and Omega, the beginning and the ending, which is and which was and which is to come the Almighty. Thus you have called, and I have answered. I am the Omega flame, called forth through this rosary and the heart of Mother Mary.

And I come to Earth to pronounce the full and final judgment of the power elite that has taken the abundant life away from the sons and daughters of God. Their day is done on this planet, through the absolute determination of the Mother of God, anchored through the absolute determination of Mother Mary – who is the highest representative of the Mother of God on this planet – and anchored in the physical through your heart flames and the heart flames of each and every one who gives Mother Mary's rosaries worldwide.

Thus I say, "This day the Lord has declared: 'Enough is enough! You who have taken the abundant life from the sons and daughters of God, your day is done! Your citadels of power will truly no longer be protected by your karma-dodging, from the just return of your karma. Thus, they will crumble under the weight of their own misuse of power. They will be ground into dust by the contracting force of the Mother that will no longer be held back.'"

This is the beginning of a new era for planet Earth, for truly the collective consciousness has been raised to the point, where the abundant life must be manifest in the physical, so that the Golden Age of Saint Germain can come forth. And thus, through the chalice raised, I have descended and pronounced this judgment this day. Thus it is done! It is finished! It is sealed. For the mouth of the Lord, I WILL WHO I WILL BE, Omega, has spoken it!

I Come in the Fullness of My Joy

Mother Mary, December 23, 2005

Only one solution to human problems

My beloved hearts, do you understand the key concept that we have being trying to give you? Jesus has been trying to give you this on the website, I give it to you in my new book. The concept is that you cannot solve a problem with the same state of consciousness that created the problem. The problems you see around you in South America and Columbia were created because the people are in a certain state of consciousness. There is no solution to these problems as long as the people remain in that state of consciousness.

So what will it take to bring about a change? It will take that some people will be the open doors for reaching beyond the consciousness that has created the problems in South America. And you, in this group, have truly proven that you are willing to raise your consciousness, to go beyond the consciousness that has created the problems around you. Do you understand how important that is? Do you understand how important it is for the Ascended Host and how important it is for God? Truly, there is no other way to solve the problems of humankind, whether it be in South America or elsewhere. Someone must be willing to raise their consciousness beyond the consciousness that created the problems.

My beloved hearts, Jesus walked the Earth in the Middle East 2,000 years ago precisely because it was the darkest area of the Earth. It is still the darkest area of the Earth because not enough people have embraced his teachings. What was his teaching all about? It was all about reaching beyond the human consciousness, the consciousness of duality, so that you could reach up for the Christ consciousness, the vision of Christ, the vision of the Christ consciousness. This truly is the only solution to humankind's problems. There is no other solution.

My beloved hearts, it is a complete illusion when people think that this political system or that political system can solve their problems. Capitalism will not solve the problems of poverty in South America, but neither will communism or socialism or any form of political ideology created by human beings who are trapped in the duality consciousness. Do you see, my beloved hearts, how important this is?

This is a concept that – if enough people could understand it – could totally change this planet almost overnight. If they, instead of looking high and low for human solutions to human problems, would start reaching higher than the consciousness that created those problems, and instead reach for the divine solution that comes to them through the mind of Christ. If only they dared to connect to the mind of Christ within their hearts, instead of expecting that the Pope or Jesus or the government or the president will solve their problems for them.

Why the Ascended Masters Sponsor Organizations

El Morya, December 29, 2005.

My beloved hearts, when Jesus walked the Earth 2,000 years ago, he said, "For judgment I am come." Who was it that needed the judgment of the embodied Christ, of the Word incarnate? Surely, the children of God did not need God's judgment. So the only reasonable conclusion is that those who needed God's judgment were those who had separated themselves out from the consciousness of oneness with God. They no longer saw themselves as the children of God, as the sons and daughters of God. They saw themselves as being more important than certain other children of God.

These then are the lifestreams that we in several organizations have called the fallen angels. They are here on Earth because while they were in Heaven they rebelled against God's plan. They refused to serve the All. They refused to give up all that they had internalized in order to serve the All. They sought to maintain their status as being above the evolutions of man. So they fell out of pride.

Truly my beloved, those angels were far more advanced in consciousness than the evolutions that were created to evolve here in the matter universe. And so it is not unrealistic for such a lifestream to recognize the fact that it has a superior understanding and attainment. Yet when that recognition goes beyond mere realism and becomes pride, then it becomes a trap. Now the lifestream cannot bend the knee, cannot accept that it needs to walk the same spiritual path as every human being on Earth.

Thus, the lifestream – after it has fallen and has embodied on Earth – wants to maintain and even increase its sense of superiority over the evolutions of man. This then perverts the light that the lifestream had before it fell, which is why the Lord Christ said, "If the light that be in thee is darkness, how great is that darkness."

So my beloved, you have a situation where those who have fallen from Heaven and who have perverted their light for selfish purposes, seeking to use their spiritual light, which is their gift from God given to them to give them the power to raise the All. Yet they have taken that light and attempted to use it to elevate themselves and their egos. And thereby, they have turned the light into darkness, and thus they are now the lowest evolutions on Earth because they are the most selfish and they have the least internalization of the path of oneness.

Misusing the light to impress others

Yet even though these beings do not have the light because it has turned to darkness, you must understand that in the material universe they can still use that darkness to impress those on Earth and manifest certain phenomena. You see my beloved, in Heaven there is only light. But on Earth you have a situation where the light can co-exist at the same time as the darkness. And since everything is energy, the fallen angels can actually use their light turned to darkness to manifest certain phenomena that can impress those who are not able to discern between the pure energies of the Christ light and the impure energies of the selfish beings, the mind and the energy of anti-christ.

My beloved, Jesus has given you the concept that the evolutions on Earth can be divided into three main sections. The top ten percent, the bottom ten percent and the eighty percent in the middle. The bottom ten percent are the most selfish lifestreams on Earth. They will do anything to achieve their selfish ends, whether it be using physical power or using the power they have from turning their light into darkness. Thus, you need to understand that even those who belong to the bottom ten percent can be very powerful on Earth. They are what Jesus called the blind leaders. And so you need to be very alert and discerning, so that you do not become the blind followers of the blind leaders. And this can only be achieved through the discernment of the Christ mind.

So my beloved, you now see a situation where there are a number of lifestreams embodying on Earth who think they are very sophisticated and more advanced than human beings. Yet in reality they are very close to going through the second death because they have misused their light for so long that their opportunity will shortly come to an end.

Now, the effect of the duality consciousness is that it tends to judge everyone according to a black-and-white standard. So while you are trapped in the duality consciousness, you will think that these fallen angels are "bad" and God cannot love them, and therefore God wants to see them condemned. Truly, some of the fallen angels are beyond rescue but some are not. Some have the possibility to be saved, to be turned around. And when there is even the slightest possibility of turning a lifestream around, God is willing to go to very great length in order to give that lifestream the opportunity to turn around through its own free-will choosing.

Why we sponsored organizations in the Piscean age

So my beloved, when Jesus walked the Earth 2,000 years ago, he came partly in an attempt to turn around the lowest evolutions on the Earth at that time—those who were closest to going through the second death. He did this by embodying the Christ light and by confronting these people, so that they could receive the opportunity to either accept or reject the Christ. And through that choice, they would be judged.

This approach had some success but only a limited success. And most of the lifestreams that Jesus judged did indeed pass through the second death. Now, as we approached the end of the Piscean dispensation, there was another class of fallen angels that faced the situation that unless they could move out of their selfishness and move on to the true spiritual path, they would have to go through the second death.

So the Ascended Host took council and they looked at what happened with the approach taken by Jesus of bringing the judgment of these angels. And they said, "Could there be a better way?" Might we create some kind of teaching and organization that might give these lifestreams another opportunity to turn around without facing the absolute confrontation and judgment of meeting the living Christ in embodiment?

It was then determined that we would try to create an organization that had a dual purpose. One purpose was to help the bottom ten percent of the lifestreams on Earth see the light, so to speak, and turn themselves around—realizing that there is an inner path beyond outer appearances. The other purpose was to give the top ten percent of the evolutions on Earth and opportunity to increase their service by interacting with the bottom ten percent, thereby increasing their love and increasing their ability not to judge, but always respond in love.

...

What is a fallen angel?

Now my beloved, I give you this teaching because I want you to understand that you need to come to a higher awareness of what it means to be a fallen angel. The key is the teaching giving by Mother Mary in her book, that the core of your identity is the "Conscious You" and you can choose to identify yourself with anything—be it in this world or in the spiritual realm or even in a lower world.

So being a fallen angel means – truly – that you identify yourself with the consciousness of separation. You are trying to raise yourself in comparison to others instead of selflessly serving to raise all of life. Yet you can separate yourself from that consciousness. And thus you need to understand that you have the option – even if you were a fallen angel – you have the option of freeing yourself from that consciousness. But you cannot do so until you recognize that you have partaken of that consciousness, that you have identified yourself with that consciousness.

And thus, you need to come to the point where you are fully willing to recognize that you have descended into the duality consciousness and that you need to separate yourself from it—and that this cannot wait for ten thousand lifetimes but that it has to happen now – not tomorrow – but now!

My beloved that is why we want you to understand that we of the Ascended Host do not judge anyone based on what they have done in the past. We are willing to raise up everyone, as they respond to us. We want you to feel that love that no one is lost if they are willing to come apart from the consciousness of anti-christ, from the consciousness of the fallen angels.

But you see, my beloved, you cannot come apart from that consciousness if there is an aspect of that consciousness that you are afraid to look at and that you are afraid to look at in your own being. And thus, it is not truly important whether you are a fallen angel or not. What is important is that you are not afraid to consider it, because you need to come to the point where being a fallen angel truly is a non-issue because you realize that you are more than that and you are willing to be that more. You are willing to separate yourself from the fallen consciousness and come into the consciousness of Christ, which is the consciousness of oneness.

Forgive Those Who Have Hurt You and Follow Me Into the New Day

El Morya, December 29, 2005

Understanding how the fallen beings can appear as spiritual leaders

My beloved hearts, you have all felt the weight today of the message I gave you this morning. And I wanted you to feel this weight, so that you could realize that the weight you were feeling was the world opposition to the message I was giving. And why is there such opposition? Because, indeed, the fallen angels on Earth have guarded the secret I told you this morning with all of their power for as long as they have been on this planet. What I told you this morning is the last thing they want you to know, because they can exist and continue to exist – they can exercise power over you – only by hiding the truth, only by taking on an appearance of being the angel of light that even Satan can appear as.

And so, my beloved, the secret they do not want you to know is that they can take the light that they were given in Heaven, the light that they have misqualified as darkness, and they can use it to create an outer appearance of being a spiritual person, of being a spiritual leader, of having contact with the spiritual realm, even contact with the Ascended Masters, or having various spiritual or psychic powers that impress those who do not have such powers—yet do not need them because they have the pure hearts. And thus, they can see God in their hearts and do not need any psychic powers or any outer phenomena.

My beloved hearts, it is a fact of life on this planet that in every spiritual and religious organization, the fallen angels in embodiment have gathered and they have tried to set themselves up as the leaders of that organization, as the prophets, as those who knew everything, as the only ones who had contact with God. But you will see, when you look more closely, that they have always done this for selfish purposes. And in most cases their main purpose was to control the members of the organization into giving them their light, the light that they needed because they have turned their own light into darkness.

So my beloved, it would shock you to hear how many of the popes of the Catholic Church have been fallen angels in embodiment, including the present Pope. But it would shock you also if you could see how many of the leaders of other spiritual movements have indeed been fallen angels.

What is a fallen angel?

Now my beloved, perhaps we should specify what we mean with a fallen angel. For as I said this morning, the key to understanding this mystery is to realize that the core of your identity, the Conscious You, can identify itself as anything. So if you identify yourself with the consciousness of anti-christ, the consciousness of separation from God above and the consciousness of separation from all life here below, then you are – for all practical purposes – a fallen angel because you act as a fallen angel. You act as one who wants control, and thus you become more and more enveloped in that consciousness, until you can no longer see that, in reality, you are more than that consciousness.

For truly, God did not create fallen angels—God created angels. And he gave them free will, which means that they had the potential to fall. But God did not want them to fall and did not make them fall. They did so by their own choice. Yet, the original blueprint of the being that God created is still safe and sound in the etheric octave, held in the universal Christ Mind. And therefore, the Conscious You of the fallen angel can, at any moment, choose to stop identifying itself with a sense of identity that it built after the fall and start walking the path back to oneness with its true identity, oneness with its God.

So truly, those who are following the outer path, those who are not willing to let go of their egos, those who are not willing to step onto the inner path of Oneness, those are the true fallen angels. Whether you fell from Heaven or fell on Earth is not important to us in the Ascended Host. It truly is not important for us what you have done in the past. What is important for us is that you are willing to let go of everything in that past.

But as I have said, to let go you must see that there is a certain consciousness that has entered your being. Therefore you must be honest and you must recognize that the consciousness of separation has entered your sphere of self, your container of self, and therefore you must separate yourself from it and come up higher, beginning to identify yourself with the divine blueprint that God created.

The problem in spiritual organizations

This, then, is the problem we have seen in virtually every spiritual organization on this planet, including the organizations that I have talked about that we have sponsored in this last century. The problem is that none of the members of those organizations were truly willing to look in the mirror and to see the beam in their own eyes. Almost every member of those organizations wanted to hide their egos and play the game of building an outer appearance of following all the outer rules, thereby doing everything right so that God would save them.

My beloved hearts, these are the ego games. And I must tell you that even though many people take those games very seriously, they are truly no fun. They are not child's play because indeed you cannot play the ego game without becoming entangled with the ego consciousness. So I ask you instead to commit yourself to letting go of those ego games, and indeed joining us on the Path of Oneness.

Surely we will talk more about this, but I want you to know that the will of God is clear. The will of God is that all life becomes one because only then can the kingdom of God be established in its fullness on Earth. Yet you, as a group, can come together in a spirit of oneness and you can establish the kingdom of God wherever you are. Yet this requires that you let go of your divisions within yourselves and amongst each other.

So my beloved, what I told you this morning was that the previous organizations we have sponsored were designed specifically to give the fallen angels – whose time was up at the end of the Piscean dispensation – one last opportunity to let go of the outer path and discover the inner path of oneness. Thus, you will note that these organizations could not escape the presence of the fallen ones. It simply was not possible to remove them from the organization. And therefore, you must realize that many of the characteristics of those organizations were indeed designed with the fallen ones in mind, not only to give them an opportunity, but also to make sure that they could not destroy the organization until it had at least had a chance to fulfill its mission.

Beyond Maitreya's Mystery School

Lord Maitreya, December 30, 2005

I am indeed Lord Maitreya and I come to greet you in the fullness of my joy. Why is my joy full? Because I can now see the proverbial light at the end of the tunnel, where we can fulfill the work that was begun so many thousands of years ago in what humankind knows as the Garden Of Eden. My beloved hearts, you know that the Garden Of Eden was Maitreya's mystery school and that I was indeed the God in that garden. Meaning not that I was God in the ultimate sense, but that I was the spiritual teacher assigned to teach the lifestreams who had come to that mystery school to learn their lessons.

My beloved hearts, many of you have wondered why there was a Serpent in the Garden Of Eden who could tempt Adam and Eve. Well I shall endeavor to explain this to you. And you know already what you have been told by beloved El Morya, where he set the foundation for what I am now going to tell you.

My beloved, the Serpent was in the Garden Of Eden because the Garden Of Eden was created for the same purpose that we have created the organizations we sponsored in this last century, namely to give the opportunity to fallen angels to rise above their fallen consciousness by interacting with those who were the Holy Innocents. My beloved, this can seem like a shock to some of you who have grown up thinking that God created the Garden Of Eden for the sake of those who were the innocent.

Yet when you consider what El Morya has told you, you will see that it is indeed logical that the Garden Of Eden was a mystery school set up to teach both the fallen lifestreams and those who had already internalized the light, so that both would have the opportunity to grow from their interaction. This surely was a sacrifice on the part of those who had not fallen from Above, yet it was a sacrifice they were willing to make out of their great love, not only for their fallen brothers and sisters but for the plan of God.

What is the true meaning of a mystery school?

My beloved, consider then what it means that there is a mystery school. Wherein lies the mystery? The mystery is indeed that there are initiations in the school that are not explained in full, so that there is something that is left as a mystery by the teacher.

Why then was it necessary to leave something unspoken, to leave something a mystery? Well it was, as beloved El Morya explained, because the fallen angels could not admit who they were and that they had fallen. They were not able to confront their pride, their egos, in a straightforward and direct manner, and that is why the mystery school had to allow them to hide who they were—otherwise we would have had no chance of reaching these lifestreams.

Do you see, my beloved, that those who are trapped in the ego cannot instantaneously overcome that ego? They cannot confront their ego all at once, so we must give them a gradual path. And in order to give them the opportunity to grow gradually, we must allow them to enter without exposing who they are, without exposing their egos and its many subtle games. Obviously, this has a cost, for those who are the innocents can easily be influenced by the fallen angels because they do not know who they are, they do not know their games. But again, as I said, this was a sacrifice that those who were in the mystery school had vowed to make, had volunteered to make, before they descended to the mystery school.

The world believes that the Garden Of Eden was the beginning place of humankind. You who are more spiritually aware know that this is not the case. Your beings were created in the spiritual realm and descended to the material universe. And although the Garden Of Eden was not in the same level of vibration, was not in the same frequency spectrum as the material universe is today, it was nevertheless in the material frequency spectrum. And thus it was in a lower vibration than what human beings call Heaven but which we today prefer to call the spiritual realm.

So my beloved, no lifestream was created in the Garden Of Eden, all lifestreams that were there had either fallen or they had descended voluntarily to that mystery school. And those who had descended voluntarily did so out of their greater love. They were willing to sacrifice, they were willing to run the risk that they might indeed be ensnared by the serpentine logic and therefore themselves fall into the duality consciousness. They were willing to take that risk because of love.

And what we endeavor to do in this day and age is to reconnect those of you who descended voluntarily to the original love that caused you to descend. So that even if you have fallen, even if you have taken on the ego and the duality consciousness, you can quickly reconnect to your original love and therefore rise above all negative feelings, all hurts, all wounds that you have received by being in this dense octave and being exposed to the ego-plays of those who have not been willing to rise above their egos, even though they have had numerous opportunities, starting with the Garden Of Eden all the way to today.

I Have Received a Dispensation for South America

Great Divine Director, December 31, 2005

The essence of Divine Direction

My beloved, what is the essence of Divine Direction? Could you see God giving opposite directions to different people, so that they would be running around hither and yon in opposite directions or even fighting each other? Truly, God has given more than one religion on planet Earth, but God never had the intention that true religions would be fighting each other instead of working for the common goal of raising the consciousness of humankind.

The division you see among religions or within religions is truly the work of the fallen angels. Therefore, Divine Direction is unified, it is oneness. This means that if you follow Divine Direction, you are working for the greater plan of the Ascended Host.

You might be doing this in different ways because you are unique individuals, but behind the outer actions there is a deeper sense of oneness of purpose. And without that oneness of purpose, you will not make the mark and change the Earth to your full potential. This is what has been missing in all previous organizations, partly because the fallen ones managed to divide them, but partly because those of the Light were not willing or able to raise their vision and come into alignment with the one plan of the Great White Brotherhood.

Thus, I trust that you who have been given much teaching on oneness, will internalize that teaching and will use it to look beyond the divisions of your own egos, the divisions of different groups and interests and factions that are pulling on you and say, "We want oneness more than we want to be right. We want to be right with God rather than be seen as being right amongst humans." For only in that rightness with God will you manifest the Golden Age.

Reach for the One Vision—the Vision of Oneness

Elohim Cyclopea, December 31, 2005

Think not that you are always right and that others are always wrong. Because I say to you, Beyond right and wrong there is a higher level, where oneness is more important than being right or finding other people wrong." Do you see my beloved, that this is what has been missing in most spiritual organizations since the beginning of time?

Which is why the fallen angels who were in those organizations had an easy time dividing and conquering the people who had the light, so that they could not come together and release that light and thereby take command over the organization. And therefore, the fallen angels retained command because they were at least somewhat united in their cause of dividing the people with the light.

This is why you so often see the fallen ones in society who are united by their greed, by their lust for power – or whatever negative feelings – to the point where they can divide an entire population and thereby neutralize that population and take power.

Chapter 5:
Teachings about fallen angels, 2006

There is only one test of chelaship—will you pass it?

El Morya, January 4, 2006

What amazes me the most about would-be chelas

Ah my beloved, if you could see the depth of the pride of the fallen angels, most of you would be shocked to the core of your beings, for their pride is almost absolute. And by that I mean that there is almost no opportunity whatsoever to turn a soul around who has descended to that level of pride, thinking that it knows better than God and certainly better than any of the representatives of God sent to this planet by the Ascended Host.

It is time to purify the heart

Mother Mary, Easter Sunday, April 16, 2006

Overcome your fears

My beloved hearts, as a final note, let me ask you – all of you – to recognize that in order to take full advantage of my new rosary and the teachings on the chakras, it is absolutely essential that you purify your beings of all fear. You will not be able to establish the figure-eight flow between the upper and lower chakras if you have fear in your beings. That fear will block the figure-eight flow and drive the light down in the lower chakras from which it cannot rise as long as fear reigns in your being. And thus you need to become consciously aware of your fears and make a special effort to overcome them by simply letting them go.

My beloved, I am aware that a number of our students have for many years been concerned about world conditions. There are indeed many students for whom this concern has been the driving force in their efforts to give decrees, prayers and rosaries. Yet I must tell you that if you are to take advantage of this new dispensation and teaching, you must not let your concern for the world be manifest as fear.

Truly, if you look for problems, you can easily conclude that the world is in a terrible state and that immense calamities could happen at any moment. But my beloved, you could have done the same at any time in the past. For if you are willing to look for the negatives, they have been there since the Fall Of Man.

Yet despite the fact that there has always been darkness and negativity on this planet, in every generation some people have managed to rise above it all and win their eternal freedom in the Light. They have done this by transcending their fears, by letting go of their fears.

My beloved, I know that fear can be a strong driving force at a certain level of the path. And there are indeed many people who need to have a certain fear for a time, so that they can put forth the effort to overcome their egos. Yet I must tell you that fear can become a trap. And it is indeed sad for me to see that so many people have been students of the Ascended Masters for decades, but they have not overcome their fears.

My beloved, no Ascended Master in Heaven has any fear in his or her being. You cannot ascend as long as you have fear. And thus, even though fear can serve as a driving force at the lower levels of the spiritual path, fear cannot take you to the top of the path. You cannot ascend by using fear as a motivation. You can ascend only when you overcome all fear. And you overcome fear only when you realize that it springs from the ego and it must be let go. You then realize that the power of God can overcome all conditions on the Earth, no matter how dire they might seem to a certain level of consciousness.

Thus, my beloved, it truly is time for you to step up to a higher level of focusing on the immaculate concept instead of focusing on all of the manifest or potential problems on this planet. My beloved, I see many of you who indulge yourselves in dire prophecies, in conspiracy theories or in watching the political process for any potential problem that might come up. I see many of you who have literally worried yourselves sick by contemplating all the problems and all the things that could potentially go wrong on this planet. This, my beloved, is indeed a negative habit, and it is time that you conquer it!

My beloved, I am being stern and direct, for I am indeed the fierce Mother who is here to defend her children against the onslaught of what in many cases are malicious demons who pound at your subconscious and conscious minds 24 hours a day in order to focus your attention on the negative portents. My beloved, I must tell you that there are people who are controlled by dark forces and who are thus used as tools to create websites or emails that focus on the many things that could go wrong, even though most of them are completely unrealistic and made up. My beloved I ask you to very sincerely consider using utmost Christ discernment to simply refuse to indulge your minds in some of the sources of negativity that you have partaken of for many years or decades.

It is not necessary to focus your attention on any negative email, website, article or book that comes along. It is not necessary to watch every TV program that spells out problems or dangers. I have need of those who will dedicate their lives to holding the immaculate concept of this planet for the transition into the Golden Age. These people cannot do this while they have fear in their beings.

In order to overcome that fear, it can be necessary for many of you to go through a period where you deliberately ignore all negative portents. I know very well that Jesus told you to be wise as serpents and harmless as doves, and part of being wise as serpents means that you must know what is happening on the planet so you can make calls for it in your rosaries.

Nevertheless, there are many of you who have forgotten the other part of his admonishment, namely to be harmless as doves. Doves are harmless because they have no fear, because it is fear that causes you to show aggression and do harm to yourself or others.

Thus, my beloved, by focusing on the negatives without the love, the perfect love that casts out fear, you only become more pulled into the dualistic mind of the Serpent. And thus, you are neither wise as a serpent nor harmless as a dove. You have become blinded by the duality consciousness and you have allowed fear to accumulate until you are pulled into a negative spiral of fear.

This causes some of you to qualify even your rosaries with fear. And this must stop! For it does nothing for you personally, nor for the planet as a whole. Thus I ask you to monitor yourself and see where you have fear. I ask you to put this fear into your rosary and to surrender it. And then I ask you to discipline your mind and your emotional body and refrain yourself from indulging in the sources of negative information that come your way.

When you have done this for a time – so that you have overcome the fear – then you can go back to selectively studying the potential problems on this planet in order to make precise calls. But I am literally asking you to go through a period of fasting from the negative news, until you have conquered your fears and can then partake in selective news without having them stir up your fears.

I need those who will walk the Path of Peace

Elohim of Peace, May 4, 2006.

Peace. Peace. The world is crying out for peace but there is no peace — or so it seems. Yet consider what is the source of peace. From where must peace come? Can it come from this world or must it come from a higher realm? My beloved, the source of peace is the God Flame of Peace. And true peace on Earth can come only when that Flame of Peace is allowed to shine its light to consume the shadows of war, conflict, even the warring in the members of God's people on Earth.

I am the Elohim of Peace. And as you might know, "Elohim" is a name used for God in the Hebrew Bible. In reality, there is more than one Elohim. For we, the Elohim, represent a level of God, a level of God consciousness, that is not the highest level of the Creator itself, but an individualization of, a representative of, the Creator. Thus we, the seven Elohim, have played a part in the creation of the entire material universe, and we did indeed create planet Earth as a platform for God's co-creators.

We, the seven Elohim, represent the seven primary God Flames, also known as the seven rays, which are simply forms of energy that have combined to build the material universe. The first flame is the flame of the Will of God. And as you – a co-creator evolving in the material universe – begin the path of self-mastery, you must begin on the first ray of God's Will. And only when you have mastered – to some degree – that flame of God's Will, can you move on to the next step of the path, which is to master God Wisdom.

Then you can move on to studying under the hierarchy of God Love. And when you have obtained some mastery of love, you can move on to the fourth ray of Purity. When your being has reached a critical mass of purity, you can move on to the fifth ray of Truth and Healing. And only when you have attained an uncompromising dedication to truth and have healed your four lower bodies, then can you move on to the sixth ray of Peace.

Why is Jesus the Prince of Peace?

My beloved, some of you will be aware that Jesus was called the Prince of Peace, and it is indeed because he served on the sixth ray of Peace and ministering service. He did indeed study under the Elohim of Peace that I AM. I taught him many things. As he, at inner levels, attended the retreat of the Elohim of Peace, located in the etheric realm over the island chain of Hawaii.

Why did Jesus study under the Elohim of Peace? Because he came to inaugurate the age of Pisces, which is the sixth age in a series of seven that are meant to take humankind and the Earth to a higher level where, indeed, the Golden Age and the kingdom of God can be physically manifest on this planet. Thus my beloved, Jesus came to inaugurate what is designed to be the Age of Peace—meaning that in this past 2,000-year cycle, humankind was designed to overcome all war.

Yes my beloved, I understand that when you look at the world today, you will see that there is much war and rumors of war going on on this planet. Indeed, one might say that the tension is building and that there is a potential for war here, there and everywhere. Yet my beloved, if you could see deeper, if you could see to the level where I see, you would realize that these are simply the death throes of the forces of war that have been ruling this planet for thousands of years. Yet their opportunity is fast coming to an end.

And thus it is time – it will shortly be time – for them to either surrender their warring ways and start the Path of Peace or to be taken from this planet, so that the Earth can continue to grow without being pulled down by the weight of these lifestreams—who have, for thousands of years, dedicated their entire beings to making war, mastering the art of war, always engaging in the dualistic struggle to destroy what they have defined as the enemy. Yet in reality these lifestreams are warring against themselves because they are trying to deflect attention from the conflict in their own beings by creating conflicts between themselves and others. Thereby, they have an excuse for defeating the enemy without instead of finally facing, conquering, and defeating the enemy within that is their own egos.

The keys to the Path of Peace

So my beloved, Jesus came 2,000 years ago to give everyone the essential spiritual keys for walking the Path of Peace and obtaining that inner peace that is the absolute necessity for bringing about outer peace on Earth. My beloved, Jesus has given you a profound teaching on how the top ten percent of the most spiritually evolved people on this planet are the ones who have the potential to take the Earth into the Golden Age.

Yet I must tell you that for this to happen, it is absolutely necessary that these top ten percent dedicate themselves to the Path of Peace, which means that they must overcome – and I say MUST overcome – the warring in their own members. For without overcoming their warring, how can there possibly be peace in their own beings? And if there is no one in embodiment to anchor the Flame of Peace, then how can there be peace on Earth?

You see, my beloved, I, the Elohim of Peace, am bound by the law of God to not cast my pearls before swine. And thus, in order to radiate the Flame of Peace to planet Earth, I must have open hearts who can be the open doors for the Flame of Peace. Yet how can you be the open door unless you have first dedicated your own being and life to the Path of Peace, to the cause of peace, so that you have been willing to overcome the warring in your members and thereby become a worthy focus in the material universe for the spiritual flame of Peace?

You see, my beloved, it simply is not possible to bring peace unless a critical mass of people on Earth dedicate their lives to becoming the open doors for peace. This is not possible because the law of God mandates that human beings have dominion over the Earth. Truly I, the Elohim of Peace, have access to the infinite supply of God's peace. My Flame of Peace could at this moment flash forth a radiation of peace so strong that it would consume all war and conflict on this planet and instantly consume those who are not willing to give up their warring ways.

Yet my beloved, this would be a violation of the law of free will, which states that you who are in embodiment have dominion. I do not have dominion because you are the ones who must decide that you will no longer accept war on this planet. And in order for that decision to carry authority and have dominion over the Earth, you must first be willing to decide that you will no longer have the warring in your own members. And thereby, you can then become a focus for the flame of God Peace. This is what Jesus had obtained. And he showed a magnificent example of how others can obtain the same.

The illusion behind war

My beloved, study some of Jesus' teachings. Why do you think he told you to turn the other cheek? Is the saying not a magnificent teaching on how to overcome war? No matter what anyone does to you, you do not respond with violence. You respond by turning the other cheek. And when you do so, you become an open door for the God Flame of Peace to shine through your being. And thus, that God Flame of Peace will consume the warring in other people. Yet, if instead you respond to violence with violence, you close your being to the Flame of Peace. You close your solar plexus chakra to the Flame of Peace. And instead you engage in – and thereby inevitably reinforce – the downward spiral of violence and conflict on this planet.

My beloved, look at history and see how – for thousands of years – human beings have created such downward spirals in any number of places on this planet. Look how individuals who are loving and kind – individuals with the best of intentions – are time and time again drawn into such a downward spiral of conflict that never ends. My beloved, how can such a downward spiral possibly come to an end? There are those who are so blinded by the warring in their own members, by their own egos, that they think the only way to stop a spiral of violence is to take it to the extreme of destroying those whom they have defined as the enemy that is the cause of the violence.

Yet this is nothing but an illusion. And Jesus gave any number of teachings to attempt to shake people out of that illusion and make them realize that you cannot combat violence through violence. There is only one way to stop a spiral of violence and conflict, and that is that some-one must decide to respond to violence with non-violence. Someone must decide to turn the other cheek instead of perpetuating the spiral of violence that can otherwise go on indefinitely, eventually becoming a self-reinforcing spiral that pulls people into it as a black hole pulls everything into its nothingness.

My beloved hearts, ponder these facts. Study the teachings of Jesus, the life of Gandhi and other people who have truly embodied the princi-ple of turning the other cheek, refusing to respond with violence. There is no other way for war to be banished from the Earth than by having the top ten percent of the people on Earth fully embody the principle of non-violence. Yet my beloved, in order to embody that principle, you must overcome the warring in your own members. You must follow Jesus' teaching and be willing to look for the beam in your own eye instead of focusing all of your attention on the mote in the eye of another.

Stop focusing on conflict!

My beloved, I must tell you that I see many very sincere spiritual seekers who have gotten themselves into a blind alley by focusing on the many problems on Earth. Truly, this was addressed by Mother Mary in her discourse, but I want to emphasize it because I clearly see that many of you have not understood what Mother Mary was saying. You have not let a word to the wise be sufficient because you have decided not to be wise on this issue.

Thus, I must tell you that there are those of you who are constantly focusing your attention on problems, conflicts and things that could potentially go wrong on this planet. You indulge in this or that article, posting on the internet or emails that spell out various disasters or areas of conflict. You are deliberately looking for something that can feed this need to feel that the world is on the brink of disaster.

Yet my beloved, consider what I have said, that you have dominion over the Earth. The top ten percent of the people on this planet have dominion over the Earth in the sense that if most of them believe the Earth is on the brink of disaster, then this planet WILL be on the brink of disaster. Yet if most of the top ten percent of the people sincerely believe and live as if the world is on the brink of a Golden Age, then this planet WILL be on the brink of a Golden Age.

Do you see, my beloved—it is all a matter of decision. It is all a matter of where you place the focus of your attention. Is the glass half full or half empty? Is the world going to go into a spiral of self-destruction, or is it going to go into a Golden Age? Well my beloved, if you believe that the world is on the brink of destruction, then obviously you cannot be at peace in your being, neither can you be the open door for the Elohim of Peace to radiate the Flame of Peace that can take the world away from the brink of destruction.

And thus, I have need of those who will stop focusing on the darkness and instead focus on the light that is within themselves. For truly, I have watched the students of the ascended masters through several organizations. And I must tell you that all of these organizations were started and sponsored as part of our process to bring forth a culmination of the Piscean Age by bringing a critical number of students to the point of mastering their individual Christhood, so that we could have a sufficient number of people in embodiment to be the open doors for the Flame of Peace.

My beloved, Jesus came to start the Age of Peace but he is not allowed to finish it. In order for the Age of Peace to come to its culmination, a critical mass of people in embodiment must decide to embody the teachings of Jesus to the point where they too become the Christ, where they too become the princes and princesses of peace. And they can take a stand on Earth and say, "Thus far and no farther. The warring in my members has come to an end this day. And thus I am a focus for the Elohim of Peace and I am radiating the Flame of Peace that consumes all war and conflict on the Earth."

Love one-another

My beloved hearts, I have need of those who will understand another of Jesus' profound teachings, namely, that those who truly are the disciples of Christ are known by the fact that they love one another as Jesus loved them. This, my beloved, is a most essential key. For truly, in order to turn the other cheek and not engage in any violence or anger no matter what other people do to you – in order to truly turn the other cheek to anything that is done to you – you must love other people as Christ loves everyone.

And how does the Living Christ love people? He loves them as he loves himself. And what is the self of the Living Christ? Well, my beloved, it is God. And thus the Living Christ loves everyone because the Living Christ sees God in everyone. The Living Christ sees God in itself, and thus it loves others as itself because it realizes that other people are itself because they are part of the one Body of God on Earth — out of which you too are a part.

The Living Christ, while seeing all imperfections, does not focus its attention on the imperfections. When the Living Christ sees another person, the Living Christ focuses on the immaculate concept and the potential for that person. It focuses attention on the positive potential and sees only the imperfections as a temporary roadblock. And then the Living Christ does whatever is necessary to help the other person overcome that roadblock and grow into the fullness of its highest potential.

My beloved, this is the essential key. The Living Christ never, ever has any desire to put down, limit or destroy any other part of life. The

Living Christ has only one desire and that is to raise up every other part of life because it knows that only by doing so does it raise up itself. My beloved hearts, Jesus himself said it, "Inasmuch as you have done it unto the least of these my little ones, you have done it unto me." The reason is that Jesus knew the oneness of all life. He saw that all other people are part of the Body of God, and therefore when you hurt any part of that body, you are hurting the whole—and therefore you are hurting yourself.

Only when you come to this realization, can you fully love others. And only when you fully love others, can you fully be a focus for the Flame of Peace. Because only when you seek to raise up others, instead of seeking to punish them, can you radiate the Flame of Peace that will consume their propensity for anger or violence.

My beloved, darkness can be removed only by bringing light. Therefore, conflict and war can be removed only by bringing the Light of Peace. And in order to remove conflict among the people of Earth, someone must bring the Light of Peace by loving everyone as God loves everyone. This, my beloved, is the key to peace on a planetary scale. But then what is the key to peace on the individual scale? What is the key whereby you personally can become the open door for the Flame of Peace?

Overcoming false expectations

Ah, my beloved, what is it that robs you of your personal peace, your inner peace? Well, it is true that everything begins in the heart. And the key to attaining inner peace is to purify the heart, a work which you have begun with this latest rosary. [Invocation for Clearing the Heart] Thus, it is indeed the work done by this rosary that has magnetized my flame and opened the door for the bringing forth of this teaching. Thus, you might consider this a work well done.

But I come to take this to another level. For I see that so many people, who are sincere spiritual seekers, are pulled away from peace because their attention is pulled away from the heart. Truly, if you could center your attention in the heart, and through that contact your own personal God Flame, you would never lose your peace.

But too often your attention is drawn away from the heart, and in many cases it truly is drawn into the solar plexus chakra that is right below the heart. This is the chakra that is the center for your emotions.

And it is so easy for the forces of anti-peace to stir up this chakra, so that your attention is immediately brought down to the solar plexus and thereby pulled out of the center of the heart.

Thus, my beloved, what is the key to avoiding having your attention drawn into the feeling body, into the wild emotions that are like waves on the ocean, whereby you too become a wave on the ocean of the collective emotional body that is driven by the wind and tossed? Well, my beloved, the primary factor that robs you of your peace is that you have an expectation of how life should be. And when life does not live up to your expectation, then you go into a negative emotional reaction that immediately pulls you out of peace.

But you see, my beloved, the problem is that during your upbringing in this lifetime – and over many lifetimes – you have allowed your ego to build an expectation that is completely unrealistic and completely out of touch with your original purpose for coming to Earth.

You see, my beloved, in the core of your being you have a memory of the spiritual realm. You have a memory of a realm in which there is peace and in which the kingdom of God is manifest. You also know that this is the way things are meant to become here on Earth. And thus, you know that you descended on Earth in order to bring your God Flame and make a personal contribution to bringing God's kingdom to Earth.

Yet what you do not realize is that even though this is a true expectation, your ego has used it – has turned it slightly, has perverted it – so that now it has become a false expectation. You see, my beloved, your ego has created the expectation that this Earth should be – already – like the kingdom of Heaven. And when you encounter conditions that are not the way that you know they should be, the ego makes you believe that it is necessary or acceptable or unavoidable for you to go into a negative emotional reaction.

The ego has come up with any number of false beliefs that seek to justify why it is acceptable for you to go into a negative emotional reaction when the ego's expectations are not met. But my beloved, you did not descend to Earth with the expectation that the Earth should already be the kingdom of God. You descended to Earth knowing that the Earth was far below the level of the kingdom of God and that you were here to help bring the Earth higher.

Do you see the difference? There is an essential difference between expecting that you come to some perfect place that is supposed to live up to the standard found in Heaven, or between expecting that you come to an imperfect place and that it will require work, effort and patience to bring the Earth to the level of the spiritual realm.

If you descend expecting Earth to be perfect, you are easily trapped into responding negatively when you encounter the fact that the Earth is not perfect. Yet if you expect that the Earth is not perfect and that you are here to work, then you are not as easily pulled into that negative reaction.

My beloved, do you see what I am trying to tell you? When you allow yourself to think that the conditions you encounter in life should live up to a certain outer standard of perfection, then you make yourself vulnerable and you open yourself up to disappointment. And this disappointment will immediately pull you away from the centeredness of peace.

Yet why do you become disappointed? So many people allow their egos to make them believe that they have nothing to do with, that they did not cause, the sense of disappointment. Why, certainly it was these other people or these imperfect conditions on Earth that caused these disappointments. But my beloved, a true spiritual seeker needs to realize that your disappointment was not caused by anything outside yourself. It was caused by an inner condition, namely that you have an unrealistic expectation of what life should be like here on Earth.

You see, my beloved, you came here to bring your personal God Flame and to let that light shine. My beloved, you came here to let the light shine during any conditions you might encounter on Earth, so that the perfection of your God Flame could consume the imperfections that you encounter on this planet.

What has happened instead is that you have allowed your ego to create a very subtle expectation that you should not allow your light to shine until certain outer conditions are met. My beloved, do you see the subtlety here? You are here to consume imperfections, and the only way to do this is to let your God Flame shine through you in the face of all imperfections. Instead, you have allowed your ego to trick you into thinking that when you encounter imperfections, you should stop your light from shining. Instead, you should look for certain outer conditions to be present before you can let your light shine.

My beloved, think back to Jesus' words. He told his disciples that those who wanted to be known to the world as his true disciples should love one another. He also told you that it was not enough to love those who loved you, that you had to love even your enemies. Do you see how this connects to what I just told you? Do you see that Jesus was saying that you should love all people no matter what they do?

Instead, the ego has tricked people into thinking that you should love other people only when they live up to certain outer requirements. Only when they supposedly deserve your love should you give them your love. But you see, my beloved, this is the lie. For truly, there is no such thing in God's mind as deserving or not deserving. Jesus told you that God lets the sun rise upon the evil and the good and the rain descends upon the just and the unjust.

So you see, my beloved, God does not create conditions. He lets his light shine upon all because he knows that letting the light shine is the only way to raise up a person. And it does not matter how much that person is trapped in darkness, for only by letting the light shine will the person be free of the darkness. So you see, my beloved, if you are to love other people as Christ loves you, then your only concern about other people must be to help them overcome whatever darkness is temporarily clouding their minds. You are here to set them free by loving them, by shining your light upon them. You are not here to judge them according to a human standard and judge who is worthy of your light and not worthy of your light.

I am not thereby saying that you need to treat all people the same, or that you need to indiscriminately let other people abuse you. For the light of God is highly intelligent, and it will give to each person what that person needs in order to be free. But in order for you to be the open instrument of this light, you must overcome the expectations, even the expectation for what other people should be like. You may look at a person and you may say, "That person is trapped in darkness and needs to be set free," but you have no need to make that judgment.

You simply remain centered in the heart, centered in your God Flame, and then you allow your God Flame to give to that person what that person needs. And for some it may be unconditional love. For others it may be tough love that challenges their illusions and calls them to come up higher by demanding that they see that there is a better way.

The Rose of Peace

My beloved, not long ago it was the anniversary of the nuclear disaster in Chernobyl in Russia. You might have read that although people cannot approach this contaminated place, nature has taken over. Even in this intense radiation, plants are growing. My beloved, imagine a rose growing in this contaminated atmosphere, yet still radiating its fragrance. It does not matter that there is no human being around to appreciate the fragrance. For the rose is not there to be appreciated. The rose is there to radiate its fragrance, and the rose is focused on doing its job.

My beloved, it was not long ago that it was the anniversary of the liberation of the Auscwitch death camp in Poland. Truly, if you want to find an example of how human conflict can reach an almost unthinkable extreme, you would be hard pressed to find a better example then the Nazi death camps.

But I must tell you that in several of these death camps the commandant, or the commandant's wife, had a rose garden. Now imagine a rose growing in proximity to the one of the darkest places on Earth. Yet the rose is not touched by this darkness. It is not concerned by it. It does not judge. Whether it be a prisoner in the death camp or one of the people who push the prisoners into the gas chambers, the rose will radiate its fragrance.

The rose does not hold back its fragrance. Anyone who walks up to the rose will receive the fullness of its fragrance because the rose is not here to judge; it is simply here to radiate the beautiful fragrance that can uplift anyone who smells it. And thus, you see my beloved, even the commandant of a Nazi death camp will receive the fragrance of the rose because that rose is only concerned about lifting up any human being by sharing its fragrance.

Thus, my beloved, I come to give you a gift. I come to give you the gift of visualizing the Rose of Peace over your solar plexus chakra. This is a rose that is pure white in appearance. But my beloved, it is not like the roses you see on Earth because the Rose of Peace is self-luminous. It radiates light. It does not simply reflect the light of the sun, it radiates brilliant white light from within itself. And thus, my gift to you is that you visualize this rose of peace over your solar plexus chakra whenever you feel that you are pulled into a negative emotional reaction concerning any condition in your personal life or on a planetary scale.

Visualize that Rose of Peace over your solar plexus chakra. Visualize how it radiates its light and spreads its fragrance of peace until your entire energy field is filled with that light and that fragrance. When you encounter conditions on Earth where there is no peace, then visualize the rose of peace over that area and again visualize how it fills the entire area with the light and the fragrance of peace.

Become a prince or princess of peace

Ah, my beloved, if you would give the greatest service for eradicating conflict and war from this planet, then commit yourself to walking the inner Path of Peace, so that you can learn from Jesus, so that you can learn from the Prince of Peace, until you too can become a prince or princess of peace. You can inherit your Father's kingdom and then give it to all.

My beloved, the sixth ray is the ray of Peace. And the seventh ray is the ray of Freedom. The Earth is destined to move from the Age of Peace into the Age of Freedom. Yet my beloved, how can there possibly be freedom until there is peace? For if you do not have peace in your own being, how can you possibly be free? You will be enslaved by the emotional thralldom that pulls you away from peace at the slightest provocation. As soon as some condition on Earth does not live up to your expectation of perfection, then you are pulled out of peace. And since hardly anything on this Earth can live up to the expectation of perfection, you are constantly in a state of non-peace.

Likewise, how can the Golden Age of Saint Germain be manifest on Earth as long as the dark clouds of war are hanging as a constant threat over this planet? How can nations truly build the Golden Age if everything they build could be destroyed in a matter of minutes through a nuclear holocaust or even through a conventional war? Look at the nation of Iraq today. How can you build a nation, how can you build a future, when at any moment a bomb can be exploded and destroy what people have built?

This, my beloved, shows you that the key to freedom is peace. And I have now given you the key to peace. Will you apply it, or will you allow the ego to continue to trick you into believing that only when certain outer conditions are met can you be at peace?

You see my beloved, the ego wants you to think that only when certain conditions are met in your personal life can you be at peace about your own life. And only when certain conditions are met in the world can you be at peace about the future of this planet. Yet I tell you, it is a lie. For the outer conditions are nothing but the reflection of your inner conditions. And thus, you will never have conditions of peace in your own life or on your planet until you make the decision to be at peace inside yourself—regardless of the outer conditions.

You see, my beloved, the essential expectation that the ego has built is that your inner peace depends on peace in the outer world. This is the illusion of the ages, for your inner peace depends on nothing outside yourself. Your inner peace depends only on one thing—your inner contact with, your centeredness in, the God Flame of Peace. And there is nothing that can stand between you and that inner contact with the Flame of Peace because, as Jesus also told you, the kingdom of God is within you. Meaning that no outer conditions in your own psychology or being, or on the planet on which you live, can come between you and your oneness with God, your oneness with the Flame of Peace.

Thus, my beloved, stop looking for peace outside yourself. Start looking for peace the only place it can be found—in the kingdom of peace that is within you, in the Flame of Peace that I AM, and that I am willing to share with all those who will dedicate themselves to being at peace regardless of outer conditions.

Thus, peace be still and know that I AM God. Peace be still and know that the I AM Presence within you is God. My peace I leave with you. Multiply it and radiate it to all life so that this planet can be at peace.

The true alchemy of the heart

Saint Germain, May 25, 2006.

Hardness of heart and abortion

My beloved, I will speak to you briefly on the issue of abortion, which as you know has been on the hearts and minds of the Ascended Host for decades. We indeed have a plan for this nation, for the raising up of America and the entire world. But contrary to the old image – that goes back decades, centuries, millennia in religions – that God or the Ascended Hosts will miraculously save humankind and bring about the Golden Age, the reality is that what will bring about the Golden Age is that a sufficient number of people in embodiment discover and follow the inner path and reach a certain level of Christhood. Where they can be the open doors – as Jesus was the open door – for bringing the immaculate concept for the Golden Age into physical manifestation.

And so for this to happen, the lifestreams that have obtained a certain level of Christhood in past lives must come into embodiment. This, of course, is a plan that has one major flaw, because the forces of antichrist are fully aware that it is people who must bring about change in the world. They have known this for a long time and they are keenly aware of it, even though most people – most spiritual people and the general population – are not aware of it. Because the power elite has created a culture that de-emphasizes the importance of the individual, seeking to turn the majority of humankind into the blind followers of themselves as the blind leaders. Thus following the currents in the mass consciousness, rather than attaining the supreme individuality that is the Christ consciousness.

Thus, they are fully aware that if they can keep out the key individuals, so that a critical mass of Christed Beings will not come forth on this planet, then they can postpone – at least for a season – the manifestation of the Golden Age, which will bring about their own exit from this planet and their loss of control. And because America is a key to the manifestation of the Golden Age, they have especially attempted to prevent the right number of Christed Beings from living in the United States.

Abortion has been one of their key strategies. And I must tell you quite frankly that it is the divine matrix, the divine plan that there should be 44 million more people living in the United States than is the case today. Many people when they hear this staggering number would say, "Oh but what would happen then to the economy, to the environment? It would be overcrowded. Think about the traffic!" [Laughter]

But you see, these are selfish concerns. And this is precisely why the forces of anti-christ have been successful in establishing abortion as the legal right for any woman with no conditions. It is because so many people in the United States have become so self-centered and so selfish that there is not room in their hearts for another person in their family or for another family down the street.

This is hardness of heart in a way that is subtle, and therefore most people do not see it as hardness of heart. They do not realize that what they see with their intellectual minds as a perfectly logical and rational argument is simply the ego's ability to justify anything, even justify the hardness of heart that would exclude a Christed soul from coming into embodiment. As King Herod attempted to kill the Christ child, and in so doing was willing to kill an entire generation of male babies.

My beloved, think of the hardness of heart of a ruler who could give such an order. Yet there are people in America today who have that same hardness of heart and therefore think abortion is acceptable.

Now, my beloved, I must tell you that the Ascended Host never look at any issue in black and white terms. We have in the past spoken out in a black-and-white way against abortion, because we deemed it necessary to portray a viewpoint that hopefully could awaken at least some people. Yet in the long run, we could foresee a society where abortion was available to a woman under certain conditions that would not jeopardize her spiritual growth.

Thus, the issue is not as clear-cut as it might have seemed from our past musings on the topic. Nevertheless, I must also tell you that the United States is not at a point yet where it is able to enact the right Christ-like conditions. And thus, it would have been better had the United States had a clear law preventing abortion over these past decades, since that fateful decision by the Supreme Court. Because there would have been millions more Americans in embodiment than there is today.

...

Back to nature versus back to God

My beloved hearts, we of the Ascended Host do not belong to the back-to-nature movement. We belong to the back-to-God movement! It is not a matter of thinking back to the "pristine" wilderness that existed when the first settlers came over here, idealizing it and thinking that America should somehow go back to this state. In which only a small number of people could survive here and only do so by being in a constant state of warring with each other over the scant natural resources.

No, it is our plan for the Golden Age that America should transcend, and establish a modern society that has pristine conditions both in the areas inhabited by man and in the areas that are left to natural conditions. Certainly, we do not desire to see overcrowded and polluted cities with slums. Certainly, we do not desire to see the entire food chain polluted by chemicals. This is not our plan for this nation.

But what you see today in the pollution of nature springs from – starts in – the pollution of the heart of the people of this nation. And again, it is hardness of heart, lack of sensitivity, lack of willingness to reach for the higher vision that there might be a better way to do things than the way that is convenient – or seems convenient – right now. Or the way that allows a small power elite to maintain their control over the majority of the wealth and resources in an entire nation.

My beloved, what overturned the rigid feudal system of Europe was a growth in the population. What will overturn the current elitist system in the United States will be only – at least on the physical level – a growth in the population, that makes it necessary to redistribute – not wealth as the Communists say – but redistribute economic and spiritual opportunity. So that all men and women can be treated as they were created, namely to be equals and have equal opportunity to raise themselves above the conditions of their own past karma. And therefore, they can experience the personal alchemy, which when it reaches critical mass will become a national alchemy and turn around a nation and raise it to an entirely new level, that is so much higher than what you have today that people today cannot even envision it.

My beloved, my vision for this nation would put all of your science fiction literature to shame. All of the things that you see [in science fiction literature and future studies] are as nothing compared to the real vision that we of the Ascended Host hold for this nation and for the world. But for that vision to come into action, into physical manifestation, a critical mass of people must be willing to let go of the old, to let the old images – the old world view, the old expectations – die as Jesus demonstrated by being willing to die on the cross and give up the ghost.

Why environmentalism is lacking love

Mother Mary, May 25, 2006.

And as I have explained many times in my teachings, the Mother Light has a built-in force, the contracting force of the Mother, which breaks down any structure that is not in alignment with the will and the vision of the Father. Thus, my beloved, those in the environmentalist movement who are acting out of pure motives to preserve nature are actually in the long run helping to destroy what they are seeking to preserve.

They stay in the closed, circular logic that does not see that the only way to preserve the Earth, even natural resources, is to bring them back into alignment with the Father's vision for this Earth. So that the conditions that are not right, that are not balanced, can be transcended and the Earth can come back to a purer state which is sustainable. Whereas the current conditions are not sustainable, which is why you see even Mother Nature herself breaking down through an increasing amount of storms and earthquakes and other natural imbalances.

This, my beloved, is one idea that if it could be embraced by enough people in the top 10% of the most spiritually advanced people, could revolutionize not only the environmentalist movement but many other movements and organizations that seek to preserve the Mother Light, the Mother's love, and express the Mother's love.

This would be my desire, to see this revelation spread like rings in the water, where people realize that we need to go beyond the old view of God as the remote, judgmental, angry being in the sky that has been portrayed by traditional Christian religion. And we need to realign ourselves with the loving Father, who loves us so much that he does not want to see us remain stuck in imperfect conditions. And thus, he wants us to transcend and come back to his kingdom, which is the Christ consciousness.

Big money and environmentalism

If people could wake up and realize this, they would indeed start seeing how the entire philosophy behind these progressive movements has been influenced by the duality consciousness. Even to the point where the entire environmentalist movement is heavily influenced – behind the scenes – by big money interests who see an opportunity to make a profit by creating an artificial scarcity of natural resources. By locking up natural resources in the name of being nature preserves or national parks or wilderness areas that are set aside, thus creating the opportunity for these big companies to attain a virtual monopoly.

This has been the dream of capitalists since the 1800s, when certain lifestreams realized that they did not want a free economy. And the only way to subvert the free market economy was to use the democratically elected government to enact laws that gave the big companies an unfair advantage over the smaller independent companies. Thus, allowing many of the big companies to do whatever they want to extract oil, timber or other resources, while shutting out the competition.

This, my beloved, is a condition that unfortunately many of the well-meaning but not spiritually alert people in the environmentalist movement are serving to uphold without understanding what they are doing. And thus, it would be my desire to see an awakening, whereby you realize that it should not be the goal of the environmentalist movement to bring this planet back to nature, but indeed, as Saint Germain said, to bring this planet back to God's original image – the immaculate concept for this planet.

And that immaculate concept includes human beings as an integral part of life on this planet. But it also envisions human beings who are not trapped in the duality consciousness, whereby they see themselves as being in opposition to the natural environment. Rather they see themselves as being one with nature, one with all life and – instead of thinking they have to fight Mother Nature for her resources, they have to subdue her and control her and rape and pillage – they realize that they can work with Mother Nature.

And then, indeed, the promise of Jesus will come true, "Fear not little flock, for it is the Father's good pleasure to give you his kingdom." But God will give you his kingdom here on Earth through Mother Nature and through the Ma-ter Light materializing the abundant life that is envisioned in the immaculate concept for this planet but which has been lost through the fall in humankind's consciousness, whereby God's co-creators have created conditions that are indeed so far from the abundant life.

I will send you to bear witness to Christ truth in this age

Jesus, May 26, 2006.

The ego as a substitute teacher

Yes my beloved, when your conscious self first decided to turn its back to the spiritual teacher – the representative of God that you had in whatever higher realm you found yourself in when you decided to experiment with the duality consciousness – when that first happened, you made a decision, and it caused you to lose contact with the teacher. And thus, you felt alone. And you could not bear that sense of aloneness, and therefore you created the ego as a substitute teacher, as a replacement for the real teacher, whether it be Lord Maitreya in the Garden Of Eden or other ascended beings in other realms and systems of worlds. For truly, many people on Earth come from far-away places in this universe and beyond.

And thus, my beloved, it is indeed true that many people believe that the ego and the prince of this world are their true teachers. There are even those who believe that the devil himself is the true liberator of humankind because as they say "Until we rebelled against the will of God, we did not truly have freedom and free will." There are those who seriously believe that it was in the act of rebelling against God that human beings attained free will. But my beloved, if you did not already have free will, how could you have the option to rebel against God? And if God really was out to control you, why would he allow you to rebel against his law and separate yourself from him?

My beloved, I know that the ego and the false teachers of this world have an array of sophisticated arguments against this simple logic. But when you look at it with the innocent mind of a child, you realize that all the sophistication is just camouflage, and it makes no sense. And thus, you can avoid following the subtle logic of the false teachers of this world who have only one goal in mind. And that is to keep the Conscious You thinking it is separated from your own higher being and from your God—and that you cannot come back to oneness with God on your own, that you need a savior from outside yourself.

Find centeredness in the heart

El Morya, May 27, 2006.

Bridging the gap

My beloved, I ask you to consider that the central challenge on the spiritual path is very simple. The path implies that you are at a particular step and you need to move up to the next step. In other words, there is a gap between where you are now and where you need to go. So the central challenge on the spiritual path is how to close that gap. And for many people it can seem insurmountable.

My Beloved, one of the major tactics employed by the dark forces and the ego, is to create the illusion that it is impossible for you to bridge the gap. They have used Jesus as a primary example in the West, but in every religion there has been created this monster of idolatry concerning the leader or leaders of that religion. Jesus was so special, was so far above everyone else that how can you possibly close the gap between your present level of consciousness and the superior level of consciousness that Jesus demonstrated. The same thing with many leaders of many organizations.

There are indeed many gurus and teachers in this world today who are not necessarily false gurus—they are well-meaning individuals, they have attained a certain spiritual attainment, perhaps even certain abilities. Yet if they do not understand the dynamics of the path, they often teach essentially by saying, "Look how advanced I am. Come up to my level!" But they do not provide a step-by-step path between where people are at in consciousness and where they are at themselves.

And thus, you see my beloved, if these individuals are not aware of this, and are yet too focused on themselves – that they have not truly let go of the self-centeredness but they have a little bit of ego left – then even though they have genuine spiritual attainment, and they actually have the ability to help people grow spiritually, they have not yet bridged the gap between their own attainment and the attainment of those they teach. And thus, even though they might give a genuine teaching, it is actually a false teaching in the sense that it discourages those who accept the teaching because they think they cannot bridge the gap between their consciousness and the consciousness of the teacher. Because they see no logical step-by-step path between their level and the level demonstrated by the teacher.

...

My beloved, the Earth has moved forward tremendously over the past century. And although you see many problems, there is an underlying progress that is indeed immense and cannot be stopped by the forces of darkness. For had they been able to stop it, they would have done so, ten years, a hundred years, a thousand years, or ten thousand years ago. And thus, the very fact that the Earth is still in existence is proof that the dark forces do not have the power to destroy this beautiful planet. For there are enough people who would not go down with them and thereby drag the Earth into their self-created hell.

Understand why civilizations rise and fall

Great Divine Director, June 30, 2006

And so, my beloved, you see in many areas of South America this longing back to the past, whether it be to the grandeur, or the so-called grandeur, of the Inca or other past civilizations or even to Colonial times. My beloved, it is necessary for the people to awaken. The Golden Age in South America cannot be brought in by an elite, for it is indeed the existence of power elites, going back through the millennia, that is responsible for the warring and the inequality that has led to the current state of poverty.

Thus, my beloved, this elitism must be overcome and it can be overcome only when a critical mass of the people themselves awaken. But they cannot be awakened through the flame of anti-peace that leads to revolution, for we cannot have South America turn to a left-wing, Marxist, communist, socialist ideology as has begun to happen in some nations. This, my beloved, will only lead to greater instability that will lead first to civil war and then war among nations.

And thus, a major war could indeed come upon this continent within the next two decades unless a critical mass of people are awakened through the flame of ecstatic, joyful peace. This is the willingness to seek peace but a peace that is based on self-transcendence, whereby the current conditions are not allowed to remain. Yet they are not allowed to lead to conflict and war but lead to a greater sense of peace based on constant self-transcendence.

...

Study how civilizations become rigid and self-destruct

My beloved, the Inca civilization that took over this place of Machu Picchu is indeed a good example to study in order to understand how an entire civilization can become trapped in a rigid mindset, a rigid culture, being so concerned about maintaining their rituals that they are not willing to self-transcend. They are not willing to go within and bring forth a creativity from within the heart that can renew their rituals, their practices, even their entire belief system and world view.

Thus, my beloved, at this place you will see certain rocks that are large and carved with great precision. On top of these huge rocks you will see smaller rocks carved with far less precision and stacked up with far less skill. This shows you that the Inca's built upon temples that are far older than the Inca civilization. It also shows you that the Inca civilization was not that creative in itself but often copied what they saw around them.

The Inca civilization was very good at organizing and that is why they grew and were successful and managed to conquer many of their neighbors who were not as organized. And this is indeed one of the necessary qualifications of any civilization. It must have organization because it creates stability. Yet stability and longevity are not the same thing. For you see, my beloved, stability without self-transcendence, without creativity, cannot create longevity, neither in your personal life nor in an entire civilization.

And that is why, indeed, you saw that the Inca's themselves – even though they had a very quick rise to power – also had a quick fall because their own rigidity, their own unwillingness to self-transcend, did indeed create the opposite force from the Mother Light itself that brought about the Spaniards who came in and very quickly conquered the Inca civilization.

Thus, my beloved, one might say that the Inca civilization is a perfect example of a civilization that – even though it reached a certain height – simply was not sustainable from the very beginning because it had too many contradictory forces. It had too much rigidity and unwillingness to go beyond rigid doctrines, beliefs and rituals. My beloved, no amount of ritual – let me say this again – no amount of ritual can ever save a human being or an entire civilization.

Why ritual cannot save you

You can pick any spiritual technique or philosophy found on this planet. You can practice it with great determination, yet the practice of ritual itself will not save you, because the practice of ritual cannot guarantee the transcendence of your consciousness. For a ritual to be effective, it must be approached as only a foundation for self-transcendence. And you must then connect to the source of creativity in your heart, thereby adding your inner creativity to the outer ritual so that you make it a living ritual.

And that is precisely what will bring about the contact between your lower being – performing the ritual – and your own Higher Being. That contact can happen only through the open door of the heart, the secret chamber behind the heart chakra that is the connecting point between the lower part and the higher part of your own Being.

Thus, my beloved, unless you open that door of the heart through creativity and love, you cannot establish the figure-eight flow in your own being that is the very key to self-transcendence and spiritual growth. Likewise, unless a civilization opens that door of the heart of its people and especially of its leaders – and especially its spiritual leaders – unless that happens, that civilization cannot have the figure-eight flow that leads to self-transcendence and thereby longevity.

The Inca civilization was not connected to the Ascended Host

My beloved hearts, if you will study the Inca civilization, you will see how the priesthood and the kings fell into the typical trap that you see in almost every civilization—where once they had ascended to power they began to be more concerned about maintaining or even increasing their power than being concerned about maintaining the connection to the spiritual realm.

My beloved, I must tell you that the Inca civilization never had a connection to the Ascended Host. Their priests needed drugs in order to induce a "higher" state of consciousness, and therefore they could not communicate with the Ascended Host, for we do not communicate with people through drugs or any other mechanical means. We communicate only through those who have opened their hearts through love.

So the Inca civilization was actually, from the very beginning, in contact with lower spirits. Yet I must tell you that even these lower spirits would have been able to promote some form of self-transcendence in the Inca civilization—if the priests had been willing to continue to heighten their contact. Yet the priests became so focused on the outer rituals and the rigidity of those rituals, and therefore they started having contact with lower and lower spirits.

And as they realized that there was no more the power in their rituals – in terms of giving them inner visions – they instead reverted to the traps seen in so many religions, including the Catholic Church and other Christian churches today, where they became more and more focused on the outer ritual instead of the inner experience beyond the ritual. And so the ritual itself became an end in itself rather than the means to an end. And that is why the Inca civilization, the Inca priesthood, became more and more rigid, which is indeed what led further and further into the downward spiral which quickly became irreversible. And the Spaniards were only the outer tool for this.

Western civilization is transcending itself

Of course, the Spaniards themselves were not a sustainable civilization. But I must give credit that the European civilization has been far better able to transcend itself than most other civilizations. Thus, you do indeed see – in Europe and in the United States today – a civilization that is very quickly transcending itself, having to a very large degree, abandoned the ritualistic rigidity of the past.

Thus, my beloved, even though you see in modern western civilization many conflicts and contradictions that do indeed threaten the longevity of this civilization, you also see the willingness to self-transcend on the part of many people. The willingness that is far greater than what you see for example in South America or in other cultures around the world.

My beloved, what I want you to understand is that the Incas were too unbalanced in terms of being too rigid and not having enough creativity. What you see in the Western civilization today is almost the opposite form of imbalance—where the Western civilization has thrown off the rigidity of the Catholic Church yet has not found anything to put in its place, to give the spiritual stability that can counter-balance the innovation you see in technology.

Thus, my beloved, you see indeed the unwise use, the unbalanced use, of technology because people do not have the inner contact of the heart—for they have no spiritual basis and foundation upon which to build their exploration of technology. Thus, what you see is a tremendous outpouring of creativity in terms of using the Mother Light in ever new ways. Yet you do not see that this happens under the guidance, under the Divine Direction, of the Father energy, the Father Light. And thus, you do not have, as of yet, a healthy figure-eight flow in the modern Western civilization.

This, my beloved, is of course the main reason for giving Mother Mary's rosaries, which are meant to help people re-establish that figure-eight flow on a personal scale and on a larger scale, that can then bring society back to a more balanced state where there is no longer the imbalance between the Alpha and Omega qualities, the Father and the Mother energies. And thus, a civilization can then use the Mother Light in the form of technology under the guidance of the spiritual truth of the Father Light.

And thus, my beloved, divine direction can come to play its intended role, where it sets the perimeters. And as long as people exercise their creativity within these perimeters, they will not self-destruct. Nor will their civilization self-destruct, as did so many civilizations in the past that did not have the proper balance.

Your mission is spiritual wholeness

God Meru, July 3, 2006.

There is only one thing that will transform the Earth into the Golden Age of Saint Germain—and that is Christhood. Namely that a critical mass of people attain and express their Christhood, wherever they are on this planetary body.

My beloved, there is no other means for bringing in a Golden Age. It is certainly true that part of bringing in a Golden Age is to bring forth new technology, new knowledge, new economic philosophies and systems, new political philosophies, new spiritual and religious philosophies. Yet my beloved, while these are necessary and are indeed the Omega aspect of bringing in a Golden Age, I must tell you plainly that no amount of technology, knowledge, political reform or social programs or religious programs can ever bring in the Golden Age of Saint Germain.

Free energy technology

For the Golden Age of Saint Germain is not a mechanical age and cannot be brought in through mechanical means. It is an age of Christhood.

For Saint Germain has no desire to see his flame of freedom be per-verted through the very technology that he has brought forth in order to give people freedom to pursue their spiritual growth—instead of spend-ing their time and energy on eking out a living from the dry soil, such as you see in this place.

Thus, my beloved, Saint Germain has decided that the release of new technology will be measured very closely to the increase of Christ-hood among the most spiritually advanced people on this planet. Thus, my beloved, the technology that can revolutionize energy production and thereby every aspect of industry and life on this planet, is ready to be released by Saint Germain himself. But that technology will not be released until a critical mass of people have manifested a critical degree of Christhood, so that they can hold the balance whereby we can prevent that this new powerful technology will be misused for war and control, as we have seen every other technology released to humankind be mis-used by the power elite.

Thus, my beloved, when you look at technology, you see how it is being used over and over again for the purposes of control, for the pur-poses of suppressing the people and concentrating power, wealth – even freedom – in the hands of the elite. This, my beloved, cannot continue, and thus it has been determined by our councils that if, indeed, it is nec-essary that the world will go through a major energy crises or a major war over oil, then this must be allowed to happen so that the people can be awakened to the dangers and the limitations of technology without Christ vision.

Yet my beloved, we would much prefer to see a scenario where those of you who are the most spiritually advanced people will make that last effort to heal your psychology, to expose your ego and to manifest and express your Christhood, whereby you can hold that balance so that before a major energy crises – leading to a third world war – will occur, we can release the technology that will make oil obsolete in a matter of a couple of decades.

The underlying cause of conflict in the Middle East

Mother Mary, July 16, 2006.

My beloved hearts, you have asked and thus I will endeavor to give you part of the answer to your questions about the Middle East. I understand that you are concerned about the situation in the Middle East and the potential for an escalation. Yet my beloved, I cannot say that I or the Ascended Host share your concern, for we look at the situation in the Middle East from a larger, broader more timeless perspective.

Thus, my beloved, let me attempt to help you step back from the situation in the Middle East and indeed gain at least a glimpse of the perspective we hold on the situation. The most important thing you can keep in mind is that planet Earth has been allowed to become a cross-roads for lifestreams from many different evolutions. Originally, this planet was conceived as a protected sphere for the descent of specific groups of lifestreams, specific evolutions, which we have sometimes called the root races. Yet after the Fall Of Man occurred and the con-sciousness of humankind began to descend into duality, it was deter-mined that lifestreams that were not part of the original root races would be allowed to embody here in large numbers. These lifestreams have come from many different places in the Cosmos, even from other plan-ets in this solar system.

Why was this allowed? Well, my beloved, it was the original plan for planet Earth that the lifestreams who embody here would never lose their conscious awareness of and their conscious contact with their spir-itual teachers. Yet my beloved, many lifestreams did indeed lose that contact and therefore they began to feel that they were abandoned by God.

Creating a downward spiral

The material universe acts like a mirror. The matter light will outpicture in physical form the conditions you hold in your mind. The potential is that a wave of lifestreams can create a downward spiral for themselves.

My beloved, this occurs because all of the lifestreams of that particular wave, of that particular root race, hold a very similar vision for the Earth and for them being abandoned by God. This vision will gradually become outpictured in physical circumstances, which is what caused matter itself to densify until it became impossible to perceive anything beyond the material universe with the physical senses.

Yes, my beloved, when the planet was of a higher vibration, people could – even with their physical senses – perceive the finer energies beyond what you today call matter substance. Yet as the consciousness of humankind became denser, the planet itself became more dense. Matter itself became more dense, and thus most people today cannot perceive anything beyond matter substance.

My beloved, do you see what happens in such a downward spiral? The lifestreams co-create their own circumstances and as matter outpictures what they co-create, they forget, or refuse to acknowledge, that they have created the outer conditions they now see around them. Thus, they become completely convinced that their vision – that they have been abandoned by God – is entirely correct. And they take their outer circumstances as proof that their vision is correct. In reality, what they see is not an objective circumstance. It is a subjective circumstance that they have created. And thus, my beloved, the only thing that can break the downward spiral is that the people change their vision.

Yet when the people have lost contact, the direct contact with their spiritual teachers, how can we reach them and tell them they need to change their vision? This, my beloved, is the central dilemma on planet Earth. The question now becomes, "Since the people have turned their backs on their spiritual teachers, what can possibly break the downward spiral?"

Well, my beloved, the only thing that can break the downward spiral is that the people change their vision. But because they will not listen to their spiritual teachers and because the matter light obediently outpictures their vision, something else is needed to break the downward spiral, the vicious circle. What is that something else? Well, one possibility is that we allow a wave of lifestreams to embody on planet Earth, a wave of lifestreams that come from an entirely different environment and therefore do not have the exact same vision as the lifestreams who are already on this planet. Thus, when these two waves of lifestreams interact, they will inevitably clash. And while this clashing will lead to conflict, it has the potential to break up the rigid mindset of both waves of lifestreams.

My beloved, do you see the essential principle I am explaining here? When you will not learn from your spiritual teachers, the only thing that has a possibility of teaching you life's lessons is the school of hard knocks. And the more rigid a wave of lifestreams become, the harder the knocks that are required to break through their shell and make them rethink their approach to life.

The Earth is in an upward spiral

Thus, my beloved, it was determined a long time ago that Earth would no longer be an exclusive sphere for the original root races. Instead, many lifestreams from other systems of worlds, from other planets, from other galaxies, would be allowed to embody here. This, my beloved, does not mean that these lifestreams traveled here in the physical octave in spaceships. They did not.

My beloved, there are many lifestreams on Earth who have a sense that they came from somewhere else, from other star systems. And while some are simply deluding themselves with fantasies, there are some who are correct. They did come from elsewhere. But their souls were allowed to embody on Earth in human bodies. They were not transported here through material, mechanical means.

Thus, my beloved, when you look at planet Earth today, you see that it is indeed a crossroads of many different lifestreams, from many different backgrounds, with many different attitudes and approaches to life. It is, so to speak, a melting pot. And the highest potential of this melting pot is that when people see the diversity, they will change their attitude, they will learn from each other, they will take the best from each evolution and build a culture that is more balanced, more centered, more harmonious.

Of course, there is always a lowest potential, which is that the different lifestreams will focus on their differences, thereby creating conflicts between them leading to physical warfare. This, of course, is what you have seen over and over again on this planet. So my beloved, why did the Ascended Host take this calculated risk of allowing the Earth to become a melting pot? Well because if it had not happened, the original root races would have continued their downward spiral until they would have destroyed themselves.

What has happened instead is that – through the breaking up of the rigid mindset of the original root races – an upward spiral has indeed been created. This upward spiral can be seen when you look at planet Earth from the perspective and with the vision of the Ascended Host. It can even be seen by those who are perceptive and are willing to look at history with the purpose of looking for timeless elements of growth and transformation.

These elements can be seen in almost every culture. In fact there are very few cultures on this planet who have not been affected by the winds of change. In some cases one might say that change has not been for the better. But as I have tried to explain, when a certain culture is trapped in a rigid mindset, any change is actually a change for the better. For only when the rigid mindset is broken up, is there a potential to reverse the downward spiral and create genuine growth. Obviously, this potential does not always come to pass and a group of lifestreams, even an entire culture, can create a new downward spiral instead of the old downward spiral.

Yet I must tell you that the entire planet has entered an upward spiral that is breaking up the rigidity of the cultures around the Earth. And when this rigidity is broken up, the people are often bewildered and distraught. They do not understand what is happening. They do not see that it is a potential for growth. Instead, they see it as a threat to their traditional lifestyle, which they have somehow – despite its obvious shortcomings and contradictions – come to believe is perfect or God-ordained and therefore should be maintained at all cost. This, my beloved, is tragic. But it is an occurrence that still cannot resist the winds of change and the wheel of time.

Those who start wars cannot stop war

Mother Mary, September 8, 2006.

The need to invoke peace

Thus my beloved, I come to congratulate you with a work well done. And as we of the Ascended Host have said for many years, the reward for service is more service. And thus, I ask you to build on the foundation that you have laid through this rosary for loving yourself and now give a vigil of these next two rosaries for peace, that we are releasing.

For my beloved, there is indeed a great need for invoking the Flame of Peace that can consume the conditions that lead to war. Yet why have we waited with these rosaries for peace until you have given the rosary for loving yourself? Because my beloved, if you do not love yourself, how can you be at peace within yourself? And if you are not at peace within yourself, how can you be a force for peace in this world?

You see, my beloved, life is really not that complicated. If you love yourself, you will love other people. And thus, you will not commit acts of violence against them nor will you respond with violence even if others are violent toward you. For you will know, through the clarity of your love, that they are more than the outer personality and the ego that commits acts of violence. And thus, instead of seeking to punish them, you will seek to raise them up out of their illusions and set them free from the energies, even the dark spirits – even the demons – of war.

Yes my beloved, there is indeed a need to invoke peace in this world. For as is clearly stated in our rosary, there can be no freedom without peace. And as you well know, Jesus was called the Prince of Peace precisely because he came to inaugurate the Age of Pisces, which was meant to be an age of peace. Thus my beloved, it was indeed the Divine design that at the end of this two-thousand-year period humankind would leave war behind them.

Obviously, as is plain for everyone to see, this goal has not been fulfilled —yet. But my beloved, this goal is far closer than you might think when you look at world events. For has not this two-thousand-year period seen an unprecedented amount of wars. And has not this past century seen an unprecedented amount of wars on a very large scale. And thus, I can assure you that there is indeed a growing realization among humankind that war MUST come to an end. And the only thing that is lacking for this to actually manifest is that people come to a recognition of the true cause of war.

The true cause of war has a personal and a planetary aspect. The personal aspect is, of course, the warring in the members of individuals, which is caused by the human ego. And the planetary aspect is the presence of a small elite of lifestreams, the power elite, who are absolutely committed to power or to proving God wrong. And thus, they will do anything to stir up conflict as a means to either control the people for their own gain or simply destroy this planet in order to thwart God's plan for the Earth.

Who can stop war?

Thus my beloved, what needs to happen is truly that people are awakened and come to see the consciousness of war for what it is. This awakening must, of course, start among the top ten percent of the most spiritually aware people on this planet. For they are truly the ones who can turn the tide away from war and toward peace. Yet the unfortunate fact is, as Jesus has pointed out in his discourse on the human ego, that many of the most spiritual people on Earth have been trapped in gray thinking. They have come to think that all that is necessary is that they love everyone and ignore every problem. For if a problem is ignored, it will surely go away by itself—or so they think.

Yet my beloved, the reality is – and history proves this for anyone who is willing to take a closer look – that no problem will go away by itself. As has been said, for evil to triumph, it only takes that good people do nothing. Thus, I must tell you that the most spiritual people, the top ten percent of the people on this planet, are the only ones who can remove the consciousness of war from the Earth. Yet they must do so by beginning to remove the warring in their own members, namely the human ego.

And this, my beloved, is precisely the problem with gray thinking, namely that it gives the ego a protected status as an untouchable part of people's psychology. For in thinking that all that is necessary is for them to be loving and kind, they are also being loving and kind to their own egos. And my beloved, you do not overcome the ego by being tolerant of the ego. You overcome the ego only when the Conscious You awakens to the existence of the ego and becomes completely intolerant of the ego, so that you will no longer allow it to run your life or to have any presence in your being.

Thus my beloved, there is indeed such a thing as the perfect hatred, which is not a hatred in the human, dualistic sense, but is the Flame of Love that burns with such brightness that it will no longer tolerate anything other than love. It will simply not tolerate anything that springs from anti-love, and thus it consumes anything based on anti-love—instantly.

This my beloved, is indeed what must happen if war is to be banished from this planet. The top ten percent of the most spiritual people on Earth must wake up and realize that they have allowed the ego to remain in their own consciousness, and thus they have allowed the consciousness of war to remain in their own subconscious minds. And as long as they allow this to happen, then God simply does not have the authority to remove the consciousness of war from this planet or remove the beings who are absolutely committed to war and thus embody the consciousness of war.

And thus my beloved, I must tell you that even though it is the bottom ten percent, the power elite, who create every war on this planet, it is actually the top ten percent, the spiritual elite, who are responsible for allowing the consciousness of war to remain on Earth. My beloved, do you see the equation?

The power elite are so trapped in the consciousness of duality that they are not likely to change their minds in the foreseeable future. It is not likely that they will be converted to the cause of peace and non-violence and suddenly destroy all their weapons and refuse to exercise power over the population. Thus, what MUST happen is that the top ten percent of the people on Earth wake up and decide that they will no longer tolerate war on this planet. They must realize that they are the ones who have the potential to bring forth God's judgment so that war can be removed from this planet.

And how do you bring forth God's judgment? Well, my beloved, you can judge the consciousness of war only when you have removed the consciousness of war from your own being, when you have removed the warring in your own members by removing the human ego.

True tolerance and false tolerance

Thus my beloved, it is indeed necessary – for planet Earth to rise above war – that there is greater tolerance among people. Yet as with everything else, the ego can pervert every positive quality, even the quality of love, forgiveness and tolerance. For the false tolerance is that anything goes, that anything should be allowed. The false tolerance makes people believe that they should not take a stand against war but that they should simply focus on being loving and kind, thinking that then war will go away by itself.

But my beloved, do you not see that if the good people do nothing, then they give free reign to those people who are committed to war? And thus they will inevitably drag nations into war, as has indeed happened over these last five years since the terrorist attacks in New York on September 11, 2001.

My beloved, do you not see that the United States has been dragged into war and conflict by those who are using terrorism as an excuse for increasing military spending and using their military superiority to supposedly bring democracy and freedom, but in reality further the cause of the power elite? Thus my beloved, even though there is a substantial number of very spiritual people in the United States, you can clearly see that these spiritual people have not been able to provide enough of a counter-weight, a counter-balance, to prevent the United States from being dragged into war by the power elite.

And this alone should show you that the spiritual people in the United States have not done their job of removing the warring in their own members. They have not been willing to face their egos and overcome those egos, so that they could have the moral authority to call forth the judgment of God upon the power elite in the United States, who are dragging this nation into war and who surely have plans to drag it into further wars around the globe.

Yes my beloved, I am being the stern mother, for it is indeed time that the most spiritual people on this planet wake up and realize that the future of this planet hangs in the balance, and they are the only ones who can tip the balance in the favor of peace. Thus, as Jesus said, "If you love me, keep my commandments." If you are a spiritual person and you claim to love God and love the spiritual realm, then keep the commandment to remove the beam from your own eye.

Stop thinking that it is other people who are responsible for the fact that there is war and violence on this planet. Yes, these people are the ones who commit violence and start wars and they make the decision to do so. But as I have tried to point out, they are simply acting on a certain state of consciousness that is dragging them into actions over which they really have no control. And so the problem is not the people, but the consciousness of war that hangs over this planet as a black cloud.

And why is this consciousness still hanging over this planet? Well, it is because God has not been given sufficient authority to remove that consciousness. Archangel Michael and his legions of Blue-flame Angels, have not been given the marching orders to consume that consciousness and remove all beings who refuse to let go of that consciousness. And why have they not been given that authority? Well, they have not been given that authority because the top ten percent of the most spiritual people on this planet have refused to overcome the warring in their own members by becoming completely intolerant toward their own egos.

Yet if those top ten percent were to awaken and make a firm commitment to overcome the ego, then in removing the beam from your own eyes, you would indeed give God the authority to remove the consciousness of war from this entire planet. And when the dark cloud of that consciousness is removed, I can assure you that even those who are now committed to war would suddenly wake up and be able to see the insanity of their actions. They cannot presently see that insanity because of what we might call the fog of war that blinds people to the existence of a nonviolent solution to their problems.

The people must stop fighting the wars of the elite

My beloved, there is indeed a small elite on this planet who are committed to war. But since when have you seen the high and the mighty of these power elite people be out in the trenches with a gun and taking the risk of being shot at? So my beloved, you realize clearly that no war could be fought on this planet unless the people allow themselves to be pulled into fighting the wars for the power elite. Unless the people allow themselves to be turned into cannon-fodder, then no war could be fought.

And what is it that allows the population to be pulled into fighting wars, even though most people are peaceful people? Well, it is indeed that the general population are blinded by the illusions created by the power elite, by the fog of war. And thus, they do not see that there is a peaceful solution to every problem, and they do not take a stand and demand that their leaders provide that peaceful solution instead of immediately going to war whenever a provocation arises.

My beloved, can you not see that the American people, the vast majority of the population, were blinded by the fog of war after 9/11, 2001? And thus, they did not have the vision, nor the determination, to demand that their government look for a peaceful solution to the problem of world terrorism. And therefore, they allowed their nation to be dragged into wars in Afghanistan and Iraq, thinking that this would be to the benefit of their own safety.

I think, my beloved, that most Americans can see today that the war in Iraq has certainly not increased the safety of the world and has not diminished the threat of terrorism. And this of course is why popular support for the war is waning. Yet my beloved, the public could not see that five years ago because they were blinded by the fog of war, by the logic of those who are committed to war and cannot see beyond the consciousness of war.

And still the American public is blinded by that consciousness, so that people cannot see peaceful solutions to the threat of terrorism or other situations. And thus, they cannot even demand that their leaders search for such solutions. This is obvious in the current situation with Iran, where the hawks in the current administration are trying to make this appear as a crisis that must be dealt with right now. They know they could potentially lose their power in the next presidential election, so they want to further their world-wide agenda while they still have a president who cannot see through their manipulation.

...

Only true emissaries of peace can stop war

Why is the public blinded by the consciousness of war? Well, it is simply because, as Jesus has explained, the eighty percent of the general population will either follow the lowest ten percent, namely the power elite, or the top ten percent, namely the spiritual elite. And precisely because the top ten percent have been so blinded by the gray thinking of the ego, they have not been willing to overcome the consciousness of warring in their own members. And thus they have not been able to act as the forerunners who could bring forth the new vision of how to actually solve the problem of world terrorism through peaceful means.

So my beloved, once again, the balance of this planet, the future of this planet, is indeed in the hearts and minds of the top ten percent of the most spiritual people. Will they choose to walk the Path of Peace, or will they choose to continue to walk the path of false peace, which makes them think that they can be emissaries of peace without overcoming their egos.

You see, my beloved, you cannot be an emissary of peace unless you first declare all-out war on your own ego. For only when you have removed that beam from your own eye, can you see clearly how to remove the mote in the eye of another. And only then can you become a true emissary of true peace. For truly, peace cannot come about through the false tolerance which says that anything goes. Peace can only come about through the true tolerance of the Christ mind, the tolerance that is based on a clear discernment of what is of God and what is not of God.

And thus, a Christed being can see that when people commit acts of violence, it is not because their real selves are evil or bad or violent. It is because the conscious self has withdrawn into a cave and has allowed the ego to act out through the consciousness of duality that always operates with two opposites. And it is this consciousness that causes people to think that they must fight the enemy, and therefore violence is necessary or unavoidable.

Thus my beloved, only when people have Christ discernment can they see the difference between the person and that person's actions. Only when they have Christ discernment can they see that the actions are caused by a state of consciousness that springs from the mind of duality, the mind of anti-christ. But behind the actions and the outer personality is the conscious self of the person, and that conscious self was created by God. And thus, all people are truly brethren and part of the One Body of God on Earth.

Only when you see beyond the outer actions, will you be able to turn the other cheek and respond to violence with love. And in that love, you will potentially set your brothers and sisters free from the consciousness of war. For by turning the other cheek, you will indeed awaken them. And those who will not be awakened, those who hold on to the consciousness of war, will then be judged and they will be removed from the planet. But even this is actually an act of mercy, for these lifestreams will then be sent to another realm, where they can receive further opportunities for overcoming the consciousness of war, opportunities that are not available to them on Earth as long as the Earth is in its present condition.

Using the new invocations

Thus my beloved, the two invocations we are releasing now form an Alpha and an Omega polarity. One, Invoking the Flame of Peace, invokes the Flame of Peace from above and it is indeed based on the dictation by the Elohim of Peace given some time ago. And I highly recommend that you study that dictation again. The other, the Invocation for World Peace, forms the Omega action of calling for specific elements of the consciousness of war to be exposed so that people can see it and separate themselves from it.

Thus my beloved, these two invocations can indeed provide an immense momentum of peace on this planet. And I can assure you that this is highly needed at this hour. For if nothing is done, then truly this planet will continue to slide further down the slippery slope of war until it passes the point of no return and a large-scale war will indeed come to pass within the next year or two.

…

Rise above all fear of war

So my beloved, it is in no way my intention to cause any kind of fear or panic in your being. I am not asking you to start acting in an unbalanced or fearful manner. I am asking you to stay in the flame of loving yourself that you have invoked during the past rosary vigil. I am asking you to let nothing disturb that state of love and that state of inner peace. And then I am asking you – based on that inner peace – to give these two invocations with the absolute knowledge and determination that when you ask for peace, you shall indeed receive it. When you call forth the Flame of Peace, then that flame will indeed consume the consciousness of war.

And thus my beloved, I am asking you to overcome all fear. And if indeed you sense elements of fear concerning war in your own being, then go after them. Use these two invocations to specifically call for all fear of war to be consumed in your own being. For it is truly only the ego that can give rise to such fear, and your ego will be hiding behind that fear, seeking to divert your attention to becoming so concerned about conditions in the world that you do not look at the ego, expose it and overcome it.

Thus my beloved, realize that whenever there is fear, the ego is hiding behind it. And thus, instead of focusing on the object of fear – as the ego would have you do – look beyond the fear itself and expose the ego. And then ask for it to be consumed by the Flame of Peace, the Flame of Ecstatic Peace, coming from the Elohim of Peace. For truly, that Flame of Ecstatic Peace is able to consume all fear. For how can there be fear when your entire being is infused with the ecstatic peace that knows nothing but peace.

So I ask you to open your heart and your chakras, to open your entire being to that Flame of Ecstatic Peace. I ask you in this coming time, as you give these invocations, to immerse yourself in the Flame of Ecstatic Peace, to allow that flame to enter your being and consume all unlike itself.

Oh my beloved, I hope that these invocations will help you recognize the essential truth that you cannot overcome war by being in a state of fear. You can overcome war only by being fully anchored in a state of peace. For as you cannot remove darkness, you cannot remove war without bringing the Light of Peace. And thus, war will be removed only when the top ten percent of the spiritual people choose to be the open doors for the Light and the Flame of Peace to stream into the material realm, into the emotional realm, into the mental realm and into the identity realm of planet Earth and consume the consciousness of war on all four levels of the matter world.

Yes my beloved, BE the Flame of Peace. BE the open door for the Flame of Peace. Determine that you WILL BE the light of the world and that as long as you are in the world, you will BE the Flame of Peace to consume the consciousness of war.

I, Mary, commend you for your love and for your steadfastness in giving my rosaries and in working to overcome your egos. I see the progress you are making individually and even as a worldwide community of those who are committed to the Path of Peace. I congratulate you and I bow to you with sincere respect and gratitude for your progress. Thus, receive the overwhelming, overflowing gratitude of the heart of your spiritual mother. For the mother of all life, I AM!

Be spiritual regardless of outer conditions

Mother Mary, September 30, 2006.

Truly, Europe is an essential key to bringing about world peace. But it cannot happen until the dark energies that were produced by the first two world wars, and so many other wars, have been consumed by the flame of peace. For only then will the European nations and the European peoples be able and willing to look at their past.

Only then will they be able to look at the past without being overwhelmed by the emotional pain of what happened. And only when they look at the past without the pain, will they be able to analyze it and be able to understand the thought process, even the events, that led to war. And then they can free themselves from that mindset and then become a force for spreading the knowledge of peace, the reality of peace, the truth of peace throughout the corners of the globe.

Truly, my beloved, as it is right now, the United States – which could have been and should have been the major force for world peace – is not capable of fulfilling that role because it is still too stuck in black-and-white thinking. This is not only limited to the current administration, but even to a large portion of the people—which is why this administration was elected.

So you see in Europe a softening up of black-and-white thinking, which unfortunately at the current time has been replaced by gray thinking, as Jesus has explained. Yet we see the potential that Europe could move out of gray thinking more quickly than the United States can move through it. And thus, it is our hope and our plan that there will be an awakening on the European continent, whereby people will understand the reality of war, the psychology of war, and then say, "Enough is enough! We have seen two world wars start on this continent, and we know the third time will not be the charm. And we are determined not to see another world war start on this continent. In fact we are determined not to see it start anywhere, including the Middle East."

This my beloved, can indeed happen. And it can happen in time. And thus, again, I say, "Be at Peace!" For it is by being at peace that you can be the open door for the Light of Peace to consume those energies that have been produced by the many wars on this continent. And that is the key to starting an upward cycle of a raising of the awareness that will lead to enlightened actions that are based on peace, based on bringing peace, rather than allowing the forces of war to continue to manipulate nations into conflicts that were never real conflicts and never had any meaning and never had any chance of being the war to end all wars, as some deceitful people labeled the second world war. For truly, no war will ever end all wars. The only thing that can end all wars is that people refuse to fight, refuse to respond to violence with violence and decide to turn the other cheek—and to challenge those who encourage war, wherever they are found.

God government versus human government

El Morya, September 30, 2006.

And indeed God's will I AM! You have known me as El Morya because I have given you that name. But I am MORE than that. And it is about the MORE that I wish to speak today, because I desire all of you to see yourself as more than these bodies that are sitting here, even more than the outer minds and the personalities that have been shaped by world conditions, by your parents and by your society. And especially those of you who have grown up in Europe, I desire you to realize that you are far more than you were brought up to think you are in a Europe that has been heavily influenced by socialist thinking, that denies the spirituality of the individual in almost every country in Europe.

Think about how many decades this has been going on, before it finally started turning after the fall of the Soviet Union. Think about how the Soviet Union had infiltrated almost every nation in Europe, had created communist or socialist parties whose entire goal was to spread a socialist-communist ideology which denied the spirituality, the inbuilt God Flame of the individual, portraying human beings as automatons or robots or mere machines that could be used by the power elite to do their bidding and be their slaves. Almost like worker bees in a beehive or in an ant hill, who had no individuality and no personality but were literally the property of the state—who were supposed to do the bidding of those who happened to be controlling the state.

My beloved, this is an ideology of anti-christ, and it is truly by the grace of God and the work of many ascended master students, that this ideology was overturned and that the Berlin Wall came down and that world communism was defeated in Russia. This, my beloved, is indeed a great turning point for Europe and for the entire world. Yet we are not out of the woods yet, as they say, for I must tell you that as there is a communist ideology of anti-christ, so there is a capitalist ideology of anti-christ. For as you well know, after having studied Jesus' discourses on the ego, there are always two extremes in the duality consciousness. And so it is not true – as many of you have also been brought up to believe in the West – that capitalism represented right and truth and freedom and was working against Communism.

For I must tell you – if you have not realized already, which many of you have – that capitalism is equally abusive and equally in denial of individual spirituality as is communism. There is no difference; they are two sides of the same coin. They are two ideologies, two systems, that sprang from the same root. And that root is the denial of the spiritual reality behind all physical appearances.

The origin of the power elite

My beloved, this denial of the spiritual reality goes back a very long time on this planet and beyond. It goes all the way back to the fall of those beings in previous realms who decided that they would not move higher when the realm in which they lived moved higher. Instead, they would deny God, deny God's will, deny God's will that all life becomes more. They would choose the path of becoming less, and they would drag as many as they could with them on that path. And as you know from Mother Mary's book, when a certain sphere ascends to a higher vibration and becomes part of the spiritual realm, then those lifestreams who are not willing to move on must then descend into a lower sphere, into a lower vibration. And yet because they have descended from a higher sphere, they not only have a sense of superiority, pride and arrogance, but they also have a certain knowledge, a certain attainment, that allows them to be very clever, very intelligent in an intellectual, logical, rational way that is far beyond many of the lifestreams who start in that lower sphere in order to work their way up.

And that is why you have the formation of a power elite who believe they are better than the people and have a right to rule the people and that the people should be their literal slaves. This, my beloved, goes back a very long time to civilizations that are not currently known. But even in your own known history, you can see the pattern and you see it few places more clearly than here in Europe, where throughout the middle ages you had the feudal lords who owned everything, even owned the people who lived on their land.

This, my beloved, certainly was not God government, nor was it the will of God. It was a totally perverted system. And it should show you that there is nothing that can be given that cannot be perverted by the human ego—as long as most of the people are blinded by the duality of the ego. For it is true that there is a potential that a king can be an enlightened ruler. And if the king is in a higher state of consciousness, he can give birth to an heir that is also in a higher state of consciousness. So the higher form of rule, the higher God government, can indeed be passed on through inheritance. But this system is not fail-proof, as is no system on Earth in the current level of vibration of this planet. And therefore, it too became perverted. And you saw throughout the Middle Ages how one insane king would have insane children that would lead on and on and on, until the God government that was meant to be, had deteriorated to the point where it was human government.

The state must not be almighty

I myself was certainly up against exactly such a king in the form of Henry the VIII [El Morya was embodied as Thomes More]. He was the embodiment of everything that is wrong with human government, the perversion of human government. You see, my beloved, it was a long time ago that the Israelites, who had prophets, demanded a worldly king. And they were given a worldly king because it is indeed a right system that there is a spiritual branch and a secular branch. This represents, in its pure form, the Alpha and the Omega, where those who are the leaders of the religion, if they have the right attunement to the Ascended Host, can serve to bring down the overall picture of God government for a particular nation or even an entire civilization. And then the secular part of the government is the one who takes care of the many day-to-day things in society. Yet when this system works correctly, the secular branch of the government works within the greater framework provided by the religious part of the government.

This can indeed work, but it can only work when the people have a certain level of consciousness. And when the people start falling asleep and are not aware of what is going on, then the power elite will enter into both the secular and the religious branch of the government, and they will start perverting it in order to obtain power. Then it is no more about truth, it is about what promotes or sustains the power of the elite. And at that point, both the religious and the secular aspects of the government will be perverted.

This is indeed what you saw in the Middle Ages. And you saw it very clearly embodied in the Catholic Church, who had imposed a man-made doctrine, a man-made world view, upon the entire continent of Europe, plunging this continent into the Dark Ages rather than the Age of Enlightenment that was envisioned by Saint Germain and other ascended Beings. So you now have a church that is unjustly limiting the population. And so you have a king who wants an heir and who cannot have it with one woman, so he wants another woman but the Church forbids divorce. And so the king goes and withdraws himself and his country from the Church, so he can make his own laws.

And you see, my beloved, there I was as Thomas More, being the king's chancellor, but I was not about to compromise what I knew to be true in my heart. Contrary to what you might think, based on history, this was not actually based on a loyalty to the outer Catholic Church. For even though I was not fully aware in that embodiment of the faults of the Catholic Church – having simply not the knowledge that you have today and have been given through our websites and other means – I still knew that there were things that were lacking in that Church.

So my loyalty in opposing the King was not so much to the Church, but to God and to the Will of God. Because I knew very well that when the secular government starts making its own rules, then that society will enter a downward spiral that can take it very far down into having one tyrant after another who is misusing his power to oppress the people. For is it not so that if any power on Earth, if any institution or individual, sets itself up as saying that we have ultimate authority and recognizes no authority beyond itself, then you have an open invitation to an abuse of power. And I can tell you that you have never on this planet, or any other planet, seen any individual or institution that could handle absolute power without being corrupted by that power.

Why it is essential to have absolute rights

And that is why it is absolutely essential that any form of government must recognize a higher authority than itself. It must recognize that there is something beyond the material realm and that that something has set forth principles, laws, that are absolute and that no authority on Earth can or should circumvent, explain away or nullify. This, my beloved, is an absolute necessity for maintaining a free society. And that is indeed why the founding fathers of the United States of America were inspired with the Declaration of Independence, whose first and foremost aim was to declare their independence of those who had taken on worldly power and did not recognize any power beyond this world. Which is exactly why the Declaration says that all men are endowed by their Creator with inalienable rights—meaning rights that no government on Earth has the power to take away or water down.

And my beloved, you should be able to see that what has happened in Europe for several generations is that the democratic freedoms that were won through such a hard fight, in many cases, have indeed been watered down by secular governments who have been influenced by a socialist ideology which recognizes no authority beyond the Earth, no authority beyond itself—and therefore believes that it can create rules without considering the Will of God and the laws of God and the laws of nature that are God's design principles that make the material universe work and make it sustainable.

Islam and the ongoing dualistic fight

Thus, you see in the Soviet Union how they thought they could create the perfect man-made system, where the economy would work and give everyone work and provide for everyone, and it could do so indefinitely. Yet in reality had it not been for loans from the West, Communism could not have survived for as long as it did. And so why did the banks in the West provide loans to their "sworn enemy" of Communism? Well, my beloved, it was because they wanted to keep the world in a dualistic fight, so that they themselves could rule behind the scenes, including making money on the entire war machine.

So what you see today is that it finally became clear, even to people in the Soviet Union, that communism was not working, and therefore the Berlin Wall came down. And for a time there was a relative calm, for even the power elite had not quite foreseen that the Soviet Union would collapse as quickly as it did, for they had not taken into account that many of our students had for many years given Saint Germain services every Saturday for the fall of Communism. So they had not in their calculations taken into consideration the spiritual force that made Communism a house of cards. And when the winds of the Spirit started blowing, that house came tumbling down much faster then anyone expected. And even the power elite was taken aback by this.

And yet what do you see today, just a few years later? You see another upcoming force that is serving to maintain the dualistic fight, the "clash of civilizations" and it is now terrorism and what is labeled as fundamentalist Islam, but which really has nothing whatsoever to do with Islam in its true form. For even Islam is clearly a religion that recognizes the Will of God and the superiority of God's law to the superiority of man. And thus, had Islam been maintained in its pure form, it could never have been what it has become today—a threat to the peace of the world.

Yet why has Islam been put into this role? Well partly because Islam itself has been perverted by those Imams, and the priests, who have taken Islam beyond what it was meant to be, who have lost the original purity of the teachings brought forth through the prophet Mohammed and who have perverted them into the concept of Jihad and many other concepts that are not in alignment with the Law and the Will of God. And so they have put themselves in this position.

But really, what has happened behind the scenes is that the power elite behind Capitalism has said, "We need another enemy so we can continue to justify military spending and our exercising power over the people. And thus we will continue to do what we have always done—create fear of an outer enemy in the people, so that they will accept the inordinate spending on military equipment and at the same time accept an erosion of their civil liberties."

Codependency between a government and the people

And this, of course, has worked very well on the other side of the pond, as they say, whereas it has not yet gained the same foothold in Europe.

And that is indeed one of the reasons why we look to Europe as having the potential to be, as Mother Mary said, a forerunner for a new awareness that can bring about world peace. For whereas Europe in the past was almost completely ruled by the power elite, it is now the United States that is more influenced by the power elite than Europe.

Although you should certainly not fall into the illusion of thinking that Europe is not influenced by the power elite. Yet I must tell you that the people in Europe do have the potential to awaken themselves and come to a higher awareness that can indeed bring about a more peaceful future, not only for this continent, but for the world as a whole. Yet before this can happen, they must analyze their past and do away with the remnants of socialist thinking that are still influencing virtually every nation on this continent including the nation in which I am now speaking.

For Sweden is a very typical example of a country where the government believes it should run every aspect of people's lives, and where the people have come to believe that the government should take care of them and that they have a right to be given what they need by the government and at the same time be told by the government how to live. And this becomes a codependent relationship between the governmental apparatus – which is huge in many nations in Europe and employs many people who in their thinking see the rest of their lives as government employees, living a certain lifestyle that is comfortable although nothing out of the ordinary. But they accept the security because it is easy for them, and they do not have to make decisions, and thus they want to maintain the governmental system that gives them that security – and the people who are dependent on that governmental system for various services, they also want to maintain it.

And you see this codependent relationship where nobody really wants to come out and say that the system is not working, that it is in danger of collapsing under its own weight, as you had in the Soviet Union before the Wall came tumbling down. So the people of Europe need to analyze their past and say, "No more of this socialism, no more of this replacing God with the state. We need to get back to a point where there is both God and man in the government."

But it needs to be enlightened man, enlightened men and women who are attuned with their God selves and attuned with God and therefore know the Laws of God, not through one religion as you saw in the

Catholic Church, for that is clearly a system that does not work. I am not talking about making one religion the ultimate religion or the only true religion in any country in Europe. I am talking about the universal realization that beyond the outer churches and religions, there is a universal body of spiritual knowledge. There is a universal teaching about God's Law and the laws of nature, and unless a government is based on these timeless, eternal principles, it simply is not sustainable. And it is just a matter of time before either internal factors or external factors will cause that system of government to collapse under its own weight.

...

Look beyond outer conditions

And so, my beloved, there are many things that need to be changed on this continent. And you might feel overwhelmed when you consider it all. But I can tell you that a breakthrough is much closer than you might think when you look at the outer conditions. And that is exactly why – time and time again – we are telling you that we have need of those who will not be blinded by the outer conditions, who will not be overwhelmed by the outer conditions, who will not think that these outer conditions are permanent and could not be changed, for after all "I am just one little person and what can I possibly do?" Well, certainly, you as a little person cannot solve the problems that your nation is facing. But you are more than that little person, and when you connect to that MORE, then the MORE through you can bring forth the solutions to every problem known to man, be it on this continent and elsewhere.

And so I can assure you, there is a solution to every problem. But that solution cannot be found through the human will. It can only be found when a critical mass of people will align themselves with the Will of God, which is not an external will seeking to put you in a straightjacket. It is the will of your own Higher Being. And when you realize that; when you accept that; when you acknowledge that and when you feel that love that you have for your own Higher Being and feel that love that your I AM Presence and the Ascended Host and your Creator have for you, then following God's Will is not a burden—it is your greatest love. For you came here to bring God's Will to Earth. You did not come here to become a human being, a robot following along with whatever the government tells you to do.

The potential for a new revolution in consciousness

For you see, my beloved, the governments have long ago left the Will of God and have elevated the will of man as the ultimate authority. And even though they claim to be democratic governments who are somewhat open to the will of the people, the reality in most nations is that it is the will of the power elite that is carried out in the politics of the day. And so what needs to happen is that someone must decide to seek for the more, as you were told about earlier. The will to become more is the first step. And then you become more, and now you become the open door for the more of the Will of God, the energy, the Light, of the Will of God to shine through you.

And what will happen when a critical mass of people decide to be the open doors is that suddenly a shift will occur in the mass consciousness, and suddenly people will wake up and realize that these old patterns – that we have been perpetuating and repeating over and over – they are not working. And we need to do something different. This is what happened in the Soviet Union. This is what happened in most European nations when the feudal system was abandoned and gave way to some form of democracy or a more enlightened form of government.

Truly, there was the French revolution, which was not the Will of God to become a bloodbath. Yet the French Revolution opened the eyes of many of the rulers of Europe, who realized that times had changed and that if they did not voluntarily let go of some of their power over the people, then the people would indeed finally rise up and take that power through force.

Yet this was in a darker age. And I must tell you that in today's age there is a potential that an equally great shift can happen in society as the shift between the feudal societies and the democratic nations. But this time it can happen without violence, without bloodshed. It can happen by a mass awakening of the people, who finally wake up and say as the little boy in the fairy tale, "But the Emperor has nothing on! The power elite has nothing on. This socialist-capitalist system has nothing on. It is not working for it takes away the initiative and the responsibility of the individual and thus denies the individual the opportunity to experiment and to learn both from its successes and its failures."

You see, my beloved, what has been created in many European nations is a welfare system, a welfare state, where there is a limit to how far you can fall because you can always go on welfare and maintain some standard of living. Yet in the focus on maintaining this bottom line, you have forced all of the people into a lower state of existence than they could have if they exercised their full spiritual potential. And so you now have nations where nobody dares to exercise their creativity, their spiritual creativity, and bring forth those ideas and inventions that are needed in order to bring the Golden Age into manifestation, even the ideas about free energy that can make the world independent of oil.

And so, because you have a nation where everybody is trying to just live what they consider to be a comfortable life, and what they consider to be the maximum that they can obtain, then you have strangled initiative. And this is precisely what the power elite wants, because they do not want the people to show initiative. They want to be able to control every new idea, every new invention, so that they can either use it to make money or to expand their power or they can stop it from creating competition that takes away their money or their power.

There is no limit to progress

You see, my beloved, there is a common misconception that is found in most of the industrialized nations, including in North America, in Europe and elsewhere. And that common misconception among most people is that the world is basically good and that there are forces that are trying to do the right thing but that sometimes bad things happen and therefore society could not be in a higher state than what we see right now.

But my beloved, this is the same kind of psychology that was perpetuated during the Middle Ages by both the Catholic Church, by the kings and by the feudal lords, the noble class. They wanted the population to believe that there was an upper limit to how far they could go in life. And thus, they should not bother to show initiative, to bring forth new ideas. And certainly they should not bother to challenge the status quo of the power elite.

And many people think that after democracy came into being, then those forces basically disappeared. But surely, you can see that they have survived and that they have simply learned how to use democracy to still further their agenda of power and privilege for the elite and of holding the people down. And this has happened in most European nations through the democratic institutions, through the educational institutions, through the media, where everybody has come to believe that there is a limit to growth, there is a limit to how much society could change, to how rich a nation could become, to how far technology could advance, to how far culture could advance.

And because of that, you see that much of Europe has accepted a lid upon the growth of this continent. Yet my beloved, I must tell you that even when you look at the European nations today – and their comfortable lifestyles, their welfare systems, the riches they have – what could be manifested on this continent is infinitely more than what you see right now. The vision that I hold, based on my oneness with the Will of God, is infinitely greater than what you see right now.

In fact if I were to tell you that vision, your outer minds would not be able to experience it. Even you, who are spiritual people, would find it difficult to experience the vision I hold for the world and for this continent. And many among the people who are not spiritual would consider me a madman if I were to tell them what could happen within just a few decades. For truly, this continent has the potential to change so dramatically that it could become the foundation for bringing true abundance to every continent on this planet.

For my beloved, is it not clear when you look at South America, when you look at Africa, when you look at the Middle East and certain parts of Asia, that these nations do not have the situation you see in Europe. They do not have the conditions, the outer conditions, nor the momentum that can allow them to transcend their current state from within themselves.

My beloved, I personally have had several embodiments in Europe, as had Saint Germain, as had Kuthumi and other masters. Why have we chosen to embody on this continent? Because we knew that despite what was going on in the Dark Ages, this continent has the potential to be – along with the North American continent – the primary forerunners for the Aquarian age, for the Golden Age of Saint Germain. And thus we have invested our own light for bringing forth ideas on this continent. And behind the scenes you see that all of the conditions are put in place for a breakthrough to occur. Yet that breakthrough is currently being blocked by the conditions I have talked about, the socialist mindset, the acceptance of an upper limit.

The potential for a Golden Age in Europe

But could that block be cleared away, then Europe could go through an incredible transformation that could then spread far beyond the borders of Europe. Indeed, this is the potential that is real, that is just behind the surface appearances. And indeed, it is the Will of God that this should be physically manifest. And as the embodiment of the Will of God, it is indeed my will for this continent. For even though there has been much darkness on this continent, I hold no negative feelings. I have let go of it all—what I experienced personally, what I have seen other people experience. Even the atrocities, such as the Holocaust or the slaughter of the Russian people by Stalin, even these atrocities I have let go of, I have left behind. And I hold only the vision for the good that could happen on this continent.

And truly, I want you who are the spiritual people to do likewise. Not in the sense that you deny the past, but that you are willing to look at the past and process it in your own beings, so that you can serve as the forerunners for your nations and you can carve a trail in the mass consciousness that other people can follow. And thereby, they too can begin to process the past and come to consciously realize why it was not working, why neither capitalism nor communism will ever work. Why indeed it was never possible to create a man-made system that would provide the ideal society. For I tell you, my beloved, there is no system that will work. What will work is only the living God government that is always in attunement with a greater picture of God's Will, so that the society, the economy, can transcend itself when the cycle has turned, and it is now necessary to come up higher rather than holding on to the old ways, the old ways of looking at things, the old state of consciousness.

Do you not see, my beloved, that when you take Jesus' discourses on the ego and transfer them to the field of government, you see that what the ego wants is to create a society that is static and that can maintain the power and privilege of the elite while keeping the population in such a state that they are not dissatisfied enough to risk their lives in a revolt against the power elite. What the ego basically wants is to create a human society that functions much like an ant hill, where the population serves to provide the privileges for the elite. And then the ego wants to maintain that society for as long as possible.

But you see, my beloved, it is not God's Will to create a static society that will remain the same for ever and ever. It is God's Will to create a society that is constantly transcending itself, so that the members of that society will be urged to constantly transcend themselves, to learn more, to come up higher, to develop their thinking, to develop culture so that everything is in a state of growth. This is the River of Life. This is how God government is.

And that is why you see so many civilizations in the past that have collapsed. And why have they collapsed? Because they became taken over by a ruling elite who, once they had power, became concerned about only one thing—maintaining their power and their privilege instead of continuing the upward growth, the self-transcendence, of society. This is the mindset of those fallen angels who rebelled against God's plan when their higher sphere, in which they lived, transcended itself and they could no longer remain.

Do you now see that this is the pattern of stopping growth, of creating a privileged position for themselves and then maintaining it indefinitely? This is the pattern that has been going on for eons on this planet. And it is time that the spiritual people realized this, that they come out of what Jesus has so brilliantly called gray thinking. And realize that it is not enough to be spiritual, to love everyone indiscriminately without Christ discernment. That you need to come to that higher state of knowing true love, the love of God, the love that is so one with the Will of God, that it loves the Will of God and that there is no greater love than the Will of God, which is self-transcendence.

Claim your Freedom in Europe!

Saint Germain, September 30, 2006.

Old records of anti-freedom

A very, very long time ago, in an age that is not recognized by current science, there was indeed a great temple of freedom on this continent. Yet, as the civilization that had built that temple went into a downward spiral, that temple of freedom was attacked from all sides by the forces of anti-freedom, and they eventually succeeded in destroying the civilization – that had decayed from within and become weak – and then moving on to destroy the freedom temple itself.

Thus, after this happened, the entire continent went into a downward spiral of anti-freedom. And it is indeed the remnants of this downward spiral that you have seen manifest so much anti-freedom on this continent in the last thousand years, especially. For have we not seen the emergence of a feudal system that replaced a much freer system in earlier ages, and thus enslaved the population in the hands of a small elite. An elite of people so insensitive to life that they would sit in their elaborate castles and mansions, eating, drinking and making merry, while the people who had provided the labor for the food and their shelter were indeed starving or dying of disease or malnutrition—or simply being over-worked.

My beloved, I know well that when I walked this Earth as the Wonderman of Europe, I worked with the kings and the queens of Europe in an attempt to establish a united states of Europe. And although it may seem like I catered to the noble class and the elite, I can assure you that I was in no way blind to the plight of the people. The reality of the situation was simply so that the people were not ready – yet – to stand up for their own freedom. And thus – foreseeing the potential of the French Revolution and even worse bloodbaths that could have taken place in other nations – I attempted to talk some sense into the royal heads of this continent.

I had little success, as I have little success today, talking to some of the same lifestreams that are now embodied in powerful positions on this continent, in North America, even in Russia and other parts of the world. For you must understand that these people are so blinded by their quest for power, by their absolute belief in their own superiority, by their belief that they have an absolute right to these privileges and that the people should simply serve as their slaves. And because of this blindness, there is no openness in their hearts to look at the people around them and be their brother's keeper.

Insensitivity to life

Truly, they have a form of the Cain consciousness, although it is not the same shade of the Cain consciousness as you see in the Middle East. For they do not desire to kill their brothers. No, they desire their brothers to work for them and give them the privileges to which they have become so addicted that they literally think they would die if they had to do an honest day's work. And in some cases some of the them would literally die if they had to do any physical work. But they have no compunctions about letting other people do that work until they die of exhaustion or overwork.

This, my beloved, is an absolute insensitivity to life. I encourage you to tour some of the places found in several nations, where you have museums that have gathered together houses in which the common people used to live a hundred or two hundred years ago. Then tour one of the royal castles that are also found in these nations. And then think about the contrast, of how 95% or more of the population lived in poverty, while the few lived in such elaborate luxury that it is almost incomprehensible how anyone could think they needed or deserved such luxury when their own people were barely surviving.

How can such a state of consciousness ever give rise to a free nation and a free people? Truly, it is inconceivable, as I am sure you can see plain as day. Thus, what needs to happen on this continent is that the people themselves become aware of the power elite and the consciousness of the power elite. For as El Morya said, there is still very much a power elite in the Western world, in the democratic world, running the world behind the scenes where the people never see it. These people, many of them, are not elected by the people.

Thus, the people have no choice. They are appointed to positions of power, be it in finance, in the banking systems or wherever it might be. And thus, they cannot easily be voted out of office or removed in other ways. Then, of course, there are the people who serve as the henchmen of the power elite in terms of controlling the information that is available to the people or in terms of serving as the henchmen who immediately execute, or ridicule, or destroy, or cast doubt upon any true idea that comes up but which is not to the liking of the power elite and their philosophy.

In the information age, disinformation is the new weapon of the power elite

Thus, misinformation and disinformation have truly become the new weapons in the war for the minds and hearts of the people. And there are people in society today who have it as their job and their life's calling to cast doubt upon the truth that is being brought out from various sources. The truth about the spiritual reality of life, the spiritual side of life, and the fact that every human being has a spiritual core and a spiritual potential that gives them the potential to rise higher in consciousness and obtain the ultimate freedom. That is the freedom from the human ego and the duality consciousness in which the power elite have been trapped for so long that they no longer see that they are trapped. And they think that their sophisticated intellectual reasoning is indeed the highest truth possible, and it is indeed higher than the reality of God and the truth brought out by the Ascended Host through many different sources.

My beloved, look how the people in Europe have systematically been programmed for several generations to look with suspicion upon religion. Yes, my beloved, I am fully aware that much of this suspicion comes from the misuse of power that has been seen on this continent, primarily through the Catholic Church. And thus, there is a reality to the fact that people should be suspicious about the misuse of power in religion. But this does not mean that you throw out the Christ child with the dirty bath water of the Church.

It means that you rise to the discernment of seeing that while there is misuse of power and misinformation and false doctrines, there is a reality behind it all. And Jesus was not simply a humble peasant or a simple spiritual teacher, nor was he the only son of God or the Lord who will save the world without you having to do anything. Because beyond all these manmade concepts, there is a reality. And you can see that reality when you are willing to go beyond the dualistic mind. Yet the power elite does not want the spiritual people in Europe to realize the reality of Christ and his inner teaching.

In fact, I must tell you that there is a power elite in Europe who is disguised as genuine spiritual and New Age organizations and teachers and gurus, who have it – behind the scenes – as their mission to destroy people's belief in Christ and the reality of Christ.

Two aspects of freedom

For again, how shall this continent manifest true freedom? There are two aspects of freedom, there is an Alpha aspect and an Omega aspect. The Omega aspect is political and economic freedom, so that the people are not oppressed through physical means. But the spiritual aspect of freedom is a freedom of the mind, the freedom to know truth, to know reality. And how shall that freedom of the mind come about? It can come about only when people attain Christ discernment, attain the mind of Christ, that allows them to rightly divide the word of truth, to separate the real from the unreal and see the unreality of the Catholic Church without going into the black and white thinking of rejecting all religion or the gray thinking of thinking that they can come up with their own spiritual truth and do not have to reach up for the Christ discernment that allows them to see the spiritual reality, rather than some man-made doctrine or concept or philosophy that is convenient and allows them to live a comfortable life while feeling that they have some kind of spirituality.

So my beloved, I, as has El Morya, have spent embodiments on this continent. I have given much light, much of my thoughts and ideas, in order to raise the consciousness of this continent, in order to bring about a Golden Age of Freedom. I have released much technology, in the Industrial Revolution and forward, that has indeed helped this continent reach a high state of political and economic freedom, where people are not as oppressed as they were for example in the Soviet Union or under the old non-democratic governments on this continent.

The technology that I have sponsored and inspired has allowed people to escape the drudgery of having to spend all of their time and energy just making a living. They have indeed attained a higher degree of freedom. And my vision for giving people political freedom and economic freedom was that by having the free time and the free energy, the free attention, they would put their minds, put their attention, on the spiritual side of life and their own spiritual growth. They would reach up for something higher.

So you see, my beloved, there has been a very deliberate attempt by the forces of anti-freedom to sabotage my plans by turning the people away from religion, completely. Or turning them away from seeking the higher truth and seeking only that form of spirituality which is convenient and which allows their egos to continue to control them while they feel they are very spiritual people.

Look at the opportunities people have today

My beloved, look at this continent. Look at the freedom people have. In many nations there is a welfare system, where people can theoretically maintain at least a basic standard of living without working at all. Now, I am not recommending that you go out and do this. But it is a fact that you could indeed justify having a certain number of people who lived off the welfare system while spending their time on true spiritual pursuits. Thus, in essence, doing what the monks and nuns did in the old days, when they lived in monasteries and focused their entire lives on spirituality.

Yet even beyond this, you have so many people who have lots of freedom. Some do not need to work full time to maintain a living. Other have pensions or other forms of income that allows them lots of free time. Just think what could happen if just a percentage of these people would use their freedom to focus on the spiritual side of life. Imagine that they gave rosaries, meditated or used other spiritual practices. Imagine that they studied individually. Imagine that they came together in groups and discussed spiritual topics. Imagine that they wrote about spiritual topics and challenged the lies of the power elite by giving people the spiritual meat that can set their minds free from these lies.

Just imagine how it was, just a couple of hundred years ago, when many people worked ten or twelve or more hours a day. At the same time as they were raising children and never had the time to sit down and contemplate the meaning of life or give a rosary or read a book, for no books were even available. So imagine what people have today, and just imagine that they started using it for something spiritual, instead of allowing themselves to be sucked in to the many addictions that are deliberately presented by the entertainment industry and so many other pursuits that make people addicted to this or that or the next thing that takes their energies down, down, down in a self-destructive spiral, that eventually ends up taking all of their freedom and imprisons them in a box of negative energy, where they are so burdened that they can barely move and they can barely raise their eyes and say, "God, there has got to be more to life."

It is, in fact, so that there are many people who have economic and political freedom, who have free time, who have free energy and free attention. Yet they are less free than many people were a century or two ago. Because their minds and their emotional bodies have been sucked into so many different addictions that there is hardly any attention left for them to ponder any deeper meaning of their existence. Yet it should be natural that when people do not have to spend all of their time on making a living, their attention should turn to the deeper topics of life, the deeper questions presented by the fact that you are alive, that you are conscious and that you have a mind that is able to ask questions and say, "Why am I here?"

Yet my beloved, so many people act as if it is dangerous to consider such questions. And in a sense one can hardly blame them for this reluctance, for have they not been fed a schizophrenic world view by, on one side, the Christian churches who hold on to doctrines that are so outdated that it is a shame to even consider that modern intelligent people could believe in some of these doctrines. And on the other side, they have a scientific establishment which pounds into their minds over and over again that life is a game of chance, that they are highly evolved animals but nothing more, and that they, their consciousness, will die when the body draws its last breath.

So, in a sense, it is understandable that people do not know how to deal with the deeper questions. But my beloved, this can change very quickly, when the consciousness is raised by people such as yourselves. And when people are presented with a teaching that actually makes sense, a teaching about God and about the spiritual side of life that makes sense. Which of course is what we are striving to do through people in various capacities who have an open mind and heart to the new ideas that must be brought in for the Aquarian Age to come into manifestation as a Golden Age of Freedom.

And you could all count yourselves among these people, even if you do not see yourselves as writers or speakers. You talk to people, and you can be who you are and share your heart flame. So my beloved, see yourselves as part of the movement that will bring the spiritual awakening that is the absolute necessity before there can be true freedom on this continent. For only a spiritual awakening will bring about the consciousness of peace that can prevent more wars, conflicts and bloodshed on this planet.

On the European Union

And thus, let me say that one of the main reasons that I have been allowed to again anchor my Flame of Freedom and give sponsorship to the European nations is indeed the expansion of the European Union towards the East, that you have seen in these last few years. For it is a fact that by reaching out to the former communist nations in Eastern Europe, the nations of Western Europe have indeed shown a willingness to be their brother's keeper and to help raise up those nations who are far behind economically and politically. And I am well aware that there is a power elite behind the scenes, who see this as an opportunity for them to expand their markets, so that people, even in a small village in Romania, can enjoy the freedom to drink Coca Cola. For to them this is the ultimate goal and the ultimate sign of civilization—that you can drink a drink that will destroy your health.

Yet it is also undeniable that there is a true willingness on the part of the richer nations in Europe to share their wealth, to reach out and to help other nations rise financially. This is nowhere more clear than in Germany, where you have seen the people of West Germany make great sacrifices after the reunification to raise up the Eastern part of that country—with great difficulty and with great reluctance from the people who had become addicted to communism.

So my beloved, I see this as a great opportunity. And I trust that if enough spiritual people will decide to raise their consciousness and do the necessary work, then this can be a positive spiral that can start— rather than being the new Europe that the power elite envisions.

How Europe can help stop war

Now for a topic that is even more serious, namely the topic of war and how the European nations can contribute to stopping war. My beloved, we have stated clearly in the Invocation for World Peace that for peace to come about, someone must start turning the other cheek. Someone must start refusing to respond to violence with violence. Someone must be the forerunner. And my beloved, who will that someone be and how will they do it?

Well my beloved, is it inconceivable that some of the smaller nations in Europe could come to a point, where they would simply abandon their military, where they would simply say, "We refuse to have a military force in this new Europe. For we will not contribute to the potential for war by acting as if we need a military in order to defend ourselves against the threat that surely is not as serious as it was in past ages."

I know that for many nations this will be a radical suggestion. But do you see, my beloved, that sooner or later someone must take this step? Some nation must decide that if we are to have peace on Earth, they must take the step of abandoning all military force. I am not saying that all nations could do this, given current world conditions. Certainly, the United States could not do this because there must be a nation that has enough military to deter certain other nations from starting a process of worldwide conquest, which is still not completely out of the question.

Yet the logic is clear. Some nations in Europe could indeed abandon the military and simply declare themselves to be war-free zones. You have seen two nations in Europe who for a very long time have remained neutral and have refused to go into any alliance. Those two nations are Sweden and Switzerland. Those two nations both maintain a fairly capable military because they feel that they need to defend their neutrality. And surely they did need to defend their neutrality, while the shadows of the Russian Bear or the Nazi Eagle were hovering over this continent.

But do they actually need a military today? Do some of the other nations need a military? Can there forever be a NATO in a United Europe, or can NATO have the form that it has today, where it is so dependent on the United States that many nations felt obligated to go along with the United States' adventures in Afghanistan and Iraq—which now virtually every nation in Europe realizes was a mistake.

So when will there come a nation that has the courage to say, "We will lay down our arms. We will refuse to fight, come what may." My beloved, is that not exactly what the people of India did when they were inspired by Gandhi. And did they not succeed in defeating the British themselves, the biggest colonial power on Earth, through non-violence. So could it not send shock waves through the world consciousness if some nations had the courage to take the bold step of abandoning their military?

My beloved, I am speaking this into the mass consciousness. For I want it to be anchored there, as a seed that can sprout and eventually set root and become a strong plant that awakens people to see that a new age has dawned, and in a new age certain choices must be made. Certainly, it was the nations of Europe that were among the first to abandon slavery and say that we cannot own other people as slaves. Well then, is it not a logical next step to say that we cannot force people into a uniform and force them to go out and kill their fellow men.

Even Gandhi himself was hesitant about the possibility of defeating Nazi Germany through non-violence. He thought it could be done but at an infinitely higher price than what had happened in India. Yet I must tell you that Nazi Germany and the Soviet Union could indeed have been defeated through non-violence. But even today the threat is far less than it was ten or twenty years ago.

My beloved, I am not blind to the fact that Russia still maintains a capable military. But I must give you a realistic assessment, that the Russian military is not nearly as capable as many people think, and certainly nowhere near the capability it had during the communist era. And even then it was overrated, as they say. For there would have been much chaos, had the Russian military, the Soviet military, actually had to engage in a war. Today it would be virtually impossible for Russia to engage in a large-scale conquest in Europe.

And certainly, by the time more nations were ready to abandon their military, the consciousness of Russia would also have changed to the point where it would be feasible to create an unarmed zone in many European nations. So this is a step that eventually must be taken, for it does not make sense to have a free democratic society which is still dependent on a military to fight off a threat that would not be there if the consciousness of that nation was raised, so that the duality itself would not create its own opposition.

You see, my beloved, it is not the people who want to fight wars. It is the power elite who want to fight wars. And that is why they want nations to have a military. It is also the power elite who want to make money out of selling military hardware and therefore wants to create artificial conflicts between nations that force them to enter an arms race that can bankrupt them, as nearly happened to the Soviet Union and the United States.

So my beloved, the people themselves must stand up and demand that their leaders find peaceful solutions to all problems. And when a nation enters the consciousness of seeking peaceful solutions, then the logical step is that a military is no longer necessary. For if you truly believe that every problem has a peaceful solution, why would you need a military to seek non-peaceful solutions?

Thus, my beloved, you may think that I have become a pacifist in my old age. And those of you who have heard me speak out against World Communism through previous organizations might especially think that I have gone soft. Yet I am simply being realistic. Times have changed. And when times change, people must abandon the old thought patterns. Otherwise, a new age cannot come into full physical manifestation but will be stopped before it breaks through to the physical octave.

And thus, those of you who are the spiritual people must realize that – in large part, by the spiritual work done by many of the ascended master students over the last several decades – the threat of war and violence has decreased to a level where it is necessary for nations to start thinking about non-violent solutions. Surely, I do not expect any nation to abandon its military within the next couple of years. But I do expect that some nations will begin to debate the necessity of maintaining all this military hardware and in essence putting themselves in a codependent relationship with the big multinational corporations who have the capacity to produce military hardware.

Multinational corporations

Surely, many nations have military equipment produced in the United States, but produced by big multinational corporations that have virtually no national loyalty whatsoever. And again, this is one of the things that needs to happen in Europe—that you realize that you cannot allow corporations that have no loyalty to a nation, or to a people, to take over behind the scenes and influence a nation's economy to a point, where they could almost bankrupt a nation because the economy of some of these large companies is indeed bigger than the economy of some small nations.

And thus, this is a situation that cannot ultimately lead to freedom. For as El Morya indeed was talking about communism and capitalism being two sides of the same coin, you must realize that the ultimate goal of capitalism is world domination, as it was the ultimate goal of communism. But instead of the state, it will become these large multi-national corporations who will eventually merge into one conglomerate, that will then be so powerful that they can dictate the course of nations, regardless of the elected representatives of the people. Obviously, this is already occurring to a large degree, but I can tell you that it could be far worse than it is at the present. And it is indeed very possible to turn back this situation by the people raising their awareness of what is happening behind the scenes and demanding that their elected representatives free their nations from this yoke.

My beloved, what sense does it make that a nation, a free democratic nation, should owe billions and billions of dollars or euros to some multinational banks that have no national loyalty whatsoever. They are run by power elite people, the very same souls who three or four hundred years ago were sitting in their castles and mansions, living off of the people, and who are still today living off of the very same people, even though the people generally have a higher standard of living.

And so, this is another thing that must happen in Europe—that people must wake up and realize that the comfortable economic situation that they have in many Western nations, the welfare system, is bought at a price and that price is their own freedom. Because they have sold out their nations and themselves to these multinational financial institutions who are pulling the strings behind the scenes. And who – for every euro spent by the people – are extracting their pound of flesh, even though they are not working for it and are providing no services and are indeed not multiplying the economies but simply hoarding to themselves by bleeding the people.

This, my beloved, is the opposite of the principle of multiplying the talents. And it simply cannot be allowed to continue, and it will be allowed to continue as long as the people do not stand up and demand a free economic system, where they do not have to pay interest to multinational banks, who should have no business whatsoever lending money, creating money in some cases out of thin air, and charging interest for that money.

This is a completely ungodly system that originated in the Middle Ages in the beginning of the Industrial Revolution and has truly prevented a far greater economic growth. It has prevented the manifestation of the vision that El Morya was talking about—much greater abundance and freedom in Europe and elsewhere.

My vision for Europe

And I must tell you that I too hold a very high vision for what could happen in Europe, not only economically but also culturally and spiritually. My beloved, this continent is literally ready for a change that is as far-reaching as the bringing forth of democracy or the industrial revolution. This can happen within a decade or two. But right now the people's vision is not clear enough and their willingness to take a stand for truth is not strong enough that they can break through the opposition, the stranglehold of the power elite, and actually get to a point where they can push aside that opposition that is holding back the growth of this continent.

This, my beloved, is a very real possibility—that if the people will wake up and realize what is going on and realize their own power, the power of their minds, the power of their voice, the power of their votes when they are cast right and when they demand the real candidates who can run their nation and have a Flame of Freedom. My beloved, the people have far more power than they realize. And it has always been so, and that is why the power elite can retain power only by keeping the people in the state of illusion, where they either do not realize they have power or where they actually deny their power to bring about change.

And this is what you see as a dark cloud hanging over this continent—that people still believe that they have no power to bring about change. And it is precisely because, for centuries, the Catholic Church told them they had no power because they were miserable sinners. And now for almost a century the scientific establishment has told them they are no more than animals, and therefore they have no spiritual power. But I must tell you that it is time to challenge that lie and that illusion. And you are indeed examples of what can happen when people are willing to challenge the lie that you have no spiritual power and come into the realization that you have power and the willingness to claim it, and the willingness to take a stand and simply demand – even if you are standing in your own room – and demanding freedom, demanding an awakening of the people as you do in the rosaries. Even this has power, but far more does it have power when people start to speak out.

And I can tell you that if the people in Europe, or in any one nation, would wake up and demand change, then you should see those people in the governments and in the financial institutions and other power elite institutions, you should see them shaking in their boots. For there is nothing they fear more than the people awakening and taking a stand. For they have seen throughout history that every time that happens, they have to retreat, for they know they cannot stand up to a united population who demands change.

Claim your freedom

So I tell you, "Claim your right to be free—spiritually, economically, politically." Start with the spiritual freedom and then radiate that light. Let your Light of Freedom shine so that other people can see it. And then share with them how you have obtained your freedom, your peace of mind. And then, as they are more open, share with them the fire of your heart that you have attained—through your love for freedom, through your willingness to challenge your own ego, to look it in the eye and say, "You have no more place in my consciousness, I want you out of my system." Likewise, you must gather, you must claim, the power to stand up and say to the power elite, "You have no more power in my nation. I want you off this continent!"

This, my beloved, is the only thing that will bring about a swift revolutionary change, whether it be in Europe or elsewhere. Someone must take that ultimate stand and say, "Enough is enough! Change must happen!" Not in a way of threatening, that if you don't change, we will kill you as they do in some revolutionary movements. No, you simply need to make the claim, to state your claim, to state your truth and then allow God to work through you and do the rest.

For I assure you that when even a small percentage of people will take that stand for freedom, then others will be awakened and suddenly there will be a popular movement, a popular awareness. And people will wake up and say, "Why have we not claimed this freedom long ago? Why have we accepted these positions for so long? It is time for a change. It is time for a new wind to blow on this continent and in this nation."

Let the people of Europe choose the Living Christ!

Jesus, October 1, 2006.

Why a democracy cannot guarantee freedom

So my beloved, what is the blindness that prevents human beings from realizing that they are creating their own reality, for better or for worse? And that the only way to create a better future for this planet is to become more aware of the power of the mind, and then make the decision to choose the consciousness of life and create the future based on the consciousness of life, instead of continuing to create the future partially based on the consciousness of death.

And so, it is the next logical step that human beings realize the power of their own minds. For my beloved, did I not say 2,000 years ago that the kingdom of God is within you? Well, what is within you? Well, surely it is your mind that is the innermost core of your being, your consciousness. And therefore, what you hold in your mind is what you create in your outer so-called reality. This is an essential truth that must be brought out in this age. For has it not been said that he who fails to learn from the past is destined to repeat it? And have you not seen this European continent be torn apart by war after war, where the one war set the stage for the next war in a seemingly endless spiral?

Thus, I come also to bring forth the judgment of the Living Christ upon the consciousness of war, the consciousness of power, the consciousness of wanting to preserve power at the cost of enslaving the people and destroying society! For my beloved, do you not see that the essence of life is self-transcendence? And therefore, nothing will remain the same. If it does not grow in an upward spiral and becomes more, then it must inevitably go into a downward spiral until it self-destructs, and in that self-destruction there is the rebirth of a new reality. This is precisely, as was explained to you, what happened with the Roman Empire, that would not transcend itself and take the power that was vested in one person and divide it up among the people as was the true matrix for the Piscean Age.

My beloved, what did you see for most of the Piscean Age? You saw a form of government where one person was at the top of the pyramid, and he had absolute power over those below him, whether it be the Pope or a king or an emperor—or a Führer. You saw the one person who had absolute power. But my beloved was I, when I walked the Earth, a person with absolute power? Nay! For the Christ has no need for power. Look at what I did with the Christian movement. I was there as the leader to bring forth a teaching and set an example, and when that was done I disappeared and I left the entire movement, not to one disciple but to twelve and those beyond.

Was the Christian movement, in its beginning days, not more like a democracy than like a totalitarian organization? Yet it was not a democracy in the sense that everybody voted based on the human consciousness. It was a democracy in the sense that people were meant to have their Christ discernment, so that they did not vote or make decisions based on the human consciousness, the death consciousness. But indeed, all had some Christ discernment, and therefore could come into oneness, could come into union in knowing what was right, what was the next step. Because they were led by the Spirit, by the Comforter, that I sent to all those who are willing to receive it.

Thus, even though a democracy is certainly a step up from the totalitarian regimes of the past, a democracy is by no means a guarantee for a free society where all have equal opportunity. A truly free society can happen only when there is a critical mass of people who have some degree of Christ discernment and are willing to exercise it by speaking out, by bearing witness to the truth that they see through that Christ discernment.

If everybody is trapped by the human consciousness, by the death consciousness, and cast their vote based on that consciousness, what do you think will happen to a democratic nation? Well, my beloved, surely only those people who are embodying the death consciousness will even be able to run for office and be recognized as candidates by the political parties. And thus, you see in every democratic nation that the leaders are a reflection of the consciousness of the people. And if the people do not have any level of Christhood, then they simply cannot attract leaders who have any level of Christhood.

And thus, the entire nation will go into a downward spiral, as El Morya and Saint Germain were explaining has happened to many of the nations in Europe, where there are more and more problems that seem to have no solution. Well, these problems have no solution precisely because the problems that are created through the death consciousness cannot be solved through the death consciousness. And therefore, the only viable solution is to reach up higher for that vision of Christ that helps you see that there is indeed a solution.

But the solution is not at the same level as the problem. The solution can be brought about only when people are willing to abandon their old ways, their comfortable ways—to let the old ways die, to give up the ghost of the old ways and then come up to an entirely higher approach, a higher world view.

This, my beloved, is precisely what is lacking in the European nations. But as both El Morya and Saint Germain said yesterday, it is close. It is right under the surface. And it just needs some final steps that can break through that ice and start it flowing downstream so that the river can be cleared. And that final step can only come from those who are the most spiritually mature people, those who are willing to honestly recognize that they are still trapped by certain elements of the death consciousness and then willing to look that death consciousness squarely in the eye and say, "Get thee behind me Satan! For you have no part of me anymore!"

The temptation of the death consciousness

My beloved, there are many people who have followed the spiritual path for a long time. There are many people who have studied the Teachings of the Ascended Masters, practiced our techniques, be it decrees or rosaries, and they have done so diligently. And they have made progress by doing so, but there will come a point where you will not make any further progress until you start to consciously make what I have called LIFE decisions.

My beloved, it is a law of God that the devil is allowed to tempt you. For in being tempted by the death consciousness, you have the opportunity to choose life and prove that you are willing to choose life. And you see the example of how I was tempted by the devil after my stay in the wilderness. And the stay in the wilderness symbolizes that I had withdrawn from the ways of the world, from the consciousness of the world, and put my entire attention on the kingdom of God within me until I connected to that kingdom.

And then, my beloved, I faced the challenge that when you connect to the kingdom of God and reach a certain level of Christhood, you cannot just sit there in your cave and meditate and be in bliss, for the world is crying in pain. And the role of the Living Christ is not to remove himself from the world, but to be in the world while not being of the world—and thus demonstrate to the people of the world that there is a higher way, not just a different way, but a higher way.

And thus, the Living Christ must go out, and in going out the Living Christ then meets the consciousness of the world as was exemplified by the devil who came to me and tried to tempt me into perverting or aborting my mission to bear witness for the absolute truth of God. The devil tried to tempt me into pursuing worldly goals or denying my Christhood or using it in frivolous pursuits of creating miracles or tempting God to save me.

This, my beloved, is a temptation, but I must tell you that although I was tempted three times, it does not actually mean that the devil can tempt you only three times. For you are the one who must decide how long you will allow the devil to keep tempting you, how long you will allow the worldly consciousness to pull you into this direction or that direction and pull you away from bearing witness to the truth and letting your light shine.

My beloved, there are people who have been on the spiritual path for decades and who are still allowing the devil to tempt them on a daily basis because they have not been willing to take a firm stand on the rock of Christ and say, "Enough is enough! Get thee behind me Satan!" When you make that decision and you are completely resolved, so that you make it with every part of your being – so that you are not a house divided, but you are of one mind, your eye is single in being focused on the one vision of Christ – then the devil will flee from you. The worldly consciousness will flee from you in the sense that it cannot touch you anymore.

This obviously does not mean that you will not encounter that consciousness. For when you interact with other people, you will encounter their consciousness. But it means that you have established a hallowed sphere inside yourself, and you know that there is a core of your being that the prince of this world, that the forces of this world, that the demons of Mara simply cannot touch. Because it is your hallowed ground. It is the meeting point between your conscious self and your I AM Presence, your God.

This is what I desire to see for each and every one of you, each person who has found my website. For my beloved, the Ask Real Jesus website is far more significant in this age than most of you realize. Think back to how it was 2,000 years ago, how many people recognized my teachings and my disciples as a significant force that would have a major impact on Western civilization. Well, my beloved, it was not very many. For there were not even any written teachings. Nor was there any way to get the teachings out, except by preaching and by word of mouth.

Think about how far we have come in being able to communicate, so that people all over the world can find a higher teaching. The outer teaching that is all they need in order to trigger what they already know in their hearts. For truly, God has written his law in your inward parts. And all you need is an outer stimulus that can help you reconnect to that inner law and that inner truth, and then you can become a spiritually self-sufficient person who has the Christ discernment to know what is real and unreal in your own psyche and in your own world.

Indeed, it will take a period of what I call magnificent confusion before you will have worked your way through the temptations of the worldly consciousness that are many and subtle. Nevertheless, by being willing to enter that state of confusion, to experiment, by being willing to make mistakes and recognizing those mistakes and learning from them, you can shorten the time it takes before you come to that inner wholeness that is sufficient for you to take the firm stand, whereby you can fully and finally rebuke the devil so that he must withdraw from you. Because even the devil realizes that when you take that firm stand on the rock of Christ, if he keeps tempting you, he will judge himself. And since he does not want to hasten his own judgment, he must run away from you.

The master key to growth is integration between your Higher and lower Being

Mother Mary, October 20, 2006.

The quintessential serpentine lie

Now, my beloved, if you will analyze what caused the fall of most human beings on Earth, you will realize that it was that they all came to believe in the quintessential serpentine lie. And that lie is that God's will is in opposition to your will, that God is a tyrant who is seeking to impose his will and his law upon you and in so doing wants to take away your free will and restrict your creativity.

This is the lie that in a disguised form was presented to Eve in the Garden Of Eden. For had not Maitreya told her that if she ate of the forbidden fruit – which represents the consciousness of duality – that she would surely die. And did not the Serpent say that she would not surely die. But in fact, there was more than what was recorded in the Bible because the Serpent made Eve believe that not only would she not die, but that she would find the real form of life, the life that God did not want her to have, the life that could only be found by rebelling against God's Law and God's Will. For the Serpent would have you believe that you can only have truly free will by going against God's Will. And this impression has, of course, been reinforced by the main religions in the Western world who are all so focused on the masculine aspect of God and deliberately deny the feminine aspect of God.

And so, what has come down to the West, including through Christianity, is the whole idea that women were responsible for the fall of humankind. But the symbol behind that outer statement is that the feminine aspect of creation and the feminine aspect of your own being is responsible for your fall and for the fall of humankind. My beloved, there is some truth to this. For the masculine aspect of your being is the spiritual self, your I AM Presence. And the feminine aspect is what I in my book have called the "Conscious You" or the conscious self.

The conscious self is what descends into the material world. It is the conscious self who is the co-creator with God, who is charged with multiplying its creative abilities and taking dominion over the Earth. And it does so by building a sense of identity through which it expresses itself. And therefore, the identity, the etheric, body is the highest of your four lower bodies, and everything that follows in your lower bodies is colored by, is springing from, is the result of the sense of identity that you have built.

And so it was the Conscious You who made the decision to believe in the serpentine lie, to leave off of your oneness with God's Will. Yet the reality is that it is also the feminine aspect of your being, your conscious self, who must make the decision – the only decision – that can bring you back into oneness, which is what Christian's call salvation.

For my beloved, it is another serpentine lie that after you have separated yourself from your own Higher Being, there will be some outer savior, some outer religion, that will save you, who will do the work for you. And it is a lie that you cannot save yourself. This is the lie that Jesus challenged when he said, "The kingdom of God is within you."

The serpentine plot

And thus, my beloved, the lie that has been perpetrated now through the Western religions for thousands of years is that the feminine aspect of your being is responsible for the Fall, is bad, can only make wrong choices and therefore must be disciplined and suppressed by—what? My beloved, this is what religions do not tell you. They do not tell you that the feminine aspect of your being must be brought into alignment with the higher part of your being, the masculine part of your being. No, they say that the feminine aspect of your being must be controlled and disciplined and restricted by some external deity, an angry being in the sky. And thus, my beloved, do you see the subtlety of the serpentine plot?

First, they get you to leave off from your oneness with your Higher Being by making it seem like your Higher Being is an external deity, who is a tyrant that is trying to impose his will upon you. And therefore, you should run away from that and exercise your free will in opposition to God's "restrictive" laws. And then they create a set of religions in the Western world who say that the only way to be saved is to submit yourself to the will of this external deity, which they first told you was a tyrant that was trying to take away your freedom.

And so, you see my beloved, they first get you to run away from the external God in the sky. And then they try to tell you that the only way to be saved is to submit yourself completely to that external being in the sky. So do you see that what has happened here is that they have attempted to create what we call a spiritual catch-22, where you are running away from something at the same time as another part of your being is feeling that it has to force itself to run towards that something?

And because you do not want to run toward the angry being in the sky, you do not want to submit yourself to the angry being in the sky and his external will, you are forever a house divided against itself. And thus, you cannot stand in the presence of the Living Christ. And thus, you cannot sense the presence of the Living Christ because you do not sense the burning in your heart, because the burning in your heart is so overshadowed by all the turmoil created by the divisions in your psyche. For that original division has mushroomed into many other divisions that take all kinds of shapes, in the form of all kinds of psychological problems or in the form of desires for the things of this world or the belief that following an outer religion and doing all its outer rituals and practices will save you.

And because of all these different things that are pulling you in so many different directions, you do not have the attention and the time to center in your heart. And that is why so many people in the world today cannot focus on the spiritual path, even though they have more free time than ever before. Yet their free time – which is Saint Germain's gift to them so they can pursue the spiritual path – their free time is being eaten up by all these outer things, all these compulsions that they cannot let go of, simply because they are so divided that they do not realize they are being pulled in different directions.

And they can never see beyond all the surface divisions to see the central division that is behind it all – and that their egos and the prince of this world do not want them to see – because once you see that central division, you can then look beyond the outer divisions and go to the core, you can take the axe and cut the tree at the root instead of dealing with the branches. And once the tree comes tumbling down, the tree of anti-life, then there will be a clearing in your mind, and you will now see the Tree of Life, which is the tree of oneness rather than the tree of anti-life which is the tree of division.

Are you awake?

Gautama Buddha, October 20, 2006.

You have a right to BE on Earth

Surely, you will be rejected by some. Surely you will be condemned by others. Surely you will be told that you are not allowed to do this, you are not allowed to be loving and kind, you are not allowed to be in peace, you are not allowed to be happy, you are not allowed to be in bliss. Who do you think you are in this world, where everything is so serious and life is such a drudgery that you can come here and radiate this peace and love and light—and thereby disturb those who are so identified with the dualistic struggle that they have convinced themselves that there is no alternative. And here you come and radiate this love and they realize that there is an alternative, but in order to attain that love they have to give up their mental boxes.

And so, they will resent you. But my beloved, as was explained this afternoon in greater clarity than you will find in any other spiritual teaching on this planet, that is part of the test. For it was because you let other people cause you to stop your light from shining that you left off the true path of self-transcendence, the path of becoming more. And thus, many of you who are the spiritual people are once again facing that initiation.

Will you let other people – whether it be your family or those that used to be your peers in a spiritual organization, or the world at large – will you let them stop from you from letting your light shine? Or will you finally become that sun and let your light shine, no matter what the world thinks about it or says about it. For after all, you, my beloved, no matter what the world says, you have a right to be on Earth and to BE on Earth all that you are Above, to let that light shine, to bear witness to your truth.

Do you hear me? You have a right to Be the Christ, to Be the Buddha, to Be your God Flame. You have an absolute God-given right. And those who oppose you and want you not to disturb them have no right to make that claim. For they have violated their free will and they seek to pull others into that violation.

But you see, my beloved, free will does not give you the right to destroy others. And that is precisely what those who are trapped in the consciousness of the fallen angels will not realize. They have no right whatsoever to kill those who bear witness to the light. Nor do they have a right to kill them emotionally and cause them to shut off their light or feeling so bad about themselves that they dare not express anything beyond the ordinary.

You see my beloved, you have a right to Be here. You have a right to disturb other people. And they have a right to be disturbed so that they are forced to face the choice—to Be or not to Be. And even if they deny it – the denial of Being, the Being they see in you – it will do something, it will start a process in their Beings. And I must tell you that in many cases a soul encountering a person with spiritual light and denying that light will not forget that experience for many embodiments. And the experience will come back and haunt that person until finally the person is willing to look at why it felt so angry. And then, in looking at this, many people have risen above it and have come up higher and have started the spiritual path, just because sometime in the near or distant past they encountered one person who dared to express their light.

Let your vision be MORE

El Morya, October 21, 2006.

Living vision or dead vision?

For my beloved, nothing that is of God stands still. Nothing that is of God stands still! God is self-transcendence! For this is how the Creator creates—by transcending his former state and becoming MORE. So my beloved, you may have a spiritual teaching, a religious doctrine, and you may think it gives you all you need to know about God's reality. But if your vision stands still – does not grow, does not become MORE – then your vision has become a graven image. And my beloved, no graven image can ever convey the reality of the Living God.

Look upon the world, look upon the religious people, for in them truly all spiritual people can see that even though they have a vision and claim that their doctrines can explain all there is to know about life, you can surely see that their vision is a graven image. Their doctrines are graven images, and they go to church every Sunday worshipping before those idols that have no resemblance whatsoever to the Living God. For how can any image ever depict the Living God? Thus, my beloved, you see so many Christians who hold on to an image of God that is completely out of touch with reality. For God is not an angry being in the sky. He is the Living, Loving God. God has no desire to punish anyone. God does not even desire to punish the devil, or Satan or Lucifer or whatever Christians name the adversary.

For my beloved, God only desires to see all life transcend itself. And this is the one thing I would like you to understand from this discourse. My beloved, God has no desire to punish anyone. For punishment as it is seen by human beings, often means that you restrict someone from growing. And God would never restrict anyone from growing, from transcending themselves. God only wants all life to be free, to become MORE—as God is constantly becoming MORE.

So you see, my beloved, the image of an angry and punishing God is indeed a false image, a graven image that springs from the duality consciousness. And it is created because human beings in embodiment are projecting onto God the qualities of their own egos. For you see, my beloved, the ego feels threatened, feels constantly threatened. And thus, the ego has a desire to control. And when someone else will not submit to the ego's control, then the ego wants to punish that someone else. And so you see, my beloved, the desire to punish, the desire for revenge, springs from the sense of being threatened. And the sense of being threatened can come only from unreality.

For my beloved, how could anything real be threatened by anything? Do you think that God sits up in Heaven and feels threatened by the devil? Do you think that God sits up in Heaven and feels threatened by anything human beings do or could possibly do on Earth? So my beloved, God is not threatened by anything, and thus God has no need to control. Nor does he have a need to punish those who will not submit to control.

...

A higher understanding of the fall

So let me now give you a higher understanding of the concept of fallen angels. For you see, my beloved, as this messenger has known for some time, God did not create fallen angels. This should be easy to see, for how could a perfect God create anything imperfect? Yet going all the way back to the Christian religion and beyond, there are many people who believe that the devil was created to fall, to sin, to be in opposition to God. There are even those in the New Age movement who believe that evil is a necessary polarity to God, and without it the universe would not be complete. There are even those who believe in the illusion that it was only by falling, by rebelling against God, that people gained their freedom and that they were meant to do so.

Well, my beloved, the reality is that God never created anyone imperfect, evil or dark. Nor did God create anyone to fall or to sin. It is not God's intention that anyone needs to fall or rebel against God's will. But because of free will, people – self-conscious beings – have the opportunity to rebel. This is an inevitable consequence of free will. So the reality is that God and the spiritual beings in higher realms never created any imperfect beings. They created self-conscious beings that were created in the immaculate concept and were given free will, so that they have the opportunity to co-create their identity according to their own choices.

Now my beloved, how is it then possible that such a being can fall? Well, it is possible because as a consequence of free will, there must be the possibility to go against the will of God. And what enables you to stay one with the will of God, with the law of God, is the Christ consciousness where you see yourself as one with your own Higher Being, going all the way up to the Creator. And in that oneness, you would never even dream of going beyond God's law. Instead, you express your creativity and your free will within the framework of God's Law, whereby you raise up all life.

Yet in order for free will to be complete, in order for there to be the opportunity to go against God's Law, the Christ consciousness must have an opposite, which is the consciousness of anti-christ. Now my beloved, please do not fall into the illusion of thinking that the consciousness of anti-christ is somehow necessary in order for the Christ to be complete. The Christ consciousness, my beloved, is completely self-sufficient and does not need an opposite polarity. The Christ mind does not need an enemy to fight because the Christ mind is above and beyond duality.

So you see, my beloved, God needs no opposite. And therefore, evil is not the opposite polarity of God. Likewise, Christ needs no opposite. And therefore the mind of anti-christ is not an opposite polarity of the mind of Christ. It is simply outside of the mind of Christ. It is outside of the oneness of the mind of Christ, removed from the oneness of the mind of Christ. And although this removal, this separation, is only an illusion, those who step into the sphere of the consciousness of anti-christ will think the separation is real, possibly even created by God.

So what makes it possible for an angel in Heaven to become a fallen angel? Well, it is that the angel refuses to step up to the point, as was discussed yesterday, of becoming self-sufficient. And that, of course, is the point of Christhood, the point of Christhood where you know the kingdom of God is within you. And therefore, you are a complete and whole and self-sufficient being who can be the sun that radiates light from within itself, because it is your God Flame, out of which you came, that radiates through you.

And this is the real definition of Christhood—that you are a spiritual sun, s-u-n. And thereby you become what has been known as the son, s-o-n, of God. Because now you know you are the offspring of God and you identify yourself as such. Yet those lifestreams in higher realms, who refused to step up to that level of Christhood, had no other way to go than to separate themselves from Christhood. And when the sphere in which they lived was raised in vibration, then they had to step away from Christhood and they had to step into the realm of duality, the realm of anti-christ.

And you see, my beloved, in the realm of duality, there is any number of states of consciousness that have been created. All of these states of consciousness were unreal. Originally, of course, they did not exist. But as beings have fallen and entered into that state of consciousness, then they have created a certain state of consciousness, a certain world view, a certain momentum that has then gradually transcended any one individual and has taken on a life of its own as a mass entity, as a conglomerate of consciousness.

And so, my beloved, what makes it possible for an angel to fall is that it steps outside of the Christ consciousness and steps into that consciousness, a certain consciousness, that exists in the realm of duality.

And it starts looking at the world from inside that consciousness. It starts identifying itself with that consciousness. For as we have explained, the core of a self-conscious being with free will is the Conscious You, the conscious self, which is the seat of free will and the seat of identity. And thus, it has the ability to either identify itself as the offspring of God or identify itself as a being who is rebelling against God.

So you see, my beloved, the conscious self is not a fallen angel—it simply is not possible. It is an individualization of God. Yet if the conscious self steps into that mold, that role, that state of consciousness, then it identifies itself as a fallen angel or as a being with a certain state of consciousness – whether it has the concept of a fallen angel or not – it identifies itself with that state of consciousness. And it expresses that in the material realm or wherever it appears. So it thinks that it could not be more than that consciousness. And therefore, it becomes stuck in that consciousness.

Judgment is the hallmark of the fallen consciousness

My beloved, my point for this long discourse is to bring you to the realization that when people are stuck in one of these dualistic states of consciousness, it is inevitable that they begin to become very critical and judgmental toward those who are not stuck in their states of consciousness.

And that is why my point here is that if you look at people, perhaps even dare to look at yourself, and say, "Do I feel a need to criticize others? Do I feel a need to judge others? Do I feel a need to evaluate others? Can I identify that in the back of my mind there is always a voice, there is always a process, of criticizing, of judging, of evaluating everything, of comparing to some standard that I am not even consciously aware of? Can I recognize in myself that there is a tendency, sometimes, to blame—to blame myself, to blame others, to criticize, to condemn, to judge, to look for imperfections, instead of looking at the immaculate concept."

My beloved, my point here is to show you that too many of those who formerly were ascended master students, or who still call themselves ascended master students, have not been willing to step up to the level of Christhood. They have instead become stuck in one of the states of consciousness that were originally created and reinforced by the fallen angels. And therefore, they have become judgmental and critical of anything that is different from that state of consciousness and its characteristics.

They are constantly judging and evaluating anything that comes to them. Because it is as if, as it was discussed yesterday, they have a mental box, and any idea that comes to them must somehow fit into that box and be put into a little drawer with a label on it, so they feel that they have the idea under control and so that their egos will not feel threatened by the idea. And so that the people themselves, the conscious selves, will not feel an urge to go beyond the mental box, to think outside the box.

You see, my beloved, what I want you to see from this discourse is that even if you have a very sophisticated vision of the spiritual side of life and have a sophisticated outer understanding of the teachings of the ascended masters, it is still possible that you can be stuck in a state of consciousness that is not the ascended master consciousness but is the consciousness of the fallen angels. And so, my beloved, whether you actually fell from above, or whether you descended on a rescue mission, or whether you evolved from the Earth, it does not really matter.

What matters is that as long as you are in a state of consciousness that has the characteristics of the fallen consciousness – the judgmentalness, the judging after appearances as Jesus said – as long as you are in that state of consciousness, you are not expressing your Christhood. And therefore, you are truly not an ascended master student. You are not truly a chela of El Morya because you are refusing to become MORE.

And instead of you becoming MORE, and constantly transcending yourself, you have accepted an upper limit. And now you are spending your attention on judging others whom you think do not live up to your standard, the standard that you have used to box yourself in—and your ego is now using to try to control everybody else and box them in, so that they will not disturb your vision by demonstrating that there is something beyond the box.

Be free as a little child

Saint Germain, October 21, 2006.

The false concept of freedom

My beloved, how can you become free? Well, you need to understand freedom, at least as a start. And so you need to realize that there are many false concepts of freedom circulating on this planet. And the most subtle of all of them is the one promoted by the false teachers, namely that freedom can only come when you can do anything you want. And my beloved, the only reason this illusion has such a hold on so many people is because the Earth is currently so dense, and humankind's consciousness so dense, that so many people do not recognize – do not experience intuitively – the direct relationship between their actions and the reaction from the universe. They do not experience directly the reality of the law of action and reaction, the law of karma.

So my beloved, how can you have an illusion that freedom means you can do anything you want? Well, you can have it only when you deny karma. For when you know the law of karma, you know that every action has an opposite reaction—at least when that action is taken from the consciousness of duality. And so, my beloved, what is truly going on is that those beings who fell from a higher realm – in their rebellion against God and against God's vision, will and law – well they have attempted to create the illusion that you can escape the reaction to your actions, that you can escape your karma.

And thus, my beloved, I must tell you that there are indeed some among the most "sophisticated" among these beings who know that karma is a reality and that you can never escape the consequences of your actions. Yet they also know that if they can get other people to accept the illusion that actions don't have consequences, that you can do whatever you want and get away with it, then they can get some of these people to go along with their schemes. And that means that the people who go along with the fallen angels, the false leaders, become partly responsible for the karma created as a result of that state of consciousness.

And that means that those who are at the top of the pyramid can avoid reaping all of the karma, because those below them take on most of it. And so they can dodge that karma and avoid having the return, because those who are below them, those who are their followers, are bearing the brunt of the burden. This is very similar to what you have seen in many cultures, such as the feudal societies in Europe, where you had a king or a duke or a master who owned – practically – the people below him. And those people were the ones who bore the brunt of the physical burden of raising crops and providing the riches that allowed the leader to sit in his castle and become fat on the labor of others.

And so, this is a physical representation of what is going on in the hidden realms, in terms of certain false teachers, false leaders, who are getting other people to follow them blindly into that state of consciousness of rebelling against the law of karma. They have created the false sense of freedom, and thus they can sit there as the leader while their followers carry the brunt of the karmic burden. So this is why these insidious lies have been spread and continue to be spread, so that someone can set himself up as a guru and have followers, who then bear the burden of the karma made through his selfish actions and through the spreading of the false teachings he is bringing forth.

When your forgiveness is unconditional, your joy will be full

Mother Mary, November 26, 2006

You see, my beloved, once you truly enter into the spirit of forgiveness – and allow the spirit of forgiveness to enter into your lower being – well then you will be in a state of perpetual forgiveness, so that you have already forgiven yourself and other people before they have done anything to you.

And thus, when they do something to you – for truly you cannot control the actions of others – well then they are already forgiven. And when you know that they are already forgiven, you also know that you can then stay free of any negative reaction, no matter what other people do to you. And thereby, my beloved, you can follow the most profound advice given by Jesus, namely that you resist not evil, but when a person smites you on one cheek, you will turn to him the other also.

My beloved, turning the other cheek can be done only when you are in a state of perpetual and unconditional forgiveness. And so, when some person does something to you, you do not go into a negative reaction. You stay in peace. You stay in love. You stay in forgiveness. And thus, you simply turn the other cheek so that you can give the other person another opportunity to see his or her own evil, his or her own imperfections.

Helping others see their illusions

For my beloved, what happens when a person hurts you and you respond negatively and seek to hurt the other person? Well, my beloved, do you not validate the other person's belief that you are a bad person? And was it not such a belief that in most cases caused other people to hurt you in the first place, namely that they believe you have done something wrong and you deserve to be punished or hurt.

And so, when you allow yourself to be hurt and respond back by trying to hurt them or defend yourself, then you only reinforce the other person's belief. And you not only reinforce the belief in the mind of the other person, but you reinforce it in your own mind. For after all, it was only because you have an imperfect belief about yourself that you allowed the other person's actions to hurt you.

And so, my beloved, when you turn the other cheek, you break the spiral. When you respond with love when someone else hurts you, you are challenging the other person's belief that you are a bad person or that you deserve to be punished. You are showing the other person that you are a person who can respond with love. And thereby, the other person is forced to reconsider his or her own actions and his or her own image of you. And this can often help people step out of their own illusions, so that they see that they are trapped in imperfect beliefs about themselves and about life. And thus, they receive an opportunity to overcome those beliefs.

Yes, my beloved, I know full well that there are persons with whom you can turn the other cheek and they will hurt you again. But you see, my beloved, when you turn the other cheek in perfect love and forgiveness – in unconditional forgiveness – and another person still hurts you, then that second act of hurting you becomes the person's judgment.

And that judgment will release a reaction from life itself that will cause that person to experience such an accelerated return of what it is sending into the cosmic mirror. And that accelerated return will either cause the person to wake up or will ultimately cause the person to be judged to the point where the person will not be allowed to reincarnate on Earth until it has changed its consciousness.

And thus, you see, my beloved, what Jesus was really saying was that if people would adopt his advice of turning the other cheek and not resisting evil, then they would allow the law of God to work in full measure. And by doing this, the law of God will actually be able to remove evil from the Earth at an accelerated rate.

For you see, my beloved, when you allow other people to hurt you while you are turning the other cheek, well then God can step in and remove those people from the Earth. And thereby, you will quickly have a situation where the most evil people – the most selfish self-centered, egotistical people – will be removed from the Earth. And therefore, humankind as a whole will simply rise up to a higher level and overcome certain states of consciousness that you today see outplayed over and over again in a seemingly endless spiral of people hurting each other and seeking revenge for hurt—thereby creating a new hurt that gives the other people an excuse for seeking revenge.

Chapter 6:
Teachings about fallen angels, 2007

Let 2007 be the year of unconditional peace

Gautama Buddha, January 1, 2007

The Buddha I AM. Gautama is my name, and I come to greet you in the lotus flame of unconditional love that is truly the flame of unconditional peace. For my beloved, how shall there ever be peace on Earth until the people on Earth begin to understand and experience that peace – true peace – is unconditional peace.

My beloved, take one look at history and see the fallacy of the human logic – the dualistic logic, the logic of anti-christ – which has made so many people believe that they must create peace through force, through revenge, through destroying their enemies. What is indeed the incredible fallacy that makes people believe in this logic?

Well it is, my beloved, very simply that there is something they are not willing to give up in themselves. There is something to which they are attached. And that something is not just an outer thing, be it a piece of property or anything else in this world. No my beloved, that to which people are attached is indeed something that is in themselves. It is a part of their egos, and they are not willing to let go of the belief that makes them feel that they have some kind of superiority, some kind of right to do what they want to do here on Earth.

Thus, my beloved, all of the outer reasons and justifications that people come up with for engaging in conflict and warfare are lies, are facades. They are nothing but pretensions and hypocrisy. For the true reality is that people wage war because they are trying to defend their egos. There is a part of the ego that people are not willing to give up. And I am not here just talking about individuals but groups of people, even entire nations or civilizations.

Superiority is the cause behind the war in Iraq

My beloved, what was it indeed that caused the American President to start the war in Iraq—which now most people in his own country realize was an ill-conceived adventure? Well, it was, my beloved, that there is something in the national psyche of America that Americans have so far not been willing to recognize and give up. And what is that something, my beloved? Well, it is indeed the entire idea of superiority. The entire idea that a certain people can be the chosen people, the most powerful people, that a nation can somehow be favored by God.

My beloved, it has been stated by other Masters that America indeed has a special place in the plans of the Ascended Host, that America was created because of Saint Germain's sponsorship and that it was his hope that America would be the bastion of freedom and the forerunner for the Golden Age. Thus, you can see that America has a certain place in the family of nations. But this does not make America superior to other nations in a dualistic sense and according to a human value judgment.

On the contrary, the sponsorship of Saint Germain is not something that should be taken lightly, and thus it should indeed be approached with utmost humility. For did not Christ say, "He who would be greatest among you, let him be the servant of all." And so is it not clear, then, that if America is meant to be the greatest among nations, America should be the servant of all of the nations.

And thus, America needs to overcome the sense of superiority, the sense that America has some kind of divine right to exercise its power in other nations. America must even overcome the belief that it has a right, or a duty, or an obligation to spread its own values throughout the world. And thus, when President Bush believed that he was spreading freedom and democracy by engaging in war in Iraq, it must be admitted that what he was truly spreading the current American version of freedom and democracy. Which is indeed not the democracy and freedom of Saint Germain but the "freedom" and "democracy" of the power elite that has taken this nation over, has infiltrated all of its institutions of power and has perverted the original ideas and democracy that were spawned from Saint Germain's sponsorship of this nation.

Thus, my beloved, there is absolutely no way that America can fulfill her destiny and her role unless Americans become willing to look for the beam in their own eye and realize that they have allowed their nation to be taken over by a power elite, who has perverted all of the original principles for which this nation stands. They have done this in the name of power and in the name of money. And thus, my beloved, American foreign policy is indeed not about freedom and democracy but about money and power.

Thus, my beloved, why has the military adventure in Iraq gone the way it has? Well, it has done so because President Bush exerted a dualistic force that inevitably created a counter force from the universe. The action of America created an equal and opposite reaction in the form of the uprising and the unrest and the insurgency in Iraq.

Now my beloved, let me make it clear that I am not in any way condoning the use of violence. But let me make it clear that I am not condoning the violence from either side, including the Americans. Yet I must tell you that the violence in Iraq is nothing but a counter-force created by the Americans themselves, by the power elite, the neo-conservatives or whatever you prefer to call the people that were behind the military adventure in Iraq.

It is indeed true that many of the insurgents or the people who commit violence in Iraq are all too willing to play their role of counter-force. And thus, I am in no way justifying or condoning what they are doing. I am simply pointing out that what you have seen in Iraq – the chaos and the violence – is something created by the Americans.

And when you look at this from a world perspective, it must actually be said that this force, this unrest, has prevented an even worse calamity. For can there be any doubt that President Bush and the people behind him did not plan to go into Iraq and stop there. Had President Bush indeed not tipped their hands by talking about an axis of evil? And is it not clear that if the military adventure in Iraq had gone as planned, then it would have only been a springboard to further adventures.

Certainly, the axis of evil was named. But my beloved, who can tell where such a momentum would have stopped, had it gotten rolling in the first place. I can assure you that if the war in Iraq had been short with no significant unrest afterwards, America would have already been engaged militarily in at least two other countries. One of them would have been Iran. The other one might not have been North Korea, for there are several other options.

Yet I can tell you that had this adventure continued, there would have been an even greater counter-force from the entire Muslim world. And this could already have started the large-scale war that we have talked about previously. Thus, one can indeed say that the unrest in Iraq has been the stitch in time that saves nine. For it has indeed prevented even more widespread warfare.

The superiority complex in the Middle East

Now my beloved, every coin has two sides and so has every conflict. Is there indeed not a similar mechanism in the Middle East, in the Arab and Muslim world, whereby they also wage war because there is something in themselves, a part of their own egos, that they are not willing to give up. And so what is, indeed, that something?

Well, my beloved, it is in fact the same mechanism, although with a slightly different disguise. Nevertheless, it is also the need for superiority, the need to feel that somehow one is favored by God because one is a member of the Muslim religion which is the highest religion on Earth, or so they think.

And so you see, my beloved, that this insane drive for ultimate superiority is indeed the most extreme outcome of the human ego that has been allowed to run rampant without any checks from people's true beings, their conscious selves. Thus one might wonder how long this insanity will go on on this planet.

And I will tell you how long it will go on. It will continue until the top ten percent of the most spiritually aware people decide that they have had enough of it. Thus, they will start by pulling the beam from their own eyes, for indeed there are many people on this planet who are truly spiritual and have engaged in spiritual activities, yet they have allowed their egos to fool them into feeling a subtle sense of superiority because they have done this or that spiritual activity. They have meditated for so long, they have given so many prayers or rosaries or decrees or what have you.

Thus, my beloved, this must indeed stop at the top by the most spiritually mature people being willing to look in the mirror and say, "We have to overcome this. We have to let go of this subtle spiritual pride and intellectual pride because we can understand spiritual concepts. We have to overcome this. We have to come together in true humility, and then we have to make the calls so that God will remove this planetary beast of superiority, so that other people can be set free from the gravitational pull of this beast that seeks to pull the entire planet into a black hole."

...

You cannot stop conflict by destroying your enemies

And thus, my beloved, what I desire you to visualize for the year 2007 is that humankind finally wakes up and realizes the essential truth that the only way to attain peace is through unconditional forgiveness. My beloved, it is the insanity of the ego to believe that one needs to compensate for the violence of the past before peace can manifest in the present. It is the insanity of the ego to believe that one can compensate for the errors of the past, that one can ever fix what was broken in the past, that one can ever put Humpty Dumpty together again after his fall from the great wall of time.

For my beloved, if you will think about this with the rationality of the Christ Mind, you will see that for thousands of years people have attempted to destroy their enemies, to seek revenge, to somehow make up for the violence and the mistakes of the past. Yet despite all of the fighting, all of the violence, all of the warfare, the errors of the past have not been erased. And the reason is simple.

Violence creates an action that generates an opposite reaction from the universal mirror. And thus, when you take action from the dualistic state of mind, you will create an opposition to your action that traps you in a dualistic struggle with an enemy. And this dualistic struggle will continue for as long as you stay in the dualistic mind.

And thus, what can break the spiral? Well, only one thing—that you stop acting from the consciousness of duality and rise to the consciousness of Christ, so that you do not seek revenge, but you forgive seventy times seven. You do not resist evil, but you turn the other cheek. You become as the Buddha, sitting under the Bo Tree, and you are unmoved by the demons of Mara who attempt to draw you into their dualistic struggle.

Thus, you realize that the dualistic struggle can go on forever and can consume your entire existence—past, present and future. And thus, you must come to realize that there is something more, something you want more, namely the peace of Christ, the peace of Buddha. And so you must say what Jesus said to his disciples, "What is that to thee, follow thou me." What are these dualistic struggles on Earth compared to following the Christ and the Buddha into the eternal peace of the Mind of God?

And so, you must decide what you want. Do you want to continue the dualistic struggle, or do you want to attain eternal peace? And if you want peace, then how can you do so? Well my beloved, you cannot attain peace by winning the dualistic struggle, for there are no winners in that struggle. You cannot attain peace by solving a problem created by the duality consciousness, for such a problem cannot be solved. You cannot attain peace by somehow compensating for creating the errors of the past, for the mistakes made through the duality consciousness cannot be corrected. My beloved, you cannot fix the duality consciousness. You can only leave it behind!

The lesson of the fact that, after thousands of years of struggle, humankind have not manifested peace is indeed that you cannot manifest peace through duality. You can only manifest peace by rising above – by transcending, by surrendering, by letting go of, by becoming non-attached to – duality and all of its appearances. Thus, you must give up the ghost of the past. You must reach for the non-attachment of the Buddha, the unconditional mercy of Kuan Yin, so that you can let go of the past. And instead of trying to fix it, you simply forgive. You forgive unconditionally. You forgive indefinitely.

And you even enter the state of perpetual forgiveness, where you are forgiving past, present and future. So that you know that whatever may be done to you in the future will be forgiven even before it is done. And in this way you can lock in to the immaculate concept of Mother Mary, where you can hold the immaculate concept – for yourself, for other people, indeed for the entire planet – that no matter what happens in the physical, it will not perpetuate the dualistic struggle. It will not draw you or other people back into or further into that dualistic struggle. But instead, people will overcome, they will rise above it, they will leave it behind. They will decide to suddenly forgive, where they have never forgiven before and to simply turn the other cheek and let the Law of God repay the wrongs committed by others.

The key to peace
This my beloved, is the essential key to peace. You cannot bring about peace through any amount of action done from the dualistic state of mind. You can only bring about peace by rising above duality. And in order to do that, you must let go of all of the appearances of duality. You must become non-attached to them so that you know that the peace of Christ, the peace of Buddha, the peace of the Divine Mother, indeed the peace of the Divine Father, is far more important than these dualistic appearances that are nothing but mirages in the desert.

And then, my beloved, when you have let go of the past, when you have let go of duality, when you have become non-attached, well at that point you might indeed take certain actions to bring about peace. But these actions will not be dualistic, they will be taken with the single-eyed vision of the Christ Mind, which is also the vision of the Divine Mother that holds the immaculate concept for all life. And thus your actions will be balanced, and they will not create a reaction, an opposite reaction from the universe, not even from other people.

And this is indeed the secret hinted at in the new Invocation for a Golden Future, namely that you can rise above the duality of action and reaction. And this does not mean that you become passive and do nothing, it means that you can perform action that is not dualistic and thus does not cause a dualistic reaction but cuts through the dualistic struggle and awakens people to the reality that there is something beyond, that there is a better way. And it is the Middle Way, the golden middle way that leads to a golden future.

Let the top ten percent of the most spiritually aware people be the forerunners for this shift of consciousness. Let them start by shifting their own consciousness, and when they have attained inner peace and non-attachment, then let them go out and bear witness to the truth and let their light of peace shine, that they might awaken others and eventually awaken the entire planet to the reality that peace can only come when you enter the state of unconditional peace. Which means that you do not let any of the conditions on Earth draw you into the dualistic struggle that takes away your peace. For there is only one way to bring peace to Earth, and that is to BE peace.

Thus I, Gautama, am peace. And I say to you, "Do not be at peace, for that is something you take on as an outer thing. Realize that the kingdom of God is within you. Go within and BE peace. BE peace on Earth!

Leave the eternal struggle and find freedom in the Eternal NOW

Mother Mary, February 18, 2007

What keeps people in the eternal struggle?

So my beloved hearts, what is indeed the blindness that blinds people to these evident truths, these truths that should be self-evident, or would be self-evident if people were not blinded so that they cannot see the obvious. Oh my beloved, so many people think that they are religious or spiritual, but they are as blind as the people who thought the Earth was flat, for they see not that which should be obvious if they would only open their minds and hearts.

And yet, my beloved, what is it that prevents people from seeing the reality and the truth of Christ and Buddha? Well, my beloved, it is that they are not mindful, that they are not awake. And why are they not awake? It is because they have allowed themselves, without realizing what happened, to be pulled into the eternal human struggle. And this is the struggle that is set up between two dualistic extremes. And these extremes take many different forms, my beloved. But there are always two extremes. And they pull you to go into one of the extremes, thinking that if only you can cross some line, you will win the ultimate victory. Yet I tell you the absolute truth that there is no victory possible in the realm of duality.

There are always those who promise you that if you shun the one dualistic extreme and come into the other dualistic extreme, you are guaranteed to be saved. And this, my beloved, is the promise of every false religion that has ever been seen on this planet. And unfortunately, the majority of humankind are still believing in this false promise of a false salvation, an outer salvation through belonging to this particular outer religion or belief system, following its leaders or practices.

Oh my beloved, it is this eternal human struggle that causes all of the suffering on Earth. And we have no other desire than to see you awaken to the reality that this struggle is unreality, and that by shunning that unreality – attaining the Christ discernment that allows you to see through it and see the reality of God behind it – you can overcome that struggle. You can pull yourself out. You can raise yourself above the eternal human struggle.

For my beloved, the Buddha truly said – as one of the four noble truths – that life is suffering. But life is only suffering when you are trapped in the consciousness of duality that binds you to this eternal struggle of seeking to avoid the one dualistic extreme, that is portrayed as bad, and coming into the other dualistic extreme, that is portrayed as good. Yet even though some people are very sincere and strive for an entire lifetime, perhaps even many lifetimes, to escape the bad dualistic extreme and come into the good dualistic extreme, they never quite make it.

And my beloved, why is this so? Well it is so, my beloved, because the duality consciousness sets up a goal that is unreachable, that is unattainable. You see, my beloved, no one has ever fully escaped the dualistic extreme that many call evil and reached the dualistic extreme that many call good. And why is this so? Because when you are trapped in duality, you have entered a realm where you are being pulled on by two opposing forces. And my beloved, the closer you get to one dualistic extreme, the more you will be pulled back toward the other extreme. And why is this so? Because as you move away from the centeredness of the Middle Way of Christ and Buddha, you are the one creating the force that pulls you back.

You see, my beloved, there are so many people who believe that when they are pulled away from what they define as good, it is because they are being pulled away by the forces of darkness, the forces of evil. And my beloved, while this is true, I must tell you that the reason why you are being pulled by the force of evil – the reason why the force of evil, the prince of this world, has anything in you on which it can pull – is that you are trapped in the realm of duality.

Being humanly good prevents you from entering heaven

You see, my beloved, if you were not being pulled away from good, what would happen was that you would go into a state in which you thought you were perfectly good, and you would stay there indefinitely. Yet my beloved, as Jesus said – when he said, that the righteousness of the scribes and Pharisees would not get them to heaven – was precisely that being humanly good is not sufficient to get you to heaven. For being humanly good is still in the realm of duality.

So you see, my beloved, if it was indeed possible for you to escape human evil and go into the extreme of human good, you would still be trapped in duality—yet you would believe that you would be saved. And therefore, you would not strive to go beyond that state. And if you did not strive to go beyond, you would never attain salvation. You will not be saved by becoming a good human being, for this is still a sense of identity that is separated from the spiritual identity in which you know you are an individualization of God's own Being.

So you see, my beloved, the force that human beings call evil is indeed evil, but it is evil in a dualistic sense. And as long as people are trapped in duality, it actually has the function of preventing them from going into the opposite extreme of human good, of relative good, and staying there indefinitely.

Now my beloved, this is a subtle point, and I do not want you to misunderstand or misinterpret what I say. I am not saying that evil is good. I am not saying that evil is part of God's plan. I am not saying that God wants evil to remain on this planet. I am only saying that as long as people insist on expressing their creative powers through the mind of duality – as long as they insist on trying to preserve the separate sense of self, the identity of the human ego – then they will be subject to the force of evil.

For people do indeed create both the relative good and the relative evil that blinds them to God's reality beyond duality. And therefore, you can never fully attain goodness or peace on Earth. This is what the Buddha knew, and that is why he said that life is suffering. For he knew that as long as you are trapped behind this veil of illusion, this veil of Maya, you cannot escape suffering. Jesus knew this as well and expressed the same truth, only in slightly different words.

      ...

Why you are in embodiment in this age

My beloved, this is why many of you are here. You came here to give Jesus his victory and through that victory of Christ set the stage for the victory of Saint Germain in a physical manifestation of the great Golden Age he envisions for this planet. For truly, unless we have the victory of Christ discernment, that Golden Age cannot and will not come about.

And unless the top ten percent of the most spiritual people wake up and accept their calling to be the forerunners for Christ discernment – to find that Christ discernment in the secret chamber of their own hearts and then to shout it from the housetops – well unless they take up that calling, then the awakening, the mass awakening, will not happen. And then the Golden Age will be delayed, possibly for centuries, if it even comes about at all.

For truly, the Golden Age cannot come about with the present level of consciousness that rules the nations. And this is something we will talk more about in our upcoming conferences, both in the United States and in Europe. For I must tell you that there is indeed an awakening that is right around the corner, that is right under the surface. But something is needed in order for it to break through, so that people can realize in their conscious awareness what is going on on this planet and how they must stand up to the forces of duality that are seeking to destroy that which the Ascended Hosts have built now for many spiritual cycles.

You see my beloved, it is possible that the power elite and the forces of duality can lose their grip on humanity within the next couple of decades. But for this to happen, someone must make an extraordinary effort. And those someone are the people who see themselves as the most spiritually advanced people on this planet, not in a prideful way, not in an outer way, but through the inner recognition of the heart that if I don't do it, who will? And if I don't do it now, then when? But you see my beloved, in order for you to come to that awakening and realization, in order for you to be willing to have dominion, you must first find the reality of Being, the reality of your Christ nature, your Buddha nature. And that reality can be found not only within yourself, but only within the Eternal NOW.

You see, my beloved, I know I am painting a picture here that we need you to make an effort. And it might seem that I am encouraging you to create a new spiritual rat race that causes you to run faster and give more prayers and decrees and rosaries and give them faster and faster so you hardly have time to breathe. But you see, my beloved, that is not what I am encouraging. I am encouraging you to step outside of the human and the human-spiritual rat race. I am encouraging you to find the stillness within, the stillness that is not stillstand in some imagined place of rest or Nirvana. No, I encourage you to find the stillness that is the stillness of the River of Life, which flows ever so gently but nevertheless is unstoppable by any of the forces in this world.

Are you serving a dead god or the Living God?

Nada, April 6, 2007.

Pursuing your original Love

And so, my beloved, how can you connect to that Allness? Well, my beloved, you must pursue Love. You must seek to understand Love. You must seek to reconnect to the original Love in your being. For I tell you, it does not matter where you are today, for you started out as a pure being in the immaculate concept. You descended into the world of form because you – the greater you that you truly are – had a true desire to serve all life, to raise up the sphere into which you originally descended, whether it be this sphere or another one. You came here out of a true desire.

You might have fallen into a different state of consciousness and have forgotten that love and that desire to serve all life. But you can reconnect to it because it is still at the core of your being. And if you will to grow beyond a certain point, then you MUST reconnect to it, for there is no other way.

You see, my beloved, the lie of the fallen beings – from Lucifer and all of the other ones who have pride – is that they actually believe that they can raise themselves up to such a point where they will become equal with God, or more important than God. But this, my beloved, can never be done as long as you are trapped in the illusion of separation. You can grow to become a God in your own right, as Maitreya explains, but you can do so only when you realize that God is the All that is in all—and you seek to serve the All, to raise up the All. You become one with God's desire to raise up this sphere until it becomes, indeed, the kingdom of God in manifestation, and all is Light and there is no longer room for any shadows or lies or illusions.

Once you connect to that oneness of the All, then you can become equal with God. But you see, my beloved, you become equal with God by becoming one with God. You can never be equal by being separate from God—for there is no such thing, for God is the All. And so, my beloved, since God is the ultimate reality, how could you become equal with the ultimate reality as long as you think you are separate from ultimate reality? There is only one ultimate reality, so you see, the logic of those beings who have fallen into the duality consciousness is fundamentally flawed. They cannot see this, your ego cannot see this, your intellect cannot see this. But – aah – the heart can see this.

When the heart is purified and opened, the heart can know the oneness of all life. And that truly is the first part of the spiritual path—to come to know in the heart the oneness of all life. And then to carry out that oneness in all your actions and words, so that you serve the One in the All. This, my beloved, is how I won my ascension so many thousands of years ago—by serving others, by serving those who were closest to me in that last incarnation, by serving without thought of self. For truly, when you come to sense the oneness, you realize, "It is not about me," me meaning the separate self. It is about the real me, meaning the All.

Why you are not forgiven for rejecting the INNER WORD

Jesus, April 6, 2007.

And so, what does it mean that the sin against the Holy Spirit shall not be forgiven? Well, my beloved, the traditional image of the Christian churches – of the remote being in the sky – makes it seem like it is God or Christ or the Holy Spirit who has to forgive your sin. But it is not so. It is YOU who have to forgive your sin by forsaking it, by changing your state of consciousness.

And the moment you change that state of consciousness, you are free of the old consciousness. And it was the old consciousness that was the real sin, not the outer actions—not even the outer actions of persecuting the Living Christ or killing him or his followers. All these things can be forgiven the moment you are willing to change yourself, to change your perspective, to let go of the false spirits—the multitude of spirits, the legion of spirits of duality that pull you hither and yon into identification with the things of this world. The moment you are willing to let them go and come into oneness with the one Spirit, well then you are free of the former self. You are no more that being.

My beloved, there is a saying that no fallen angel has ever been redeemed. And it is true. Because as long as you see yourself as a fallen angel, you cannot redeem yourself, you cannot enter the kingdom of God. So therefore, you must let the identity of a fallen being – or a sinner – you must let it die, so that you – the Conscious You – is reborn into a new identity. Do you see the reality here?

Understanding the elite and the counter-elite

Saint Germain, April 6, 2007.

The second law of thermodynamics and politics

You see, my beloved, as one of the masters who sponsored science on this planet, I would like to bring you a scientific perspective. What is the problem in America today? Well, it is a problem that has been described by physics in a law that has been known for centuries. And it is called the second law of thermodynamics.

Some of you are familiar with it through our releases. But unfortunately most people in the world and in America are not familiar with this law. And if they are, they see it as something that applies only to science but not to other areas of life.

And this, my beloved, is indeed part of the problem—that everything becomes so compartmentalized. And as Jesus, Nada and Mother Mary have talked about, people become so blinded by the filter in front of their eyes that they can no longer see beyond it. They cannot see the greater perspective, they cannot see themselves from the outside—and therefore they cannot see that they are heading straight for the abyss.

Therefore, my beloved, what is needed is an integration of the philosophical implications of the second law of thermodynamics, where you understand what this law actually means for a civilization, a nation, a group of people or even an individual. So for those not familiar with this law, it states very simply that if a system becomes closed, becomes isolated from anything outside itself, then disorder will increase in that system, until the system breaks down to the lowest possible energy state. Which we also might call the lowest common denominator, where things are so bad, so flat, so dead that they simply cannot go any lower.

And so, my beloved, what exactly does that mean for a civilization, for a nation? Well, it has been said that those who do not learn from history are destined to repeat it. So let us look at history. Let us look at the Roman civilization, as a perfect example for many reasons. One is that at its time Rome was close to being as dominant in the ancient world as America has become after the so-called collapse of the Soviet Union.

Rome could do almost whatever they wanted with their armies, as America today thinks they can do almost whatever they want. Yet, this great civilization – that had conquered most of the known world back then – collapsed. And why did it collapse? Well, it collapsed because it fell victim to the second law of thermodynamics! Because Rome, especially those who lived in the city of Rome and directed the Roman empire – or the emperors, wherever they lived – they isolated, they insulated, themselves from anything outside their own little mental box.

And as a result, their mental box became narrower and narrower. It became more and more focused on themselves, and they became more and more blinded by their own logic, by their own filter through which they were looking at the world. And so they were absolutely convinced that they were right and that their way of looking at the world was the only possible way of looking at the world. And they were so convinced that Rome was so mighty and so powerful that it could not possibly collapse.

And, my beloved, what was it that caused that collapse? Well, it was precisely because they had been blinded by their logic—they refused to change themselves, they refused to transcend themselves and come up higher. They wanted to expand the empire militarily but they did not want to expand their minds. They did not want to expand the empire in a spiritual way, in a spiritual capacity. And once the emperors had gained power, they wanted to maintain power, rather than using that power for the benefit of their own people or for the progress of civilization as a whole.

My beloved, the Roman empire collapsed first and foremost from within, through corruption, through decadence, through neglect, through denial. And it was this corruption, this division from within, that made the empire vulnerable to invasion from without. But truly, the invading forces were only instruments of the people's own divisions and their inner turmoil. They simply finished the breakdown process that the people themselves had started, led by the power elite of the Roman civilization.

But do not believe that the people, as suppressed as they might have been, were without responsibility in this matter. For what did the Roman people do during those times? Well, they wanted to live the good life—to sing, dance and make merry, to be entertained in the forum by the gladiators, to entertain themselves with the power and the greatness of Rome, thinking that they were so sophisticated and had such a wonderful civilization, the likes of which the world had never seen.

. . .

The power elite is always divided

For my beloved, I must tell you – as we have tried to explain now, through the books, especially Mother Mary's and Maitreya's books – there are always two dualistic extremes. And when we talk about the power elite, we are not talking about one homogeneous body on this planet. For if the power elite were united, they would already have controlled every aspect of life on this planet.

And, my beloved, you might think that they already have a lot of control. But if they had this planet under total control, I would not be able to speak through a physical messenger and speak this message. And so you see, there is still an opening, there is still freedom for the Living Word to flow. And this is indeed the potential for turning around a nation and a planet.

But, my beloved, the two dualistic extremes that are set up by the power elite, the two different factions of the power elite, are first of all those who are trying to keep people asleep, to prevent them from waking up because they are in total denial of the forces described in the second law of thermodynamics. They truly believe that they can create a civilization where they are in control and that they can maintain that control indefinitely. This is what the Romans believed, the leaders of the Roman empire. And they were the last ones to wake up and realize that things had shifted and they could no longer maintain control.

Then there is the other faction of the power elite, and they will move in once the control of the first power elite begins to slip. They will then come in and try to take advantage of the situation in order to create a panic and a downward spiral that goes out of control, so that they can break down the old order and then set themselves up as the new power elite that holds the position of the old power elite.

If you want a typical example of this, look at France before and after the revolution. The old power elite were the kings. And again you see the typical example, where they had isolated and insulated themselves, created a mental box that they thought was unassailable. And yet, the force of the second law of thermodynamics eventually created a shift. But then what happened was that the counter elite moved in and caused the French revolution to spin out of control, until so many heads had rolled that there was no rhyme or reason for it whatsoever. And they then set themselves up as the new power elite. And they quickly became as tyrannical and as controlling as the old one.

Another typical example is Russia before and after the Bolshevik revolution. The czar is another example of a leader who had insulated and isolated himself, not being willing to see reality. And then, after the revolution had taken hold, the Bolshevik forces moved in and set themselves up. And I dare say that anyone looking at history will see that the communists in Russia were responsible for far more atrocities, killings and suppression of the Russian people than the czars ever were.

With the Flame of Victory, one person can indeed make a difference

Elohim Victoria, April 7, 2007.

One person can make a difference

Yet, my beloved, I must say to you that – as is the case with the Living Word – the flame of Victory is a two-edged sword. For if you take it into your being, it will expose all elements of anti-victory that are left—where you sometimes defeat yourself. Or you excuse yourself in various ways, saying, "But how could I possibly make a difference? How could one person make a difference in the world, or in a nation as big as America?"

And, my beloved, I would remind you of the old story of a man walking down the beach, and ahead of him he sees another person. And on the beach are millions of starfish that have drifted ashore in a storm. And the person bends down, takes a starfish, throws it back in the ocean, and then he moves on to the next one, throws it back in the ocean. And the person taking a walk comes up to him and says, "What are you doing? Look at the beach, there are millions of starfish. You cannot possibly throw them all back. What you are doing won't make a difference." And the other person looks at him, bends down, takes a starfish, throws it out and says, "It made a difference for that one." [Laughter]

And so, my beloved, do not ever fall prey to the lie – the ultimate lie of the power elite – that you cannot make a difference. For I tell you—if everybody believes that lie, then indeed they will not make a difference. But if one person here and one person there decides to reach for the Living Word and align their consciousness with it, then as enough people do this, there will come that critical point, where suddenly you have that shift—and the shift in the national consciousness, where now America can wake up and realize her faults without being plunged into the anti-victory of berating herself, taking herself down instead of saying, "Aah we have faults that must be corrected, but we are willing to do it. And therefore, we will use them as a stepping stone for Victory, for coming up higher than we ever could have reached before, because now we are wiser, because we have been willing to look at the beam in our own eye. And by recognizing that beam, pulling it out, throwing it back into the ocean where it came from, we have risen higher. And therefore, we can take our nation higher than we could ever have done in the old consciousness—where we were not willing to recognize our shortcomings and pull that beam from our own eye."

Passing through the screen door to heaven

Jesus, April 7, 2007.

Understanding the WORD incarnate

And what you have seen throughout history is that – truly – most people in the world have followed the outer path and very few have discovered the inner path. But I am telling you that we are now at the fortunate point, where there is the potential that a much larger group of people can awaken to the inner path and truly understand the universal nature of that path. But we must give them assistance to be awakened. For it will not just happen by mere happenstance or by some divine force forcing people to awaken. And that is indeed why the Living Word incarnates on Earth. And, my beloved, the WORD incarnate is not a limited phenomenon that could only happen through one particular person 2,000 years ago.

The Living Word can embody through anyone who is open and willing. But you see, my beloved – as I explained – in order to become the open door for the Living Word, you have to be willing to first go through the purging process of being willing to allow the WORD to purify your own being from those imperfections that could cause you to either block the WORD or color the WORD with your own mindset, your own dualistic filter.

And so, the question really is whether people, those who are the spiritually evolved and mature people, are going to be willing to step up and let go of the ancient mindset that by following certain outer directions you can qualify for salvation. Will people be willing to acknowledge the reality that unless you change your inner being, unless you change your consciousness, you cannot qualify for salvation? Which means that you have to take total responsibility for yourself.

You see, my beloved, the reason why official Christianity turned me into an idol, turned me into the savior who is up there on a pedestal saving all people, is that not enough people were ready to understand the inner path. And then the blind leaders – who have rejected the Living Word for eons – stepped into the Christian churches, took over and set themselves up as the authority, which is what they always do. The power elite set themselves up as the only ones who know how to interpret the Word.

And so, they do exactly as I said of the scribes and Pharisees: they turn the Word of God into no effect in their tradition. They teach for doctrines, the commandments of men (Mark 7:7), because they take the Living Word and they project their own dualistic filter onto that WORD. And now they interpret the word through that filter, setting up outer doctrines and outer rules which they then claim are infallible. And then they will use that outer tradition to judge anyone who comes representing the Living Word, in their attempts to either silence that person or prevent the people from following the true leader who represents the Living Word instead of the dead word.

Do you see, my beloved, that as soon as a word has been expressed in this world, in a form that can be copied and interpreted, as soon as that happens, the Word becomes the dead word. My beloved, as I explained before, the Bible, the written Bible that you pick up, is the dead word. But if you read that word and allow it to enter your heart and reach for the Comforter who can breathe new life into that word as you study it, well then the word that you read can become the Living Word in your heart. But it cannot become the Living Word in your head, where you interpret it with the analytical, linear mind.

And so you see, my beloved, in order to truly accept the Living Word and accept yourself as the open door for the Living Word, you have to be willing to let go of the outer tradition and the mindset behind that tradition, which really is an attempt to create a guaranteed path to salvation: "If I follow these outer rules, God has to save me—even if I have not been willing to change the condition of my heart, to pull the beam from my own eye. Even if I still have all these lies and imperfect conditions in my heart, God still has to save me."

How can America be one nation under God?

Saint Germain, April 7, 2007.

Most gracious ladies and gentlemen—and anyone else who might be present [Laughter]. For truly, there are many angels present here who are above the duality of sex on Earth. For they have attained oneness with the LOGOS, the reality of the Christ mind, that is set up to establish and maintain oneness between all aspects, all expressions of the one God in the world of form.

So, my beloved, I, Saint Germain, congratulate you for the work you have accomplished so far, culminating in this latest rosary that you have given. You see, my beloved, the film you have seen about the power of vibration should give you some visual sense of what can be attained when you give your rosaries and decrees.

For you see an inert, passive substance that is stirred into various patterns by the application of sound. And I can assure you that as you give a rosary, you are sending the vibration of sound into the mass consciousness and the four levels of the material universe. And my beloved, I can assure you that the effect of your rosaries is far more dramatic than what you saw on this movie. And I might add, it is far more beautiful as well. For when you come into unison, when you speak with one voice, you create a very powerful unified and harmonious pattern.

And you see, my beloved, one of the greatest problems on Earth is the multitude of sound waves that are crisscrossing the ethers—that are chaotic, uncoordinated. And this is precisely the uncoordinated sound that breaks down the organized, beautiful structures that are sustainable.

And so part of the task of giving rosaries and invoking the Light is to counteract the chaos. And how can you counteract the chaos unless what you send out is more than chaos, is more harmonious, unified, and therefore sends out a unifying vibration. For I tell you, my beloved, what science can also teach you is that you can have a substance, such as a gas, where all the molecules are oriented in all different directions in a chaotic pattern. And yet when certain types of energy are applied, there comes a point where – suddenly – a phase transition occurs and now the molecules line up and there is oneness.

Unity in Spirit does not override individuality

And you see, my beloved, this is what needs to happen for this nation of America to be one nation under God. There must be a certain unison in the consciousness of the people. For as they say, "United we stand; divided we fall." And so, indeed, America has fallen far below the immaculate concept that I hold for this nation. And what will bring her back, except there is some unifying force, even beyond what people are aware of at the conscious level?

And that force is not just the sound that is expressed. For it to have the full effect, the sound, the Word that you speak, must be infused with the Spirit so that it becomes the Living Word, rather than a rote repetition that really is not infused with the Spirit and therefore doesn't have the power and the momentum to cut through the chaos of the mass consciousness.

You see, my beloved, that is why we have talked about the importance of the WORD, the Living Word. For when you come together as a group, the effect of your rosaries and your being together is in direct proportion to the degree of unity and oneness you can attain. And how can you attain oneness? You can do so only when a critical mass of people in the group reach for the Living Word within themselves.

For you see, my beloved, as everything else in this world, the concept of unity and oneness can indeed be perverted by the duality consciousness—as you have seen in many civilizations, where the power elite attempts to create uniformity by turning the people into virtual robots who blindly follow the blind leaders. And while this might give what from a surface standpoint seems like unity, it is not the true unity of the Spirit.

For you see, my beloved, God does not want you to blindly follow God, or a spiritual leader, or an outer religion. God created you – each one of you – as a unique individual. And God has no desire to have you extinguish your individuality in order to attain some state of uniformity in a spiritual group or community. What God truly desires is for you to express your individuality, even while you are coming together.

And yet, my beloved, the individuality that needs to be expressed is obviously not the false individuality of the ego—who is always seeing itself separated from other people and most of the time seeing itself in competition with those other people. And so, it cannot attain any kind of oneness because it wants to set up various measures, whereby it can maintain the illusion that it is better than others because it is doing this or that outer thing—as you saw with the scribes and Pharisees—and, if you will be honest, have seen with many other religious and spiritual groups. Where there is always the formation of some kind of clique or elite, who thinks that because they are doing all the outer things a certain way, they are above the rest of the congregation.

...

The separation of church and state

Now, my beloved, one thing I would address here is the topic of the separation of church and state. For it is essential for you to understand what we are really talking about, when we talk about one nation under God. The essence of the problem is that if there is no recognition and respect for something that is beyond the duality consciousness, then a nation will inevitably deteriorate and be taken over by the power elite— thereby becoming a closed system, becoming subject to the forces of the second law of thermodynamics, as I explained yesterday.

And you see, my beloved, there is no surefire way to ensure that a nation will not slip into that state. For you have indeed seen governments, you have seen nations, that were ruled by a religious authority and yet that religious authority became influenced by the duality consciousness, whereby you had a tyrannical priesthood and pretty soon the entire civilization started spiraling downhill.

And so, when we talk about one nation under God, we are not talking about a nation that is ruled by some priesthood, be it the Catholic church or any other church. We are talking about a nation that has some mechanism for reaching beyond the duality consciousness and bringing forth the Living Word. And the Living Word can serve as the tuning fork used by musicians to set the proper key, whereby an entire orchestra can tune their instruments so they can play in harmony without creating discord.

And so, it is not that the entire nation needs to be in the same church, and needs to consciously – in the outer awareness – recognize a certain religious authority as the ultimate authority. But it is that a critical mass of people must come to the awareness of the Living Word within themselves, so that they can attune their own individual consciousness to that Living Word. And so that they can recognize it when someone – somewhere – comes up as the spokesman who can verbalize that Living Word in a particular situation. And I can tell you that that someone is almost always outside the established system, for that system is controlled by the power elite. So the voice of truth is almost always the voice crying in the wilderness—and not inside the halls of power.

And yet if a critical mass of people recognize that voice, accept it, start talking about it to other people, start writing about it, start writing to their congressmen and demanding change, then the shift can begin to occur that brings the entire nation into alignment. And suddenly, you see a shift in the national consciousness, where they now recognize the unreality of a former policy or a former law. And suddenly, there is an awareness that things have to change. And then, gradually, even the inertia found in the bureaucracy and in the government will be forced to comply.

Government is a two-way process

For when the will of the people is united, then the government must follow. For I tell you, when we talk about a government that is of the people, by the people and for the people, I can assure you that even though America is currently far from the free democracy that we would like to see, there is certainly a two-way process between the government and the people.

And I can assure you that there is a limit to how far the power elite behind the government can actually take things—and that limit is set by the consciousness of the people. Which, by the way, is the only reason why you have not seen a further erosion of civil liberties after the 9/11 event. It is also why you have not seen further manipulation of the economy and why you have not seen another military excursion in some part of the world.

So you see, my beloved, there is always a two-way process. And even though the government might be controlled by the power elite, there is a limit to their power—as long as the people are still relatively free and relatively informed, as is the case in America today.

And so, the key here is not that we create some almighty church in America that suddenly becomes set up as the ultimate authority. For I tell you, truly, that America is not a static society. And it is not meant to remain today the way it was when the constitution was written. For change is the order of the day, growth is the order of the day, self-transcendence is the order of the day. And so America must transcend herself. And how is that transcendence meant to occur? Well, my beloved, it is meant to occur by more and more people discovering the Living Word within themselves, using that as the absolute measure for what is real and what is unreal.

And then, as more and more people come into that attunement, a shift will occur in the outer consciousness. And that, my beloved, is why the American government, the American Constitution, the American laws, must be refined, must grow—so that the nation can grow. Yet the importance here is that this change does not happen by the power elite manipulating the constitution to give themselves more power. It must happen because a critical mass of people have come to the realization that a change is needed.

The difference between a republic and a democracy
And so, to comment on your discussion yesterday of the difference between a republic and a democracy. Well, my beloved, America started out as a republic mainly because the consciousness of the people was not ready for a more free society. They were not ready to have all responsibility put on themselves. And thus, there had to be some safety measures that could keep the government within certain boundaries.

Yet as the nation grows, America must face the challenge of becoming a democracy, where the majority does rule. And where the majority is now faced with the challenge that either they align themselves with the Living Word and bring their nation up, or they refuse to align themselves with the Living Word and then witness the deterioration of their nation.

For my beloved, I can assure you that in the Aquarian age, governments need to be free. And freedom can only happen when the people take responsibility for their nation. It cannot be forced upon them. And so you see, in the Aquarian age – in the Aquarian age consciousness – you need to refine your concept of freedom. For there does come a point where people must be set free to either stand or fall by their own consciousness.

And again, freedom can be perverted by the dualistic extremes. And at one dualistic extreme is the consciousness that anything goes—and if it feels good do it, for there is no real truth. Everything is relative, so my truth is as good as your truth, which is as good as the next person's truth. On the other fence, in the other extreme, you have the lie that the people cannot govern themselves, and therefore they need an elite who can protect them against themselves. And this, my beloved, is what has been used by the tyrannical power elites for eons as an excuse for them controlling the people, taking away the people's freedom, all for their own good—or so they say, for truly it is only for the good of the power elite.

And so, my beloved, true freedom can only be attained when you have some guideline, some lodestone, that reaches beyond duality. And that lodestone is, of course, the Living Word. And, as I have said, it only takes a critical mass of people to get an entire nation to come into alignment behind a particular issue—that may not be the ultimate truth but it is the practical, realistic measure that needs to be taken right now so that the nation can rise to the next level. And then, when you are on that level, you can begin to reach for an even greater understanding that might eventually transform your present level, but you have to take it one step at a time.

A Buddhic perspective on how America can represent Christ in the world

Gautama Buddha, April 8, 2007.

You are not here to change the world

So my beloved, how can you walk the tightrope of being the Living Christ in action without going too far into any of the dualistic extremes? Well, you see my beloved, you must first of all keep one truth in mind: As the Living Christ, you are not here to produce a specific outer change on Earth!

You are not here to raise up America to recognize the ascended masters. You are not here to produce world peace. You are not here to expose the power elite and their manipulation of the economy. You are not here to overthrow the international banking system. You are not here to overturn Roe vs. Wade.

Take note that I am not saying that some of these things are not worthy goals that need to be attained, that need to happen. But you are not here to make it happen. For my beloved, what is to happen on this Earth must happen through the free will of the people. And thus, you see my beloved, how the American form of government – how the Constitution, the Declaration of Independence – how they incorporate the concept of "we the people."

What you can do as the Living Christ is to awaken the people, so that they can make the best possible choices. But the Living Christ is not a dictator who comes in and takes power, and takes power away from the other dictator who is identified as the real bad guy, as the real villain in the play.

For you see, my beloved, when you fall into the trap of thinking that you are here to produce a specific result – when you are here to overthrow the rule of this or that other group of people or these or that dark forces – what have you then done? Well, you have done what Jesus described when he described the world as a stage and life as a play with separate roles.

Do you see, my beloved, there are many roles defined in this world based on the consciousness of duality. And there is a role created by the serpentine mind to specifically trap those who have been awakened to the path of Christhood but who have not yet attained balance. And so, they go into that role of thinking that as representatives of Christ, they have to fight and destroy the representatives of anti-christ, and produce a specific result by overthrowing this or that action taken by those they identify as the representatives of anti-christ.

Do you see, my beloved, how subtle this trap can be? How easy it is for a person who has become awakened to the spiritual path – who is all on fire to serve God, to serve the cause of Christ – to step into that role without noticing what has happened. And then people can go off on a tangent, sometimes for decades, thinking they are working for God, they are working for the Ascended Masters, yet in reality they are simply outplaying another dualistic role that does virtually nothing to further the true cause of the Ascended Host, which is to raise the people above the consciousness of duality.

Do you see, my beloved, what I am saying? We are not primarily concerned with creating world peace, getting America out of Iraq, overturning Roe vs. Wade, overthrowing the monetary elite. Our primary concern is to awaken the people from the blindness caused by the duality consciousness, because when the people are awakened from duality, they will make the right choices. And thus, once duality has been conquered, all other things will fall into place. Do you see? As the Christ said, "Seek ye first the kingdom of God and his righteousness, and all these things shall be added unto you."

...

The complete blindness of the power elite

And you see, of course, that those who exemplify – who embody that state of consciousness to the ultimate degree – are those who are members of the power elite. For I can assure you, my beloved, that the vast majority of these people are absolutely convinced that they are doing the right thing. Many of them are even convinced that they are doing the work of God or serving the cause of Christ. For they truly believe that they are superior to the people, and therefore they should rule the people and rule this nation.

But you see, my beloved, this is completely contrary to the true goal that I described earlier, that we have the goal of awakening the people, whereas it is the forces of anti-christ, the false teachers of anti-christ, who want to force the people into the fold of what they define as the true kingdom of God according to their dualistic standard.

And so, my beloved, you have indeed attained a victory at this conference, a victory of softening up that hardened mindset that has imprisoned Washington D.C. and the entire Federal Government in the United States, thereby blinding them to the Middle Way, the Middle Way that could have avoided the national embarrassment of Iraq. So you have cleared the way that has made it much more likely that the American government will start coming back to – or rather will start finding for the first time – that Middle Way.

...

So the dispensation I will give you today is that I will anchor my presence in the Capitol building, in the rotunda of the Capitol building. And those around the world who are willing, can anchor a portion of their God flames there, expressed through my heart and my Presence. So I ask you who are here now – and those who might hear or read this dictation later – to visualize that in the center of the Capitol building, I am sitting in the lotus posture. And you are sitting around me in the lotus posture. Pay no attention to the senators and congressmen who pass by and find this to be a peculiar spectacle [Laughter]. Be non-attached, for we are here in the Eternal NOW. And my beloved, I shall remain there in the Eternal NOW, which is beyond time and space.

So visualize with me that we are seated there in the perfect peace of the Buddha. We are not concerned by what is going on in the House of Congress or the Senate. We are not concerned by the illogical musings of the representatives. We are not concerned with their decisions. We are concerned with remaining in the Peace of the Buddha, simply anchoring that light in the Capitol building as a counterbalance.

For you see, my beloved, although there are certain representatives who certainly could be said to have embodied the consciousness of anti-christ, there are indeed many of the elected representatives of this nation who have the best of intentions and who represent the consciousness of the American people in the state it is in today. And it is no easy job to come to Washington D.C. and be exposed to the intense pressures that are sent at the representatives from every corner.

So we are not here to make those representatives make certain decisions. We are here to anchor the Peace of the Buddha that might set some of them free from the pressures that pull them into the dualistic extremes and may indeed allow them to experience an inner stillness that reconnects them to the original purpose, the original dream they had when they decided to run for office.

Perhaps reconnects them to the true tradition of the American Founding Fathers and the spiritual principles of this nation, so that they realize that they do not have to fall for these pressures of the lobbyists, of the special interest groups, of the media, of other senators, of their own party that wants them to follow the party line and play party politics rather than doing what is right. They can go within.

They can take a stand for what they truly believe in, the true principles of this nation, and they can say, "I have had enough of party politics. I know in my heart what is right and that is how I will speak my mind in the assembly and that is how I will cast my vote. For I was not elected by my people to be a puppet for the power elite. I was elected to represent "we the people" and I have not forgotten that I came from "we the people." And I am here to represent the people and not the power elite and their manipulation. So I will take my stand, come what may. And I will take this government back from the power elite and give it to the people where it belongs. For I am a true representative of Saint Germain."

Thus, my beloved, you are true representatives of Saint Germain. And now visualize how the Flame of Freedom and Saint Germain in his Presence descends from above through a shaft of light, anchoring his Presence also in the rotunda of the Capitol building. And then arching that Presence as the arc that you see [in Saint Louis] to the Washington Monument, as an arc of light—thereby creating a double focus of the Alpha of the Washington Monument and the Omega of the Capitol building. Truly representing what we have talked about at this conference, of the coming together of God government, where you have both a government that connects to God and a government that is the Omega polarity, that is of the people, by the people, and for the people. Yet still one nation under God. For we are one people under God.

Find bliss beyond your expectations

Ascended Master Patrick, May 18, 2007

How they destroyed the Church of Ireland

And so my beloved, I give you this image to inspire you. But also to give you a realistic assessment of what it was like to be Patrick. For you see, my beloved, when you look back at my life today – after 1,500 years of idolatry and idolizing – you do not see the real Patrick—for how could you? You see, my beloved, you see the Saint Patrick that the Catholic Church – especially the Catholic Church of Ireland – has wanted to pass down to you. They do not want you to know the real person as I was back then or as I am today as the ascended master.

You see, my beloved, they want you to accept their graven image, for their graven image is carefully crafted to give you the impression that I was so special and so far above you that you could not possibly walk in my footsteps and make a difference for an entire country. Do you see, my beloved, they do not want you to realize that if you are willing to let God in you flow, to let your light shine, then God in you can make a difference for your country. If just one person is willing to be God in action, to realize the truth in Christ's words that, "I of my own self can do nothing, it is the Father within me. He doeth the work."

Then that one person, God through that one person, can plant a seed, can start a new movement that will gradually grow and change an entire nation and a mindset of an entire nation. Yet I must tell you that unless more people pick up and create a movement that is sustainable, well then the change will not last.

For surely, if you look at the history of my life and the history of Ireland, you will see, that yes Ireland was changed by my presence, Ireland became a Christian nation, but surely you will see – given the open-minded people that you are – that after just a century or so, Ireland started going the way of the rest of Europe, where the Catholic Church became increasingly rigid and focused on outer doctrines and rituals, and started burning as heretics anyone who dared to speak the Living Word of God.

For my beloved, I can assure you that I did not convert the closed-minded people of Ireland by speaking the dead word and reading from a scripture. I spoke the Living Word, for I let the River of Life flow through me, so that that river could speak what the people at that time needed to hear. And so my beloved, what happened was that those who were in the serpentine consciousness, those who opposed me openly as the Kings and the Druids and their priests, they reincarnated as the Catholic priests and Bishops who then took power in the Church in Ireland and then quickly followed along with those in the Catholic Church throughout Europe, who shut down the Living Word and shut down those who dared to speak or write the Living Word as did so many, even some of the early Church fathers, such as Origen.

And my beloved, you can see this if you care to look at history, how what they were after was to shut down the Living Word, so that all that could be preached from the Catholic pulpits was the controlled Word, the dead word, that would not ignite the heart flame of the people so that they would wake up and become the Christ in action—after those that had inspired them by demonstrating Christhood.

The eternal plot of the power elite

Do you see, my beloved, that this is their eternal plot? They would prefer that no human being on Earth ever dared to express any kind of Christhood, but they know that realistically they cannot prevent this, for once in a while there will be one who dares to speak out and demonstrate that Christhood. And so, although they do all manner of things to keep the population down, they know that once in a while there will be the rare few that will defy them and the programming of the mass mind. And so that is why – when that happens – what do they do?

Well, as soon as that person has passed from the screen of life, they start idolizing that person, putting him up on a pedestal so that none dare follow the example. And so that even though one person had demonstrated Christhood, it will not become a trickle that will spread through others, eventually becoming a powerful waterfall that sweeps away and wears away the rock of those who have the consciousness that is not the rock of Christ, but the immovable rock of the serpentine mind.

And so, they did this with me, when it became apparent that they could not prevent the people of Ireland from revering me as someone who had inspired their country. Well they turned me into a saint, and not only that, a good Catholic saint who follows all the rules and directions of that Church for what a saint should be like. For my beloved, once I was out of embodiment, I could not well challenge them, could I? So they could do with me whatever they wanted, as they have done with Christ whatever they wanted.

And so my beloved, I can assure you that while I was in embodiment, I was following the inner guidance of my Higher Being, of my Lord Christ, of my Christ Self. I was flowing with the River of Life, letting the Holy Spirit flow through me. And I can assure you that what I preached was not "good Catholic doctrine" as it is seen today or as it was seen back then by those who had attained powerful positions, such as the Bishop who presided over me until I obtained independence through the grace of God and the enlightenment of one Pope who was not in the serpentine mind.

And so, my beloved, it is even a misunderstanding to say that St. Patrick was the one that not only brought Christianity but brought Catholicism to Ireland, for what I truly preached was a teaching that was far more universal than what has ever been preached by the mainstream Catholic Church. For I am sure you realize that in those days, communication was much more slow and much more primitive. So it was not possible to have an Internet broadcast of my sermons given in the mountains, so that the Pope in Rome could have some censor sit there and say, "Ah! That Patrick guy up in Ireland said something wrong! We have to reign him in!"

My beloved I am sure you realize that had this been possible then, that is exactly what they would have done. And before long they would have had somebody come in on the airplane and put me in my place, as the Bishop in England tried to do several times.

For you see my beloved, I was surely up against those in the serpentine mind in the Kings and the Priests of the pagan religion, but I was also up against those in the serpentine mind in the Catholic Church itself, for they were surely there from the very beginning of the formation of that Church, as indeed Constantine himself was a primary example of a person who is completely identified with the serpentine mind.

It is time for a revolution of thought in Europe

Saint Germain, May 18, 2007

The greatest need in Europe today

So my beloved, what is indeed the greatest need in Europe today, what is my highest hopes, what is my highest vision for this continent? Well my beloved, let me assure you that even though I have spent a considerable amount of time, energy and attention on establishing the United States, I still have a very great love for this continent, and a very great hope that Europe can once again become the open door for bringing forth new ideas in every area of human endeavor.

For was it not so, my beloved, that during the Renaissance and beyond, Europe was indeed the birthplace of many new ideas. Some of those ideas were surely from the dualistic, serpentine mindset, but still there were valid ideas that came forth and transformed Europe and eventually the world. But my beloved, look at history again. Look at the Renaissance and how there was an explosion of new ideas, new inventions, new thoughts. Yet they were brought forth primarily through science—not in the area of religion. And once again, was not the reason that there was one Church that claimed to be the only true Church of Christ and therefore felt justified in using whatever power it had to suppress innovation in the area of religion? Truly, there was the Reformation, but as I am sure you, of all people, can see, the Lutheran, Protestant churches and their offspring did not bring out the true teachings of Christ. For they took out some of the artificial elements added by the Catholic Church, but they did not go back and put back in what had been taken out by the Catholic Church or even earlier.

And so you see, my beloved, the greatest need in Europe is the restoration of the Word because the word affects every area of society. The Word is the key element to setting the people free. Why is this so, my beloved? It is so because the word, the perversion of the word that creates illusions, is the primary means used by the Power Elite to suppress the people, to prevent the people from having the knowledge, the truth that will make them free.

Surely, there are few better historical examples of this than the Catholic Church and how it suppressed the Word, even the written Word, so that for centuries the Bible could not be translated into any other language but Latin, meaning that the majority of the people in the Christian world back then could not understand and read the Bible for themselves. They had to rely on the interpretation given by their preachers and priests. And so my beloved, can you see that when the people do not even have access to the written Word, well then the institution that took away that access can control the peoples' thoughts, which is indeed why the same institution managed to keep Europe locked in the Dark Ages for nigh a millennium.

Learn from the history of Europe

Oh my beloved, think about where Europe and the world could have been today if the scientific revolution could have started 500 years or more earlier than it did. Well my beloved, the reality is that either the Golden Age would have been manifest or the world would have blown itself up through the misuse of technology. And so the real, realistic assessment of the situation is that everything happened for a reason. And the reason is simple: the consciousness of the people was not ready for the scientific revolution to start any sooner than it did.

For had the consciousness of the people been ready, they would have thrown off the yoke of the Catholic Church sooner. And therefore, if somehow the technology had been brought out, then you can see, my beloved, how the war between Protestants and Catholics could have been fought with far more devastating weapons. And therefore, you could have indeed seen both sides of the conflict using nuclear weapons in the name of God. My beloved, can you image the karma that would have been made on this continent if a nuclear war had been fought in the name of God, killing tens of millions of people and polluting the environment for decades to come?

So indeed, we can say again: everything happens for a reason and according to cycles. Yet the co-measurement I want to give you is that those cycles are not set in stone but are indeed dependent upon the willingness of the people to come up higher. And that depends on their willingness to look beyond the watered-down, dead word that they are presented by every institution in society, be it the religious institutions, the political institutions, the governments and the scientific establishment.

Can you see, my beloved, that today in Europe you have a situation where the scientific establishment is claiming that it has set Europe free from the tyranny and the yoke of religion. Yet they are not willing to admit that they have simply created another tyranny – of materialism, secularism, relativism – that is as dangerous and as oppressive as what was established by the Catholic Church.

And so we must look beyond the establishment, for history shows us clearly that the establishment will not voluntarily let go of their power—unless they sense that the people have finally risen up and mustered the determination to say, "Thus far and no farther, for we will take a stand for what we know in our hearts, and we demand more freedom than we have today." And so, you saw how the French revolution was the text-book example, as I have described before, of the aspiring power elite finally getting the better of the established power elite and becoming as oppressive as the old elite, only in a different way with a different justification.

And my beloved, this back-and-forth fight can go on indefinitely, but I must tell you that I have great hopes that the people of Europe – within the foreseeable future – will wake up and say, "We have seen too many wars on this continent and we now see that the real cause of war is the dualistic, relative thinking that makes people believe that they have the only truth and that they have a right to kill those who oppose them, be it for religious or political reasons, or even to maintain the power over the people, the privilege of those who are so rich that they can suppress the people totally and absolutely."

My beloved, in the history of the world, few societies have indeed been so oppressive as what you have seen in the feudal societies in Europe, where the peasants were simply the property of the noble men and could not do anything without their permission. Well, they could do one thing without their permission, they could die, but that was about the only option they had.

And so my beloved, given its history, I believe – I envision – that it is indeed possible for a critical mass of Europeans to be awakened to the reality that the only way to end this dualistic struggle in Europe is to reach for something that is beyond duality. Something that is beyond the dualistic way of thinking, the relative way of thinking, where there is no absolute truth or where people take a relative truth and elevate it to the status of an absolute truth, as you have seen both in the Catholic Church, in the communist block and in materialism today.

...

Claim the true authority of the Living Word

Do you see, my beloved, there is a way to claim authority without going into the dualistic tracks that you see in the churches and the scientific and political establishments. Do you see, my beloved, that when you stand up to – challenge – status quo, those in the established power elite will immediately say, "By what authority do you say this? What authority do you have to challenge the Catholic Church, or the Lutheran Churches, or the scientific establishment? Who are you, what is your background? Ah, you are not a scientist. Well then we don't need to listen to you. Ah, you have not been willing to bend the knee and submit to the Catholic indoctrination. Well, then we don't need to listen to you."

But you see, my beloved, this is the intimidation that has been used successfully by the power elite for a very, very long time—to suppress the people and prevent them from bearing witness to the truth they know in their hearts. They have established a culture that truly is a world-wide phenomenon. But I must tell you that within the last 1000 years, that culture has been more powerful in Europe than anywhere else, and the culture is precisely this: that unless you have some kind of earthly authority – given to you by the establishment – then you have no authority and no right to speak out.

And so my beloved, is this not likewise what you saw by the scribes and the Pharisees and the temple priests, those who represented the Jewish establishment, and how they challenged Christ and his right to be in embodiment and speak the Living Word and the Living Truth? And so can you not see, that you need to completely rise above any need to have any outer authority.

And how do you do this, my beloved? You do it precisely by heeding the profound teachings given earlier by Mother Mary and Patrick, about overcoming your expectations of a certain outer result. For you are simply here to bear witness to the truth. And when you dare to speak from the heart—and when they ask you by what authority you speak, you simply say, "I speak the Living Truth, I speak the Living Word that I know in my heart."

And when they say, "Well then, how can you challenge our authoritative version of truth that we can trace back 15-1700 years?" And you can say, "I challenge it because I know in my heart the Living Truth, as Christ knew the Living Truth in his heart, and as he indeed said that the Kingdom of God is within me. I have dared to look for that Kingdom—I have found it. I have dared to follow the call of Christ that God is a Spirit, and them that worship him must worship him in spirit and in truth. I have gone into the inner Kingdom, and I have discovered the Living Truth and I speak what I receive in my heart, what I receive from Above. I do not speak of my own self, I have no desire for power or position. I want no recognition. I simply speak what I know in my heart, what I receive in my heart. And I speak to those who also know truth in their hearts when they hear it. And therefore, I need no outer authority, nor will I allow any outer authority to keep me quiet, to prevent me from witnessing to the truth that I know, and from letting my light shine. For indeed, I have light whereas you have only outer authority, for if you had the light, why would you need the outer authority?"

You see, my beloved, this is precisely as the dynamic with Jesus and the temple Priests and the scribes and the lawyers. They had to claim an outer authority because they had not the witness of Christ, they had not the Light of Christ. And they did not have that light because they had not been willing to enter the inner Kingdom and obtain the Key of Knowledge. But you who are willing can have that Key of Knowledge, that Spirit of Truth, that Living Word. And then you can speak by the only authority that counts in Heaven.

And my beloved, as was said by Patrick, take note that in order for you to truly win your ascension from this planet – at its present level of development – you have to dare to bear witness to the Truth in front of those who have destroyed that living truth by refusing to enter the inner kingdom.

You are here to help manifest the Golden Age of Saint Germain

For my beloved, it is not enough to balance 51% or more of your karma. We have never – ever – said that this was the only requirement for your ascension. For as we have said before, you did not come here to make karma, balance that karma and then leave. You came here to bring a gift, to fulfill your divine plan by helping to set the people free.

And you who are in embodiment at this time came here because you wanted to be part of the Aquarian Age of Saint Germain. And you wanted to be part of the process of breaking through the opposition to that age, so that the power elite cannot hold it back but that it will break through as it broke through in the Renaissance. And suddenly the established power elite of the Church could not hold the floodgates closed and could not prevent the new inventions and thoughts from coming up.

And surely, those new scientific ideas have been taken over by the aspiring power elite that has now become the established power elite in science and politics. Nevertheless, we just do the same thing again, we leap-frog them – as they say – we jump beyond them, we rise above them, we cut through their walls because we become so transparent that we can walk right through their barriers. They can no longer hold back our thoughts and our minds, and therefore we can march, we can be on the road to freedom because we simply do not accept any conditions on Earth that can stop our forward movement.

It is time for a second revolution of thought in Europe

My beloved, what is true freedom? It is what Mother Mary explained when she talked about the conditions that hold you back. It is the conditions that you have accepted that are taking away your freedom and imprisoning you in a mental box that has no reality whatsoever. No reality in God and not even a reality in the material world, because it is a smokescreen that is only upheld by peoples' belief that it is reality and in its ability to hold them back. It has no true reality, my beloved. Do you see what I am saying?

Next door is a castle with thick stone walls. That castle has a certain reality in the same vibrational realm as your physical bodies, and currently you cannot walk through those stone walls because there is a certain vibrational correspondence between your body and the stones. But what I am telling you here is that the illusions created by the serpentine mind have less reality than those stone walls. Because they are not in the physical, they are in the emotional and the mental – primarily – even though some have made it to the lower etheric.

So it is only when your minds resonate with that level of vibration, that you think that these conditions can hold you back and imprison you. But I tell you, you certainly can raise the vibration of your bodies so you can walk through the walls. But that will take a greater effort and a greater attainment than it will take to simply realize that the ideologies and the illusions created by the power elites of Europe have no reality and cannot hold back your minds.

And thus I say to you, come with me as I lead the way in this coming decade and beyond to awaken those people who can be awakened in Europe, in America, in Latin America, in Asia, in Russia and even beyond in Australia and to some degree in Africa. Come with me as I march throughout this planet to awaken those who can be awakened to the new winds of freedom that are blowing, so that people will simply wake up as if they have been sleeping and say, "We no longer need to accept these illusions, for we see that the emperor has nothing on. We see that this is all a lie, it was never real to begin with. And we will no longer follow the mass consciousness, no matter how many people will cling to the illusions. We will take a stand, we will stand on the housetops and shout the Living Word that goes beyond the illusions and exposes them for what they are."

My beloved, truly this is the universal change that needs to happen in Europe. It needs to happen world-wide, surely, but I have confidence that as I stand on this continent, there will be an awakening throughout Europe, not only through this initiative and movement, but through many others. There will be an awakening that this is unreal, and we will no longer give it reality. We will rise above it and we will make obsolete not only the illusions but the institutions that are supporting them and upholding them because they could not exist without them.

We will move beyond individually and we will form a critical mass that will force, that will compel, that will blow the winds of the Holy Spirit so our societies will also rise above the old mindset as most European nations did during the Renaissance when – suddenly – people simply let go of the old worn-out ideas and beliefs of what could and could not be done—such as that the Earth was flat and that there was nothing beyond the horizon.

Well my beloved, it is now time for the second revolution of thought that makes you realize that the human mind is not flat and that there is something beyond the mental boxes created by the power elite—who think they have a monopoly on truth, but certainly do not have a monopoly on the Christed Beings on this planet, those who are willing to take that stand for Christ, to take that stand for Saint Germain, to take a stand for the Age of Freedom, and claim, "We have a right to be free in mind and Spirit, we have a right to be spiritual people on this continent, regardless of the old religions and the new scientific pseudo religion, that claims it knows there is no God. We have a right to claim our spirituality, and to pronounce that spirituality from the housetops, and from the housetops of cyberspace."

Freeing Europe from the misuse of the WORD

Jesus, May 20, 2007

How the Catholic Church distorted the WORD

So, my beloved, when I came as Jesus, I came to restore the WORD to Israel and to the world. For they had lost the true understanding of the WORD and they had lost it precisely because they had become the victims of the plots of those who are the fallen beings who have entered the serpentine consciousness, and who have sought to control humankind, as Maitreya explains in his book. [Master Keys to Spiritual Freedom]

And the primary means for this control is to pacify the people so that they do not believe they have access to the Living Word inside themselves. And therefore, their entire world view – their entire belief system, their entire concept of themselves, of God, of life – is determined by outer teachings—be it a religious teaching or a political ideology or a scientific mindset and world view.

Thus, my beloved, I came to restore the Living Word to Israel. But most people were not ready for it. And as Christianity began to spread throughout Europe, then certainly the fallen beings saw that this would spell their doom—unless they did something to stop the spreading of the Living Word and the understanding of the Living Word.

And so what did they do? Well, when it became apparent to them that they could not stop the spread of Christianity – although it was not Christianity as you see it today – that they could not stop the spread of the early Christian movement, well they did what they have always done: "If you can't beat them, join them!"

And so, they joined the Christian movement, and, through the help of one of their primary henchmen, Constantine, they turned it into an official religion that very quickly became as rigid and closed as the religion that persecuted and killed me when I walked this Earth in a physical body.

And so you see, my beloved, dating back to the "conversion" of Constantine, Western civilization was set on a specific track that first was dominated by the Catholic Church—that for many years had a grip on the WORD in Europe. Do you see my beloved? The Catholic Church ruled the population in Europe by controlling the WORD, controlling access to the WORD.

They had set themselves up in a position, where they had the physical power to suppress or kill or ban as a heretic anyone who dared to speak the Living Word. And they had defined a doctrine that completely shut out the Living Word, having instead turned it into a dead outer scripture. But not even the outer scripture, for the Catholic Church did not want people to read the scriptures themselves. They only wanted them to have an interpretation that was in accordance with church doctrine.

My beloved, even though the scriptures that were written down are no longer, strictly speaking, the Living Word, there is still so many clues in the scriptures that people who read them can connect to the Living Word—if they are willing to go beyond the letter of the outer teaching. And so it was indeed a travesty that people were prevented from reading the scriptures.

How pacifying religion serves the elite

So, my beloved, you now see that what the Catholic Church represents in Europe is precisely what I call "pacifying religion." A religion that seeks to pacify people by promoting the belief that the people are as nothing and cannot save themselves. They need an external savior and they need an external institution and its priesthood in order to be saved. In the Catholic Church this became the doctrine that you are a sinner by the very fact that you exist—for you were born in sin.

And so, by just the mere fact that you have existence on this Earth, you are a sinner. And that means that you cannot save yourself but need to be saved by the vicarious atonement, where I do all the work for you, therefore completely pacifying people. And my beloved, do you see that this does not only pacify people on an individual level, it pacifies them in the entire society, so that the population at large becomes susceptible to the domination by the power elite?

Do you see, my beloved – in the history of Europe – how the power elite took up positions in the Catholic Church, took up positions in the noble class. And even though you had some rivalry between the two power elites, I can assure you that even the noble class was quite happy with the Church, because they knew that it was because of that pacifying element in the very deepest aspect of life, namely religion, that they were able to control the people and maintain their physical hold over them.

So that is indeed why you see, my beloved, the wisdom brought forth in Maitreya's book, where he says that if we can change the religious debate on this planet then everything else will begin to fall into place after it.

Europe as the birthplace of pacifying ideas

And so, my beloved, when you look at the history of Europe, you see the cradle of a number of ideas that have been used around the world to pacify and suppress the people. First and foremost, of course, in the religious arena, as I have explained. But then see what happened when the religious domination of the Catholic Church began to crumble and the people began to say, "We have had enough. We want to have our freedom to think. We want to have our freedom to look at the reality of the physical octave and what it tells us, instead of being fed these infallible doctrines that truly are out of touch with reality."

My beloved, it was an incredible expansion of the mindset of Europe, when it began to be generally known that the Earth was not flat and that it was not the center of a very small universe. But that it indeed revolved around the sun and that the sun was the center of the solar system.

My beloved, what you had before that time was a mindset where the general culture and world view of the population was almost completely out of touch with reality, divine reality. For what you had seen in the preceding centuries was that the leaders of the Catholic Church had created a world view that was entirely man-made. So they had made the

Word of God of no effect in their tradition (Mark 7:13). They had indeed created a world view that was so removed, from the reality of God that there was hardly any reality left. And you can see this clearly by the fact that the Catholic Church promoted the idea that the Earth, this little planet, was the center of the entire universe—although certainly they believed the universe was much smaller than today.

So can you see, my beloved, that when it first became apparent to people – and greater numbers of people, namely the top 10 percent – that it was possible to make an observation through a simple telescope – and see that the movements in the heavens did not correspond to the doctrine that the Earth was the center of the universe – that this, my beloved, was an incredible expansion of the mindset of Europe. For certainly, then it once again connected to the fact that there is a reality beyond man-made ideas and beliefs.

And, my beloved, this was indeed the very central element of the bringing forth of the Renaissance and the many new ideas and inventions that sprung up in Europe. But of course, as always happens, it was not only true ideas that were promoted. For it is inevitable that when there is an expansion of creativity, there will be both true and untrue ideas. And so you did see several ideologies that were brought forth here in Europe, such as Karl Marx and Marxism and Darwin and the theory of evolution.

Now, my beloved, I must tell you that there are some elements of truth even in these ideologies. They are not completely lies. There is indeed a reality to the fact that a country cannot bring forth a just society while allowing those who are the most aggressive people to attain whatever power they can take through force. And therefore, there must be some way to stop this. But of course, it is not the socialist way, where the state owns and controls everything. It is the spiritual way, where the people are awakened, so that they are subject neither to the privately owned companies nor to the state. And my beloved, that is why communism is not a solution to the problem of the power elite, for it gives the power elite a perfect vehicle through which to attain and maintain power, namely the state itself.

And so you see that capitalism and communism form a dualistic polarity that both work towards the same goal, namely a society with centralized control. Either you have a society controlled by the state, as in the communist countries, or you have a society that is controlled by one company that has eventually absorbed all the other companies and therefore in effect has become the state. Or you can have what you had in Catholic Europe, where you had a society that was controlled by the religious authority which had taken over all areas of society.

And so, my beloved, it should be possible for you to see that Europe is indeed an interesting continent, where so many of the ideas that have shaped the world have been born. And therefore, again, as Saint Germain has said, there is an incredible potential on this continent of people rising up and saying, "Enough is enough! We want something more. We want something better."

And that is indeed already beginning to happen, as it is beginning to happen in other areas of the world. And it can and will – by the grace of God and the willingness of the top 10 percent of the most spiritually aware people – become an unstoppable movement that will sweep away the old mindset, the old ideas and bring forth precisely what Saint Germain talked about when he said that we need a universal spiritual awakening so that we can overcome the ideology of materialism that denies your spirituality. For it is only through spirituality that the world can be righted and set on the right course.

How both religion and science pacifies people

You see, my beloved, what I would like to expound upon now is the transition from the Catholic domination of Europe to the current domination by science and the scientific mindset. During the Catholic era, people were presented or viewed as sinners. They were as nothing. They had no inbuilt, inherent divinity. For there was divinity in only one man—Jesus Christ. This of course, is a continuation of the Roman Empire, where they saw that there was divinity in only one man—the Emperor. And thus, after Christianity became the Roman state religion, I became the substitute for the Emperor, the symbol that there can only be one man on Earth who has divinity, whereas all the people are below him and fundamentally different from him. And so, you now had a self image among the people that they were nothing, that they were sinners by their mere existence.

As I have said, the scientific revolution did indeed start a process that was highly beneficial in expanding people's mindset and making them see beyond the traditional view of themselves and the world. Yet, what happened was the same thing that happened to Christianity, my beloved.

After just a few centuries the power elite began to use science in their eternal quest to suppress the people. You will see that many of the early scientists, including Darwin himself, were indeed religious people and did not believe there was any inherent conflict between science and religion—and that indeed science would simply work within a world view that accounted for the existence of a supreme being and a reality that was beyond human manipulation.

Indeed, many of the early scientists were driven precisely by an understanding of how the Catholic Church had created an entirely false view that was out of touch with reality. And their desire was to use science to bring back some reality in the world view of the people, realizing however that there was certain limitations to what science could discover. For truly, Galileo and others realized that they would never be able to see God through a telescope because God was not located above the sky, as was believed in the old world view.

So my beloved, in the beginning science was a beneficial movement, expanding the mindset of the people. But then it very gradually turned into a materialistic philosophy instead of a spiritual philosophy. And so what happened in that process, my beloved, was that now the people were no longer portrayed as worthless sinners, but they were portrayed as only slightly more highly evolved than the monkeys and therefore as nothing more than animals that had come into being entirely by chance.

Do you see, my beloved, that whether you consider yourself a worthless sinner or whether you consider yourself an animal—it really is not progress, is it? So the reality is that science has not freed the people's minds and given them a higher or a more realistic world view. Science has indeed become just another tool in the almost endless string of tools used by the power elite to suppress and pacify the people. So that they can continue to dominate society and attain extraordinary privileges for themselves, while the general population toil and work to support the lifestyle of the elite.

Why the top 10 percent are the key

My beloved, the greatest potential for an awakening in Europe is that the top 10 percent of the people realize the existence of this power elite, realize what they have always been doing, realize how they have been using any means available to them – including any ideology or belief system – and stand up and say, "We have had enough of this! This cannot go on on our continent. We will not see our continent be responsible for the spreading of these false ideas that have been used to suppress the people."

"We will instead turn our continent into a cradle for a new, universal spiritual mindset that will finally free the people from the domination of the power elite by bringing forth the truth and the reality that every human being is not simply an animal or a worthless sinner, but is indeed a son or daughter of God, is an individualization of God, come here to be a co-creator and bring God's kingdom to Earth—rather than this kingdom of man that we have seen in so many versions that it is nauseating to look back at the pages of history."

My beloved, what can bring about this awakening? Well, as I said, it has already begun. And if you hold the vision and do your best, then you will do all you can do to bring it about and others will pitch in as well. And it will happen.

But I will tell you that it has been a clear strategy and goal of the power elite – not necessarily those in physical in embodiment who did not have the awareness of what is going on, but certainly, as I talked about yesterday, the greater conspiracy in the etheric, mental and emotional realm of those who are the fallen beings in the serpentine consciousness exposed in Maitreya's book – it has been their strategy for a long time to suppress the top 10 percent by making them believe, as we have talked about, that they have no right, they have no authority, to take a stand – they cannot take a stand – and divert them into believing that they are nothing more than animals and that life has no meaning whatsoever.

My beloved, the ideology and belief system of scientific materialism is indeed the primary means used today to divert the attention of the top 10 percent of the people on this planet—those who at inner levels have the spiritual maturity to be part of the awakening but who in their outer minds have been so misled by the scientific world view that they have come to believe that they are only animals, that life has no real purpose and meaning, that there is no life after the death of the body. And therefore, there really is no other purpose, no long-term purpose, to life, so it is just, "Enjoy what we have right now, for tomorrow we die."

So you see, my beloved, there are many people on this continent – and of course throughout the world as well, but especially on this continent – there are many people who have the maturity already to be forerunners for this awakening. But their outer minds have been so twisted and misled that they do not even dare conceive that they could be part of the spiritual awakening of the same momentous proportions as the awakening brought forth by my mission in Israel or by the Buddha's mission in India.

Do you see, my beloved? The world truly has examples of how, suddenly, one person started something but others picked up on it, and suddenly a shift occurred in the mindset of an entire area, eventually spreading to the entire world. This can happen again, but as we have said, it must be many people who drive it this time, not just one person. And that is why the power elite have indeed sought to create a belief system that makes people unable or unwilling to even conceive that they could truly make a difference.

Understanding how the power elite seek to destroy individuality

My beloved, you must understand—the reality is that each person on Earth has infinite value in the eyes of God, because each person is an extension of God's own Being. The conscious self of each person is an extension of God's own being. Therefore, we of the Ascended Host, and the Creator of this universe, place infinite value on the individual, on individuality. Certainly, we desire to see all live up to their highest potential – namely your spiritual identity and individuality – rather than the so-called individuality of the ego, which truly is not individuality for it is simply out of the mass consciousness.

Yet you must understand that the power elite have no respect whatsoever for individuality, at least not an individuality beyond their own. They want to destroy your individuality. They want to create a race of mechanized people who are like robots that will passively do whatever they are told by the elite. Or that they will at least be passively misled into creating the kind of society that allows the elite to stay in control.

And so, many of you will know from growing up in Europe – as certainly this messenger has come to realize – that from very early childhood, you were exposed to very subtle beliefs that suppressed your individuality, that caused you to feel that you had no inherent worth, that you could not truly make a difference. And so you look at some of the people throughout history who have made a difference and you say, "They must have been special. I could not do this. What chance do I have? I am worth nothing, for I have been told this by my society from a very early age. I have been treated like cattle, like a sheep that should be herded into the fold and then not make any trouble after that."

And so, my beloved, this is what you need to come to a greater awareness of. And you need to come to a determination where you reach for that spark – that spark of divine fire in your own being – and you recognize that you do have a God-given individuality. And by the very fact that you exist, you have the authority to express that individuality on Earth.

For my beloved, I can assure you that the truth that, "Without him was not anything made that was made" means that you were made by God. And therefore, God gave you opportunity to be embodied on Earth, and that means that God has given you the right to express your divine, spiritual individuality on this planet. And, my beloved, you who are spiritual people should be able to recognize that there is no higher authority than God. And therefore, no authority on Earth has the right to take away what God has given. And you have a divine right to express your individuality—and do not let any authority on Earth – be it the state or a scientific establishment or the Catholic Church or any other religion – do not let them take it away from you, my beloved.

For if you do, you violate the first two commandments—thou shalt have no other gods before me and thou shalt not take unto thyself any graven image. For I tell you, that when you take unto yourself the graven image of the fallen beings, well then you begin to worship that image as reality, thinking there is nothing beyond it. And then you make that image and the people who promote it your god. And then you start worshiping the false gods who have set themselves up, claiming to be the true God.

This, my beloved, did indeed happen to the people at various times during the Old Testament era. As you will see when you realize that there were times when the people believed they were told by their God to massacre other tribes that they had conquered. This certainly could not be the true God of Abraham, the true God of infinite and unconditional love.

And so you see that throughout the history of the world, many people have worshipped the false gods—as many people in Europe today worship the false god of scientific materialism. For, my beloved, scientific materialism is not what it claims to be—it is not a scientific ideology. It is a religious philosophy that simply denies God, instead of worshiping a false god, like the many orthodox religions throughout the world.

Dare to go beyond the false gods

So dare to go within. Dare to seek first the kingdom of God and his righteousness. Dare to seek that kingdom within yourself. Dare to connect to what you know in your hearts, that there is a truth that is beyond the man-made doctrines and belief systems. Dare to recognize that even though you have been exposed to this manipulation from early childhood, even from early childhood you had an inner sense that there was something more, there was something beyond it. So dare to recognize, my beloved—you are more than cattle, you are indeed the sons and daughters of God, you are indeed the spiritually mature people who volunteered to come into embodiment to drive the awakening that is simply just waiting to happen.

So, my beloved, dare to connect to your divine plan. Dare to Be who you are and dare to stand up and let that light shine. Dare to express it so that other people can take courage and inspiration from your example and see that perhaps we really are more than animals, perhaps we really are more than sinners, perhaps we all have a divine spark, a potential to follow in the footsteps of Jesus and other spiritual saints and sages who have found a higher way of life. Perhaps we all have the potential to rise above the human condition and bring forth a new philosophy, a new day, a new era in human society that finally breaks the stranglehold that the power elite has had over the people for so many thousands of years.

My beloved, dare to take responsibility for yourself, and for your nations, and for your continent and for your world. And you will inspire others beyond what your outer minds can even conceive is possible. For I tell you, even beyond what you do on the outer, there is an immense power in you making the inner decision to accept your spiritual identity. For that, my beloved, will spread like rings in the water in the collective consciousness. For surely, you know that all people are connected through the mind, through the collective mind. And so the real battle for planet Earth is not fought in the physical, it is fought in the mental, emotional and etheric realms. It is fought in the mind, for it is a battle for the minds of the people.

For did I not start out saying, my beloved, that it is through your beliefs – through the WORD – that you hold in your mind that you impress images upon the ma-ter light and therefore co-create the physical conditions you encounter? So we have now come full circle, where you realize, my beloved, that the physical manifestations – even the existence of the power elite and their suppression – are simply an outpicturing in form of what is going on at the mental, emotional and etheric levels of the mind. And therefore, it is at these levels that the battle is truly fought and won.

And that is why I want to impress upon you that even when you make that decision in your own mind – to accept who you are – you are doing something to raise up humankind, especially when you hold true to that decision. And when you are willing to be aware that the onslaught from the mass consciousness will come to you to try to weaken your resolve, to tear down your decision. But when you are willing to stand up against that onslaught – to openly look at your own consciousness and see what beliefs make you vulnerable to the mass consciousness, and overcome those beliefs – well then by you doing this individually, you are actually resolving part of the collective consciousness, the illusions in the collective consciousness. So by freeing yourself, you are not only freeing yourself but many other people.

Understanding the pyramid of consciousness

For I tell you, humankind can be put on a scale of consciousness that is like a pyramid, where there are various levels, just like you see at the Great Pyramid of Giza that has levels and steps. And so each of those levels represents a certain state of consciousness. And at the lower levels of consciousness, the pyramid is the widest, meaning that there are more people at that lower level of consciousness. And as you go up higher, you find more and more aware people, until you reach the apex of the pyramid where you find the highest—the top 10 percent, or even those who are in the top 10 percent of the top 10 percent.

Yet, my beloved, the entire pyramid is connected, and you will know that if you could lift up the pyramid of Giza by lifting at the top, you would lift the entire structure. And that means that when those in the top 10 percent raise their consciousness, they are not just pulling up one person below them. For below you is a greater number of people, and below them at the level down is an even greater number of people, for the pyramid widens as you go down. So when you pull yourself up, you pull on everyone who is below you, and therefore – suddenly – a shift can occur when enough people raise their own consciousness.

This is the magic, my beloved, of individuality and the interconnectedness of individuals. And this is why the fallen ones, the serpentine mind, wants you to deny your individuality so you do not even try to raise yourself up, so you believe that nothing you do could make a difference.

But I tell you, my beloved, all of us who have made a difference in the world have started out from this simple premise. We changed ourselves. And once we had overcome the duality consciousness, well we could then go out and do outer things. But I tell you, there are many people around the world who are unknown to history who have never been known to the public and have never done any outer manifestation, but they have still raised their own consciousness and thereby raised up many other people who were below them in the pyramid of life. And this, my beloved, is the greatest potential that cannot be stopped by the power elite—unless they can manage to stop the individuals at the top from starting the chain reaction by changing themselves by getting them to deny their individuality, their spiritual potential.

Thus, my beloved, deny not the God that is within you. Reject not that God. Do not take unto yourself the graven image of an external God, an external word, and worship that image as the true God. Instead find the kingdom within you. Find the true God in that inner kingdom, and realize that your conscious self is an individualization of that God. And therefore, you have the potential to become more of that God in manifestation and thereby bring the kingdom of the true God to Earth. Even the awareness of the true God, where people begin to see the reality that God is beyond any religion or man-made belief system.

Let us rise above the fighting over land!

Saint Germain, May 20, 2007

How can people claim ownership of land?

What is your land? Well, is it a physical manifestation, is it a physical place around which you can draw a border, or is it more than that? For my beloved, what I desire you to look at this night is the very fact that one of the major causes of war on this continent – and indeed throughout the world – has indeed been the fact that so many people have allowed themselves to feel ownership of a piece of land. And in order to protect that land – or to expand it by moving a line on a map a few kilometers this way or that – they have been willing to kill untold numbers of their fellow men.

My beloved, what folly is this that human beings develop ownership of a piece of land and call it theirs? My beloved, does not the entire planet belong to the Earth Mother? For is not the entire planet an out-picturing in form of the Earth Mother herself? And so who can draw a line on a map and say, "This is now our land. We own it, and if someone wants to move here, we will kill them before they kill us."

So my beloved, why does this sense of ownership develop? Well, there are two reasons, as there are two reasons for everything. One is the personal reason of the ego of each person that needs the sense of security and being in control. And so when you feel that you own a piece of land that is yours, personally yours, and you can draw a border around that land, then you begin to think that no one can take it away from you, and so the ego feels secure and in control. And on a larger scale a group of people will develop a national identity, draw a border around a piece of land, and then again, their collective ego will feel a sense of security and control.

But my beloved, there is the greater issue behind the human level. Namely, as Jesus talked about when he talked about conspiracies, that in the higher realms – the mental, emotional and etheric – there are fallen beings who are plotting to control this world, and control the people thereon. And my beloved, how do they control the people on Earth?

Well, they do it primarily through the divide-and-conquer method, the divide and conquer philosophy, the divide and conquer strategy. You see, my beloved, in Heaven we are all one because we know individually that we are one with the Creator—and thus we know that everything came out of the Creator and therefore we are one with each other.

Truly, the people on Earth are meant to manifest the Body of God on Earth, to see themselves as part of the one body of God. And when they do so, well there will be no room for darkness and duality on this planet. For how can there be warfare when all people see themselves as one? Who can be foolish enough to see their right arm as an enemy, and cut off that right arm when they truly realize the arm is part of their body and without it the body will suffer, potentially die.

And so, you can only kill another human being when you do not see yourself as part of the Body of God and therefore cannot see other people as part of that same body. And so in their strategy to prevent the emergence of the consciousness of Oneness on this planet, the fallen beings have plotted to divide humankind.

And certainly, there are many ways they can do this, but I would bring to your attention that one of the primary ways is precisely to divide them up in groups that live on a particular, well-defined piece of land with borders around it. And then make them believe that they have some kind of obligation to defend that land, or to expand it by killing other people when necessary.

How to look upon and deal with the power elite

Truly my beloved, this is one of the primary strategies of those who control humankind. And with that I truly mean, the principalities and the beasts in higher realms as Maitreya explains. For you see, my beloved, it is not truly the power elite on Earth who is consciously and deliberately doing this, for they simply do not have the sophistication or the awareness to plot such an overall strategy. And the reason is that those who are in embodiment are, of course, susceptible to the same mechanism that you all experience—that when you are in a physical body, you experience everything from inside the material realm, and thus you lose the larger perspective.

So even though there are various power elite groups who are plotting behind the scenes, I must tell you that they do not have the awareness to consciously carry out the overall strategy hatched in the minds of those who are not in physical embodiment. Thus, the embodied power elites simply act as puppets on a string. They are pulled hither and yon by those beyond the physical whom they have made their masters.

And so you see, my beloved, there are indeed many among the power elite who are completely attached to a particular plot of land, and who are willing to wage war with those in the next country who have also formed a power elite in that country. And so that is indeed why, my beloved, this planet has not been taken over by one, centralized power elite—for they are warring amongst themselves and cannot come together in oneness.

And my beloved, they will never be able to come together in oneness as long as they cling to the consciousness of separation, the consciousness of duality. And were they to rise above that consciousness of separation, well my beloved, what would happen? Well, they would enter the spiritual path and come closer to Christhood and thereby leave behind their need for power and control.

So you see, my beloved, I ask you to consider the planetary history and the history of Europe from a greater perspective. For what I would give you is the sense of realism, that although we do talk over and again about the power elite, we have no desire to induce any sense of fear or hopelessness or even anger or animosity in you against that power elite. In fact there is a very good reason why we talk about the power elite without being too specific, for we have no desire to see our most mature and balanced students enter into a dualistic struggle against particular individuals or groups or institutions on Earth.

For my beloved, take note of the fact that Jesus Christ himself did not enter into a physical battle with a power elite of his time, be it the leaders of the Jewish religion or the Roman empire. Surely, there were those who wanted him to be the warrior king who would free Israel from the Romans and bring the power of God into battle. But Jesus knew full well that he was meant to set forth a higher example, and bring forth a teaching that is beyond duality.

Being aware of the power elite without giving them power

And so, even though we do want you to be aware that the power elite exists – even though we want you to make the calls that will authorize Archangel Michael and his legions to remove some among the power elite from Earth – we do not want you to focus attention upon this. For as we discussed earlier, when you put attention on something – with a negative emotion such as fear or anger – well my beloved, you misqualify energy. And that misqualified energy is then directed by your attention towards the people towards whom you feel anger.

And my beloved, what happens to that emotional energy? Well, even though it might affect the people in some way, the beasts and principalities behind those people will suck up that energy and use it for their nourishment. So you see, it is indeed true – as some among the New Age people have said – that what you resist persists, and what you place your attention upon, you magnify. But it is only true if you place your attention upon something with a negative emotion, or a sense of hopelessness or despair.

And that is indeed why we ask you to find the middle way of the Christ discernment that allows you to recognize that there is a power elite on Earth, that they have influenced society in many ways, and that you need to be consciously aware of this and expose it where appropriate. But you do not enter into the dualistic consciousness, where you personally think you have to fight that elite and do battle with them. For you realize that it is not truly the physical elite that is the problem. The real problem is a state of consciousness, namely the false beliefs and ideas, and the beast and principalities beyond the physical.

And so, when you realize this, you realize that the real enemy is never people, it is indeed a state of consciousness. And it is even treacherous to say that there is an enemy, for in reality there is no enemy. For when you are centered in the mind of Christ, you realize that the consciousness of anti-christ is not your enemy. For you are not really concerned about the consciousness of anti-christ in the sense that you believe it has any power over you and therefore you need to fight it to protect yourself against it.

No, my beloved, you have followed the call of Christ to come to the point of surrender, where the prince of this world comes and has nothing in you. The duality consciousness comes and has no elements of duality, no illusions whereby it can control you and force you to enter into that dualistic struggle, whether it be over land, whether it be over which religion is right, or whether it be over which nation is superior to another.

The key to the ultimate victory is ultimate surrender

Elohim Victoria, May 20, 2007

The illusion that problems are too big to be solved

My beloved, you may see the most powerful army on Earth. You may see them arrayed with their nuclear weapons, but what can they do to the far-flung galaxies of the cosmos? And this should then give you the sense of co-measurement that the Creator who could create such a vast cosmos, has a power that is infinitely greater than any power on Earth. And thus, you should realize that when that power of God is allowed to flow through those who have opened themselves to be the open doors for that power, well then, "With men this is impossible, but with God all things are possible." There is not one single condition on Earth that cannot be resolved or consumed or transformed by the power of God.

My beloved, one of the foremost plots of the fallen consciousness and the beings who embody it, is precisely to make you believe that you are so insignificant and the problems facing this Earth are so great, that there is nothing you can do to change status quo. There is nothing you can do to overthrow the power elite. But my beloved, this is nothing but an illusion, designed to do one thing only, namely to prevent you from letting the Light of God shine through you, the Light of God that is already anchored in the kingdom of God that is within you.

And so my beloved, their greatest fear is that a critical number of people will stand up and say, "Come what may, we will pursue the path of individual Christhood. We will follow the example set by our supreme teacher, Jesus Christ. And we will dare to do the works that he did because we realize that WE are not doing the works—it is God within us who is doing the works."

This is their supreme fear, because they know that there was nothing they could do to stop Jesus, to stop Gautama, to stop many of the other people who have awakened to the reality that they are individualizations of God on Earth and that they can allow the power of God to shine through them. And therefore, they know that if a critical mass of people were to manifest that Christhood, well then they would lose their control over this planet. And they would then be faced with a choice of either changing their ways or going to the second death. This they are seeking to avoid or postpone, by causing the people to take on the karma they have created.

Yet my beloved, through your willingness to come apart from that consciousness of hopelessness, of paralysis, of despair, of worthlessness, you have shown, you have demonstrated, that they will not win, they will not endure. For God will be victorious on Earth.

Dare to leave the dualistic struggle behind

Thus, I come to commend you. For you see, my beloved, it is not a matter of fighting some gigantic, epic battle against the forces of darkness, defeating them in a giant explosion. No, the true revolution that will change the Earth is an inner revolution, where you dare to be who you are and rise above the dualistic struggle, thus refusing to feed it.

This is the true victory we are looking for—those who will overcome and be who they are in God. You have dared to start that process. And you can surely continue it. Yes, my beloved, I sense how some of you have your doubts. But I am not asking you to attain the Christ consciousness in the next five seconds. I am asking you to continue to do what we have talked about, namely put one foot in front of the other. Take one step at a time and simply determine in your mind that come what may, you will – for the rest of your lifetime – continue to take one small step at a time, always looking for the next step. Never allowing yourself to be held up by the sense of comfortability, or the sense of fear or the sense of hopelessness.

My beloved, all I am asking is this: Always look for the next step you can take. Look for how your ego is trying to come up with an excuse for why you should not take that step. And then realize that it is nothing but an illusion and determine to not let it hold you back but to take that next step anyway. That is what I am asking, my beloved. For that is what will win your victory.

Do you see, my beloved, some of our students in the organizations we have sponsored have sometimes had a somewhat naive and black-and-white perspective, where they thought that what they were doing was engaging in some epic struggle where there would be glory in the end because they had defeated the enemy. This, my beloved, is the remnants of a consciousness that has permeated this planet for a very long time, causing many people to actually want to go to war because they thought that war was some glorious activity that would give them honor.

My beloved, it is time that the spiritual people abandon this state of consciousness of wanting and needing to fight an enemy. It is time you realized that there is a higher form of victory than the dualistic victory that requires you to defeat an external enemy, namely by killing or conquering other people. It is time to realize that the true victory is a spiritual victory, namely that of rising above duality. You do not win the ultimate victory by destroying other people that you have defined as your enemies. You win the ultimate victory by you rising above the consciousness that causes you to see others as separate from yourselves, thereby potentially converting your enemies into your brothers and sisters in Christ.

Rising above the possibility of defeat

This is the ultimate victory. And that requires you to overcome the sense that it is possible for you to lose. You see, my beloved, you might have your doubts of whether you can manifest your Christhood, whether you can overcome this or that condition. But I tell you, my beloved, Henry Ford was indeed right when he was inspired to say, "Whether you believe you can, or whether you believe you can't—you're right." For it is the belief that precipitates the reality. If you believe you cannot win, then you cannot win. But if you believe and accept and determine with all of your heart, that you can and will win, then that will be your reality.

So do you see, my beloved, I am imparting to you the true Flame of Victory that is not in opposition to defeat, for it has and needs no opposing polarity—for it is the unrivaled victory of God. And in that Flame of Victory there is no possibility of defeat. For you know that if you keep taking one small step at a time, then you can only win.

For victory, my beloved, is not a static state of no change. What is victory? It is self-transcendence, coming up one step higher than you were yesterday. That is victory!

It is not a matter of attaining some ultimate state of supposed perfection, where there is no longer any growth or change possible. No, those who have ascended beyond the human state are those who have discovered the reality that life itself – that God itself – is eternal, perpetual self-transcendence. And so when you determine that you will continue to transcend yourself – for as long as you have awareness – well then my beloved you have entered the Circle of victory, the Flame of victory.

You have stepped onto the path of victory where there is no possibility of defeat. It is not a matter of "if" you can make it. It is only a matter of keeping on taking one small step at a time. And if you find that you have slipped back, then you do not condemn yourself. You simply surrender and then move on. If you always move on, if you always take the next step, you cannot lose.

For my beloved, did not Jesus give his wonderful parable about the talents? And the servants who multiplied the talents they had been given were rewarded. For did not the Lord say, "Thou good and faithful servant, thou has been faithful over a few things. I will make thee ruler over many things."

So you see, my beloved, when you come to that determination – that you will keep taking one small step at a time – then you might say that the small steps that you can take are not enough to win the ultimate victory or to reach some state of Christhood or to manifest the Golden Age. And you are right. The small steps that you can take are not enough, but the small steps that you can take are enough to bring forth the multiplication from above. And that multiplication will manifest your Christhood, will manifest your victory, will manifest the Golden Age.

Understanding non-dual Victory

Thus, my beloved, you see that as with everything, there is dualistic perspective and there is a higher supra-dualistic perspective. And when you reach for that higher perspective, you see that there is a different approach. Even an approach where you do not need to be forceful or powerful in order to win. For my beloved, I have earlier spoken with greater power through this messenger, but I choose to tone down the power in order to impart to you a different aspect of the Flame of Victory, a more quiet aspect of that flame that is based on an inner knowing that there is only victory.

For my beloved, when you read Maitreya's book, you can read between the lines that there has never been a sphere that has not ascended—that there never will be a sphere that will not ascend. For there is no question that God's vision and design for this world of form will be manifest. It is only a matter of how long it will take before the beings who have used their free will to separate themselves from God will either realize the folly of their ways or run out of opportunity, so that the sphere in which they have lived will ascend without them.

Thus, my beloved, the force that drives the spheres to ascend is simply this: constant self-transcendence. And my beloved, you are never in a situation that you cannot transcend—IF you are willing to transcend yourself. For have we not said over and over again that your outer situation is a manifestation of your state of consciousness? And so even though you might feel right now that you have no power over your outer situation, I must tell you that you do have power to change your state of consciousness one small step at a time, one illusion at a time.

And thus, the sense that you are paralyzed and can do nothing has no reality to it. For my beloved, you can always surrender. And it is precisely in unconditional surrender that you win the victory. For as has been explained by Maitreya in his book and by Jesus and Mother Mary before, you cannot perfect the human consciousness. You can only rise above it. And in order to do that, you must surrender it. You must let it go.

And so my beloved, do you see it has been said that it is better to conquer yourself than to conquer a city? And indeed, conquering yourself is not a matter of fighting a battle. It is not even a matter of fighting your ego or the different divisions of your ego that cause a warring in your members. It is only a matter of surrendering them, leaving them behind—realizing that you are more than this. And therefore, accepting that you can rise above any condition—when you are willing to look at it, to understand why it is unreal and then simply let it go.

Thus in the softness of the Flame of Victory, I seal your hearts and I express my gratitude as well. For you have set forth another movement, another momentum, in the consciousness of Europe, namely that of VICTORY THROUGH SURRENDER.

I come to awaken those who volunteered to bring in the Golden Age!

Mother Mary, July 12, 2007

Victory is in giving

My beloved, it is not a matter of evaluating whether other people want your gift. It is only a matter of radiating that light, of giving that gift. The Victory is not in other people's responses or lack of response. The Victory is in radiating the Light.

My beloved, the Sun does not evaluate its own success based on what people on Earth do with the Sun's rays. The Sun only evaluates success based on the amount of light that it is radiating and the quality of that light. For the Sun is not here to be concerned about people, for they have their free will. The Sun – or rather the spiritual beings who serve as the hierarchs for the physical Sun – are here to radiate Light. You are here to radiate the Light that you are – the Light of your God Flame – by Being who you are—even right here in the physical universe where there are so many forces that are arrayed against Being.

For my beloved, do you not see even in this movie [October Sky], how an entire town has been so locked down by a certain consciousness that they can only work in these dirty, dangerous jobs underground in order to make a living? And yet, my beloved, who owns the mine? Who makes the profit off the sweat and the risk that these people are taking? Is there not somewhere someone who forms an elite who is reaping the profit off the people's labor? And is that elite not dependent upon keeping the people in a state of consciousness where they will keep walking that treadmill of thinking that this is the only way to make a living.

And so, my beloved, look around you here in California. Surely, you have a much better economy than they have in that little mining town in West Virginia. Surely, you have many job opportunities, you can have even better pay and a better lifestyle. Bus is there still not someone who is reaping the profit off what you are doing? Whether you are working for yourself or whether you are working in a job, there is someone somewhere who is reaping a greater profit than you are because they have somehow managed to get an entire state, an entire population, locked in a mental box, in a mindset that allows them to reap a profit of other people's labor without giving anything in return.

This, my beloved, is a completely ungodly principle that you will see throughout the history of this planet, where there have always been those who want to receive without giving in return. Yet the principle of God is what was described in Jesus' parable about the servants who received ten, five and two talents. And two multiplied them and one buried them in the ground. For you see, my beloved, the principle of God is simple: If you multiply what you are given, you will receive much more in return. For when you are willing to multiply in your own life, you are multiplying the abundance that is available for everyone on Earth. But those who bury the talents in the ground – and not only bury them in the ground but seek to receive from others rather than multiplying their own – they are the ones who form an elite, who are seeking to take advantage of others.

And this is precisely the consciousness that must be overthrown for the Aquarian age to manifest—where people realize that they do not need any overlords in the physical octave, in the material realm. They do not need a priesthood who tells them they can only be saved by following the priesthood's every command—or they will burn forever in hell. Neither do they need a political priesthood who tells them that unless they vote for them, or allow them to do whatever they want once they are elected, calamity will happen, the economy will fail, the stock market crash, or this or that. Nor do the people need an economic elite behind the scenes who are pulling the strings of the politicians – the political marionettes – who are simply dancing to the tune of the hidden power elite.

The people have the power to thrive without an elite

My beloved, I can assure you that if you removed the power elite from the state of California tomorrow, the economy would not collapse. Surely there would be an adjustment—there would be a major adjustment. But the economy would not stop to function. The economy would not collapse. The political system would not collapse. For people would step up to the plate and fill the roles that are now being filled by the elite or those who are controlled by the elite.

You see, my beloved, the elite can survive only by beating down the people, by making them believe that they are as nothing, that they cannot govern themselves, that they cannot run their societies or their communities. This is the lie that has been perpetrated upon humankind for a very, very long time, as described in Maitreya's book.

My beloved, it is as big of a lie as when it was first released in this world. There is absolutely no amount of argumentation – no matter how subtle, no matter how seemingly sophisticated – that can make it any less of a lie. It is a lie for the simple reason that God is in everyone. And as Jesus said, "With men this is impossible, but with God all things are possible." And therefore when the people are not beaten down by an elite, God in them will step up to the plate and they will be able to govern themselves and to run the economy and their families.

My beloved, this is an absolute truth that I am telling you. The people have power, and the power elite can survive only by preventing the people from unleashing the power that is found... where? Well, my beloved, the power is found in the Kingdom of God that is within you, within every human being.

Thus, if you will take another look at the teachings of Jesus, you will see that he was anti-establishment, anti-elite, from the very beginning. And he came to set the people free from the elite who had managed to make the people believe that they needed the elite in order to be saved and in order to run their society, in order to keep law and order, in order to keep the government going, in order to keep the economy going— whatever you have.

This is the lie that is daily being perpetrated upon the people through the mainstream media, who are also subject to the lie. Thinking that they cannot survive without the elite and therefore they must promote the mindset and the belief system of the elite. Even though many of them know that it is a lie that they are writing in their newspapers or broadcasting on their television stations.

The Golden Age requires an all-encompassing shift in consciousness

Saint Germain, July 13, 2007

The elite as the "saviors" of the people

And what you have seen over this last year is a steady decline in the American people's support for the war in Iraq and support for the president. And what that really signifies is that the people have stopped supporting the agenda behind the war in Iraq. And that agenda was not the war on terror, was not to fight the terrorists on foreign soil instead of fighting them at home, as Bush has said over and over again. The real agenda was the agenda of the power elite which has many facets that I will not here go into. But what I want you to realize is that because of the clearing of consciousness, the clearing of the heart, the American people have begun to realize that they will not support their president when their president is not their president but is the president of the elite.

Because the people are beginning to realize that they can no longer allow their leaders to follow the agenda of the elite instead of following the agenda of the Ascended Host—who are really behind the people. And thus, our agenda is what is best for the people of this nation.

And so, my beloved, to return to my concepts that everything in nature, even the balance of nature, is affected by the consciousness of humankind, one of the subtle beliefs behind this idea is that there are certain aspects of life on this planet that are beyond the power of the people and thus you need someone outside yourself to do something for you. This is the lie that Jesus has exposed in such detail, such richness and with such eloquence on his website. Where they elevated his example to an idol that he is the only Son of God and everybody needs him in order to be saved. But in reality his true mission was to show everyone that they can find the kingdom of God within them and thus do not need an external savior.

But what the fallen beings who came to this planet, and who as I said are attempting to set themselves up as gods on Earth – getting the people to worship them as gods on Earth – what they have attempted to do from the very beginning, my beloved, is a very simple strategy. Through their fallen consciousness, through their dualistic consciousness, they create a state of imbalance on the planet, and then they set themselves up as those who can save the people from that imbalance. You see it today—they are the ones, my beloved, who have misused science and technology in their greed to create multinational corporations that have no respect for the environment, no respect for the people they employ. These are the ones who have created the pollution that is threatening the ecosystem on this planet.

If anyone is responsible for global warming, they are the ones who are responsible for it. Of course, we have given teachings already on the reality of global warming but what I want you to realize is that pollution is first and foremost created by the elite. But now that the problem is there and has been recognized by the people, well then the power elite comes in with the second part of their strategy, which is to set themselves as the saviors who can tell the people how to overcome this problem.

Do you see, my beloved, that for nigh a century they were trying to hide the fact that pollution could have an influence on the environment so that they could continue to have the biggest possible short-term profits by polluting? And now that the consciousness of the people has shifted – where they could no longer get away with this – they are trying to use the new environmental awareness to their advantage by setting themselves up as the saviors of the people.

This, my beloved, is what they have done over and over again. Every single problem on this planet is created through the consciousness of duality. And although many of the people have fallen into duality, it is first and foremost the elite – of the most rigid and closed-minded fallen beings – who are upholding that consciousness as the dominant state of consciousness on Earth.

So through that consciousness, a problem is created and then the elite comes in and says "Ah, but we have the only solution—and that is that you, the people, give us more control over you and then we will solve the problem and take you to heaven on Earth." My beloved, this is of course a complete fallacy. For obviously, you cannot solve a problem with the same state of consciousness that has created that problem. And so how can those who are the most blinded by the duality consciousness solve the problems created through the duality consciousness? And thus, obviously the elite will never save the people.

But you see, my beloved, for a time a particular elite will be able to use the problem to control the people, until the people start seeing through the illusion. And then what happens? Well, what happens is what I explained in Virginia, that now an aspiring power elite begins to form. And they say, "No, the established power elite is wrong, but we are the real saviors. We have the real solution. So follow us instead of following the old elite."

But my beloved, is it not time for a critical mass of people to awaken to the reality that you have come into embodiment to rise above this dualistic game, to totally leave it behind, to expose it for what it is and to stand up and say, "The emperors of duality have nothing on!"

The secret about the rise and fall of Golden Ages

Saint Germain, July 14, 2007

So, my beloved, you see, once again, the pattern that human society, the economy and all aspects of human society have become unbalanced because of the dualistic state of consciousness. And especially because of those who are the most trapped in that state of consciousness, namely those who form a power elite. They have become so trapped in duality and separation that they believe that they – in their separate sense of identity – know better than God how things should be done on planet Earth, or even in the entire universe. And so they have set themselves up as those who know best.

Yet in their duality they inevitably create imbalances that lead to problems. And then, as I said last night, we have the ongoing pattern of an established power elite creating a problem and an aspiring power elite coming up, claiming that they can solve the problem created by the old power elite, even though they are still in the consciousness of duality. And therefore, they must inevitably create another imbalance that leads to another problem, and so on ad infinitum.

What, my beloved, can be done to break this cycle, to break this spiral? Well, the only thing that can be done is, as I said last night, that those who are my own, those who are loyal to the cause of Freedom, awaken to who they are, awaken to their potential and decide to hold the spiritual balance for the awakening of humankind. This has an Alpha aspect, where you raise your consciousness and hold the balance for many. It has an Omega aspect, where you speak out the truth that you know and demand change in society.

Why are those who misuse power allowed to reincarnate?

You see, my beloved, one of the questions that many of you have is why certain lifestreams – who are completely stuck in duality – are allowed to incarnate again and again on Earth. Why these same lifestreams are allowed to ascend to leadership positions time and time again. And lifetime after lifetime, they repeat the same old patterns of creating problems and they seem to be the only ones who cannot see it. They cannot see how disastrous it is to keep doing the same thing over and over again, and expecting that one day paradise is going to descend on Iraq, or on the Third Reich, or whatever ideal society they claim can be manifest on this planet, based on their dualistic ideologies.

So, my beloved, why do we allow such lifestreams to continue to reincarnate and to continue to become leaders of the people? Well, the reality is, my beloved, that we of the Ascended Host are not allowing these lifestreams to reincarnate—you are! Humankind is allowing this and here, my beloved, is precisely why. You see, as Maitreya explains in great detail in his book, there are two ways you can learn, my beloved. The highest way of learning is that you learn from the Ascended Host because you recognize that there is something beyond your own consciousness – something beyond duality, something beyond the ego – and thus you are willing to listen to a true teacher who has no selfish motives whatsoever.

Yet, as Maitreya explains, if you are not willing – anymore – to listen to that true teacher, then what happens? Well, you lose contact with the true teacher, and then the false teachers become your teacher. And so you see, my beloved, if the people had been willing to listen to the Ascended Host, we could long ago have raised up a critical mass of people who could then take leadership positions and lead from the level of the Christ mind—rather than from the mind of anti-christ.

And thus, they would have replaced the power elite people who are trapped in duality. However for this to happen, it would require that the people had reached a certain level of consciousness, where they were actually able to recognize the difference between those who lead from the consciousness of Christ and those who lead from the consciousness of anti-christ. And my beloved, the people of the world have not yet reached that level, even though they are very close to breaking through to a realization that there is a higher reality and that not everything is a matter of argument and counter-argument.

So you see, my beloved, when the people are not willing to reach for something beyond the consciousness of duality, then the fallen beings – those who are trapped in duality – become the teachers – by default – of the people. We allow this to happen because we have respect for free will. And also because we see that there is still a potential that the people can be awakened. Because, after all, we see very clearly that these lifestreams who are stuck in duality are not likely to change their ways. So when they ascend to positions of power, they will inevitably misuse that power. And we see that when that abuse of power becomes severe enough, there is the potential that the people will finally wake up.

Obviously this is an awakening that is the hard way, and we would prefer to see it the higher way. But again, we bow to the free will of the people who are in embodiment and therefore are the ones who determine what is allowed to occur and continue to occur on Earth. The people are the ones who must wake up and say, "Enough is enough!" It is, as Jesus has explained and as Maitreya explains, there is a top 10 percent and a bottom 10 percent. But what really determines the fate of the planet is whether the 80 percent of the general population will blindly follow the blind leaders in the bottom 10 percent or whether they will wake up and open their eyes to follow the leaders in the top 10 percent.

Overcoming the grand illusion of the scarcity of resources

Saint Germain, July 14, 2007

My beloved, I Saint Germain come to give you the next installment of my discourses for this conference. What then is the next thing that needs to be reconsidered? For as I said yesterday, in order to bring the Golden Age, you need to rethink everything that has been part of life in the old age, which we might call the dark age of Pisces.

For my beloved, we are about to shine a light on this planet so that there will be no shadows left. There will be no one and nothing that can hide, there will be no illusion and no lie that could possibly hide from the light – the Christ Light of Aquarius – that will shine upon this planet through those who are willing to re-think everything in their own lives, and therefore be the catalysts for an awakening in the mass consciousness.

So, one of the things that needs to be rethought is the entire concept of scarcity of resources. My beloved, from very early on, you have been programmed to believe that this planet Earth has only limited resources and therefore can sustain only a limited number of people. My beloved, this is a one hundred percent lie. It has no reality to it whatsoever. This planet does not have a scarcity of material resources. It has a scarcity of the love of the heart, which has enabled some people to form an elite who are the haves, as opposed to those who are the have-nots.

This, my beloved, is what they have desired to create on this planet from the very moment they were allowed to embody here. Namely a planet where they can form a privileged elite who have abundance and privileges and power beyond the majority of the population, so that they can feel that they are special. Thus, it is the selfishness – and the self-centeredness that kills the love of the heart – that is directly responsible for what seems to be a lack of physical resources. My beloved, there is a saying in some of the old countries that if there is room in the heart, there is room in the house. Well if there is room in the heart, then there is room on the planet.

Scarcity is not inevitable

My beloved, if the consciousness changed and we saw the spreading of the consciousness of Aquarius – as I have full confidence will happen – then you will see that suddenly the scarcity of resources that today seems inevitable and insurmountable will simply evaporate like the dew when the morning sun rises. There is no scarcity of resources, there is only an illusion of scarcity put upon the people by the elite who need to have scarcity so that they can have more than others.

Do you see, my beloved, the inevitability of this? You cannot have an elite who has more than the population if there is an abundance of resources. You must create an artificial situation, where the people are prevented from reaping the just reward of their labour. Because the elite has managed to steal the fruits of the people's labour, concentrating it in their own hands instead of allowing it to remain in the hands of those who are doing the work, those who are putting the seeds in the ground and are therefore entitled to reap the harvest.

This, my beloved, is a state of consciousness that needs to be challenged before the Golden Age can manifest. For I can assure you that in the Golden Age there will not be a scarcity of resources, nor will you have the majority of the population on this planet living below the so-called poverty level, which I, by the way, consider to be a completely artificial construct. For I can tell you that I want everyone on Earth to have the abundant life, materially and spiritually. And that means an entirely different consideration than what they currently consider the border between poverty and non-poverty.

Nevertheless, the reality that needs to dawn upon the people is that scarcity is a complete illusion; abundance is the reality—the real potential for planet Earth. Did not Christ say, my beloved, "Fear not little flock, for it is the father's good pleasure to give you the kingdom." And truly, it is so. The people can only fail to have the kingdom if they reject that kingdom. And they will only reject the kingdom if they have come to believe in the lie – promoted by the elite – that there is not room in the inn, there is not room in the kingdom, for them to sit at the same table as the elite.

My beloved, the Bible states clearly, "God is no respecter of persons," and thus you can see – when you look back at history – that the entire idea of elitism is out of touch with the reality of God. God is in everything and in everyone. Every single person on this planet has infinite value in the eyes of God. Thus, God wants everyone to have the abundant life. This does not mean that there will not be some who are willing to work harder and therefore have a little more than others. But it does mean a society in which you simply cannot have a state where there are a few people that are so unnecessarily affluent while many people live in abject poverty.

Be MORE than normal!

Saint Germain, July 14, 2007

The greatest threat to your freedom

And so my beloved, we have now reached the point where I can ask you to consider the greatest threat to your freedom and to the freedom of humankind, the greatest hindrance to the bringing forth of the Golden Age of Aquarius. This, my beloved, is a factor that has always been the greatest obstacle for the spiritual growth of humankind, for the awakening of people. What is the factor I am talking about?

It is the very subtle, very insidious, programming to which you have all been subjected from the very moment you first took embodiment on this planet, and certainly for your entire lifetime. It is the programming that you are supposed to be normal, a normal human being. Yet my beloved, what does it mean to be normal? Is it not, my beloved, an attempt by the dark forces and the power elite to put you in a box, where you are so focused on following the norms defined by your society that you do not dare to challenge those norms—and therefore do not dare to challenge the status quo that keeps the elite in control?

For as long as you fit into the mold of a normal human being, you will not dare to fulfill your divine plan, and certainly you will not dare to express your Christhood. For my beloved, there has yet to be a society on this planet – at least in recent history – where being the Christ in action was considered normal by the powers that be.

Thus, my beloved, those who are my own – who have come into embodiment at this time to help bring the Golden Age of Aquarius into manifestation – well my beloved, certainly part of your divine plan is to speak out about conditions in society and to challenge the lies and the illusions. But the very deepest thing that you can help me with is by being willing to challenge the ultimate illusion, the illusion of normality. For my beloved, if you will look at the life of Christ, you will see that he too was challenged to be normal, even by his own mother and his brothers and sisters who came to him while he was preaching, being disturbed by the fact that he had shattered their conception of what it meant to be normal.

My beloved, it is so easy to look at those who do not follow the norm of your particular society and label them with some fancy medical term, be it bipolar, insane, schizophrenic, depressed, having boundary issues or this or that. But my beloved, I can assure you that there are people in mental hospitals in this nation who are actually more in touch with reality than the average person. Certainly there are also people in mental hospitals who are out of touch with reality and do not know what is real and unreal. But what I want you to see here is the fact that the average human being on this planet – the "normal" human being – truly has no conception whatsoever of what is real and what is unreal—and has indeed been programmed to think that this material world and the conditions that you see right now are real and normal, and therefore should be preserved.

Dare to go beyond the norms of your society

This, of course, is the programming of the power elite who wants people to uphold the status quo that maintains their privilege and their power. For once they have set themselves up in those positions of privilege and power, their main concern is not to lose it. And that is precisely why, my beloved, they seek to stop progress, they seek to stop new inventions, new ideas, new philosophies, new concepts. And when they cannot stop the emergence of new ideas, such as new ideas in spirituality and religion, well they seek to prevent the population from embracing those ideas by using the weapon that you have to be normal—and this new idea is not normal. It is a cult, it is bad, it is dangerous.

And so my beloved, the message I want to get across here is that if you are to fulfill your divine plans, if you are to manifest your Christhood and do what you came here to do – namely help Saint Germain bring in the Golden Age of Aquarius – well then you have to take a long, hard look in the mirror and say, "Where am I attached to being normal, to following the norms defined by my society, my family, or even by my own outer mind or my ego?"

You must evaluate whether you are more concerned about being seen as being normal by society or whether you are concerned about fulfilling your divine plan. Certainly, I am not talking about manifesting something that is clearly insane, for being the Christ does not mean that you are insane in any sense of the word. But it does mean that you are willing to go beyond the norm, and even to do things that for "normal" people might appear to be a little bit "out there," as the popular saying goes.

...

Challenging the concept of a "normal human being"

For you see, my beloved, what does it really mean to be normal? Well, it means that you accept boundaries for who you are, what you can be and how you can express yourself as long as you want to be an accepted member of society.

And so the job of the Living Christ in embodiment is to challenge people's sense of what is normal, which is what you saw Jesus do with his miracles and his words. Look at how even in the scriptures it is portrayed how people wanted him to be normal, to follow their standard, to not go too far beyond, to not push the envelope, push the limits for what was considered possible for a human being.

And so you see, again, the incredible depth in the statement of Christ, "With men this is impossible, but with God all things are possible." For you see that with men – with their human consciousness, with a standard for what is normal – well when you are in that state of consciousness, you must accept that there are boundaries and limitations for what can be achieved. And that is precisely what the power elite uses to maintain status quo by getting people to believe in the lie that there are certain problems that cannot be solved, or even certain conditions, my beloved – as I explained in my earlier discourses – that you have come to believe are natural, are normal, because nature simply is that way and there is nothing that can change it.

And so you see, my beloved, in reality there is no norm, there is no standard. Why is this so, my beloved? Because the Creator has created billions of expressions of itself, each one of which is unique in God. And so if everyone is a unique individual with a unique God-given individuality and identity, well then how can there be a standard? How can there be a norm? How can there be norms in individuality? How can there be a standard in uniqueness?

Politics and education in the Golden Age

Saint Germain, July 15, 2007

The need to overcome division in society

My beloved, the message that I want to speak this morning is to comment further on the potential for the spreading of a new awareness from this area of California. The one area where there needs to be a new awareness in the United States is in the fact that in a Golden Age there is no division in society. In a Golden Age, precisely what makes it Golden is that there has been attained a state of oneness in society.

This, of course, has many facets and many aspects. But of particular importance is the realization in the people that the power elite has always used the divide-and-conquer strategy to divide the people into warring groups and set them up against each other. And this division of society takes many forms. But one of the most important ones to expose and transcend in this age is the division between science and religion—between spirit and matter.

For you see, my beloved, this nation is founded on the principle that all people were given inalienable rights by their Creator. Meaning that there is a higher authority than any authority on Earth, be it the President or the Congress or the hidden elite that seeks to rule society behind surface appearances.

...

A new understanding of elitism as a driving force in history
And so, my beloved, precisely because, as I have explained earlier, there are so many people embodied in the state of California who are close to the level of consciousness that is needed, well, then there is the potential that California can become the forerunner for this new awareness, this new mindset, this new way of looking at life.

It can even come in the form of a new analysis of history, where you simply look at history and recognize the existence of a power elite that are blinded and controlled by the human ego—and therefore through the outplaying of this psychological mechanism have attempted to dominate the population for thousands of years. And by the population becoming aware of this mechanism, well even that in itself will bring forth a new day where the power elite cannot rule behind the scenes.

And I tell you that the power elite can only rule when they can stay hidden from the people. For once they are exposed, well then the people will no longer accept the elite, will no longer accept the lies that allow the elite to stay in power by manipulating the situation.

...

Let go of the dream of an ultimate system
So you see, my beloved, once again, I hurl the challenge at you to be willing to question everything. And I tell you that even the spiritual people – and especially the Ascended Master students – can have a tendency to become rigid and thinking that now we have found the highest expression of truth, and thus we do not really need to dip into the universal stream, the River of Life, to bring forth an even higher expression, or an even higher application of it for practical matters in society.

You see, my beloved, as I have explained, there is no standing still. The River of Life moves on. There is no ultimate system of government or education that could ever be brought forth on this planet. For my beloved, as I attempted to explain yesterday, when those who are the leaders of a Golden Age society begin to believe that they have found some ultimate system – and that they are the elite who are now seeing it as their job to maintain the system – well at that point the Golden Age society begins to stagnate and the collapse is only a matter of time. Thus, let go of the dream of an ultimate educational system, an ultimate state of the economy, an ultimate political system! It will never happen on Earth!

It is a dualistic dream projected onto the people by those who are trapped in the serpentine consciousness and are attempting to take heaven by force and establish paradise on Earth. When in reality this cannot happen as a static society, but only by creating a society that is constantly transcending itself, thereby raising up the Earth to become part of the spiritual realm, as the entire material sphere ascends, as described in Maitreya's book. This is a fundamentally different approach than chasing the pipe dream of some static state of perfection in this realm.

Thus my beloved, my closing thought for this discourse is to hurl at you the challenge to recognize that in a golden-age society, nothing stands still. And thus, you cannot be attached to anything. You cannot allow yourself to believe that, "Oh if we only achieve this particular state of education, or this particular state of a religious movement, or this particular political system, then we don't need to be alert anymore."

My beloved, the reality of it is that there is no stillstand in Christhood. There is no getting comfortable in Christhood. For my beloved, Christhood is an ongoing process of flowing with the River of Life. And when you accept this, you can find peace in constant self-transcendence, rather than seeking to establish the false peace of stopping the growth and maintaining status quo—thinking that status quo can give you peace when in reality it is only by being in – and being one with – the River of Life that you will ever find peace.

I challenge you to rethink the concept of ownership

Saint Germain, July 15, 2007

The world is designed to give you abundance

For you see, my beloved, you have been sent into a world that is very well designed for giving you the abundant life. In fact, God has designed this world to give you anything and everything you want. However, if you seek to own something, you will limit your possessions to that which you can currently conceive instead of flowing with the River of Life.

Do you see, my beloved, that you have been given free will by God? And you have been given the ability to impose images upon the Ma-ter Light, causing the light to take on form, whereby it will temporarily stagnate in a certain form. As I said, you have the right to do this, to create any form you desire. Yet what God desires to see for you is that you do not settle for the forms that you can currently conceive, but that you are part of the ongoing movement of the River of Life. So that, instead of holding on to one limited form, you are constantly transcending yourself, constantly transcending your former mental images so they do not become graven images. And therefore, you are not seeking to hold on to one particular form, for you are willing to transcend that form, allowing that form to become more.

And do you see, my beloved, this is what the human ego and those who are trapped in the fallen consciousness cannot fathom? For they believe that if a particular form is changed, they will lose that form. And you see, my beloved, in a sense this is true. For if you have ten dollars in the bank and they accrue interest and now you have twelve dollars, well in a sense you have lost the ten dollars, at least the sense of having ten dollars in the bank. But is it really a loss, or have you received something more?

Challenge the sense of ownership

Thus you see, my beloved, you who are the spiritual people have the opportunity – not only in your own lives but also in the collective consciousness and even by speaking out about this in society – you have the opportunity to challenge the sense of ownership, the very subtle programming that has programmed almost everyone, at least in the more affluent nations on this planet, to believe that one of the main purposes in life is to own something and to accumulate what you own. And this very subtle programming is the primary factor that prevents the manifestation of the abundant life on this planet.

And with the abundant life I mean a state where every human being on this planet has enough to eat, has a decent place to live and has a standard of living that gives that person free time and energy to pursue spiritual goals.

You see, my beloved, this planet is perfectly capable of sustaining 10 billion people in a state of affluence. But obviously it is not doing so right now. And the reason is that the bottom 10 percent of the people – the power elite – are so trapped in the sense of ownership and the fear of loss that they have accumulated the world's wealth and resources to themselves, concentrating it in their own hands—thereby taking from someone else.

This is, as I said, partly a completely unconscious drive that springs from the fear of loss and the illusion that the separate self can own anything. But it is also a desire to be better than others because they have more gadgets, more things, more possessions. So this is what prevents the shift—whereby even nature itself would change so that it could produce the abundance that would feed even more people than are currently living here.

And so, again, I look to those in the top 10 percent, those who are the more aware people, to come to a higher understanding of this and to demonstrate it in your own lives. My beloved, demonstrate that when you give up the need to own something for the separate self, well then you become one with the River of Life. And, my beloved, this does not mean that you do not have personal possessions. For there is a certain validity in having certain possessions, but you do not have those possessions in order to have them, to have the sense of owning them. You have them as tools for fulfilling your divine plan.

For you have now transcended the consciousness whereby owning something has become an end in itself. And instead, you realize that ownership of anything in this world is simply a means to the greater end of fulfilling your divine plan, helping to manifest God's kingdom on Earth.

...

Challenge the illusion of lack

But you see, my beloved, in order to sell their illusion of ownership and the false belief that those who own more are better than those who have less, well the power elite and the false teachers have had to sell another subtle illusion. Which is again, as I have said before, that the consciousness of lack – that lack and limitation – is unavoidable.

But you see, my beloved, when you merge with the River of Life, there is no need for lack. For you see, when you truly merge with the

River, you not only become one with the River, you become the River. Which means that you are now – through your Being – directing a part of the flow of the River of Life. And thus you can direct it – the very Light of God – into manifesting whatever you need to fulfill your divine plan.

And so you see, my beloved, that what I am talking about here is not a superficial psychological mechanism that you can easily overcome by giving a few affirmations or going to a psychologist for an hour or two. This is a very deep-seated mechanism that will require you to do some serious contemplation and soul searching, so that you can finally come to see it for the illusion that it is. And you can come to believe the reality that when you are willing to transcend your expectations of what life should be, when you are willing to confront and overcome your fear of loss, well then you will not lose anything. For the River of Life will gladly give you more—as you become More. And as you become More, instead of seeking to own and control everything, you will – because you are in the flow of the River of Life – freely give what you have freely received. Whereby you spread the wealth, you spread the abundance. And thereby everyone will have more.

For my beloved, do you not see that it is only the illusion of the fallen beings that makes it seem as if there is a limited amount of resources— so if you spread those resources to every human being on the planet, nobody would have enough? This is what they want you to believe. But the reality is, my beloved, that when those who have start freely giving what they have received, well then everyone will become more affluent. The entire economy will grow to a higher level. And therefore, economic opportunity and the collective amount of wealth in a society will increase dramatically and exponentially.

...

And I must tell you that there is a power elite on this planet – who have been reincarnating again and again and again – who, if they could, would have been perfectly content to keep the total amount of wealth available in the Western world at the level that you saw in the feudal societies. They do not care about expanding the total amount of wealth as much as they care about staying ahead of the population.

There is, of course, a few members of the power elite who are trapped in another spiral, where they are not even concerned about having more than the people. They are only concerned about having more and more and more, for they have been trapped in a never-ending cycle that can never be filled.

There IS MORE to Life!

El Morya as Master MORE, October 26, 2007

The missing link in history

For what is it that the elite has done to suppress the people? Yes, you will look back at history and say that the king had some real physical power and he used it ruthlessly. Nevertheless, let me tell you that there never has been a regime on this planet – be it the British monarchy, or the Communist Party in the Soviet Union, or the emperors of Rome – there never has been a regime that had enough physical power to suppress the people with physical power alone. For had the people come together at a critical mass and stood up against that physical power, then the powers would have fallen. And this you have seen in a number of nations around the world.

So therefore, physical power is not enough to suppress the people. And that is indeed the missing link in history, where historians tend to look back, and they look only at the material circumstances, thinking that the cause of everything that happened in the world must be found in the material realm. But I tell you that the cause of everything that happened in the material realm is found in the consciousness of the people, the collective consciousness. And thus, my beloved, I tell you – truly – what they have used to suppress the people is the Word, the perversion of the Word of God.

The Word of God is the consciousness of Christ that allows you – as I started out this discourse talking about – that allows you to discern between what is real and what is unreal. And so, in order to suppress the people, they must take away that key of knowledge. They must create this false reality, where they have now created two dualistic polarities that seem to be inseparably linked in a dualistic struggle for supremacy. Yet both of them are lies.

And so this, my beloved, is one realization that needs to be brought out at this time in Britain and elsewhere, for it is the essential realization that must be spread before a Golden Age can dawn—namely the whole nature of duality. And this, my beloved, is of course why we of the Ascended Host have brought forth the new book, The Art of Non-War, which is written in a way that is more universal than any other book we have brought forth through any dispensation whatsoever. Thus, it has a potential to reach the people and awaken them to the basic dynamic of the duality consciousness and how it prevents them from discerning what is real and what is unreal. So every action they take, every idea they believe in, does not really lead to change because it merely perpetuates the dualistic struggle which is the very root of their suffering and their limitations.

But that dualistic struggle starts in the consciousness, for the elite themselves could not perpetuate the dualistic struggle unless the people responded. And that is why you see the unholy alliance between those in the power elite who want power, and those among the people who do not want power but want to give away their power and have other people make decisions for them. So that they do not have to face the potential of making wrong choices, but can criticize those who make choices no matter what choices they make. And yet even this can shift almost as in the blinking of an eye. And it will shift when enough of the top 10 percent process that state of consciousness in their own beings and overcome it once and for all.

Understanding power and love in the roles of men and women

Mother Mary, October 27, 2007

Abuse of power springs from lack of love

And so, when you have this complementary interchange, this complementary interplay between the transcending love and the nurturing love, well then society will be propelled beyond the old concepts of love and power. For do you see, my beloved, what Master MORE was talking about—the people who have formed a power elite, how they have perverted power and abused power? But do you see, my beloved, that those who abuse power do so for one reason only—namely, that they do not have love.

So they do not have real power, the power of God, and therefore they must take power through force here on Earth and seek to force other people into submitting to them—and if they will not submit, then kill them. This is a complete abuse of power, and it is only possible for people to do this to other people when they have no love for those other people.

But, my beloved, how can it be that a person can have no love for other people? Well, as Jesus said, do unto others as you want them to do unto you, which can be switched and mean: what you do unto others is a reflection of your state of consciousness. And therefore, what you do unto others, you have already done to yourself in your own mind. So if you have no love for other people, it can be for only one reason, namely that you have no love for yourself—for you do not love yourself, you do not believe you are a loving person, that you are worthy of love.

And yet, my beloved, how can people come to feel this? Well, it is possible only because they have been completely blinded by, and absorbed in, the consciousness of separation from God—the consciousness that was started by those beings who, in a higher realm – in a higher sphere, as Maitreya explains in his book – decided to rebel against God and therefore separated themselves from God. Do you see, my beloved, that these lifestreams have separated from God, and thus they cannot experience God's love for them?

...

So my beloved, I give you these teachings for several reasons. One is that you should not allow yourself to fall into the old trap of engaging in the dualistic struggle. Surely, you need to be aware that there is a power elite on Earth. You need to be aware of their methods and how they have influenced society and the mass consciousness. You need to be aware of their subtle lies. In some cases, you do need to be aware of who they are in order to stand up and say, "We need to question those people who are representing a certain state of consciousness."

Yet you do not fall into the trap of seeing yourself in opposition to this power elite, or to particular individuals. You do not feel fear of them, nor anger towards them. For when you unconditionally love yourself, you can only unconditionally love other people, and the unconditional love is what the Bible calls the perfect love that will cast out all fear.

Those who abuse power are consumed by fear

And so you see, my beloved, when you have unconditional love, you are not afraid of the power elite. You do not feel threatened by them. In fact, you realize the truth that those who are the most powerful people are the most afraid. For if they were not afraid, why would they need the power?

You see, my beloved, when you separate yourself from God, it becomes possible that a lifestream can cease to exist, that it can go through the ultimate spiritual death, that we have sometimes called the "second death," because it is the death of the lifestream itself, and not just the temporary death of the physical body. And so, my beloved, the inevitable companion of the sense of separation is the fear of annihilation, the fear of the cessation of self.

And for those who are in the duality consciousness, it is a real potential, but only because they remain in the duality consciousness instead of stepping outside of it, which they can do at any time. And again, as it is difficult for people to live with the sense that they are not lovable, it is difficult for them to live with the sense of fear. And so the more fear they have, the more they have a need to compensate. And how do they compensate? They compensate by taking on power on Earth, by taking power through force. Because if they can make millions of people in a country believe that they are powerful, well then they can ignore or gloss over their inner fear, to the point where they almost don't feel it anymore.

But you see, my beloved, why is it that some of these powerful people need millions of people to confirm the illusion that they have power or that they are fearless? Because if they really knew in their own beings that they had power and they had no fear, why would they need other people to confirm their power? So you see, they are also the lifestreams who have the greatest doubt, and that is why, only when millions of people follow them, revere them as powerful, only then can they believe it themselves and therefore push aside their doubt, their fear, their sense of not being lovable.

And so, this of course holds true for the men that you see take on the image of being tough men. They also are driven by fear and they compensate for it through violence because violence is always a way to make other people fear you. But truly, it can never have a permanent effect in helping them overcome their fear, for it will always surface again.

And so these people are on an impossible quest that often accelerates until they lose control of their lives and end up destroying themselves. And you see this in so-called ordinary people who enter a negative spiral of anger and violence until they either get themselves killed, or end up in jail. And this is certainly what you have seen in these boys who committed the school shootings. It was again their fear, their lack of self-love. But you have also seen it in some of the "great leaders" of history, my beloved, such as Hitler, Napoleon, and others, who in their insatiable quest for more and more power to cover over their fear, ended up destroying themselves.

Using the power of love to transform society

And so my beloved, the real key to transforming a society is not that the people use power against the elite who is abusing power and suppressing the people. The real key is that a critical mass among the people wake up and realize that the true power IS love. And they connect to the love they have in their own beings – their love for higher principles, for higher truth – and then they express that by simply stating the truth that society needs to change, that the old ways are no longer working, that it is time to come up higher.

You see, my beloved, when you are still in fear, what you see is that the people will start a movement, and to some degree it is driven by a true desire to see improvement in society. But because of the fear, it always ends up being a scape-goating effort, where the people appoint somebody as the scapegoat who is responsible for everything that is wrong in society. So if we only get rid of the scapegoat, we will solve all of our problems.

This certainly is what you saw in the French Revolution, where the aristocracy were named as the scapegoat. But in reality, they were just one expression of the people's unwillingness to take responsibility for themselves. And when the aristocracy was removed from power, another power elite emerged and took over, and thus the people were hardly freer than they were before.

And the key to breaking this pattern of one power elite taking over from the existing power elite, is that the people must awaken their love so they do not need a scapegoat. They do not need to make it seem like the queen is so bad and that's why we should get rid of the monarchy. Instead, they just state the truth that it is time to change the monarchy in its present form, to ask the questions that need to be asked.

Because it is a question of recognizing that there is a progressive movement in the world, as Master Morya talked about, with the River of Life. And that when society has moved forward to a certain point, well then the old clothes no longer fit and it is time to throw them away and get a new wardrobe. And so, there will come a point where the monarchy in its present form has outlived its purpose. And we do not need to say that it is wrong, that it is bad, that it should be destroyed. We need to transform it. Perhaps that will mean that we no longer need a particular institution, but perhaps we need something else as a symbol for the nation.

Likewise with the Church, it is not necessary to go out and make the Church seem like an evil institution. But it is necessary to say that the Church of England is no longer fulfilling the spiritual needs of the majority of the British people, and that is why they no longer go to church and they no longer feel that they get the answers they need. And so, it is necessary to seek for a new approach to spirituality that can meet the needs of the people in this age.

Likewise, you do not need to single out the upper class. You do not need to be negative towards anyone who has more money than the average. But you do need to challenge the consciousness that some people are inherently better than others, and you can challenge that only when you tune in to the unconditional love of God. For my beloved, when you realize the nature of unconditional love, you see that unconditional love cannot love some people more than others. For that would be conditional love, would it not?

Poverty is NOT the will of God, nor mandated by the laws of nature

Saint Germain, December 14, 2007

Science's role in upholding poverty

Now then, as there is always two sides to the coin, there is of course the other side—the perversion of the Mother aspect. And that perversion has come through science and the philosophy of natural selection, and the philosophy that everything in life is an outpicturing of the struggle for limited resources, thereby causing some to be more fit than others. And again, this has been used by those among the power elite, those among the forces of anti-christ who would not accept and would not submit to the authority of the Catholic Church. For they were the aspiring power elite who wanted to take power away from the established power elite, who had been in an alliance, an unholy alliance, with the Catholic Church for centuries.

And so the aspiring power elite saw that the emerging philosophy of materialism, especially boosted by the theory of evolution, was their vehicle for setting themselves up as the unquestioned rulers of this world, through their philosophy of materialism that there is nothing beyond this world. And that, again, elitism and the fact that some people are rich and that many people are poor is simply an outpicturing of the laws of nature, where those who are more fit have a right to rule, have a right to take unto themselves privileges, such as abundance, and keep the majority of the population in poverty.

My beloved, not only is this a complete fabrication. It is actually a perversion of the reality and the laws of nature. For you see, my beloved, if you were to carefully analyze history on this planet, even by using the knowledge that has already been brought forth through science itself – including the science of physics and the science of biology – if you were to perform such an analysis and read between the lines – look beyond the official doctrines of science, and refuse to listen to the priesthood of science – well then you would find that the theory of evolution is based on an utterly and completely false premise.

First of all, it is based on the consciousness of lack, the concept that this is a planet with limited resources. This is, as I have spoken about before, a complete lie. For the only real resource is the knowledge of people in embodiment, combined with the will to let God's light flow through them, thereby bringing forth more abundance than is in existence today. The will to become MORE.

And so, my beloved, it is not true that this planet has limited resources. For as Jesus said, with men this is impossible—meaning that when you are in the human consciousness and you deny the power of God within you, well then this planet does have limited resources. For it is not possible to bring forth greater resources through the power and the wisdom of man. And thus, those who have become completely identified with the consciousness of anti-christ and their identity of separation, well my beloved, they are indeed cut off from that power, so to them it seems as if this planet has limited resources.

But, of course, the reality is that when you exercise the potential, that all people have, to find the kingdom of God within you, well then it is possible to increase the amount of abundance on this planet. And in fact this is, despite what science says currently, this is precisely the force that is driving evolution on a planetary historical scale. As Maitreya explains in his book, the drive to be more, the drive to grow that is built into life—this is what causes species and the entire planet to transcend itself and come to higher and higher levels, greater and greater levels of complexity. And more complex life forms, of course, being an expression of abundance.

So you see, historically, that if it had only been the consciousness of lack and the competition for limited resources, well then this planet would not have been in an upward evolutionary spiral. It would have been in a downward evolutionary spiral and would long ago have disintegrated under the weight of that spiral. So the reality is that it is indeed possible to bring forth greater and greater resources, thereby overcoming poverty and giving the abundant life to all people. This is perfectly possible within the laws of nature.

Yet, what has been programmed into the collective consciousness through the philosophy of science and materialism is precisely that this is not possible, causing millions if not billions of people around the world to accept that this is simply their lot in life, and there is nothing they can do about it. For after all, my beloved, resources are limited, so how could all people be rich? How could all people have a certain standard of living?

...

The will of God always overcomes the anti-will

So it takes courage, it takes will, it takes determination to stand up against the mass consciousness and the elite who will use whatever power they have in society to ridicule and put down those who question their basic paradigms. Nevertheless, if you have the will, you will succeed. For you will stand up and the power of God working through you will turn back the opposition from those who also have will, but it is the anti-will that can never be as strong as the will of God. And why is that, my beloved?

Because the anti-will is based on the consciousness of separation and the consciousness of separation has built into it fear. My beloved, when you separate yourself from oneness with the Infinite, as we say in the new book The Art of Non-War, then it is inevitable that you become vulnerable to fear. For only in oneness with God do you escape fear.

And so do you see, my beloved, that the power elite on Earth might appear mighty because they have the outer weapons of power. And they seem to have great determination, even to use those weapons to destroy anyone who opposes them. But you need to look beyond it and say, "Why do they hide in their palaces? Why do they hide in their fortresses? Why do they hide behind their weapons?" It is because they have fear, and the greater the weapons, the greater the fear. For it is the only way they can keep it at bay so they can continue to exist without disintegrating into insanity because of the fear.

So, my beloved, look at them and see that their willpower is hollow. It goes only to a certain point. And when you overcome the consciousness of fear and lock in to the will of God – the will of God that is not based on fear but is based on love, my beloved, the unconditional love of God – well then you will know that their willpower and their determination and their weapons of power are simply conditions in the material universe. And they are not as powerful as the unconditional River of Life, where there are no conditions.

And thus, when you have that unconditional love, you will not accept any conditions on Earth as causing you to hold back the power of God from flowing through you. And when you allow that unconditional love to flow through you, you will seek to raise up all life, even those who are trapped and who are forming a power elite. You will not seek to destroy them, as some have done in the past, where they became the aspiring power elite seeking to destroy the established power elite because they wanted the position of the power elite.

Nay, it will not be so. You will walk the Middle Way where you will not seek the power, because you will seek to bring that power to the people, by bringing the abundance to the people. First of all by giving them spiritual abundance of ideas and awakening, and then also the material abundance.

So you see, my beloved, true willpower is not based on fear, but is based on love. And that love is God's Love, which is unconditional. And thus it is able to sweep aside and consume any conditions on this Earth that would hold back the changes that are mandated by the will of God, mandated by the laws of nature—namely that this planet transcend poverty and manifest the abundant life for all of the 10 billion souls that are meant to find a home on this planet and find the abundant life on this planet. For I tell you that this planet has the potential to sustain 10 billion people in a state of abundance, spiritually and materially. For if they have the spiritual abundance, then the planet will gratefully and lovingly outpicture the material abundance as well.

Overcoming poverty through the second ray of God Wisdom

Saint Germain, December 15, 2007

Why capitalism does not work

And, my beloved, from a realistic perspective you can look at the Western world and see that through capitalism there has been an increase in material wealth in many Western nations. And from this one might say that capitalism must work. But the reality is that capitalism does not work, but capitalism in the West has given greater freedom to individual initiative than was given in the communist countries. And therefore, there has been more of an opening for people in the West to express their creativity—and this is what has brought forth greater abundance.

The problem with capitalism is that it has allowed a small elite to exploit the creativity of the individual people, and use it to generate profit for big multi-national corporations instead of spreading the abundance to all people in society. And thus, my beloved, if you analyze the capitalist economy, you will see that it also has built-in limitations for how much abundance can be brought forth. And in fact, you will see that many of the older nations in Europe have already gone through a period where their economies started to stagnate.

The United States has started on this process but has not gone as far as the European nations had gone a decade or two ago. But you will still see a stagnation beginning. And what has kept this from being even accelerated further is only that capitalism has expanded to other areas of the world—and has therefore been able to spread the exploitation of the working people to those in other countries who – because they were living at the starvation level – have now been willing to work for wages that no sane person in the Western world would work for.

And this has then allowed the capitalists to continue to exploit the people, whereas the people in the Western world have become educated to how the economy works and how the labor situation is and thus would no longer allow themselves to be exploited to the degree that these people in other parts of the world are allowing themselves to be exploited, thereby providing cheaper goods to the Western world.

And, my beloved, what do those cheaper goods allow? Well, they allow the people in the Western world to feel that they still have some sense of material abundance. For they can buy inexpensive goods imported from China and elsewhere, which gives them the illusion that they can maintain their standard of living, perhaps even expand that standard a little bit. But in reality this only serves to maintain status quo, where a small elite in the Western world are becoming increasingly wealthy, whereas the people, the general population in the Western world, are actually seeing a lowering of their actual standard of living compared to what it was a decade or two ago.

The value of your labor

So you see, my beloved, what is it that determines your actual standard of living? Well, it is the value of your labor and your ability to express your creativity in bringing forth more abundance. But the value of the labor of the people in the Western world has actually deteriorated over the last few decades. And it has only been offset by the import of inexpensive goods from countries where the value of the people's labor is even less. And thus, the people in the West have been duped into thinking that they have expanded or maintained their standard of living, whereas in reality the value of their labor and their ability to express their creativity has deteriorated.

If they were aware of this, if they knew what was happening, they would have revolted against capitalism and they would have overthrown the capitalist system that allows a small elite of international financiers to keep the people in a state that is in an economic sense almost the same as the feudal societies of the middle ages—where the international power elite own the means of production and the means of exchange just as the feudal lords in the middle ages owned the land that back then was the only source of abundance.

Now, today the source of abundance is the means of production, the means of transportation, the means of exchange, including the money system. And that system is virtually owned as a monopoly by an international power elite that manipulate corporations, that manipulate countries, that manipulate currencies and the money system to their own benefit. Including, of course, what you see right now, where they have manipulated the price of oil, using crude oil as a way to extract inordinate amounts of money from the people, almost as a form of artificial taxation. Only that taxation does not even go to the government elected by the people, but goes to the international financial institutions and the big corporations who answer to no government elected by any people in any nation.

So you see, my beloved, there was a former American president who said that if the people understood how the money system works, there would be a revolution tomorrow. And I can assure you that if the people in the Western world understood how the money system truly works – and how it is set up in very subtle ways to allow the elite to maintain a monopoly on the means of production and on the money system – if they truly understood how they are being exploited by that system, well then they would indeed create a revolution tomorrow and demand a total reform of the money system on a planetary scale.

The Alpha and the Omega of ignorance

Thus, my beloved, do you see how the only thing that prevents an overthrow of the status quo in any society, in any historical period, has been that the elite has managed to keep the people in ignorance?

This ignorance has, as everything else, an Alpha and an Omega aspect. The Alpha aspect is that the people are kept in ignorance of their true identity as spiritual beings, as co-creators with God, who have the ability, my beloved, not to simply create abundance through what is already in the material realm. But they have the ability to draw forth spiritual light from their own higher beings, and use that light to bring forth a greater amount of abundance than is currently manifest in the physical realm. Thereby increasing the amount of resources and abundance available on Earth to truly create the abundant life for all people.

Yet the Omega aspect of this ignorance is that the people are kept in ignorance of how society works. And thereby, they do not clearly see how they are being exploited by the power elite. Go back to the middle ages, my beloved, and see how the Catholic Church in Europe served to keep the people in ignorance in the Alpha aspect by telling them that they were miserable sinners who did not have the ability to co-create with God—and who were not sons and daughters of God because Jesus was the only son of God and they were created as sinners.

And yet at the same time there was the Omega ignorance, where the feudal lords would not allow the people – that they believed they owned – to be educated—even to learn how to read and write, so that they had no possibility of truly understanding how they were being exploited. Nor did they have any opportunity to organize with other people and therefore put up a united front, as I talked about yesterday.

So you see, my beloved, what has changed in the modern world is, again, that you now have the possibility of spreading knowledge and information around the world. And thereby you have an unprecedented opportunity of awakening the people to both the Alpha and the Omega aspect of how they are being deliberately kept in ignorance—in order to prevent them from rising up and demanding a change in the status quo.

So you see, my beloved, what we of the Ascended Host desire to see happen is that the people realize that physical poverty, poverty that is based on a lack of money is only the effect of a deeper cause. And part of that cause is the spiritual poverty that comes from a poverty of knowledge, a lack of knowledge, a lack of understanding of who people are, a lack of understanding of how society works.

...

What really enslaves the people

Do you not see, my beloved, that what has kept the people in ignorance for thousands of years is that a small elite have prevented the people from realizing and accepting their built-in divinity and their Christ potential to escape any limitations, to go beyond any institutions on this Earth by connecting to a reality that is beyond the material universe and therefore can never be subject to, or restricted by, any institutions in this world?

And do you not see, my beloved, that the only way for the people to be truly free is to connect to something that cannot be controlled by any philosophy or institution on this Earth, something that is beyond any philosophy or force that springs from the consciousness of anti-christ?

My beloved, only by reaching beyond this world can the people be truly free. And they can reach beyond this world only when they discover, understand and fully accept the reality that Jesus attempted to teach humankind 2,000 years ago, namely that the Kingdom of God is within you.

Poverty is hatred of the Mother

Saint Germain, December 20, 2007

How Lucifer fell

For in hating the Mother, you can avoid looking in the mirror—seeing your own impurity. Instead of recognizing that the impurity is inside your own mind and energy field, you do what the ego does best—you project the impurity outside yourself, projecting it onto the Mother light, saying, "Oh this planet Earth is such a low place. There is such a lack of resources. There is such an imbalance in nature. Our bodies are so limited and manifest disease so easily. There is not enough money for everyone. There is not enough resources. There is not enough oil. Everything is so limited and restricted. And this is the Mother's fault, this is the fault of Mother Earth because she will not give us the abundant life."

And so you see, my beloved, you have an entire class of lifestreams that fell on the initiations of the fourth ray. Most of them fell in higher spheres, but it was the same basic initiation. And thus, you may know that Lucifer himself fell on the fourth ray, and he fell because of the pride of not being willing to look at his own impurities and therefore projecting those impurities on the Mother light, building up hatred of the Mother.

And you see, my beloved, this is where you need to understand how ingenious God's universe is designed, and how ingeniously the law of free will actually works. You see, my beloved, when a lifestream refuses to voluntarily look at the beam in its own eye, well then that lifestream has put itself beyond the reach of the true spiritual teachers of humankind. We cannot reach that lifestream, for we work exclusively within the framework of the law of free will. And thus, my beloved, you realize that there is no point in that lifestream remaining in the mystery school. And that is why the lifestream then falls or descends into a lower sphere, or outside of the mystery school. And what happens to that lifestream is that it descends precisely into a sphere that corresponds to its level of consciousness.

So you see, my beloved, when a lifestream has hatred of the Mother, it will descend into the most dense level of the world of form, which is currently the material universe, where it encounters the lowest vibration of the Mother light—and therefore has an opportunity to learn by encountering precisely that which it has come to believe is responsible for all of its problems. And so you see, that by being forced, so to speak, to face that which it was not willing to face in the mystery school, the lifestream has the only remaining opportunity left open to it to pass its initiations—and overcome the false beliefs that caused it to fall in the first place.

The question, of course, is whether the lifestream will actually do so or whether it will continue to build upon the momentum of denial, thereby building up more and more hatred of the Mother—until its time runs out and there is no opportunity left for that lifestream to become MORE, making it necessary for the lifestream – the separate lifestream – to be dissolved in the final act of dissolution in the Court of Sacred Fire. Where the intensity of the white light of purity burns away all impurities that have been built up over what would be corresponding to millions of lifetimes on Earth.

...

Understanding that the power elite are the most poor people

Yet, my beloved, as I have said, no matter how little you have you can always do more. But the reverse of that is, of course, that no matter how much you have, you can still refuse to do more with what you have. And thereby, you will see that some of the richest people in the world – in terms of money and material possessions – are in reality as poor spiritually, mentally, emotionally as those who are poor physically.

And thus, my beloved, I can assure you that when you look at the wealthiest people, the members of the power elite, you will see that if they are not sharing their wealth – seeking to raise up all life, but are using that wealth to control life – well then I can assure you, my beloved, that they have taken that wealth by force. And although a lifestream can build up a momentum that allows it to gather material wealth through force, I can assure you that by doing so a lifestream will diminish its spiritual wealth.

You see, my beloved, precisely because of the time delay built into the material universe, as Mother Mary explains, it is possible that a lifestream can misuse its co-creative abilities to take material abundance from other people by exploiting those people. The lifestream can get away with doing this for several lifetimes. And that is why many people have come to believe that there must be some injustice in the universe that allows certain people to be very rich or inherit great riches, even if they have done nothing to help other parts of life.

But you see, my beloved, the law of God is unfailing. And it works two ways. If you have little but do more with what you have, it is unfailing that the law will in the future give you more. But the reverse, of course, is that if you have much and refuse to do something for others with what you have, then in time – as cycles move on – well it is inevitable that what you have will be taken away from you.

And that is why you see, my beloved – when you look at the history of the world – you will often see that there have been societies that had a power elite who seemed to be untouchable. For they were simply so above the ordinary population that it seemed like their power and privileges could never be taken away from them. Yet, suddenly things shifted in that society. And through some natural occurrence or a revolution or other occurrence in society, well suddenly some of the richest people lost all they had, and now stood with nothing.

But they were worse off than the people, for they had never had to work for what they had and thus were not able to handle that situation psychologically—often going to pieces, as they say, instead of picking up the pieces and starting the path of initiation. The path of doing more with whatever you have, no matter how little or how much you have.

Without vision the people perish, but with pure vision they manifest a Golden Age

Saint Germain, December 24, 2007

The origin of inequality in society

And thus, you see in many past ages it has happened that those who were the dualistic leaders managed to create a society in which they had set themselves up in leadership positions. And positions that were untouchable, because the people could not challenge them—either because they did not have the physical power or because they believed that they could or should not challenge the leaders.

As was explained earlier, the Jews of Jesus' time had created precisely such a society. And this was a society, my beloved, in which they were very comfortable. And even though they had the concept that a Messiah would come, they were not actually looking forward to the coming of the Messiah. Of course, they would not have admitted this consciously, but subconsciously they were not willing to lose their comfortability, to lose their mortal lives in order to follow the Messiah. And thus, subconsciously they were happy to believe that the Messiah would come sometime in the distant future.

So when suddenly Jesus appeared and said, "I AM the Messiah and I am here NOW," they came up with all kinds of excuses for ignoring him. And they allowed the fallen leaders to kill his physical body in an attempt to prevent that he would overthrow status quo by overturning those tables of the spiritual money-changers—who had taken away not the money of the people but the consciousness of abundance of the people. Thus separating them from the flow of the River of Life, so that no one among the people could gather enough light, enough Christhood, to stand up and challenge those fallen beings in leadership positions.

A subtle secret about fallen beings

So you see, my beloved, I will now give you a very subtle truth that very few people on this Earth have understood. And I do not say this to cause any kind of pride in your being, although I do say it with the intention of giving you a test of whether you will respond with pride or not.

So, my beloved, what exactly is it that happens when a culture or society or a lifewave separates itself from the flow of the River of Life? Well, my beloved, they obviously are cut off from the creative forces of God, namely the expanding force of the Father and the contracting force of the Mother. They cannot be the open door for this creative force, and thus they cannot bring more abundance into their sphere, into the sphere of their planet. But more than that, you need to understand exactly what is going on in the minds of such beings.

Now, my beloved, to illustrate this let me ask you to imagine something. Imagine, my beloved, that you had a gun as you know them on Earth. And imagine you were walking in the forest – and you were starving and your family and community were starving – and you saw a deer that could provide nutrition to your community. And you took aim with the gun and fired the gun, and then the gun would fire and the deer would be killed. But if you flew into anger and raised that gun to shoot one of your fellow men, then the gun would refuse to fire.

Now you see, my beloved, this is how it is with the creative power of God, the flow of the River of Life. If you co-create with a pure intention and pure vision, then the power of God and the love of God – in perfect balance – will gladly and lovingly flow through you. They will flow with the eagerness of the God who wants to express itself through all of its sons and daughters. And thus, you will have the power of God for which nothing is impossible.

But you see, my beloved, when you try to express your co-creative abilities with impure vision, an impure intent, well then the power of God will not flow through you. We might say that the cosmic gun will not fire, and thus you will not have the power of God. You will only have the power you have garnered in your own being through your initiations on the first rays before you fell.

And so, my beloved, those who were the original fallen beings – who realized this mechanism after they had descended into the matter spheres – realized that they would soon run out of power if they did not do something. And so here, my beloved, is the plan they came up with in order to prolong their own existence in the matter realm for as long as possible.

You see, my beloved, we might say that the River of Life – the creative force of God – is creative, and by creative I mean something that is not predictable, that is not mechanical. And this creative force will work only when you have pure intention. And thus, it will not work for those who are trapped in duality and seek to limit other forms of life and raise up themselves. And so what they decided to create was a sphere in the material realm – not limited to planet Earth, but including planet Earth – where they had created a mechanical force in imitation of the creative force of God. A force that allowed them to express power with impure intentions.

The mechanization consciousness

And so this, my beloved, is precisely the beginning of what we of the Ascended Host have called the mechanization concept. So you see, my beloved, to return to my previous analogy of a gun, you know that a gun is a mechanical device. And if it is properly loaded and functioning, it will fire anytime you pull the trigger, whether you are shooting to get food, or shooting to kill another human being, or shooting for the mere sport of killing an animal even though you do not need the nourishment.

And this, my beloved, is precisely what the beings trapped in duality love—something that allows them to express their power without any of what they would call restrictions. For you see, my beloved, when you are separated from the flow of the River of Life, you think that the laws of God are restrictions of your creativity. But in reality they are not restrictions of your creativity, for what you are expressing is not creativity, it is a mechanical display of power, a dualistic display of power, my beloved.

And so, my beloved, you must understand that this concept, this consciousness of mechanization, has permeated virtually every aspect of life on this planet. And it is a clear perversion of the fifth ray. For the fifth ray of God Vision is precisely what is meant to empower beings to use their powers in a creative manner, by tuning in to their Higher Beings, thus expressing their creative powers in accordance with the laws of God so that they multiply all life.

And so, as a perversion of that, you have the creation of a mechanical device, which does not even have to be a physical device, where you do not have to be in alignment with the laws of God. You do not have to have pure intention in order to express power and force the Ma-ter light into an impure matrix, into an impure form. This, my beloved, is a consciousness that is very subtle, that has been given many subtle disguises and that in today's world – especially in the more technological part of the world – truly has deceived the majority of the population into believing that it is necessary, that it is good and that there is no alternative to it, my beloved.

And this is why you have an entire group of leaders on this planet – not only political leaders, but leaders in science, in the media, even in religion, my beloved – who believe in, are blinded by – and thus are continually promoting – an approach to life that springs from the mechanization consciousness. Where they are attempting to maintain their positions of leadership, privilege and power by keeping the people in a state of consciousness, where they are not being co-creators with God, for they dare not or cannot express their true creative powers.

And thus, they are literally living as mechanized beings, as a kind of biological robots who are doing the same thing over and over, never breaking out of certain boundaries. Because they have, like computers, like robots, been programmed to stay within their program and do what they were programmed to do and nothing more, nothing beyond it, nothing creative, but mechanically repeating the same actions, the same beliefs, the same patterns over and over and over again.

Discernment about technology

And so you see, my beloved, this, of course, is most clearly expressed in technology, where you have grown up from you were "this big," with technological devices that are entirely mechanical in nature. When you push the switch on the wall, the light will come on. And if it does not, well then you know there is something wrong that has to be fixed somewhere.

And this, my beloved, is where you need to use the discernment of the Christ mind. For I am not saying that all technology is wrong. For at this particular stage in the unfoldment of the growth of humankind and of this planet, technology does give many people freedom from the drudgery of physical, mechanical labor.

So you see, my beloved, if you go back to older times, you will see that many people lived in an agricultural society, where they were literally having to work night and day to scratch out a living from the meager conditions provided by the unbalanced state of nature. And thus, most of their time was caught up in simple survival, so they had little left over for spirituality of any kind. And thus, in my embodiments as Roger Bacon and Francis Bacon I did indeed set the stage for the emergence of modern science, which has brought forth much technology. And so you see, my beloved, what I realized those centuries ago was that humankind was so trapped in the mechanization consciousness that it would not be possible to bring them out of it through spirituality alone. And thus, I determined to – for a time – literally fight fire with fire by bringing forth the scientific method and thereby creating technological, mechanical devices that could set people free from the mechanical labor of scratching out a living from the Earth.

But, my beloved, it – of course – was not my plan or my intention that people should be trapped in this technological wonder age. Being so used to, so addicted to, technology that they would refuse to develop the creative powers of their mind to the point, where they no longer needed technology. Or where they could use technology wisely, to bring forth only that which could not – at the time – be brought forth through the powers of the mind alone.

Turning a spiritual teaching into a mechanical doctrine

So you see, my beloved, it is necessary for you who are the spiritual people to realize that there are many of the things you see on this Earth that are by no means ideal whatsoever. And thus, even we of the Ascended Host have to adapt our efforts to free humankind to what is possible to bring forth at a particular time, in a particular culture. And one aspect of this is, of course, that when we bring forth a spiritual teaching it is adapted to the consciousness of the people of the time. And thus, it is not meant to be turned into an infallible doctrine that can stand for all time.

For you see, my beloved, when human beings turn a spiritual teaching into such a fixed dogma, well then they turn a spiritual teaching into a mechanical "device." And now – instead of using a mechanical device to produce food or take them from one place to another on the Earth – well, my beloved, they now seek to use a mechanical device to take them from Earth to heaven. And they believe that the outer path – what Jesus called the broad way that leads to destruction, the outer religion

– can lead them to salvation. But they fail to see that it will never lead them to salvation because it is a mechanical path, my beloved.

And you must understand that this concept of a mechanical, outer religion that will guarantee your salvation was developed by a very small minority of the people in embodiment and the disembodied beings who are controlling them, as Maitreya explains in his book. And it was not developed, my beloved, because these beings actually believe that they can force their way into heaven through a mechanical path. For they – in their pride – have no intention of going to heaven. They do not want to have anything to do with God. They want to stay separated from God for as long as possible. And how can they do this, my beloved? Well, they can do this only when they turn the majority of the population into mechanical people, and especially when they do this to the top ten percent—those who have the greater connection to their Higher Beings, to the spiritual realm.

So you see, my beloved, the top ten percent are those who still have some connection to their Higher Beings, who have a pure intention of doing what is right for the All. But they have been tricked into expressing that pure intention through an impure vision that is affected by the mechanization consciousness. Whereby they believe that if they do what is prescribed by an outer religion, then they will not only be doing what is right to raise up other people, but they will also be securing their own salvation.

And thus, you see, my beloved, the fallen beings do not believe that a mechanical religion will work. They have only created a mechanical religion in order to trap especially the top ten percent but also the majority of the population into approaching salvation in a mechanical manner, thereby expressing whatever light they have through the mechanization consciousness. Thereby misqualifying that light with a dualistic human vibration that allows the fallen beings – who are cut off from the flow of light – to steal the misqualified light, use it to sustain their own beings, their own existence, use it to sustain their own leadership positions. Use it to secure their position as the money-changers in the temple who control the people because they have managed to make the people believe that the people cannot enter the kingdom of God without going through the outer religion and its leaders.

Growing up in a mechanistic society

My beloved, you have been brought up in a society, in a religion, that is almost completely inundated with this mechanization consciousness. But it is time for you to come to a higher level of understanding of the spiritual path. It is time for you to make a sincere effort, an all-out effort, to shake off this yoke of the mechanization consciousness.

It is time to take a stand and say, "I am not a robot. I am not a mechanical being. I am a son or daughter of God. I am a spiritual being. I am a creative being. I see who I AM and I am willing to purify my vision so that I will no longer express the power of God from my heart through the impurities of this mechanization consciousness that causes me to use my co-creative powers in a way that seeks to maintain a society, and a culture – and even nature – in a state that is less than the actual potential for this Earth."

This is keeping the Earth cut off from the flow of the River of Life, serving to maintain status quo that allows a small power elite to control the population and to keep this planet in a state of poverty – physical, material, spiritual, emotional, mental poverty – that causes the majority of the population to live at a much lower level materially and spiritually than is necessary, in order to make it possible to create the illusion that the elite is raised above the people.

Even though the reality is that the elite are more poor than all those below them – for they are more trapped in the consciousness of poverty, the consciousness of mechanization – than any of the people that are being led by these blind leaders who are truly heading for the ditch of duality, either the ditch on the one side of the road or the ditch on the other side.

True service means acceleration into unity

Saint Germain, December 25, 2007

Service and the removal of poverty

You cannot overcome poverty, my beloved, by re-distributing the amount of wealth that is already in the world, as the socialists believe. You can overcome poverty only by increasing the amount of wealth available in this world! So that there is enough for everyone and so that the power elite cannot continue to monopolize it because there is simply too much for them to control. And also in that you have spoken out and awakened the people to the existence of the power elite, so that they will not allow them to continue with their monopolization of the wealth, or by creating wars or by sustaining the consciousness that precipitates natural disasters.

My beloved, creative service is the need of the hour if we are going to have the Golden Age on this planet in the foreseeable future. And that is why, I, Saint Germain, use this opportunity – having set the foundation in my previous five discourses – to send forth the call into the mass consciousness, to all those who are a part of the top 10 percent, all those who are engaged in some form of service to others. I say to you now: "I Saint Germain, who is your sponsor, I call you to step up your vision, your approach, your attitude to service, where you realize that there is more to service!"

My beloved, what is the goal of life? It is to accelerate this planet until it outpictures the kingdom of God, and this can be done only when people are willing to become More. Thus, my beloved, you do not give service to life if you administer to some earthly need but basically leave the persons in the same state of consciousness in which you found them. You give service to life only when you demonstrate – clearly and un-equivocally, my beloved – that there is more to life. And that you do whatever is necessary by allowing yourself to be the open door for the light of God to accelerate that person so that they are shaken out – or inspired out – of their old state of limited consciousness and realize there is more to life, there is something to reach for, there is a goal.

Freedom means surrender into oneness

Saint Germain, December 29, 2007

Understanding the power of "One"

You see, my beloved, many years ago this messenger was very concerned – at a young age – about nuclear war. He went deep into meditation one night and cried out to God – feeling a greater degree of oneness with God on the issue of nuclear war – he cried out to stop this. And he felt a return current, a reassurance that there would not be a nuclear war, at least a large-scale nuclear war on this planet. But that was because – unbeknownst to his outer mind – he had vowed to play a part in holding the balance so that there would not be such a war.

Yet, my beloved, one person cannot necessarily hold a balance if millions of people pull in the other direction. Because, again, the law of free will must outplay itself in giving people the lessons they need in order to change their consciousness. And so, you will know that, in the previous dispensation, I gave warnings about the potential for a nuclear war. And that was because, from a realistic assessment, not enough people had made that determination, that a nuclear war could completely be avoided.

And so you see, my beloved, while there is value in one person shifting his or her consciousness, there is in most issues a certain critical mass that must be reached, so that there is a counter-balance between those who are willing to raise their consciousness and those who are not, including those who are simply indifferent without knowing better.

So when I say that it only takes one ascended master student to change a planet, this is true in the sense that one person making up his or her mind will shift the collective consciousness. But it takes a certain critical mass of individuals to prevent certain outer manifestations. For if one person, or just a very few, could remove some ungodly condition from this planet, well how would the majority learn the lesson and come to the point where they have decided that they too have had enough of this or that manifestation?

So you see, my beloved, the power of one must be understood at different levels of consciousness. And so, you see that there is value in YOU making up your mind, but that it is also necessary that you realize that you are not a separate individual living in a world with six billion other separate individuals. It is necessary that you contact the oneness in your own Being, which gives you the sense of oneness with your own I AM Presence, but also takes you to the next step of realizing your oneness with all other people.

And thus you realize, my beloved, that it is not always enough for you to come to an inner determination based on oneness with your own higher being. It is also necessary for you to fulfill the Omega requirement and go out and seek to awaken others, so that they can come into oneness with their own higher beings. And so that, eventually, a critical mass of people can come together in oneness on a particular issue, and therefore shift the collective consciousness.

...

Save the world by saving yourself

My beloved, what we desire you to see is that there comes a point, where focusing on the problems and the negatives actually becomes an excuse that the ego will use to get ascended master students to focus so much on changing world conditions that you simply say, whether subconsciously or consciously, "I do not have time to work on my personal psychology, for I have to save the world for Saint Germain."

But you see, my beloved, how do you save the world for Saint Germain? You do so precisely by starting with yourself, by overcoming your own ego, so that you come into that oneness with your own higher being. So that instead of running around doing, doing, doing, you are instead centered in the peace, the higher bliss, of Being.

And therefore, you are the open door which no human can shut, because you have decided not to allow your ego to shut that door that is your connection to your higher self. And therefore, the light of that higher self, the Being of that higher self, can radiate through your lower form and anchor its light, its vibration, here in the physical octave. And this, my beloved, has a far greater impact than anything else you can do, including any amount of violet flame decrees or rosaries.

This is not to say that you do not need to take outer actions. But what we desire to bring you to is the point, where your outer actions do not spring from the outer mind, and the outer will, and the outer determination. They spring from the inner reality of who you are, so your outer actions are based on Being. You are Being as you are doing. That will have the maximum impact on this planet!

The peace that passes understanding

At the same time it will also give you that deeper sense of peace that passes understanding, my beloved. Think about this expression from the Bible, the "peace that passes understanding." What does it mean, my beloved? Well what is understanding? It is the outer mind, the logical mind, the intellect. And the intellect is an analytical faculty that always operates with two dualities, two polarities. And so peace that can be understood by the linear, analytical mind must have an opposite in the form of anti-peace. Which is why many, many people – even many intelligent people on Earth – currently believe, even at subconscious levels, that there is no way to eradicate war on this planet. That it simply is not possible to be free of the ghost of war that will always haunt humankind.

Yet I tell you, my beloved, it is entirely possible to remove war from this planet. It is a completely realistic and attainable goal. And humankind is actually much closer than you would think by looking at the headlines here or there around the world. For as happened with slavery, there is a potential and a momentum built that could very quickly break through, where a majority of the people suddenly come to see that war is not necessary, that war can be avoided and that it is time for them to stand up and demand an end to war. Because they will no longer allow themselves or their children to become cannon fodder for the endless ongoing struggle precipitated by a small elite who are absolutely dedicated to destroying this planet and the Golden Age I have planned for Earth.

And thus, my beloved, we desire you who are the ascended master students to rise above that dualistic consciousness. Not that you isolate yourself from the world and suddenly no longer pay attention to the news. We desire you to know what is going on, but we desire you to be in a state where what is happening in the world would not disturb your inner peace, your inner connection to your higher being. So that no matter what might happen, no matter what conflict there might be, you can Be in that situation. And thus, you can be the anchor for the spiritual light that will prevent even a situation like you see currently in Pakistan from escalating into a more widespread conflict.

And thus, my beloved, you will have a situation where the power elite have planned a conflict, and they have set all of the people in motion to blow up this or that, to create this or that conflict. And they start executing their plan, but suddenly – to their surprise – the ball stops rolling, so to speak. Because the people who should have been drawn into the conflict refuse to be pulled into the vortex of negativity and conflict. Instead they stand back and say, "We will no longer engage in these energies."

And thus, the carefully orchestrated plans of the power elite come to naught. They just die out. And the power elite stand there and cannot understand how this could happen, "Why did our plans not work, as they have worked so many times before in the past? Where we just needed to create a tension and then provide the one little spark that lit the powder keg, and everything would blow up and people would be killing each other in the streets. And now they are not doing this."

Well, my beloved, it can very well be because one person – in a state of Being, in a state of Oneness – is holding the balance for tens of thousands or millions of people. So that they are not drawn into a conflict, but so that they finally stand back and say, "No we have to find a higher way, a higher approach to problems. We have to find a non-violent solution to our problems."

Diversity and tolerance are keys to a Golden Age society

Gautama Buddha, December 31, 2007

Why Golden Age societies deteriorate

And yet my beloved, why is it then that there have been several past golden ages that had attained a state where there was growth and abundance, yet they could not maintain that state and stay in that growth pattern? Well my beloved, the hidden explanation for this fact is that there has not in any past Golden Age been a sufficient awareness of the fact that there are lifestreams on this Earth who are so trapped in the duality consciousness that they simply cannot see any value in diversification and growth.

They do not want a society that grows, for in such a society all are becoming more, and thus there will be less of a difference between the low and the high. In fact, in a truly Golden Age society there will be no people who are seen as better or higher or more valuable than others. For all will be seen as being of equal value, being appreciated not for their standing or their rank in some hierarchy on Earth, but for their willingness to allow their built-in, God-given creativity to express itself through them, so that the most creative people are – not the most valuable – but the most appreciated.

And this, my beloved, is precisely what those who are trapped in the consciousness of duality do not want to see in a society, for in such a society, my beloved, they have no possibility whatsoever of attaining high positions. For the very fact that they are blinded by the duality consciousness means that they are cut off from the flow of the River of Life and thus cannot express their built-in creativity. They will not let that creativity flow, and thus in a society that rewards creativity they cannot attain high positions and thus cannot attain positions that give them the illusion that they are better than other people.

And since they are bent on attaining such positions, my beloved, you see that such people – who are driven by power – must stop creativity, for they see it as a threat. And thus, my beloved, how do these

lifestreams – which we might call the blind leaders of the blind as Jesus
calls it, or we might call it the fallen lifestreams – how do they manage
to destroy the Golden Age society and take it into a downward spiral?
Well my beloved, they do it, of course, by perverting the very driving force behind that society, which is creativity that expresses itself
through diverse manifestations.

And so, they take the diversity and they process it through their own
dualistic consciousness. And therefore, they come up with a thought
system, a philosophy, or even a popular culture that suddenly portrays
diversification as a threat, as a source of conflict. Where they manage
to get one distinctly separate group of people to see themselves as separated from the rest of society and see that those who belong to a different group are a threat to themselves, or a threat to society, or a threat
to progress, or a threat to God or whatever appeals to the people in that
society and culture.

So you see, my beloved, because there was not a sufficient awareness of the duality consciousness and how it affects the people who are
blinded by it, well because of that very reason, many past Golden Age
societies eventually went into a downward spiral. Where the people –
instead of seeing diversification and creativity as the very cause of their
abundance – now entered into the consciousness of seeing it as a threat
to the stability of their society.

They came to believe, my beloved, that maintaining a Golden Age
society, maintaining the kind of society and culture they had, necessitated the clamping down on the creative flow because the creative flow
was seen as the threat that could bring forth something that would upset
status quo and therefore threaten society. When, in reality, the fact is
that diversification and creativity is the only thing that can secure the
long-term survival of a Golden Age society, for that is the only way a
society can flow with the River of Life instead of becoming a closed
system that deteriorates through the forces described in the second law
of thermodynamics.

...

Understanding the false hierarchy

Thus, my beloved, we have sometimes talked about the fact that there
is a certain percentage of lifestreams who have been allowed to embody on this planet, and that they form – together with lifestreams in

the mental and emotional realms – a hierarchy which we have called the false hierarchy. Now my beloved, this is the force that I earlier said has destroyed many previous Golden Age civilizations.

And so, you who are spiritual people have gone through a phase, many of you, where you saw the necessity to make calls or decrees or call forth the judgment of the false hierarchy. And this was a necessary step, not only in the planetary unfoldment but also in your own personal growth. But many of you, my beloved, have reached a point where you are, as again was discussed earlier, ready to truly free yourself from the last very subtle remnants of the duality consciousness. And thus, I, as the Lord of the World – who truly holds the spiritual balance for all lifestreams who embody on Earth – I have determined to give you a teaching that is beyond what we have released earlier.

Thus my beloved, let me take you through a little bit of a thought experiment, an exercise of your imagination. You might, my beloved, start out with the image that was given in the books and movies that were popular in the recent time about the little hobbit Frodo who received the ring and had to bring it back to its creation point [Lord of the Rings]. And in so doing had to fight against this dark force that seemed to be permeating the universe and seemed to be emanating from a central point, where supposedly there was an evil emperor or sorcerer who was directing not only the force, but who was directing millions upon millions of orcs or other beings who were doing his bidding and were under his control.

Yet my beloved, I desire to give you a twist on this story. Now imagine, my beloved, that you look at the world and see that there are certain people who are seemingly committed to destroying peace and prosperity in the world. And you see deeper and realize that they are committed to this because they are in a certain state of consciousness. And you see, my beloved, that they are in this state of consciousness primarily because they are afraid. They are afraid that if they do not pursue a certain course of action, well, some calamity will befall them, such as burning forever in the hell that is the worst thing they can imagine.

So out of that fear of going to hell, they are afraid of going against those who command them to kill others in the name of God. And thus, you see that on Earth there is a certain hierarchy, as you have seen for example in past ages, where the leaders of a particular religion – even the supreme leader, such as the pope of the Christian religion – would command those below him to make war with the members of another religion. Thus killing other human beings in the name of their god, which they at the same time claim was a god of love who had given the commandment, "Thou shall not kill." And who had sent his only begotten son into the Earth, who gave the commandment to turn the other cheek and to love your neighbor as yourself.

Yet somehow, the logic was that if you killed in the name of this god, you would avoid a fiery hell that would otherwise come upon the Earth—if those of the other religion were allowed to spread their religion unhindered. And so my beloved, you have an earthly hierarchy but when you are a spiritual person and see deeper, you see that there is a non-material hierarchy that is actually pulling the strings, so to speak, of the marionettes that dance around on the Earth. But even those who seem to have great power, such as popes and emperors, are truly robots who are doing the bidding of some greater force behind them.

Facing your fear of the false hierarchy

And so you might, as some of you have done, open your awareness to the fact that there is a force beyond the material. And in the beginning, you might feel some fear about this force. And you might think, my beloved, that as there is a hierarchy of darkness on Earth, well there is an even greater and more powerful hierarchy in the higher realms – in the nonmaterial world – so that that false hierarchy has unlimited power, or almost unlimited power, over those who have been pulled into their sphere of influence.

And this, of course, has given many people on Earth – from various religions including ascended master students – a great fear of being influenced by this false hierarchy, my beloved. So that in that fear of being influenced by the false hierarchy, you become so concerned about keeping your consciousness pure that you actually – without realizing it – shut off the flow of the River of Life through your own being, shut off your own creativity by thinking that you need to be so afraid of experimenting with your own creative ability for fear of opening yourself to the false hierarchy.

So my beloved, many spiritual people who have gone beyond the "ignorance is bliss" of "seeing no evil, hearing no evil" have come to believe that there are these dark forces. And indeed, there are dark forces—I am not in any way denying that. But the image I want to give you here is that there truly is a false or dark hierarchy, a dark force that is organized into a hierarchy, my beloved. And so you can look on Earth and you can see that there are individual people who are driven by this evil force, who are blinded by it and some of them, for example, become serial killers.

But there is also a more organized form, where at certain points an entire society can come under the spell of the false hierarchy, so that they now unite their forces in seeking to kill the members of another society. And of course, if you want an obvious example of this, you can see the Nazi force in Germany as one modern example. But if you dare to look a little more closely, you can see that many societies have elements of this. Even modern-day America has certain people who are in high positions of power, who have come under the spell of this false hierarchy and thus become instruments for precipitating war and conflict on a planetary scale.

And yet, my beloved, when you look beyond these people on Earth – who have been blinded or taken over by the false hierarchy – you see that beyond them is a non-material hierarchy. And you might think of it in terms of evil spirits, demons, discarnates, entities, whatever you want to call them. But the main image here is that there are beings who are completely blinded by the consciousness of duality and thus are completely focused on and committed to expressing some form of darkness—even though they often believe it is for some greater good.

And so my beloved, if you conceive of this false or dark hierarchy as a pyramid, where the physical manifestations you see are the lowest level of the pyramid and beyond it is another level, and beyond that is another level—and all of it leads up toward the top of the pyramid. And you know, my beloved, of course that the pyramid ends in one single point. And thus, you have the popular image that at the top of the pyramid of the dark hierarchy is the devil or Satan or Lucifer or whatever that being has been called in various cultures and religions.

A journey into the illusions of darkness

Yet my beloved, now imagine that we put on the full armor of Archangel Michael, so that we are invulnerable to the dark forces, and we set out on a journey like Frodo who traveled to the depths of Mordor, the depths of darkness. We are traveling now through the different layers of the false hierarchy, the forces of darkness. We are traveling higher and higher towards the apex, the very top point of the pyramid.

And as we come closer and closer, we encounter various manifestations of darkness, as Frodo encountered on his journey towards Mordor. And we expect, of course, that as we come to the very top, we will find the ultimate temple of darkness, the ultimate building that houses the dark lord himself, who is at the very top of this dark hierarchy. And indeed, my beloved, as we penetrate through the deeper levels of darkness, we do see such a temple, a structure constructed with all kinds of evil or ugly manifestations of figures, of dragons, of gargoyles of whatever you can imagine on Earth.

And yet my beloved, as we get to this very temple itself, we see something peculiar. We see that surrounding the temple are beings who worship the temple, but those beings are so afraid to enter the temple that they never, ever enter the temple. They always reside outside. But we see that these beings form, so to speak, the top level of the dark hierarchy that we can see from our position outside the dark temple. And we see that they are so hypnotized, so focused on promoting or perpetuating a particular idea that they believe has been given to them by the dark lord himself. But we realize that none of these beings have ever seen the dark lord, they have never actually received that philosophy or matrix from the dark lord.

They believe it was given in the distant past, my beloved, to their forefathers, and they are simply continuing to carry out the instructions that they were given in the past. And they pass those instructions on to the next level of the pyramid, to those below them. And so those below them blindly carry out the instructions of their overlords, which they believe came directly from the dark lord himself, and so on down through the levels of the pyramid.

And now my beloved, we look at these that are – so to speak – the most advanced dark beings we have encountered on our journey, and we see that although they have great power over those below them, we see that they are actually driven by fear themselves—rather than being the powerful beings that their followers see them to be.

We see through them and see that they are hollow shells because they are driven by fear. And in their fear, they are actually mechanically carrying out what they believe to be the instructions of their dark lord. And although they believe that the dark lord is the counterpoint to God

– and thus as powerful as God – they really have no proof of this, for they have never seen the dark lord himself, my beloved. So when we realize this fear – and again, of course, being protected by the full armor of Archangel Michael – we say, "Well, perhaps we should do what they are afraid to do. Perhaps we should walk into that temple and take a look at this dark lord, who is supposedly as powerful as God himself."

And now my beloved, we gather our courage, and we walk through the temple gates and we encounter a great hall, and at the end of that hall is a great throne. But to our surprise we discover that there is no one sitting on the throne, save a little mouse, my beloved, who has snuck into the dark temple looking for food, but has found none and thus quickly runs away as it hears us coming. And thus, we stand there in front of that dark throne—and suddenly it dawns upon us, my beloved, that there is no dark lord!

Stop giving power to what is not real

There never was a dark lord! There never was an evil being who was the counterpoint of God and who was thus as powerful as God. You see, my beloved, what we realize in an instant is that all of the different levels of the hierarchy of darkness are worshipping a complete illusion. They are worshipping something that is not there, something that has no reality. And thus, we see something very profound.

The beings at the lower levels of the pyramid are afraid to disobey those above them because they believe those above them have power over them. And to some degree this is true, for when you are at the lower levels, well those above you have certain powers of black magic that they can use against you.

But we also see that the entire hierarchy leads towards the very highest level of the beings who are outside the temple, and we see that those beings are worshipping the dark lord that they think resides in the temple. But they do so because they believe that the dark lord is there and that he has real, actual powers over them, and thus will destroy them if they do not do his bidding. But we see that those beings – even though they have power over all of the beings below them in hierarchy – they are actually the most to be pitied—because they think that the dark lord above them has power over them. But since the dark lord is not there and the temple is empty, there is no power over them and thus there is no one who can destroy them if they do not do the bidding of the dark lord that is nonexistent.

And thus we suddenly see, my beloved, that this false hierarchy – which might appear to have power on Earth, or in the mental or emotional realms – actually has no real power. It is all an illusion, and that which is unreal cannot have power over that which is real—unless that which is real has fallen into the illusion of believing that the darkness is real, thereby – by affirming the reality of the darkness – giving the darkness power.

So do you see, my beloved, that we suddenly realize that those on the lower levels of the hierarchy of darkness are using their own energies to feed the illusion. And in so doing, they are sending their energies into a false matrix, and thereby they give their own energies to create a force which those at the next highest level of the pyramid can then use to control them.

In other words, those who are being controlled are themselves giving their own energies to those who control them. And thus, if those who are being controlled would stop feeding the energy to their overloads, well then they would take away the power that the overlords have over them. And when you see that this is repeated at each level of the pyramid, you see that it is not actually true – as you see portrayed in many myths around the world – that those who are immediately below the dark lord are receiving power from the dark lord himself.

For you see that there is no dark lord, so how could those who are at the top level of the pyramid receive power when there is nothing above them but emptiness? And so, you see now that the entire superstructure of the false hierarchy are not fed by the dark lord. They are fed by those below them, going all the way back to the human beings in embodiment who are not completely empty of light but still have some reality, some light in them. But who have been tricked into misqualifying this light through illusions and thereby feeding the entire superstructure of dark beings and the false hierarchy.

And so we suddenly realize that evil is not real and its appearance has no actual power over human beings—except what human beings give to darkness by misqualifying their own light with the illusions created by darkness. The illusions that people believe are real.

Overcoming the illusion that darkness has power

Now my beloved, you who are the spiritual people, many of you are right at that point where you are ready to fully integrate this truth that I have given you. Where you are ready to take that step, which finally and fully brings you out of the reach of the forces of duality. Which brings you to the point, my beloved, where the prince of this world will come but have nothing in you, whereby he can force you to go into a negative reaction that feeds your light to the darkness.

You are right at the point where one more step will set you free, so that you can sit as the Buddha under the tree and be confronted with the demons of Mara, the forces of this world. But no matter how they attempt to attack or tempt you, there is no attachment in you, whereby they can cause you to give power to their illusions. For you see through the illusions, and thus you are unmoved through your own perpetual surrender of all that is unreal. And do you see, my beloved, that many of you are at the point, where a slight turn of the dial of consciousness will suddenly open up your vision to see the complete unreality of all that is dark and evil? This my beloved, would not instantly remove that darkness from the Earth, for the law of free will allows that there are still many people who believe in the illusions of darkness. But there are two important aspects of you overcoming that illusion.

First of all that you, of course, are free of the pull of duality, free of the fear of the false hierarchy. You are anchored in the infinite peace of the Buddha, the infinite peace of Christ, the infinite peace of the Divine Mother, the infinite peace of the Divine Father, the infinite peace of the Holy Spirit. And by being anchored in that peace, well then you can step up to an entirely new level of holding the balance for the Earth, so that you can serve as a counterbalance to the people who are still blinded by duality and still think they have to do the bidding of the evil lord and those above them in the dark hierarchy. Which they often do not see as a dark hierarchy but see as the hierarchy of their own religion or the hierarchy of their political party. Or whatever illusion you have on Earth that is designed to trick people into giving their obedience and energies to the dark forces while thinking they are working for God or some ultimate cause.

And this, truly, is how you hold the counterbalance, my beloved, against the forces of darkness—when you realize that there is no dark lord. There is no reality to the forces of darkness, but you also realize that too many of your brothers and sisters are still blinded by that illusion that darkness is real and that is has actual power over them. And so you recognize that there are many people who are not yet ready to let go of that illusion. And why are they not ready my beloved? Because they are not ready to take a look at darkness. They are not ready to acknowledge that if they are engaged in the dualistic struggle – even though they believe they are fighting for a good cause – they are actually working for the hierarchy of darkness. They are afraid to acknowledge that—because they would feel such remorse and self-condemnation that it would take them lifetimes to heal from that wound. And even those who are willing to acknowledge that fighting can never come from the hierarchy of light, they still are afraid to take a close look at the hierarchy of darkness, following it all the way to the top and then finally seeing that there is nothing at the top and therefore it can have no power.

And so you see that it is necessary that there is a certain percentage of people who will hold the balance that gives the rest of humanity more time to build up the maturity and the courage, where they are then able to look at the darkness, to see it for what it is and thus use their free will to abandon it. And you see that it is necessary that some will hold the balance, so that the people who are blinded by the darkness will not plunge this Earth into a negative spiral of violence that will prevent the manifestation of the Golden Age.

Hold the vision of an awakening from the illusion of darkness

So what you need to hold the vision for, my beloved is that humankind will be pulled out of violence and will be raised gradually into the Golden Age consciousness. And the vision you need to hold, my beloved, is that this happens by more and more people being awakened to the value of tolerance the value of diversity, the value of creativity—and that it is through creativity that humankind will solve its problems, not through control. That it is through finding creative solutions rather than repeating the mechanization consciousness of thinking that it is by enforcing one particular solution, one particular belief system, that supposedly has the solution to all problems but in realty does not have the solution to any problems but will only reinforce the dualistic struggle.

And so my beloved, I desire you to hold the vision that this awakening will spread like rings in the water. And that when you fully awaken to the reality of light and darkness – seeing the unreality and darkness, and seeing the reality of God and the reality of the statement of Christ that with God all things are possible – and therefore, truly, the Golden Age can manifest and emerge as the phoenix bird that rises from the fires of the conflicts you see in the present world.

I desire you to hold the vision for that awakening of humankind, my beloved, to the value of creativity, the value of their own built-in creativity—that they can all play a part in bringing forth creative solutions or supporting creative solutions to the problems that for thousands of years have caused conflict. Including, my beloved, creative solutions in the field of religion and spirituality, so that religion will no longer be the trigger for violent conflict that will set the world ablaze. And thereby create a spiral that people cannot free themselves from, where they mindlessly and mechanically kill those who belong to a different religion, becoming like robots that are completely taken over by the dark forces who want to kill and destroy.

Chapter 7:
Teachings about fallen angels, 2008

Freedom is found only by forgiving everything

Kuan Yin, March 22, 2008

What Balance Could Have Done for America

And so, my beloved, had there been a greater balance on both sides, a greater integration; you would indeed have seen a very different nation that would have had a greater balance between Father and Mother. And thus, you would not have seen many of the manifestations that have taken place in American society.

For example, you would have seen a greater respect for the value of the individual, for the value of all people, and the need to spread abundance among all people. As you indeed saw in many of the native tribes, where they did not have anyone who was particularly rich and above the rest. Nor did they have anyone who was particularly poor and below the average, for they took care of each other. Many of the early settlers did likewise in their small communities, for they needed to stick together to survive.

But as America grew, you saw a moving away from this. And you saw how the power elite started to gradually gain an inroad in the American government, so that they undermined the value and the respect for the individual. They created a mentality that was so alien to the first

American revolutionaries and their desire to create a society with equal rights for all.

They created a society that was much closer to the feudal societies of Europe, where you now have – not a noble class that is noble by birth – but you have a rich power elite, many of whom are born into their positions. But you do have some openness that someone can move into the power elite by accumulating enough money and thereby becoming a member of the club. Although, perhaps not as valued as those who come from old money, as they say.

And had this development of the power elite and the power elite mentality been averted, then many other calamities could have been averted. For example, the United States would not have entered into the First World War at all. For it was truly the power elite who manipulated the United States into that war for the sake of monetary gain and increasing their power over American society. Likewise, the Second World War might have been averted or it could have taken a different form with the killing being much, much less than it actually was.

Envisioning the money system of the Golden Age

Saint Germain, March 22, 2008.

Understanding the divine economy

You see my beloved, as we have explained, there is indeed a power elite on this planet who want to enslave the people and have the people work for them as worker bees to create privileges. And so you see, my beloved, what you are dealing with in the economy is two different states of consciousness that are opposing one another.

You see my beloved, in Jesus' parable about the servants who received different numbers of talents, you see the principle for how the divine economy works. You are given certain talents through your ingenuity and your labor and your willingness to take initiative. You multiply those talents, and then you receive more in return because you have been willing to fulfill your role as a co-creator with God on this planet.

For as Jesus also said, "Fear not little flock, for it is your Father's good pleasure to give you the kingdom." It is your Father's good pleasure to give you the abundant life. So you see, my beloved, when all people take what they have been given – whatever talents that may be individually – and they make the best of it, they multiply what they have. Well, then, they bring forth more abundance than what they were given.

And this then opens up the doorway to heaven, where we can multiply what you have multiplied and bring forth even more abundance, whereby the total amount of abundance available on this planet is increased. And this then opens the possibility that the entire economy can grow, whereby all people receive more abundance. Not necessarily in the way of the communist dream, where supposedly all are given an equal share, but in the way of the money system and the economy becoming another tool for the path of individual Christhood, where people are rewarded according to their willingness to multiply their talents.

And as I said, there are three ways you multiply the talents:

- Through your ingenuity of bringing forth new ideas, new inventions, better ways of doing the same old tasks.

- Through your willingness to take risks by taking an initiative by doing something that no one has done before—and therefore you cannot know what the outcome will be.

- By your willingness to put forth the labor that is needed in order to get the economy to run.

So these are three legitimate ways to multiply your talents, my beloved. And truly, when you look at history, you will see that the majority of the people on this planet have been willing to multiply their talents in at least one of these ways. The majority, of course, choosing the role of doing the actual labor but yet many other people also being inventors or taking the initiative.

The perverted economy

This then is the consciousness of multiplying the talents and thereby increasing the amount of abundance. And this is, of course, the Christ consciousness, or aspects of the Christ consciousness. In contrast to this consciousness, my beloved, is the consciousness that springs from the mind of anti-christ, and it is the consciousness of wanting something for nothing. Or as a variant of that, the perversion of wanting to reap the reward of other peoples' labor.

This then is the perversion of the father-mother element, where wanting something for nothing is the perversion of the Mother, where you seek to reap without sowing. And wanting to reap the reward of the other peoples' labor is the perversion of the Father element, where you seek to control and suppress others and set yourself up above them because you have created the division of separating man from God. And therefore, all cannot be equal in God, for as I said, only through the connection to the spiritual realm can you have true equality.

So when that connection is lost in a civilization, you inevitably open up for the creation of an elite, who will then suppress the people and reap the rewards of the labor of the people. Which is what you saw, my beloved, in the feudal societies of Europe, with a noble class who had the physical power to suppress the people and make them work for them.

Yet when people are physically suppressed, it is very difficult for them, of course, to fail to notice that they are suppressed. So when the feudal societies collapsed, there were those among humankind who realized that this was not the ultimate way to suppress the people—that there was a much better way to suppress and control the people, namely in hidden ways so that the people did not realize they were suppressed.

What is real money?

And some among these fallen beings, my beloved, realized that with the growing economy that actually resulted from the collapse of the feudal societies – giving rise to better trade and the Industrial Revolution – well then, the creation of this new medium of money gave them an opportunity to control the people by controlling the money system, my beloved.

And thus, they realized that the money system, if they could manage to pervert it, would give them incredible opportunities for suppressing the people and stealing the value of their labor—without the people understanding what was happening. And my beloved, this has now been going on for a long time, and the people still are not realizing how the value of their labor is being stolen through a manipulation of the money system. And so you see, my beloved, without going into a long and overly complex discourse, I will give you the few highlights you need to understand.

What you need to understand, my beloved, is that when money is used correctly as a medium of exchange, well then you have only a need for the amount of money that is needed to exchange the total amount of goods and services that are produced by a society. There is, so to speak, a one-on-one relationship between the amount of money and the amount of something that has real actual value, be it goods or services. Or even, in the case of gold money, that the gold itself has a certain value. So you see, my beloved, the direct relationship between money and something that has real value.

Then, when people actually multiply their talents, they can, as a result of that multiplication, accumulate a certain amount of money which they can then choose, if they will, to store for times when they may not be able to make the money. Even this is legitimate, as long as the money was created as a result of providing a real service to life, be it an invention, taking the initiative, or performing physical labor.

There is nothing wrong with then storing that money, although, of course, when it is put to use in investing, then it will help the economy grow. And thus, savings should really only be a temporary thing and should not mean that the money is permanently taken out of circulation. For money is indeed meant to flow and thereby help the entire economy grow.

But you see, my beloved, when there is a direct correspondence between money and something of real value, well then it is not possible to create money out of nothing, money that has no real value associated with it. And that means, my beloved, that even though the money supply can grow, the value of money is not degraded, for you still only have the money needed to buy goods and services.

And therefore, you can actually have a society that has a steadily growing economy and a steady increase in the money supply without actually having an increase in the prices of goods and services. For what is the need of such an increase, when you do not have excess money that has no correspondence to real value? You still only have the amount of money needed to exchange goods and services, which means that the value of the money – what you can buy for that money – will remain constant.

When money is disassociated from real value

Perhaps it is even possible that as productivity increases – as new methods for producing goods and services cheaper and with less labor are invented – well then prices can actually decrease. Or you could say that the value of your labor goes up, so that you can buy more for the same amount of labor put in. And thus, everyone experiences an increase in abundance.

This, my beloved, is the divine economy, which we might also call the spiritual economy or even the natural economy. For you see in nature that if you take even the theory of evolution, as flawed as it is, it does point out the very fact that nature itself has a built-in force that produces greater and greater abundance of life forms and more complex life forms and greater numbers in different species, so that every niche in nature is filled and there is nothing wasted. And so you see that nature has a built-in force that leads towards greater abundance for all life.

Yet my beloved, how do you then get away from this divine economy? Well, you do so very simply by perverting the money system, so that you disassociate money from something that has real value. This has been done in various societies – starting in Europe – over time. And why did this happen, my beloved? Well, if you look at the history of this, you will see that it started with some of the kings in Europe who needed money to wage war with each other. And therefore, they needed excess money, more money than could be raised through the production of goods and services.

For you see, my beloved, war cannot produce something of value. It can only destroy something of value. So even though there are those who will say that war leads to economic growth, this is actually a fallacy. War can only lead to a loss through the destruction of something that has real value, including the killing of soldiers who could have otherwise been put to productive work and therefore produce something of value instead of killing each other.

So what you see is that the very kings that I attempted to work with during my sojourn on the European continent as the Wonderman of Europe – the very kings that rejected me and rejected the idea of the United States of Europe – well those very kings were the ones who in their greed for money – more money that they could tax from their subjects – set the stage for the emergence of a money system that was perverted.

You see my beloved, even though the kings of the Middle Ages and later had great power, even they had a fear of their own people. And thus, they knew that if they raised taxes in order to finance their wars, well then the people might actually revolt against them and they might lose their power and privilege. So they saw that they needed to find some other way to finance their wars.

And thus, they entered into an unholy alliance with the emerging bankers of Europe who started out as the goldsmiths who stored the excess money that people had legitimately earned. And they stored the gold in their vaults, my beloved, and they started realizing that they could make money out of lending that gold and charging interest. And since it was very rare that all of the people would demand all of their gold at the same time, they started lending out the money that people had deposited in their vaults, even though it was not theirs to lend. And so you see the beginning of the banking system.

And thus, my beloved, the kings of Europe were open to the suggestions of the bankers, who suggested that instead of having money that was based on gold or silver – thus the money had an inherent, indigenous value – you created a new type of money, called fiat money—that was, money by decree. Where the king issued a law that this newly created money was now the legal tender, the legally approved form of money in society, and all people had to accept it as payment for goods and services. Whereby, my beloved, the bankers could create this money, lend it to the king, who could then use it to buy the goods and services needed to finance his war.

The deception of fractional reserve banking

And so you see now the beginning of a money system, where there is no longer a direct correspondence between the amount of money and the amount of goods and services. There is now a disconnect between the money and something of real value, which means you can now create excess money – money, my beloved, that is not the result of someone multiplying their talents, but is literally created out of nothing by the bankers lending money, charging interest for it, but actually lending more money than they have reserves for in their vaults. Thus, the emergence of the system called fractional reserve banking, which is what your banking system in the United States and most of the civilized world is based on even today.

And so, you see now the emergence of a money supply that is disconnected from real value, which means that the kings and the bankers can now increase the money supply beyond what is needed to trade goods and services that have real value. Yet, my beloved, what happens when you increase the amount of money?

Well, suddenly there is more money in circulation, and what does that mean? That means that the first people who get a hold of the newly issued money, those people who did not have to work for it, they can now spend it, and in so doing they will inevitably bid up prices of goods and services, including real estate. And therefore, they increase prices, which gradually filters through the economy until the prices of all goods and services have gone up.

And so, to simplify this process for you, if you have a certain amount of goods and services and you have a certain amount of money needed to trade those goods and services, well, my beloved, if you doubled the amount of money by creating money that is not backed by precious metals or other things of value, then eventually – in fact in a short period of time – this will result in the fact that the prices of most goods and services will also double. Or at least go up to some degree to adjust to the fact that there is now more money in circulation.

Inflation steals the value of your labor

But you see, my beloved, what has happened in this process? Well, what has happened is that the value of the labor of the majority of the population has now been reduced because you still only work x amount of hours, and you are still paid x amount of whatever the monetary unit is. But you need more money to pay for the goods and services you need in order to survive.

And this then leads to a spiral, my beloved, where in the beginning, of course, of the Industrial Revolution – when this new money system started becoming the norm – well the people who did the actual work, the value of their labor was degraded to the point where they could hardly maintain a living. Which necessitated that the workers started organizing into labor unions, who then demanded higher wages, which then the employers were forced to pay. But in so doing they created a spiral where, again, those in the power elite simply created more money out of nothing to pay the higher wages. And so for a time the workers were happy, but as the filter-down effect on prices took place, then again the value of their labor was degraded. And this has continued, my beloved, to the present day.

How the people uphold the system of the elite

Now of course, you will look back at history and see that if you compare what an ordinary laborer is paid today, to what a laborer was paid a hundred years ago, you will say the laborer today can buy more goods and services and has a higher standard of living than they had a hundred years ago. And this is true, my beloved. But why is this true?

It is true because part of the money that was created out of nothing has been, so to speak, absorbed into the system, through the fact that people have continued to multiply their talents. They have taken initiative, they have brought forth new inventions, better methods for fabrication, and they have become more productive in their work. So that the average worker today can produce much more than the average worker could a hundred years ago.

So you see that those people who are still functioning in the state of consciousness of not wanting something for nothing – but being willing to work to earn a living – well they have, so to speak, underwritten the system of the elite by adding real value to the economy. And this has prevented the inflation created by an increase in the money supply from reaching such proportions that the economy literally would collapse because the money had no value.

As you have indeed seen in certain circumstances, such as Argentina and Germany, where you needed a wheelbarrow full of paper bills in order to buy a loaf of bread because the money was worth next to nothing. In fact, there have been periods where the value of the money, where the money itself, literally was not worth the paper it was printed on. So it was cheaper for people to light the fire with money than to use the money to buy firewood, my beloved.

Inflation is a hidden form of taxation

And so, you see that the money system – the fiat money system based on fractional reserve banking, based on creating money out of debt – has a

built-in inflationary factor that inevitably will cause the system to collapse. Because those who are in charge of such a money system cannot
contain their greed, my beloved. The king will want more money, the
bankers will want to make a greater profit. And why not, when all they
need to do is roll the printing presses and print more money?

And therefore, they inevitably become blinded by that greed, and
they set the economy into an inflationary spiral that will destroy the
economy—if it is not balanced by the real people performing real labor, real goods and services. And therefore increasing the amount of
services so quickly that the money supply, the money system, does not
collapse, does not go into the tailspin of an inflationary cycle that cannot
be stopped.

So do you see that even though you can say that the average worker,
the average citizen, is better off today, this is true—but this is only true
because they have been willing to multiply their talents. But what I want
you to understand here is that through the money system, the people
have not reaped the natural God-given reward of the multiplication of
their talents. Because through the increase of the money supply and inflation, they have, in fact been taxed, my beloved.

For inflation is indeed a hidden form of tax, where the people do not
realize they are taxed because they do not see it on their tax bill or their
paycheck—that x amount of dollars have been taken out of their paycheck. What they do not see is that the value of the money, and thereby
the value of their labor, has been reduced.

Concentrating wealth in the hands of the elite

So what I want you to understand is that if there had been a divine
economy over this last century and more, then the standard of living that
you see today would have been even higher. And if that economy had
been truly divine, then you would see a state where there would not be
any poverty left for any people in the western civilized nations.

And indeed, you would also have seen a worldwide economy, where
the standard of living would have gone up tremendously in what you
today consider the poor nations—where, indeed, so many people must
exist on less than two dollars a day. This would not have taken place in
a divine economy, because the value of the abundance would have increased so greatly that there would have been enough to pull everybody
up to a decent standard of living.

And so, what you see here is that the power elite – through the perversion of the money system, and through eroding the value of the fiat money that they have created – well then they have managed to actually delay the God-ordained growth in the economy and the manifestation of the abundant life that should have come about by now—if it had not been for this intervention of the power elite.

And so, what has happened instead, my beloved, is, as I explained, that the first people who can spend the newly created money – the money that has no correspondence to real value – well they can, of course, buy goods and services with that money at the old prices. Because only as the new money circulates through the economy will prices go up.

So what you actually see here is that over the last century and more, you have seen a greater and greater concentration of wealth in the control of a smaller and smaller elite. So that you now, literally, have five to ten percent of the population in the United States who control the majority of the wealth in this nation. And my beloved, even the top two percent control the majority of that wealth. And this, of course, is not the divine economy, where there is abundance for all.

How today's "kings" finance their wars

And so you need, as the spiritual people, to educate yourself to how this works, and we will indeed provide more instruction on this. But certainly, I encourage you to come to understand this by studying at least the basics of how the money system currently works. And you will see that this is an absolute perversion of the abundant life of God. This is nothing more than the power elite – those who are trapped in the duality consciousness – seeking to control the people through the money supply. And you will know, my beloved, that one of the original bankers that created this system said, that if you allowed him to control a nation's money, he did not care who made the nation's laws, for he knew that the nation could be controlled through the money system.

And so, you need to see this – even in today's world, my beloved – that this is still going on. In the United States, for example, you have the unholy alliance between the federal government – which is at least a federal agency – and the Federal Reserve, which as most of you know – but which most Americans do not know – is not a federal agency. And therefore is not answerable to the people in a direct manner by the people being able to vote.

So you see, my beloved, what is happening here is that the government of today also faces the situation that they want to spend more money than they know the people are willing to pay in taxes. And so where to do they get the money from? They create it, or they let the bankers create it out of nothing, thereby eroding the entire value of the money—and thus taxing the people without the people being aware of this.

So take a modern example of this, my beloved, and imagine that President Bush in 2003 had said to the American people in his State of the Union Address: "I have decided to go to war against Saddam Hussein, and my people tell me that this will cost each American family 2,000 dollars over the next year, so expect to see an increase in your tax bill."

Well, my beloved, do you think the American people would have been very positive towards such an announcement? Many of them, surely, would have revolted against this—a war that they from the beginning were not really sure was necessary and would rather have avoided. So what did the president do? Well, he simply set the money machine in motion, and the Federal Reserve created the money out of nothing, lending it to the federal government so that they could spend it to buy the goods and services that were needed to start the military invasion in Iraq.

The magical money machine

And this, my beloved, is not only done for war. It is done for many other aspects of the economy, where the government wants to spend more than they think the people are willing to pay in taxes, so they simply camouflage it as inflation so that the people pay it anyway. But now they do not notice and thus they do not object.

And of course, the bankers and those in the top financial elite, they make the money off of it, because you the people not only have the degradation of the value of the money but you also pay the interest of the federal debt, my beloved. Or perhaps you do not pay it, but your children or grandchildren might end up paying it—unless, of course, they continue the scheme indefinitely.

For the bankers are not necessarily concerned about having you pay back the debt—as long as you keep paying the interest and allowing them to create more money out of nothing, so that they can keep their money machine rolling. Yet, my beloved, you do need to educate yourself to the connection between war and money. For even though I said that the kings were open to creating fiat money to finance their wars, you should not be so blind that you do not see that the bankers quickly realized that there was no better way to earn a profit than to set nations against each other in Europe so that they went to war.

For once two nations are committed to war, my beloved, well is it not so that suddenly they feel a need to spend whatever money is needed to defeat their enemy? And thus, they spend more money than they ever would have done in peacetime. And so who makes the money off of it? Well, certainly the bankers, who in many cases in Europe financed both sides of the conflict, my beloved, and also opened the weapons plants that produced the weapons used in the conflict. And thus, they made a profit all around, while the people paid not only with their blood in the war but also with their sweat and blood as they worked to produce the real value that was needed to keep the system going.

The modern form of slavery through money

This, my beloved, then is a form of slavery that is far beyond the physical slavery that you have seen with the native peoples of this continent being sold into slavery, or people from Africa being imported into slavery. For again, this was a physical slavery that the people were surely aware of.

But the slavery that you are under is a slavery that most people do not understand, and therefore they cannot object to it because they do not even know. They just notice that they have to work harder and harder, and they do not understand why this is so. But they do not muster the will to be more and to educate themselves as to why they have to work harder, as to why it seems their dollar is not stretching as far as it used to.

And so you see, my beloved, again, that you have the situation that Kuan Yin explained—that everything that happens in the material realm is an outpicturing in matter of the consciousness of the people. So the people themselves – by not being willing to take responsibility for their society, for their money system – well they draw unto them those who are willing to pervert the system and take advantage of the people.

And this then, my beloved, becomes a vicious circle that only has two potential outcomes. Either the people wake up, educate themselves, and demand the return to a divine economy with a sound money system. Or the power elite will inevitably keep increasing the money supply in their greed and their blindness and even their spiritual pride, where they think they will never have to suffer the consequences of their actions. For they are so used to the people bearing the karma and the consequences of their actions that they think they can get away with anything.

And thus, you cannot expect the power elite to stop this downward spiral. And thus, if the people do not put on the brakes, then it is just a matter of time before the money machine will run amok, my beloved. And as you see with a train that runs faster and faster and faster – until the wheels start coming off and everything flies apart and the whole system collapses – and then you will be faced with the necessity to return to a sound money system.

Do you want an economy for the people or an economy for the elite?

Saint Germain, September 21, 2008

I am indeed Saint Germain. I hold the Flame of Freedom for the Earth. But what exactly does that mean? It means that I have become completely and utterly one with the God Flame of Freedom. And I have vowed to radiate that Flame of Freedom to this planet for the next cycle of the Aquarian Age. Thus, my beloved, I have earned the title of the God of Freedom for the Earth, as I have become one with that God flame.

Yet, I prefer not to use this title, as it can easily be misunderstood and mistaken by human beings as an excuse for building idolatry, my beloved. And thus, I would speak, in the beginning of this discourse, about idolatry. For indeed, idolatry is one of the main lessons that humankind was meant to overcome during the Piscean Age.

And what they have done instead, my beloved—they have built an even greater idolatry of Jesus, who came to set all people free from idolatry. Not only the idolatry of self but especially the idolatry of the fallen beings on this planet, those who are entirely trapped in the duality consciousness, because they have become completely blinded by their own egos. And thus firmly believe the illusions of the ego, believe those illusions to be an absolute, undeniable and unquestionable truth. Thus having the ultimate idolatry of having elevated a lie to a truth, and thereby thinking that by adhering to the "absolute truth," they have elevated themselves to some ultimate status compared to other human beings.

And thus, my beloved, you see, indeed, that idolatry is the veil of ignorance, the veil of illusions, that keeps the majority of the population trapped in the illusion that they need an elite to stand between themselves and God. Was this not, my beloved, what Jesus challenged when he challenged the scribes and the Pharisees and the temple priests and money changers—who had set themselves up as an elite between the people and their God, perpetuating the illusion, the lie, that people were not free to go within their own hearts and find God directly. But that they could contact God only through the outer religion and its priesthood.

. . .

Idolatry and the economic crisis

And why, my beloved, do I choose to start talking about idolatry? Well, is it not because it is precisely idolatry that is the central problem in the current economic crisis? What have you seen perpetuated by the press and the media, by government officials, by leaders in various economic organizations such as the Federal Reserve or big banks? Well, my beloved, is it not the consciousness that certain organizations, companies and institutions are "too big to fail," and thus the government must step in and prop up those colossuses so that they do not tumble?

You see, my beloved, what is this if not idolatry? And the underlying truth here is that it is the idolatry of the people, perpetuated throughout the Piscean Age and earlier, that they cannot exist without the power elite of fallen beings. This, my beloved, is precisely the problem that you see on Earth. It is the illusion that prevents the people from standing up and taking back their God Power, the power of God within each and every one of them. And it is the illusion that is being perpetuated by the elite itself - the elite in the media, the elite in the government, the elite in businesses and finance and banking.

For they desperately cling to their positions of power and privilege. Yet, underneath it all, some of them are beginning to realize that their days are numbered. And that the days of their power and privilege over the people—those days are numbered too, my beloved. For they see that this cannot go on forever. And that it is only a matter of a relatively short time before the people will rise up, as they have done before against the feudal system, and other examples of the power elite having attained almost total control over the people.

Many among the power elite are, of course, still blind to this. But some of them are beginning to see it. Thus, my beloved, what I desire you to be aware of, what I desire you to envision and what I desire you to make calls on, is that the people are awakened from this idolatry of thinking that they need an elite. An elite of selfish and self-centered people in order to continue a society with stability.

For you see, my beloved, we of the Ascended Host are not in any way, shape or form attached to stability. We want growth! And sometimes, growth means that you must throw off the old, by letting it become shattered—if that is what is necessary, because the people cling to it to the point of almost insanity, of not being willing to let it go.

So you see, my beloved, we certainly prefer a smooth transition from the current economic system to a Golden Age economy. We prefer to minimize the suffering and the loss. Nevertheless, we do not prefer this to the point where we are willing to prevent the people from learning their lesson. And thus I trust that you will see, that it is not appropriate for you to make calls for the stabilizing of the economy. It is not appropriate for you to make calls for the propping up of the institutions created by the fallen beings. It is not appropriate for you to make calls that support the power elite.

You need to make the calls and hold the vision that the people learn their lesson. And that those who will not learn receive the judgment of Christ, so that they can be removed. This, my beloved, is what will bring progress. And if it requires a few bumpy turns of the road, then so be it. For I tell you, it is a necessity that the people learn what can be done to misuse the economy before they will be ready to accept the economy of the Golden Age.

For I tell you, my beloved, that if I had an instrument that could right now present the Golden Age economy to humankind, well the vast majority of the people on this planet simply would not accept it. They would reject it as a hopeless, utopian pipe-dream, that simply could never come to pass. For they are so steeped in the consciousness of lack, again perpetrated by the fallen beings as a result of their idolatry, my beloved. For what is the essence of idolatry? It is the desire to raise yourself and your own group above other people. But how can you raise yourself compared to others unless you are in an environment infused with the illusion of lack? For in order for some to have more, others must have less, my beloved. And this state of an unequal distribution of wealth and privilege cannot exist in the abundant life of God. It can only exist when that abundant life has been rejected by a critical mass of human beings, so that it cannot be physically manifest.

You cannot overcome the past without looking at the past

Master MORE, October 31, 2008.

Economic crisis and war

For I tell you – not to induce fear here – but I ask you to be realistic and see that there is a connection, as St. Germain has said, between war and money. And you will see that there was a great depression, so to speak, in the 1930s, and then came the Second World War. And we, of course, do not desire in any way to see that pattern repeat itself in this day and age.

Again, this is not to induce fear, but to give you a sense of realism that it is indeed necessary with a breakthrough in consciousness – a breakthrough in a greater sense of oneness – so that those in the power elite who have a plan to precipitate first a financial collapse and then another war, will not get away with this. Because the people will have overcome enough of their sense of separation that they simply will not allow themselves to be pulled into this age-old pattern of building hatred against another group of people, who have been portrayed as the scapegoat and a cause of all their problems, so that they eventually go to war with those people, seeking to destroy them.

This is the pattern that can only be overcome by the people rising above it, and saying, "Enough is enough." And my beloved, this has happened many times in the past—slavery one example, democracy, another. "It is enough. We will not stand for this any more!" And therefore we look forward again to this breakthrough where you say, "We will no longer stand for this hatred. We will no longer stand for this separation. We will see ourselves as one people!"

Only Oneness between masculine and feminine can stop war

Mother Mary, November 1, 2008

Why most wars are started by men

For my beloved, if you look at the situation on Earth, is it not true that most wars are precipitated by men? This is a universal reality seen throughout history, at least, known history. I am not saying there have not been exceptions from this rule in the past. But certainly, in general it is those who represent the male energy who go to war.

And why is that, my beloved? It is because it has not found expression in a balanced manner. For, you see, the very nature of the masculine energy is that it wants to express, it wants to break boundaries. It wants to go beyond and transcend. That is indeed the driving force in creation. And there is nothing wrong with this, as long as it is expressed in a way that raises the All. It is indeed the very force that brings the creative process forward.

Yet, my beloved, when that force is suppressed, when it is held back in an unnatural way, well then the force will not die—the force will not go away. So, it will keep building pressure upon pressure. And sooner or later the pressure becomes so great that those who are under that pressure see no other way to relieve the pressure than through some act of violence and aggression.

Which, of course, is a phenomenon that is known by the false teachers, who have come to this Earth. And who know that if they can make people believe in the illusion, as Master MORE explained, that one other group of people is the cause of all of their problems, well then, it is inevitable that as the pressure keeps building, there will come a point where people are motivated to go to war with those who have become the scapegoats. And so you see the pattern here that it is the male energy – unbalanced – that creates or sets the stage for war. For, of course, what truly creates war is the free-will choices of human beings.

...

How women prevent war

But you see my beloved, unless there is that greater balance between masculine and feminine, well then there cannot be true peace. And certainly, those who are in a feminine body can – and have for generations – been holding a certain balance that has actually prevented even more wars than have taken place. For many times the women in a society, in a nation, have provided that balancing aspect that has prevented that nation from going to war.

In some cases they have not been able to hold that balance. But what I am expressing to you here is that in this day and age women are not meant to hold the balance for men. Women are not meant to compensate for the fact that men are unbalanced in expressing the masculine energy. It is indeed the responsibility of the men to get in touch with that feminine aspect of their beings and allow it to balance the masculine outgoing, expressive energy.

And so it has indeed been necessary for women to step back, or rather to transcend the traditional feminine role. When they are not just the passive ones who stay at home and take care of the man when he comes home, whether it be from work or war or whatever activity – such as going to the pub and worshipping the gods of beer or wine as some have done for generations, to the point where one must wonder, how many lifetimes does a soul need in order to fully have explored any effect that beer can have on the mind and body and come to a point where one says, perhaps there is more to life than blowing the foam off a glass of beer. And so you see, women have stepped forward in society to take up positions that just a generation or two ago could have been held only by men.

...

Only the female polarity can stop war

For do you not see that if Europe is to be united in peace, then people must transcend the self-images based on division and separation that caused them to follow the blind leaders into the collective blindness that is war? For do you not see, my beloved, that there is no greater example of blindness, spiritual blindness, than when nations go to war?

Generals on a battlefield talk about the fog of war. For once the battle has started, it is impossible to know what is going to happen or understand everything that is happening. But do you not see that even on a greater scale, beyond the individual battles, as soon as two nations or many nations go to war, there is a cloud that hangs over them and blinds them. And many times it is only after things have gotten much worse than they ever thought they would get, that they wake up from that blindness and see, and ask the question, "Why are we doing this? Why are we continuing to kill and allow our own people to be killed? When must we stop, when CAN we stop?"

And that, my beloved, is where the female energy is the only thing that can stop the male energy from running amok. For once the male energy has gone down the path of war, it cannot stop itself. It must be the female, because the female, my beloved, is what is in touch with what is happening in the Earth, what is in touch with the consequences of war. And therefore, it is the female that knows the suffering and the pain inflicted upon the children and all who participate in a war. I do not mean just the physical children, but all are, in a sense, children. And they are suffering, both the soldiers on the battlefield and the civilians in their homes, waiting for the next bomb to drop.

So you see, my beloved, the female is the only thing that can stop war, the female energy, the female perspective. And therefore, it is also the female that can prevent war—that can prevent the masculine from being unbalanced, so that it keeps building tension until violence seems like the only way out to the masculine, because they do not see beyond their own cloud of energy. But the female can see beyond. The female can see that there is always a way out without violence. There is always an alternative to violence. There is always an alternative to war. And indeed, the female can see what the male cannot see. For the male believes that once you have started on the path to war, you must continue in order to maintain your honor.

Ah, my beloved, how many people on this continent of Europe have been killed because of this idolatrous image of honor? How many people around the world have been killed based on this idolatrous image that we must save face. We must maintain the illusion that we are somehow superior, even if it means killing those who threaten that illusion—or being killed ourselves. This is something that seems perfectly logical to those who are unbalanced in the male energy. Sometimes it even seems logical to women who have become unbalanced in the feminine energy. But for most women it seems illogical, and even often ridiculous, when men posture and challenge each other, whether it be in ordinary arguments over the dinner table or between nations that eventually lead to war.

We shall use the trees to purify the European psyche

Kuan Yin, November 1, 2008

Mercy prevented a third world war

And so, we have spoken about the need to reunify Germany and Europe, to create that sense of oneness that was broken when certain representatives of the power elite – blinded by the duality consciousness – decided to artificially divide the German nation into two halves. And make one of them capitalist and one of them communist, so that they had the perfect laboratory for seeing how the conflict between communism and capitalism could outplay itself on a grander scale.

It was indeed their intention, my beloved, to let that conflict blossom into a full-scale third world war. And why did it not come to pass? It did not come to pass because there were many people in Germany, in the Soviet Union at the time, in Eastern Europe and in Western Europe, who had had enough of war. There were even many who embodied shortly after the war in order to hold a spiritual balance, so that the Second World War would not set the stage for the third, as the first has set the stage for the second. Again, as an experiment by the power elite of how to continue to create this continued string of conflicts, that would keep the world in a state of perpetual war.

Well, my beloved, they did create a state of perpetual war in the form of the cold war. But even that did not last and could not blossom into a hot war—a war that was so hot that the heat can come only from a nuclear explosion. And so, back to my question – why did this not happen? Well, it did not happen because those people who have vowed to hold the balance that this would not happen became the open doors for the Flame of Mercy.

Mercy is masculine, forgiveness is feminine

Mercy has a slightly different quality than forgiveness. Mercy is actually the masculine aspect, whereas forgiveness is the feminine aspect. Mercy then carries a certain power, a certain expansiveness, as it represents the expanding force of the Father—mercy you extend to others. And you can do this when you are in a position of power, but do not wish to use that power to take from them their lives, their possessions or whatever it may be.

And so, mercy then becomes the oil that calms the waters of the emotional body and infuses the entire continent with a sense that we will not let this war, this kind of war, happen again. And so, mercy is an integral part of progress, of growth. For without mercy, how can there then be the feminine aspect of forgiveness? For there is always a winner of a conflict – a seeming winner of a conflict – and that winner must decide to not press the advantage but to extend mercy.

And so, you saw that the quality – among other qualities, but one of the important qualities that drove the reunification of Germany – was indeed that people in Western Germany extended mercy to their brothers and sisters in the East, who have been under communism for so long that they did not have the will or the vision for what the reunited Germany should be like. And thus, there was an honest effort—not to dominate but to truly reunite and bring Germany into what it should have been all along, a coherent whole that could fill its place in the family of nations in Europe.

And so, what is one of the qualities that can accelerate the unification of Europe, that can heal the psyche of Europe, so that there can be not only a physical, economical, political or even military oneness, but a spiritual oneness that will truly bring peace and not a forced state of oneness through other means? Well, the quality is, of course, mercy — mercy that allows all nations to feel as one, because the stronger nations extend mercy in helping the weaker. And the weaker receive it, and in receiving it extend forgiveness to the stronger nations, even also forgiving themselves.

And so you have the flow of Alpha to Omega, but back again to Alpha so that the figure-eight is complete. And thus, does not become that broken figure-eight flow.

How can Europe be free when the minds of the people are imprisoned by illusions?

Saint Germain, November 1, 2008

Is your country truly free?

And thus, be honest then and look over here in Europe as well – to the countries that claim to be free societies – and then consider whether they can truly live up to that high label, my beloved. Are you really free in the western part of Europe? You may have democracy, you many have human rights, you may have freedom to move around, but are you truly free if you have been brought up in a culture that is so infused with duality, that they cannot even give you a clear, concise image of who you are and why you are here?

How can there be freedom when a society is trapped in a dualistic struggle between the traditional, orthodox, mainstream religions that have been used for centuries – nay for millennia – to control the minds of the people and make them believe that they are not sons and daughters of God, that they are not anything more than sinners, that they do not have a Christ potential? And on the other hand of the battle field is the materialists – the aspiring power elite, seeking to overthrow the established power elite of religion – promoting their idolatrous image that you are nothing more than a sophisticated animal and that life has no purpose beyond the material realm.

Ah, how can this be freedom? How can people be truly free when they do not even know who they are and cannot answer the questions, "Why am I here? Where did I come from? Where am I going? Is there a God? Is there something beyond the mental box created by the ego?" But they cannot even ask that last question, because they are brought up without any awareness of the ego, of the duality consciousness, of the illusion of separation. Being brought up to believe that what they see in this world is real—has some ultimate reality. And because it has this ultimate, objective reality, then it exists independently of their own consciousness—meaning that they have no power over material conditions.

The grand conspiracy of anti-freedom

And so, right there, you are brought up to be unfree, because you are brought up not to accept full responsibility for your own life. Always thinking that your life, your state of mind, your feelings, your life experience is determined by these outer conditions. And that you are but a slave, who when you are exposed to certain outer conditions can only react a certain way—for you do not have the freedom to choose your own reaction. You do not have the freedom to choose to be non-attached, to be unaffected by anything that anyone does to you, instead remaining at peace no matter what goes on around you.

Do you see that there are so many subtle illusions that you have been brought up to take for granted, and they limit your self-image? And what limits your self-image will also limit your self-expression. And this is indeed part of the plot of the false teachers, who are the blind leading the blind.

Take note of what I am saying. There are those who think that there is a grand conspiracy, which is consciously plotting to take over the world. But you must understand that anyone who is involved with the power elite in the control of the people—well, they are the most trapped of all people. For while they might seem to have some power and control over the people who are blind, well they themselves are even more blinded by their own ego, by the dualistic illusions, by the sense of separation—that they can attain privileges for themselves and it will not affect their greater selves. They can do to the people whatever they want without ultimately limiting themselves.

They truly believe that they can get away with this. They believe they are superior, because they are separated from "the people" and better than the people. For the people cannot govern themselves, and therefore, need the elite to govern for them.

Many forms of anti-freedom

So you see, my beloved, there are many forms of prisons. There are many forms of anti-freedom. And when you do not recognize who you are as a spiritual being – who is beyond the religions of this world and the political ideologies of this world and the scientific philosophies of this world – when you do not recognize this reality, then you are led to follow one of these systems of thought that claims that they have the ultimate reality, the ultimate truth, and can take you to whatever promised land they conjure up.

Or you will be trapped in the opposite polarity, where you are not promised something better, but where you are driven by fear, trying to get away from something even worse. As you have seen used cleverly in the past on this continent, my beloved, where you have seen various dictators and totalitarian machines ultimately promising to bring forth a better world through control. Or scaring the people into trying to avoid some greater calamity by making you follow them blindly without asking questions, without taking charge, without understanding what is going on in the economy or other parts of life. So you see that this is the pattern that has occurred over and over again on this continent.

There was an alternative to the Second World War

Take a look at Europe in the years leading up to the Second World War and how the people on this continent gradually became blinded by this cloud of war that caused them to believe, that there was no other alternative to the current situation than all-out war. Both the people in Germany and the people in other nations were led to believe in this illusion—that they had no other option for dealing with conditions. But you see, my beloved, there is always another option. And let me, then – to provoke you to think beyond traditional interpretations of history – let me take you through a thought experiment.

Let us envision, my beloved, that the rest of Europe had not resisted the Nazi expansion plans and had indeed allowed the Nazi troops to roll into their countries and control them. It is easy to see that pretty soon every country in Europe would have been under the Nazi banner, with Hitler as the supreme Führer standing on top of this false pyramid. Nevertheless, my beloved, how long do you think Hitler would have survived in that position? How long do you think it would have taken before infighting in his own inner circle would have destroyed the Nazi regime?

For you see, it was an extremely dualistic regime. And you see, also, that duality will always create an opposite polarity to itself. Action creates reaction. For every action, there is an opposite and equally strong reaction. And so the extreme action of the Nazis created its own opposition. Now, in this case, the other countries in Europe and the United States chose to step into the role of out-picturing the opposing force to the Nazi action. They became the reaction. But do you see, my beloved, that if those countries – most of whom claimed to be Christian – had heeded the call of Jesus, they would have refused to resist evil; they would have turned the other cheek? And what would then have happened?

What would have happened was that since there was no external reaction to the Nazi action, well then the reaction – which could not be held back, for it is universal law – and when the reaction does not come from without, it must come from within. It is as certain as if you throw a rock into the air, it will fall back down to Earth. Do you see, my beloved? There was an alternative to war. There is always an alternative to war.

A truth many will resist

This is a truth that many will resist. They will say, "But we had no other alternative. We had to resist or the whole continent, the whole world, would have been under totalitarian forces." But you see, they say this in order to justify their own dualistic illusions, which made them believe that they had to respond to violence with more violence. This is indeed an unpopular truth, but it is the truth that can set you free—that WILL set you free, if you accept it.

For you see, while there would have been some suffering if the Nazis had been allowed to take over Europe, on an overall scale less people would have died than died in the Second World War. There would have been less suffering overall than there was because the world repeated the old pattern of all-out war, of refusing to turn the other cheek, and instead, responding in kind.

Now you may know, my beloved, that in a previous dispensation I, Saint Germain, gave special decrees to resist the spread of communism. I encouraged the building of certain defense measures to defend against communist aggression. But you see, I am here talking about two slightly different things. For I am not saying that the nations of Europe could have responded with non-violence to the Nazi aggression. They could not have responded, given the state of consciousness they were in at the time, and given the fact that they were unwilling to transcend that state of consciousness.

And likewise, during the cold war of the '70s and '80s, there was a potential for a nuclear confrontation between the Soviet Union and the United States. And on the one hand there was always the alternative that the West could have chosen to turn the other cheek to communistic expansion. But given the state of consciousness of the West, this was not a realistic alternative.

And therefore, the best that could be achieved at the time was that the West had enough of a defense to provide a deterrent for an all-out Soviet attack. And so you see, I am on the one hand talking about the highest potential, but I am not denying the fact that we of the Ascended Host have to be practical realists, who work with the people of the world in whatever state of consciousness they are in.

The way to make wars stop

But my hope is that you can see here that there is always an alternative to war and that, in fact, wars will never stop coming until a critical mass of people do choose to turn the other cheek, instead of responding in kind. For as long as people are in that state of consciousness of feeling threatened, of feeling afraid and of being ready to strike back at the slightest provocation, well then how can war stop? How can you be free of the threat of war that hangs over this planet as a Damocles sword ready to drop at any minute?

So how then do you free yourselves from the consciousness of war? Well, it goes back to what I started out talking about—that you need to know who you are. You need to know that you are a spiritual being, that you are more than any earthly conditions. And therefore, you have the power to choose how you respond to any condition you face in the material universe.

So when you are faced with a threat, you have the power to choose that instead of focusing on the splinter in the eye of your brother, you can look at the beam in your own eye and say, "Why have I attracted to myself this situation, where I am being threatened by an external force? What is the action I have set in motion, perhaps in past lives long forgotten, that has precipitated this reaction from the cosmic mirror? What is it I must learn in order to free myself from this dualistic ping pong match with the universal mirror that will always shoot back to me what I send at it?"

You see, my beloved, you may miss the ball in a ping pong match, but the universe will not. It will always return to you what you send out. It is not possible to escape the reaction to your action. It is not possible to be free from that reaction. All you can do is to create another type of action by changing your consciousness and then, when you change your consciousness and send that other action into the universe, well then with absolute certainty the universe will send back another reaction. It cannot be any other way, my beloved.

Choose ye this day the parallel universe in which you want to abide

Jesus, November 2, 2008.

Christ is beyond any authority on Earth

It is not God who wants to control your thoughts and your behavior. It is those who have attempted to set themselves up as gods on Earth—or as the only representatives of Gods on Earth. Inserting themselves as the High Priests of the temple – as the Alpha perversion of the power elite – and the money changers in the temple—as the perversion of the ego, the perversion of the feminine, the Omega polarity.

So my beloved, you will see that there have always been two main groupings in the power elite, in the false teachers. Those who pervert the expanding force of the Father, those who pervert the contracting force of the Mother. And in many cases they have formed an unholy alliance, my beloved, and this can be seen out-pictured here in Europe, going back many centuries.

For go back to the song you have just heard, "King of Kings and Lord of Lords." [The Hallelujah Chorus] Well my beloved, that original statement was meant to signify that Christ is beyond any ideas and graven images created by the consciousness of anti-christ. And therefore, Christ is beyond any authority on Earth—whether it be the king, or the emperor, or the Lord, or the Pope, or the priest, or the cardinal or the bishop. It matters not, for Christ is beyond all of them.

For Christ cannot be corrupted by the dualistic consciousness, Christ cannot be forced into a mental box created by the consciousness of anti-christ—which is – as we have said many times – based on the illusion of separation, whereas Christ is based on the reality of oneness, the oneness of all life.

In oneness, no one is Lord or King over another

So you see; when life is one, no one is in control. No one is lord over another; no one is king over another. And do you then see that when the ancient Israelites demanded a king, well then they only reinforced the illusion of separation—and it was not truly the people who demanded a king.

It was the aspiring power elite at the time; those who lusted after the power held by the high priests and wanted their own share of that power—out of their perversion of the Omega aspect of wanting to control the people's daily lives, whereas the high priests wanted to control their minds. And do you then see that here in Europe the concept that Christ is King of Kings was perverted to the point, where the kings started claiming that they were representatives of Christ—that they were standing between the people and Christ, and that they had the ordination of Christ for their kingship and for the fact that the son of the previous king, the oldest son, would always become the next king.

Well my beloved, if you go back to ancient times, they had kings but the kings were not simply appointed in succession. You were appointed through some agency of the spiritual realm, be it an oracle or in other manners whereby the Spirit could appoint the king. Often raising up a person who was born and raised as a commoner to be the next king, so that that king knew what it was like to live among the people and had not been born in a royal castle, far removed from the ordinary people, growing up in this closed environment, and therefore naturally becoming halfway insane, so to speak, being brought up to be insane in the sense that he was insensitive to the plight of the people. This then is indeed one of the great problems; perhaps one might say the great problem on Earth, especially here in Europe.

Find the Living Christ in the kingdom within

You see, my beloved, Europe is in many ways intended to be what it to some degree has been, the cradle of new ideas, of new inventions, of new philosophies and ideologies that can bring progress and freedom to the people. And precisely because this is the divine intention for this land, those of the power elites – the two power elites – have congregated here and have attempted to divide the people amongst each other and divide the people from their God within.

This then is the pattern that you will see on this continent, over and over again, successfully completed by the Catholic Church who used my inner teachings about the inner kingdom to set themselves up as the spiritual representatives of Christ on Earth. Claiming that you could only be saved and reach Christ through the hierarchy of the church.

Now my beloved, it is true that you can only reach Christ through a certain hierarchy—you will see that we have often talked about you seeing yourselves as part of a certain hierarchy of Light. But you see, as I came to demonstrate 2000 years ago, you do not need a hierarchy on Earth in order to claim your oneness with the hierarchy of light.

For the kingdom of God is within, and you have the key of knowledge, you have the ability to know truth in your own heart. And therefore, you do not need an outer authority to define dogma and doctrine for you, based on some literal interpretation of a scripture that was outdated before it was even written down, my beloved.

...

Consciousness on a scale of higher or lower frequencies

This, then, very much ties in with the teaching I have been giving for some time, where you can divide the population into the top 10% – or the most spiritually aware people – the bottom 10% of the most self-centered, ego-centered people, and the 80% of the general population who are somewhere in between those two. So, what I desire you to understand here is that it is the level of consciousness that determines where people fit into this scale—it is not their outer power.

Obviously, the most powerful people on Earth are not necessarily – and in fact are rarely – in the top 10%. The top 10% are not somehow superior to others, for in order to enter the top 10% you must overcome duality and the need to feel better than others. You must not go into the false humility that is the opposite, but the realism that we have talked about in previous dictations at this conference, of simply realizing who you are, as a co-creator with God. That is what determines your entry into the top 10%, so we are not here giving a teaching that the ego should be allowed to turn into a teaching of superiority giving rise to pride, for then you have not understood the teaching.

It is indeed a reality that there are those who have attuned their consciousness to higher frequencies, to the higher radio stations that are broadcasting the truth from the Ascended Masters' octave. And they, then, have raised their consciousness to the point, where they can attune to a different radio station than the general population, and certainly the lowest 10% who are often attuning to the radio station that has traditionally been called hell.

For you see, hell exists in the emotional realm, where those beings who have become completely self-centered – have become so eaten up by the their own anger against God, and their anger against themselves – that they have formed the realm where the anger has become so intense, so hot, that it will be experienced as a hell with flames that burn you in eternal torment. For these beings that are trapped there, are in eternal torment, even though they do not always see this because they are so focused on their anger against God that their anger is consuming their awareness to the point, that they cannot even realize that this is uncomfortable to them and that they wish they could get out of it.

Consciousness as a gravitational force

So you see, when you look at the scale of the bottom 10%, the top 10% and the 80% in the middle, you see that there are many different levels on that scale. And you can then can go to the people who are in embodiment and who are part of the lowest 10%, and you will see that there are people at the very lowest level who embody a certain state of consciousness, and they are forming a gravitational force that seeks to pull the minds of everyone else down to their level of consciousness.

They do this not only through their minds; they do it through their actions, where they have attempted to embroil people into war so that when people are trapped in war, trapped in battle, some people will rise in honor, whereas others will descend to the very animalistic tendencies of killing anyone who seems to come in their way. Or conquering a village and raping the women, or otherwise displaying complete disrespect for life. And thereby they pull them down to that level of being an animal. And they pull those down who look at these atrocities and become angry and seek revenge, and so they create this downward spiral where people are pulled down more and more and more.

And so, you see that there are those in the lowest 10% who are living in a particular universe that you who are spiritual people can scarcely imagine. And I do not in fact encourage you to try to imagine how these people experience life. For I myself descended into hell – meaning I descended into their level of consciousness to seek to raise them up – but I did not do this until I was resurrected, and therefore had shed the body and the human consciousness. And certainly, I do not encourage you to descend to that level while you are still in a physical body.

This will only be reserved for a very few people, and so you strive to raise your consciousness rather than lowering it. Unless, of course, you need to go down and look at something in your psychology from past lives and undo a decision that you made at a lower level of consciousness. But you do not attune to the consciousness of others, for you do not need to undo the decisions made by others—as only they can do that.

The top 10% must bring positive change

Now, my beloved, the message I want to get across here is that God gave human beings dominion over the Earth. You have people in the lowest 10% who are the blind—they are the blind seeking to lead the blind of the general population. They are aggressive, they are completely self-centered and focused on themselves. My beloved, you cannot expect these people to suddenly awaken and start raising their own consciousness and that of the 80% of the people.

I am not saying that people from the lowest 10% have not been awakened; it does happen but only a small percentage. So what I am saying is that you cannot expect positive change on this planet to come from the lowest 10%. So where must positive change come from? Well, if you look at the 80%, they tend to be followers; they do not have a strong enough sense of self to go against the grain, to refuse to fit into the mold defined by society. And so, who must then bring positive change? Well, it can only be the top 10%, my beloved, and this is what you need to realize.

As an example of this, look at Europe during the Second World War. It was a conflict that killed millions and millions of people on this continent. Millions of people lost loved ones, millions of people saw their homes destroyed, their cities destroyed—even a nation destroyed. Yet if you go to other parts of the European continent, you can find people who lived almost normal lives during the five years of the Second World War. And why is that, my beloved? Because they were at a different level of consciousness than the people who were directly involved in the war!

My beloved, do not believe that things just happen to happen a certain way. Everything is a manifestation of consciousness. There is a reason why certain people had congregated and embodied in the same areas, the geographical areas, where they became embroiled in the direct war. There is a reason why other people had embodied in other parts of Europe where they were not so directly involved. There is a reason for this, and it is their level of consciousness. So what I am endeavoring to explain is that even in a conflict as serious as the Second World War, you will see that people at different levels of consciousness had very different experiences of the physical events.

Parallel universes in consciousness

And what I endeavor to explain is that you too, today – as the spiritual people – you are, so to speak, living in a parallel universe compared to the greater population and those in the lower 10%. Consider the very fact that you are sitting in a room here, in a monastery of a particular Christian order that has existed for a very long time, and has a very set, rigid organized tradition. Consider that you are sitting here listening to a person who claims to give voice to the real Jesus Christ, whereas right below you are the monks of this order who are sitting doing their Sunday service, claiming that they are worshipping the real Jesus Christ and would be shocked to really understand what is happening here. Do you see that even though you are in such physical proximity, you are living in parallel universes in the mind?

So the idea from quantum physics of parallel universes is not wrong, only they are not physically parallel universes – they are not parallel universes in the material vibrational spectrum – they are parallel universes in consciousness. And this is the magic of planet Earth in the material realm—that it allows people to exist – as Maitreya explains in greater detail in his book – in the same physical location yet be in parallel universes in consciousness.

Christhood shifts the entire spectrum of consciousness

Now, what that means is that there is a correspondence between the parallel universe that you live in as the spiritual people, and the parallel universe of the lowest 10%. For you see, my beloved, it is a law of God that before a certain manifestation of duality – a certain manifestation of darkness, of evil can be removed from the Earth – before that can happen, there must be those in the top 10% who have raised their consciousness to a certain level, where they have freed themselves from those aspects of the ego that are being out-pictured as that manifestation of darkness.

They must free themselves, but they must also then take a stand and say, "This manifestation of evil is no longer acceptable in my world!" And only when you stand on the Rock of Christ – because you have been willing to remove the beam in your eye, that aspect of the ego which is being out-pictured as that manifestation – only then, when you stand on that Rock of Christ, will you then have the authority – or we might say, you will give God the authority – to remove that manifestation of evil from this planet and remove those who will not voluntarily raise their consciousness beyond it.

Do you see that this is how progress occurs on this planet? There must be some in the top 10% who have reached the level of Christhood that corresponds to the perversion of that level among the bottom 10%. And only when we have those – a critical mass of people at that level of Christhood – can the perversion of that level be removed. And that way the entire spectrum of consciousness is shifted upwards.

If you look at the spectrum of human consciousness that you find on this Earth, then you will see that the way progress happens is that the entire spectrum is shifted upwards. It is now possible to go one step higher for the top 10%, but those in the bottom 10% cannot go below a certain level or they will be removed from the Earth.

This is the only way that progress can happen; it cannot happen in any other way, my beloved. It cannot happen through force. It cannot happen by one totalitarian nation conquering the world and establishing the kingdom of God through force. It cannot happen through one religion conquering the world. It cannot happen in any other way but a shift in consciousness, whereby those who have the potential must rise, claim their Christhood, purify their own minds of a certain manifestation of the duality consciousness; and then declare with one voice, with one mind, with one heart, that this must stop, for enough is enough!

Can any man-made system bring the Promised Land to Earth?

Lanello, November 2, 2008

Learn from history—or repeat it

Well, my beloved, if we had only understood the reality of the inner teachings of Christ—that there is no way to defeat evil by fighting it but that we must turn the other cheek. How much bloodshed, how much warfare, could have been avoided on this continent, if more of us had had that understanding in past lifetimes. Certainly, as an Ascended Being, I AM not lamenting the past, but nevertheless when one is on a continent such as Europe, it is necessary to recognize that this continent does indeed have a past—a long and somewhat bloody past, my beloved.

And so, for the people of Europe, who are embodying here today, to rise above that past, it is indeed necessary to look at the past, to learn the lessons from history. For has it not been said that unless you learn those lessons, you are destined to repeat the mistakes of history.

And how many times have we seen that outplayed on this continent, where one conflict sets the stage for the next. And where the emergence of one power elite created a conflict that then – when they became the established power elite – they attracted the opposite polarity and a new conflict was born. Ah, what a pattern, what a pattern has been repeated so many times that it is nauseating if one looks at it.

There is only one conflict on Earth

And thus, I do indeed intend all of you to look at it, whether it makes you nauseated or not; for there comes a point where you go beyond it—you go beyond that sense of hopelessness and despair. For when you dare to actually look at what has been going on – when you dare to look at why it has been going on – you see that even though there is a seemingly endless stream of conflicts on this planet and this continent, you see, my beloved, that there really is only one conflict that has simply been repeating itself over and over again in different physical circumstances.

And that conflict is, of course, the conflict between what we have called the power elite and the people of God. It is the conflict between those who have fallen, as Maitreya explains in his ground-breaking and magnificent book—that I dare say, I wish it had been possible to bring that forth while I was still a messenger in embodiment, for it would have explained so many things; so many questions that were left hanging by the teachings that could be brought forth at the time.

Nevertheless, reality is reality, the now is the now, and so when you see that these fallen beings fell because they honestly, seriously, sincerely – or should I just say naively – believed that they were smarter than God and knew better than God how to run an entire universe. And so they fell into the duality consciousness, ended up on Earth, have embodied here over and over again ever since. And they have repeated the same old pattern of seeking to attain ultimate control over the people in the mistaken belief – the absolutely naïve belief – that that could prove God wrong and prove themselves right.

As if, my beloved – when you consider what you know today in the modern world about the vastness of the material universe – as if what happens on one little planet such as Earth would actually prove God wrong—the God that strung the Pleiades, that strung the galaxies. How could what happens on this little planet ever be significant in the grand scheme of things? But such is the intense blindness of the human ego—that it actually believes that it has the power to change the fate of the universe. What folly, what folly I might say.

God cannot be mocked

This is what must be seen by the people—that it is completely, utterly naïve to believe that God can be mocked by human beings. And only when you have that realistic sense of reality of the Law of God – the actual, absolute immovability of the law of God – only then will you see that you need to escape that illusion.

And you need to stop following the blind leaders, those who are trapped in that illusion. For if you do not stop following them, then you are like a ship without a rudder that is being carried by the current down the Rhine and will be wrecked on the Lorelei Cliff, as a representative for the rock of Christ. For do you not see that the very force that is at work in the second law of thermodynamics is the Rock of Christ that breaks down all closed mental boxes. It breaks down all closed systems and reduces them to the lowest possible energy state, for without the constant infusion of the life of Christ nothing is sustainable.

And thus, those who in some higher sphere chose to cut themselves off from the eternal stream that is the life of Christ, well then they have only a certain time. Their days are numbered, my beloved, and there does indeed come a point, where they are ready to be taken because they have had enough opportunity to be expressed.

The need for Christed ones

But then there is – as we have spoken about – that condition that someone must be raised up to the level of Christhood out-pictured as a perversion by these self-centered, egotistical beings. And unless there is someone who dares to step forward and accept that they are the Christ – accept that they are a son or daughter of God – unless that happens, well then they cannot be taken.

And I can tell you that there are right now a number of these beings, who have had their lawful opportunity, and they are simply being sustained on this planet by the fact that nobody has dared to claim their Christhood. Which, of course, is the very plot that they have engineered from the very beginning—even while Jesus still walked on the Earth. And they attempted to set the stage, thinking that they could kill him physically. And then, of course, when that did not work, going to Plan B and killing his teaching and example—that no one dare to step forward.

And thus, some of you have indeed realized – and had a conversation just before this release – that this is a dark cloud that hangs especially over the European continent. Certainly, every other continent has its own version of what suppresses the people, but here on this continent of Europe – because the Catholic Church was here, because Christianity spread here first – there is indeed a stigma that you can do or say almost anything you want to do or say—except that you are the Christ or a representative of the Christ on Earth. For the very beings who have embodied the consciousness of anti-christ have claimed that as a monopoly for themselves.

Oh, my beloved, it is indeed time that people wake up all over Europe and realize this is a complete lie. It is a complete and utter denial of the very mission of Christ, the very mission of Christ to free the Christ in every human heart and to make every human being acknowledge their Christ potential, my beloved. This has always been the goal of Christ, this will always be the goal of Christ, and it is time that the people on this continent wake up.

...

You have dominion over the Earth

We are indeed not human beings, and you are indeed not human beings—unless you think you are. For then we must, of course, bow to your free will and allow you to think that the power elite has power over you—while in reality you are the co-creators. You are the ones who have been given authority by God to have dominion over the Earth. Do you understand this, my beloved?

The fallen angels were never given the authority by God to have dominion over the Earth. They may claim that they were given that authority—some of them believing that the entire material universe was created for their sake; but this is not the case. It is simply another reasoning of the duality consciousness. They were never given authority over this planet. YOU were given authority over this planet.

But when you did not take that authority, then the fallen beings were allowed to embody here. And that, then, became the problem, where the people now became even more embroiled in the consciousness of not wanting to take responsibility and authority. Instead wanting the blind leaders – who claim to have some ultimate authority – to lead them to the promised land—failing to realize that they would never get to that promised land. For by the time they got into embodiment again, they had forgotten the futile search for the promised land that they went through in the past 30 embodiments or more.

Remember the point of stillness within you

Gautama Buddha, November 2, 2008

Looking at your universe through the vision of the Buddha
For you see that even though we talk about fallen beings and dark forces, we know – and we desire you to know – that they have no ultimate reality. I know that this can be difficult to grasp for some of you. For in the parallel universe in which your mind is currently focused, they seem to be very real and they even seem to have power over you. But that is where I can offer my assistance, if you will only spend a little bit of time and attention tuning in to my Presence.

Do not fall prey to the temptation to turn this into an elaborate ritual. Simply create a very simple visualization in your mind of you sitting under the Bo tree with the presence of Gautama superimposed over you. And then ask me to show you how your parallel universe looks from my state of consciousness, or at least from the state of consciousness right above yours, so that you may grasp it and free yourself from the illusion that this Mara is real and has any power over you. This will require you, my beloved – as Jesus expressed – to tune in to the silence, the silence within.

My beloved, how many of you as children played with a top, a spinning top? Probably all of you did, or at least you know how it works. It spins around on its axis, and when you look at the periphery of the toy, you might focus on a particular point on that periphery, and it is constantly spinning at great speed, never standing still. But that point is on the periphery of a circle, and the circle has a center. And my beloved, no matter how fast the point on the periphery is spinning, the point in the center is always standing still, is it not?

And so you see, from a surface perspective, things on this planet may seem very confusing and chaotic. But that is because your attention is focused on the surface of the Earth, which is indeed spinning around at thousands of miles per hour. So direct your attention to the axis, to the center, and realize that no matter how much turmoil is going on on the surface, there is a point within that is always standing still. And in that stillness you can find your own center, and there you will find me—for I am the center for all life on Earth. That is my office as "Lord of the World."

Thus, I sit in complete peace and Oneness, and although I see the surface appearances – although I see the demons of Mara in their distorted form – I see beyond them and see that everything is made from the Ma-ter Light. And the Ma-ter Light is the Buddha Nature. It is so one with that Buddha Nature, that it is longing to out-picture the perfect images that are stored in that Buddha Nature, as an infinite potential to express creativity in a way that raises up all life, rather than raising that separate self.

...

For even though the Buddha is the center of stillness for all life on Earth, I am not standing still, as many who claim to be Buddhists conceive of me—as being beyond needing to grow, expand and self-transcend. But you see, my beloved, if that idolatrous vision was correct, then how could the Earth rise if the Lord of the World does not transcend himself? You see that everything is a hierarchy, and that which is below in hierarchy cannot rise unless that which is above also rises.

Which is precisely why the continent of Europe cannot rise if those who have the potential to be the top ten percent do not rise. For how then can the others go beyond a certain level of consciousness? How can they transcend that parallel universe in which there is still struggle and suffering and a potential for war on this continent? How can they rise to the higher realm, to the higher universe, where war has been transcended once and for all, and where the consciousness of war has been banished from this continent?

And so you see, it is so easy for human beings to create these graven images of what a spiritual being is like; but you cannot know a spiritual being through any image based on the illusion of separation. You can know a spiritual being only through gnosis, through coming into oneness with that flame. As Saint Germain said, "How can you be free but by coming into oneness with the Flame of Freedom?" How can you be the Buddha without coming into oneness with the Presence of Buddha? How can you be the Christ without becoming one with Christ, by drinking His body and blood in a spiritual sense and absorbing it with every fiber of your being?

Chapter 8:
Teachings about fallen angels, 2009

Communicate that life is MORE

Mother Mary, January 3, 2009.

Control means stopping creativity

And thus, of course, you see the entire plot of the fallen beings who seek to control humankind. How can you control humankind? Well, only by seeking to stop creativity, for creativity is unpredictable. And how do you attain control? Well, only if you can make everything predictable, by making it mechanical—as opposed to creative.

And thus, so many of the philosophies and thought systems in this world have been designed specifically to cause the individual to shut off the creative flow through its being. Thereby, of course, paying the price of feeling unfulfilled. Yet many are trapped into thinking that they can still find fulfillment by hoarding and possessing something from this world, or even by attaining fame or fortune, or even by working for some greater cause.

Then, again, many have been fooled into believing that they should not seek fulfillment in this world, for this world is somehow sinful or lesser. No, they should work their whole lives – being satisfied with being dissatisfied – and then hoping for that ultimate fulfillment and satisfaction in the next world. Thus, again, making sure that God's creativity cannot come in and overturn the tables of the moneychangers who have inserted themselves into the temples of people's very beings and cut off that flow of creativity—instead demanding that they be paid by people giving them their spiritual light, my beloved.

Do you see that when Jesus overturned the tables of the moneychangers in the temple, it was a symbol for the living Christ coming into your being and overturning the tables of that which is untruth in your being and thus keeps you trapped? Because you do not dare to bring forth the creative solutions that can take you beyond any problem and any limitation you face in the material universe.

What is truth, my beloved? It is that the material world is entirely created from the energies of the Ma-ter light. The Ma-ter light – being spiritual – therefore cannot be confined to the form that it has taken on. It can – at any moment – break the bonds of that form and transcend itself into a higher form. But it will do so only when God's co-creators set it free from the old form, for it has vowed to maintain that form for as long as the people on this planet maintain their limited images in their databases—and then project a limited form onto the Ma-ter light through those limited images.

The force of liberation

And thus, my beloved, what happens when you hold on to those images in the database and will not question them? Well then, there is a built-in force in the Ma-ter light that we have talked about as the second law of thermodynamics – as the force of Kali – that breaks down all imperfections. Even what the Hindus call Shiva, the God of destruction, the destroyer of all that which has become, so to speak, set in stone and has taken on the form of a graven image, meaning any image that does not change.

You see, that force itself will break down those towers of Babel that people have built – and that they think can reach into the heavens and that are not changeable or that could never fall apart – those institutions in finance that they think could never fail or should not be allowed to fail. So that they think that when the institutions are in danger of failing, the government should step in. And I tell you, when the government does step in to prop up those institutions and prevent them from failing, well then there is a real possibility that the government will have to fail in order to set the people free from the illusion behind it.

You see, my beloved, there will always be that force of the Mother light – out of the unconditional love of God – that will not allow God's co-creators to be trapped forever in a limited sense of identity. And thus, it will come in and it will indeed overturn the moneychangers and their tables, overturn the illusions. It will upset the apple cart, my beloved, until the souls are free—free to bask in the light of creativity that is the very force of life itself. For what God – you might ask logically – would allow his own co-creators to be forever trapped in that lesser sense of identity, when he knows that they are so much more?

The end of nation states and the beginning of the Golden Age

Saint Germain, April 12, 2009.

Truly, my beloved, what will it take to manifest Saint Germain's Golden Age? Well, it will take that the people of this world are willing to rise to a higher state of consciousness and overcome the division created by the artificial, man-made concept of nation states. Am I thereby saying, that there will be no nation states in The Golden Age? Indeed, I am.

The progression in consciousness

For within a century or two, the current nation states will dissolve and merge into a higher unity—or they will self-destruct in warfare and conflict. You see, my beloved, when you look back at the history of humankind, you will see a clear progression in consciousness. Go back thousands of years, where there were only scattered tribes living in the harsh environment, having no means of communication, no sense of awareness of what existed beyond their own small territory and their own tribe. Perhaps coming in contact with a few neighboring tribes, often being in conflict with them over territory or hunting rights.

Gradually – very slowly – the population grew and the awareness grew. Yet, if you go back to the time of Jesus, as Mother Mary mentioned yesterday, there was not the sense of awareness that you, today, take for granted as nation states. Consider the consciousness of the people before you had maps, my beloved. You have grown up from an early age being shown maps of the world and of your own nation. And so, you have grown up with the concept of a bird's-eye view of this planet and what it looks like from above, seen from great height or even from space. And you have been used to seeing the lines drawn on the map that mark the boundaries of your own nation.

But that was not there only a few hundred years ago. People could not even imagine what the earth looked like from above. Only a few souls started drawing maps, but most people did not have the awareness that you take for granted. What I desire you to see is, my beloved, that people started out with a very primitive tribal consciousness which then gradually grew to a greater awareness, where many tribes might merge into the sense of a people, a greater people that lived in a certain area or migrated from area to area. But when the bible, for example, talks about the land of Egypt, it is not the Egypt as the nation state you see today. For that awareness was not there.

Yet, the concept of nation states was a step forward in the growth – in the broadening – of awareness from the tribal level. Yet as you clearly see – especially in this past century, but also in previous centuries – the concept of a nation state can also be misused by the ego to create conflict and warfare. And thus, you will clearly see with all of the warfare that the concept of nation states has given rise to, it can only be a temporary stage in the growth of the consciousness of humankind. For there must be a higher level, there must be something beyond, my beloved.

Four nations are forerunners for taking the world beyond nation states

And I can assure you that it is not the old model that one nation conquers the world and rules the world. The age of colonization, the age of spreading communism – even the concept misunderstood by the former American administration of spreading freedom and democracy – surely must come to an end before The Golden Age can unfold.

What, then, can replace the concept of nation states? It is a more universal awareness that human beings come from the same source, a spiritual source—a source beyond the material world. And therefore, the material world is a means to an end, namely the growth in consciousness. And it is not an end in itself. For when it becomes a closed system, it will break down.

Thus, I come to give you a vision of the potential for starting this movement of overcoming nation states. Obviously, I attempted to start this here in Europe, centuries ago, as the Wonderman of Europe. And you see that it is now beginning to manifest more clearly in the European Union, which – as its highest potential – can be a polarity to the United States. Where even though you have a strong national consciousness, the individual states are at least unified and not in direct conflict with each other—at least not, since the Civil War.

So you see, my beloved, something must begin to break down that national consciousness. And when you think about this logically, you see that one nation cannot do this alone. Thus, the vision I wish to give you is that the greatest potential for a stepping up into a higher awareness, a more universal awareness, is indeed that there are four nations in Europe that are prepared to be the forerunners for this.

One of them, of course, being this nation, the Netherlands. But we might say, that the core of the Netherlands is indeed what you would call Holland. Where the greatest population is, and where there also is the greatest density of the spiritual people who have volunteered to embody here, to bring about this and other changes. Holland, then, represents the Mother element. But as you know, there are always the four elements— the Father, Mother, Son and Holy Spirit.

So although I know it will surprise many, the Father element is, indeed, Germany. Germany, of course, has the history of having a very strong national awareness that led to – or at least was the flash point for – both the first and second World Wars. But Germany was broken up after the second World War, and therefore the old sense of national awareness, in a sense, died. And even after the reunification, it was never recreated.

For the German people do indeed have – at least the many spiritual people who have embodied among them – a desire to leave the past behind. And they want to grow away from that national awareness based on the sense of superiority, that they have so clearly seen out-pictured in their own nation—and that they truly desire to transcend.

Thus, you have Germany as the largest country, but Germany in itself cannot make that transition. And so you see that Holland is a smaller nation right next to Germany, on the West. On the South you have Switzerland and Austria that represent the Holy Spirit. Where the highest mountains reach towards the heavens and the energies can descend, even the waters that become the rivers that run through Germany and out through Holland to the sea.

And then on the North, you have the small country of Denmark that represents the Son, the Christ element. Which is why this messenger was born there, having the mission to restore, in this age, a true vision, a true understanding of Christ and the mission of Christ.

Equality is essential for the Golden Age

So you see how these four countries – the three bordering the center of Germany – have a potential to bring forth a new awareness. And you will even see that these countries have for a long time had that awareness of the equality of all men—and, of course, women as well. This is ingrained in their constitutions, in their national psyches. Especially the three smaller countries who can then help Germany overcome the last vestiges of the sense of division.

For you see, my beloved, even though in all of the three smaller countries you will see a certain perversion of the principle of equality, it should be obvious that for there to be a Golden Age, there must be true equality among human beings. We cannot have a Golden Age as long as the majority of the population are suppressed and controlled by a small elite, my beloved. And you will indeed see that in some of these smaller countries there has been a strong awareness in the population of the dangers of the elite, or the noble class of the middle ages and even the big industrialists and bankers and financiers. And so, you see that there is an awareness in the people of the need to establish equality, where all people are valued and all people are given equal opportunity, equal freedom.

Yet, my beloved, you will, of course, also see that this principle of equality and freedom can be taken too far, as it has been both in this nation and others. For as you discussed yesterday, my beloved, freedom does not actually mean freedom to do whatever you want. For if you exercise your so-called freedom to do whatever you want, well then the material world becomes a closed circle. And then, the contracting force of the mother – or the second law of thermodynamics, as science calls it – will begin to break things down and this will take away your freedom.

This can be seen clearly in this nation, it can be seen clearly in Denmark. It can be seen clearly in Switzerland. And of course, it can be seen most clearly in Germany and in its past, where Nazism was the extreme example of taking away the people's freedom in the guise of some greater, "noble" cause. And so you see that it is necessary for the people to be awakened, to realize that there must be a new awareness and understanding of the true nature of freedom.

The nature of freedom

Freedom, my beloved, is the freedom to reach beyond the separate sense of self and realize you are more than that separate self—and then express that more in this world. That, my beloved, is freedom.

What has happened in many nations is the perversion of this, where the power elite have taken away – through subtle and sometimes obvious means – people's freedom to express their spirituality, their creativity. And therefore, they have given them a substitute of material freedom. Which of course is not material freedom at all, but they have then sought to use both religion and science to make the people believe that the consequences of their "free" choices is not really the consequences of their choices, but something that happens that shouldn't be there, that should be masked and camouflaged, as you see in the health field.

Where you see that people have been given the impression that they can live any way they want, eat anything they want, and then when the body breaks down, they just go to the doctor who can supposedly give them some kind of remedy or cut out some part of the body to take away the symptom without even approaching the cause. The cause, of course, being consciousness, my beloved. And so you recognize, my beloved, that the people are not aware that the material world is not material, the material world is mind—the basic substance of the material world is mind, is consciousness. And thus the entire world is a projection of an image upon the Ma-ter Light. That image held in the consciousness of a self-aware being or many self-aware beings.

The earth, then, being created by beings in the spiritual realm called the Elohim, projecting a pure and balanced image upon the Ma-ter Light to create the planet as a platform for the growth of self-aware beings, who had not yet risen to that point of Christ-awareness, where they see the oneness of all life. Thus, giving them a platform for experimentation with their free will, even through the sense of separation but also, of course, giving them feedback by having nature itself and their bodies out-picture the images and beliefs they hold in consciousness.

Yet, because this very basic fact of life has been taken away from the people, how can the people exercise freedom when they do not know that every material circumstance they experience is nothing more than a projection of the images held in their consciousness, individually and collectively. This then is the awareness that must be brought forth, that must be spread abroad, through the people, for many are ready to understand this.

The new message to be spread

You may find that they will reject traditional religion. You may find that some cannot tolerate the mention of the word God, but I tell you, it is because they are rejecting the traditional theistic view of God as the remote judgmental being in the sky. Yet many of these people know within their hearts that there is a spiritual component to life, and it is only a matter of finding a way to express this that helps them go beyond the traditional images of God and the spiritual side of life, to where they see the true universality of it, my beloved.

And one key to this in Europe – that has been so dominated by Christianity for so long – is, of course, to restore a true understanding of the nature and mission of Christ, so that they can see in their outer minds what they already know in their hearts. So that they can see just how far the outer official Christian churches have strayed from the inner reality, mission and message of Christ. There is such a crying need for this to be spoken freely by those who are willing to acknowledge who they are and why they have come. For you see, my beloved, there is absolutely no way to manifest The Golden Age of Saint Germain without restoring – or we might say spreading for the first time – a true understanding of Christ.

The Golden Age is not something that can be brought forth on its own, independently of history. The Golden Age must be built on a foundation. And that foundation, my beloved, is that at least the top ten percent of the population need to understand and know that the central message of Christ was to be the example for all people to show that they have access to their own higher beings—that they have access to God, directly within themselves. They do not need an outer intermediary, be it the state or political party, or a church. For the Kingdom of God is within you, as Christ said so many years ago.

That statement was never taken out of the official bible. For those who attempted to manipulate the bible could not even comprehend it themselves and thus did not see it as necessary to remove it. Yet it is the very center of the message of Christ. And it is the very key to establishing what I talked about earlier, the true equality among men, upon which the political system of The Golden Age must be built.

The master key to freedom and equality

For you see, my beloved, only when each person knows that he or she has access to God directly within themselves, only then can there be true freedom and true equality. If the population believe that they cannot access God directly but must access God through an external mediator of some kind, well then they will be subject to being dominated by that external mediator and whatever institution this might be will inevitably be taken over by those people who lust after power. And therefore will use that external institution to control the people, as indeed the Roman Catholic Church – from its inception by the Emperor Constantine – was meant as an instrument to control the people.

This must be seen. Someone must cry out that the Pope has nothing on. And that the institution that he represents was flawed from its inception, was a deviation from the true mission of Christ. Where are those who dare make that cry? You, of course, have the potential to be among them, my beloved. As some of you have already done, at least in your own minds and among friends. But I tell you, there is a need to bring forth this awareness and to challenge not only the Catholic Church – for certainly we are not seeking to single out the Catholic Church – but to challenge the very institutionalized nature of Christianity—be it Protestant or Catholic or Fundamentalist or whatever you want to call it.

Look at the very idea that you are born in sin, my beloved, and therefore are fundamentally flawed from the very beginning, fundamentally different from Jesus, who had an immaculate conception. I tell you, my beloved, you all had an immaculate conception in the mind of your spiritual parents when your lifestream first descended to this Earth. Therefore, you can reclaim that birthright and say, "No, I was not born in sin. I do not accept that I am fundamentally different from Christ." For do you not see, my beloved, that the principle of equality cannot be completely understood or espoused as long as there is in the consciousness of the people the concept that one person, even though he walked the earth in a physical body, was fundamentally different from all others?

Right there, you have, in the Christian religion, a concept that undermines the very reality of the mission of Christ and the very reality of the true principle of equality that all men, all self-aware beings, all co-creators were created equal in the mind of God. Not in the sense that they were created alike, for each one is a unique individual, but in the sense that they are of equal value in the mind of God. Or rather, we should go beyond even the concept of value and comparison and recognize that each lifestream was created out of the unconditional love, the unconditional mind of God.

A non-linear view of karma

Master MORE, April 17, 2009

Honesty is the foundation for true healing

Thus I tell you, my beloved, in order to restore true healing, we must begin with a solid foundation. And thus, of course, we must begin with the first ray of the will of God. And what, then, is the quality of the first ray? You may think of it as the will of God, you may think of it as the power of God. But how about another quality: honesty.

Honesty, my beloved. Is that not a quality of the first ray? Is it not an expression, then, of the will of God and the power of God? For you see, my beloved, what is the core of honesty? Is it not oneness with the will of God? For truly, God is the ultimate honest being—for God cannot hide anything from itself.

You may have heard the old question – asked by the linear mind – "If God is almighty, can God create a rock so big that God cannot lift it?" Well, my beloved, God is One, so God cannot create anything that is hidden from itself—and thus the honesty. For my beloved, consider the very core of dishonesty. It is the belief that something can be hidden, that it is possible to say or do certain things while thinking something different within. As indeed, the serpent, to Eve, portrayed itself as the liberator, come to set her free from the shackles of the command of the spiritual teacher in the garden. And thus, you see – right there – where the foundation of disease is laid—in the dishonesty, in the illusion that something can be hidden.

And then, consider honesty and my previous message of your free will right to have any experience you want, to enter the theater of life and put on any costume that you desire to experience, my beloved. Do you see that there is nothing wrong, sinful – or whatever you want to call it – in trying on many different costumes on the stage of life. This is what God has given you a right to do.

Yet, my beloved, when you begin to create the belief that you are trapped in a particular costume and that some external force is preventing you from moving on, well then, dishonesty enters the picture. Why do I say dishonesty? Because when you consider this from a realistic perspective, you realize that God has given you complete freedom to try on any costume you like. God does not force you to try on any costume whatsoever. Which means what, my beloved? It means that you, yourself, you are choosing which costume to put on.

And thus, when you build the belief that you have not chosen your current situation – that your situation is not the result of your own choices, past and present – well then you put yourself in a situation where you are trapped in what we have called the catch-22. For you see, my beloved, when you imagine that some external force has put you in your current situation, well then, who can set you free from that situation? Logically, it must also be an external force, must it not? And that means, then, that you have given away your power to change your situation. You have put yourself in a passive mode, my beloved, of waiting for some external force to do it for you. And thus, you have done what you also have a right to do—you have given away your free will to an external power.

Again, my beloved, God has given you free will. You have a right to do this. You have a right, as Maitreya explains in his book, to decide that you no longer want to decide – to make the decision that you no longer want to make decisions – and therefore create the graven image that there is some external power that is ruling your life.

Beware the subtlety of free will

And you see, my beloved, the serpent will whisper in your ear that you have a right to create that role, that costume, and to try on what it feels like to be disempowered. And from the perspective of the linear intellectual mind, it will seem that the serpent is right. But the subtlety here, my beloved, is that when you do give away your power, then how can you step outside of the costume? How can you just leave it behind and walk away from it? Do you see, the subtlety?

One cannot necessarily say from a linear, analytical perspective that the serpent is wrong. But you see, God has given you complete freedom and does not limit your choices. You may try on any costume, but no matter which costume you take on, God accepts you for the being that God created as an extension of itself. Which means that any time you desire to put off the old man and put on the new man in Christ, the new man in Oneness, well then God will welcome you with open arms. So God does not limit your freedom to take on a costume or to take it off again.

But do you see that the serpentine logic does indeed limit your freedom? For when you accept the lie, the illusion, that some external force – such as the angry God in the sky who has caused you to be born in sin – has precipitated your situation, well then you cannot simply believe that you can just take off the costume, put off the old man and be reborn and become a new being in Christ. And so, while God has given you power and the freedom to exercise that power, the serpent and the serpentine consciousness aims to take away your power.

And of course, I, as the representative of the Will of God, will say that the overall will of God is that you exercise your free will, create any experience you want, so that you have an opportunity to learn. And thus, that is why you have the potential to separate from oneness and to believe in the serpentine lie and to follow that false path, the downward path, of separating yourself further and further from oneness.

This is your right. I champion it. But my point here, my beloved, is that it is not in any way, shape, or form the will of God that you should suffer or be stuck in a limited sense of identity. It is not the will of God for you, personally, that you should become less, in the sense that you see yourself as less than the pure Being that God created.

The Alpha and the Omega of healing

So you see, there is an Alpha aspect of the will of God, which has given you complete freedom of choice. And there is an Omega aspect of the will of God, which desires you to use your freedom of choice to become MORE, not less. And so, what is the lesson, then, in terms of true healing? Well what is true healing? It is self-healing!

For what is the purpose of life? It is the growth of the self, the growth of your self-awareness, my beloved. Which is the entire purpose for the world of form. Where you might start out with a very localized sense of identity – being identified with some material form, such as your physical body – but yet, no matter how limited that identity might be, you have the potential to grow in self-awareness until you reach the consciousness of the Being out of which Being you are. Yet this growth is self-growth. It is not forced upon you by God. For self-growth cannot be forced.

And thus, the beginning of true healing is indeed when you recognize that you have chosen to separate from Oneness. The reason why your physical body or your mind needs healing is that you have made choices that limited yourself, rather than expanding your sense of self. You became trapped in the illusion, whereby you have come to see yourself – not as a spiritual being who has temporarily taken on a particular role and costume in the drama of the material universe – you instead think that you are trapped in this universe, trapped in a particular role. This then, is giving away your power to heal yourself.

How can you exercise that power? Well, my beloved, when you truly understand free will, you recognize that it is free, completely free, my beloved. God has given you a will that is completely free. Which means that as you can choose to take on a particular costume – no matter what that costume may be like – you do, at any moment, have the complete freedom to separate yourself from the costume—to just take it off, to let it drop from you, to let the old man die and to be reborn in a new sense of self. This is recognizing the power that God has given you. And thus, you recognize that it is the ego and the false teachers, those in the serpentine consciousness, who are seeking to take away your power by making you believe that you either are that costume, that role, or that you cannot simply just take it off.

Opening up to a new view of karma

For you see, my beloved, when you look at humankind there is indeed a dividing line that you might observe, namely that many are still completely identified with the physical body and their growing up in a particular circumstance of family, culture, nationality, religion, ethnicity, race or whatever division you have. Yet the more spiritual people have started to awaken from that illusion and realize they are more than these outer identities and labels and divisions. But still, when you begin to awaken and realize you are more, well then you are faced with the lie that you cannot simply walk away from your old identity. For you have made mistakes, you have sinned. And somehow your sins must be repaid, your karma must be balanced.

But you see, my beloved, may I ask you to partake of a little thought experiment here. Let us take the old teaching given in the East – even a teaching that we have found it necessary to give in previous dispensations of the Ascended Host – namely, the teaching that karma is some external force. You have committed errors in a past life and you owe some kind of debt to life and the scales must be balanced. The energy you have misqualified needs to be rebalanced, my beloved.

Now, this is not necessarily incorrect. You have free will to do anything you want. But what is it that allows you to do anything in the material world? Well, it is that you are receiving a portion of spiritual light from your own I AM Presence, which you then express through your four lower bodies. And you are, of course, responsible for what you do with that energy. For you cannot permanently leave the Earth behind until you have at least raised up all energy that you have qualified with the vibration of non-love, thus limiting all life.

You must come to a point where at least your presence on this Earth is a balance—you do not pull life down. Of course, you did not come here to pull life down, nor did you come here to struggle for hundreds of embodiments only to come back to a balanced point and then leave. You came here to bring a positive gift, to shine your light in the darkness of the material universe and to ultimately raise up this sphere, as Maitreya explains, to where it can ascend and out-picture the kingdom of God.

Yet, let us then consider that you are a co-creator who has experimented with free will over many lifetimes. You have taken on a certain role, identified yourself as a separate being, and you have used the energy given to you by your I AM Presence to seek to own and possess things for that separate self. Perhaps seeking to raise it up in comparison to others, thereby attaining some prominent position in society that enabled you to put other people down, so that you would seem more important.

There are, of course, many ways to make such karma, as we call it. But now look at this realistically, my beloved, and recognize that there is nothing that can be said with words that cannot be twisted and turned by the serpentine consciousness and the serpentine logic. For this is the essence of the serpentine logic—that when you eat of the fruit, you become "wise as God," you become as God, "knowing good and evil," which means that you enter into the duality consciousness, my beloved. Where you now think – your ego thinks – that it has the right to define good and evil in an ultimate sense.

Which is why you see that there are religions on this Earth that define themselves as being the only true religion, thereby defining the absolute belief that all non-members will burn forever in hell. There are those who have espoused a particular political philosophy as superior to any other, therefore giving rise to the belief that it is justified that they seek to suppress any other philosophy, imposing their own system upon the rest of the world.

And so, you see now how the serpentine consciousness entraps you in this belief—that the forms you see in the material world have some ultimate reality. And thus, you cannot simply walk away from them. You are crucified, by the form, by the image, by the consciousness. And so, as was out-pictured by Jesus, you enter into the drama of life, and they may indeed "crucify" you. And it seems like there was, even for Jesus, nothing he could do but play that role.

Look at the stations of the cross out-pictured here in this place [Lourdes, France] through the Catholic tradition. Jesus is condemned to death. Jesus accepts his cross. However, even that is a passive act of accepting what others want to put upon him. Jesus falls, someone helps Jesus carry the cross, someone wipes his tears, someone attempts to tell him not to go through with this. He is nailed to the cross, he dies, he is taken down, he is put in the tomb. All passive things, my beloved.

And so, what is missing from the steps of the cross, the stations of the cross? Well many things, but for one, my beloved, the reality that Jesus chose to enter into Jerusalem, knowing full well what might happen. And most importantly, while hanging on the cross, he chose to give up the ghost, thereby in an instant putting off that sense of the separate self, my beloved, showing the potential that all of you have to instantly let the old being, the old self die. And thereby not cease to exist, as the false teachers and the ego would have you believe, but indeed being reborn into a greater sense of self, the self that you still are in the eyes of God.

A revolutionary view of karma

Now, my beloved, there is a deeper reality. And so, returning to the concept of karma, what is the illusion superimposed upon the concept by the serpentine mind? Understand that the serpentine mind is based on separation, and when you are separated from your source, what must you believe about the power of God?

You must believe that it can only come from outside yourself. For when you see yourself as a separate being, you cannot accept that the power of God can come from inside yourself. And thus, you are susceptible to the belief, my beloved, that in one extreme you need an external savior. In the other extreme that you need to do something down here, on Earth, as a separate self, in order to be redeemed of your sin or to balance your karma.

Now, my beloved, beware of what I am telling you. Be alert now, and perhaps even step back and see how your own outer, analytical mind will seek to play tricks on you, so that you either do not hear my words or do not hear the true meaning. What was said earlier? That you have come to accept that there is something wrong with you, something particular, some particular problem that blocks you from entering the kingdom of God. But you see, my beloved, what is truly wrong with you is the concept that there is something wrong.

And where does that concept come from? From the illusion of separation, from the creation of the separate self! There is indeed, one might say, something wrong with the separate self if one wants to think in dualistic terms. But there is nothing wrong with you, the being that you truly are.

From a greater perspective there is not even anything wrong with the separate self, for God does not think in terms of right or wrong. God only thinks in terms of what is real and what is unreal. And only that which is created in oneness, as an expression of oneness, only that is real. Whereas anything created out of the consciousness of separation is not real and thus cannot affect that part of you which is real—cannot limit it, cannot encage it in a particular role, or costume, or form or sense of self.

Do you, then, begin to see, my beloved, what karma truly is? You have been so accustomed, so conditioned by the dualistic mind, that you have come to believe that there really are two opposites—and that one of those opposites is God, and the other opposite is that which is anti-God. This, my beloved, is the arrogance of the fallen beings, who in their spiritual pride believe that by rebelling against God they actually had an affect on God and the spiritual Beings who have not separated from oneness. But you see, my beloved, God is not in the opposite polarity of separation. God is One, undivided, indivisible, unconditional. How can any condition oppose that which is unconditional?

Do you see that in oneness there can be no conditions? So how do you separate from oneness? By creating conditions! But how can you create conditions? You must create two conditions, at least two, that oppose each other. For if there is not the opposition, then you still have oneness, and so you have no separation.

My beloved, I AM the master of the Will of God. I have my beloved friends on the other six rays. Am I in opposition to Saint Germain because I am on the first and he is on the seventh, thus on opposite ends of the linear scale? How could this be possible? How could the Will of God oppose the Freedom of God, when it is the will of God that all beings be free—and that you become free by being one with the will of God that raises all life?

So do you see, my beloved, that you may think that in a past life you created bad karma and that in order to ascend, you must balance that karma by creating good karma. But good and bad are dualistic conditions. You cannot neutralize, balance or negate one dualistic condition by going into the opposite. You cannot overcome a problem with the same state of consciousness that created the problem.

So what is karma? It is that you use your creative power through the filter of a separate, dualistic self. My beloved, anything you do through that filter creates karma that separates you from oneness. Do you see that it was because you came to see yourself as a separate being, that you became focused on the self, and therefore might have done something that was egotistical or selfish according to the standard definition—thus creating what most people see as negative karma? It was the illusion that you are a separate being that caused this.

Well, then, how can you counteract that by doing something else through the separate self? Do you see that the very concept that you have created negative karma as a separate self and that you have to balance it as a separate self is illogical, contradictory? For as long as you are striving to balance the karma that you see as being made by the separate self, you are reinforcing the illusion that you are a separate self.

...

A faster way to rise above karma

So while you can make some progress from the consciousness of the separate self, consider another route. Consider that instead of focusing on balancing karma, as some external force, you instead listen to the words of Christ, my beloved. For did he not say, "Seek ye first the kingdom of God and his righteousness and all these things shall be added unto you." What is the kingdom of God? It is indeed the Christ consciousness based on oneness, where you have the righteousness – the right use – of your creative power—that you use it to raise up the All instead of the separate self. And so, consider that instead of focusing on an outer, somewhat mechanical, act of balancing karma, you focus on switching your sense of identity, switching your self-image, switching your perspective. Going through that seismic shift in identity, where you no longer see separation, but see oneness.

What will happen in the process, my beloved? What will happen is that you take back your own power, you reconnect to the Higher Being you are and now you can say with Jesus, "I and my father are one. My father worketh hitherto and I work." And so, my beloved, when you come into that state of oneness – at least some degree of oneness although not yet the full Christhood, but still some degree of oneness – and you see that you still have some karma left, my beloved, how hard do you think it is to balance that karma when you have the power of God flowing through you to do it?

Do you see, it is much easier to walk the path by first seeking oneness than by seeking to fulfill an outer requirement of balancing karma, and then thinking that oneness will come automatically? Thereby limiting yourself – perhaps for the rest of this embodiment – to only exercising the power that comes through your separate self, instead of the power of the greater being that you are.

Illusions, my beloved—illusions! How subtle is the logic of the serpentine mind? How subtle it is, when you look at it from inside the separate self. How obvious it is when you reach for the Christ mind and gain that unconditional perspective, where you do not see truth as expressed in a particular word or teaching, but you have followed the call of Christ: "God is a Spirit, and they that worship him must worship him in Spirit and in truth."

And when you know this Spirit of Truth, you know the vibration of truth, and you have the ultimate co-measurement, the ultimate guiding rod, the staff of Moses, my beloved, that will part the waters of the dead sea—as a representation of the duality consciousness. So that you may walk across safely and yet, when the hordes of death come behind you, the waters of their own dualistic consciousness close upon them. And they are swept up in the turmoil, while you walk to the other side, to the land of Israel, that which Is Real.

Balancing the scales of life

Lady Master Portia with Saint Germain, April 19, 2009

Many people think that if you have committed evil in the past, even in a past life, and your scale is pulled down to one side, that if you commit good in this life, you will put weight on the opposite side of the scale and you will gradually balance them. But you see, my beloved, you may commit many good acts and raise up the other side of the scale, but you cannot hold it in balance. You cannot hold the balance, the scale will immediately begin to move down on the other side, until you have another unbalanced situation. For you are now moving from the extreme of relative evil to the opposite extreme of relative good, which is not God-good, because it is not unconditional good.

There is, of course, no unconditional evil, my beloved. And that is why, in order to balance the scales, you must empty both cups, so that you have no conditions on either side—neither the side of relative evil, nor the side of relative good.

...

Matter is infinitely changeable, but only when you are willing to change the cause behind the effect of matter—namely the mental image, the condition of the mind. Thus, my beloved, if you have the subtle belief that your illness is a punishment for some error committed, that you deserve the punishment, and that you need to suffer for a time in order to be saved and go to heaven, well then how can you accept that you can instantly be free of the illness? How can you accept healing? How can you accept wholeness, my beloved?

Overcoming the consciousness of death

This is, indeed, a test that all must face. It is a test that Jesus had to face in order to attain that level of mastery, where he could be the open door for the light of such a high vibration that it could instantly change matter and therefore manifest what people have called the miracles of Christ. They are not miracles in the traditional sense, they are simply the out-picturing of a higher law. For as I said, it is not possible to change the vibration of matter through the dualistic consciousness. As Jesus expressed it, "With Man, this is impossible"—with the manly, the human, the dualistic, the separate, the mortal state of consciousness, it is not possible to change matter through the power of mind.

It is only possible to change matter through the force that can be exercised through the physical realm. And that is why you indeed see medical technology seeking to increase its power to change disease by force, by destroying the disease, even destroying the body in the process. And so, you need to come to that true realization that Jesus came to, towards the end of his training period, the true realization that it – truly, honestly, absolutely, realistically – is possible to change any condition in matter in an instant—when you switch the mind.

What is it that pulls you away from that knowing, that acceptance? It is the consciousness that has been called "death." Death has been called the last enemy, for death is the sense that matter is permanent, difficult to change. But behind that, the sense that matter is real, that it has some independent existence, my beloved. This, of course, is based on the illusion of the fallen beings who have rebelled against God and who have created the illusion that separated themselves from God and God's kingdom, creating a world where God is not. Therefore, they seek to spread that death consciousness to all people, so that they reinforce it. And through their acceptance of death as inevitable, the acceptance of matter as real and separated from God, they give their light to the fallen beings who have no light, for they cannot receive it from within.

Why? Because they have chosen to go into the ultimate state of separation. There are degrees of separation, and until you reach that ultimate state, you still receive some light from your I AM Presence that sustains you. But when you come to that ultimate state of separation, then you can no longer receive the light, for you are not willing to accept it. It is not that the light is not there, that God withholds his light. For I tell you that even the darkest being that you can possibly imagine, be it Lucifer, Satan or whomever, God is not withholding light from them. For God still only desires to see them come back to oneness, but you can come to a point, where you absolutely reject that you have the ability to receive light or the willingness or the worthiness or whatever it might be.

And from that point you can sustain any form of self, any form of awareness, only by taking light from others—who are still receiving it from above, but who are misqualifying it through fear, anger or whatever lower feelings that are not of love. And thus, my beloved, you will indeed see that this world is enveloped in a black cloud of the death consciousness. And that is why death is the last enemy. Because it is so difficult to overcome that illusion that matter is real.

For after all, your five senses are telling you that matter is real. And even your outer, analytical mind is telling you that matter is real. And therefore, it cannot simply be changed in an instant. For you cannot see with the outer mind and the senses that behind the matter that seems so solid, there is only light—consciousness. And consciousness can change in an instant.

This you have all experienced—how you can change your mind in an instant, from a state of sorrow, to a state of joy, or the other way around. Consider how simple it is to change your mind in an instant. Consider, my beloved, how women are often accused of changing their minds a thousand times. But realize that the reality here is that women are more in tune with the reality that you have a perfect right to change your mind at any time. For God has given you free will. So who says that because you have chosen to be in a certain state of mind – for a day, or a decade, or ten thousand embodiments – you have to continue to be in that state of mind indefinitely?

This is the death consciousness, my beloved. The death consciousness says that once you have made the mistake of eating a forbidden fruit, of partaking of the duality consciousness, you can never overcome that duality consciousness. As one person explained to this messenger yesterday, the Church of Satan says that once you have accepted membership, you can never renounce it, for you have given your soul to the devil and you can never take it back. But the reality is, of course, that there is no such thing as any permanence in the material realm. That which is unreal cannot permanently affect that which is real.

And so, when you see that you are real, you know that no promise made, no curse put upon you, no illusion can ever hold you any longer than the moment when you decide that you are no longer the person who made the promise or made the mistake or accepted the death consciousness. You have been reborn, and thus you are free. You are free to Be what you want to be. For God within you will say, "I will be who I will be. And now I choose to be MORE than I was before." And in that choosing, you are reborn, you are free.

The tenth ray of transparency

Gautama Buddha, May 9, 2009.

The reality is, my beloved, that everything is consciousness—everything is awareness. Thus, you are a co-creator with God. You are a self-aware being. But how do you co-create? You co-create by using the only reality there is, namely, what we have called the Ma-ter light. We have also explained that the Ma-ter light has consciousness, although few of you have truly pondered this. What exactly does this mean, my beloved? It means, that whatever is created, whatever is envisioned, whatever is imagined, is done with this basic consciousness of the Ma-ter light.

And so, that consciousness of the Ma-ter light takes on a particular form. Yet, because it is conscious, it is possible to create enough intensity that eventually that which is conscious now becomes so concentrated that it develops a rudimentary form of self-awareness. And thus, what has been created is a particular, conscious, living entity.

You have been so used to growing up in a society that presents everything in the material world as inanimate forms and objects. This, of course, is an inaccurate image, as I explained earlier, that even quantum physics itself has proven to be incomplete. Consciousness is the underlying reality, my beloved. And so, when you, as a self-aware co-creator, impose a mental image upon the Ma-ter light, you are not simply projecting an image upon the inanimate object of a movie screen. You are projecting it upon the basic awareness of the Mother light.

And when you infuse that image with enough life force, through your attention, through your awareness, well then the image will reach that intensity, that complexity, where now it begins to take on a life of its own. It is somewhat like the old dream, where people believe they can create life, out-pictured, for example, in the movie about Doctor Frankenstein—who took various body parts, stitched them together, infused them with a higher force, and then it came alive.

This is essentially what all of you do when you co-create, for that is the power of your consciousness. You have the power, through your self-awareness, to impose that self-awareness, that life-force, upon the Ma-ter light, until it takes on enough of the life force, that the image that you have imposed actually comes alive. Almost like what you see in a cartoon, where the drawings are still images, but when played in sequence it seems as if the character comes alive.

Co-creating from oneness

So, the question now becomes, how do you use your co-creative power? Is it through the state of non-duality or through the state of duality?

You see, when you use your co-creative power from that state of equilibrium – of oneness, of knowing the oneness of all life – then you can create distinct life forms that do take on a life, but not a disconnected, separate existence. They become part of the River of Life that is created out of the thrust and the Being of all the self-aware co-creators who have gone before you in the different spheres, as Maitreya explains. So as long as you are one with that River of Life, anything you create becomes part of the River of Life. For the purpose of this discussion on transparency, we might say that anything you create from the state of oneness has transparency—which means that the pure light of God can shine through it.

Consider how you look at a window in a house. If the window was not transparent, would it have any value whatsoever? Of course not, for you want the light to shine through. And that is precisely what happens when you create from oneness. You create a life form that may take on life, but it is not separated, disconnected. And you can see that that life form owes its life, owes its existence, to the flow of life that comes from a higher source—even though it comes through your consciousness, it comes from a higher source. And therefore, you recognize that you are a co-creator, "I can of my own self do nothing. The father within me, he doeth the work."

For you are using the light, the life force, of God, streaming through your mind. You cannot produce that light from your conscious self or your lower mind. You can only receive it from a higher source, from your I AM Presence, and from the hierarchy of light stretching all the way back to the Creator. "Stretching," of course, implying great distance, which is not the reality, but yet, there is a certain reality in the different levels of vibration and frequency.

Now then, as long as you create from oneness, there will be transparency in what you create. Meaning that no one can actually look at what you have co-created and think that it can exist on its own. You know that nothing can exist without its source, that everything owes its existence, its life, to the source beyond it. And thus, no one can become trapped in that particular world of form, for they will know that there is always something beyond—for the light is shining through.

Co-creating from duality

So then, what happens when you begin to co-create from the state of separation, the illusion of duality? Well, what happens is that what you create is also a life form that takes on, in this case, a life of its own, a separate life.

You may have heard in various spiritual teachings, there is talk of entities, of demons, of various dark beings. Well, my beloved, such beings are created through the duality consciousness.

But do not be naive and think that what is created through the duality consciousness can only appear as dark or scary. The reality is that people have created many beings, many entities, that are seemingly good and that they believe are good or necessary or beneficial or even serve God's purpose. Yet they are based on the sense of separation, the illusion of separation.

You see, what is the illusion of separation? As we have explained, God is everywhere and in everything. You cannot be separated from

God—it is impossible. It is like a drop in the ocean claiming to be separated from the ocean. Yet, because of free will, you can create the appearance, the illusion that you are separated. And how can you do this? You do this, my beloved, because you live in a universe, in a sphere, that, as Maitreya explains, has not yet reached the critical intensity of light. If your universe had reached that intensity of light, the light would be so intense that it could shine through anything and everything. And thus, everything would be transparent, nothing could block the light, and the illusion of separation could not exist.

But because the intensity of light is yet below the critical level in the material universe – at least in certain pockets of that universe, such as your solar system – well then it is possible to use the co-creative powers of the mind to go into a lower vibration – a vibration that vibrates below the frequency of love – and use one of these lower vibrations – be it fear, anger, hatred, judgment, criticism, or whatever you have – to co-create something. And it is almost as if that something becomes so dense that the light cannot shine through it. The reality, however, being that it becomes so dense that when you look through that screen, you cannot see the light.

The light is still there. There is still light everywhere in the material universe. But when you, the conscious self, step into an environment created from frequencies below a certain level, then the conscious self cannot see the light. For you have used your free will to create a sphere that has no real existence, but it has existence in your mind—so that it forms a screen that you see through. It is as if you put a piece of colored paper onto your window, and it reduces the light intensity that can shine through and it gives that light a certain coloring. And if you keep putting enough paper on the window, eventually you will block the light entirely.

Yet, take note of what I said. You co-create by directing the life force that is streaming through you. You have the right, according to the Law of Free Will, to impose any image, any mental image, upon that light, as you project it onto the Ma-ter light.

If you want to connect to what I said in the previous discourse, you may say that the Ma-ter light represents the Mother aspect of creation. And the expanding force is the Father aspect, which streams through your consciousness and is directed onto the Ma-ter light, where it then causes the Ma-ter light to take on the form of the image you hold in your mind, as the light flows through it.

You have the power to create a living entity

But because everything is consciousness, what you create is not just an inanimate form, it is not just a dead form. It will eventually start to take on life, and the more it is infused with the life force through your attention, the more life it takes on, the more of a survival instinct it begins to develop. Which is why you can have an ego that has a survival instinct, and as such seeks to control the Conscious You. And you can have mass entities that have enough of a survival instinct to seek to control people, and pull them into an addiction – such as tobacco – that forces their light so that the entity can absorb it and use it to survive, and even grow in intensity.

So what you see is that ever since the first beings in a higher realm descended into duality – because they were not willing to transcend themselves – they have used their co-creative abilities to co-create through the illusion – the filter, the maya – of the duality consciousness. But what they have created are these entities, these beings that do not have self-awareness as you do – as an extension of the Creator – but they have enough awareness that they exist and that they need something in order to continue to exist.

Thus, they are sort of like an animal life form that, while not having a sophisticated self-awareness that you see in humans, they have at least some rudimentary self-awareness that causes them, then, to seek to control anyone that can be controlled by their particular frequency. For all of these entities that have been created, form what Jesus called the "prince of this world."

And if they have something in you, they will pull upon it in order to force your attention into certain patterns, into certain images, so that you misqualify the light and keep feeding the life force to these entities—that have a hold on you and essentially milk you, as if you were a cow, ready to be milked twice a day by going into a certain state of consciousness.

And so, this is what you see, not only with physical addictions, but with so many people who go into anger or fear, or judgmentalness, or criticalness—of criticizing or always judging and analyzing everyone and everything, using the analytical mind, but imposing that value judgment of the ego upon it. Which then causes the misqualification of the light, causes the light to take on a lower frequency, according to this dualistic relative value judgment, where something is good and something is bad.

Whereas, in the transparency – the purity of the transparency, my beloved – everything is an expression of the one, so nothing can be good in a relative sense to something that is bad. It simply IS.

The initiation of the tenth ray

So then, when you come to the tenth ray and the initiations of the tenth ray, you need to become aware of this. A topic that many people, even many spiritual people, would rather not know about, would rather not think about, would rather not talk about. For it is uncomfortable to them to recognize that perhaps they could have used their co-creative abilities to create something that has taken on a life of its own and is now seeking to control them—and is even seeking to control other people. And perhaps they could even be controlled by a mass entity created by humankind over thousands and tens of thousands and millions of years—so that that mass entity has become so strong that it is very difficult for the individual to withstand its pull.

Which, precisely, is why, as you go through the initiations of the seven rays, you need to create that momentum that keeps you going beyond the downward pull of the mass consciousness. But it is also why you need to go back, as Mother Mary explained, and recover any aspects of your being that are trapped in these lower states. But you cannot, in most cases, fully recover this until you go beyond the seven rays, go into the eighth, go into the ninth, come into that equilibrium. For you see, my beloved, the equilibrium forms a foundation. When you know that there is equilibrium, beyond the struggle, well then you have a foundation for taking a closer look at the struggle. And that is when you can realize that the struggle is not really what it seems to be from a surface awareness.

It is actually a struggle between principalities and forces that are not visible to the senses and the outer mind—it is between all of these entities that have been created. And precisely because they are created out of the duality consciousness, they must be locked in a struggle with each other. For you see, the pure light of God that remains transparent, that remains at the vibration of love, is unlimited. But when the light takes on a lower vibration than love, it becomes finite, it becomes limited.

So now there is only – even though six billion people on this planet are constantly misqualifying light – there is still only a finite amount. Which means that all of the entities that inhabit the forcefield, the energy field, of Earth must fight. Just like you see, when an animal dies on the African Savannah, the hyenas and the vultures immediately start fighting over the carcass, my beloved. For they know that it will only last a short time, and if they don't get it, someone else will. And this is the real cause of the struggle.

Why are people struggling

You may look at people and say, "Why are they struggling?" And you may look at what so many people that are well-meaning have done—trying to find a psychological cause, looking at the individual, looking at a particular group, looking at their beliefs. For example, you will see a wave of people who have come to conclude that the real cause of all warfare is religion and religious beliefs. And so, they think that if only we can get rid of religion and get people to disavow their belief in religion, then we will have peace.

But they fail to realize that it is not religion that is the cause of war—that religion is simply being used as a tool to agitate people, so that they misqualify their light. Whereas the real cause of the struggle and the war is that there are entities beyond the physical, who need the constant misqualification of light in order to survive. And if people do not misqualify that light, well then, they will die out.

Which is why they must continue to keep people in that grip, so that they will continue to fight each other in a senseless struggle—as you see in the Middle East and elsewhere. This surely can never be construed as being the will of the real God, but could only be the will of a graven image of God, projected upon God through the duality consciousness.

And so, again, there are numerous of these living entities—born from a certain image of God, a certain image born from duality. The most dangerous of these entities are precisely the ones that relate to a graven image of God. Because those are the ones that people find it most difficult to abandon, my beloved.

You may take an entity, such as the tobacco entity, and see that it is obviously very dangerous for the people who are addicted to tobacco.

Nevertheless, it is becoming increasingly easier for people in the modern world to see the dangers of smoking. Which is why more and more people have given up this habit, after realizing that it destroys their bodies and perhaps even sensing that it has negative spiritual ramifications as well. Yet, look at how many people are still trapped in believing that there has to be one superior religion and that this religion is given by God. And therefore, it is mandated by God that this religion must take over the world, for it is the only way to save people. And all non-believers will not be saved but will be condemned to live in eternity in hell.

And so, consider how difficult it is for people to give up this belief, this illusion, so that they will stop feeding their light into this mass entity—whether it be the mass entity of Christianity, the mass entity of Islam, even the mass entity of Buddhism, my beloved. For each religion, each belief system, has created such a mass entity that is struggling with the mass entities of other religions—even feeding an even greater entity that simply feeds on the struggle itself and will use anything to create the struggle. Certainly, my beloved, materialistic science has created such a mass entity that is also seeking to strengthen itself and take over, even to the point of taking the light from the mass entities of religion, by getting people to distrust religion and give up their religious beliefs.

So those scientists who believe they are working for a greater cause are simply working for the same cause that they see religious people working for. Thus, they see the fallacy of religious people, feeding their light into this beast, but they do not see that they, themselves, are doing the same thing—simply working for another beast. And that they, too, have this belief in the supremacy of their own world view and the drive to impose it and enforce it upon others—which cannot come from God, my beloved.

How to create unity among people

Why can this not come from God? Why can you not truly say that the one God has created one true religion and wants all people to go into it? Well, because the true God, the Living God, has given complete free will to all extensions of itself. And thus, the true God does not want people to come into unity by being forced to adhere to a particular outer belief system.

There is only one way to create true unity and oneness among people and that is to increase the transparency, so that more and more people can begin to see that they come from a higher source. And when you see that you come from a higher source, you will eventually come to see that all other people must also have come from that source, and that, then, is the foundation for true unity—based on transparency.

And as the consciousness is raised, then the light will shine through the screen of people's consciousness. And as more and more light shines through, then the light is the unifying factor. Not a particular religion, not a political ideology, not a scientific world view – or rather, belief system – but the light is the only unifying factor. The light that exposes the darkness for what it is—unreal, temporary, impermanent.

For when you see the light, you see that only the light is real—and only that which is real can be permanent. Whereas anything else must be temporary, a fleeting image projected upon the screen of the Ma-ter light. But only sustained as long as enough self-aware beings are feeding it through their attention, through their identification with it—seeing it as part of their identity. Instead of seeing the transparent reality that they are more than anything on Earth. For they are spiritual beings, and they can instantly withdraw from these patterns of unreality. They can instantly rise above them, walk away from them and refuse to keep feeding them their light.

The lie that you cannot transcend

Do you see how the prince of this world has attempted to create a belief that says that once you have created this entity, you cannot simply walk away from it? But you can, my beloved. How else will you stop feeding it your light?

Consider my previous discourse on action. You take an unbalanced action—how do you undo it? You cannot undo it by taking another un-balanced action. You can take one action through one dualistic polarity, but you do not undo it by taking an action from the opposite dualistic polarity. You undo it only by rising above duality, so that you no longer feed it through your attention. You neither feed this dualistic entity, nor that dualistic entity. You simply transcend it. And you then allow the second law of thermodynamics, or the wrath of Kali, or the dance of Shiva, to consume it.

Do you see, my beloved, your Creator was not ignorant. This is one of the greatest traps of the duality consciousness—that it creates a world view, which it believes is perfectly logical. And thus, it believes that it is smarter than even God, and God could not possibly have foreseen this sophisticated world view. But God did foresee exactly what would happen by giving self-aware beings free will—that some would go into the duality consciousness and become trapped there.

And thus, God set up a perfect system for making sure that it was as difficult as possible for a being to become trapped in duality so long that it would eventually face the possibility of a second death. Thereby, giving people as many possibilities as anyone could possibly want to transcend and come back to the reality of oneness. And that is why, indeed, the system is such that when you go into an unbalanced state, you will create the struggle. You will create from the realm where the struggle is inevitable, and thus your creation will break down, will be threatened, will be opposed by others—and so you can never have permanence in that creation.

You cannot step into the same river twice

But now let us take this one step further and consider why you want permanency, my beloved? For as we have said before, the ego was created because the conscious self perceived that the ego could give it some advantage. And so, consider the saying, "You cannot step into the same river twice."

For what is a river? It is a stream of water that is constantly moving. And if you step into the river, you are stepping into certain water molecules. If you step out and step back in, other molecules have moved into the place of the previous ones. And thus, you are not – technically, in reality – stepping into the same river.

So it is with the River of Life, my beloved. The River of Life is constantly moving on. It is set up so that those who are willing to be part of that forward movement are constantly becoming MORE, instead of standing still or becoming less. Why is this so, my beloved? Well, because the goal of a self-aware being is, of course, to start out with a limited, localized self-awareness and expand it to the level of the Creator itself. We might say – by using images with which you are familiar – that God thought that you might be bored by being the same being over a long period of time. And thus, God gave you the option of being in the River of Life where everything is constantly new.

So, you will see that even though God has given you the right to create any experience you want, when you are in the River of Life, every experience is new. There is growth, there is transcendence. And so, there can be those, my beloved, who cannot fully accept or adjust to this constant flow and transcendence. They want to own something, they want to own an experience and keep it for a time, instead of transcending it.

And thus, the only place where you can own something is in the realm – the sphere, the illusion – of separation, where things can be perceived as standing still. The reality is, of course, that nothing stands still, neither in the realm of oneness, nor in the realm of separation. For in the realm of oneness, you have the constant drive to become MORE, to transcend. And in the realm of separation, you have the contracting force of the Mother – the second law of thermodynamics, the power of Shiva – that breaks down everything. And so you see, you can either transcend, which is life, or you can attempt to stand still, which is death. There is truly no other choice. Choose ye this day whom ye will serve. Choose life!

For, unless you choose life, you will choose death. And you will suffer loss. You will be less, until you eventually forget who you are and believe that you truly are a lesser being, be it a sinner or be it a sophisticated ape.

What you think you own owns you

So, the desire for ownership can be very subtle. It is what I called an attachment, when I walked the Earth. It is the desire to own or posses something, to pull it out of the constant self-transcendence of the River of Life. And you can create the illusion that you own something, but that which you own is precisely an entity created through the power of your attention. And that entity wants to survive. And how can it survive? Only when you keep feeding it your light, which means that the entity wants to own you.

And as long as you believe it is real, as long as you allow it in your sphere of identity, then it does own you. What you create in separation will own you, my beloved. You may think that you own it, but it is the other way around.

What is the beginning of the spiritual path? It is when a person comes to the point – whether it is consciously aware of this or not – but comes to the point of deciding, "I cannot do this anymore. There must be a better way. There must be more to life." And thereby essentially saying, "I do not want to be owned by my own miscreations. I want to be free. I want to be more than this." And thus, it begins the upward climb, where it gradually shakes off the snakeskins of that lesser identity, until it can stand free and recognize that, "I AM a spiritual being. I am a co-creator with my God."

The eleventh ray of transcendence

Gautama Buddha, May 9, 2009.

Transcendence is the key word for the eleventh ray. Transcendence of what? Transcendence of your present sense of self—whatever that sense of self might be. You can always transcend and become MORE, as even your Creator is becoming MORE by creating you.

So you see, transcendence is, again, a concept that the linear mind finds it impossible to categorize and put in a mental box. For the linear mind wants to go to the ultimate extreme and say, "There must come a point where no more transcendence is possible. There must come some end, where you have reached a state of perfection that cannot be transcended."

Says who, my beloved? The linear mind may not be able to fathom that there is no end to self-transcendence—and that is precisely why the linear mind must be left behind by the student who comes to a point of wanting MORE, more self than what it has experienced so far.

There is no linearity in the spiritual realm; there is a spherical reality. And once you step out of the linear mind, once you transcend it, then perpetual self-transcendence becomes a living reality. You are not concerned about what might come in some future time. You are flowing with the River of Life, existing in the eternal NOW—that is perpetual self-transcendence. You are not projecting into the future what should or should not happen. You are not analyzing the past of what should or should not have happened. You are simply flowing with the River of Life. Something that the ego cannot do, for the ego wants to own and possess.

So, the question becomes, "Do you still want the experience of owning something, owning a particular experience, a particular sense of self?" And by so doing, also being owned by your own creation of that separate self, which then, in turn, wants to own you—wants you, as the unlimited, infinite spiritual being, to limit your self, your sense of self, your sense of identity to that particular limited belief from which the ego was born.

The descent into duality

How, my beloved, did all of this descent into duality begin? It began, as Maitreya explains, when a sphere had come to the point of ascension, where it could ascend and become a part of the spiritual realm. Where it had reached the critical intensity of light that made it possible to accelerate the entire sphere into the higher vibrations of the spiritual realm—the vibrations of unconditionality, of love. And yet, what was the condition for that acceleration to take place? Well, you see, my beloved, you had a great number of beings who had applied themselves in a very concentrated effort in order to raise their sphere to that level. They had made great efforts. They had truly worked selflessly, so to speak, on raising all beings in their sphere to that point.

But you see, even in so doing, some of them had retained a remnant of the separate self, thinking that by working so hard to raise up their sphere, they would receive what they perceived as some ultimate reward by God for their efforts. And so, it was a great shock to them when all of the beings who had been the forerunners for raising the sphere were called, and they were shown that the next logical step for them was not to enter the spiritual realm as some kind of superheroes – receiving position and recognition in that spiritual realm – but instead, their next logical step was to lay down their lives, their attainment, their self-awareness and give that momentum and self-awareness and attainment as the foundation for creating the next sphere that would start out as an unenlightened sphere—inhabited by beings with a limited sense of self-awareness. Thereby, the sophisticated beings in the ascending sphere would, so to speak, let their beings descend, and now they would become the ones who allowed the beings in the next sphere to do with their light according to their free will.

This was a logical step because in the sphere that was ascending, that sphere was created out of the beings of those in a higher sphere. And so, the beings who were now at the top of the ascending sphere were simply being asked to do for others what others had done for them. Many of these beings were ready to ascend – to shed the last remnants of the separate self – and gladly embraced this opportunity. Which is why the next sphere was created—leading to your own. You would not be here unless someone had volunteered to lay down their lives to give you the opportunity to have a sphere in which you could grow in self-awareness. Thus, it is only logical that as you come to having made maximum use of this opportunity, you are asked to extend that opportunity to others, my beloved.

Yet, there were a small number, among the beings that had the opportunity to ascend, who did not want to give up that last remnant of the separate self. So they rebelled against God's plan. And they wanted to keep owning what they saw as a superior position in their sphere, which they believed they had earned, and therefore they were entitled to keep experiencing that superiority for a time longer. And so, they demanded to be exempt from this—to set themselves apart as their sphere ascended. And in so doing, of course, they automatically fell into the next sphere that was created. For they could not maintain an existence in the ascended sphere, and thus could only go into the sphere that was not yet ascended and therefore had room for the separate self to continue to exist.

And yet, these beings were not stripped of their attainment. And so, they did, indeed, come into the next sphere with a far greater attainment and awareness than the beings who were just starting out in that sphere. And so, naturally, they set themselves up as leaders—as precisely what Jesus called the blind leaders of the blind followers. Some of their followers actually having followed them from the ascended sphere where they had leadership positions. And those of their followers who were not willing to let go of their obedience to their leaders, they had to fall as well.

The initiations of the eleventh ray

And so, when you come to the eleventh ray, it is indeed the challenge you face to transcend, to let go of the last remnants of the separate self. And thus come to what we might call a sense of ultimate reality, ultimate realism, of knowing that the separate self is unreal. And only when you know that your separate self is unreal – and only when you see this from within your sphere of self – can you then see that everything that was created out of duality is likewise unreal.

This, then, is the state of reality, of realism, of asking yourself, "Why am I here?" And so far, especially during the initiations of the first seven rays, you might also have asked yourself that question many times. Such as, "Why did I come to Earth? Why did I volunteer to descend here? Why did I come back to Earth?" And it is always that you are here to do something, to bring something, to achieve some kind of result. But you see, when you come to the eleventh ray, you need to transcend the very concept that you are here to achieve any particular result.

This will be a shock to the ego. It will be a shock to the remnants of the separate self. Which is precisely why I give this teaching in such a manner as to shock your separate self into objecting to the teaching, thereby giving you an opportunity to see those remnants of the separate self.

Consider how we have, several times now, said that what brings you to a certain point will not bring you beyond that point. You cannot then rise beyond the challenge of the tenth ray unless you are willing to consider the question of, "Why I am here?" from an entirely new perspective. You need to ask yourself not, "Why am I here," but, "What is the 'I' that is here?"

Is it an I that still sees itself as separate from its source, as separate from other self-aware beings? Do you think you are here to do something for God, for the Ascended Masters, or even do something for other people—saving them, setting them free, awakening them, or whatever it might be? Why do you need to consider this, my beloved? Because only the separate self can have the sense that it is doing something that affects others.

Do you see the subtlety? So many well-meaning spiritual people believe they are here to affect positive change on this planet. So many religious people believe their goal is to convert others to their religion. But even those who have transcended this need to convert others to a particular outer religion can be caught up in wanting to awaken others to the spiritual path, wanting to change them, wanting to change society, wanting to change the Earth and humankind.

But you see, my beloved, why does the world need changing? Why do people need saving? They need saving because they are trapped in the separate sense of self. The world needs changing because people have co-created numerous problems through the separate sense of self, thereby, reinforcing the illusion that the separate self has some kind of reality, some kind of permanence, some kind of real existence. And so, do you see that there comes a point on the path – when you go into the secret rays – where you need to come to the realization, the sense of ultimate realism, that you cannot fulfill the true goal of raising your sphere as long as you maintain even a faint remnant, even a shadow, of the separate self—as long as you think that you, as a separate self, are here to affect some kind of change to the separate selves of other people.

…

There is no shortcut

You may think, my beloved, that we of the Ascended Masters should be able to come up with a shortcut that could help you pass this initiation on the eleventh ray. But there is no shortcut. This is the point on the path where you must face your own demons—the demons, the entities, that you have created by giving the life force to certain images that are not springing from oneness, but from separation. You must face them. You have created them.

You must face what you have created, and you must separate your real self from your own creation and the creation of others. You may think it sounds illogical that you have to give up the separate self, but at the same time I talk about you separating yourself from the mass consciousness. But they are one and the same. You separate yourself from the mass consciousness by giving up the separate self. It is the only way to separate yourself, for it is the separate self that pulls you into the mass consciousness.

And so, at the lower levels of the path, you build that upward momentum, where you actually hold on to a part of the separate self, even turning it into a spiritual persona that takes on the characteristics demanded in your spiritual environment. But that is what must go, that is what must be left behind for you to be free and be free to express your Higher Being, the being that is the real you. So there is no shortcut. You must wrestle with this, until you come to the point, where you are no longer wrestling with the demons, for you see through the illusion that created them. And you simply let it go, let it fall away from you.

What am I talking about here? There are many demons, my beloved, many entities that have been created. And you may, as ascended master students, have thought of them as being somewhat evil or dark in appearance. But it is time to face reality that there are also demons and entities that are disguised as being benevolent, spiritual, religious. What you have created, as you have walked the path up until this point, is an entity. That is what the separate self is, an entity that has spiritual characteristics, that seeks to appear so good that God simply has to accept it into its kingdom.

But it can never be accepted. Only you, the real you, can be accepted. No man has ascended to Heaven, save he that descended from Heaven. What descended from Heaven was the conscious self. And only the conscious self can ascend back. But it does not ascend back as the same that descended, but as the greater being it has become through its experiences in this world. Yet, the greater being that it has become is not the separate self. It is the being that has transcended separation by seeing through it and thus gaining a different perspective on oneness—that you could not have if you had never been outside of oneness.

The twelfth ray of rebirth

Jesus, May 10, 2009.

The prince of this world is a finite being

Do you see that the prince of this world is not an infinite being; the prince of this world is a finite being. Meaning, that even though there are some who think that the devil has great power, the devil has only finite power, because the devil has only a finite sense of self, and therefore only a finite awareness.

Do you see, my beloved, that what the devil wants is to come to you and cause you to accept the fixed sense of identity that holds you back at a certain level—so that he can now run out and start working with other people, getting them to accept the fixed sense of identity? And he wants that when he has made his rounds and comes back, you are still in that fixed sense of identity.

But you see, if you transcend that sense of identity, and the devil comes back, he will be shocked, "He is no longer there, where is he?"

And now he will have to try to catch up with your new sense of identity and try to turn that into a fixed sense of identity. And that takes his attention away from all the other people that he has to entrap—and all of a sudden, when enough people transcend their former sense of self, the devil becomes so scattered, the prince of this world becomes so confused, that he can no longer keep his sense of control. And thus, even the prince of this world must somehow transcend his old sense of identity in order to keep up with the people who are accelerating, my beloved. And thus, you see, everything is pulled up.

"I, if I be lifted up, will draw all men unto me." This also means lifting up the mass consciousness—which is just one expression of what has traditionally been called the devil. For as Gautama explained last year, at New Year's, my beloved, when you go into the temple of the dark lord, you see that there is no dark lord there. It is all an empty shell, it has no ultimate reality.

But do you see that constant self-transcendence is the key to accelerating yourself out of this pull of the gravitational pull of the mass consciousness? So that you simply – whatever they send at you – you use it to transcend your sense of identity, to be reborn. You accept that you are reborn, and thus, you are a new being in Christ. And it will take time for your ego, or the false teachers, or the mass consciousness or other people to catch up with you. And when they eventually catch up with you, as they probably will while you are in a physical body, you just immediately allow yourself to be reborn again. And now they have to play catch-up.

And therefore, you come to the point where they are always playing catch-up, my beloved. For you have now turned the tables on the moneychangers, so that they are the ones that have to catch up to you. Because you are no longer allowing yourself to remain in that fixed sense of identity, where they think they have you under control.

And so you see, my beloved, that this becomes sort of a cat-and-mouse game, that you might even for a period find some enjoyment in. Where you realize that you are no longer playing the dualistic game of seeking to destroy the opposite dualistic polarity, but you are playing a sort of a higher version of the game of trying to outfox and outsmart and out-transcend the forces of this world, the prince of this world.

And you can do so very easily once you truly lock in to the process of being reborn. Of course, there will come a point where you are ultimately reborn to the point, where you do not even find enjoyment in outfoxing or outsmarting the prince of this world because that prince has simply become irrelevant to your sense of self. And you are now focused on other things, you are now focused on raising up others and awakening them from the consciousness of death by demonstrating to them how it is possible to be reborn. And by teaching them that they, too, can be reborn—challenging their present sense of self.

The thirteenth ray of creative flow

Saint Germain, May 10, 2009.

Lucifer as the thirteenth archangel

So, my beloved, now let me take this in a slightly different direction by talking about the very fact that Lucifer has been called the thirteenth archangel. Lucifer was, indeed, a representative of the thirteenth ray in a higher sphere. He fell through a perversion of the thirteenth ray of creative freedom, creative flow.

This can take several subtle – very subtle – perversions. But one is the thought that if I have total creative freedom, then why should I not be able to create a form and maintain it? And as we have said, you have the right to seek to maintain your form, but you cannot do so in the creative flow. For, when you stop a particular form, you are no longer flowing, and therefore you must separate yourself out from it.

The other perversion, of course, is the idea that God's decision to give people freedom can never lead to the end result—namely the manifestation of the kingdom of God. For people will misuse that freedom to go all over the place and work against each other. And so, therefore, freedom needs to be restricted, freedom needs to be forced. And people must be forced into the fold, where the devil thinks that he can guarantee their salvation, if they follow what he sees is the only true path to salvation. But it is the path of separation, my beloved.

The true path to salvation, the true path to the manifestation of the kingdom of God in the lower sphere is, indeed, the creative flow that brings forth higher solutions. You see, my beloved, it does not matter how low, how dense, a particular sphere is when it is first created. If the self-aware beings in that sphere are willing to constantly transcend themselves, they will eventually bring that sphere up. It cannot be any other way.

Self-transcendence will lead to the manifestation of the kingdom of God. It has always been so; it always will be so. It is the only way to manifest the kingdom of God—when you realize that God is the Living God and that God is transcending itself. There comes a point, my beloved, where you need to come into that creative flow of saying, "I will be who I will be!" Meaning, that you will, at any point in time, be more than you were before. The perversion of that is when you say, "I will be what I am, I will stay where I am at right now. I will stay here for a period of time." Then, you have separated yourself from it.

And this ties in with what the Buddha said, for, again, Lucifer himself was asked to pass the initiation that Gautama talked about, the initiation in a higher sphere of laying down his life and his attainment for those in the next sphere. But he did not want to do so, for he said, "I want to stay in this superior position, for I am looked up to by those below me. I do not want to go down and lay down my life for those who are not yet at a level where they can even recognize my attainment." And so, you see the desire to stop the creative flow, to step outside of it, to maintain a certain position. For again, you cannot maintain a position in the flow, my beloved.

Abraham's God was the Living God— not a dead god

Master MORE, October 25, 2009.

Understanding Abraham's God

So my beloved, let us now go back to the time of Abraham, considered to be one of the Patriarchs of the Jewish faith, one of the patriarchs of both Christianity and Islam, as the three monotheistic religions. My beloved, did Abraham actually preach what you today call today monotheism? Well, yes and no my beloved, depending on how you understand and define monotheism. For you see, at the time of Abraham this entire region was a mixture of various tribes, each having their own tribal gods, usually having some idol carved in wood or stone or gold or whatever, but some physical object, where they believed that the God that they were worshipping was indwelling in that physical object and not elsewhere in the realm of matter.

So what you had was not only conflict between the various tribes competing over land for their flocks, but you also had conflict based on the tribal gods and the idea that each tribe believed that their God was stronger than the God of the other tribe, my beloved. And so, when I was young man in that embodiment, I pondered this. I pondered why there had to be this conflict between the tribes, and I realized that if the tribes were ever to overcome their conflicts, they needed something to unite them, something greater than the tribe. They needed to have a vision of something that was beyond their own tribe, beyond the mental box – although I certainly couldn't have used that word at the time – for their own tribe.

And so you see, the vision I had as a young man was that it was clearly the tribal gods who were blocking the vision of something greater than the tribe and the tribal consciousness. Now, even then my beloved there was indeed some exchange of goods and ideas between this region and the East, and so I was fortunate indeed to meet a traveling merchant who had grown up in the East and was familiar with the Vedas and the Vedic world view. I learned from this traveling merchant-sage, as you might call him, the view that beyond the many gods of Hinduism – the specific gods with different characteristics – there was the One Supreme God, Brahman, the originator of all that has formed.

Yet Brahman is beyond form, for how can the originator of form have form in itself? It must be beyond, it must be transcendent, my beloved, for if something has form, it cannot be the Supreme Source of form. This was immediately logical to me.

I know full well that those trapped in the duality consciousness can and will debate this point endlessly, as you see people today endlessly debating whether God is like this or like that, whether he is like that described by their religion or in some other way. But you see, God is not a he or a she because the God who is beyond form has not taken on anything that can be compared to masculine and feminine, male and female.

And so, I saw in a vision – on an early morning in the desert as the sun was rising – I saw in a vision that even beyond the sun there had to be some source that was driving the sun; driving the light, creating the light, generating the light. And I knew that that God, that formless, transcendent, never-changing eternal God—THAT was my God. And that is the God I preached, my beloved; the God that is beyond form, and therefore cannot be, my beloved, the personal God, the angry judgmental being in the sky that has been portrayed throughout the Old Testament.

For certainly, you can see that Abraham cannot be responsible for what happened after his time, where the concept of the transcendent God not only was not understood, but was interpreted to mean a God that had certain human characteristics, where again human beings projected onto that God what they wanted to see, so that they could feel, my beloved, that this God was partial to their people, although it had grown beyond to not just one tribe but the Jewish people.

Yet they still wanted a God who was simply larger than the old tribal God but was partial to their people. And so they took the concept that I preached of the transcendent God and made it into a material deity that they gave human characteristics, first of all by projecting their male chauvinist, their male dominated, world view and mental box upon that God.

Those who wrestle with God

And so, then you have the creation of the Old Testament God, which became the God of the Israelites—the God of Israel after Jacob. And my beloved, you should know that the word Israel means "he who wrestles with God," the name given to Jacob after he wrestled with the Angel of God for the entire night, refusing to let the Angel go until he had been blessed.

My beloved, what does this indeed symbolize? It symbolizes an attitude, a world view, where you want Spirit to fit into the mental box you have created in matter. Thus, you wrestle with Spirit, you demand that Spirit come down to your level of consciousness and express itself through that level of consciousness, instead of being willing to do what I did – what Jesus did, what Moses did on ascending the mountain and what all other true teachers and prophets have done – namely raise your consciousness beyond your mental box and move outside of that mental box, as even symbolized by the fact that I had to leave my homeland and move on to other pastures, move into the unknown in order to prove to God that I was willing to transcend my mental box. Even being put through the extreme test of being asked to physically sacrifice my son in order to again prove that I was willing to step out, even of the mental box of that ancient society, where your sons were seen as your seeds, your offspring, the key to your future, to the future of your family tree and name.

Do you see my beloved, how I was asked not only as recorded in the scriptures but asked many times to transcend that mental box and the next mental box and then the next and the next? And do you see that this is the sign of those who are willing to flow with the River of Life? For as Jesus has recently explained in his latest discourses on the ego, as long as you are in embodiment, there will be some mental box, for you cannot be in this denser realm of the world of form without looking at it through a particular box, a particular filter, that you then seek to project upon the Ma-ter light, and the Ma-ter light must obey and take on the form that you project through your mind.

Do you see that this is the test that all spiritual students have faced throughout the Ages? When will you come to the point where you stop projecting onto Spirit and thereby rejecting the flow of the Holy Spirit that is here to take you beyond your mental prison? When will you stop projecting and open your mind and heart to the guiding hand of

Spirit, who may speak to you from deep within your heart, speak to you through another person, even speak to you between the lines of a scripture or speak to you in a more direct manifestation such as the appearance of what people call Angels but which are truly the thoughts of God, sent to you to awaken you to the need to look beyond your mental box?

For do you not see – when you look at history – that any religious or spiritual teaching has always become a mental prison for many of those who have claimed to follow a particular religion? There is no exception to this, although certainly there are religions that have become more rigid than others, with hardly any becoming more rigid in the entire world history than the three great monotheistic religions of Judaism, Islam and Christianity.

For do you not see my beloved – when you walk through the streets of Jerusalem, when you walk on or around the Temple Mount, when you ascend the Mount of Olives – do you not sense the rigidity? The rigidity of consciousness, the intolerance toward those who have other ideas, other ways of looking at God, other ways of worshipping God. And thus, my beloved, you will know exactly the same consciousness that I contemplated in that lifetime as Abraham, where I saw the consciousness of the different tribes.

And so, you see now, so many thousands of years later in what is called the modern age with the immense expansion of knowledge, of awareness of the universe; you still have that same consciousness of intolerance toward those who dare to be different from yourselves or who are born different through their skin color, race, ethnicity, or what have you.

Do you see why you have the old saying that there is nothing new under the sun? For human beings are still prone to go into those same mental boxes, always projecting from that mental box that other people should conform to my mental box, and when they do not, I will reject them! I will reject their right, I will even reject the very possibility that I might learn something from others. Or that I even might learn tolerance towards others and therefore learn tolerance toward my own way of life, that I might actually transcend that way of life and reconnect to the fact that I am a spiritual being that sprang from the formless God. And I am meant to return to formlessness and I can do so only by transcending those form-based mental boxes, created here on Earth to trap the Spirit in a lesser form and therefore prevent that Spirit from letting its light shine and therefore raising the collective consciousness.

The mental box of intolerance

My Beloved, contemplate for a second the immense expansion of knowledge brought about through science. Contemplate how astronomers have created stronger and stronger telescopes that can look deeper and deeper into the material universe. Contemplate how they have discovered that the universe is so vast that the human mind can barely fathom it, that there are billions upon billions of stars, billions of solar systems. Contemplate this immense vastness my beloved; this immense vastness of the material universe.

And then perhaps even look beyond it and contemplate the vastness of the spiritual universes beyond the material that you cannot see even with the best telescopes, for the telescopes merely extend the mental box that science is currently in. Because they not been willing to go beyond and construct telescopes that can show other realms beyond the material, even though they have actually constructed certain instruments that can show forms of energy that are not in the material frequency spectrum, only the discoveries have not yet been interpreted correctly to show that scientists have looked into other dimensions already.

Nevertheless, my beloved, contemplate this vastness that science has discovered, and then project your mind to the narrow streets of the old city of Jerusalem – even to the Temple Mount and to the Mount of Olives – and then realize that here you have a flashpoint between the world's three great monotheistic religions, and realize that they claim to be worshipping the same God yet they cannot exist side by side in peace.

They cannot worship that God in different ways in peace, and then consider what that says about the people of this region and their unwillingness to transcend that tribal consciousness that I experienced so many years ago, and that has been propagated here from generation to generation with so few people in this area being willing to transcend it that it almost defies comprehension.

For my beloved, I have been willing to transcend that consciousness, which is why I am today an ascended being. And I assure you that if I could reach that level of consciousness, well then so can everyone else. This much I know for sure, for I started out from very humble beginnings. I was not by any means a saint, even in that embodiment as Abraham and in succeeding embodiments, where I was still somewhat trapped in the warring consciousness. And so you see, my beloved, that there is nothing in the material realm that cannot be transcended by that which is Spirit.

As Jesus said it, "No man shall ascend back to heaven, save he that descended from heaven." And the man that descended is your conscious self that is beyond any form that you might have chosen to identify with in this realm. And thus, you can throw off those shackles of matter, those shackles of form no matter what they are—you can throw them off, you can transcend them, you can go beyond them my beloved. This much I can promise you with absolute certainty, for I have proven it to myself and I know that my brothers and sisters in the Ascended Host have proven it as well.

The cause behind the ongoing conflict

And thus, I say to you, it is time, my beloved, to look at this area of the Middle East and to see what is the true cause behind the conflict, my beloved. The ongoing incessant conflict that is always there, almost like the explosive gas you see in a mine, that is lying there, filling the tunnels only waiting for that one spark to ignite, so that it explodes into conflict. As you even saw this morning, where this little band of my disciples could not go to the Temple Mount for some conflict – meaningless, nameless – yet a proof of how the consciousness is always there, simply looking for an excuse to burst out into violence, yelling, screaming, hatred. That then is propagated onto the innocent children who chose to embody here to give the adults an opportunity to encounter the innocence of the childlike mind, and therefore have an opportunity to evaluate, "Will they pollute that childlike mind with the anger and hatred that they have come to absorb into their beings?"

Or will they say, "No, my children deserve a better future than I have had myself. And how can they have that better future unless I do not put upon them that same heavy burden of anger toward other people, of hatred towards those who are different that was put upon me when I was a child?"

My beloved is this not simply sanity? And is the denial of this simple fact not thus insanity? And yet, you yourselves should not sit wherever you are when you hear or read this and feel that you are that much better, for you too have your mental boxes, you too have your personal dramas. And I dare say that there are very few spiritual students – especially those who have been in contact with Ascended Master movements – who are not also affected by the epic dramas that Jesus has described.

Contemplate this and the other discourses that will be forthcoming, for as a spiritual student I can assure you that there comes a point on your path, where you will be stopped dead in your tracks unless you seriously contemplate the existence of the epic drama and how it is your own personal drama that has given an inroad into your consciousness to the epic dramas—that are not only hanging over this planet like clouds but have been turned into, over the millennia, beasts in the astral, in the emotional realm, in the mental realm, even in the lower etheric. Beasts that are constantly seeking to get their psychic hooks into your being, so that they can milk you of your energy by stirring up your sense of identity, your thoughts and your feelings to play out the drama to where you believe in the essential lie of these epic dramas—that the only way to stop the conflict is to manifest the physical outcome that the drama claims it is working towards.

My beloved, it is time to wizen up and realize, first of all, as Jesus has explained, the drama itself generates an equal reaction to its own action. And thus, it is simply a lie that there could ever be an outcome to any drama. There cannot be peace through war! There cannot be peace by exterminating those of another race or religion or political ideology. It cannot happen, my beloved, there will only be peace when people turn their swords into ploughshares by refusing to play the drama of war and conflict, by refusing to play any of the dramas that simply seek to reinforce the dualistic struggle that allows the forces of darkness to milk people of their spiritual light and energy.

The ongoing spirals of ascension towards the White Cube

Lord Ling (Moses), October 26, 2009.

Moses also preached the transcendent God

For there are always those trapped in that linear mind, trapped in the pride of the ego or the fear of the ego, of not daring or not wanting to give up the sense of superiority that they have the highest, most important teaching that ever has and can be given on this planet. Thus my beloved, as my beloved colleague, Master MORE, has explained, he preached as Abraham the transcendent God. Well my beloved, what do you think I preached as Moses?

Well, indeed, it was, too, that same transcendent God who – when I asked for a name – would not actually give me a name, but would only give me the words "I will be who I will be" as a meditation for those who are willing to realize that the Living God can never be captured by a name, by an image, by a scripture or by anything else in the material world. For there is indeed nothing in the world of form that can contain the formless. This is an eternal truth, an eternal idea, contemplated by those who are willing to know the Living God, rather than wanting to worship a graven image of their own making or of someone else's making.

The psychology that wrestles with God

And who might that someone else be, but precisely those beings who – as Jesus has recently explained and as Maitreya has explained before him – who have fallen through several spheres—falling into this one with that sense of superiority that they know better than God. Thus, my beloved, you will see that Abraham was a true man of the Living God who was willing to transcend all outer images of the tribal Gods. I too was a man of the Living God, but my beloved, was the third patriarch, Jacob, a man of the Living God? Indeed why would he wrestle with the Angel of God if he was?

For I tell you that the hallmark of the fallen beings is indeed that they wrestle with God about anything and everything. For you see, my beloved, what is the difference between those who know the Living God and those who will not know the Living God? It is indeed that those who know or are willing to know the Living God will let nothing on Earth come between them and a direct experience, a direct encounter with the Living God. Thus they are willing to overcome any mental box, any graven image that they or others have conjured up here on this little planet. They are willing to reach beyond it all, to continually transcend their state of consciousness in order to have even a brief glimpse of that Living God and the Presence of that God.

Thus, my beloved, those who are not willing to go beyond, what do they do? Well, they turn God into a player in their epic dramas. You will not find, my beloved, a more profound teaching than the one given recently by Jesus, and given by other Ascended Masters in the recent book, about dramas [Master Keys to Personal Wholeness]. You will not find a more profound teaching anywhere for explaining the psychological dynamic that has been going on on this planet for eons.

You see my beloved; this teaching can liberate you from being a blind follower of the blind leaders who are the fallen beings—who are wrestling with God, who have been wrestling with God in previous spheres and therefore have been doing it for what is even beyond the beginning of time in this universe. And my beloved, from a realistic perspective, most of those beings will probably continue to wrestle with God until they face the final judgment and the end of their opportunity as self-aware beings who have any power to express themselves in the world of form.

My beloved, these beings have turned the Living God into a graven image that fits within their epic dramas, whichever drama they have conjured up and have come to believe themselves is the absolute truth about God and this universe. They are not likely to give it up. They could potentially give it up, but I tell you, that that should not be your concern for that is up to their free will, and the Law of God is indeed set up to give them that opportunity for the appointed time.

You may shorten the time they have here on Earth as you have been instructed by other Masters, but you need not concern yourself about whether these beings will be converted to the true Living Path for it is indeed not your job to convert them. It is your job to let your light shine and to set forth an example of those who are willing to reach for the Living God, who are willing to look beyond and question any graven image created by the religions of this world, by political philosophies or even by the ideology; the religion if you will, of materialism.

Beyond a literal interpretation of the exodus

Now my beloved, going back to my opening remarks about those who want to take any teaching literally. Well let me tell you that it is possible to take the Bible – the New Testament, the Old Testament, the Jewish version, the Muslim version, any version you like – it is possible to take it and interpret it in a linear, literal fashion. This is indeed possible. And it is not necessarily wrong that some people do so, for they are at a level of consciousness where they are not able to do anything else. They are not able to look beyond the outer teaching, for they still need something outer to follow, they need a religion with a clearly defined scripture, a clearly defined set of rules, so that they can follow them for a time, until they become more mature and able – actually – to think about religious matters. For many of the new souls cannot.

However, there is a distinction that must be made here, for there are many souls who have come to the level of maturity, where they should have long ago started to take responsibility for themselves and thinking about religious matters. Going beyond the outer teachings, the outer scriptures, the outer dogmas and traditions, so that they could reach for the Living God. For my beloved, you cannot experience the Living God if your mind is closed and fixated on some outer religion that you think you must follow blindly. You simply will not encounter the Living God this way, for there must be an openness of mind and heart. For the Living God respects his own Law of Free Will and will not intrude, will not intrude, my beloved, if your mind and heart is closed.

And so we now have on this planet billions, literally billions, of souls who have come to that level of maturity but who are still blindly following an outer religion created by the fallen beings as a part of their epic dramas. And these people are, so to speak, held in a no-man's land, in a catch-22, where they have been given certain beliefs but also been infused with a fear to ever question or look beyond them, for the fear of some calamity coming upon them, such as enduring eternal torture in some fiery hell.

Oh my beloved what a lie! What a lie perpetrated upon humankind that the real God, the Living God, could ever condemn you to such a fate. For what does the Living God want? Well as Jesus said, "It is the Father's good pleasure to give you the kingdom" so what is there to fear? Indeed, I too came to preach the same message.

For you see, there WERE certain people captured in the land of Egypt by certain powers that be. I did serve in some capacity to lead them out of that on a search for the Promised Land. But if you take the Bible the way it is written and interpret it with the linear, literal mind, then you will miss the deeper meaning, my beloved. For what is the true symbolism here, the deeper symbolism that can unlock the keys to your understanding?

Well my beloved, what does the captivity in Egypt symbolize spiritually? Is it just a matter of physical captivity my beloved? Nay. It is a captivity of the mind, a captivity of the mind, my beloved. The Israelites were not so much imprisoned by physical powers as they were imprisoned by a set of illusions in the mind.

The mistake of Jacob

What does Pharaoh represent, my beloved? He represents the Fallen Beings, and what was it that had imprisoned the minds of the Israelites? Well, it was indeed the epic dramas, my beloved, the epic dramas that the people had come to believe. And why did they believe it? Because they followed the patriarch Jacob who did not follow the path outlined by Abraham of seeking the formless God but wrestled with the Angel of God until, as the scripture says, the Angel relented and gave him a blessing.

But was it a true blessing my beloved? Or was this simply an illusion? And what really happened was that the Angel wrestled with Jacob to help him see beyond his mental box of the need for a graven image of God. And when the Angel could get nowhere, he had to withdraw to respect the free will of Jacob. And thus Jacob faced that choice that is the judgment—will you follow the representative of God sent to you or will you remain in your mental box?

And so, because Jacob wanted to stay in his mental box, he indeed interpreted the event to mean that he had been blessed by the Angel, who had confirmed his view of God, his idolatrous view of the external God, the personal God that favors the Israelites and is therefore simply, as has been said before me, an extension of the tribal Gods. For do you not see, my beloved, that the Living God cannot possibly have one people on this little planet that is his chosen people over all others?

Think back to the visualization given yesterday of the immensity of this universe and how small this planet is. Do you not realize that the Living God is the originator of all this expansive world of form? And now consider how infinitely small this Earth is, how your scientists have already revealed millions of planets that could potentially have life. And I tell you, my beloved, there are millions upon millions of planets in this universe that do have life; most of them are far more advanced and sophisticated forms of life than what you have on this planet, certainly a much higher state of consciousness than what you see in humanity today.

And thus, does it make any sense whatsoever that out of the vastness of this universe, the Real God would have one small group of people wandering around in the desert in this parched part of the planet that were his favorite and chosen people? And that they were the only ones who would be saved and all other inhabitants on this beautiful planet would perish in some fiery hell—or whatever hell you want to envision.

The pride of those who wrestle with God

It makes no sense whatsoever and can only be believed by people who are so blinded by their own epic drama that gives them this need to feel superior to all others that they will believe almost anything that seems to affirm that sense of superiority. And so, why were the Israelites driven into exile? Because what else could be done to shake them out of the mental box that they had entered into—that they were God's chosen people? What else could break that arrogance, that pride but persecution after persecution?

But did it break the pride? No, my beloved, for there is no sure way to make people wake up against free will. There is nothing that the duality consciousness cannot interpret to mean whatever it wants it to mean. And therefore, you see that the Israelites did not take the persecution as an opportunity to say, "What is God trying to tell us, is he perhaps telling us that we have misunderstood something—that we need to look beyond our mental box, and what is indeed that mental box?"

Well if you look beyond it, you will see that you are – your conscious self is – an extension of God's own Being—but so is the conscious self of every other human being. And thus, it makes no sense to take racial or religious or ethnic differences and turn them into some epic struggle, where everybody else is against you and you are the favorite people. For all are extensions of the One Living God. And when you know that you are an extension of that God, you see that all others are too. And thus, you know what Jesus was trying to tell the Israelites—that you are all extensions of the Living God, that there is no favorite son except those who hear the Word of God and do it! The Living Word of God that they are willing to embody.

And thus, you see the symbolism of the Israelites being driven into exile in order to shake up their mental boxes, including the mental box, my beloved, that there is one piece of land on this entire Earth that is holier than others, that is chosen by God for them and that therefore they have some divine right to take and defend at all cost. And so, what happened was that prophets were sent to the Israelites as, indeed, prophets have been sent to all other people and civilizations on this planet to give them the Living Word; some teaching, some revelation, some progressive revelation that could take them out of their mental box.

And thus, I was simply one of them. One that was sent to show them that the power of the Living God is indeed greater than the abuse of power symbolized by the magicians in the court of Pharaoh. And in Pharaoh himself and the institution he represents, which is indeed the government of man, a worldly government as opposed to God Government.

Wandering in the desert

And so, because the Israelites somewhat responded to my calling and my message, they were at least somewhat – even though they grumbled and wrestled with me – they were at least willing to leave the comfortability they had built in their state of slavery. For even slavery, my beloved, can become a source of comfortability, for now you have someone telling you what to do, and you do not have to take responsibility for yourself and think for yourself. And so, you see why many among the Israelites would rather have stayed there, but when a critical mass were willing to leave, they all felt compelled to follow.

And so we left the court of Pharaoh; we left the land of Egypt to wander in the desert. And again, the symbolism is not necessarily a physical wandering in the desert, but the symbolism of a journey in consciousness from that false, idolatrous religion that worshipped a graven image of the extended tribal God, until you come to the point where the people can begin to grasp that there is a Living God. But my beloved, could they grasp it? For do you not see the symbolism of me ascending the mountain to get the Laws of God, leaving the people down below — leaving them in their current state of consciousness after having given them teaching and examples that were plenty to help them see that they too could reach beyond that state of consciousness.

Do you not see that this was a test my beloved? A test as to whether the people would accelerate out of the old state of consciousness or whether they would cling to the sense of the comfortable. And so, indeed, you see again that the Israelites started to argue amongst themselves, and instead of being willing to transcend, to go within and reach for an experience of the Living God, they wrestled with God, with their image of God and came up with the need to have some physical representation symbolized by the golden calf.

And so, when I came down from the Mount and saw that they had started worshipping an outer symbol, instead of seeking the Living God within their own hearts, well it was obvious that they were not ready for the higher law that I could have given them based on my state of consciousness. The state of consciousness to which I had ascended, as a symbol for my ascending the Mountain of God and encountering the Living God who appeared as a burning fire—that was willing to burn away the last remnants of the personal and epic dramas that had lodged in my consciousness.

The symbol of the promised land

And so, indeed, I did respond with a certain state of disappointment and passion and anger, when I saw them having descended. And I had to withdraw again and meditate again on what could be given to them; given that they were not willing to rise above that lower state of consciousness and reach for the Living God. And so, even though other teachings may have been given in previous dispensations, I desire you to understand that the deeper meaning here is that although we wandered for a long time in the desert – and although I was not allowed to enter the Promised Land – the deeper meaning is that the real, true promised land was not a physical area on this planet.

My beloved, the Promised Land in its pure form is a symbol of a state of consciousness, a state of consciousness that Jesus later called the Kingdom of God. And where did he say that that kingdom was to be found? Well, "within you," my beloved. And I knew this full well. I knew that the real Promised Land is within, is a state of consciousness. And thus, when the Israelites were not willing to reach for that state of consciousness, once again they were allowed to go their own way. For I could do no more for them, and thus again they came to believe that they had to find a physical land and enter it. And I had to stay without, for I could not follow them into that lower state of consciousness.

My victory over my drama

I had to remain true to the vision and to the level of consciousness I had attained. And so, thus I stayed outside, I left the people behind, I left my physical body behind, I left even the drama behind that I had created as a necessity for my playing the role that needed to be outplayed for the people. For I, indeed, played that role to some degree, so that I thought I could save them, I could do something for them. Just as you see Jesus himself had taken on a certain drama of thinking he could help the people, he could awaken the people. And indeed, he had to give up that ghost while hanging on the cross before he could be resurrected.

Well my beloved, I was not fully able to give it up after that embodiment as Moses, which is why I had to re-embody in a completely different spiritual tradition, where I finally was able to let go, was able to let go of the seriousness and the tendency to take life and my mission and myself so seriously that I had become attached to the drama in which I had assigned myself. This epic role that I thought I had to take so seriously, for the fate of the people hung in the balance.

And thus, I thought I had failed. And in my thinking I had failed, I created an attachment to the drama, my beloved. For you see, when you play a role – when you play a role in a drama that is enacted to give people the opportunity to see their own dramas, to see their own reaction, as Master MORE so profoundly explained – well, when you play such a role, my beloved, the test for you is to not become attached. For you are not here to force anyone; you are not here to force their free will. You are only here to give them an example so they have an opportunity to choose.

All is vanity in the epic dramas

And thus, as this messenger knows himself from his own tests – his own playing a role in one of these dramas – you see, he must also face that test of being nonattached to those who will not look at their own dramas. And so you see, we have the personal dramas, we have the epic dramas created by the fallen beings and we have the cosmic dramas created by the Ascended Host, who enact these dramas in order to give certain people an opportunity to see the inconsistency, the contradictions, and the pure ridiculousness of the epic dramas!

So that they can see the falsities, see how unnecessary it is, see how pointless it is, how it is all vanity. Vanity my beloved, "all is vanity" in the epic dramas, for it can never lead to any outcome of any consequence in the reality of God. You see, the epic dramas claim that there is a final solution, as indeed Hitler believed there was a final solution to the Jewish problem. But you see, as you have heard various myths and legends of those seeking to reach some marker, yet just as they are about to reach it, the marker is moved forward and now they have to keep going.

Well, that is the nature of an epic drama, beloved. It promises you some reward when you reach an ultimate goal, but the goal can never be reached. So when you think you have reached it, you see that this was not so, but then there is the immediate promise that if you just keep going, perhaps changing a little bit and adjusting a little bit here and there, there will be the ultimate goal, the ultimate end, the ultimate outcome.

My beloved, you have free will. Play these epic dramas for as long as you want—it is your right. But I am here to tell you – as one who has ascended – that they will never lead you home, they will never lead you to the promised land, they will never lead you to the ascended state of consciousness. They will only lead you round and round on the merry-go-round, where the devil is turning the wheel and laughing. For as the wheel goes round, you give him your light.

Enter the fire of God

This of course is again your free-will right. But should you come to the point, where you have had enough of wandering in the desert, then I say, "Come with me, up on the Mountain of God, where you will see the eternal fire of the Living God, ready to burn off the dross, the remnants of the drama, the imperfect energies in your consciousness. But that which is real, that which is the real you, is like the bush that will burn with fire but will not be consumed."

And therefore, when you have had enough of dancing around the golden calf forged by the fallen beings, then come up and enter into the fire of God. Not the fiery hell, but the true fire of the resurrection and the ascension that will burn away all elements of the human consciousness, the fallen consciousness. And thus, you will stand naked in your original purity before the Living God. And that Living God will appear to you in the form of Alpha and Omega, the first expression of the God expressing itself, the formless God expressing itself, in form.

And they will welcome you home, that you may sit, once again, at your point of origin – as this messenger was once privileged to experience – sitting on the White Cube between Alpha and Omega. And you may know that this is the point of origin of all beings who have journeyed into the world of form, and that you can return to it, when you are ready, when you are willing, when you have expanded your sense of self to the point, where you are willing to step up and become a Creator of your own world, instead of being a co-creator within the world of form created by your Living God.

Thus, you may know, when you ascend from Earth, your true origin. And you may choose from the ascended state to still journey through the many levels of form that are now open to you, before you finally return home to the White Cube from which you can accelerate your Being out of the world of form—to the point where you are now no longer the co-creator, but the full Creator God. This is the potential. This IS the potential.

My beloved, I can assure you that this journey from the ascended state is far more rewarding than the false rewards promised by the fallen beings in their epic dramas—for it is a real journey. It has a real destination, namely your total awakening to the ultimate state of self-awareness. This is indeed the ascension beyond the ascension, the ultimate ascension.

Transcending the energies of the accuser of the brethren

Elohim Astrea, December 17, 2009.

"And there was war in Heaven. Michael and his angels fought against the dragon, and the dragon fought and his angels and prevailed not. Neither was their place found any more in Heaven. And the great dragon was cast out, that old serpent, called the Devil and Satan, which deceiveth the whole world. He was cast out into the Earth and his angels were cast out with him.

And I heard a loud voice saying in Heaven; "Now is come salvation and strength and the Kingdom of our God and the power of his Christ, for the accuser of our brethren is cast down, which accused them before our God day and night.

And they overcame him by the blood of the lamb and by the word of their testimony, and they loved not their lives unto the death. Therefore rejoice ye Heavens and ye that dwell in them. Woe unto the inhabitors of the Earth and of the sea, for the devil has come down unto you having great wrath for he knowest that he has but a short time."

The consciousness of the accuser

Now then, where does this energy come from? Where does this consciousness come from, of wanting to be right, of wanting to prove other people wrong, even the energy of wanting to accuse others of this, that or the next thing? Go into the courtrooms of the world and see how in some nations it has become a pastime, a form on entertainment, a form of addiction, to sue someone and to accuse them of having done this wrong, because of which you are entitled to a monetary compensation.

You can read the words that are written in the court papers. You can see how someone will accuse someone else by using certain words. But if you are willing to use your inner sight, to read beyond the words with your heart, you will see that beyond the words is a particular energy, an energy of accusation.

And thus, why did I have the messenger read the quote from the Book of Revelation about the accuser of our brethren, which accused them before their God day and night? Who is the accuser of our brethren? Well, those of you who have studied Maitreyas book are familiar with the concept of the spheres. And thus, you can grasp the true deeper meaning behind this quote, which – considering the level of consciousness of 2,000 years ago – could not be given in the highest possible form, for it had to be adapted to the state of consciousness and the words that were used back then.

It simply was not possible for people at the time to understand the concept of different spheres. To them anything beyond Earth was either heaven or hell. Anything beyond what could be seen with the physical senses was either heaven or hell. And thus, they could not understand that the quote in Revelation, even though using the word "heaven," was not referring to heaven in the ultimate sense, in the sense of the spiritual realm. For surely, in the spiritual realm, how could the devil exist there, for the spiritual realm is pure, and thus it would not be possible for anyone in a lower state of consciousness to exist in that realm of purity. And so, you understand that what is hidden behind the word "heaven" is a higher sphere, a sphere that is higher than the Earth, but still a sphere that had not yet fully ascended, a sphere that had entered into the process of the ascension.

And therefore, it had become clear to certain lifestreams in that sphere that those who were not willing to accelerate their beings into the purity of the ascension coil, those lifestreams would be left behind as the entirety of the sphere ascended. And thus, those lifestreams would – seen from the perspective of inside that sphere – they would be lost. They would not be part of their original mandala, destined to ascend together. They would be left behind, as the rest of the sphere and the lifestreams within it accelerated into the purity of the ascension coil.

And thus, those lifestreams who were in leadership positions suddenly had a complete change of mind. They flipped, as it would not be possible for a spiritual being to do, but as it is indeed possible for any unascended being to do. They flipped into the opposite polarity of suddenly deciding – mind you, deciding – that the plan of God was flawed, that free will was flawed, that the possibility that lifestreams could be lost proved that the Creator had created a flawed design for the ascension of the spheres. That free will was a risk too great to take, that it was a liability, that it simply could not be right that these lifestreams could be lost.

Now behind this reasoning, however, was the unwillingness, as Maitreya explains, of these lifestreams to humble themselves and to let go of their lives as exalted beings, as leaders with power, and make themselves the servants of all. For indeed, these lifestreams did love their lives unto the death. They loved the position they had in that sphere, that unascended sphere, and they loved it to the extent that they felt that stepping up to the higher level of service, of being the servants of all, was a degradation for them, a degradation of their rank and position. And thus, they were not willing to lay down their lives for the all. And as an excuse for not having to lay down their lives, they latched on to the fact that some lifestreams would be left behind. They used this to come up with the reasoning that this was a flaw in God's plan, and that it was their role to prove God wrong.

And in the new consciousness that they entered into – the consciousness of separation, the consciousness of duality – they actually thought that they could prove God wrong, that they could set themselves up in opposition to God. Yet the moment they entered into duality, they were deceived by duality. They now looked at the universe from inside a dualistic polarity, and therefore to them it looked perfectly real, perfectly logical, that there had to be an opposite polarity to their own polarity. And therefore, they now believed – as a man wearing yellow glasses believes that the sky is green – that God simply was an opposite polarity to themselves. And therefore it was possible to prove God wrong, to prove God's plan wrong.

Yet why could they believe this? Because they had lost the Word and had now been enveloped by, embroiled in, the consciousness of words, the divided word, where words are now not used to convey, to communicate, an infinite vibration. They had now been taken down to a level of duality.

Communication via thought

Yet be careful here to realize that that sphere – even though the majority of lifestreams had not yet ascended – it was still in a much higher level of vibration than what you currently see on Earth. Therefore, when I say "words" I do not mean spoken words that can be written down. I mean words as a symbol for at state of consciousness.

For you see, when a sphere comes close to the ascension point, then the inhabitants of that sphere have raised their consciousness to such a level that they can communicate by thought alone. And the advantage of communicating by thought is that you can communicate directly at the level of concepts and ideas.

You will know the old saying that a picture is worth more than a thousand words. That is because a picture can convey more than can be described in words. It conveys a wholeness of a particular sight. You can describe that sight with words, but it will take many words, and the words themselves will actually never convey to you the same experience you get from looking at a picture for one second. Certainly, words written by a poet can convey a deeper meaning, a deeper experience to those who have open hearts and minds. But the words themselves cannot do this in a mechanical way, but only by the people reading them being willing to go beyond the words and open up their hearts to an experience that is more than the words. And thus you see, that one look at a picture can convey and open up for an experience that a thousand words could not give you. For the words are representations of the picture—they are not the picture. As the old saying goes; you cannot through words give someone the experience of the taste of an apple.

So in a higher sphere communication takes place at a higher level, where the people have developed the faculties of their minds to the point, where they can project images, concepts, ideas directly into each others minds and therefore communicate at that level. And of course, as a sphere ascends, people get better and better at communicating with concepts. And as they raise the collective consciousness, they of course communicate in a more and more pure way, where the concepts and ideas that they project into each others minds, are more and more pure, more and more elevated, more and more directed towards raising up other lifestreams, raising up the entire sphere by bringing forth more sophisticated, more pure concepts and ideas.

Proving that free will was God's mistake

And so, what did actually happen when those first beings in that sphere decided to rebel against God's plan, decided they would not lay down their lives for a friend—they would not lay down their positions in order to rise into an even higher position of serving the All, they loved their lives to the point where they were willing to die for them, spiritually speaking, by going into duality? What happened was that they decided that they wanted to prove God wrong by proving free will wrong. And how could they do this? Well, they knew that they themselves would indeed fall into the next sphere that had already been created. And they realized that the more lifestreams they could pull down with them, the more they had a chance of proving that free will does not work, because free will carries too big of a risk that people will fall rather than ascend.

And so they sat there, a group of them, and held a council and said; "How can we in this last stage, where the ascension spiral has already been formed, how can we cause as many lifestreams as possible to fall with us by causing them to go into the duality consciousness? And the plan they came up with was very simple. "We will do something to them that has never been done before in this sphere. We will accuse them in all manners possible. We will accuse them of not being pure. We will accuse them of not having will-power or not using that will-power correctly. We will accuse them of having false wisdom. We will accuse them of not being loving. We will accuse them of not having truth, but of being liars. We will accuse them of not being peaceful, and we will accuse them of wanting to take the freedom of others. Whatever God-quality they have mastered to the point where they are almost ready to ascend on that God-quality, we will accuse them of having perverted it. We will accuse them of not having it in purity. We will accuse them of exercising it in the wrong way. And thus, we will see how they respond to this new energy of accusation that they have never encountered before."

And do you see that this is how they became the Devil and Satan, not as one being but as a group of beings who formed within themselves what we have recently exposed as a downward spiral, the exact opposite of the upward spiral, the ascension spiral, that had been formed by the majority of the lifestreams in that sphere. And so, within the totality of that ascension spiral, they formed such an intense forcefield of negative energy, of impure energy, that they created, so to speak, a black hole within the white hole of the ascension spiral.

And they now used that energy, they built up the intensity of the energy, by perverting their own light. For did not Jesus say, "If the light that is in thee be darkness, how great is that darkness." And these beings did have light, they did have momentum, they did have attainment that they had gathered over their long service, where they had been serving the light. But now, as they flipped to the opposite side of opposing the light, instantly their light, their momentum, their attainment became darkness and a momentum of darkness. And thus, they could use that attainment, that momentum – that momentum of darkness – to direct a very intense energy of accusation at other lifestreams.

Imagine the shockwave that was felt, when suddenly those who were the holy innocents – who had worked selflessly, selflessly, for the ascension of their sphere, for the raising up of all of their brethren – suddenly were now accused of doing the exact opposite of what they were doing, of being the exact opposite of what they knew they were. Just imagine how this was experienced by these innocent lifestreams. They had never encountered an energy like this before. They had never encountered lifestreams who were willing to lie in order to accuse them of something they had not done.

How did the accused respond?

Do you see what a temptation this was? Do you see how subtle was the temptation? Do you see how powerful it was when imbued with the immensity of this negative energy? Do you see that there were lifestreams who were literally blown over by the energy directed at them and by the thought, "What have I done wrong? Could I have done something wrong? Are they really right? How could they be right? How could they accuse me of this? Here I have been working selflessly to raise up the All, and they accuse me of having done the exact opposite. How could they do this? How could they be allowed to do this? How could God allow them to do this?"

Do you see a myriad of possible reactions of how these beings – innocent – suddenly embroiled in this energy, how they reacted to this shock, this total shock to their beings? Do you see that the strategy of the rebellious beings worked very efficiently in causing many of the innocent beings to go into various states of consciousness that were contrary to the ascension spiral?

On an overall level, some beings went into the accusatory energy and accused the accusers back, accusing them of having done everything they accused other beings of doing. Others went into the opposite of the accusatory energy. For you see, do you not, that the accusatory energy is an outgoing energy and thus a perversion of the expanding force of the Father. As such, it is also possible to have an opposite polarity as a perversion of the contracting force of the Mother, namely that of wanting to defend yourself, even to the point of wanting to destroy the arguments of the accuser or the accuser himself.

Yet beyond these two overall negative spirals, the beings who had attained mastery on one of the seven rays could go into a perversion of those seven rays, as was explained at Wesak, where each ray has a masculine and feminine perversion that you can go into. And therefore seek to deal with this shock in some way or another according to your ray, seeking to defend yourself by will-power alone or by using wisdom to argue against the accusers and their accusations—or perverting one of the other rays, as the case might be.

But do you see the central realization that I am seeking to convey? Do you see the reality here that what the rebellious beings had done was to create a situation – a challenge, a test if you will – where there was only one way to avoid being pulled into a negative spiral, and that was by remaining completely non-attached to the accusations themselves and to the energy behind them. The moment you reacted – either by seeking to defend yourself or argue with the accusations themselves, or by seeking to throw back the energy directed at you – the moment you reacted, you were caught in a negative spiral. And the more you reacted, the more you would begin to misqualify your own light, until that misqualification of your own light had formed a negative spiral, that could now overpower your conscious mind and will to the point, where you were sucked into the spiral. And now, all of your light became darkness, for you were seeking to use your light to defend yourself against the accusers by reverting their negative energy.

But you see, how can you push back energy that vibrates at the level of duality? Only by using another form of energy that vibrates at that level. And that means you must then pervert your light by giving it a lower vibration, a vibration that is less than love, that is less than purity.

This then, is how the accuser of our brethren were successful in causing a third of the stars of Heaven to fall to Earth as the saying is in Revelation. This is not necessarily a literal measure; it does not mean that a third of the lifestreams in that ascending sphere fell into the downward spiral, but it does signify that a substantial number of those, who had already entered the ascension spiral, were indeed tempted to react to the accusations and the accusatory energy, and thus were pulled into the downward spiral created by the rebellious beings, so that they indeed fell altogether. Certainly, some of those who fell, fell out of their loyalty to their leaders, and they thought their leaders were right and were doing the right thing. But many more fell because they were pulled into reacting to the accuser of the brethren.

So then, this fall has continued through other spheres, until the current sphere, where you also see that even a small planet such as Earth has this consciousness of the accuser of our brethren.

The Battle of Armageddon

Now again, 2,000 years ago people had a much more limited world view than you have today. They thought the Earth was, really, the entirety of the material universe and that just beyond the sky – which they saw as a dome above the flat Earth – was Heaven. They could not conceive the vastness of the physical universe, and thus naturally they thought that the Earth was the center, the entirety of the world. And thus, of course, if some beings were cast out of what they saw as Heaven, those beings had to be cast down to Earth, meaning that the battle of Armageddon in its entirety was taking place here on Earth, and that the Earth is the battleground that will decide the fate of the universe.

This, of course, has been taken by many fundamentalist Christians, who take the Bible literally, so they also have the inflated belief that the Earth is the center of the battle of Armageddon, and that the fate of the entire universe is determined by what happens on this little planet. This of course, is vastly inaccurate, is a view that can be held only by some of those who are in the fallen consciousness, where they want to think that they are so important that they can determine the fate of the universe and therefore even challenge God. Or even that they can correct the flaw in God's design by forcing people to ascend.

Yet the reality is, of course, that Earth is a very small planet in a very large universe. And as you will know that the gravitational force of Earth pulls on the entire universe, but certainly does not have the power to pull the entire universe up or down, you should be able to see that the spiritual force generated by the lifestreams on this Earth certainly cannot pull the entire universe up or down. But what the Earth can do is serve as a testing ground, as a proving ground, for whether it is possible for the Ascended Host to be instrumental in empowering a sufficient number among the top ten percent to pull the Earth into an ascending spiral, to pull it out of the descending, downward spiral created by the number of fallen beings that have been allowed to embody here over the ages.

And thus, indeed, some among the fallen beings have been cast down to the Earth, and they have great wrath. Not only do they know they have a short time, but they also feel a great urgency to continue on the very same track that was instituted several spheres above yours— that of seeking to get lifestreams to enter a downward spiral by accusing them of anything that these fallen beings can think of, anything at all. There is no limit to what the fallen consciousness can come up with in terms of accusing the innocent. For the fallen consciousness, as Jesus said of the devil, has no truth in it, and thus anything goes, the end can justify the means.

You see, for a person who is trapped in the fallen consciousness, it is no longer a matter of what is right and wrong, what is true and false. It is not even a matter of what is logical or what is consistent. Such a being has no compunctions about saying something today that contradicted what it said yesterday, because the aim is not to be consistent, to be truthful, to be logical. The aim is to accuse others by inducing doubt in their beings, by overwhelming them with this accusatory energy, that has now been built up through several spheres and has therefore formed a downward spiral, a black hole, of very high intensity. And although there is only a certain, smaller black hole associated with the Earth, it is nevertheless so intense, that it is extremely difficult for human beings to withstand it, to withstand the attack of this accusatory energy, without reacting to it—just like the lifestreams in that higher sphere, by trying to push back the accusation or the accusatory energy or by trying to defend yourself by destroying the argument or the accuser.

The central dynamic on Earth

Do you see this dynamic? It is the central, underlying dynamic that will determine whether the Earth will indeed be pulled out of a negative spiral and enter into an ascending spiral that will raise it above these accusatory energies, to where the inhabitants of the Earth will raise their consciousness to the point, where the accusers of the brethren will be cast down from the Earth. And must then descend to an even lower place, where they can continue to accuse those around them—or even resort to accusing each other, for they simply cannot stop. They are so overpowered by this downward spiral that if they have no innocents to accuse, they will indeed accuse each other, which is precisely the safety mechanism, that makes it impossible for them to form a coherent power elite that could control the entirety of planet Earth.

For you see, the Karmic Board is not made up of unintelligent beings. In allowing a certain fallen lifestream to embody on a planet like Earth, there is a very simple formula. The momentum of the fallen lifestream cannot be beyond a certain limit that is related to the size of the Earth, to the number of lifestreams embodying here and to the level of their consciousness. In other words, one fallen lifestream must not be able to pull the Earth down by itself. It can do so only in cooperation with others, and given that these fallen lifestreams are in the accusatory consciousness, it is virtually impossible for them to fully cooperate to the point where they can take over the Earth and control society. They will always have warring factions – an established power elite, one or more aspiring power elites – and thus they are not only accusing the innocent, but also accusing each other and thus dividing their strength and their power.

And so my point is simply this; we are at a crossroads. We have entered the countdown to the year 2012, as Gautama Buddha explained at New Years. We are nearing the end of the first year of that cycle, the year of the Father. And so, those who are the top ten percent of the lifestreams on this planet are now facing the initiation, where they are ready to ascend into a higher understanding and application of the correct use of the expanding force of the Father. In fact, an ascension spiral has been formed.

The question is: will you enter that ascending spiral, will you reinforce that ascending spiral, will you stay in it? Or will you be tempted to leave it in order to fight some battle with the accuser of our brethren, who are accusing you before your God day and night by accusing you of this, that or the next thing?

Will you recognize this energy? Will you recognize it in yourself? Will you be honest and look at yourself and look at your life and say; "Do I have a tendency to accuse others? Have I been in these negative spirals described by the messenger? Can I honestly say that I have never in my life entered a negative spiral? Am I in a negative spiral right now? Am I focused on changing other people, accusing them, because of the splinters I see in their eyes, while I have not been willing to look at the beam in my own eye? Thus you must ask yourself: "Have I made myself an instrument for the energy that accuses the brethren?"

Or you must look at yourself and say; "Have I been tempted into defending myself against accusations? Can I look at my life and see that I have a pattern of feeling unjustly accused and thus go into a spiral of defending and justifying myself, whether I do this openly to other people or whether I do it inside my own head, having a martyr complex, where I feel that I have been unjustly condemned, but I dream that one day, one day, I will be elevated and the world will see that I was unjustly condemned. Or that I had this talent that no one ever saw, even though I had never expressed it, for I felt that I could not express my talents; I could not shine my light because of this or that impure or unjust condition in the world. Or because I thought that I would be accused by shining my light, or that I would scare other people or overwhelm them or that it would be too much."

Do you see how you don't even have to be accused to have taken on this energy in past lives, so that you have such a momentum on this that you are either accusing yourself, putting yourself down, or you are anticipating how the force of the accuser of the brethren will accuse you, if you take any stand for truth or stand out from the crowd. Do you see how many subtle games there are that have sprung from this consciousness of accusing and defending, accusing and accusing back, feeling unjustly condemned, seeking to justify yourself, waiting for the point where you are finally recognized as being just or having a talent. Always waiting for something outside yourself, instead of simply daring to step forward and be the open door for the Word.

There is no room for judgment in the ascension spiral

Serapis Bey, December 18, 2009.

The energy of the accuser interrupts the ascension spiral
If you are willing to see truth, then listen to the words, but listen beyond the words. Life is an ongoing process. Nothing is static. Nothing can stand still. You are either moving upwards in the ascension spiral or you are spiraling downwards in a negative spiral. There is no standing still.

Take note of the teachings given yesterday by Astrea, of the energy of the accuser of the brethren and how it was this energy that started the original downward spiral in a higher realm. Those of you who have studied the Kabala will know that there is a teaching that the judgment started when a group of fallen beings wanted to be the judgment without having the judgment tempered by mercy.

Well, mercy is not the highest understanding; neither is judgment, for both words have become too colored by the duality consciousness. Mercy is not mercy but realism—the reality of seeing that there is no impurity – no matter what level of vibration it is at – that cannot be raised back into purity. For no matter how impure a manifestation or form might seem, it is still the Ma-ter Light that has taken on that form—and the Ma-ter Light can always be raised back to its original purity, shaking off all imperfect images.

Do you see that when you have this sense of realism, it is not possible to divide human beings or any form of self-aware beings into those who are good, those who are bad, those who are within hope, those who are beyond hope, those who can be saved, and those who cannot be saved? One cannot think that way with the Christ consciousness. One cannot think that way with the ascended consciousness. It is not possible. For if one thinks that way, one will not enter the ascension spiral. One will stay in a negative spiral created by the original fallen beings, who used exactly this kind of mindset to project their accusations upon the innocent, accusing them of having done this or that wrong and therefore being so bad that they did not deserve to ascend as the rest of their sphere was ascending.

Do you see that the essence of the accusatory energy is precisely this—the division into those who are worthy, those who are not worthy, the accusation that you – or you, or you – are not worthy? You are not worthy to face your God. You are not worthy to face your spiritual teacher or to go back to your spiritual teacher after you have eaten the forbidden fruit.

And when a lifestream comes to believe in this unworthiness, then it falls into the downward spiral. And then it becomes susceptible to the epic dramas, which say that if you do this or that outer thing – if you belong to this or that outer organization – then you will automatically become worthy without having to look at the beam in your own eye. The beam being the decision that caused you to believe in the accusation that you are not worthy because you did not live up to this or that condition defined by the duality consciousness.

Do you see what I am saying here? The false accusation is that is order to be worthy to face your God, to ascend, you have to live up to certain conditions defined by the duality consciousness. And when you believe this, you think that in order to fulfill those conditions, you must participate in some epic drama and bring about this or that change on Earth, whereby you will automatically fulfill the conditions for your salvation or ascension.

And what is the epic drama in which you must participate? Well it is one that is based on the idea that there is a division between those who are saved and those who are not saved, based on dualistic conditions. And therefore, if you can then raise up your religion as the only one or condemn or judge these other people or kill them all, well then you will fulfill the condition for salvation, and you will be among those who are saved based on outer conditions. Ah, it cannot be done. It cannot be done. It cannot be done.

...

It is indeed only those who have entered a negative spiral – who have come to believe in the epic dramas created by the fallen ones – who think that they can decide who is worthy and unworthy, that they can single out one person and say this person should not be allowed to be in embodiment, this person should be sent to the second death, this person is in their last embodiment and will never be given another opportunity. If you cannot see that this is simply the judgment, the value judgment that springs from the fallen consciousness, then certainly you are not ready to enter the ascension spiral. For in the ascension spiral you are not seeking to condemn or put down any part of life. You are seeking to accelerate every part of life, so that you can reinforce the collective ascension spiral for your particular area, such as planet Earth, and thereby you will pull up all life.

What did Jesus say when he contemplated entering the ascension? He said, "I, if I be lifted up, I will draw all men unto me." He did not say, "I will draw unto me the good men and destroy the bad men." For if he had said so, he would not have been lifted up into the ascension spiral, for he was still not ready to let go of the epic dramas and the struggle. We in the ascended realm are not sitting around wanting to put down any part of life, not even the devil himself.

If the devil himself – although the devil, as conceived by most people on Earth, is not one single being – but nevertheless, if any of the original fallen beings that fell in that first sphere, if they came to us and sincerely applied to raise up their consciousness, then they would receive our help. Of course they would. Any being who sincerely applies, will receive the help of the Ascended Host to accelerate beyond their present level of consciousness. This is also your hope of redemption, of salvation, of the ascension.

So in order to enter the ascension spiral you must focus on raising up life, and you cannot do that if you are focused on judging, on dividing people into those who are good and those who are bad. It simply is not possible. You cannot enter that ascension spiral if you still have that need, that desire, to judge based on the value judgment. All life is worthy to be accelerated into purity. No impurity can be so impure that it is not worthy or capable of being accelerated into purity. That is the extreme realism of the fourth ray, and of those who are in the ascending spiral and those who have passed through it and ascended.

Overcoming your dramas by going from reacting to acting

Gautama Buddha, December 31, 2009

What is pure perception?

You have heard the story of how I started out as the son of a king, having grown up in an environment where my perception was protected from seeing decay and death. I therefore grew up with a limited, a one-sided, perception that could be said to be more pure than the perception of most people on this planet. You have heard how it was my perception of an old man that caused me to realize that my previous perception had been limited. And although it may have been purer than the average person's perception, it was not ultimately pure because I had simply ignored certain things that are temporary realities on this planet. And this is not truly pure perception.

Truly pure perception is not attained by ignoring imperfections but by seeing through them, seeing beyond them, and seeing there is something beyond the perception—even the perception that life is a struggle. And so, you know that after this realization, I withdrew from my life in the palace, I withdrew into the forest; living an ascetic lifestyle, punishing my body and mind, seeking to discipline my mind. Until I finally came to the realization that even that would not lead me to pure perception.

And so, what caused me to go beyond that level and reach the level of Buddhahood? It was that I came to the point, where I was willing to question EVERY aspect of my perception—the perception that I had grown up with, the perception of the ascetic lifestyle and philosophy. I was willing to question everything. And when I began to question everything, I began to see the patterns of how the polluted perception is an endless cycle that leads nowhere. And that was when I began to experience the pure consciousness that in Buddhism is called Samadhi, or Nirvana. And that, then, gradually allowed me to maintain that pure awareness even while I was engaged in certain activities and therefore could now perceive the world from the level of pure awareness.

And thus, I saw, I began to see, that the polluted perception is the dualistic perception, where there must be two opposite polarities. And they are seen as if they are ultimately real, that one could not exist without the other. And therefore, one is, in a sense, as real as the other, thus giving the impression that evil is as real as God, that the devil has power—permanence, reality. And so, I began to see beyond the dualistic perception. I began to see that there was a way to engage in life – even an active life in this world with all its imperfections – and still not be pulled into the dualistic perception—where you have to label everything on a relative, dualistic scale with two extremes, one being good, one being evil; the other one being right, one being wrong; one being true, one being untrue or false; one being beautiful, one being ugly; one being pleasurable one being un-pleasurable.

Do you see that what happened to me was that I began to see that there is something beyond this dualistic perception, and that this is polluted perception, where you perceive something, but you are not just perceiving because your perception is polluted. And therefore, you cannot separate the act of perception from the act of labeling, of evaluating, of judging. "Judge not, that ye be not judged, for with whatever measure ye measure out, it shall be measured out to you." Do you see that you will be judged by yourself through your own consciousness, and thus the way you judge others while you are in embodiment on Earth is the way you will judge yourself when you go out of embodiment and have a life review—where you now look at yourself through the consciousness with which you have looked at others.

And so, I began to see that beyond this perception – that makes it seem like you have to judge and label and evaluate everything – there is pure perception. A perception where you do not ignore the imperfections on Earth, the unreality on Earth; but you do not judge it, you do not label it. And therefore, you do not react to it in an emotional way by feeling threatened by it, or by feeling disgusted or repelled by it, or by feeling that it should not be there. You in fact see beyond it, you see that beyond the outer form is the Buddha Nature, the Ma-ter light; the PURITY, the reality that everything is created out of God's light. And therefore, it has the potential to shake off the impure image, the impure form, and be accelerated into purity—the purity of the Christ Consciousness, the purity of the Buddhic consciousness, the purity of the God consciousness.

And thus, you come to that point of the Buddhic consciousness, where you can maintain Nirvana, maintain Samadhi, even while you are engaged in activities. You do not have to sit there with closed eyes and meditate in order to be in Samadhi or Nirvana. You carry it with you and you see through that pure consciousness. You still see the imperfections in this world, but you do not label them, you do not judge them, you do not react to them. You just see them, but you see them as temporary, you see them as unreal. And thus, you do not react to the unreality, the imperfection. Instead you ACT, based on the realization that every imperfection can be accelerated into purity, into a higher state. And therefore, you go out and act in order to raise up all life, instead of seeking to condemn certain aspects of life and then seeking to destroy them.

The lie behind all dramas

Do you see, this is the lie of the accuser of the brethren? This is the underlying lie behind the epic dramas we have exposed so carefully now. The epic drama makes you believe that there is something that is bad or evil and that that something must be destroyed. But when you seek to destroy evil, you enter into a reaction to evil—and this cannot remove suffering from the Earth but will only increase suffering. And therefore, the only way to "remove" "evil" is to transcend the dualistic consciousness, so that you can act from the non-dualistic consciousness and therefore seek to accelerate the conditions that others call evil, accelerate them into purity by lifting up all life instead of seeking to condemn, to put down, to destroy. This is the difference between those who have ascended and those who have not. This is the difference between those who have taken a love-based approach to life and those who are still stuck in a fear-based approach, where they feel a need to judge, condemn, to put down and destroy.

How do you ascend? By accelerating yourself and by coming to the point where you say with Jesus: "And I, if I be lifted up from the Earth, will draw all men unto to me." Did Jesus say, I will draw only the good people unto me and send the bad people to hell? Nay, he did not. He said "I am willing to accelerate, to lift up all life" and that was why he could ascend. Because he had accelerated himself beyond the accusatory consciousness that divides the undivided, indivisible oneness of God into two polarities and labels one as good – that can enter the Kingdom of God – and one as bad – that cannot enter the Kingdom of God – and therefore must be destroyed by those who want to enter the Kingdom of God. For in destroying evil, you will supposedly qualify yourself to enter the Kingdom of God.

Such is the lie of the epic dramas. And how many people have believed them, and still believe them and still think that they can find some way to qualify to enter God's Kingdom by still maintaining that consciousness of duality—and therefore not putting on the wedding garment, of being completely non-violent, by being non-dualistic, non-judgmental and simply seeking to accelerate all life into purity, for you do not judge or condemn or put anything down.

Do you see that I am not asking you to be blind. I am not asking you to ignore the many impurities you see in the world, but I am asking you to not make them permanent in your mind. For when you react to them, what is it you do? Well, if you know that something is unreal and that you are real, you do not have any need to react to it or against it, do you? Why would you need to react to something unreal? And so, you do not react with a sense of being threatened, or angry, or afraid, or having any other negative emotion. You simply look at it, and then you act based on—not the outer appearance, not the outer form, but based on your inner creativity that comes forth spontaneously from your own higher being, from your I AM Presence, from the lineage of spiritual beings that stretches from you all the way to the Creator.

You act out of that wellspring of creativity instead of reacting. And by not reacting to the form, you do not give it permanence, you do not give it reality. And thus, your action is not geared towards putting something down and destroying it. It is geared towards accelerating it into the purity that you see beyond the outer form. This is pure perception, where you can look at something and see it as an unreal manifestation without going into the reaction of labeling it as ugly, or bad or evil—as most people do.

Chapter 9:
Teachings about fallen angels, 2010

It is time to face hatred of the mother

Mother Mary, February 8, 2010

The desire for control

What do I mean, when I say that life is a process? I mean that is it is an ever-moving, ever-flowing state of change. But not just circular change; a directional change where everything transcends itself in the eternal dance—that is not at dance in a horizontal way but a dance in a vertical way of transcendence, where everything becomes MORE. Not "more of," but "more than."

Becoming MORE is indeed the mandate of the world of form. You can – seemingly – maintain a form for a time, but, as even the short history known to man on Earth has proven over and over again, nothing can be maintained forever. In fact, one would – if one were to take a neutral look at history – have to conclude that nothing can be maintained for very long. And thus, if one is an astute student of life, one would conclude that there is no point in seeking to maintain anything in any particular state. For the second law of thermodynamics, the contracting force of the mother, will break it down as fast as you can seek to lock it into a particular matrix.

Thus, the question is: Why do human beings seek to lock everything into a particular matrix, why do they seek to stop the flow of life? Well, they do it, of course, because they want to maintain a particular form, a particular experience of life. But what is the deeper motivation behind this drive, this obsessive-compulsive drive to maintain something in a particular state, where you have it under some form of control? Well, it is – precisely – the drive to feel that you have life under control, that you have your own life, yourself, under control. But also that you have your surroundings, your circumstances under control.

Yet behind this is an even deeper desire for control that does not truly come from any individual co-creator but came from the original fallen beings who, in their anger and rebellion against God, decided that they wanted to control God. Truly, they were so arrogant, so unrealistic in their assessment of life, that they believed they could control God. And when it was proven, after a short while, that they could not control God – they could not control anything above their own level – well then they decided that if they could not control God, they would seek to control God's creation.

Denying that God is also mother

So then, what is the God they saw as the God that they wanted to control, as the God that they thought had made the mistake of giving co-creators free will? Well, it was the God that they saw as above them in the hierarchy of the spiritual realm, meaning that they saw this as God the father. And so, indeed, it is relevant to say that there is a God who represents the father aspect, the masculine aspect. Yet, what the fallen beings were not willing to recognize was that that God is everywhere present, meaning it is present within its creation as well. And thus, you will see that, in the mindset of these fallen beings, the only way they could maintain their illusion of being in opposition to God was if they denied the presence of God where they are. And thus, in order to deny that God is everywhere present, what is it that you must deny? Well, you must deny the mother aspect of God.

For truly, the father aspect, in its ultimate sense, is the unexpressed, formless Creator that has not yet divided itself into the two polarities of Alpha and Omega, father and mother, Spirit and matter. And so, you see that what you deny, what the fallen beings denied, was that the mother aspect of God is also God—that God is present within the mother as well as within the father. For the formless Creator expresses itself as both Spirit and matter, but it creates both of its own Being, meaning that the formless Creator is equally present in both Spirit and in matter.

This is the truth, the reality, that the fallen beings had to deny, and they have been denying it ever since, seeking to get all of God's co-creators to deny it as well. And on planet Earth – as is the case in certain other places throughout the cosmos – they have been remarkably successful in getting people to deny that God is within themselves. This is the entire concept behind monotheism, where you create an image of God as a masculine figure who is not found on Earth but is only found in a remote Kingdom up there in heaven. And then you say that God is only up there and is not down here among human beings—who are all sinners or somehow deficient in other ways. So that they need some external assistance from an external religion in order to enter that external kingdom that has now been defined and as the ultimate goal for the process of life.

…

Do you see, my beloved, that in the original design, you are created as a spiritual being. You are not meant to adapt to the world of form, for you are meant to be a co-creator who can bring the etheric, the higher etheric, thoughtforms into physical manifestation. Thus, you are not meant to look at any state in the world of form as permanent or unchanging. You are not meant to descend into embodiment on planet Earth, look at the conditions found here at the time you descended, and accept them as permanent or accept them as having any power over your Spirit. You are meant to retain the connection to your I AM presence, so that you continue to superimpose the etheric images and thoughtforms upon the Ma-ter light, never accepting that the current images and forms are permanent or real in the sense that they are more real than your Spirit.

And so, you see that in the original design, you are not meant to create a sense of identity based on the conditions that you find on Earth, using these conditions to reason that you are only a human being, that you have certain limitations and that the power of your mind cannot override what has already been manifest as material forms. And thus, you need to build a self based on the inevitability, the permanence, the reality of the material forms that you see already manifest on Earth. How can you be a co-creator who brings God's kingdom to Earth, if you look at the present conditions and accept them as permanent or real or as having power over you? Or if you see yourself as not having power to change them, for you have somehow come to accept the idea that with God all things are not possible on Earth—at least not for you.

Two ways to progress, one way to be stuck

Yet my beloved, were you even to go to the ultimate opposite extreme of totally identifying yourself with form, then even that might actually be a way to progress spiritually. As you would eventually come to a point, where you would be so tired of being limited by form that you would begin to long for something more. And thus, it is indeed correct, as they say in the East, that there are two ways to progress spiritually. One is to focus on Spirit and withdraw from the physical realm to some degree; the other is to immerse yourself in the material world and indulge in its pleasures, until you have had enough of that experience.

But you see, my beloved, what the fallen beings have attempted to do is to fixate most human beings in a no-man's land and no-god's land that is in between these two, where you neither renounce the material world nor immerse yourself in it. For you, instead, seek to attempt to control the material world, rebelling against the basic design of it, the purpose behind it, but yet not fully accepting it either. Therefore being neither accepting nor withdrawing from it but seeking to make it conform to the images in your mind, the images that are based on the illusion of separation that can never truly have power over matter.

Do you see that this springs from the desire to control, the desire to be proven right—even over God the Creator, the desire to prove God wrong. And so, what you see on this Earth is indeed that most people have come to believe in one of the many subtle illusions created by the fallen beings that there is a flaw, some fundamental evil in the material world that must be overcome, that must be corrected, that must be destroyed, my beloved, making it necessary to destroy the forms, even the people, that our epic mindset has defined as being the embodiment of that evil, that flaw.

Free will is not a flaw

My beloved, there is no fundamental flaw in the material world, for the fundamental law that guides the forms that you see on Earth is free will, and free will is not a flaw. It is the very essence of the purpose of life, namely the growth in self-awareness through experimentation with your co-creative abilities, and an expansion of your sense of self from a localized to a universal viewpoint.

This is not a flaw, even if it results in taking the original pure design of the Earth into the state you see today, with a myriad of imbalances and impurities. Yet even though you may look at the conditions currently found on Earth and see that they are surely below the original vision of the Elohim – when they created the physical planet – still this is not a flaw. There is no flaw in the Creator's design, for even that which is imperfect, even that which is below the vision of Elohim, can become the basis for a learning experience that leads to an expansion of consciousness.

You see, the essence of the fallen consciousness is that it imposes a value judgment that says that this is bad, this is good, this is evil, this is God. When I, as the representative of the mother flame – the mother aspect of God for planet Earth – when I look at the Earth, I do not see good and evil, good and bad. I see only expressions of a certain state of consciousness. I also see that any state of consciousness, any sense of self, that is based on duality and separation, can only lead to suffering.

And thus, as the Buddha said, if you speak or act with polluted perception – because you see through the filter of separation – well then suffering will indeed follow you all the days of your life. Yet I also see that behind this sense of self based on form are pure spiritual beings who can at any time return to and rediscover their pure awareness, the pure awareness within them—what Saint Germain called the point of stillness within them. And thus, they can return to that stillness, that pure identity and begin to express it. They can do what Jesus said: let the old sense of self die and be reborn into a pure sense of self.

I have no value judgments

And thus, when I look at the Earth, I see no epic need to correct, to destroy some evil. And thus, I am not tempted to enter into the epic dramas, the epic consciousness, the epic mindset of the fallen beings. I wish you could see the Earth through that immaculate conception, that immaculate concept that I see it through. I wish you could see yourself as I see you, as the pure spiritual being that was created. I wish you could see what I see, namely that you are a pure spiritual being and that that external sense of identity based on form is simply unreal.

Thus, you would see that you do not belong to a particular spiritual movement. You do not belong to a particular religion, to a particular nationality, to a particular ethnic group, a particular race or even a particular sex. Your pure spiritual being is neither male nor female, for it is in polarity with the male aspect of the Spirit, your I AM Presence. Thus, there is no male or female spiritual beings, as you conceive of male and female on Earth. For surely, many people on Earth – even if they were to accept reincarnation – would think that if you are a female spiritual being, you can only express yourself and embody in a female body. But it is not so. Your conscious self is neither male nor female in the sense conceived by human beings through that filter of separation and distinction that must set male and female apart from each other—and therefore can give rise to a conflict between the two. As you indeed see the conflict between men and women.

The deepest conflict on Earth

And this, my beloved, is indeed the deepest division found on Earth— that between men and women. It is a division that has been used by the fallen beings from the very beginning to create conflict, irreconcilable conflict on Earth. For as I said, as we explained last year, there is indeed no possibility of peace in society if there is not peace in the home, peace between man and woman.

And thus, what do you see, my beloved, when you look at the world? You see a suppression of women in almost every culture and society. Can we say that women are only suppressed in monotheistic cultures? Nay, we cannot, for surely women are even more suppressed in India and China and other cultures influenced by Hinduism and Buddhism; where women are considered to be of no value, so that they will abort female fetuses, kill female babies or abandon them, give them away. Or force them to marry at a young age, that the parents might gain some kind of advantage—for the girls are seen merely as property to be traded for some short-lived material advantage.

Hatred of the mother

What then is the very basis for this universal suppression of women? It is a concept that I would like to call "hatred of the mother." What, my beloved, is hatred of the mother? In order to explain it, we need to again look at the original fallen beings. They thought that they could control the Creator and cause the Creator to change its design for the material universe, for the world of form, for their particular sphere. They thought they could get the Creator to withdraw free will from co-creators and make the co-creators the subjects, the underlings, of the fallen beings themselves; so that the fallen beings would be allowed to force co-creators to enter into what they conceived of as the proper state of consciousness—that would allow the co-creators to enter the kingdom of heaven.

Now, this was from the very beginning a fundamental misconception. The fallen beings did not even understand the consciousness that allows you to enter the ascended state. For if they had understood this, they would realize that you cannot come up with one image that defines the ascended consciousness. It is not so that all beings who ascend become alike or even live up to a particular standard or norm. This is a misconception, even held by many who call themselves ascended master students, yet base their image of the ascension process on what was given through previous dispensations. Yet in reality the image of the ascension process is not based on the teaching given, but on a particular interpretation of it, filtered through the consciousness of duality and separation.

There is no standard for ascended beings, and the reason for this is that a being who has ascended is one who has become one with the River of Life, and therefore is expressing its God-given creativity in full measure. Do you think that I, as an ascended being, that I am expressing myself the same way that Master MORE, or Gautama, or Saint Germain or Jesus are expressing themselves? There is no norm, there is no standard—unless you want to call it a standard that each ascended being expresses its God-given individuality and creativity by constantly transcending itself. If indeed you think this can be called a standard, then I wish you good luck in trying to define it. But I would suggest that you give up trying to define it, and instead focus on your individual creativity, allowing that to be expressed through your outer form. For that is how you will qualify for your ascension.

As long as you think that you have to live up to some external standard, defined based on how other beings have ascended in the past, then you cannot win your ascension. You may make spiritual progress, which is why we have given certain external definitions in the past, for students whose consciousness could not yet fathom what I am explaining here. You may make progress towards the ascended state by raising your consciousness according to certain criteria, according to a certain path that can indeed be defined. But you will not make that last step into the ascended state until you have become one with your higher being, and thus naturally and effortlessly express your individual creativity and being through your outer form.

The desire to judge others

This is what the fallen beings could not understand, could not fathom. And the reason for this was that they wanted to judge others, they wanted to raise themselves up as being superior to others. And how can you do this? You can do it only by creating a standard, a graven image, and now setting that graven image before the true God of constant transcendence, the living God. Now you elevate that graven image to some absolute authority or standard, saying that only those who live up to this image will enter the kingdom of heaven, whereas all others will be denied—and therefore condemned to the opposite of the kingdom of heaven, namely hell. But you see, in defining an opposite to the kingdom of heaven, you must first define the kingdom of heaven based on separation. And thus, what this "absolute" standard gives entry into is not the real kingdom of heaven, of the ascended state. It is a false, man-made concept that does not have any actual existence or reality.

And so, that is how the fallen beings set up an impossible goal of seeking to get people to strive to qualify for entry into a non-existent kingdom of heaven by living up to a standard that either cannot be defined or cannot be fulfilled. How many people can give a definition, a clear concise definition, of perfection? And how many could live up to it, if they could give a definition? And so, you see the impossibility of what the fallen ones have set up as the ultimate goal of life. Yet it is set up precisely to keep you trapped in the state of consciousness I described earlier—that is neither this nor that. For it is based on an attempt to control the matter realm, to stop the flow of life and to force the Mater light to take on and maintain a certain form indefinitely, even forever. Or so the arrogance of the fallen angels would have you believe, for they have come to believe it—that it is actually possible to maintain their fallen state of consciousness forever.

And so, when you go into this frame of mind – of judging everything based on an impossible standard – then it is inevitable that the safety mechanism built into the world of form will seek to shatter your illusion. What we have called the second law of thermodynamics or the contracting force of the mother will break down the graven image that you seek to superimpose upon the Ma-ter light.

The Ma-ter light will indeed take on the image for a time. For according to the Law of Free Will you must be allowed to create any form, any experience you desire. So if you desire to create the perfect empire on Earth – as for example the Roman civilization, or the Greek civilization, or the civilizations of the Middle East or many other civilizations have desired – well then you must be allowed to create that empire. But of course, in creating it, you make it subject to the second law that will then break it down. And you must then continually struggle and struggle to maintain it, which means your life becomes a process of suffering.

And so, as you then experience that some force is seeking to break down this perfect kingdom that you created on Earth, what is the inevitable result? Well, it is that you come to hate the force of nature that is breaking down what you have created. Therefore, you come to hate the mother aspect of God, the world of form, even the Ma-ter light. And so, what is hatred of the mother? It is hatred of the ongoingness of life, it is hatred of the demand of life – the underlying principle of life – namely that of growth, change, self-transcendence. You hate the process and love a particular result, and you want to freeze the process on that particular result and maintain it indefinitely. This is hatred of the mother; the unwillingness to change, the unwillingness to transcend, the unwillingness to flow with the River of Life.

...

This is the next task for our work—to shake up those remnants of these megalithic power structures that indeed Jesus came to overthrow 2,000 years ago. For it was one of the goals of the Age of Pisces that humankind would finally free itself from this dream of creating an earthly empire, an earthly kingdom, that was an outpicturing of the kingdom of God. And therefore guaranteed entry into the kingdom of God to those who submitted themselves to it and to the image upon which it was built. It was the hope that humankind would acquire the discernment to see through the fallen consciousness and its attempts to build these earthly empires, these structures that can guarantee your entry into the external kingdom of heaven. And thus keep you so focused on defending or building these earthly empires that you forget to seek the kingdom within you—that is the true entry of the kingdom of heaven.

You have your own entryway to the kingdom

Do you see, my beloved, the essence of this? Every self-aware being has his or her personal entryway to the kingdom of heaven, located within your heart. Yet you will not find that entryway as long as you are looking for it outside yourself, and thus the entire plot of the fallen beings is to create the epic dramas that make you think that you have to fight for some cause, for some empire, for some kingdom on Earth. And therefore, you will qualify – through that external activity – you will qualify for entry into the kingdom that you see as external to yourself.

They will do anything they can think of to get you to forget to look inside yourself. And what is, indeed, the main tool? It is the hatred of the mother that you then turn against yourself, as hatred not only of your physical body, but hatred of your self. For when you see your self as separated from your heavenly father, then you cannot see your self as truly an expression of that father.

So you think you are confined to the mother realm. You think that the mother realm is separated from God and therefore has some fundamental flaw—that therefore there is something fundamentally wrong or evil about matter, there is something fundamentally wrong or evil about your physical body, there is even something fundamentally wrong or evil about your soul. For you were conceived in sin and you can only sin—unless you are saved by some external savior. And thus, you come to hate yourself, for hatred of the mother can only be hatred of self.

For what is – truly – the mother? It is the expressed God. You are an expression of the unexpressed God, but you are an expression and therefore you are in the matter realm, the mother realm. And thus, when you hate the mother, you hate yourself—and hatred is not the doorway, the entry, the key to the kingdom of heaven. Love is, oneness is, acceptance is.

How a limited imagination blocks peace in the Middle East

Saint Germain, February 3, 2010.

Stillness is a Presence. It is pure awareness. Not an awareness of this or that or the next thing on Earth, but pure awareness. If you have not experienced it or recognized it for what it is – recognized the contrast between pure awareness and what human beings call normal awareness – well, then you will not go beyond a certain level of the spiritual path. You will get stuck at that level. And therefore, you will become more and more focused on – more and more attached to – something in the material world. And you will begin to believe that that something is the key to your entering heaven—the kingdom of God, or whatever you want to call it.

You will think that perfecting this outer activity, performing it to a certain quantity – such as doing so many decrees, doing so much violet flame, doing so much meditation, prostrating yourself on the floor so many times, lighting so many candles or doing this, that or the next thing – you will think that this outer activity not only is the key to your entering heaven but in fact can guarantee your entry into the kingdom. For you have become a slave of the ancient epic drama that defines an activity on Earth as the key to heaven. And then says that when you perform that activity a certain number of times, your entry into heaven is guaranteed.

This, of course, is one of the oldest epic dramas used by the fallen beings to trap God's co-creators and prevent them from fulfilling their role to be co-creators on Earth. The effect of this drama is twofold: it focuses you on what happens after you are no longer on Earth, taking you focus away from the Earth and what you are here to accomplish in the Earth. And then it focuses you on a repetitive, mechanical activity that takes your focus away from the reality of who you are—a co-creator who has access to the infinite fount of creativity right within yourself.

And what is that fount of creativity? It is stillness—but you have no need for stillness, you think, for all you need to do is to perform this external religious activity and then you will get out of this limited realm and into this wonderful kingdom that awaits you beyond the veil. Yet why did Jesus say that the kingdom of God is within you? It is because until you find the kingdom within yourself, you will not find it. Until you find the kingdom in the present moment, you will not find it.

As long as you see the kingdom as being outside yourself, and as being achievable in some future time, you will never, ever find it. The kingdom is within you—here and now. And until you find it in the here and in the now, it will remain far from you—or so it seems to the mind that has forgotten stillness and has been trapped in doing. Even thinking it is free because it has certain powers on Earth—and can supposedly do anything it wants, which in reality means anything it can imagine from the limited human level of imagination. For if you go beyond that level and into the point of stillness, you will contact God's imagination, which is infinitely greater and can imagine things for the Earth that hardly any human being on this planet can imagine right now.

...

If you cannot imagine peace, you cannot create peace

What is freedom? Is it freedom that your inner state of consciousness is tied to and depends on – is a slave of – your external conditions? Is that freedom? Nay, it is slavery—bondage, the oldest and only form of bondage known in the world of form. This is the bondage that the original fallen beings entered into when they separated themselves from the kingdom of God within them – from the point of stillness - and then started using the external, dualistic imagination. Thereby making themselves the subjects of the second law of thermodynamics, that will break down organized structures, until you reach the lowest possible energy state. And is this not precisely what you see in the barren sand dunes in the desert, where nothing can grow?

I, Jesus, withdraw my light from Christianity

Jesus, February 11, 2010.
This dictation was given in Saint Peter's basilica.

Get thee behind me, Satan. For thou art an offense to me. Thou savourest not the things that be of God, but the things that be of men.

These are the words I spoke to Peter on that fateful day, when he set the pattern that has become the pattern of the Catholic Church—and through the Catholic Church for all of Christianity. The pattern was that of using your built-in ability to recognize Christ – that there is something unusual about Christ or those who have the light of the Spirit – but you are not willing to let them take you out of your mental box. You want them – you want the Living Christ – to come into your mental box and conform to it, therefore confirming that box and all of the beliefs within it, all of the mental images, the graven images, the idols that you have built in your desire to avoid taking responsibility for yourself and changing your life to follow Christ.

For you are not willing to let the old identity die and be reborn. You are not willing to give up that old identity in order to follow Christ into the unknown, where for a time – for a split second – it will seem as if you have no identity—for you have allowed it to die. And indeed, you have, for you must let the old die before the new can be reborn of the Spirit. That is the law, that is the eternal law that everyone who has ever ascended has faced. You must be willing to let go of the old, not knowing if there will be any self-awareness behind that point of letting go. Not knowing what it will be like, not knowing whether you will go to heaven or hell—or whatever you envision might come after the surrender of that mortal self that you have come to deify, or idolize, and see as the graven image that you have set before God.

This is the initiation that Peter failed, and he failed it to the end of his days, and he has failed it to this day. That is why the soul of Peter has not ascended. Yet, truth be told, Peter is not the only one of my personal disciples that have not ascended. For the reality of it is that two-thirds of them were among the original fallen angels that fell in the first sphere and have kept falling until they ended up in this sphere, here on planet Earth. They were assembled here over a long period of time, they were put together in embodiment after embodiment, and I descended to give them that final opportunity to confess Christ or to deny Christ. And they have all denied it, with the exception of one who is now in the process of ascending. Which one it is, is immaterial. But I give you this realization – that it is possible for even the original fallen angels to rise above that fallen sense of identity – if they are willing to let it die. And if they are not willing, well then they will continue the downward spiral until they end up at the second death, where their opportunity runs out.

The fallen consciousness in the Catholic Church

This, my beloved, is precisely the consciousness that is permeating the Catholic Church. For the fallen beings who form the false hierarchy on this Earth, for this Earth, they were quick – when they saw that Christianity could not be eradicated and would not die out on its own – they were quick to follow their own old axiom, "If you can't beat'em, join'em."

And so, they joined the Christian religion at an early age, and they attempted to influence it and pervert it by inserting what I have called toxic ideas. Toxic ideas that took Christianity – in subtle and seemingly unrelated ways – into a downward spiral that has created what you see before you, this Cathedral of Saint Peter, this Basilica of Saint Peter, this monument to the death consciousness, starting with Peter and being traceable all the way down. For this is the truth behind the apostolic succession, of which the Catholics are so proud.

The truth is that what they have maintained from Peter is exactly the Peter consciousness, the death consciousness that they have maintained in an unbroken line. And why is it an unbroken line? Because that which is of the death consciousness can be maintained in an unbroken line in the physical, whereas that which is of the Spirit cannot be maintained in an unbroken line—for the Holy Spirit bloweth where it listeth. It cannot be confined to any system, any mental box, any particular structure, such as a church or an organization. There cannot be an unbroken line of the Spirit, for some will have the Spirit only for a time. Others will have it for a lifetime, but then, when they are gone, where will the Spirit land next, who will be open to the flow of the Spirit?

The Spirit cannot be captured by any organization

This is indeed the question, and that is why you will see the impossibility of having an organization that has the unbroken flow of the Spirit. It simply cannot be done, for when you start an organization and when that organization reaches a certain size and complexity, it is inevitable that the people who created that structure, that complexity, will have endowed it with enough of their consciousness that they have created a living entity, a living beast. And that beast will seek to maintain itself, to survive. And therefore, it will use the outer organization that created it in order to sustain itself.

And if the people in the organization are not willing to let their mortal identity die, even letting the organization seemingly die – that it can be reborn again continually – well then they will give in to that beast, and they will give it the continuity that it seeks. For it has no reality in Spirit, and therefore must seek immortality in the physical octave by getting people to worship it, to worship the beast rather than to worship the living Christ—who does not need to be worshiped, but needs you to become one with me.

I have no need for worship. I have a need for those who will be one with me in the continual regeneration, the continual self-transcendence. Yet those who will not transcend, who will not let the old die, they will want continuity in the physical octave in the form of a structure, an organization, a church. And this is precisely what you see in this mausoleum of the dead popes, who have no Spirit whatsoever, for they have no connection to the reality of who I am or why I came to this Earth. They have perverted everything that I stood for, everything I stand for today. There is absolutely nothing in here that vibrates with the reality of who I am.

There is no room for Christ in the church

As this messenger, walking around here, realized that there was hardly even a depiction of me, but even the depictions of me found here are not representative of me. And thus, as he was walking, he finally noticed a sun beam shining through a window, and he realized that that was the only true spiritual light in here—coming from outside this structure that has no life in it, that has no Spirit in it—for it has no room for me.

There is no room for me in the structure, in the organization—there is no room for me. Even though many people who come here have a great devotion to me in their hearts, the devotion they have is so colored by the graven images produced by this Catholic Church – and other mainstream Christian churches – that they truly do not have room for the Living Christ. They only have room for the dead Christ that lives up to their image. And if I did not live up to their image, well they would shun me instantly. They would withdraw from me, they would even call me of the devil, as they did when I walked this Earth and the scribes and the Pharisees said that I was a false prophet or of the devil. So they would say the same thing in here, if I allowed this messenger to stand up and create a spectacle. They would instantly reject the Living Spirit flowing through anyone, for they will not recognize that anyone can have the Living Spirit, for they think the Spirit has been encaged, encaged in this structure, so that it rests only on this one person, the Pope.

But look at him and the sermon and the service he gave this morning. Was there any Living Spirit in that man? I tell you "nay," there was not a spark of it, there was not a spark of life, my beloved. There was no willingness to flow with the River of Life, with the joy of life. There was only a whitened sepulcher, which looks beautiful on the outward with all the pomp and pageantry that you find in the structure, but it has no reality within it—it is filled with dead men's bones. The dead men's bones that are stored here as the dead bones of the past popes.

The judgment of the beast of mainstream Christianity

Thus, I say to you – I, Jesus, the Living Christ – raise the right hand of this messenger to use the scepter of Surya to bring forth the absolute and final judgment of this beast of orthodox Christianity and the Catholic Church. The beast that began even before Peter, for he had worshiped it in many embodiments before he met me in the flesh. And he is still worshiping it today, refusing to let it go. My beloved, this beast has come to an end this day.

Certainly, it will be re-created almost instantly by those who cannot, who will not, let it go. But yet the momentum that has been gathered over these 2,000 years, that momentum is dead—now at this very instant; it is gone. And thus, people have a new start, a new white page on which they must now write. And everyone who is here, every one of the billion plus people who call themselves Catholics – and the many millions more who claim to be following another mainstream religion – well, they will sense it this instant at inner levels, even though most of them will be unwilling to recognize it consciously. They will sense that a shift has occurred, that a cycle has come to an end. For this is the year 2010, that marks the end of the Piscean age and the beginning of the Aquarian age.

And thus, I tell you I, Jesus, am withdrawing my light, the light that has allowed so many Christians over these 2,000 years to be able to call themselves Christians while worshiping the idols of anti-christ. That veil, that dispensation, has been withdrawn. I allowed this because I wanted to give people as much time as possible to build the inner discernment, from within their hearts, that would allow them to recognize the reality of Christ within themselves. Yet, I can no longer maintain this dispensation, and thus it must be withdrawn—that people must stand on their own, their own momentum without having any of my light, any of the grace that has supported them. And thus, they will have to deal with their own karma, with their own thoughts, their own idols, their own dualistic images that they are constantly superimposing upon the Ma-ter light, and thereby superimposing upon themselves, their outer minds, their physical bodies.

The suppression of women must come to an end – in the Church and in the home

Mother Mary, February 13, 2010. This dictation was given on the square in front of Saint Peter's Basilica.

My beloved hearts, they come here by the thousands. They come here, many of them, with pure hearts, with pure devotion to Jesus my son and to myself. Yet I, Mary, must say – in the interest of truth in the interest of healing – "You do not honor me if you come here and take in the mindset that is the antithesis of the mindset of Christ, of the Christ mind that sees the oneness of all life the oneness between the Creator and its creation."

And what is the Creator's creation? Did not Jesus say in the Book of Revelation, "I am Alpha and Omega, the beginning and the ending?" And thus, does this not signify that the one Creator divided itself into the two polarities of expanding and contracting, of masculine and feminine? And so, it must be understood, in the interest of truth, that the original perversion of the fallen angels – the original plan of the fallen angels to create a downward spiral on Earth – was precisely to pervert the original act of creation in the minds of those who are open to the lie of separation and duality.

The plan to separate male and female

When the Creator divided itself into two polarities, those polarities were not opposites. They do not cancel out each other, they complement each other, they form a new whole out of which new life is created. This is the reality. This is the reality that must be known by all who claim to honor Jesus and myself. For you cannot honor me and the office I hold, the office of the Divine Mother for Earth, without honoring the union of male and female. Not in what is normally seen as the sexual union – that has the purpose of physical procreation or the satisfaction of base sensual desires – but as a higher form of union, where male and female, man and woman, come together and transcend the consciousness that they are opposites, that they are in opposition to each other, that one must be put down and the other be the head of the household.

This is the consciousness, the division of the original polarities of God, created by the fallen angels and the fallen consciousness. For they knew – they knew – that because it is inevitable that men and women on Earth are different sexes, then if they could insert a wedge of untruth that divided the sexes – that created suspicion, animosity and opposition between them – well then, there would be very little possibility of the Earth rising into such a high state of consciousness that they themselves would no longer be able to embody here. And so, their plan, their entire purpose, is indeed to set men and women apart—that they cannot come together in that union, that transcends sexuality and procreation, that transcends traditional roles, where the man is the head of the household and the woman is the subordinate, but finds a higher union, where they come together in complete equality. For they have transcended value judgments, the relative scale, where there is two extremes that are in opposition to each other, neither have they come together in any point near the center of that scale, forming a compromise between them that is not true balance.

Male and female relationships without relative value judgments

You see, my beloved, the reality that we have attempted to teach you – so many of us in so many different ways through this messenger over these last couple of years – is that everything on the dualistic scale is outside the oneness of the mind of Christ. And thus, it is not a matter of raising up one side of the scale or lowering the other. It is a matter of transcending the scale, whereby you form such an upward magnetic pull that you pull the consciousness of all mankind up.

As I showed this messenger only very recently, you cannot raise up one part of life by seeking to put down another and at the same time be in the mind of Christ. You cannot desire to be right among men by making other people wrong or by judging them according to some standard that you have created or accepted and at the same time be in the oneness of the mind of Christ—that seeks only to raise up all life. "Judge not, that ye be not judged" means, truly, "Transcend the dualistic scale that you will not judge yourself through that dualistic consciousness as you pass from the screen of life."

Indeed, when you look at this enormous basilica – supposedly built to honor Christ – you see that it is in its entirety an expression of the duality consciousness, the desire to raise up one part of life and portray it as being superior to all others.

This my beloved, started a very long time ago, after the original fall in the Garden Of Eden, where there were those – even in the Garden – who would not follow Maitreya into transcending that state of consciousness, transcending the dualistic scale. For they even desired to be better than others in the mystery school, to be more advanced students, to be given special initiations and special privileges, even to be set up as leaders for the new students, who had not yet reached a certain level— or so they thought, those who love to judge according to a standard that they had created or accepted from the fallen angels themselves.

The choice to put women down

And so, you see how this tendency to divide, based on a man-made or a relative standard, can be traced throughout cultures and religions on this Earth. As you see it in the Garden Of Eden, where it indeed was the forbidden fruit, the forbidden fruit because once you partake of that duality consciousness – and are trapped inside of that mind state created by the dualistic perception – you cannot see beyond the perception. You cannot see anything wrong with the perception, you can see no need to transcend it, for everything looks so perfectly logical and rational, according to the dualistic filter through which you see everything.

You are blinded, but you do not know you are blinded—you think you see supreme truth. And thus, you see it in the Bible in Cain and Abel, you see it in the tribes of Israel, you see it in the Egyptians, and the Jews, and you see it even among Jesus' own disciples, where they had to compete as to who would be the most important among them after Jesus took his leave. And thus, in going into that entire argument, they demonstrated that they had not understood, they had not locked in to, the consciousness of Christ that Jesus had demonstrated to them on so many occasions—and that he demonstrated later to them by allowing himself to be crucified by that consciousness of dualistic judgment.

And thus, my beloved, do you see how the fallen angels made a choice? They made the choice that because women are physically not the stronger of the two sexes, therefore not the ones who are likely to go out and wage war, they would put women down as the weaker sex. And not only the weaker sex, but they would put upon them this burden that they were the ones who ate the forbidden fruit, that Eve was the one who sinned, and therefore Eve is responsible for the fall of all of mankind.

This is such a subtle perversion that has so many ramifications, such a subtle state of consciousness, that it permeates the very relationship between the two sexes from ancient days and all the way forward. Yet as Jesus himself said inside the basilica, I now express it outside the Basilica. This consciousness of the animosity, or the rivalry, or the guilt and the blame between men and women, this must be transcended in the Aquarian age—if the Aquarian age is to become the Golden Age of Saint Germain.

. . .

The need for a higher vision of sexuality

Certainly, it is understandable that spiritual people throughout the ages have looked at some of the perversions, or the base aspects of human sexuality, and have concluded that this cannot be congruent with the spiritual path or a spiritual lifestyle. But this does not mean that you have to jump into the opposite extreme and say that the only alternative to base sexuality is no sexuality at all. For as Jesus himself said, how can there be balance, how can there be a restoration of balance, when you jump from the one extreme to the other.

And thus, I too echo what Jesus has already said. Celibacy is not a mandate from God. It was not an inspiration from God or the Holy Spirit that caused the Catholic Church to institute celibacy. It was indeed because the Catholic Church from its inception was based on the fallen consciousness, the consciousness of Peter, the desire to control, the desire to raise up a structure on Earth that is of such magnitude, that lives up to such a standard on Earth, that you can create the illusion – and people will believe the illusion – that this structure will give you access to heaven.

For how could God turn you down, how could God turn down something that is so honored among men? Yet I tell you—what did Jesus say to the devil when he was tempted? "What shall it profit a man that he gains the whole world yet loses his own soul." Or what shall it profit a church if they gain the whole world and the membership of the whole world yet loses the original soul of Christ. And thus, they have nothing but an empty shell—nothing but an empty shell, my beloved.

Shiva clears the records of the Roman Empire

Shiva, February 13, 2010.

Wanting to be gods on Earth

As Mother Mary just said, what is the entire problem of the Catholic Church? It is, indeed, that they have created a mindset, a perception, through which one is supposed to look at life. It is completely based on the consciousness of anti-christ, yet they believe it is completely based on the consciousness of Christ, even that the Pope himself represents Christ. As indeed, many Romans believed that the emperor represented some higher authority, be it this or that God. But they literally wanted to be gods on Earth – the emperors – and that is, of course, exactly the desire of the original fallen angels, who wanted to be seen as gods on Earth, who wanted to be seen by men as having the authority on Earth that only God has.

But God does not exercise that authority as human beings conceive of authority, for God is not the ultimate tyrant—even though many people make him out to be so. This is not the case. I, indeed, Shiva, I know Brahman. And I know that Brahman is the formless God, and therefore is no tyrant. Brahman has given you free will. What can be tyrannical about it—you are the one making the choices. If there is a tyrant in your life, you are that tyrant. If there is a judge in your life, you are that judge. If there is a murderer in your life, you are that murderer—by having murdered your own creativity and imagination, allowing your imagination to be entombed in one of these structures built by men, the structures that must come tumbling down for the Age of Aquarius to become the age of the Holy Spirit.

Don't be like the Romans—be the Christ in you

Archangel Michael, February 13, 2010.

Michael, the Archangel, I Am! Let me ask you to participate with me in a little exercise of your imagination. Even if you have not been there in person, you have certainly seen pictures, perhaps even movies about the Colosseum in Rome, and the games with gladiators and the slaughter of animals. And thus, I ask you to envision that it is a day of the games.

The Colosseum is full, with tens of thousands of people, crowded in there—even more than the official numbers says that the stadium can hold. They are all ready for one thing: Blood—drama! What they desire to experience is a simulated warfare, where they can experience the drama and the bloodshed of war without being exposed to the risk that they will be maimed or killed themselves. This is a consciousness that – although not the originator of war – is certainly the consciousness that has allowed war to continue to exist on this planet. And although it is greatly exemplified in the Roman empire, it certainly is not unique, as you even find it in the world of today.

Yet let us not get ahead of ourselves. Let us stay with the vision of the Romans sitting there, waiting for the gladiator games to begin. And for a time, they have various warm-up events: various fights among gladiators, wild animals being let loose to kill criminals or to fight against the gladiators. But everyone is waiting for the main event, which is rumored to be something special on this day. The noise is deafening, the vibration is that of a mob that is aroused to extreme anger and anxiety—and the desire for blood.

As you may know, in the later stages, the Colosseum had an elaborate system that allowed the upcoming events to be staged underneath the arena itself. And a part of the floor in the arena would then be lowered, and the next event would be raised up literally through the floor, thus appearing in the arena in front of the people. Finally then, as the excitement reaches a crescendo, the main event is about to take place. The roar of the crowd reaches an all-time high, and now the floor moves and rises up. And what comes up through the floor is indeed myself. I come in my full stature, over 12 feet high, clad in blue armor that shines as neon lightning, an intense blue, such as no man has ever seen before with the physical eyes. I bring a sword that radiates blue flames. And suddenly the crowd falls silent—for this was not what they expected. They have never seen anything like it; they do not know what to make of it. And in their silence, they look at each other.

They start to mumble amongst themselves, as I stand there holding up my sword. And then, after a few minutes of silence, they start yelling. For now they want some action; they want some blood. They imagine that this fearsome looking creature must be able to beat any of the other gladiators. And they are expecting that all the gladiators will be let loose against me. They obviously think this is some kind of trickery, that perhaps this is a man made to look bigger, made to look more radiant.

Yet, as they begin to raise the noise level again, I point my sword against the crowd. And as I slowly turn around, blue flames, like blue laser beams, shoot out of the sword and hit all of the people in the stadium. And as they are hit by this intense light, they instantly fall silent. And as I go around the stadium, the silence follows the sword—until I have reached all the way around. And now the crowd is reduced from an angry mob lusting for blood to a silent crowd. Silent because what they are seeing is what they have not been willing to face in themselves. And suddenly, they have a sense of co-measurement, of what is the momentum, the illusion, that each person has that stands between that person and entry into heaven. They also have a sense co-measurement, that makes them realize that there is absolutely nothing they can do to cheat or force their way into heaven, as I am absolutely, completely, totally immovable.

I did not fight the dragon

You see, there are many illusions among men. But no one, no illusion, is more dangerous or more subtle than the idea that you can somehow force your way into heaven, that you can enter the kingdom of heaven through some kind of force, as Saint Germain described earlier today. Take the expressions from the Book of Revelation, where it is described how the original fallen angels rebelled against God, accused the brethren and finally, as the saying is, "There was war in heaven. And the dragon fought against Archangel Michael, and prevailed not." (Rev.:12.7)

My beloved, it is so very easy for you – even those of you who have been ascended Master students for a long time; decades in this lifetime, perhaps even in previous lifetimes – it is so easy for you to still have remnants of the duality consciousness, that you project onto this expression from the Book of Revelation. Yet that particular formulation was chosen to challenge those in the duality consciousness, to see whether they would project the dualistic images upon the description or whether they would be willing to look beyond them.

For you see, you have been told, by Maitreya in his book about the different spheres. And so, you know now that it was not in heaven that there was rebellion—if with heaven we mean the spiritual realm, where you only find beings who have passed the initiation of the ascension or who have never fallen into duality. Thus, what you know is that it was a previous sphere in which the fallen angels rebelled. And that sphere had not yet fully ascended, even though it had entered the Ascension spiral. And that is, indeed, why it was possible for the angels to rebel, as it is not possible for an ascended being to rebel. For that being has already passed the initiation of potentially misusing your free will to go against the will of God. And this, of course, does not mean that when you choose not to go against the will of God, you give up your free will. It does mean that you learn and choose to use that free will in a way that raises the All. Instead of, as Portia has talked about, raising only one part of life—and therefore inevitably doing so by putting another part of life down, so that the scales are raised: one up, one down.

My beloved, knowing this, you should be able to take the knowledge we have given you about the duality consciousness and transfer this to the situation, where I supposedly fought the Dragon, represented by the consciousness that rebelled against God. But more than that, the consciousness that was already split into two polarities that can only oppose each other; one seeking to destroy the other. And therefore, the dragon being really an expression of that warring consciousness, the consciousness of those who want to be in the epic mindset, who love the epic mindset. For they want to fight for what they think is a good and just cause, to fight to destroy others that they have labeled as the scapegoat, as the enemy or even as the enemies of God that must be put down by any means available. For, to the dragon, the ends can fully justify any means. The end for the dragon is not to manifest the kingdom of God, but to destroy the opponent. For it is the lust for blood, the lust for murder, the lust for destruction that is the consciousness that is described as the Dragon in Revelation.

And so, it is so easy for you – if you have not given up the duality consciousness – to look at this description and think that I, Archangel Michael, fought the fallen angels and their legions in heaven—that I fought against them, that I fought against them to kill them or destroy them, that I fought against them in anger or wrath, or whatever you might envision by projecting graven images upon God. Yet I am an ascended being. I am holding a spiritual office. I am not trapped in the duality consciousness. I have no anger. I have no desire to destroy any part of life. Thus, we might even say I am incapable of destroying any part of life.

Yet, what I am capable of doing, and what is indeed my office, is to defend those who are seeking to raise the All against those who are the Spoilers, those who are simply seeking to destroy and tear down the ascension spiral. And how do I defend? I defend by being absolutely immovable. The dragon fought against me; I did not fight back. I was simply immovable.

My immovability is a mirror

And in being immovable, I form that mirror that sends back the aggression, the anger, that is sent against me. And thus, those who attack me will meet their own momentums sent back to them. They will, of course, fail to see that I am mirroring back what they are sending out. And thus, they will actually experience that I am sending these rays at them, as my illustration of the people in the Colosseum experiencing, perceiving, that I was sending laser beams of light at them. But what is sent at them is their own consciousness, mirrored back and in some cases, if it is deemed constructive, magnified by the power that I am, so as to cut through the density of people's consciousness and give them an opportunity to see what they are not willing to see.

I have no anger against the devil, against the Dragon. I am an Archangel. How do you become an Archangel in the spiritual realm? Only by transcending all duality, all separation. And thus, in becoming one with the will of God, the power of God, I am one with the will to raise up all life—and with the power to defend those who are willing to raise themselves against those who are seeking to tear them down. But in defending, again, not fighting but providing that co-measurement, that here there is something that is absolutely immovable to the duality consciousness. And so, you see that those fallen angels who were part of the Dragon that fought against me, they carried deep within their beings an inner knowing that they cannot move Archangel Michael, they cannot move the forces of heaven. It is as if you would try to knock down a concrete wall by bumping your head against it.

And thus, this is indeed why – when they were cast down to the Earth; or rather, when they descended themselves – they came with such great wrath. What does it mean that they descended instead of being cast down? Well, they experienced that they were cast down, but this is again because they perceived it this way. They were not willing to face what they needed to face in themselves. And in not being willing to face this, they projected upon the situation that I was the one who was sending anger or aggression towards them. And thus, the reality is that while they experienced being cast down, they were cast down by their own momentums being returned to them—through the immovability that I and my legions are.

How co-creators differ from fallen angels

And thus, if you could take a fallen angel in embodiment or a co-creator who has become trapped in the duality consciousness, you would then – by comparing the two – see a difference. If you go deep within the psyche of the fallen being, you will come to a point, where that being knows that heaven is immovable. This of course has been covered over by layers upon layers of illusion. But it would be there, for that being has experienced the immovability of heaven. Yet if you take a co-creator who has been ensnared by the duality consciousness, that co-creator has never come up against the immovability of an archangel and thus has no co-measurement in its inner being that this truly is immovable. And that is precisely why the co-creator is susceptible to the belief, the toxic idea put out by the fallen beings, that it is possible to find some way to force your way into heaven. And this is, indeed, why so many co-creators – who have a potential to ascend, who have a potential to transcend the fallen consciousness – that is precisely why they are so often trapped in this dream, as Saint Germain described it, that an outer structure will take them to heaven.

Now then, if you also look at a comparison between the psyche of a fallen being and a co-creator from a different perspective, you see that

in the psyche of the fallen being, you also have a point of absolute rebellion against God and of complete unwillingness to see something in
yourself. Whereas a co-creator has never encountered that higher level
of the God consciousness, and therefore has not had the opportunity
to rebel against it. Therefore, the co-creator has not gone through this
deep-seated inner denial. And therefore it is easier, far easier, for a co-
creator to see through the illusion of the fallen beings. The co-creator
has a potential to transcend the fallen consciousness – the dream of
the outer salvation – but it is trapped by not having the sense that there
is something that is immovable in heaven, and that you cannot enter
heaven in any way through force.

And so, it is possible that a co-creator can be trapped in the lie for
many, many lifetimes. Where it for several lifetimes pursues one particular religion, or one particular approach to spirituality, thinking that this
particular approach will allow it to get into heaven without confronting
and transcending the duality consciousness, without looking at the beam
in its own eye. And so, co-creators, then, can be trapped in this lie that
even if something didn't work in the past, there must be another way. If
we can't force, maybe we can cheat, maybe we can hide from God—for
we think we can hide from other people or from ourselves. Maybe there
is some way to persuade God – to make him feel sorry for us – or to
make it seem like we are so good because we are doing all these things
on Earth.

Awakening from the lie that you can cheat your way into heaven

And this is what a co-creator can be trapped in, and that is why the co-
creators are so susceptible to following the fallen beings, the blind leaders of the blind, as Jesus called them. Yet there is also the potential that
the co-creator can be awakened from this illusion. However, this will in
almost all cases happen in only one way, and that is that the Conscious
You of the co-creator must awaken to its own inner reality as an extension of the pure awareness of God.

For when you experience that pure awareness – when you experience awareness without content, the formlessness of God – then you experience immovability. You know that the consciousness that is beyond
form can never be confined to – or moved by – that which has form.
When you connect to the pure, formless awareness in yourself, you ex-

perience an aspect of your own being over which the outer mind – the human mind, the ego, the separate identity – could not possibly have any power. You experience this directly. And thus, you gain that same sense of co-measurement that the fallen angels had by rebelling—and therefore meeting up against my immovability.

And once you have that co-measurement, because you have not gone through the denial, then it becomes much easier for you to switch your consciousness, to suddenly see—to turn the dial of consciousness those few degrees that allows you to see the fallacy of the lies of the fallen angels. You can literally awaken gradually, where it is almost like you feel the wheels of your mind turning, and everything gradually clicks into place. Now you see this illusion, now you see the one behind it. Now you see the next layer behind that, and then the next, and the next, and the next, and the next. And suddenly you have gone around the cosmic clock, the cosmic wheel of the 12 lines. And then, it even clicks further and you see beyond it to the 15, that we have described, as the seven rays, the eighth ray and the seven secret rays. And you see the layers of illusion, falling one after another.

However, you will only see this if you are also willing to look in the mirror and look at what it is in your own consciousness that caused you to believe in these illusions. For as long as you project, that it is the devil – or the fallen angels, or the leaders of this or that church – that have forced you to accept these illusions, well, then you cannot see the choices you made to accept these illusions—because the illusions seem to offer you something, some justification for not taking full responsibility for yourself. And thus, if you are not willing to see this in yourself, you will remain in the illusion – pursuing this or the next illusion – thinking that this is a means for you to enter heaven, that the perversion of the God-quality on that particular ray must surely allow you to enter heaven.

Understanding the mob consciousness

So, what I would describe to you next is to return to the concept of the mob, the mob that sits there in the Colosseum, or that sits out there in society—even the mob that is assembled on a regular basis in front of the TV screen, where all those who watch the same program partake in that same collective state of consciousness. And what you see is that once the co-creators have been trapped in the duality consciousness –

precisely because they have no inner sense of the immovability – they are susceptible to blindly following their leaders, or blindly following the mob itself, the mass consciousness itself.

This happens because when you choose not to take full responsibility for yourself, you are in reality refusing to express your individuality, your creativity. And thus, in accepting an excuse for suppressing your life force - suppressing your creativity, denying your individuality – you are creating the ego that has no creativity, has no individuality—and therefore can only follow something; it cannot create by itself. And if you are not using your individuality and creativity, you cannot create an ego that has individuality and creativity. And if you were willing to use your individuality and creativity, you would have no need to create the ego to make decisions for you.

So you see that – by definition, by its nature – the ego is neither creative nor has much individuality, certainly not the true individuality of God, given to you by God. And thus, the ego is susceptible to following either a strong leader or following the crowd, following the mob. There is nothing more destructive for spiritual growth than partaking in the mob consciousness. There is nothing more anti-spiritual on Earth than the mob consciousness. The mob consciousness is the antithesis of spiritual growth.

For what is the ascension? As we have explained recently, it is an individual process. You pass through the gate to the ascended state alone, by your own momentum—you pass through as an individual. And thus, you see, the extreme individuality that is needed to ascend is the exact antithesis to the mob consciousness, where the minds of the individuals in the mob have been taken over – have been overridden, so to speak – by the collective mind that is formed whenever a group of people come together. And with a group, I mean anything more than one person.

Do you see how the mob overrides individuality? The mob will not allow expressions of individuality. It wants all members of the mob to follow the mob and the mob consciousness. Dissent is not allowed, for then you will not only be an outcast from the mob, but it is likely that the mob will turn on you and destroy you, if they can.

And so, you see the mob that attacked Jesus, that scorned him, even as he was carrying the cross through the streets of Jerusalem. Even the mob that cried out for him to be crucified—that would rather see a convicted murderer set free than to see the living Christ set free. And this is precisely because the mob could identify with the murderer, for the murderer had the consciousness that is the consciousness behind the mob—the murder consciousness. The consciousness that wants to murder individuality and absorb the individual into the mob—and keep absorbing more and more individuals, until the mob has taken over the entire world.

How to create a mob

This is, again, a deliberate strategy by the fallen beings. How do you create a mob? There must be two elements. One is the perversion of the Father aspect, through creating and perpetrating a toxic idea that gives the mob something to focus on. A toxic idea is one that is based on duality, where there is a clear-cut division between what is right and wrong, good or evil. And now there is a division, so that there is a clear scapegoat that represents evil, and then there is the mob which is on the side of good, and therefore must take action against evil. But do you see that the deeper reality here is that the mob consciousness is that which wants to murder individuality? And thus, any individual is evil to the mob because it is a threat to the mob.

If one individual can refuse to be moved by the mob, that one individual can shatter the matrix of the mob consciousness—and therefore set people free from it, so that they suddenly switch from the mob consciousness to being individuals again. And as individuals, they have human feelings—they have a human sense of responsibility, of morals, of ethics, of right and wrong at a higher level than that defined in the mob consciousness. You see this out-pictured in the situation, where Jesus faces the angry mob who is ready to stone the woman caught in adultery. By being immovable – and by asking an awakening question – he manages to shatter the matrix of the mob and turn them back into individuals, so that they walk away one by one—instead of attacking the woman as that unity of the mob.

And so, how is the mob created? By putting out the toxic idea, and then the second element – which is a perversion of the Mother – which is the desire to create oneness in the matter realm, in the world of form. This is a subtle distinction that fools many spiritual people, for you think that oneness is supposed to be good, is supposed to be spiritual— for through oneness you can have peace. But you see, you cannot create true oneness in the material realm; you cannot create it from the duality consciousness. For you cannot create oneness through force.

True oneness through individuality

So you see, you cannot have oneness between people – true oneness between people – who deny their individuality. Oneness can only come about through individuality. Certainly, this sounds like a contradiction. But instead of seeing it as a contradiction, may I suggest that you see it as an enigma—that is an enigma only because you see through the filter of duality. For when you see beyond duality, you see that true individuality is that each self-aware being is an extension of the Creator's Being.

And so how is true oneness achieved? By each individual being realizing its oneness with its source—and then realizing that all other self-aware beings are also extensions of that source. And that is how you have true oneness—through the connection to the one source. The fallen beings, of course, have set themselves apart from this oneness by denying their connection to their source—and by seeking to deny that every other being on Earth is connected to the source. And that is why they have attempted to create the oneness here below, the false oneness, that is created through force, namely that of the collective mind taking over and forcing into submission the individual mind.

And so what they have done, in any number of ways, is putting out these toxic ideas, and then, as a perversion of the mother, putting out the idea that you need to accept and submit to this overall goal in order to show solidarity, to work for the greater cause, to even work for God's cause.

So you see: first you put out your overall goal, and then you put out the belief that the good people will submit to this goal, will participate in it—and will be willing to set aside their individuality in order to achieve this common goal, as it is defined. And so, once you have a population that accepts this, they have essentially become like a mob—for they are no longer thinking or feeling like individuals.

And I started out by giving you the example of the mob in the Colosseum, for I trust, that most of you will be willing and able to see this as a clear expression of the mob consciousness—that is ready to destroy, ready to destroy anything that will not submit to it. And thus, by seeing it in this extreme form, it is my hope that you will be willing to see it in its more subtle forms. For there are many of such subtle forms.

Hatred of the mother – unwillingness to face changing conditions on Earth

Portia, through Helen Michaels, February 13, 2010.

Jealousy

Behind the judgmental mindset, that the fallen ones have practiced on earth for so long, is the jealousy of the fallen consciousness. In this judgmental mindset, the emperor has the sense that he can do whatever he wants on Earth, even decide if a person on the arena will die or survive. Yet, I have to tell you that it was not only the emperors in Rome who embodied this consciousness; it was the Roman population who magnified their emperors.

Going back in world history, you see that the hatred of the mother energy did not start in Rome. It started from the fallen consciousness, which was jealous of any lifestream that had spiritual light. This light was the Presence of God that the fallen consciousness did not manifest and also could not control in any other way than by creating the structures and games on Earth, that had the purpose of taking the attention away from spirituality—and force upon the population the standards (if in Rome, do like the Romans), that if you behave like others, you are accepted in heaven.

You see, this jealousy of the fallen consciousness manifested already during Jesus' lifetime – as you see written in Mary Magdalene's gospel – namely how the other disciples were jealous of Mary Magdalene because Jesus had given her teachings that he did not give to the others. Instead of raising up all of Jesus' teachings – and raising up each other – the disciples, especially Peter, immediately went into a downward spiral, seeking to put Mary Magdalene down as they felt that she had received something that they did not.

What you have seen happen in Judea back then – and over many eons before – is that the fallen consciousness makes every possible effort to keep the illusion that God the Father is separated from God the Mother. And therefore, every situation that shatters this illusion – and every person who dares to shatter this illusion by expressing the real,

Living God – becomes a threat to the fallen consciousness—as Peter felt threatened by Mary Magdalene, who manifested a certain amount of Christ consciousness and had passed the initiations that Peter himself had not.

Thus, the threatened Peter sought to put God into his predefined limitations or structures and tried to convince everybody that if God really does not fit into those limits, then it cannot be the real God or the manifestation of the real God. Peter back then – and the Catholic Church today – outplay this gladiator game with everyone who does not fit into their limitations or predefined structures—and thus will be identified as the cause of the fighting or resistance.

I withdraw space from the consciousness of anger against women

Gautama Buddha, February 14, 2010.

Not being willing to call a spade a spade

Yet there is another aspect that I will address here, for there are indeed those on Earth who have been willing to see something in themselves. There are millions of people who have come to the point of being willing to look at the beam in their own eye, as Christ put it, and at least see some aspect of the duality consciousness. Yet I must tell you that this awakening is being held back by a certain state of consciousness, that has been put upon humankind by the fallen angels in a last-ditch attempt to hold back a widespread awakening.

You see, when you come to acknowledge an element of duality in your own being – what you might call a fault or a flaw in your own mind or character – then, even though you work through it, surrender it and raise yourself above it, it is very easy to begin to believe in a toxic idea put out by the fallen ones. And that is that if you have had a flaw in your own mind – even though you may have raised yourself above it – you should still be tolerant towards those who have that flaw. And thus, you should not speak out against it, if you see it displayed in your society. It is, so to speak, a variant of the old saying, where you think that two wrongs can make a right. And you now think that if there is a wrong that you see in society, yet if you have had some wrong in yourself, then the wrong in you should cancel out your willingness to speak out against the wrong in society.

Thus, there are many, many people who are honestly working on themselves and have made great progress in terms of removing at least part of the beam in their own eyes. Yet these people have become so reluctant to speak out, either against other individuals or against some collective problem, that they are not having the impact upon society that they are meant to have, here in the Age of Aquarius. I must tell you straightforwardly that you will not see the manifestation of a golden age as long as those who are working on themselves are not willing to speak out and openly address what you see in other people and in society.

This is something that almost all of those who are the non-aggressive, non-forceful people – those who are the honest people, those who are the meek, that Jesus talked about – that all of you have. You can see in the description by this messenger of how he went through his transformation in Israel, of realizing that there was something that he had not been willing to see in the Jews, something he had overcome in himself and thus was able to see, but he was not willing to use that ability.

For you see, as Jesus said, first remove the beam in your own eye— and then you will see clearly. And when you have removed the beam in your eye, then you will see that beam or that splinter in the eyes of others or in society. For when you have been willing to face something in yourself, you are no longer in denial, and thus are no longer projecting that anger or whatever it may be upon others. And when you no longer project out, then your perception is not polluted by the projection, by the denial. And thus, you can see clearly what is going on in the minds of other people, what is going on in society.

How you can come to "know" ultimate truth

Pallas Athena, May 4, 2010.

Goddess of Truth. Is it not an imposing title, meant to be impressive—but to whom? For surely, I, Pallas Athena, the one to whom this title is attached by men, am not easily impressed by the antics of men, am I? Thus, it is meant to be impressive to men only.

And so you see, there is a consciousness among men of wanting to elevate something to an ultimate status, and that status is, of course, that of God or Goddess. Or in a monotheistic religion, as the supreme God, the male God, yet it is always a distant God, an objectified God. And this is the one secret that men cannot or will not understand. Yet you see this theme in all cultures, in all civilizations that have existed on this planet—that have existed on this planet, for they do not exist anymore.

And why do they not exist anymore? Because they will not let go of the consciousness that objectifies their God or their gods. Do you see, this is the very consciousness of the fallen angels, the consciousness of separation, of separating out from oneness. For when you separate out from the oneness of God, then what happens? You are not in oneness with God, and therefore you are not in God. And therefore God becomes an object outside of yourself.

God becomes something that can be reduced to an object, that you can know through certain characteristics that are defined either through words or images, but they are words and images created by men who have fallen into the duality consciousness. For surely, those who experience oneness with God know that there are no words or images in the material world that could possibly convey the fullness of God's Being.

And thus, what you see here behind the messenger's physical body is indeed this temple, erected by the ancient Greeks to me, Pallas Athena—or rather to their image of me, their false God, their graven image that they wanted to worship instead of the real Goddess of Truth. They did not want to truly worship me, for what does it mean to worship the real, living Goddess of Truth? It means to come into oneness with me; there is no other way.

So they wanted to worship me, and worshiping implies that you are worshiping a distant object, a separate object, something that is outside of yourself. For, if you know that God is inside of yourself – if you have entered the kingdom of God that is within you, as Christ said – then you do not need to worship God. You just need to let the inner God express itself through you, do you not?

This then is the only form of worship that the living God – and those who are the representatives of the living God in the form of the Ascended Host, whether you call us gods or goddesses matters not to us – desire. We desire to be expressed through you, not worshiped as distant objects, not studied as distant objects that you think you can know with the linear, analytical mind, because you have attached certain characteristics to us. And therefore, you have entombed us in those graven images that you have created.

Think back to when this monument was erected so many years ago, when the Pallas Athena statue – meant to be the most magnificent statue ever created by man, put inside the most magnificent building ever created by man – think about the mindset of the people who created this monument. And then, ask yourself: "Was it a monument to the Goddess of Truth, Pallas Athena, or was it a monument to the egos of the people who erected it?" And you will see that it was indeed a monument, the size of which reveals the size of the egos and the desire of those egos to write themselves into history by creating a monument that would stand for a very long time.

And so far they have been successful, in the sense that although the ancient cult to Pallas Athena has largely vanished, the monument is still here. And it is even connected with a movement that became known as democracy, although even democracy as conceived by the Greeks was not the true democracy that we hold the vision for in the ascended realm—a democracy that has not yet fully been manifested in any nation on Earth.

And so you see, my dear students, if you are the eternal, the perpetual student – who thinks you have to study at distant topic and that I, Pallas Athena, can be reduced to a distant topic, an object that you can study and come to know with the outer, linear mind – well, then I must tell you, you are not true students. In essence, there is a period on the spiritual path, where you do need to study, for you cannot come into oneness, you have not reached that level of maturity. But there comes a point where you need to go beyond being a student of truth and instead come into oneness with truth.

You need to stop seeking for truth in ancient books or in new books, even in newly revealed teachings, such as what we have given through this messenger. For do you see the reality that we cannot say anything through a given messenger to which the mind of the messenger is not open and is not accepting? And thus, if this messenger had a desire to set himself up as some ultimate source of truth – to be venerated and to be thought impressive among men – well then, I could not give the teaching I am giving. Then indeed, I would be forced to either not speak at all or to speak in a way that would perpetuate the image that has been given of the ascended masters through previous dispensations, where there was not the openness, neither in the mind of the messengers nor in the minds of the students.

And thus, you see, progressive revelation is progressive only when the students of what is given take what is given, multiply it in their hearts, use it to come up to a level of consciousness beyond that at which the teaching was given. And then they can become the open door for bringing forth the progressive teaching that takes the progressive revelation one step further up the ladder of what we of the Ascended Host desire to reveal. And thus you see, indeed, coming into oneness with the Ascended Host is the logical step up from being as student or chela of the Ascended Host. You do not honor me if you see me as distant from yourself, if you see me as above yourself, if you see me as some remote object up in heaven, that you have objectified because are still stuck in the linear, dualistic, analytical mind. This mind wants to see me as a distant object because it does not want to have its own duality, its own inconsistencies, its own contradictions be exposed.

And thus, what will it take for you to step beyond being a student? It will take that you are willing to not have anything hidden from me, the Goddess of Truth. For I will come into your being and help you rise to a higher level of consciousness, but what is the acceleration in consciousness that I, Pallas Athena, can offer you? It is an acceleration into the vibration, the characteristic of God, that I embody and represent to the Earth, and that is the living truth. And in the living truth, of course, nothing can be hidden. There can be no contradictions, there can be no inconsistencies in your views or beliefs. And so, how do you then go beyond inconsistencies in your views, and opinions and beliefs?

My beloved, you go beyond in only one way: by giving up all of your viewpoints, your opinions and your beliefs. Yes, I said all of them—they must all be given up. For you see, as long as you see yourself as a student – as long as you are in the consciousness where you think I am a distant object to be studied and revered – well then, all of your opinions, and viewpoints and beliefs spring from the duality consciousness, the consciousness that objectifies God instead of coming into oneness with God. This is a simple truth, a simple truth to state in words, but will it have any meaning to you?

Well, that depends on whether you have reached the point, where you have had enough of the merry-go-round of your own ego and the egos of the fallen beings—who are taking you through this labyrinth, this maze, where they promise you that there will be exciting revelations around every turn and that in some distant future, you will arrive at the ultimate summit, where the Acropolis is built and where Pallas Athena is waiting in the inner sanctuary. No my beloved, I am not waiting for you in the inner sanctuary in the Acropolis or any other building or any other place. I am waiting for you in the inner sanctuary of your own heart.

When you stop looking for me outside yourselves – because you realize that I am not an object to be studied, worshipped or revered; I am indeed, a living, breathing Presence of God to come into oneness with – then I can accelerate your own being. Not that you become something you are not, but that you cease to be something you are not, you cease to be the not-self, you cease to be identified with the not-self. Because through coming into contact with my vibration, you see the alternative to the not-self, and therefore you can no longer maintain the illusion that you are that not-self and that the not-self is all that there is and that the illusions of duality represent some kind of infallible truth.

For this is, indeed, the promise spread through the world through so many thoughts systems, belief systems, political systems – what have you – philosophical systems, as the ancient Greek philosophers sat in this place and endlessly debated this or that system, while none of them had the ultimate truth and reality. None of them had that reality, my beloved, because they were not willing to see what I have just explained. You see, those Greek philosophers who sat here to gather students and to be thought wise among men; that is exactly what they wanted—they wanted to be thought wise among men, and they were, thereby, raising their own egos and the egos of those who objectified the philosophers, as the philosophers had objectified the gods and goddesses.

There is no ultimate reality that can be spoken or pictured in the material universe. The ultimate truth, the living truth, is something you can come into oneness with—if you are willing. If you are willing to go beyond the man-made so-called truths that are spread out there by so many philosophers, so many authority figures that want to set themselves up as being more than this other authority figure, that want to gather a following among men instead of coming into oneness with the reality of God. This is the stark reality.

You can go to any philosophical system, and you will not there find the living truth. You can go to the teachings of the ascended masters, you can go to the AskRealJesus website, and you will not there find the living truth; you will find an expression of truth. It can be at guiding post for you to come into oneness with the vibration of truth, with the vibration of Jesus and other ascended beings. But it can do so only if you are willing to go beyond the outer expression of that truth, instead of objectifying it and elevating it to some ultimate status, seeing it as better or more important than other expressions of truth. For certainly, there are other expressions of truth that can take you into at direct encounter with the Spirit of truth—but only if you are willing to transcend them, as you should be willing to transcend everything.

Even the words I speak are only words—unless they are endowed by you with a flow of the living spirit from your heart. And then you follow that flow, you follow it beyond the words to the Living Spirit that I am. And when you make contact with that Living Spirit, then you know the living truth of Pallas Athena—only then. You will never know it by watching a statue, by reading or listening to a dictation given through this or that messenger. You will only know it when you know it in your heart. And you will know me in your heart only when you come into oneness with me and no longer see yourself as separated from me. For you are not afraid to have my light of truth shine upon every nook and cranny in your being, every aspect of your thoughts, feelings, actions, beliefs, your self-image, your world image, your image of God—all of these structures that you have created in your mind, as Jesus so clearly expressed it in Saint Peter's Basilica.

Dare to imagine a Golden Age in Russia and surrounding nations

Archangel Michael, June 10, 2010. This dictation was given in Saint Petersburg, Russia.

Yet what does it mean to transcend division? It means to transcend the very key that created division in the first place—and that key is doubt! Thus I, Archangel Michael, come today to this place in the Russian nation, and I come with a dispensation from the Karmic Board of planet Earth to send millions of my angels to Russia and to every nation that was part of the former Soviet Union or was under the propaganda of the Soviet Union or the physical power of the Soviet Union.

I come with a special dispensation to bring forth the Light of God in a specific measure that will challenge the very mindset behind communism, which sprang out of the very fallen consciousness itself. Thus, I ask you to visualize millions of my angels descending, descending from the God Star Sirius – where they have received special instructions before this assignment – descending in a spiral, like an infinite spiral, like a spiral staircase, whereby they descend to Earth and go to the farthest corners of any nation, any area, that has ever been affected by the consciousness of communism—which is virtually everywhere on Earth.

They go and they do not go to fight anyone or anything. They go to take up their position there and to demonstrate the very flame that I AM, the Flame of the Will of God, but the immovability of the Will of God, that will not be moved by the will of man, or by the will of the fallen beings who see themselves as being in opposition to God. This is the Flame I embody. This is why I am with Earth: to provide a frame of reference that there is something that will not be moved by any force in this material universe, that will not be moved by the fallen consciousness.

For I AM so one with the Will of God, and so are my angels, that there is no force on Earth, no argument on Earth, no lie of the serpentine mind that can cause us to doubt the Reality of God. We are immovable to any form of doubt! And thus, we are here to provide that frame of reference that will enable those who are willing, that will empower those who are willing, to step up higher to also overcome the very doubt that makes you vulnerable to the tempter, the serpent that comes with its arguments that make you doubt what you get from the Spirit within yourselves.

Take note of exactly how this doubt started. You have read the teaching given by Maitreya that the original fall took place in a higher sphere. This sphere had been brought close to the ascension point by a majority of the beings being in a positive spiral. Then came the test that those who had risen to a certain level, where they saw themselves as the leaders, were now asked to go down to the seemingly lowest point and allow their beings, their momentum, their attainment to be used to create the very next sphere.

They were not willing to bend the knee; they were not willing to do what they saw as a degradation of their position. For some of them had been working – although they had been doing positive work to raise up the sphere – they still had some leftover of the consciousness of thinking they were doing this to reap a reward in heaven. So that when their sphere was ascended – they having been among the forerunners, or so they saw themselves – would surely be rewarded with a high position in Heaven.

Yet, I come to reveal to you another understanding, another layer of understanding, of our unfolding, progressive revelation on this topic of the fall and the fallen consciousness. For you see, those who thought that they were the leaders were actually not the ones who had brought their sphere to the ascension point. As Jesus said, the meek shall inherit the Earth. There were billions of lifestreams in that sphere who had truly embodied selflessness because they had transcended the separate consciousness. They had no desire to be in a superior position to anyone else. Some of them did serve in leadership positions, others did not, they simply worked selflessly at whatever they felt was their calling, their divine plan, their desire to express their God-individuality. So the reality is that those who were allowed to be among the leaders were not necessarily allowed that position because they had attainment.

For some of them had indeed not overcome all remnants of the separate self, the separate consciousness, the force-based consciousness. They wanted to set themselves above, and they were allowed – mind you "allowed" – to be in leadership positions because by acting out this desire for superiority, they received another opportunity to overcome it, to have had enough of the experience, so that they could in the end choose to let go of that remnant of the separate self and merge with their divine individuality and thus truly become part of the Ascended Host.

For we have all gone through the process of completely letting go of the separate self. For how else could we enter the ascended realm where all is oneness? Letting go of the separate self does not mean letting go of your divine individuality; it means letting go of the separate individuality, the separate self that you have built in the world of form. So you see, there was a group of beings who had been allowed to assume superior positions, leadership positions in that sphere in order to give them an opportunity to let go of the need to feel superior, to accept that all self-aware beings are individualizations of God and therefore none can be superior to another. For it makes no sense that one expression of God is superior to another.

Thus, when the turning point came – when the point of no return came, where the sphere was ready to ascend – these beings were faced with this ultimate test. Could they now let go of the separate identity – in which case they could have stepped up and perhaps been assigned a leadership position in the spiritual realm – or would they not be able to let go of the separate self? And they were given this test by being confronted with the need to be the servant of all. And yet, they were not willing to be greatest among you by being the servant of all. They wanted to remain in what they thought was a position of being greatest among their peers while still being a servant of the separate self, seeking to elevate that self to a superior position. And thus, of course, they fell.

Yet after having fallen, they felt they had been unjustly treated, for they saw that some of their peers, some of their former peers, were indeed raised up to positions in the spiritual realm. Yet they were not able or willing to see that this happened because those lifestreams had indeed let go of the separate self and were willing to be the servants of all. So they thought – the fallen beings thought – they had been unjustly treated. And that is when they decided to deliberately and consciously oppose God's plan by seeking to draw as many lifestreams with them into the fallen state as they possibly could.

And how did they determine to do this? We have earlier spoken about the consciousness of the accuser of the brethren that accused the beings in the sphere that was ascending, yet had not fully ascended. And thus, there were beings who were open to this accusation. Why could this happen? Why was this allowed? Because, again, there were beings in the ascending sphere who had not come to the point of fully becoming spiritually self-sufficient, of accepting and expressing their divine individuality, because they also had remnants of that separate self. And so, these beings also needed the initiation, the test: could they let go of the separate self and step up into oneness, or would they seek to retain some aspect of the separate self because they were not willing to take full responsibility for themselves. They were not willing to express their God-given creativity to the point where that God-given creativity could propel them to the ascended state.

Do you see, again, how these lifestreams had not understood that the ascension is not a collective process? Do you see that when a sphere is in an ascending spiral, those beings who are part of creating that spiral do form an upward momentum? That upward momentum can pull up higher all beings in the sphere, and thereby all get the opportunity to become self-sufficient; to internalize the Ascension Flame. Yet the question is: Will a Being come to see that the Light of God is within itself? Or will it see it as coming from an exterior source?

As long as you think the Light comes from outside yourself – whether it be in a leader, in a messenger or in some spiritual guru – then you are not spiritually self-sufficient. And as long as you are not spiritually self-sufficient – by knowing that the Light of God is inside of you and thus you need nothing from the world of form – well then you cannot ascend. For the ascension is a process where you individually ascend because you have become spiritually self-sufficient.

You have become the rocket that Serapis Bey talked about that is now ready to take off, break free of the gravitational field of the Earth and go into orbit. And thus, when a sphere does ascend, those who have not yet become spiritually self-sufficient must also receive the initiation. Can they ascend, can they let go of the separate self, or must they take another round in the world of form and therefore descend into the new sphere that is being created?

And so, these many lifestreams that had not become spiritually self-sufficient received this initiation precisely by being confronted by the "higher" lifestreams – those who had set themselves up in leadership positions – by being confronted by their rebellion against God. And what exactly did the fallen beings do in order to pull other lifestreams with them? Well, they only had to do one simple thing and it is essential that you understand this.

In an ascending sphere there is a greater and greater sense of oneness. All beings in that sphere are at least aware of this oneness. All have not come fully into the oneness, but they are aware of the energy of oneness. And so, all are aware of the need to come into oneness and that oneness is the underlying reality. Yet those who have not yet experienced it, will see it more as a theoretical possibility, something they need to come into in some distant future.

Yet when the turning point comes, that distant future is no longer distant. It is NOW. Now the choice must be made. You can only have a certain time to grow towards the ascension in a particular cycle, in a particular sphere, and then there comes a cut-off point where you must now make the choice. For you cannot have forever to postpone that choice, or free will would not be truly free. And so, there are those who have not internalized oneness, and therefore oneness is still somewhat of a concept that they understand with the mind but do not yet experience fully with the heart.

And that is why, when the fallen beings came out and demonstrated that they were in opposition to oneness, well then all of a sudden they provided a frame of reference that had not been there before; namely that there was something that was not only outside of oneness but was in opposition to oneness. And this then became what we might call a negative, or a separatist, frame of reference, as opposed to what I talked about earlier that my angels and myself provide the positive frame of reference that we will not be moved from oneness. And so, you see that when the fallen beings projected their opposition to God through the consciousness of the accuser; those who had already come into oneness – those for whom oneness was no longer a distant external concept – they were not moved. They saw immediately, they read the vibration that this was not oneness, and thus they were unmoved by the fallen beings.

Yet those more innocent lifestreams who had not yet come into oneness, many of those were indeed shocked by this demonstration of anti-oneness. And what did it do? Well, in their minds it caused doubt. Doubt crept into their minds. Is oneness really the underlying reality? If oneness is the underlying reality, how can these beings be allowed to separate themselves from oneness? Are they really right in what they are saying that God was wrong, that free will is not the ultimate way to salvation, that free will can only lead to disaster? Are they right, that maybe I am wrong?

Do you see, my beloved, if you are not totally anchored in yourself, if you are not spiritually self-sufficient, then you do not have the frame of reference inside yourself in order to know what is real and unreal, in order to know that oneness is real. For if you do not experience oneness inside yourself, then you cannot fully know that oneness is the underlying reality. You may understand it intellectually but you do not "know" through gnosis, through oneness between the subject and object, between the knower and the known.

And then, when you do not have this firm inner frame of reference, your mind is open to an external frame of reference that then makes you doubt yourself. And through that doubt you then become open to the fallen consciousness, to the consciousness of separation and all of its lies and arguments and very subtle turning on its head every teaching you have been given before. Making you therefore doubt not only the teaching but first of all your own inner ability to know what is real and unreal by referring to something inside yourself.

You are pulled into focusing your attention on something outside of yourself, and then you think that external thing is or should be your absolute frame of reference for what is real and unreal. And that is how people are led into following a particular outer guru or a particular outer teaching, such as the Catholic Church. And thus you see again, the Peter consciousness represents precisely this: the desire for an outer frame of reference that you will not give up even though you are faced – you are face-to-face – with the Living Christ.

Even though you walk and talk with the Living Christ in the form that you can see, as Peter did, you will not give up that external frame of reference, you will not let it die. You want the Christ to validate your frame of reference, to conform to it, to come into your mental box. This is what Peter attempted to do to Jesus, it is what the Catholic Church has attempted to do to Jesus, to God, to Reality ever since. This is what every other system on Earth has attempted to do, including the communist system that you are familiar with as students who have been affected by the Soviet Union in any way.

Communism is nothing but an attempt to create a system, and it is based on the very essential doubt created by the fallen beings. It is attempting to pervert something that all people know in themselves –

namely oneness – the need to come into oneness in a "community" not a "commune." Come ye into unity! How can you come into unity? Only when you individually have reconnected and become one with your divine individuality. When you have vertical oneness with your Higher Being, then you know you are an extension of God. Then you know that your brother is an extension of God. And therefore, you can now come into horizontal oneness with your brothers and sisters, for you all see each other as extensions of God—none being superior, none being inferior. That is true unity.

What communism attempted to do was to create unity through sameness by destroying, by suppressing, individual expression, by turning people into mechanized beings who would blindly follow what they were told. This is not unity! You cannot create unity through force. You cannot create oneness through force. For force can only force apart. You cannot force together. What brings things together is not a force that is projected out, but magnetism that pulls together, and that magnetism is love. But it is not human love that so often seeks to control and therefore is expressed through the force-based consciousness. Instead, it is Divine Love, which is Unconditional Love.

Those who do not experience oneness with their Higher Beings cannot fathom unconditional love. For you see, you cannot understand unconditional love; you can only experience it. And thus, what the mind can understand is not Divine Love, it is a conditional force-based love that seeks to control. You cannot argue against unconditional love. If you argue against unconditional love, you demonstrate that you have not experienced it. And thus, what you are arguing against is not unconditional love; it is conditional love. And thus, you are not speaking a higher truth by arguing against unconditionality or by arguing against oneness.

You are instead demonstrating that you have set yourself outside of oneness, outside of unconditional love, because you have not been willing to let go of the separate self. You are still seeking to glorify the separate self to the point where it can feel superior, where it can feel that it is right, because it has this absolute truth or this absolute system that has such power on Earth by having such a following.

What is the superiority behind the Catholic Church? It is that they feel they have such a following that backs them up. What was the superiority behind Soviet communism? It was also the feeling that they were powerful and that they had suppressed other countries and that they thought they were on the way to suppressing the whole world. For the force-based consciousness can never feel at peace, but it thinks it will be at peace when it has forced all beings on Earth to come into its own system, and therefore it must seek to expand its control, to expand its power indefinitely—it cannot stop.

This is what you saw in Adolf Hitler and his desire to conquer the world. This is what you saw behind Soviet communism and the desire to conquer the world. The force-based consciousness must expand until it feels it has total control. But you see, because of the second law of thermodynamics – and because of the size of the Earth and the number of people and the complexity of suppressing people – it simply cannot be done. And therefore any system that attempts to expand itself to conquer the entire planet will inevitably self-destruct. It cannot be otherwise, because of the Law of God that you cannot move. No matter how powerful of a system you create, you cannot move reality! You cannot change the Law of God!

And this is what the fallen ones already know deep within their beings, even though few of them will admit it with their outer minds. And that is why they are still trapped in this endless quest of seeking to get all people on Earth to agree with one of their systems, so that they can feel they are secure and they have superiority.

This is precisely the illusion that my angels and I have come to provide a frame of reference for, so that people can sense that there is no system on Earth that will change the reality and the Law of God. As this messenger is fond of saying, even when all people on Earth believed that the Earth was flat, it was as round then as it is today. Even when the Soviet Union was at the height of its outer power – even when a large portion of the people on Earth believed in some form of communism or socialism – nothing that was done had changed the Law of God one bit! Nothing had changed the Reality of God.

This is precisely the change that needs to happen before Russia can move on from its current deadlock and move closer to the Golden Age. There must be a realization that "nothing we do will change reality, so we better find out what reality is. We better learn the Laws of God, realign ourselves and our society with those Laws of God, and then we can move forward."

…But again, this would not have been possible, for I assure you that the leaders of the Soviet system were not high spiritual beings, many of them in fact being fallen angels, some even among the original fallen angels at least in the past. For surely I must tell you the absolute truth that Lenin and Stalin and Trotsky were fallen angels, as were Marx and Engels. You see thus that the communist system was created by fallen angels in embodiment. This is a truth that must be stated here on Russian soil, that people may do with it what they want.

Yet precisely because there were so many spiritual beings in embodiment, they could hold the balance, so that even the leaders of the Soviet Union could awaken. For I tell you that even though there are some fallen beings that are beyond being reached, there are indeed some that will respond to hard reality. When they acknowledge that they cannot move a mountain, then sometimes they can be awakened and realize that they need to change, for otherwise they will destroy themselves.

Hard realities! Hard lessons in the school of hard knocks. Yet consider as spiritual people embodying in Russia and the surrounding republics or states that you have volunteered to embody here to give the majority of the Russian people, and the smaller groups of the Russian leaders, an opportunity to awaken from one of the systems created by the fallen consciousness. Consider that you did this out of love and that you need to reconnect to that love, so you can overcome any sense of regret, any sense of bitterness, any sense of sorrow about the past, but recognize that whatever happened in the past was part of the learning process.

You volunteered to be part of it out of love. If you reconnect to your original love, then that love can take you beyond anything you have experienced in this very difficult, very extreme situation that was the Soviet Union. Truly, even if you go beyond the annals of known history, but go back to past ages, the Soviet Union was one of the more extreme examples of how far the fallen consciousness is willing to go in its insensitivity to life, that leads to an almost total willingness to suppress any opposition, to destroy that opposition by killing people by the millions or by doing anything else possible to suppress their individuality, their divine spark, their creative potential.

There is nothing in the past of any nation that the Light cannot purify

Elohim Astrea, June 10, 2010. This dictation was given at an event in Saint Petersburg, Russia.

Indeed, Elohim Astrea I am. For the call compels the answer, and thus I am with you. For you have come to this great city of Saint Petersburg, the largest city closest to the Elohim of Astrea's retreat over the White Sea. Indeed, it was the magnetic pull of our retreat that inspired Peter the Great to found this city and to move the capital of the Russian empire to this place, thus opening up Russia to the rest of the world, especially to Europe, that it might be put on a path that made it part of Europe, part of the family of nations. Thus, you might surmise, and correctly so, that Peter was working with the light, was open to inspiration from above as were several of the Russian leaders who followed him and indeed built up not only this city but built up the Russian empire to become a nation that was at the time fully as modern, fully as creative, as any nation in Europe.

And thus, you see that there was indeed a realistic potential for the Russian nation to flourish and blossom and find a way to be part of a new age that could indeed have taken the world to a higher level than what you saw instead during the twentieth century. What then was it, indeed, that happened that this development did not come to pass? Well, it was a deliberate act of those who are part of the international power elite, those who saw the potential that a Golden Age was beginning to emerge, because there was such creativity – including the emergence of democratic nations, including the emergence of new technology – that they could not maintain the control that they had attempted to build as a result of the freedom, the economic freedom, that they had received after the abolishment of the feudal system and the establishment of the United states of America.

Do you see how this is the classical example of what Saint Germain has explained with the established power elite and the aspiring power elite, the established power elite represented by the Catholic Church, the medieval Kings and the feudal lords that had near total control over society. Yet, again, in their total control, they created the opposition to their own rule, and the second law of thermodynamics inevitably caused their system to break down. And although there was a movement towards freeing the people, you also saw the emergence of the aspiring power elite, another faction of fallen angels who had been lusting after the power they had seen in the old elite. A power which they could not share because the old elite was such a closed system that it was difficult for fallen angels of a different band to force their way into the system.

Thus, they felt shut out from power. And when the old power began to crumble, they seized the opportunity to now enter the fray and become the new power elite that used the economic freedom and the industrial revolution to – instead of establishing national empires, or a religious empire – they established financial and industrial empires. This was something that the old power elite did not understand, for it did not fit their mindset. Yet, the new elite came to understand this very quickly and took advantage of it, thus creating some of these industrial empires that are the forerunners for the multinational corporations you have to this day. This power elite understood money, financial markets. They understood how to exploit the people while giving the people an impression that they were part of a greater cause, or that they were part of a free society that would give them opportunities. Yet indeed, it only exploited the labor of the people without giving them equal rights or equal opportunity.

You know well the names of some of these industrialists and international bankers. You also know that they had a desire to establish monopolies. This is something that is generally not understood in the West, where they have been exposed to a century or more of so-called capitalist propaganda that makes people believe that capitalism is the same as free enterprise or a free market economy. Nothing, of course, could be further from the truth, for capitalism has one goal: that is to establish more and more monopolies until the corporations merge together and form the ultimate monopoly. Which then, by the fact that it owns the means of production, also owns the state.

These industrialists saw that the western system was not necessarily the fastest or the most sure way to establish this ultimate monopoly. For they needed to maintain the illusion of a free market economy, and thus there was a limit to how much control over the economy they could establish or how fast they could establish it, given that the people were aware of at least some of the dangers of too much control of the economy. Thus, when Karl Marx formulated his philosophy of Marxism, they began to see that this could be another way to establish their goal of the ultimate monopoly. And so, some of you will know – and all of you should know – that it was indeed these international financiers that financed Lenin and the Bolshevik revolution.

Without the directive and the financing from Wall Street, from these financial corporations, the Bolshevik revolution would not have been possible and would indeed either never have taken place or have failed in its early stages. Thus you see, the power elite of capitalism deliberately establishing what seems to be a system that is opposed to capitalism. And indeed, the two systems are in opposition to each other, but do you see the deeper reality that they both work towards the same end? So that, whether communism had taken over the world or capitalism had taken over the world, it would ultimately lead to the same end, where one state or one corporation had total control over the economy and therefore over society.

This then is what you need to understand: that this is the consciousness of the power elite and their desire to establish total control. You must understand that it was not the power elite's desire to see the Soviet Union collapse or crumble as it did. They wanted to maintain the Soviet Union as a viable opponent to the West. Not only because they could profit from selling technology to both sides and keep the arms-race going, but also because it fit their overall strategy of leading to greater and greater control. So indeed, as Archangel Michael talked about, the Russian people, the spiritual beings who have embodied in Russia and held the balance for the abolishment of communism, have indeed served in a great capacity to foil the control schemes of the power elite, the international power elite. They have, as the saying is in America, thrown a monkey wrench into the machinery of the elite.

This has then caused this elite to reassess its strategy, and although they still think they have control through the financial instruments, even this control is beginning to crumble. Some of them have already seen the handwriting on the wall, others are still blinded. Yet many people, both in the West and throughout the planet, are beginning to see that the real problem that underlies every problem seen in history is elitism and the elitist mindset, the desire for a small group to establish superiority through force, through control.

What then does this have to do with the base chakra of the planet and the retreat of Purity and Astrea, which focuses the base chakra and the base chakra energies for the planetary body? Well, if you look at Russia before the Bolshevik revolution – even if you take a walk in this city of Saint Petersburg and look at the buildings that were built since the foundation of this city – you will see with your own eye the immense creativity present in the Russian people. You will see the elegance, even the lightness of some of these buildings, if you were to compare them to some of the buildings you see in the West that are older, that are from the Middle ages, such as the buildings in the Vatican, or in Rome or in other older cities. You will see there a darkness, a heaviness in the architecture itself, whereas in this city you see more of a lightness, more of an elegance, more of a devotion to beauty, a willingness to try new things, to express creativity, without predefined conditions or limitations.

This was the potential for the Russian nation. Yet then, compare to what has happened to architecture and art under the Soviet Union. Look at the buildings built during communist times, and you will notice the tremendous difference. There is no focus on beauty; there is no desire to create beauty. Why not? Because there was no desire to allow creativity to be expressed. What was the outer excuse? It was that all of the buildings built before communism were an expression of the ruling elite. They were elitist, they were of the Bourgeoisie, and this was not what was the new goal of the Soviet Union, which was supposed to be of the people, but was not of the people at all.

Nay, what was expressed in Soviet communism was the desire to reduce the people to mechanical beings who dared not express creativity and individuality. Therefore, they would be the perfect mindless followers of the elite, the perfect worker bees that the elite in the West had dreamed about but could not produce in sufficient numbers because of these dangerous ideas of democracy and self-determination and economic freedom and opportunity. So do you see that Soviet communism even went beyond the principles of Marx and created a system that was so based on force that it could only be put in place through a complete and merciless suppression of the people. And it could only be kept in place through this forceful suppression, even the willingness of killing any number of the Russian people, as you saw in Stalin.

This willingness to destroy anyone who could be a threat; not even the ones who were a threat, but the ones who could potentially become a threat. This is almost similar to the consciousness that caused King Herod to kill all male babies in order to make sure he had killed the one Christ child that could be a threat to his rule. This is a symbol for being willing to kill anyone who has the potential to manifest any degree of Christhood, so that all you have left are those who are not yet at the point where they can manifest the Christhood and the individuality that is essential for Christhood.

This then, is a deliberate attempt to abort the very life force itself at the very point where it first flows into the material universe, the physical octave, namely at the base chakra. In the base chakra you have the fount of creativity. The question becomes: will it be allowed to rise and illumine the other chakras, until they all light up in a full flowering of the creative potential of the individual? Or will that life force be stopped at any point of its ascent?

And of course, the power elite know that the earlier they can stop the life force, the better. And thus they have attempted, through many different schemes throughout history, to stop the life force right in the base chakra itself. This is what you have seen in the Soviet Union, of the willingness to kill life, to kill those who expressed any kind of creativity or individuality. They would simply disappear; go to Siberia, concentration camps, death-camps, never to be heard from again.

You see, of course, the same attempt in the West, although with different means. Here you have seen an attempt to squash the life force through poverty, and when poverty began to recede, then came the perversion of the life force through music, through rhythms that beat the life force down into the base chakra, where it cannot rise and therefore is easily led into various perversions such as sexual perversions, but many other perversions in art or materialism, or a lifestyle that says: "Let us eat, drink and be merry, for tomorrow, we die."

This then, is the perversion of the very life force itself, the perversion of the creativity that, if it is allowed to flow, will inevitably overthrow the control schemes of the power elite. They know this, and therefore they know that the only opportunity they have for establishing and maintaining this ultimate system of control is to seek to squash the life force, to suppress it either by killing the people who are creative or by suppressing them or by misguiding them into taking their creativity out into forms that do not raise up society, but simply keep society at a certain level or even take it down into a downward spiral.

This then, is what you have seen. And you will see how there is only so much control that can be imposed by the power elite to squash the life force. For a time, indeed, it is possible to kill off all the people who try to express creativity, but you cannot do this forever unless you are willing to see your country fall behind other nations where there is more room for creativity. Why is it that it seems like the western world was more advanced than the communist world? It was because the suppression of the life force was not as total, not as efficient in the western world, and thus, there was more room for creativity. But certainly, if the power elite had not suppressed or misdirected the life force in the West, there would have been even more creativity, and the West would have been far closer to the Golden Age.

So what you see is, indeed, as we have said many times, there is a safety measure built into the design of the material universe, so that no power can attain total control, and no power can maintain a high degree of control for an extended period of time. Time will eventually grind down the power elite and their control. And the primary example of this is, of course, what has happened in Russia, but also in the surrounding nations and republics.

...

Do you understand, my beloved, the real purpose behind the widespread killing and torture and other atrocities that took place in the Soviet Union? Do you understand that those who are the darkest fallen beings had a clear purpose of establishing such an intense downward spiral through these atrocities that nothing on Earth could overcome it, that it could not be reversed, that it could not be stopped. And that therefore, the Soviet Union would continue to go down until it even pulled the entire planet into this third, all-consuming war that Archangel Michael talked about.

This was their goal. And their goal now, their hope now, is that even though the war has not come to pass, that they can still create a widespread war, and that they can still maintain the downward spiral created by these atrocities. Yet, I tell you, regardless of what has happened in this nation of Russia, the Power of the Elohim of the Fourth Ray, the Archangels of the Fourth Ray, and the Chohan and the Masters of the Fourth Ray can clean it all up in an instant.

We are, of course, not allowed to clean it up in an instant, for that would deprive you, who are the spiritual people, of the experience, of experiencing yourselves as the open door for the Light of Purity. And we would not want to deprive you of that experience, for it is an essential experience on your path to Christhood and the ascension. Truly, what more powerful impetus on the path to the ascension can there be, but experiencing how you are the instruments, the open doors, for lifting an entire nation beyond the darkness of its past.

Thus, I encourage you to begin the shift in perception for how you see yourselves, that you first throw off the yoke of this darkness in yourselves. And then see how you can become the open doors for transforming the collective consciousness of Russia into an upward spiral, releasing that old creativity and the joy that is the inevitable, eternal companion of creativity. For where can true joy come from? It can come only from the free flow of creativity that is your very reason for being as co-creators with God, who have volunteered to come here to raise this planet into the perfection of the kingdom of God. This is the ultimate joy—allow yourselves to feel it.

...

The biggest hindrance to the Golden Age, as far as the spiritual people is concerned, is precisely that they have in their minds this fallen belief that in order to serve God or the Ascended Masters you have to live up to some outer standard of perfection, which is up there and you are down here, and you don't know how to cross and close the gap. But the way to close the gap is simple. Look at what you have and multiply what you have, and then, when you have multiplied what you have, you will be given more.

...

At any given stage, multiply what you have, and you will move on. And you will then allow yourself – if you are willing to shift your mind – you will allow yourself to feel the full joy that comes from having multiplied the talents. And then knowing from within that you are the good and faithful servant who can come into the joy of the Lord, as Jesus said 2,000 years ago—but as hardly anyone who called themselves Christians have fully understood and embraced. But do not let that stop you. Embrace it, prove it in your own lives, "Prove me herewith, saith the

Lord, that I shall pour out a blessing that there shall not be room enough to contain it."

You will, when you multiply your talents, receive a blessing that your chakras and your being cannot fully contain. But then you will see that you have the opportunity to step up higher, that you may contain more and be given more and more, thus creating your personal upward spiral that must start at the base by you being willing to be creative with what you have instead of always saying, "Oh, whenever I get more, whenever some Master appears to me and gives me a jewel, then I will be able to serve God." No, you can serve God right now by multiplying what you have, and this is the difference between those who are the true servants of God and those who think they are superior, think they have some superior truth, but they are not willing to multiply their talents.

So what do they do? They become jealous of you and your light, and so they sit there, and they mock you, and they mock the creativity, as they have mocked this messenger now for almost a year in any way they can think of, while failing to see that this is not multiplying your own talents. For when you truly multiply your own talents, you have no need to criticize or mock anyone else, for it is not a threat to you what other people do. You have no desire to control, you have no desire to suppress. And thus, you see that the mocking and the anger is just another expression of the fallen consciousness that wants to squash creativity.

And you will see throughout the ages, how there has always been a consciousness, an offshoot of the accuser of the brethren, that wants to mock those who dare to be creative, who dare to think outside the mental box of their society, or their family, or their group, whatever outer characteristics define the group. There is always the mocking, there is always the putting down. And what you will notice is that this mocking consciousness will send arrows of doubt into your mind, that are meant to make you doubt.

But what you will notice is, if you are alert, that these arrows of doubt, these curses, always take the form of some mocking statement that makes a derogatory statement without explaining it. Thus, it is meant to bypass your logical, rational mind. For you see, when you start looking at these arrows of doubt with the rational mind, you see how unfounded, how unreal, how sometimes contradictory and ridiculous they are.

But they are constructed in such a way that they bypass the mind and go into the emotional body, where they make you feel whatever you have that is unresolved, be it doubt, be it guilt, be it shame, be it fear or whatever. So you go into this emotional reaction, and now you are not able to step back and look at this with the rational mind and say: "Why should I accept this statement, why indeed should I allow it into my mind at all. For I see the motive, I see the rationale behind it, and I have no desire whatsoever to allow this impurity to enter my energy-field or my mind." And thus, you can reject it, based on the higher reasoning of the Christ mind, you can reject these arrows of doubt or mocking that come from the serpentine mind.

Entering the ascension spiral requires you to overcome the great projection game

Serapis Bey, June 11, 2010.

For as they say, "It is lonely at the top." And surely the one that is ultimately superior to others has no peers and therefore must feel alone—so is the justification of the ego of those people who have allowed themselves to feel superior to others. When you feel superior, you cannot relate to other people on the same level. You can relate only when you feel superior to them and when they validate your sense of superiority. And therefore, those who will not validate that – because they know they are sons and daughters of God and therefore refuse to feel inferior to you – well those people become a threat to you, so you have to ban them from your circle of influence so that you can maintain that fragile equilibrium of superiority.

Do you see, my beloved – when you take an honest look at the history of this planet – do you see this pattern and how many times this pattern has been repeated in human society? Do you see that Adolph Hitler was an example of a person who had this ultimate need of superiority? He was at the top. His authority could not be questioned. If anybody dared to question that authority, they would be dealt with, they would be imprisoned, they would be intimidated. If they would not be intimidated, they would be killed. There was no in-between. Dissent was not tolerated.

Do you see here in Russia how this was precisely the mindset that ruled the Soviet Union. Dissent was not tolerated. Do you see that Joseph Stalin was another example of such a being who needed to feel superior, to be ultimately in command—and therefore did not tolerate dissent. Those who would not submit were killed by the millions.

Do you see, if you go further back, that you have other examples in Russian history; Ivan the Terrible being one. And thus you see indeed, as was said yesterday, that Stalin, Lenin, Marx and Engels were fallen angels, so you see Ivan the Terrible likewise being a fallen angel, displaying all the characteristics of the fallen mindset that will kill, without even thinking, those who will not submit.

You see this pattern throughout history. You see it in the Catholic Church, most notably in the Inquisition, where indeed it was fallen angels who presided over the Inquisition and who – without thinking, without having second thoughts – would kill those who would not recant their so-called heretical beliefs. Do you see that this is the very mindset that you can find behind every conflict, every dictatorial system that you see on Earth. Again and again and again you see this mindset. You see how often two beings in this mindset would clash with each other, as you saw in the medieval kings of Europe, as you have seen in many other parts of the world.

But you have also seen the pattern where these fallen ones would recognize that if they ultimately fought each other, it would lead to their mutual assured destruction. And thus, they established this sense of equilibrium amongst themselves that you saw for instance at the Yalta Conference at the end of World War II, where Stalin, Roosevelt and Churchill met to, so to speak, divide the world between them. Three fallen angels coming together, my beloved. Not the heroes that many people see them as being, but another example of the fallen angels having no sensitivity to life, no sensitivity to higher principles.

Thus, you see, what has been allowed to be outpictured in the world is indeed this consciousness, how far this consciousness will go to destroy what it sees as a threat to its own superiority, to its own feeling of being right—and having not simply a perception but having this superior truth, this superior thought system. There is, as we have attempted to explain many times, no superior system. There is no superior truth that can be expressed in the words and images and concepts and philosophies found on this planet at its current level of cosmic unfoldment. It is simply not possible to bring forth a truth that is absolute, infallible or superior.

…

The beginning of wisdom is when you recognize a simple fact. God does not look at the world through your perception. The Ascended Masters do not look at the world through your perception. Your I AM Presence does not look at the world through your perception. You will not change us, no matter what you project out. Therefore, your only option – if you will to make progress – is to change yourself. Seeking to change all other people will not change us. You might change every human being on Earth and make them agree with you, but it will only mean that all human beings on Earth will remain outside the ascension spiral until they change their perception. You cannot force your way into Heaven. It is not possible. I could say this a million more times. But I trust that I have said enough that some will understand.

Projection is the bane of the fallen consciousness, it is the one thing that, more than anything else, prevents the manifestation of a Golden Age. For why do you not have a Golden Age? Because you are projecting images upon the Ma-ter light that are based on the separate self and its perception. How can you manifest the Golden Age? Transcend the perception until you see the images based on Oneness and then project those images. Or rather, realize what I have explained: that there is a way to transcend perception and the need to project anything.

For you see, when you do indeed transcend the entire projection game, it does not mean that you become as nothing, it does not mean that you are now a pacifist who sits in a cave in the Himalayas. You can still go out and take active part in society, but you are not doing it by projecting your perception of the separate self. You are doing it by being the open door for the perception of your I AM Presence, the vision of your I AM Presence and the light of your I AM Presence to stream through you. And this is true co-creation. You are not creating a mental image and projecting the light through that image. Your Conscious Self has no image that stands between it and the I AM Presence. You are the open door, a clear pane of glass.

But what you do do is, you focus your attention. So, you are in physical embodiment. You focus your attention on a particular location, on a particular problem or issue. You do not project an image upon it of what should happen or what is wrong. You simply focus your attention, and then you allow the light and the vision of the I AM Presence to flow through you, flow into the situation and perform whatever changes can be performed according to the Law of Free Will and the higher vision.

Do you see the essential difference between projecting and simply focusing attention, experiencing in a neutral non-attached way? You are not projecting. You are simply being the clear pane of glass that provides the frame of reference. This is what you saw when Jesus encountered and challenged the scribes and the Pharisees. He did not project, he simply allowed the light of God to flow through him and challenge their perception.

This is your ultimate role as well. We are not seeking to raise up an army of people who think they have the infallible truth and will go out there and do battle with all those who perceive the world differently and therefore have a different mental image. We are seeking to raise up the Christed ones who acknowledge that they are here to be the open door, that there is nothing to project.

Let the cosmic wrecking ball shatter the structures that limit your Spirit

Kuan Yin, June 12, 2010.

The conditions that existed during the era of the Soviet Union started as mental images in consciousness. Yet, once those mental images had crossed the line and had become outpictured as physical forms, then those physical forms affected the human beings who lived under and experienced those conditions. And thus, the physical forms affected the consciousness of the people, depending on their spiritual development, their identification with form. The more they were identified with form, the more they thought these conditions were real, permanent, or perhaps even the only way that things could be. And thus, the external conditions affected or reinforced their sense of identity as material beings, or their sense of identity as powerless beings who did not have the power to change their own destiny.

And thus, you see, the question becomes: how can, then, an individual or an entire nation rise above its past, rise above the conditions that it has come to believe as real or permanent? This, then, is the very mechanism that makes it possible for a downward self-reinforcing spiral to be formed. And this is what makes it possible that an entire planet can fall below the level at which it was created, or fall below the level of a Golden Age. This makes it possible that an entire planet can go into a downward spiral that the inhabitants of this planet cannot stop, and therefore the entire planet self-destructs.

This is the very mechanism that the fallen beings, the false teachers, have understood, and have made use of in order to create a downward spiral that put themselves in positions of power, and made it very difficult for the people to stand up to the elite, to overthrow the power elite. For once the people had come to accept that they had no power beyond a certain level, how could they then believe that it was possible for them to stand up to the elite whom they perceived to have greater power than themselves? This is essentially the very consciousness that you saw during the Middle Ages, where the people actually believed that the noble class or the kings had some super-human power against which they could not survive.

And thus, you will even see here in the former Soviet Union, how many among the people were almost hypnotized – mesmerized – by the power displayed by the apparatus, the power machine. And they thought they had no power to rise up against this machine, for surely it would kill any individual that attempted to oppose it. This, then, is how you can create a situation, where the people cannot stand up to the elite precisely because the people cannot imagine or believe that they have the power to stand up to the elite.

And so you see, as has been explained earlier, that you have the perversion of the Father as the perversion of power, meaning that the power elite demonstrates a willingness to kill anyone who stands up to their power. Then you have the perversion of the Mother that divides people amongst themselves, even within themselves, because they never know who will listen, who is spying upon them, and who will tell the authorities.

Yet beyond that, you also have the perversion of the element of the Son, in the form of a combination of withholding information and propagating false information as propaganda. And thus, the people do not know what reality is, they do not know there is an alternative to the present system that they see. And they do not know everything that is happening within the system, for everything is so compartmentalized that virtually no people in the system have the full picture of all activities taking place in the system.

This is what you saw in Nazi Germany, where very few people, even in the highest ranks of the Nazi government, were aware of the full extent of what was happening in the concentration camps. You had a very similar situation in the Soviet Union, where very few people were fully aware of how all aspects of the system were functioning. And even in many cases, the leaders themselves did not know exactly what was going on in all of the compartments of the system.

And then, of course, to complete the suppression, you have the perversion of the Holy Spirit, where the people are never allowed to build any kind of momentum, for everything is frozen. Everything is so slow and seems so impossible that changes seem beyond what can actually take place. And thus, everyone believes that the system is so closed that there is no possibility of moving the system in any decisive direction.

And so, they just give up trying, for what is the use? Better to submit and make the best of it, than to stand up to the system and be ground into dust by the machine itself.

And so, my point is to help you understand that what happens to a people who are exposed to such a closed system is that their sense of imagination, their sense of identity, can be affected so deeply that even after the system itself is no more, they still cannot quite dare to believe that it is possible to affect deep and lasting changes in Russia. They still feel powerless to take command over their destiny, they still do not dare to imagine a better destiny for themselves. And that is why they become subject to various forces that then claim that they can fill in the vacuum left by the system.

That is why you see a percentage of the population that longs back to communism. That is why you see some people, a large group of people, who long for a strong leader who can present them with the kind of certainty that they were used to during the age of the apparatus—that always had unquestionable answers to everything, even though these answers did not really answer questions or solve problems. Nevertheless, they gave the impression of certainty, which people have come to crave, for since they cannot connect to the creativity within themselves, they see creativity as a threat rather than as an opportunity for improving their lives.

You also see a tendency of the emergence of oligarchs that also, even though they may be using some form of capitalism, are actually acting much like those in the political system of the communist regime. You also see the emergence of criminals who likewise have no compunctions about suppressing the people and misusing power. You see the emergence of corruption and a bureaucratic system that, again, seems immovable and insensitive to the people, that again sees change as a threat—and therefore, in order to survive and propagate its own power, wants to suppress change.

So, what I am endeavoring to explain here is that even though Russia no longer has a communist system, it still has a communist conscious-ness to a very large extent. The people have not freed themselves from the communist consciousness that was put upon them over so many de-cades. They have not fully seen this consciousness for what it is. They have not fully seen beyond it, and therefore they cannot even imagine or cannot believe in the alternative to the communist system and the communist consciousness.

Yet what is the core of the communist consciousness? It is precisely as we have explained before, the suppression of individuality and individual creativity. It is the denial that you are a spiritual being and that because you are a spiritual being, you are not bound by or limited by anything in the world of form.

You do not need to feel that you are bound by or limited by anything that you experience or perceive in the world of form. You are not bound by the objects of your perception, for you have the ability to project yourself outside of what you perceive through the physical body, the physical senses and the outer mind. You can connect to the greater reality that you are, the individuality anchored in your I AM Presence. This is the path of Christhood. And of course, the communist system and the communist consciousness is just one example of how the fallen beings have attempted to create a system that completely suppresses the drive of the individual to attain Christhood. They have attempted to create many such systems, that either denies Christhood or defines it out of existence by defining a system according to which Christhood is impossible.

Other systems are, of course, various religions, including the Catholic religion itself—which claims to be the only true church of Jesus Christ, yet denies the very core of His teaching, namely that all people on Earth have the potential to attain Christhood. Of course, you also have capitalism, scientific materialism, which denies the power of the individual, or at least the power of the individual that has Christhood, while in some ways deifying the power of those who do not have Christhood, as you see the CEOs of large corporations have an almost totalitarian power over all of the people who are part of that corporation.

So what you see is that the fallen angels have attempted to create a system that denies christhood, and therefore denies true individuality, but it does not deny the false individuality that comes through the ego. For it raises up the ego of certain beings to the status of a god, so that their word cannot be gainsaid, as you see in every dictator throughout the world, even in those who had risen to some power in the communist system. Even though in the communist system no individual had ultimate power, for the system itself would – at least in the time after Stalin – have power even over the supreme leader of the system.

And this, then, is a lesson to be learned. For indeed, when you create such a system, you may think that you have power over the system, but in reality, the system begins to own you as well. For the system will see any individual only as a tool to its survival, and therefore it has no room for the individuals who will not go along with the system.

So then, my beloved, when you understand these mechanics of how the fallen system works, you can then begin to realize that the system works only through deception. It is built on a lie. And it can survive only as long as the majority among the people accept the lie, as long as they do not see beyond the lie. For once they begin to see the lie and refuse to submit to what they now see as unreal, then the system will being to crumble.

And thus, you can begin to see that even when you look at the Soviet Union, it was not the physical power that kept the system in place. This can be difficult to understand, but you have experienced the near total power and the total disregard for human life displayed by the system. Yet the reality is that even the Soviet Union could not have killed an unlimited amount of people, for the system itself cannot kill anyone. It needs representatives who have become so insensitive to human life that they are willing to do the bidding of the leaders of the system. And where will it get those representatives? It can only get them from among the people. And so, there will come a point where it will not be possible to find enough people who have the total insensitive to life that they are willing to kill a large number of the population in order to keep the system in place.

You have heard about the balance of power, and this is precisely the balance. How many people are available that will act as the henchmen of the system, compared to how many people are willing to disobey and challenge the system? Once the number of people who are willing to challenge the system goes beyond the number that the henchmen are able to kill or imprison – or even that the prisons can hold – well then the system, the physical power of the system, will begin to crumble. And that is precisely why the threat of power is a necessary ingredient, but it is not the power itself that maintains the system, it is the deception the lie, the illusion, that maintains the system.

And that is also why – even after the physical power is no longer there – the deception, the consciousness, can still hang as a black cloud over this nation of Russia; and can still serve to suppress the people, their knowledge, their awareness, their imagination, and their belief in the possibility of a better future. And as long as that illusion hangs as a black cloud, then the people are not free to embrace a new and better future. And thus, they cannot magnetize the kind of leaders who could bring about that future, for they instead magnetize the kind of leaders who are also blinded by the illusion and therefore cannot see how to take Russia beyond the current state with all of its chaos and limitations.

They do not have the vision, for the vision can only come when the old consciousness is not suppressing the imagination of the people. And so then, the question I am asking you to consider is how this old consciousness can be shattered, how it can be diluted to the point where people can see through the fog, and see through the clouds and see the reality of the possibility of the Golden Age.

...

What then is the ultimate demise of the Soviet Union or of the Nazi regime? It is that those regimes are forgotten by the people. Why, my beloved, do you think that the veil has been drawn, so that there is no memory and no records of past ages where there has been as great, if not greater, of a warfare and atrocities as what you have seen in the last century? It is out of mercy; for if people still maintained the memory of the past, they would continue to be affected by that past and could not rise above it and imagine and believe in a future that was free of the past.

And how do you become free unless you forgive? For until you have forgiven those who have harmed you, you are maintaining an energetic tie, not only to the people or to the institutions, but to the consciousness behind it. And that means you are giving your life force to that consciousness, and you are serving to maintain the consciousness, to keep the beast alive, to keep the structure standing, even though it may be an empty structure. So do you see the absolute necessity of complete and unconditional forgiveness?

How can you forgive? By realizing that most of the people who were part of the Soviet apparatus were not evil. They were simply blinded by the illusion. And it was the same illusion that you were blinded by, for as I said, had you not been blinded by the illusion, you would have challenged the illusion. So forgive yourselves and forgive others, and realize that what you have witnessed was a lesson for humankind, a lesson in how consciousness co-creates physical reality. And then, what you create can limit your imagination so you cannot free yourself from your own creation. In other words, when you co-create from the consciousness of separation, the consciousness of duality, you will become a slave of your own creation, as the monster created by Doctor Frankenstein turned upon him and destroyed him. This is the ancient story of the ego and what is created through the consciousness of the ego.

Now, of course, comes the question: How can you then forgive the fallen angels and the consciousness behind them? Well, you can forgive by again realizing that there is a difference between the consciousness and the being who is identified with the consciousness. The fallen angels were not created as fallen angels. They were created as God's angels. Before they fell, they were genuine angels. And they fell only because they became blinded by the consciousness of separation. That is why we have said earlier that a fallen angel cannot be redeemed. For the consciousness of the fallen angel is the consciousness of separation, and the consciousness of separation cannot come into Oneness. So as long as a being is identified with the consciousness of separation, it cannot be redeemed. But if a fallen being can separate itself from the consciousness of separation, then the being that was created by God, the man that descended from heaven, can then indeed return to heaven.

And then, when you separate the being from the consciousness, you can see that the consciousness is unreal. And therefore, even the original fallen beings, even those who are the most identified with the fallen consciousness, they still fall under the category that Jesus talked about when he was hanging on the cross and said, "Father forgive them, for they know not what they do."

You may see that these beings, or even people who embody the fallen consciousness, are completely unreachable; that you cannot reach them with reason; you cannot reach them with the Christ mind. And this is true. But why can you not reach them? Because they are blinded by the illusion. They are the most blind because they believe an illusion is the truth. They believe that a complete illusion is an absolute and infallible truth. And that is why they are actually the most ignorant, the most blind, the most to be pitied. And when you realize this, you can see that even they are acting out of ignorance, and even the consciousness that they express is unreal.

And then, when you begin to connect to the reality that you are a spiritual being, then you can realize, as Jesus has said in the Christhood course, that that which is real cannot be affected by that which is unreal. And then you can begin to experience in your own being that the fallen consciousness has no power over you, your Spirit. For you begin to realize that matter, that form, has no power over Spirit. For Spirit is beyond matter, Spirit is beyond form. And when you realize and experience this, you have no fear of the fallen consciousness. You have no fear of the beings who are blinded by it, the beings who might accuse you and seek to create doubt in your being.

You will know that they have no power over you, as Jesus knew they had no power over him. And therefore, you can say with Jesus, "Father forgive them, for they know not what they do." And when you can say this and truly say it with all of your being, then you have forgiven, and then you are free of the consciousness. For can you see that as long as you think that a particular consciousness or a particular form has power over your Spirit, you are not free of that form? You are not free of that consciousness. How can you be free, if you think anything has power over you?

And of course, if you think that you are a being that has form, then you will think that the forms in the material world have power over you as a being with form. It is only when you connect to the reality that the Conscious You is a formless being—that is when you realize and experience that nothing in the world of form has power over you. It only seemed to have power over you because you were identifying yourself with a lower consciousness. For you are a formless being, which means that you have the power to immediately, instantly stop identifying yourself with a limited consciousness—and indeed withdraw yourself, withdraw your being, from that consciousness and return to the formlessness that you are. Whereby you know that you are an extension of your I AM Presence and that nothing in the world of form can touch you.

My beloved, this was the essence of the discussion you had earlier about whether a particular ascended master can change his name just because it was said in a previous dispensation that this is not possible. An ascended master is a formless being; cannot be bound by anything in form. Any statement made by words is made in the world of form. If you allow yourself to believe that such a statement should stand for all time, then you have made yourself the subject of the fallen consciousness itself, the very consciousness of the false hierarchy. For they are constantly trying to make you believe that you are limited by some kind of form, that you should submit to that form, to that structure, to that system. And therefore, you should limit the expression of your Spirit according to that system.

My beloved, there is an old question that has been asked for a long time. It is this: If God is omnipotent, can God create a rock that is so heavy that God cannot lift it? Many people have spent a considerable amount of mental energy trying to figure out this riddle. But I can solve it for you by pointing out that this is the perfect example of how the consciousness of duality projects an image upon everything, including God. For you see, what makes this riddle seem impossible to solve is the concept that God has some kind of form and therefore can be limited by form. But God is not a being with form; God is the source of form yet God is beyond form. Therefore, any form that can be created, any rock that could be created, can only exist in the world of form. And therefore, that form cannot limit the formless God.

Do you see, it is not a matter of answering a question in a linear fashion with a yes or no. Yes, God can create a rock that is so big that God cannot lift it, but then God is not omnipotent. But if God cannot create a rock that is so big that God cannot lift it, then God is not omnipotent either. But you see, there is no omnipotence in the world of form, for in the world of form everything has limitation—or it would not have form. So you see, the way to solve the riddle is to realize that the riddle is a product of the dualistic state of consciousness, and when you transcend that state of consciousness – and realize that you are formless being who are an extension of the formless God – then you can experience the formlessness of God. And then you know the riddle has no meaning— and then you are free of the consciousness behind it.

Do you understand a deeper truth here, my beloved? If you look at all the philosophies and religions in the world, there is not one among them that is not affected by the fallen consciousness. This does not mean that they are necessarily created by the false hierarchy, but they are affected by the fallen consciousness. The fallen consciousness says that form is real and that form should have power over Spirit. And therefore, it is possible to create a philosophy on Earth that can accurately describe God.

But it is not possible to create anything that has form which can capture the fullness of the formless God. That is why those who that are wise may use a system as a stepping stone, but there comes a point where they know they have to go beyond the system if they will know the real living God. So you see, there are so many people, even those on the spiritual path, who have questions, questions about this, questions about that. But do you understand that in order to formulate a question, you must have a foundation for even formulating the question. And in having a foundation you have already created a system, and now you are looking for an answer that fits within the system—and therefore validates the system you have created.

Yet, how will you ultimately be free, how will you ultimately ascend? When you let go of any and all structures and systems that have been created in the world of form, whether they were created by you personally or by other beings. You must let go of all structure before you can ascend into the formlessness of Spirit. And so, as long as you keep asking questions based on a particular system, as long as you keep looking for a spiritual teacher who will answer those questions within the system, you will not find truth, you will not find the living truth.

Imagination, acceptance, oneness: A new formula for alchemy in the Golden Age

Saint Germain, June 12, 2010.

Do you see, as Kuan Yin attempted to explain, that what was attempted in the Soviet Union was indeed to destroy the potential that someone would make this kind of unpredictable choice, this kind of creative choice. The fallen beings behind the creation of communism, especially Soviet communism, wanted to destroy individuality and creativity, so that nothing could overthrow and overturn the system, so that the system, like a machine, would keep grinding away into the distant future. They attempted to create a system that was immortal, just as individuals attempt to make their egos immortal.

This was an attempt to do on Earth what only God can do. For only God can make things permanent, and yet, that permanence cannot be manifest in the material realm, in the world of form, but only in the world beyond the material, in the ascended realm. And yet, even then things are not permanent, for they are constantly ascending, transcending themselves.

So you see, the attempt to create something permanent on Earth is the ultimate dream of the fallen beings. For they think that if they could manage to create this system that could not be overthrown – but would keep sustaining itself – then they would have created, they think, a viable alternative to God's creation. This is their logic. It is, of course, not the Christ logic, for in the Christ logic you know that nothing in the world of form can be permanent. Nevertheless, this is what they believe in their duality consciousness, in their sense of separation from the reality of God, but they cannot fathom the reality that even God is transcending itself. And therefore, they think that God is permanent. And they think that it is possible to create something in this world that is permanent, because they think that they have created a permanent graven image of God that can be maintained.

So then, what is the deeper reality? How do you break out of this closed system of the separate self? How do you become free? Well, only by realizing that you are a formless being—that therefore cannot be trapped in, cannot be limited by, any form whatsoever. For you are more than any form in this world, and therefore, you cannot be bound by any form. And therefore, no matter that you have grown up in a repressive system, such as Soviet communism – that has hammered into your mind and being that you are nothing but a material being, that you have come from dust, that you will return to dust – no matter all of this propaganda, all of this brainwashing, nevertheless, you are the Conscious You. And you can at any moment leave behind that limited sense of identity, for you have not become that identity. You have only projected your being into it, so that you look at the world through the filter of that identity.

...

What would be the point in bringing the Golden Age into manifestation in heaven, where everything is golden already? So what would be the point of getting all spiritual people to ascend, and then the Earth is left in some lower state? Then the Earth would self-destruct. That is not the plan of the Elohim, that is not why the Elohim focused their attention for many, many cycles in order to create the physical platform of this

Earth. They wanted to see not so much the Earth ascend but the inhabitants of Earth ascend [in consciousness] so that the kingdom of God would be manifest on Earth, not in heaven.

For when the kingdom of God is manifest on Earth, then Earth becomes a magnet that pulls up the entire sphere to a higher level, instead of being a dead weight that pulls it down, as it has been for some time. So you see, it is indeed a deliberate plot of the fallen beings and the false teachers. They know that there are certain people they cannot prevent from discovering the spiritual path. When you look at the Soviet Union, when you look at many of the initiatives in the West, such as materialism, you see how they have attempted to create these systems and structures that suppress spirituality. But they know they cannot work for all people, so what do they attempt to do? They attempt to create a diversion, so that those who are spiritual or religious think that salvation only comes after life on Earth.

And what does this do? It leaves the Earth in the control of the fallen beings, for there is none who attain Christhood, whereby they can challenge the fallen beings right here on Earth. And then, of course, the Earth will not progress. It will go in a downward spiral, and the second law of thermodynamics will cause it to self-destruct.

...

For as we have attempted to explain to you, everything is a creation of consciousness. And when you change the consciousness, the outer conditions WILL change. It cannot be any other way. This is, of course, again one of the things that the fallen beings and the false teachers are doing all they can to prevent you from accepting. They do not want you to truly believe that if you change your consciousness, and help others change their consciousness, then your society will change. They want you to think that the only way to bring change is to engage in the dualistic struggle. They are even willing to have you struggle against themselves in order to keep you and others in duality.

For some of these false teachers do indeed understand that if enough people raised themselves beyond duality, then their power over that society would quickly come to an end. That is why they are so anxious to destroy the potential for people manifesting their Christhood. That is why King Herod killed all the male babies to kill the one Christ. That is why the Catholic Church has done everything it could to kill Jesus' example. That is why the communist system did everything it could to kill individuality, so that no Christed being could rise and challenge them.

You, women of Russia, are all daughters of God!

Mother Mary, June 13, 2010.

So you see, we are not here talking about some sinister ideology that everyone recognizes as sinister. But do you understand, my beloved, the false teachers, the fallen ones, the false hierarchy are cleverer than most people think. Most people think that it is easy to identify the devil, for he looks like the devil. But you see, the images of the devil, the images of evil, the images of false teachings have been set up precisely to serve as a camouflage, so that you do not see that the opposite polarity of the ego is actually also of the duality consciousness. You think that that which appears to be good, or benign or benevolent is good, benign and benevolent. You think it is of God, of the Light.

But it is not; it is simply a camouflage, where those who have inserted themselves as leaders, or thinkers or philosophers may appear to be benevolent, but they are nevertheless interjecting in the collective consciousness ideas that are still based on duality and therefore still seduce the people into giving them some kind of elite power over them.

Therefore, you need to become wise as serpents while remaining, or becoming, harmless as doves. This can be seen no more clearly than in the Catholic Church or the Eastern Orthodox Church, that both claim to represent Christ. Yet none of them represent Christ; they represent two different perversions of the teachings of Christ. And they are, quite frankly, not that different when you take a closer look. They are perversions of Christ, for they raise up a structure and they seek to use that structure to suppress individual Christhood—that none dare follow in the footsteps of Christ.

It is time to accelerate yourself beyond psychic projections

Mother Mary, October 15, 2010

The origin of psychic projections

What, then, do I mean, when I talk about something psychic? Surely, the general definition of this word pertains to the abilities of the mind, of the psyche. This may be related to thoughts and feelings, or it may be related to deeper abilities to sense something beyond the material world, such as people who are sensitive and can serve as mediums for communicating with dead relatives, disembodied spirits—or other phenomena that are often labeled as psychic.

This, however, is not the way we of the Ascended Host prefer to use the term. When we talk about the psychic, we are talking about a specific perversion of your psychic abilities, not be higher and correct use of these psychic abilities. So let me endeavor to explain the difference.

As Maitreya explains in his book, there was a point in a higher sphere, when a certain group of lifestreams decided that they were not willing to transcend their level of consciousness and lay down their lives to be the servants of all. Thus, they rebelled against God's plan for salvation through free will—which really was not, in God's eyes, a plan for salvation but a plan for the raising up of all self-aware beings to the level of self-awareness of the Creator out of which they came. Thus, in God's original plan, there was no need for salvation, for there had been no fall, there was no cosmic accident that caused self-aware beings to descend into a separate sense of identity.

God, of course, knew this to be a possibility, a consequence of free will. Yet God had also defined the universe, and the laws of this universe, in such a way that no being could possibly sink so far into the illusion of separation that it could not come back to oneness by reaching for the mind of Christ, that is the universal unifying agent behind all form and within all form—and thus accessible from anywhere in the world of form.

Thus, the deeper reality is that there was no flaw in God's plan. There is no flaw in giving self-aware beings free will; on the contrary, free will is the means to the expansion of self-awareness. For how can self–awareness be expanded in a way that is imposed by an external force? The growth in self-awareness must come from within the self, through the experiences of the self and the decisions made by the self.

Yet when these beings rebelled against God's plan, they separated themselves from the flow of the River of Life. Instead of ascending with their sphere, they were then lowered into the next sphere that was created. In their minds they perceived this as being cast down forcefully by beings in what they then called the heaven realm. Thus, you have even in the Book of Revelation an impure view, that presents the fall as a great war in heaven, where Michael fought the dragon. But it was not so, Archangel Michael, as he has explained himself, did not fight the devil. Archangel Michael was simply immovable, and thus it was the devil who fought and in fighting separated itself from the oneness of God—and thus confined itself to a lower level of vibration than the ascending sphere, thus being left behind by that sphere and all of the inhabitants that were willing to transcend.

Now then, what was it that happened in the process of the fall, when the, shall we call them "fallen" beings, rebelled against God? Well, they realized that in order for them to have any chance of proving themselves right and proving God wrong – as they had decided was their desire, their life's goal – they would have to pull as many lifestreams as possible with them into the lower sphere. They knew that they would descend, and they wanted to drag as many beings with them as possible, thinking that if enough beings were dragged down with them, then God would have to do something to change the design and the plan for the universe.

And how, then, did they manage to drag a great number of the beings in the ascending sphere with them into the fall? They did so by using their abilities of the mind, abilities that most people in the ascending sphere had never used and had never encountered. For you see, when you are in the Ascension spiral and know that you are being raised up, you have only one desire and that is what was expressed in the words of Jesus, when he said, "And I, if I be lifted up from the earth will draw all men onto me."

You are not seeking to raise yourself out of selfish reasons, you are not seeking to elevate yourself in comparison to others. You are not in any way seeking to set yourself apart from others or above them. On the contrary, you are only seeking to raise the All, you are seeking to raise yourself that you might be an instrument for raising the All. And in this pure motive, you are indeed elevated, which is why Jesus said that the meek shall inherit the Earth.

And so, most of the beings in that ascending sphere had only encountered other beings who also had these pure intentions. Yet, when those who thought they were the high and the mighty in that sphere realized that they were not willing to lay down their lives in service to the All, they then went into a different state of mind than even they had been in before. For up until that turning point, they too had attempted to raise the All, although with a hidden motive of thinking that it would elevate themselves in the end. Yet when they realized that the only way to progress and ascend with the sphere was to lay down their lives without knowing what would come after, then they rebelled. And now, in their rebellious state of mind, they decided to attempt to drag as many other beings with them as possible.

And they accomplished this by using the abilities of the mind. These are the very co-creative abilities, but in a perverted form. We have explained in many different ways that you have the ability to formulate a mental image and to superimpose the image upon the Mater light. As we have recently inspired this messenger to write, you do indeed have a right to experiment with this creative ability. You do have a right to formulate any mental image you want, and to project it upon the Ma-ter light, for the Ma-ter light will gratefully take on the form you project upon it, thus enabling you to experience what you have created. And in experiencing these consequences, you can then evaluate whether your mental image was indeed one you wish to repeat or whether it was one you wish to transcend.

Yet of course, in having this ability to formulate a mental image and project it outside yourself, you also have the possibility of not only projecting it upon the Ma-ter light but indeed projecting it into the inner sanctuary of other beings with free will.

How to make the maximum amount of karma

You will see, my beloved, that on planet Earth you have the possibility of physically – through physical force – forcing someone else to do what you want them to do. This is, of course, a violation of free will, but it is not the most severe violation of free will possible. Indeed, even killing another human being is not the way to make maximum karma on planet Earth.

A much more severe violation of free will is when you use your psychic abilities to project images, beliefs, emotions and energies into the inner sanctuary of another human being, thereby interfering with that person's state of mind and its ability to make free choices. And thereby in subtle ways, often unseen by the recipient, forcing the other person to make the choices you want that person to make. So even though you will make a severe karma by physically killing another human being, you will make an even more severe karma by projecting psychic projections into the mind of another person, so that that person kills himself.

Do you see my point? It is one thing to physically violate the free will of others by seeking to force them by what they see, clearly, as an external force. But it is an entirely other thing to project psychic projections at them, so that they do not realize they are being forced but nevertheless you are controlling their will, or at least interfering with their ability to make free choices. This then, is precisely what the original fallen beings did in the sphere that was close to the ascension point.

They used the energies of the accuser of the brethren, as we have explained before, to create mental images that were limiting to the ascension process. Then, they used very intense fear-based emotions, such as anger, fear, resentment or what have you, to project these images into the minds of other beings. And because they had never been exposed to this, many of these beings, in their innocence, had little defense. They were harmless as doves, but they were not wise as serpents, for they had never been exposed to the serpents, or the serpentine lies or the serpentine energies. So many of them reacted to these projections in various ways that caused them to also go into a lower state of consciousness—where they attempted to either refute the accusations or attack the accusers back. And thus, they became, as the fallen beings had foreseen, pulled into the dualistic struggle.

And of course, when you are in the mindset of the dualistic struggle, you cannot ascend. And thus, when the sphere ascended, these beings were left behind, plunging into the newly created sphere, attempting to restart the process of the ascension from there. It was not, as the Book of Revelation says, a third of the stars of heaven that fell; it was indeed a much smaller number. But it was a third of the stars in a particular system, where Lucifer and the original fallen angels resided.

The difference between psychic forces and ascended masters

Thus, what you see on planet earth today is indeed a continuation of this process, where you have a great number of forces that are seeking to direct these psychic projections into the minds of all human beings, for the purpose of keeping them trapped in this dualistic struggle that prevents them from entering the ascension spiral. These forces exist, not in the physical realm but in the emotional realm, the mental realm and even in the lowest level of the etheric realm. These are spirit beings, dark spirits we might say, but many of them are indeed able to masquerade themselves and appear as benign spirits, or even spirits with a certain light and power. For they have learned to mirror back to you your own light, so that you see it and think it is their light. Yet of course, these beings do not work only from the realms that are beyond the material, for indeed there are many people on earth who have – without knowing it, and in a few cases by knowing it – become tools for these psychic forces, these sinister forces, if you will.

What then is the essential difference between these psychic forces and the beings in the ascended realm? Well, I have already expounded upon it by saying that as you enter the ascension spiral, you overcome all desire to raise yourself in comparison to others but only seek to raise the All. But how do you come to that point? You come to that point by purifying your intent, your motives, your beings, your chakras your auras, your inner sanctum from all lower energies.

You see, there is an essential distinction that must be known by those who are serious spiritual students and aspire to the ascension. It is indeed the ability to sense the difference between the vibrations that vibrate above a certain critical level and those that vibrate below that level. The vibrations that are above a certain level cannot easily be described by the words you currently use on Earth, for almost any word that you can use can be interpreted and misinterpreted in various ways by various people. That is why, given the limitations of words, we have used the word "unconditional" or the word "infinite" to describe these vibrations. But it is a vibration that seeks to accelerate and raise up life, and does not seek to put down or limit life.

Thus, let us take the vibration that most people call "love," and let us realize that in the ascended realm, we experience and express a form of love that is completely beyond what most human beings call love. It is a form of love that is completely without restrictions, without conditions and that only seeks to raise up life. This does not mean that this love is always soft and gentle and always agrees with people and seeks to make them feel good. Unconditional love is the love that accepts no conditions for its flow. It wants to flow, it wants to be expressed, and when it encounters a person who has conditions for its flow, it will challenge those conditions in a way that is most suited to awakening the person from those conditions.

Now then, take what happens when love is lowered below the critical threshold and thus becomes the kind of energy that most people call love, yet it is a conditional love, a possessive love that seeks to control others in order to make you feel good. There are many of you who have experienced this kind of love from parents, spouses and many other people. These people love you only if you live up to their conditions, so that they can feel secure, or feel comfortable, or feel that they don't need to change—or that you will not change and therefore upset the apple cart. This is clearly a form of love that is not the higher love. It is a possessive, controlling love that seeks to interfere with your free will and get you to make choices that will make the other person feel comfortable, or feel in control, or feel superior or whatever the need might be.

And thus, this is not a love that seeks to raise up and accelerate you; it seeks to hold you in a certain matrix, in a certain limitation, in a certain mental box. This, therefore, is what we might call psychic love, although it truly becomes psychic only when it is projected into someone's mind with a deliberate and aggressive intent of controlling their free will. So we might say that there is even a form of human love that is, although selfish and self-centered, not be aggressive love that is expressed in a psychic projection.

Thus again, there is a distinction between lower energies and energies that are directed into other people's minds for the specific purpose of influencing their free-will choices. Now, if you think back at your life and your own path, you will most likely see that you have encountered a number of people who had an aggressive intent. And although they were not able or even willing to force you through physical force, they were both able and willing to attempt to force you through psychic means, by making you feel bad if you did not live up to their expectations, by making you feel obligated, or by making you feel afraid—or even by engaging you in arguments, so that they would be able to steal your energy.

My beloved, have you ever met a person who attempted to engage you in an argument, and after the argument had gone on for some time, suddenly – even though no outer resolution had been reached – the other person stopped arguing and was now suddenly nice and conciliatory. Why do you think there was this sudden shift? Because the person had managed to direct psychic projections into your mind, into your mental and emotional bodies, and to get you so agitated that you released energy that the other person – or the demons, discarnates and entities controlling that person – were absorbing. And when the person or the entities had had enough light to be full, there was no need to continue the argument, and so the argument stopped—until, of course, they became hungry the next time and thus attempted to engage you once again.

Can you see that even in society you encounter an almost infinite amount of psychic projections? Consider how, from the womb to the grave, you are bombarded by advertising that seeks to get you to buy certain products. Or you are bombarded with political ideas and ideologies, seeking to make you vote for certain parties or certain people. All this, if it has an aggressive intent, is psychic projections. Anything that aggressively seeks to invade your mind and being, your inner sanctuary, and seeks to influence your free will is a psychic projection. It comes ultimately from the psychic forces, but it often comes through other people, people who are not aware of what they are doing—and therefore might think they have the best of intentions. But ignorance of the law is no excuse, as they say.

How to free yourself from psychic projections

Those who are the open doors for these psychic projections will indeed be responsible for what they allow dark forces to do through them—as you, of course, are responsible for the psychic projections you have directed at others. And again, if you are honest and look at your life, you may see that you have also had a tendency to want to – in subtle and "nice" ways – force other people to comply with your expectations. Yet,

I am not here to find fault with you, I am not here to blame you, I am not here to create fear.

I am only here to awaken you to the willingness to acknowledge this phenomenon of psychic projections and decide that you are willing to rise above it, so that you stop directing psychic projections at others. And as you stop doing unto others, then you will also make yourself invulnerable to their doings unto you. For it is indeed whatever beliefs or energies you have in your own being – that are below the threshold of the psychic – that will make you vulnerable to the psychic projections from other people or dark forces.

Only when the prince of this world has some psychic energy or belief in you, will he be able to affect you by directing psychic beliefs or energies at you. This is the truth that I trust almost everyone open to this teaching that we are giving, can see and acknowledge. And thus, it is absolutely necessary that you take a look in the mirror, look for the beam in your own eyes and look at how you might have used your psychic abilities to project something into the minds of other people. When you see this honestly, then you do not need to feel guilt, for have I not said that this world has been deeply infused with the fallen mindset and that these psychic forces have been around in this world for a very long time?

Thus, there is no need to feel guilty over the fact that your body gets dirty and starts smelling after I while. You simply take a shower and accelerate your physical body into purity. And thus, there is no need to feel guilty when you realize that, after having lived for a certain amount of time in the density of the psychic projections found on earth, you have also become dirty in your inner sanctuary. Do not feel guilt, do not feel fear but sense the willingness in you to accelerate your being into purity, by taking a cosmic shower of invoking higher energies that will purify your being from these psychic energies and projections.

And to this end, I indeed come to release to you this latest invocation, [Freedom from Psychic Projections] specifically designed to help you attain freedom from psychic projections. Certainly, there is an almost infinite number of such projections, and we could not possibly incorporate all of them in one invocation. But there is enough in this invocation to put you in the accelerated spiral that will eventually free yourself from the hold of these forces, especially when you combine them with our other rosaries and invocations, such as the ones for clearing the heart, loving yourself and many of the others.

...

The fallen angels believe there is a flaw in God's design

My beloved, let me give you one more key to understanding the psychic forces and why they are so detrimental to the ascension spiral. I have already said that there was no flaw in God's plan. Yet after the original beings fell, they have, now for very long time, continued to project the image that there is some kind of flaw in God's plan, that something went wrong, that some cosmic accident happened. Even in the Jewish Kabbalah you will see the concept that at a certain point in the descent of light, there was a cosmic accident that shattered the vessels and the shards were lost in the lower realm. Thus, even the Kabbalah makes it seem like there must have been a flaw in God's design, for otherwise how could such an accident happen?

This is, therefore, the essence of psychic projections. A psychic projection is based on a very simple dynamic: something has gone wrong and it needs to be corrected. You have done something wrong, and you need to correct it.

Yet, do you see the subtle, underlying mechanism? If you can define what has supposedly gone wrong, then those who accept this definition will have their choices controlled by the condition. If you think there really is an angry and judgmental God in the sky – who will send you to an eternity in hell if you do not live up to certain conditions, defined by an external religion on earth – well then you will condemn yourself to using your free will in an attempt to live up to those conditions, so that the angry and judgmental God in the sky will accept you into his kingdom—that is supposedly more wonderful than the fiery hell that is the only alternative.

Yet what would be so wonderful, my beloved, about spending an eternity with an angry and judgmental God? Is that really the future of you look forward to as the highest expression of your potential as a self-aware being? For I can tell you that it is not my ideal of how I would prefer to spend eternity, for I prefer to spend it in oneness with the loving Creator that is beyond all conditions that can be defined in any unascended sphere, that can be defined by the mind of anti-christ.

So do you see, my beloved, I am not here saying that you can do anything you want and it will have no consequence. You are, of course, responsible for what you do with your free will and with God's energy. But God's law, God's design was perfect from the very beginning and is still perfect. The fact that a number of beings have fallen into separation and duality is not a flaw in God's design. It is all foreseen in God's design that this could happen, and God has designed a perfectly functioning mechanism that will return to any self-aware being what they are projecting out. And therefore will eventually cause the vast majority of self-aware beings to decide that they have had enough of kicking against the pricks, of pounding their heads against the concrete wall of the cosmic mirror, and that therefore THEY are willing to change—instead of projecting that the change needs to take place outside themselves.

Can you see, my beloved, that the original fallen beings were not willing to change themselves, and ever since then they have attempted to make all other beings think that "The flaw cannot be in me; it must be out there somewhere, in other people, in dark forces or even in God's design for the universe. I could not be wrong, I could not possibly have to change. Thus it must be those other people who have to change. They are the problem, they are the threat!" And thous you have the classical mechanism described by Jesus, when he told you to stop looking at the splinter in the eye of your brother and instead look at the beam in your own eye.

Do you see that the cosmic mirror, in returning back to you what you are projecting out, is perfectly capable of giving you ample opportunity to eventually reach the point, where you are willing to look at the beam in your own eye, instead of projecting out and therefore receiving back – again and again and again and again – exactly what you are projecting?

There is no flaw in God's design. There is no need for you to correct that flaw by projecting psychic projections at other people, in order to make them live up to whatever standard you have accepted. The way to deal with the current imperfect conditions on Earth is to stop looking at the splinter in the eyes of your brothers, to stop projecting anything into the minds of other people, but to instead look at the beam in your own eye and transcend that beam. And as you continue to transcend the beam, you will enter the ascension spiral. And thus, by you being lifted up from the Earth, you will draw all of the people unto you, as Jesus himself has done, as any other ascended master has done. And thus, you will be part of creating the ascension spiral for Earth, that will make it easier and easier for people to transcend the illusion of separation and duality.

This is your contribution, this is your contribution to correcting, so to speak, the current problem on Earth. Because this problem is not the result of a flaw in God's design; it is the result of choices made by a number of beings who are not willing to take responsibility for themselves and thus projected that other people or God are at fault.

Fallen angels and Fallen co-creators

Question: Dear Jesus, I have a question regarding fallen angels. I understand that the Bible and the Book of Enoch say that some angels fell through lust because they desired to incarnate in order to have sex with the beautiful daughters of men. Since angels know and love each other, could some angels close to those who fell through lust have chosen to come to earth to try and bring their friends back home and then gotten caught in duality and forgotten why they were here? I realize that this rescue mission would probably have violated God's will, since angels were not created to incarnate. If some angels did fall through a misguided rescue attempt and were caught in duality and the incarnation cycle, how would they grow to come back home? If angels were not created to incarnate, would they have an I AM presence? Would they also have spirit guides assigned to help them on their path back to God like souls created to incarnate do? Most of what I have read about fallen angels seems to depict them as being hostile to God or full of pride. I am just wondering whether some could have fallen out of misplaced love (putting their fallen comrades ahead of God's plan), which I guess would be loving something more than God. I really hope you will answer this question.

Answer from Jesus - November 30, 2010

The Book of Enoch and the Book or Revelation are correct in that angels fell, but it is not correct that these were angels in the spiritual realm. Because neither the Bible nor the Book of Enoch discern between ascended and unascended spheres, it has become a common misunderstanding that angels exist only in the spiritual or ascended realm. People have therefore assumed that the fallen angels must have been in the spiritual realm, and as a result many people have wondered how angels in Heaven could possibly fall. This is, of course, only made more confusing by the Book of Revelation and its statement that there was a war in heaven and that some angels were cast out.

The reality is, as we have explained elsewhere [Chapter 2], that the world of form consists of a number of spheres. In the first three spheres, no beings fell. It was in the fourth sphere that beings fell for the first time, and this happened before that sphere ascended and became part of the spiritual realm. Beings have also fallen in the succeeding spheres, up until the seventh, in which you live.

My point is that there are many beings – both angels and co-creators – who have fallen and they fell for different reasons. Some did fall because of pride, some fell because of rebellion and some fell for other reasons. Certainly, beings have fallen as a result of perverting each of the seven rays.

It is correct that there were certain angels who fell because they desired to take on physical bodies and have sex. However, the statement that they fell because they lusted after the daughters of men is not entirely correct. Angels do have polarities, but they do not have what you see as male and female sex—for the simple reason that angels are not designed to produce offspring through a sexual union. So it is more correct to say that certain angels desired to descend to the level, where they could take on male and female bodies and thus have sex. The Book of Enoch makes it sound like it was male angels that fell, but that is simply a product of the male bias found in the society of the time. That is also why God is portrayed as a masculine being.

Angels were, of course, not created to take on physical bodies, so it was a violation of their original design and the greater plan for the raising of their sphere. However, it is not – in an overall sense – a violation of the Law of Free Will. If a being is capable of making a certain choice, the Law of Free Will gives it the right to make that choice—as long as the being does not violate the free will of others. In other words, the angels had a right to descend and take on bodies in order to have sex—with each other.

Yet the angels who fell for this reason were not content to have sex with each other but also wanted to have it with other evolutions, such as co-creators in embodiment. The fallen angels could not have sex only with each other, for the simple reason that as they fell, they were cut off from receiving more than a minimum of light from above. Thus, in order to continue to survive, they had to steal light from other beings, and they obviously did this through sex—the cause of their fall.

If you look at sex on this planet, you will see that virtually any kind of sexual perversion originated with the angels who fell because they wanted sex. They came up with these perversions in order to get other beings to give them their light. This goes for everything from pornography to rape. Any form of sexual activity that forces light out of the lower chakras was originally conceived by the fallen angels. This is in contrast to sex that raises the light through the heart to the upper chakras, and thus generates an experience of oneness between the man and woman having sex.

So when you look at people who are very skilled at seducing others or who are willing to force others – such as through buying sex, coercion, rape or rape drugs – and who have a considerable momentum on doing so, they are likely to be from the angels who fell out of a desire for sex. This is also true for anyone seeking sex with children.

Now back to your question. It is correct that for each group of beings who fell, there were others who followed them. In other words, what I will say here does not apply only to the angels who fell because of a desire for sex but to any angels that fell. We can talk about three groups:

- The angels who initiated the fall. These were the beings who made the decision that caused the fall, and at the time they had at least some awareness of what they were doing. After the fall, they had great pride and also a denial that they had done anything that needed to be changed. They were also extremely focused on themselves.

- Angels who were serving under the angels who fell. They were used to following their leaders, and they did so without making or understanding the decision that caused the fall. After the fall, they had little understanding of what had happened, but they usually had some sense that something had gone wrong. They also had a tendency to follow leaders blindly, and they were more focused on serving others than fulfilling their own needs.

- Angels who after the fall decided to descend on a rescue mission in order to help the above two categories get back to the Path of Oneness. After the fall, they had a strong sense that something had gone wrong – possibly even that something had gone wrong with God's plan – and they had an urgent need to save others. They were so focused on changing others that they rarely stopped to look at their own psychology.

Do you see what I am saying? The very decision that an angel wanted to descend in order to save others did indeed cause that angel to fall. It was not that the angel took embodiment and later became entangled with duality and then fell. It was fallen from the moment it descended below the level at which it was designed to serve. An angel was not created to take embodiment and thus cannot do so without falling.

This obviously does not mean that each angel in embodiment is evil, as popular belief might imply. Many co-creators have fallen as well, and most beings who fell did not do so out of bad or evil motives. There is no reason to place blame or feel guilt; all who have been blinded by duality simply need to awaken from that illusion. So here is what each group has to do in order to get on the true path:

- The initiators of the fall will have to admit what they did and decide to completely change their ways. They must take the focus off themselves and serve others selflessly. This can theoretically happen at any time, especially when a being realizes that it has had enough of the experience it desired before the fall or when it is faced with extreme consequences of its actions. However, in practicality it often happens only when a sphere is ready to ascend and the fallen beings realize they must either change or fall into a denser sphere.

- The followers must stop blindly following leaders and take responsibility for their choices. They must take their focus off serving others, and they must instead focus on themselves. Not in the sense that they become selfish, but in the sense that they take responsibility for thinking on their own and changing their psychology. Incidentally, many of these beings have stopped following their original leaders and have instead started following the ones who fell out of a desire to save others. Thus, they are now serving in ways they think will help others, but if they still refuse to look at themselves, it will not bring them home.

- The angels who wanted to save the others have an almost more difficult task than the original fallen angels. They must admit that they have fallen, regardless of their belief that they did it for a good purpose. And they must admit that they did this *not* because God wanted them to but because they – pridefully – thought they could reform others or that God's Law needed their help. Thus, they must completely surrender all need or desire to save or reform others or to save or reform the world. They must overcome all sense that something has "gone wrong" or that there is a flaw in God's design. They must let go of all sense that they know better than God, and they must acknowledge that they are not responsible for the choices made by other beings, and as such they can have no desire to change those choices. They must stop focusing on changing others and instead seek to change themselves.

Do you see what I am saying? The angels who fell out of a desire to experience something in a lower realm did so out of pure selfishness. And it is sometimes easier for them to come back home, because their return depends only on their own decisions. For example, if such a being realizes that it has had enough sex, then it can relatively easily make the decision that it wants to return to a higher sphere. Yet the angels who fell out of wanting to serve others, feel that they cannot return home until the others are saved. Meaning that their choice to return home depends on the choices of others—and this obviously puts them in a bind.

For the sake of completeness, there is a concept called "avatars" which are beings who descended voluntarily in order to outpicture a higher state of consciousness and thus make it easier for beings in the material world to ascend. Yet these beings did not descend out of a desire to save others or correct a flaw in God's design. They did so out of a desire to express their God-given individuality and thus give others an example, a frame of reference. The angels who fell want to change the choices of others and are often willing to use force in order to accomplish this. The avatars have no desire to change others, but only want to give them a choice that they did not have before, leaving people completely free to choose. As an example, an avatar will never blame others, whereas fallen angels routinely do so—and feel fully justified in doing it.

In closing, angels can fall only in an unascended sphere. Any being in an unascended sphere has an anchor point in the spiritual realm in which the blueprint for that being is stored. This is what we normally call the I AM Presence. An angel that falls also will have spiritual guides that will seek to help it get back to higher realms. However, fallen angels are not guided by other angels, as that would increase the risk of those angels falling. Thus, fallen angels are guided only by ascended masters, which explains why the Serpent – as a symbol for the fallen angels – was allowed in the Garden of Eden, namely Maitreya's Mystery School.

It also explains why organizations sponsored by the ascended masters allow fallen angels to enter. Incidentally, you will in such organizations see somewhat of a concentration of the angels who fell out of a desire to save others. This desire causes them to be attracted to our teachings, but it also causes them to often misunderstand the true purpose of the teachings. They will often interpret our teachings in such a way, that it validates their obsession with saving others. Thus, you will often see them using our teachings to reform, control or judge others, instead of using them to remove the beam in their own eyes.

As I have said many times, the Law of Free Will says that you are the only one responsible for your choices, whereas you are never responsible for the choices of others. When you understand this, you will be able to let go of all desire to save or change others and instead focus on the only thing that can secure your own ascension: changing yourself. Again, study my discourse on the true path.

Chapter 10:
Teachings about fallen angels, 2011

The choice is yours: increased resistance or increased transcendence

Gautama Buddha, January 1, 2011

Understanding the reality of time and space

What is time? What is it that time has done? What is it that the veil of matter has done, the veil of Maya has done? Well, as Jesus has explained in his latest discourse, everything – everything – follows the law of free will. What did the fallen beings say when they rebelled against God? They said: "We demand to have a place where we can feel separated from God and the stream of consciousness that is God, that is the rest of our sphere." And so, in order to give them that, there had to be created a world where there was the illusion that matter is real, that matter hides Spirit and that time exists. So that it is possible to postpone self-transcendence and uphold your current sense of self for a period of time.

When you separated yourself from the guru, when you refused to define your own role – as Jesus has explained – when you hid from Maitreya, you demanded the same as the fallen beings demanded: a place where you could believe that you were separated from the teacher, separated from your source. A place where you could believe that you could uphold your current sense of self for a length of time. This is what you demanded—not consciously, but in order to make the choices you made, you subconsciously demanded this.

If this is the way you want to continue to exist, then I, the Buddha – as all members of the Ascended Host – bow to your free will. I accept that choice, but I also say – as I said last year at new years – then you are not ready to be in the Sangha of the Buddha. And thus, I have nothing further to offer you.

I have something to offer only to those who have come to the point, where they are willing to begin to question their previous choices, their current sense of identity, their current perceptions. Those who are willing to say: "I no longer want the space where I can believe I am apart. I no longer want to uphold my current identity into the future for a period of time. I want to transcend my current identity and come closer to oneness with my source. This is my desire, this is my choice and I am willing to take responsibility for the fact that I am the one who must choose. And I am the one who must be willing to let the Wheel of the Dharma roll back that veil of illusion that has allowed me to uphold the sense of separateness, the sense of a separate self that can exist in time, or that can even exist at all."

Time is Mother; space is Buddha. Do you see that the Mother in her love allows the children to uphold the illusion that they can create something – a separate self, a form of life on a planet – and that that something can endure over time? Even the illusion that the separate self could gain some sense of permanence or immortality or be accepted into the kingdom of God. This is the illusion that the Mother allows you to uphold, so that you can experience it until you have had enough of the experience and is ready to make the choice to transcend it.

Yet on an even deeper level, how can you have the illusion that the matter world is separated from Spirit or that there is no Spirit? What allows this illusion to exist? It is the fact that the Buddha holds the balance for you. The Buddha holds the balance for space, the space between where you are now and where you would have been if you had followed the background acceleration rate of the world in which you live.

It is the Buddha consciousness that allows this to happen, again so that you may have the experience of separation until you have had enough of it. And then you desire and decide that you are willing to let it die, to let that illusory sense of self die, that you may catch up to where you could have been had you accelerated at the same rate as the rest of the universe—as indeed the Buddha has done.

But he has allowed himself to be put in between, that he might fill the space between where you are and where you could have been. Only the Buddha's love allows that space to exist. And if the space had not existed, you would either have had to follow the acceleration rate or cease to exist in the second death. And thus, the Buddha creating space is the background for the Mother giving you the illusion of time. Time truly is not.

Space is not real in the sense that the space between where you are and where you could have been is not real. But the deeper reality is that space is indeed real, as that is what allows forms to exist and what also allows them to transcend by moving closer and closer to the ultimate acceleration rate that will cause your entire sphere to ascend and become a permanent part of the spiritual realm.

The key to being the open door in the Year of the Mother

Saint Germain, January 4, 2011

Do not allow freedom of some to limit the freedom of others
Do you see that freedom to be the open door in one situation should never be used to create a resistance or a structure that restricts your freedom in coming situations. This is also the challenge, that I spoke about through my feminine messenger, about the corporate world and the governments.

There has been now, for a very long time, this tendency to divide the world into the unfree world and the free world. And the West, and especially the United States, sees itself as the free world. And the United States prides itself of being the leader of the free world.

Well, if you aspire to be the leader of the free world, should you not look in the mirror and make sure that you are free, before you attempt to lead the world into greater freedom? For how can you lead the world into a state of freedom that you have not attained yourself?

And so, indeed, the question that needs to be brought out into the open in this coming year is: "Can we claim to be the free world, can we claim to have a free enterprise economy, if we allow certain entities, and conglomerates, and corporations to use the freedom we have given them to limit the freedom of the people?" Can we be a free society, if we allow a small elite the freedom to take away or limit the freedom of the people? Is this a free society?

And if you apply that evaluation to the world today, you will see that the United States of America is indeed one of the least free nations in the world. For there are few nations where a small elite has greater control of the economy and the government than in these United States.

Let the era of fiat money come to an end

Paul the Venetian, February 9, 2011.

Do you need a money system?

Why do you need a money system? Just let the money be regulated by the people themselves. Sure, this will lead to some turmoil, but is that not the only way that people will ever learn? How will they learn, if there is a government that seeks to protect them from the consequences of their own choices? And in so doing, becomes an instrument for the elite, who are really trying to protect themselves from the consequences of their own choices by getting the people to bear the karma for the choices of the elite.

This is one of the fundamental problems of democracy, of any democratic nation. But in few nations is it more important than in these United States, for how can the government be of the people, by the people and for the people unless the people do two things:

- Number one: Educate themselves to the existence of the elite and take a stand for freedom and against elitism.

- And number two: Become willing to bear the consequences of their own choices, instead of expecting the elite to make decisions for them, and their own government to protect them against the consequences of their choices.

What is the purpose of these United States? Is it to provide some physical structure of a great civilization? Is it to provide some degree of welfare or wealth? Or is it to be a path of initiation for as many people as possible?

How then will anyone learn in the current system, where the elite have encaged themselves in these mighty fortresses, where they are so insulated from the consequences of their choices, and where they can use the intellectual reasoning to always explain away or outright deny those consequences? How will the elite learn from this, when the people protect them by bearing the consequences of the choices of the elite? How will the elite learn?

And how will the people learn, when the elite has set up a system that also seeks to protect a large part of the people from the consequences of their choices? Do you not see, that this is why the elite has allowed the growth of the middle class, so that they can get more and more people to feel that they are invested in the stock market or the financial system? So that they will go along with the government, when it says that these financial institutions are "too big to fail."

Do you not see what Lanto said about the elite being like the gentleman farmer Thomas Jefferson, who sat at his comfortable estate and was not willing to give up his own slaves, for he did not want to lose his comfortable lifestyle? The elite is like that, but can you not also see, that a large part of America's middle class are like that as well?

They have now invested for so long, that they think they have all this wealth on paper or in numbers on a computer screen. And they do not want to lose this good comfortable life. And so they are willing to let a large number of their fellow citizens go into the uncertain future of unemployment. Just so that they can continue to sit there and enjoy the benefits of the system that is now protected by the government at the cost of increasing unemployment, and increasing inflation. So that those who have less will have even less, whereas those in the middle class also have less, but it really does not matter for they can still be comfortable.

Do you see, that as long as there is not that solidarity from the middle class to those who are not as fortunate, well then the United States cannot be One Nation Under God? For what is needed is that those in the middle class, who have the comfortable lifestyle, dedicate themselves to the spiritual path, so that they grasp the higher vision of equality, equal opportunity among all people. And so that they are dedicated to this, and so that they are willing to sacrifice some of their comfortable lifestyle in order to, so to speak, spread the wealth and give all a more equal opportunity.

...

The intensity of the Ruby Fire

Let those who have so far not been willing to listen, let them be awakened by the intensity of this Ruby Fire, that is so intense that it is difficult to ignore it. And thus, I speak directly into this building, where you sit there, hidden behind your security guards. And you think they can protect you against the people, but your henchmen are also of the people. And there will come a time, where you will no longer be able to trust them, as you have already seen in the leaking of documents by those who have access – and must continue to be given access – if you are to be able to continue to run your system.

For systems do not run themselves, they must be run by people. And this is the eternal dilemma of the fallen beings and the power elite. They know they cannot trust people, so they attempt to build machines and computers that are mechanical and that will carry out their bidding without any conscience. Or they attempt to reduce people to being functionally robots, the mechanized man who has no conscience, who has no heart. And therefore would carry out orders blindly without any humanitarian considerations, or any spiritual consideration.

A golden age view of what it means to be President

Gautama Buddha, February 13, 2011.

Will the United States be an empire or an example?

There is no office that is more difficult to hold in the entire world than that of being President of the United States. And this is, of course, because the United States currently has such a dominant position in the world, where it can be either the next empire that will attempt to take over the world, or it can be, truly, an example of a nation that will not be an empire, that will not have a king or an emperor. And was it not precisely this example that George Washington set for this nation, when he resigned his military commission and refused to run for a third term as President, refused to be President for Life. Do you not see that this is the example that must be understood, that must be upheld even by the current President?

For indeed, it is absolutely necessary that this nation "Under God" does not become an empire that pursues a human ambition, the ambition of the power elite, who can never get enough power. And who will, as Godfre also explained, continue to use the power available to them in a blind pursuit of their goals; their selfish, self-centered goals. And so, indeed, what has happened since the time of George Washington is that the power elite – who have attempted to manipulate the United States behind the scenes – have indeed attempted to gradually, and not noticeably, inflate the powers of the President.

How to manipulate the President

Do you not see – if you study the history of this nation – that when the original delegations formulated the division of power between the Presidency, the Congress and the Supreme Court, they gave far-reaching powers to the President. But they did this partly because they had in mind a President of the caliber of George Washington, who had already shown his willingness to surrender his ambitions relating to exercising power. And thus, they felt comfortable in giving the decisive powers to the President, without limiting them as has indeed been done in many European nations, where in some cases they do not even have a President but only a Prime Minister.

And so, you see that although Washington was able to exercise these powers in a balanced manner, other Presidents have not been equally able. And since then, what has happened is, that the Office of the President has taken on far greater powers than is healthy. And this, of course, was made even worse during the Bush presidency, especially during the so-called covert efforts of the Vice-President, Dick Cheney. Who attempted to take the use of Executive Orders and Executive Powers far beyond what is actually constitutional, or at least beyond what is the intention of the Founding Fathers and what is good for the nation.

And so, you might ask yourself: why it is that power elite have attempted to inflate the Office of the President? Well, is it not simple, my beloved? It is far easier to manipulate one President than to manipulate hundreds of Congressman or a larger number of Supreme Court judges than the one President.

Can you not see that, throughout history, there are many examples of how – when power was vested in just one person – that person was so easily deceived by his or her personal ambition into making precisely the wrong choices? And this is what the power elite knows, and thus they know that if they set up a political machinery that is simply a sorting mechanism – that sorts out those who are not willing to compromise in order to achieve their ambition – well, then they can make sure that anyone elected to the Office of President is willing to compromise in order to achieve his personal ambitions. And thus, they know they can manipulate that individual into making decisions in a crisis situation that are not good for the all.

And thus, what has happened since George Washington's time is, that the Office of the President has morphed into a position in the collective psyche that is different from what it was back then, where they often compared the president to a king or an emperor. But now the Presidency has taken on a life of its own in the American psyche, and they now look to the President as almost a god-like figure who has, they think, unlimited power.

Make an effort to stop making an effort

Elohim Purity, September 23, 2011 in Arkhangelsk, Russia

Accelerate into purity! (9 times) … the purity that I AM. Indeed, I am the masculine counterpart of Astrea, the Elohim of the fourth ray, we are. Inseparable, we are. Although Astrea has traditionally been the one speaking for the Elohim of the fourth ray, I will put in my two cents worth, as they say. Or perhaps, I should say my four cents worth.

Thus, what is it that can enable you to lock in to the flame of purity? Well, my beloved, take a look at this area, where you, little flock, have gathered, in Arkhangelsk in northern Russia, which is close to the location of the etheric retreat of Purity and Astrea. Take a look at this town, which is like an empty shell, compared to what it was in its heyday under the Soviet Union, where it was an important naval base and military center. Yet, even go back further, where it was a prosperous trade center as the only port to the Russian nation, at least the only port from Europe.

So, see then today, how there is a heavy cloud of hopelessness hanging over this area. And you may see, if you look carefully, that this cloud is indeed impurity, a special form of impurity that takes away the hope that the people can accelerate the condition they are experiencing in matter through their own power.

Control by taking away hope

This, of course, is one of the primary conditions of the fourth ray, and you will indeed see that the Archeia of the fourth ray is named Hope. And thus, those who are seeking to control humankind through a perversion of the fourth ray of purity, will always, as their primary order of business, seek to take away hope, the hope that you can transcend the current conditions by your own power.

It does not matter if people believe it is possible to transcend current conditions, if they believe it can only happen through some external power. For this will still keep the people trapped in the bind between the rock and the hard spot, meaning the rock as the matter world and the hard spot as the power elite.

And thus, you see so many societies – in so many historical periods, in so many parts of the world – where the common man, so to speak, the broader population have always felt that they were limited between these two elements, the matter world itself, which seems to be inflexible and beyond their power to change. For so they had been told by the power elite who was ruling their thought world, their identity world, the way they looked at themselves and their opportunity to transcend their current sense of self, and thereby transcend their current state in the matter world.

For, as we have explained many times, it is indeed your sense of self in the identity body that filters down to the mental body, where you think what you can and cannot do in this world. And then filters down to the emotional body, where you begin to feel hopeless, because you think you cannot do anything to change your situation. And this, of course, then filters down into your actions, where you submit yourself to some external authority or another.

Christianity and Soviet power

And thus, see how in this area you find a peculiar mixture of both Christian Orthodox churches and these monuments to Soviet power. Go back before Soviet time, and you will see that the Eastern Orthodox Church was indeed one of the primary factors that limited the people, their sense of self and their sense that they had power to improve their condition in matter.

What did the traditional Christian churches in both East and West give to the people? They gave to the people the sense that they could not transcend their conditions in this world. And thus, they had to submit both to the conditions in this world and to the power elite that had taken over the church, or at least was in a peaceful coexistence with the church and its hierarchy.

And thus, you see that Christianity has been used as an effective tool by the power elite to suppress the people, by getting them to focus on the next world. You might say that people had some hope under Christianity, that there could be an improvement of their situation. But it was a hope that was inevitably linked to the future, to an existence beyond this world.

And thus, the people did not think they had the power, nor that it was even their obligation, to improve conditions in this world. And thus, they did not speak out against their overlords in this world, be it the church or the Tzar, or the king or the emperor—or whomever it might be that was in an alliance, an unholy alliance, with the church.

So then, look at what happened with the communist takeover of this nation. You will see that most people did indeed have their faith in Christianity erased. Yet, you will also see, that even the Soviet Union allowed some existence of Christianity, because they realized that those who will not believe in Communism, would indeed still be pacified by believing in the next world and improvement of their situation in the next world, rather than in this world.

The creators of the Soviet Union had no higher principles

And so, what you see here is indeed a very simple realization, that most people in Russia have simply not come to, as of yet. And it is the fact, that those who were behind the Communist takeover and the establishment of the Soviet Union, did not have any higher principles. They did not believe that there were higher principles behind the philosophy of Karl Marx, as even Karl Marx did not believe so—even though he to some degree was so in love with the product of his own mind, as he thought it was, that he believed in at least some of it. Yet those who formulated the Soviet Union: Lenin, Trotsky and later Stalin and other leaders did not believe in Communism. They simply used Communism as a tool to suppress the people.

And if the Russian people, at least the spiritual people among them, could come to this realization and begin to consider what it truly means, then they could at least begin the process of separating themselves from the communist mindset, and therefore becoming the forerunners for allowing the Russian people to throw off the subtle thoughtforms that have been put into the collective consciousness during the years of open Communism. Whereas today, of course, you have a more hidden, a more camouflaged form of Communism.

For as many people will know, there is still very much a power elite in Russia, and even though the church has now become more prominent in society, we are actually not moving forward. We are just moving backwards to the old era, where the church and the power elite formed an alliance that suppressed the people very effectively.

And so, what I endeavor to explain here is that when you look at this from the perspective of the fourth ray of purity, you realize that what the power elite will always do, is to seek to take away the hope that the people can affect change in their material situation by their own power. And thus, they will seek to take away the belief by the people, the realization by the people, that they are more than matter, that they are spiritual beings who can be the open doors for a higher power, a higher vibration, to stream through them.

The true power to transform the world

Truly, as has been said over and over again by both Christianity and Communism, the people do not have the power on their own to transform material conditions. As even Jesus himself recognized: "I can of my own self do nothing." Yet the people do have the potential to become the open doors for the power of God, that can indeed transform material circumstances.

They can indeed transform what has become realized in matter, but has not thereby taken on any permanent reality in the mind of God. And thus, when the people embodied in matter realize that they are more than matter, then they can become the open doors for the process of true materialization, whereby matter is realized according to the thought-forms of God, and therefore transcends the thoughtforms of the fallen consciousness, that seem to have reality and permanence. Yet they are nothing more than mirages, that could be whisked away by the power of the Spirit through the fourth ray and the other rays in a surprisingly short period of time, as you measure time on earth.

Thus, if you were to look at the invocation [Loving the Divine Mother - Part 2] that you gave before this dictation, and some of the ideas expressed in it, and then compare it to what the people in this area and the people in Russia – and for that matter the people in many nations of the world – believe about themselves and the world, you would see, that they would scarcely be able to fathom the concepts encapsulated in this short invocation. For the concepts are so revolutionary, compared to both a materialistic thought system and the closed religious thought system, represented here by Christianity and Communism, but having many outer representatives throughout the world.

And thus, the people would scarcely be able to fathom the reality that they are spiritual beings, that matter does not have power over them. And that therefore, no matter what conditions they face in the matter world – or in their physical bodies, or in their personal situation, or in the national situation on the world scale – no matter what conditions they face, they always have the potential to become the open door for the power of Spirit, that can accelerate those conditions into a higher state.

The catch-22 of purity

Yet of course, how shall the people become the open doors? For here we have another example of the typical Catch-22. How do you become the open door for the stream of purity? Well, indeed, when you are trapped in the consciousness of duality and separation – when you are trapped in the impure self-awareness of thinking you are a product of matter or trapped in matter – then you cannot be the open door for the stream of purity. And how will you ever transcend that self-awareness, unless indeed you encounter the energy of purity, the Spirit of Purity?

So you see, once you have lost the experience of purity, you cannot even believe that you could be an open door for the stream of purity. And if you do not believe you can be an open door for the stream of purity, how can you then experience purity?

For you will see many spiritual people, who have followed the spiritual path for many years, even decades. And they give rosaries and invocations and decrees and do other spiritual exercises, and they think that one day they will become open to this flow, to this experience, of a higher form of energy. But they do not realize that this experience will not come from some external savior or their guru, who claims to be the embodiment of some deity. Nay, it will never come from an external source.

You can experience this flow of the Spirit, only when you experience the Spirit flowing through you, by you becoming an open door. And so again, how can you cut that Gordian knot, how can you escape this Catch-22? Well, you can do so only by coming to an understanding and acceptance of some teaching that portrays you as what you truly are. And this teaching has been given by the Ascended Host in many variations over the years and millennia. But it has always been in a veiled form, although in some cases very thinly veiled.

We recently directed this messenger to find a teaching by, Padma Sambhava, [Self-Liberation through Seeing with Naked Awareness.] given in the eighth century, where he at that time talked about concepts that are strikingly similar to what we have given through this messenger today, namely the concept that when you still the thoughts, when you go beyond the outer identity created by your mind, created in your mind, then you see that behind these outer confusing thoughts, there is only pure awareness. This of course, is an expression we have used recently through this messenger, and before it we have even used the concept of a Conscious You, that is also simply pure awareness—and therefore is the open door.

So you see, the fallacy of so many religions and spiritual movements is that they think, that in order for you to experience the flow of the Spirit, you have to perfect be outer self, you have to perfect the self that the mind has created. But as Jesus himself said, no man can ascend to heaven save he that descended from heaven. Thus, what can be the open door is not the outer self, no matter how sophisticated or spiritual you think it might be, no matter how well it lives up to some standard created here on earth, a standard that will inevitably have originated with the fallen beings and their attempts to deceive humankind.

There is only one way to experience the flow of the Spirit, and that is to realize that you need to return to your original form as pure awareness. And then you can realize, that even though you have built an outer self, that you have to a large degree identified with, you can still at any moment – if you can find a way to transcend your fixation on the outer mind – you can still step outside of that identity and experience glimpses of pure awareness.

And once you experience even a glimpse of pure awareness, then you have a new frame of reference, and then that pure awareness becomes your frame of reference. And this will then allow you to gradually – and perhaps through many intricate and subtle steps – free yourself from the standard of the fallen beings, where your frame of reference for escaping what the fallen beings have defined as impurity is a standard that they have defined as purity.

So in order to transcend one form of impurity, you are striving to attain another form of impurity, that the fallen beings have simply called purity, because they have captured what might be called the privilege of formulating the problem. Which is certainly something that Karl Marx, Hegel and many of the early communist philosophers understood and made use of.

Marx defined both Communism and Capitalism

And so, you see, again, what did Marx do? He defined Communism as an ideology that was locked in a battle with its polar opposite, namely Capitalism. But who was talking about Capitalism before Marx? It was not a common understanding, and thus you see that what Marx did was not simply define Communism as opposed to something that was already existing. Nay, he defined both opposing polarities, both Capitalism and Communism.

And if you look honestly at this, you will see that even in the West, there are many people who will swear all day and night that they are true–blood capitalists. Yet they are still trapped in the dualistic thought system of thinking that Capitalism is opposed to Communism. Which of course it is, because Capitalism has no reality, it has no existence in the mind of God. It is entirely a creation of man, namely the power elite. And so, what you see, when you look at this honestly, is that the power elite have defined both Capitalism and Communism and the struggle between them, in their attempts to pacify the people, so that they will submit to the elite.

My beloved, why did Communism fall, so to speak? Well, this is not a question that is truly relevant. The relevant question to ask is why was Communism allowed to fall? Well, it was simply because the power elite, the global power elite, realized that Communism was not the most efficient way to suppress the people.

Communism was an attempt to suppress the people through direct force by state control, where the state was clearly seen as the controlling agency. Capitalism, on the other hand, was an attempt to suppress the people in a subtle way, where the state is still the controlling agency but the people do not see this. They even think that the state is there to protect them against the capitalists. But in reality, of course, the capitalists control the state behind the artificially created façade in the theater that the fallen beings have created on Earth.

So you see, for decades it was an open question who would end up ruling the world. Would Communism be able to forcefully take over most of the world, or would it eventually self-destruct? And so you see, that after the fall, so to speak, of Communism, it was believed that Communism had failed. And it was believed by many in the West, that this had proven the superiority of Capitalism.

Yet beginning with the financial crisis in 2008, would it be unreasonable to say that Capitalism is also in the process of failing? And thus, can we really say that Capitalism proved its superiority to Communism, or should we rather accelerate the entire debate and realize that both Capitalism and Communism are impure expressions; they are perversions of the Alpha and the Omega, the expanding and the contracting forces.

A new approach to the economy

And thus, it is necessary to step away from this fixation on the polarized dualistic debate and realize that you are pure awareness. And thus, those of you who know a little about the economy can, by making contact with that pure awareness at your core, become the open doors for the bringing forth of the ideas that will accelerate the economy beyond Capitalism and Communism—and thereby have an opportunity to finally set the people free from being dominated by the elite through money and the entire financial system and the production apparatus of society.

This then, would certainly be a great gift for those, even though they may never hear this dictation, who have the knowledge and the experience of the financial world and who also have the ability and the willingness to tune in to their own pure awareness, regardless of what they call it, regardless of whether they have any spiritual understanding or framework in their outer minds.

Thus you, who do have an awareness of your spiritual nature and of the Ascended Host, might volunteer to hold the immaculate concept, to hold the vision, that the very people who have the potential to bring forth these new financial realizations, will indeed be able to tune in and will indeed have the courage to speak out. And that they will indeed be heard by those who have the potential to spread these ideas in the fields of science, in the economy, in the media and in the political field—even among the people. Who will finally have had enough and stand up and demand more, by using their own built-in power to know, that if they are pure awareness, they are not bound by the material conditions they face, they are not bound by the overlords of the power elite, for they have the potential to be the open door. Whether they have any outer expertise, they can be the open door for the light, and as the light increases, there will be transcendence in society—it cannot be any other way.

And thus, I Purity hereby release a mighty impetus from the Astrea and Purity retreat. We release it throughout the world; we release it to all of those who are open to the fourth ray. And there are many millions of people on earth, who are open to the fourth ray.

Stop thinking you are more sophisticated than others

Thus, let me give you one final thought, that will enable those of you who are willing to transcend your current image, to be an open door for the stream of purity. For you may look at the people throughout the world, who are not spiritual and would never be open to spiritual teachings—or so you think. You may look at those, as I said, who would find it extremely difficult to even fathom the concepts given in this rosary, for they are so far away from their common beliefs about life. And you may think that these people are at a lower state of consciousness than you are. You may think they are not as sophisticated, because they do not have your spiritual understanding.

Yet my beloved, I can assure you, that if this world is to be accelerated into a Golden Age, it will not be done by the people who know about the AskRealJesus website alone. It will not be done by the people who know about the ascended masters alone. It will not be done by the people who know any spiritual teaching. There are not enough people who have an outer knowledge of spiritual teachings, that they can accelerate society by themselves.

For the law of free will would not allow it, unless a critical mass among the 80% of the general population are likewise accelerated. And thus, the vision you can hold is this: no matter how sophisticated you think you are, no matter how sophisticated you think your knowledge and understanding of ascended master concepts might be, you are not more sophisticated that any other person on this planet.

Why is this so? What is it that could be considered sophisticated compared to someone else? My beloved, it can only be your outer self, the outer self you have built in this world—and that most of you have even used a spiritual or even an ascended master teaching to build, making you think you are sophisticated because you can explain this or that concept. But what have I said is the key to a transformation? It is the stream of the Spirit. What is the key to being the open door for the stream of the Spirit? It is that you return to the pure awareness with which you descended.

And I can assure you, that the pure awareness with which you descended is no more or no less sophisticated than the pure awareness of any other human being. Do you see: in pure awareness there can be no comparisons? So how can you even talk about the Conscious You of one person being more sophisticated, or more evolved, or more spiritual than the Conscious You of another person? It is not possible; it is not meaningful for those who have begun to see beyond the veil of duality.

And thus, as spiritual people, you can hold the immaculate concept that all people on earth have pure awareness at their core. And you can hold the vision, that they will gradually come to a realization, or that they will have a spontaneous contact, a spontaneous experience, of this pure awareness. And thereby, they will, even if they do not consciously understand it, be the open door for a measure of light to flow into the physical octave. And this is what will bring about the change.

For you see, what you have the potential to do – those of you who have a spiritual understanding – is that you can hold the vision for how the light should be directed into specific conditions on Earth. But even though you can also be open door for the light, you are not allowed by the Law of Free Will to provide the entire impetus of light that will accelerate society. It is only when a critical mass among the population also become the open door, that society will truly be accelerated. And of course, I am not saying that this has not already happened to some degree, which is why you have seen positive change in society.

Incomparable self-worth

Nevertheless, I encourage you to ponder these ideas, for I tell you, that far too many spiritual people, far too many ascended master students, are still trapped in the superiority game of seeking to establish some sense of self-worth, by feeling they are more sophisticated than others spiritually. Yet, when you begin to experience yourself as pure awareness, you establish a natural sense of self-worth. Because you realize, that you do not need to live up to any conditions on Earth, any standard defined by the fallen angels, in order to have self-worth in the eyes of God. God is holding the immaculate concept for you with infinite, incomparable self–worth.

And the only way to have true self-worth is to accept yourself as that Conscious You, that is simply pure awareness—and therefore cannot be defined by any conditions, by any words, by any images, by any standard. There may be those who think they can apply some standard to the Conscious You, to pure awareness. But it is only because they have not understood it, and they have not understood it because you cannot understand it.

You either experience it, or you do not experience it. If you do not experience it, you think you can understand what it is by projecting your own standard upon it. But that only proves, that you have not experienced it. And those who do not experience, do not actually understand—even though they think they understand. But they understand only according to their own standard, or to the standard they have accepted from the fallen beings.

So once you begin to experience pure awareness, you have that ultimate frame of reference. And now you begin to see how unreal, how impure, the standard of the fallen beings truly is. For this is, of course, the essence of purity, that there is no standard that can divide purity into two spheres: what is pure, what is impure. It has been said for many centuries, that to the pure everything is pure, and it is because everything is a matter of perception.

When you see, when you perceive, the world through the separate self that is trapped, defined, by the dualistic opposites, then you see the world with polluted perception. And as the Buddha said so many centuries ago, then suffering will surely follow. Only those who see with pure perception, will not be suffering. But what does it mean to see with pure perception? It means that you see with the purity of being the open door, where you see that all of the conditions in this world are ultimately unreal, impermanent. And thus, they have no power over you.

It is not a matter of avoiding what is impure and striving to outpicture what is pure. It is a matter of dropping the whole ball of wax of the fallen beings. And this is indeed what the Buddha explained 2,500 years ago, what Padma Sambhava explained in the treatise that I mentioned earlier. For those who have eyes to see, this truth has been there in a physical form for thousands of years. Thus, make an effort to stop making an effort to become a sophisticated spiritual being.

Instead, step back from all your desires to make an effort, and realize that what it takes is the non–effort of stopping the outer mind that always wants to make an effort to reach some goal. And thus, allow yourself to just be the open door, and then flow with the Spirit, as it flows through you. For this is indeed the highest form of purity you can express in this world.

Let the Latvians be wise as serpents, without becoming indecisive

Lord Lanto, October 30, 2011.

The international power elite created the Iron Curtain

This, of course, is not to say, that this is the only course. For there are indeed some nations that could and will benefit from being merged with others, or even being split up into one or several regions. Nevertheless, the vision we give for the Baltic region is indeed one of cooperation across national borders and boundaries. It is one that will bring together East and West, and that will truly accelerate the process of merging East and West that has been going on since the Iron Curtain came down.

For truly, as we have mentioned before, this was an artificial division of the European continent. And it must be stated bluntly, that this division clearly was not in the better interest of the people. It was designed and perpetrated by the international power elite, who at the time had a strong influence on governments in both the Soviet Union, England and the United States. And thus, what happened at the Malta Conference, between Stalin, Churchill and Roosevelt was indeed not in any way the design of the Ascended Host.

It was the design of the fallen beings, to divide and thereby weaken Europe, and thereby delay the process of unification and cooperation, that is indeed the design of the Ascended Host, and has been so since Saint Germain took physical embodiment for the purpose of establishing a United States of Europe. Again, his attempts back then were thwarted by the fallen beings – the kings and the international elite – that had already then begun to think that it was able to run the world behind the scenes, without ever being noticed and therefore held accountable by the people.

The financial crisis was an accident by design

And so, it must be stated also that the financial crisis was not just an accident that happened. It was indeed an accident by design, for it was the international power elite that again precipitated the bubble economy in their attempt to delay the process of a unification of Europe. For they knew that by artificially pumping money into some of the new developing economies in the eastern european countries, then they could precipitate a crash that would delay the true unification and cooperation between East and West.

For you see – with all we have said about the duality consciousness – that the power elite must seek to create these artificial divisions wherever possible. And certainly, the Soviet occupation of Eastern Europe was by their design. And even powerful people in the United States thought that this would be in the interest of the U.S., in order to prevent a united Europe from becoming stronger economically and politically, even militarily, than the United States.

For back then, the leaders of the United States thought they were so far ahead of the Soviet Union, that they could hold them in check. Yet they did not realize how the power elite behind the scenes manipulated events, so that the Soviet Union very quickly could develop nuclear weapons and therefore attain, not necessarily military parity with the United States, but certainly a strength that guaranteed that the Cold War would go on for decades and decades.

Just imagine, what would have happened if the Eastern European nations had remained independent after the Second World War. Just imagine how much greater abundance there would have been in these nations, if personal initiative had not been destroyed by the Soviet brainwashing machine. Just imagine how the attempts of unification that you have seen in Western Europe with the EU, could have spread East of the Iron Curtain decades ago. And how by now, the poverty that you see in the eastern european nations could have been completely unknown, as these nations would have been almost on parity economically with the western nations.

This would have been a great advantage, not only to the continent of Europe but to the world as a whole. For Europe has the potential to be the balancing factor between East and West. Thus, it was indeed the fallen beings who saw the necessity of precipitating the Bolshevik revolution, so that the Soviet Union would be formed and thereby Russia would be shut out from becoming part of Europe, as it was envisioned by Peter the Great so long ago.

Seeing the skull and the rose with naked awareness

PadmaSambhava, November 27, 2011.

The fallen beings have an easy task

For do you not begin to see, with all the teachings we have given, that the fallen beings had a very simple task before them, when they decided to oppose God and pull everyone down into this seemingly endless spiral of actions and reaction? Do you not see that they had to do only one thing: they had to create an action that was beyond what you, as a newly incarnated being on earth, were expecting?

Once they had shocked you with something you did not expect, then it was so easy for you to feel that you had to react to this. And in the beginning, you reacted slightly. But as the actions from them kept coming relentlessly, you eventually crossed a line, where you did not even react. But now you started thinking, that because what they were doing was wrong, you had to take action to stop the wrong, to right the wrong.

And thus, you started projecting out your own action. And then other people started reacting to your action. And this shocked you even more, because you felt that you had only the best of intentions. So why were they reacting to you telling them what to do? Well, my beloved, they were reacting for the same reason that you started reacting. And it is a very simple mechanism, once you understand—once you see, once you experience, once you have the frame of reference from the true guru, who is not in duality, and thus can give you that transfer of light that is the only antidote to the poisons of duality.

The simple fact is this: You were instructed by the true guru, that when you venture into the realm where free will is the ultimate law, you cannot allow yourself to have expectations of what should or should not happen. Yet what happened to many – and my beloved, it is perfectly understandable that this happened – do you perhaps sense strictness in my voice? It is because I am intending to cut through the density of the layers that have been built in the mass consciousness. But that intensity is also the Ruby Ray fire of love, and originally there was only the most tender love.

For we understand, all of us, how difficult it is to go into this realm. We understand how subtle the temptation is presented by the dualistic mind. Nevertheless, I am here not to condemn and put down, but to give you the key to escaping duality. And there is only one key, and it is to recognize the following: You were instructed by the guru that in this realm, free will reigns supreme. Thus, you have a sphere of your free will, and that is your mind.

Creating an action to influence the choices of others

Nevertheless, it is possible to use your mind to create an action and to project that outside your mind, for the deliberate purpose of influencing other minds. You knew that you could not allow yourself to expect that you would not be exposed to this. For it was virtually inevitable, that you would be exposed to someone outside of your mind, outside the sphere of your free will, who would project an action against you, for the deliberate purpose of changing something inside your sphere of free will, of changing your mind, of changing your choices, of influencing your choices.

And thus, what happened to so many was that they gradually forgot this instruction. And again, there is no blame here. It is simply something that happened. It happened because you made a choice. As Maitreya explains in his book, for each lifestream there was an individual reason for why you made the choice. No reason was wrong, no reason was better than another—it was your reason.

When you discover that individual reason, you have the option to change it. But you will not be able to discover it, unless you start looking inside yourself. And in order to start looking, you must break the cycle of action and reaction. And therefore, you must realize a simple truth, taught by the Buddha and all who are of the lineage of the Buddha: Whatever other people do to you, there is no natural law, or spiritual law, that says that you have to react to this.

This must be understood as being solely in the mind. It is entirely possible, if someone attacks you, to take evasive action or even to protect yourself. But this outer action still does not mean that you have to react inside your mind, by creating mental and emotional patterns that remain in the mind, even when the outer action is no more.

You see, it is entirely possible – as demonstrated by the Buddha, as demonstrated by Jesus – to be in the world but not of the world, to experience the actions that come at you from other beings without having an internal reaction—that creates a pattern in you that gradually builds a momentum. Until the pattern, the emotional and mental energies, become so strong, that you lose control of your mind. You lose control of your reactions.

And now you begin to think, that either in order to protect yourself, or in order to protect God's plan, or promote some ultimate cause, you have to take action. You have to change the people who are seeking to change you, for you have now come to believe in the lie that something is right and something is wrong. And thus, what you experience them doing to you is wrong, and you must right that wrong.

Being deceived by good intentions

Do you see, how is it possible that so many people throughout the ages have had the best of intentions of doing God's work, but they have been trapped into still using methods that were clearly against their own religious scriptures, or the universal knowing of what is right to do to another? For, of course, you all know that in some sense it is not right for one being to interfere with the free will of another. But you also need to know, that in this realm, where free will reigns supreme, it is inevitable that you will be exposed to this.

And so, what you need to do is, instead of trying to change the choices and actions of others, you focus exclusively on yourself. And you focus on not reacting, not creating a reactionary pattern. And when you have created patterns – as of course all of us did, when we were in embodiment, dealing with the physical realm – then you strive to immediately unravel the pattern.

If you will reach enlightenment, if you will make your ascension in this lifetime, if you will attain peace of mind, if you will fulfill your highest potential, you need to make a choice, a decision, to start unraveling the patterns of action and reaction. You think you have to react, when other people do or say certain things. You think you have to act, even in a long-term way, where you think that doing God's work means seeking to influence others. And thus, YOU project an influence out from your mind.

You need to ponder the subtle distinction, for you need, of course, to come to the realization, that the fruit of the knowledge of good and evil precisely symbolizes the main feature of the dualistic mind: that there is no absolute statement, no absolute argument. You can take words and twist them to argue for or against any viewpoint, any issue.

Do you not see, that the scribes and Pharisees twisted words to argue against the living Christ, when he stood before them in the flesh? Do you not see, throughout the ages, that all true gurus have faced some among their supposed students, who came only to argue at the level of words, to twist words, to project out an interpretation.

So you cannot truly discern truth and error based on words. You cannot judge a person, you cannot discern a person, based on the words that they say, and especially not the words that they write. And thus, you need to look beyond the words, and you have the ability to tune in and sense not only people's vibration, but their intent. You can, when you begin to become aware of the pattern of action and reaction in your own mind, you also begin to build the discernment where you can sense this in others.

Attracting a false guru

You can instantly sense when someone comes at you, and perhaps they speak seemingly neutral or kind words, but behind it is an intent of influencing your free will, of tying in to whatever patterns of action and reaction you have in your mind, and seeking to use it to get you to react—and therefore take a certain action, that they want to project into your mind. Thus, do you not see, that as long as you are trapped, fully identified with this pattern of action and reaction, you will – according to the age-old law that when the student is ready the teacher appears – you will inevitably attract to you, or attract yourself to, what we might call a false guru.

For the saying that when the student is ready, the teacher appears, of course, means that the student is always ready for some teacher. And the teacher that appears is the teacher, that the student can see with its present level of consciousness. And so, when you are trapped, fully identified with the pattern of action and reaction, you can only see a guru who is also in this pattern, but who has taken it to a more extreme level than yourself. And therefore, he is willing to project at his students what they should do, what actions and reactions they should have to his teachings—or to some problem in life that he projects that they need to solve.

And thus, it is only when you begin to see this pattern of action and reaction in your life, that you can magnetize yourself to what we might – of course, with an artificial choice of words – call a true guru. In other words, a guru who has at least begun to see and dis-identify from these patterns. And this is, then, when you can become open to a teaching that comes from the lineage of the true gurus, the gurus who are not teaching because they have a pattern of action and reaction that they need to project. They are teaching because they are not projecting; they are sharing their Presences, like the sun is sharing its light.

The sun is not shining upon earth for the purpose of influencing human beings. The sun is the sun; it would shine even if there were no planets orbiting it. For it is a self-luminous orb, the open door between the material and the higher realms. It simply shines, for that is its joy. The teacher teaches, for that is his or her joy. It is an expression of who they are.

And that is why one of the subtle traps of many students is to look at a certain teacher, look at the outer teaching, look at the words or the choice of words, look at the concepts, look at the teacher himself – his looks, his dress, his manners, his this, his that – and they focus on the outer form of the teacher, instead of realizing that the outer form is just a vehicle and that the outer form is not nearly as important as the fact, that this form is transparent enough to let something from beyond shine through.

And even if the outer form of the teacher appears to be less than perfect according to your standard, then your standard is a product of the patterns of action and reaction you have in your mind. So if you seek to project your standard upon the teacher, how can you make use of that teacher? For the only way to make use of a teacher is to see, that there is a light shining through the outer form of the teacher—and then reach for that light, follow that light. Follow the light, my beloved. You know how in the world they say: "Follow the money," but I say: "Follow the light!"

Look beyond the outer form of the teacher and the teaching, whatever teaching or teacher it may be. Follow the light that is shining through. And it is through that light, that you will have a frame of reference, that will empower you to transcend the patterns of reaction and action that keep you trapped at your current level of consciousness. For it is only when you sense that there is something beyond, shining through the teacher, that you are able to step outside of those patterns in your mind—and thus, suddenly, experience that moment of pure awareness.

The importance of pure awareness

And what is the importance of you experiencing pure awareness? It is because when you experience pure awareness, you become the open door for the light. And thus, you can realize, that the light that you have so far seen shining through the teacher, can now shine through you. And thus, you have made the ultimate use of the teacher, by realizing that when you follow a teacher to the point where you embody the teaching, you embody the light, then you become the next link in the chain of the true gurus.

You become a teacher yourself, even if you are not perfect. For when you have at least glimpses of pure awareness, going beyond this reactionary and action pattern, then you become an open door to the light. And then you can give some measure of that light to someone else.

Anchoring a mighty Pillar of Freedom in Central Asia

Saint Germain, December 29, 2011.

Why the capitalist system is failing

It is not a truly good intention, if you think you want to set people free, but you think this can only be done by forcing them into a system. You see, my beloved, I am not sitting up here in the spiritual realm with a plan for the coming Golden Age that is a closed system. It is not my goal to get everyone to follow a certain system, even a certain outer teaching. As it is of not our goal to get everyone on earth to follow an ascended master teaching, whether given through this messenger or any other messenger, past, present or future. The coming Age of Aquarius the coming age of Saint Germain is the age of the Holy Spirit—and the Holy Spirit blows where it listeth.

It cannot be predicted by the linear, analytical, human mind, it cannot be fit into any system created by the analytical, linear, human mind. And thus, those who seek to come up with the ultimate system, will simply fall away from atunement with the Freedom Flame that I am. And thus, they will be left behind, when more and more people become willing to flow, flow, flow, with the Spirit, flow with the light, my beloved.

What is it you see in the financial crisis, that is rolling around the world? It is simply this: the capitalist system is no longer working. Neither, of course, could the communist system have solved the current economic problems. There is no system that you can apply, for you must flow with the Spirit without knowing where you are going next. And this is, of course, what the power elites of the world do not want to see happen.

For what is it they have been trying to do now, in the capitalist world for so long? They have been trying to create a hidden system, whereby they could control the economy, they could control the stock market, they could control the currencies and make them go up or down at their will. So that they had control: when there was an upswing, when there was a downswing—and thus they could profit from both the upswing and the downswing.

In fact, they could only profit by creating these artificial upswings and downswings, for they – the power elite – do not profit by a steady growth that is indeed the highest potential of the economy. And thus, what you see is that those economies, those nations, that seek to hold on to the old ways will indeed find it almost impossible to solve their financial situation, to solve these problems. And only those who are willing to think beyond the old patterns, who are willing to flow with it, will be able to weather this financial crisis and come out stronger in the end.

The economy of the Holy Spirit

For of course, when the systems fall, then the power elite will always cry out. And they will try to make the people believe, that the systems are too big to fail, that they must be propped up with the money from the people in order to avoid some calamity or other. But I tell you, it is all a smokescreen. For when the systems created by the power elite fall, then the Holy Spirit has room to flow. And there is no better economy than the economy of the Holy Spirit. That is: there is no better economy for the people than the economy of the Spirit. For it is, of course, not the best economy for the elite—for they cannot predict where it will go.

They want something for nothing, and that is a principle that does not work in life—nor does it work on the spiritual path. We of the Ascended Host are surely seeking to raise humankind to a higher level of consciousness, but we are not seeking to do this by releasing so much light from our octave, that it would force people to raise their consciousness. That is why we respect the Law of Free Will, that is why we will only release light through the hearts of those who are willing to apply themselves to a spiritual path and a spiritual practice.

...

The toxic ideas of the fallen beings

For what the fallen beings have been doing, for eons of time on this planet, is to seek to entrap the people, by radiating certain ideas into the mass consciousness that have much the same effect in consciousness as nuclear radiation has in the physical body. Where the radiation breaks down the very structure of the atom itself; the very building block of the physical body is rent apart by the nuclear radiation.

And yet, you have a parallel in the emotional, in the mental and in the etheric realm, where you have certain ideas that spring from the serpentine mind that have the same effect as physical radiation. They shake apart the fabric of the emotional body, of the mental body, of the identity body. And thus, you lose that inner sense that you are more than mechanized man, that you are more than a mechanical robot, more than a human, material being. You forget; you do not dare to believe—and thus you come to doubt your origin. And you believe that these toxic, nuclear, radioactive ideas have some kind of power over you or your society, or that you owe them some kind of allegiance, my beloved.

And so, there is no argument, there is no reasoning that could be presented, that would counteract the effects of this radiation, this fallout in the mind. The only antidote is the light itself, the light of freedom. And that is precisely why, as I have been speaking these words in the physical, I have anchored a mighty pillar of the Freedom Flame precisely at the center of the nuclear testing site, so that it will begin to consume the effects in the four lower bodies of the earth, and begin to radiate out the antidote to the effect in the consciousness of the people in this area.

Is there any injustice in the universe?

Portia, the Goddess of Justice, May 30, 2011

Vajra Vajra Vajra Vajra Vajra!

Thus, let it be known, that, I, the Goddess of Justice, have taken up my abode on this Earth in a more tangible manifestation than ever before. For I have decided that it is time to add a momentum of divine justice – the flame, the living flame, the streaming flame of divine justice – to this Earth. For indeed, one of the major challenges facing humankind, and facing individual spiritual seekers, is to solve the enigma of justice, to find out what is justice and what is injustice. And indeed, to ponder the larger question: "Is there are any injustice in the universe?"

The Goddess of Justice is the office that I hold. Portia is the name you have been given, but I am, of course, far more than you can fathom by hearing a name or by hearing the title of an office. For indeed, is it not so that one of the things we have attempted to help you see – in the releases we have given through this messenger now for quite some time – is that the major challenge on Earth is indeed the fact that people's perception has distorted their view of reality. Because people have come to believe that a limited, a colored, a biased perception is the same as reality.

Thus, one might indeed talk about the spiritual path as a process that has several turning points. And one of the major turning points is when you come to that level, where you are willing to begin pondering the question: "Is what I see truly reality? Or is what I see, a distorted image?" And then, beyond this, the even larger question: "Can my current perception show me reality? Or do I need to go beyond my current perception in order to know reality?"

How can you know reality?

And as we have attempted to help you see, the answer to these questions is, indeed, that your current perception is not showing you reality, and that you can never know reality as long as you think you have to look only through your current perception. For it is, indeed, your perception that you have to overcome before you can know reality.

For how do you know reality? You do not know reality through the outer mind, through the separate, linear, analytical mind, that can only operate with objects that it sees as being remote and separate from itself. The outer mind can only know at a distance. Yet in order to truly know, you must come into oneness with what it is you seek to know. But you cannot come into oneness with an object.

You can come into oneness only by you letting go of the outer mind – the separate sense of identity – and coming back to the state of pure awareness. And from that state of pure awareness, you can come into oneness with the consciousness behind objects or with the consciousness that is beyond objects. And thus, you can know through gnosis; not through perception and understanding.

So then, how would you come to know divine justice? Well, only through gnosis, through becoming the open door, whereby this spiritual flame of divine justice can stream through you into this world. But you see, becoming the open door for a spiritual flame requires you to completely empty yourself from the outer perception, based on your view of the flame that you are seeking to come into oneness with.

What is divine justice?

So, let us take a look at the concept of justice, even the concept of divine justice. The image that most people have in their minds concerning divine justice, is of a female figure, in flowing robes who is holding the scales, one being lower than the other. And then, this female figure has a piece of cloth wrapped over her eyes, for she is supposedly blind.

Well, my beloved, is this an accurate depiction of divine justice? Am I, the Goddess of Justice, really blind? Do I not see? Oh indeed, I do see everything that is going on on Earth. It is, indeed, the dream of the ego, that divine justice should be blind, so that the ego can hide itself behind an outer facade, an outer definition, a mental image of what is divine justice.

From the very moment that the first beings fell in that fourth sphere, they have attempted to set themselves up as the ones who define what is divine justice and what is not. And thus, it is their dream – the dream of the fallen beings – that the Goddess of Justice should be blind.

But I am not blind. I see all, and there is nothing that you or anyone else can hide from me. Do you really think, I can be fooled by anything on Earth? Oh yes, my beloved, there are many people in embodiment who believe that I can be fooled—who believe that they can hide from God what they can hide from each other. This is a state of consciousness that colors your perception, because you think you have become as a god defining good and evil.

Do you not realize—well perhaps you do not realize, but then it is time, that you begin to question, whether the Bible is the infallible word of God. For indeed, I can tell you, that the story in Genesis about how the serpent tempted Eve into eating the forbidden fruit was not written by God. It was written by the fallen beings. It is the fallen beings who have attempted to create man in their image and likeness. For, if you take on the image and likeness of the fallen beings, then you too are trapped in the duality of knowing good and evil, of thinking you are a God who can define what is good and evil—what is just an unjust.

Yet, this is a state of consciousness that is based on separation and duality, and therefore it is fundamentally different from divine justice. For what is divine justice? Well, you cannot understand divine justice unless you understand free will. And yet the fallen beings have done everything they could think of – and in fairness they can think of quite a lot – to make sure that no one on Earth understands free will.

It is essential to understand free will

Again, of course, you cannot truly understand free will as a remote concept. You can come into oneness with the River of Life, so that you are flowing with it. And then, you will know that free will truly is free. It is free to express whatever the Presence wants to express on Earth, and it is free from all the constraints created by the fallen beings, by the mass consciousness and by your own ego.

You cannot be free to express your will freely, as long as you think you have to live up to any standard on Earth. And of course, when God first gave self-aware beings free will, it was not the Creator's intention that they live up to any standard on Earth, as the Earth was not even in existence. And as the first beings had not fallen, and so there were no beings in the fallen consciousness to impose any standard upon the beings with free will.

But do you not see, that it is only the dualistic mind that can create, that can define, a standard for what is good and evil, just and unjust? It is only the separate mind that creates a standard.

This is what we have attempted to help you see, since Mother Mary first released her wonderful book about the abundant life, where she gave the concept that you are not a self that can be defined according to any standard or mental image on Earth. You are a self that has no earthly, no worldly, no form-based definition. For, you are pure awareness. You are designed to be the open door and nothing more.

You see, my beloved, as a wise student on the path, you need to come to another turning point, where you realize that words have inherent limitations. Read the beginning of Maitreya's book if you are not fully familiar with the limitations of words. Any word can be twisted and turned, and you can use words to support just about any argument you desire.

There are those, my beloved, who love to use words as weapons against their fellow man, playing some power game of trying to convince them or force them. You will see these throughout history, you would see Jesus being up against them, you will see the Buddha engaging them somewhat without engaging them at all. And you will see that they always come up, whenever the Living Christ appears in any form. There are the wordsmiths, the word twisters who will seek to use clever interpretations of words against the Living Christ. You find them everywhere, you find them anywhere, where the Living Christ appears.

So you have a choice to make: will you twist and turn words, or will you go beyond words? Will you become the open door, that you may experience the reality of what it is you seek to know, such as divine justice?

Is there any injustice in the universe? How can there be, when the ultimate law of the world of form is free will? Do you not understand that free will is free? And it is individual.

You are an individualized extension of the Creator—you were not created as a separate being, but as an extension of the Creator. Yet, the moment you were individualized, you were given completely free will to experience anything you desire to experience. And you were then sent into a world, that has the potential to give you any experience you desire, because the Ma-ter light can take on any form that is projected upon it. And the Mother – the Divine Mother – has vowed to take on any form, so that you can have any experience you desire. This is the simplest, the most basic form of divine justice.

No choice without consequences

You are free to create any mental image you like, and to project that image upon the mother light, and then the mother light will reflect back to you circumstances in the world of form, that reflect the image you have projected. This is the most basic form of divine justice—what you sow that shall you also reap.

Can it be any more simple? Yet, those of you who have been willing to study and apply the teachings on non-duality, that we have been giving now for several years, should be open to understanding a secret that very few people have understood. It is the essence of how the fallen beings – or should I even say: the fallen consciousness – has tricked self-aware beings into the endless struggle.

Do you not see, what I have just told you? You can take two different viewpoints, my beloved. You can look at life from the inside of your current situation, your current state of consciousness, your current perception. Or you can use your ability to return to pure awareness, so that you can see the big picture and look at life from the outside.

So let us then step outside of the mental boxes and look at the big picture! What have I just explained about how free will and the universe works? You have completely free will, but how do you actually exercise your will? You exercise your will by making choices! But what are choices? If you are walking down the road and you come to a point, where the road forks into a Y, you are now facing a choice: Should I take the right or the left road.

Yet, what if this road simply forks for a time, goes through two tunnels that are exactly alike, and then the two branches of the road merge back into the same point. In that case, do you actually have a choice, given that following either road gives you the exact same experience and brings you to the exact same place. In other words, whether you choose the right or the left, there is no difference; it has no consequence! And in that case, do you really have a choice?

Yet, if the roads now go off in different directions, give you different views, different experiences and take you to different places, then you can indeed be said to have a choice. But why do you have a choice? Because there are different consequences, depending on which road you take. So what makes it possible for you to exercise your will, is that there are consequences of whether you do this or do that. If there were no consequences, you could not exercise will!

And so, how do you produce consequences? You make the choice, to form a certain mental image, then you project it upon the Ma-ter light, and the matter light takes on the form of your image. Thus, you produce your own consequence, my beloved. This is a truth that is very difficult for most people to accept.

It is completely impossible for the ego and the separate self to accept this concept. For the ego will never – ever – take responsibility for producing consequences. And in a sense, you cannot blame the ego for this, when you understand why the ego was created. So, let us take a look at this.

How planetary units evolve

Of course, it is all well and good for me to say that you have individual free will and you produce your own consequences. Yet, as the old saying goes, no man is an island. The reality is, that you were not created as a single individual, sent into an entire world, where you are the only being and therefore you are the only one making choices. You were created as part of a large group of beings, that were sent to some planetary system in the material world. And thus, you would exercise your free will within the context of a larger whole, where there were many other individual beings also exercising their individual will.

This is actually a mechanism that ensures more rapid growth, because if you were all alone in your own separate world, it is very possible that you would get yourself into a state of mind, where you were highly comfortable and you could stay there for an indefinite period of time. And thus, how would you fulfill the original purpose for creating you, namely that you grow in self-awareness until you reach the level of God consciousness? And so, in the infinite wisdom of the Creator, it was clear that by creating many individual beings and putting them together in some greater whole, such as on a planet, then they would make more rapid progress by observing each other or even, if they chose to enter a certain state of consciousness, clashing with each other.

And so, what has happened in most of these – should we call them planetary units – that you find in this material universe, is that after a long period of experimentation and conflict, a certain coherence has emerged. There are, of course, millions and millions of planets with intelligent life throughout the material universe. And the vast majority of them have indeed gone through this period of initial, what scientists like to call chaos. But which is truly just the outplaying of free will, until you have seen, as scientists have even observed can happen in certain gases, that the molecules, the individual molecules, gradually or even suddenly come into alignment.

And this is what has happened on most planets, where beings have experimented for a time, clashing with each other, challenging each other, conflicting each other, but then they have gradually realized, that there is greater joy in working together on a higher union, a higher vision. And so, they have come into coherence, and now they have put their planetary unit in an upward spiral, in an ascending spiral.

So you see, indeed, that the entire material universe is in an ascending spiral? Yet, when you look at this universe, you see that there are still some planets – not a large number compared to the total, but a large number if you look at just the number – that have not entered this Ascension Spiral or have not passed this point of the phase transition, where coherence emerges. Planet Earth has entered an ascending spiral, but humankind has not yet come to this point, where there is the phase transition, that aligns the consciousness of most people to a higher vision, a higher oneness, a higher unity. And so, what is it you see, then, on these planets, where there is still chaos, where there is still conflict between people?

How the ego projects responsibility

Well, what you see is this: the conflict is a product of the mental images, that the beings on the planetary system are holding in their minds and projecting upon the Ma-ter light. The Ma-ter light is simply taking on the form of what is projected upon it, and thus creates a planet with physical conditions and a society with certain conditions that outpicture these mental images.

Do you see, what I am explaining here? You, as an individual, have created a mental image in your mind. You are projecting that mental image upon the Ma-ter light and the Ma-ter light is simply reflecting back to you the consequence, that you have chosen to produce by the way you have exercised your free will.

Now, of course, you may say: "But I have not single-handedly produced the situation that exists on Earth!" And you are quite right. Humankind has collectively produced the current situation, but why are you on Earth? Well, because you have taken on the same kind of consciousness, shared by the majority of the people on this planet.

And thus, you will see that you have been part of creating the current situation on Earth. What you see on Earth is a consequence of the exercise of free will. Yet, of course, this might be possible to see when you project yourself outside of your current state of consciousness, your current sense of self as a separate being. But it is not possible to see this, when you are looking at life from inside your separate mind, your separate sense of self.

When you are looking at things from the inside, you will think that the situations you experience on Earth is not the result of your own free-will choices, or even the choices made by humankind. You will be susceptible to believing in the lie projected by the fallen beings, that what you are experiencing is something that was forced upon you by an external force — be this the angry, remote God in the sky or other people or some immutable laws of nature created by mere chance.

How the fallen beings trap you in the dualistic struggle

Do you not see, that the main thought systems – be they religious or scientific-materialist or political – found on this Earth, portrays you as a victim of circumstances beyond your control? And what does this victim consciousness cause you to do? Well, it causes you to think that the only way to improve your situation is to seek to change the outer conditions, to change the consequences.

And thus, the most simple mechanism – applied by the fallen beings in their attempt to tie you into the ongoing dualistic struggle – is indeed to get you to struggle against consequences. Yet, do you not see why this will never give you peace of mind?

My beloved, imagine that you are in a movie theater. You are looking at the movie that is playing on the screen, and you decide that you do not like the movie. But since the movie is appearing on the screen, you now get it into your head that the only way to change the movie is to change the screen. So, you get out a bucket of black paint and a paintbrush, and you start painting the screen black. And yes, that does change the movie somewhat, but it is still the same image that is being projected at the screen. So, how much can you really change the movie by changing the screen?

For is the movie not produced away from the screen? Is it not so, that the image on the screen is a consequence of a cause that is found somewhere else? And in a movie theater, that cause is the film strip in the movie projector. But, do you not see the parallel? What you experience on Earth is a consequence of a cause. And the cause is found in your consciousness and in the collective consciousness.

If you think you have to fight the consequences – instead of changing the cause – you will inevitably turn your life into an ongoing and potentially never-ending struggle. Although the struggle will certainly end at some point, as mandated by the law of free will, that although you have free will to have any experience you want, you do not have the right to have that experience, to remain in a certain experience, forever.

And so, divine justice is simply that you have free will to make choices, but that you will experience the consequences of your choices. Because when you go into a certain state of consciousness, you will magnetize yourself to a planetary unit on which a majority of the beings have that same state of consciousness. And thus, you will inevitably be tempted to go into a struggle against other people with the same state of consciousness, struggling against consequences produced by the collective state of consciousness on that planet.

How planets are pulled up by the universe

Yet, it is also divine justice that no planetary unit is an island. And therefore, the inhabitants of a planetary unit cannot do whatever they want without being connected to the whole of the material universe. And so, if the entire universe is in an accelerated Ascension Spiral, then the inhabitants of a planet like Earth, will be connected to that spiral. And thus, in order to resist the Ascension Spiral, they must exert greater and greater force. And this again intensifies the struggle.

Now, you may say – if you look at this from inside the struggle – that this is then forced upon you by this external God, who is forcing you to be connected to the Ascension Spiral. But things are not quite that simple. For the reality is this: if a planetary unit was an isolated unit, and if the inhabitants of that unit really could take their planet into a downward spiral without being connected to a greater whole, well, then that downward spiral would very quickly accelerate to the point, where the planetary unit would be destroyed. And the beings who were then responsible for that spiral, would have no other way to go than through the dissolution of their individuality in what has been called the second death.

And thus, if the Earth was not connected to the whole, then the Earth would long ago have self-destructed, and the beings who brought in into that spiral would have destructed with it. And thus, they would no longer have free will, the opportunity to choose.

And so, you see indeed, there is no self-aware being that can exist independently, for it is an expression of the Creator's own Being. And of course, the Creator prefers that all expressions of its Being go through the Ascension Spiral. The Creator has given you an incredibly long time span, and has given you free will to decide which road you want to travel on the way to the ascension point. But there is an underlying law that states, that you must go either up or down, that you cannot stand still. For that would be against the purpose of creation itself. And it would indeed be against the purpose for which you have chosen to enter this spiral that is creation, that is the world of form.

For regardless of the images created by science or various religions, the world of form is not static. It does not stand still, nor is it cyclical in nature going from one state to another and back to the first, back to the second and so forth indefinitely. The world of form is an upward spiral that has a clear direction and a clear purpose. You may fight against it – that is your choice – but you are not fighting against God or God's plan. You are fighting against the consequences that you have created and that those on your planetary unit have created collectively.

The definition of Satan

And thus, do you not see what is the simplest definition of Satan? It is the consciousness that causes you to fight against consequences, instead of taking the Christ perspective of simply changing the cause and thereby also inevitably changing the consequences.

And so, what has happened to those who have gone into this consciousness of fighting consequences, is that they inevitably get sucked into the epic mindset created by the fallen beings. Which is indeed, that something has gone wrong with God's plan, with God's original design. And this, of course, can exist only when you believe that there is a standard for evaluating what should or what should not happen. And that you are the one who can define that standard, or that those whom you consider to be the ultimate authority on Earth can define that standard for what has gone wrong with God's plan.

And once you accept that there is such a standard, you are easily sucked into the epic struggle of now seeking to change what has gone wrong according to your definition. And this inevitably leads you to the conclusion that what has gone wrong is that some people have exercised their free will in a way that threatens God's plan for the universe. And thus, it is your job to change these people, either through direct physical violence or through persuasion, of seeking to in any way persuade or manipulate them into conforming to your standard—your mental image of how the Earth should be.

This, then, is the consciousness of Satan, that Peter attempted to put on Jesus in that crucial situation described in the gospels, where Jesus turned to him, looked him sternly in the eye and said: "Get thee behind me, Satan!"

For Jesus was committed to the greater process of God's plan for the universe. Jesus had volunteered to take on the role of the Living Christ, to come into embodiment and to let people trapped in the dualistic consciousness do with him whatever they wanted, yet demonstrating that whatever they did to him, they could not change him. For he refused to see himself as being bound by consequences, ever remaining true to the reality that you as an individual being are not a consequence. You are a co-creator, which means you have the potential to be a cause and to change the consequence on Earth.

But how do you truly change the consequence on Earth? You do not change it by fighting current conditions. You change it by taking responsibility for yourself and saying "I am an individual, existing in this planetary unit. I do not have the right to violate the free will of others, but I do have the right to not let their choices violate or limit my free will. And therefore, I have a right to take responsibility for my own state of consciousness and to change my state of consciousness and to express a higher state of consciousness, regardless of what the majority on this planet are doing. So that I may be a light in the world—a light that is set on a hill and cannot be hid. So that those who are willing may see it as an example and be inspired by it, without me having to fight them or force them or persuade them in any way. I am simply the light of the world. I am the open door for the light to shine through my being, and thus I am the open door for the flame of divine justice." Or whatever flame you desire to be the open door for that will stream through you.

And it is not that the light goes in and becomes some specific teaching that challenges other teachings. For, as I said, that which is expressed in words has its limitations. The entire teaching, given by the Ascended Host throughout the ages, has no value in itself, for once it becomes a disconnected teaching that exist only in the form of words, then it is just another teaching, and words that can be argued against indefinitely. It has value only when people go beyond the teaching and use it as only a tool to attune themselves with the consciousness of the Ascended Host and then become the open door.

How to know divine justice

For how will you know the Goddess of Justice? Not through an outer teaching formulated in words. You will not know me as long as you see me as an object that you can know from a distance. You will know me only when you go beyond your mental images; become pure awareness, that you become the open door through which the being that I AM – the stream of consciousness I AM – may flow through you and express itself on Earth.

And then, you will know me, then you will know the Goddess of Justice. But I am an ever-flowing stream, and I will be who I will be at any moment. And in any situation, I will express something different, for my goal is not to express some ultimate truth. My goal is, in any situation where I am given an entry into this world, to challenge people to come up higher, to transcend their current state of consciousness, their current mental box.

And thus, my expression will be adapted to the current mental box and adapted in such a way that it gives them an opportunity to transcend it, to take the next step. Not some ultimate step, that they are not ready to take because it is far beyond them. This is how the Living Christ expresses itself on Earth.

Whenever someone becomes the open door, then the greater consciousness that is the Ascended Host, will express itself according to the situation, always seeking to raise up all life, never seeking to put down any form of life. Do you not see, that there are so many people who are attempting to put down others? First, they are attempting to control others, and then, when some people will not be controlled, they attempt to put them down, even destroy them or punish them. And this is, indeed, because the fallen beings have projected this false image of divine justice which says, there is a standard for how you should exercise your "free" will.

Well, if there is a standard, then your will cannot be truly free, can it? And so, they have even projected that God has set a standard for how you should exercise your free will. And thus, they say that if you do what is wrong according to the standard, then you deserve to be punished. And thus, you will see that on planet Earth the concept of justice is inextricably linked to the idea of punishment.

Yet, God has no desire to punish anyone. For God has no need to punish anyone, because God has given you free will and God has set up the Ma-ter light to reflect back to you the consequences of your own choices. So, who is punishing you, my beloved? You are! You are punishing yourself! Who is punishing humankind? Humankind is collectively punishing itself through the choices made.

And until a critical mass of people awaken to this reality – and decide to stop fighting the consequences and instead change the cause which is their own state of consciousness – well, until that happens, humankind will not reach that coherence point, where they can unite around a higher vision. Instead, they will remain in the current state, where they will continue to struggle against each other. Only, of course, given that the entire rest of the universe is moving on, the struggle will become intensified, until it eventually becomes so much that people say: "Enough, we have had enough of this, there must be a better way."

The cause of all human conflict

And of course, many people have already reached that point. And thus, we are indeed optimistic that, as the planet moves forward in the coming years and decades, we will get ever closer to this turning point. Yet of course, there may be some very serious confrontations that will take place before then. For there certainly are many people on this planet who are blinded completely by the consciousness of Satan, where they think they have to fight the consequences of their own choices, instead of changing the consciousness that led to those choices.

And therefore, they think they have to fight other people and seek to change other people's state of mind, instead of changing their own state of mind. Do you not see, that this one mechanism is the cause of all human conflict? You think you have to change other people's minds instead of changing your own mind. Right there, my beloved, you have the cause of all conflict and the cause of all so-called injustice on this planet.

For do you not see, that the law of real, free will mandates that you have no right to seek to change other people's minds? When you do so, you are violating their free will, and they will feel this as a violation of their free will, even if they do not understand the Law of Free Will. And thus, if they cannot escape your violation of their free will, then they will sense this as an injustice. And of course, this is all designed by the fallen beings to trap people in this endless struggle of fighting against each other, because they seek to force each others will, thereby violating each others free will and creating the sense of injustice. And so it goes on and on and on.

How will it ever change? Only by those who are the spiritual people, coming to see that you are not here to change the minds of anyone else. You are here to change your own state of consciousness, until you become a light that is set on a hill and cannot be hid. Let your light so shine before men, that they may see that this light cannot come from you; it must come from a greater source. You have not produced it, you have become an open door for it.

Ahh, my beloved, this is the true goal of a Christed being! It never has been and it never will be, the goal of a Christed being to fight against others, to punish others, to put down others, to expose others according to your standard, to judge them or to change their minds in any way. If you will experience the greatest form of personal freedom that can be experienced on Earth, then you need to give up the idea that you are here to change anyone else. This is an incredible freedom, my beloved!

I give you an opportunity to escape the struggle

Do you not see that I, Portia, have also been called the Goddess of Opportunity? What is the greatest opportunity for you? It is that you let go of the desire to change others. For when you have a desire to change others, where does your attention go? It goes outside yourself! But where did Jesus say that the kingdom of God is to be found? Did he not say that the kingdom of God is within you?

So, as long as your attention is directed out, seeking to change others, how can you find the kingdom within yourself? And thus, giving up the desire to change others is the greatest opportunity for you to go within and realize this simple fact: you have been given individual free will, and the ultimate meaning of this is that you have complete freedom to choose your state of mind. Because your state of mind does not depend on anything outside yourself!

Yes, you are living on planet Earth, yes there are many things on this earth that are impinging upon you, even seeking to force your free will! But you still have the potential to go through those things and retain your peace of mind. But you cannot attain this peace of mind as long as your attention is directed outwardly, seeking to change others.

You will attain peace of mind only when you direct your attention inward and seek to change yourself—your own state of mind. That is when you have the opportunity to manifest Christhood. And then, when you become the open door for the light to shine through you, then you will give other people an opportunity to see that light and either accept it or reject it. But you are not giving other people an opportunity by going out there, trying to force them, trying to enlighten them, trying to make them see, what you think they should see.

This is not giving them an opportunity to escape the struggle, this is only enveloping them or yourself more deeply in the struggle. Become the light, become the open door, then you give people an opportunity—and then you have the opportunity to be in the world without being affected by the world but truly being the open door for the joy and the love of the Presence to flow through you, whereby you will feel at peace. You will feel fulfilled in expressing and experiencing the God quality of your Presence flowing through you. This is your greatest opportunity!

And yet, we of course know, that this is not simple to attain for people who have been in embodiment for many lifetimes in the density of this struggle consciousness. Those of us who have been in embodiment know this full well. For many ascended masters have indeed spent many lifetimes in the consciousness of the struggle, even thinking that they have to work for some ultimate good by struggling against other people, as you see in the lives of several masters. Nevertheless, how did they become ascended masters? They did so by coming to the realization, that you can never win the ultimate battle, for the struggle will never end until you transcend the consciousness that created the struggle.

And so, in order to give you an opportunity to transcend that consciousness, we have decided to release these latest four invocations. [Loving the Divine Mother - Part 1-4] Here, as we are coming to the halfway mark of the Year of the Mother, to give you an opportunity to sail through the rest of this year, without being involved with the struggle. As you may indeed likely see, that the rest of humanity will become more and more involved in the struggle in the last half of this Year the Mother.

And so, look upon these four invocations as a supreme opportunity for you to pass the initiations of the Year of the Mother, and also to make a contribution to helping the rest of humankind pass these initiations and indeed transcend the consciousness that needs to be transcended in this year. This is our hope: that you will look at them this way, that you will make use of them and that you will allow these very intricate invocations, very intricate statements, to change your state of consciousness.

For truly, it is one thing to read a book or a dictation, but it is another to have a teaching expressed in the form of an invocation, where you do not read it with the intellectual mind, but it goes into your consciousness at a deeper level, and therefore has a much more transformative effect than anything you just read.

For again, you will not be enlightened by thinking that enlightenment is some object that you can study at a distance. You will be enlightened only by becoming first pure awareness and then the open door, whereby the stream of consciousness that is enlightenment can flow through you. For enlightenment is not a static state, despite what many spiritual teachings portray it as. It is indeed the living, flowing River of Life that is ever-changing ever self-transcending, because it is always in the process of being more—at any moment being more than it was before.

This is life! Life is constant self-transcendence, death is stillstand! Therefore, I say as has been said before: CHOOSE LIFE! For if you do not choose life in the Year of the Mother, then it will become much more difficult to do so in the Year of the Holy Spirit and in succeeding years.

Thus, choose wisely and use these invocations to help you transform your state of consciousness, until you are not making this choice with the outer mind—you are connecting to the deeper choice that brought you into embodiment.

And thus, you are not actually making that choice with the lower mind, you are flowing with the River of Life. You are flowing with a choice already made by your higher being and with those of your brothers and sisters in the world of form who have also joined this River of Life.

Thus, my release is complete! Make use of it as you see fit. For I give you complete freedom! Yet, I will let you know, that I have also given you – with this release and these four invocations – a complete opportunity to escape the consciousness of the struggle—the consciousness of Satan. So that you can come to the point, where you do not even need to say: "Get thee behind me, Satan!" For Satan is no longer in front of you. For what is in front of you, is your I AM Presence and beyond that the Ascended Host and the hierarchy of beings, leading all the way to your source—the Creator itself.

Epilogue

I officially inaugurate the Aquarian age—catch my enthusiasm

Saint Germain, March 22, 2010

I have been known for some time now as the ascended master Saint Germain. Yet, Saint Germain is but a name, and I am more than a name—for I am a Living Spirit, constantly transcending myself as an expression of the Flame of Freedom that I have chosen to merge into, to become one with, to become the embodiment of for planet Earth. This is how I earned the office of the Hierarch of the Aquarian age—by being willing to transcend myself until I had raised my self-awareness to the level, that is required for one to serve in the position of being the main hierarch for a 2150 year cycle on Earth.

Jesus had done so before me, likewise raising his sense of self-awareness to the point of being able to serve as the hierarch of the Age of Pisces. I received great inspiration from Christ—not from the outer life of Christ that was preserved in the image given by the official Christian churches, but I received inspiration from within, through my own ponderings over many embodiments on the true inner message of Christ. A message that I tried to express, as best I could, through various embodiments, including through the works of Shakespeare and the writings of Francis Bacon, seeking to always instill that drive for self-transcendence as the very key factor that will bring about a new and better age—no matter where you are.

There if a forward progression to life

For is it not so – and is it not obvious to those who have opened their minds and hearts – that the key to growth is always self-transcendence?

Life is transcending itself; everything is constantly transcending itself. You may look at nature, you may look at the cycles of winter, spring, summer, fall, winter and so on, and you may think that this is but a repetitive cycle. But look at history down through the millennia, down through the eons, and see that it is not just a cycle that repeats itself, for there is a forward progression. There is a progression that brought forth, gradually, more complex life forms, until a physical body had been brought into existence with a brain and nervous system sophisticated enough to support the embodiment of the living spirits, the individualizations of the Creator's Being, the co-creators that we are.

Look even at the Earth revolving around the sun. Look how you might have grown up with the image that the Earth simply moves around the sun, and when it has moved around the sun one time, it returns to the same position that it was a year ago. This is the common perception — or rather the common misperception. For my beloved, you do not seriously believe, do you, that the sun is stationery in space? Have not your scientists told you that the universe is constantly expanding, have they not told you that your sun is one star in a larger system, called a galaxy, and that it moves along with that galaxy? Even the entire galaxy is moving in space, so you see – when you think more deeply about this – that when the Earth has revolved around the sun one time, it does not come back to the same position in space. For the sun has moved, meaning that the trajectory, the path, of the Earth around the sun is not an elliptical orbit: it is a spiral that moves in a clear direction.

And such it is with everything in the material universe. Everything is moving, not in circles but in spirals—spirals that have a clear direction. It is either upwards or downwards. It is either an expanding spiral or a collapsing spiral, for there is nothing in between. The dream of the elliptical, stationary orbit is but a dream. Where does this dream come from? It comes from the human ego, which wants to preserve itself by stopping the forward progression of the entire universe, if it could. And given that I cannot, it seeks to create the impression of something stationary. And because of free will and the density of the matter realm, it is indeed possible to create the image that something is stationary, something can be preserved, something can survive for a time in its present form. Indeed, this is the central challenge of life but it is especially the challenge faced by humankind right now.

This marks the official beginning of the Aquarian age

For I, Saint Germain, come with great joy to tell you that this day, March 22, 2010, marks the first day of the Aquarian age. The changeover from the Piscean to the Aquarian taking place at midnight, between the 21st and the 22nd of March, 2010. And thus I, Saint Germain, greet you as the Hierarch of the Aquarian Age on this first day of the Aquarian age.

What is the significance of this day? Well, this can be viewed from two different perspectives. First, the overall perspective; the significance is simply this: everything has changed. Everything has changed. Everything on Earth has changed in an instant, and nothing will be the same.

Yet will people notice that everything has changed? Not for a while—for some of them for a long while. Let me take you back, if you will, to the day before I, embodied as Columbus, discovered America. After a long struggle with the crew on my ships, I was relieved to wake up to the discovery of land. When you look back, you will see that that day, October 12, 1492, truly marked the beginning of a new era, with the colonization of America and everything America stands for in the world today. Nevertheless, the day itself hardly seemed significant at all. It was a day that most people did not notice as being any different from any other day.

I, of course, noticed it, chiefly because through the discovery of land there was less risk that I would be thrown overboard by my own crew. And that was a fate I preferred to avoid at the time, being somewhat attached to my physical body, even being somewhat attached to the desire to make a significant discovery. For I was, of course, back then an unascended being and not free of ego. There was a certain amount of ego in the entire desire to discover new land. There was even a certain amount of ego in the desire to prove the old mindset wrong, to prove once and for all that the Earth is not flat, even to prove the fallacy of the Roman doctrines—that I was not much in favor of in that embodiment. Having, of course, suffered from the abuse of the Christian churches for several embodiments, and having clearly seen how – during those times of the Middle Ages – it was indeed the Catholic Church that was the major hindrance to progress in Europe and to the dawning of a new age.

Nevertheless, beyond a certain ego involvement, a certain desire to prove them wrong, there was also a deeper desire to be part of the River of Life that brings civilization forward. And so it has been with many other people throughout history that have brought forth new ideas, new ideas that brought civilization forward. In some cases the people were driven by selfish motives of fame or fortune or writing themselves into history. Yet they were still open to being the recipients of a particular new idea that brought society forward. And this is indeed how civilization has progressed, in the past 2,000 years, from the stage that you saw back then to the stage that you see today.

And so let us look at the civilization of 2000 years ago, and let us look at the dominant civilization of the time, namely the Roman Empire. It is of course no coincidence that we have sent this messenger and his companion to Rome, right before the dawning of the Aquarian age. For indeed, you will see that the Roman Empire and the Roman church have provided the major challenges – they illustrate the major challenges – that humankind must transcend – were meant to transcend – during the Piscean age—and must transcend in order to move into the aquarian age consciousness, and therefore manifest the golden age that is the highest potential for the Aquarian age.

What is it indeed that the Roman Empire and the Roman Church represent? They represent the consciousness that started with the original fallen angels, when they fell in a higher sphere, out of the arrogance of thinking they knew better than God how to run God's creation. They thought that they formed an elite with special powers, with special wisdom and insight and intellectual prowess. And therefore, they thought that they deserved to rule the people. They deserved to rule the new co-creators in the sphere into which they had fallen, after they refused to self-transcend and ascend with their original sphere. They thought that in their sophistication, they were better suited for ruling over the co-creators, who were yet new and yet experimenting. Yet the co-creators were simply the children of God, and as Jesus said: "Unless you become as little children you shall in no wise enter the kingdom." And so, they were not nearly as unsophisticated as the fallen angels thought—and as they think to this day.

You see, what the fallen angels did was they created a standard for sophistication that was based on themselves and their own state of consciousness. This was not a universal standard, it was not a logical standard, it was not a natural standard, it was not a standard set by God; it was a standard set by the fallen consciousness, the consciousness of duality and separation. It was a standard that attempted to make a virtue out of necessity, the necessity that you are in when you enter duality, and therefore cannot be one with the River of Life—and therefore must take everything by force. For it will not come to you easily, when you are not willing to surrender yourself, your separate sense of self, into that flow of the River of Life.

And so, this is the very consciousness of taking by force, and the fallen ones had no other option. And thus, they attempted to make it seem like taking by force was a virtue, and that those who were the best at forcing others were the ones that were best suited to rule, and were indeed the ones that should be seen as the most sophisticated—even as the representatives of God on Earth. This is the height of their arrogance. The Roman emperors proclaimed themselves as gods on Earth, requiring the people to worship them as such and accept that everything they said or did was infallible.

Ahh, the dream of infallibility. Is that not also the dream of a stationary orbit, that something stands still and can be preserved. For the emperor's word is always infallible, no matter what it is and no matter what the consequences. And this is precisely the consciousness that was carried from the Roman Empire, and as the Roman Empire began to crumble was transferred to the Roman church, the Roman Catholic Church. Where it also was declared that the Pope was infallible, that he was speaking for God, that he was the only true representative of Christ on Earth.

Understanding the challenge that Jesus hurled at humankind

So then, this is the consciousness that humankind has been up against for these past 2,000 years. Certainly they have been up against it before, but they have not really been up against it; they have been subjected to it. For it was only 2,000 years ago that humankind received a true opportunity to see and transcend this consciousness. And what gave them that opportunity to transcend the fallen consciousness, the consciousness that something on Earth can be infallible, can be permanent? Well, it was, my beloved, the incarnation of Jesus as the living Christ. When he walked the Earth those 2,000 years ago, he hurled the challenge at humankind: there is a higher reality than the fallen consciousness. "Ye are of your father the devil, and the lust of your father will ye do, for he was a murderer from the beginning." He murdered truth, the fallen ones murdered truth, murdered innocence, murdered the very transcendence of life.

For life is transcendence. Without transcendence, there is no life. Life is not in a stationary orbit; life is constantly transcending and re-newing itself. And a species that will not adapt and renew itself, will become extinct. That is the one valuable lesson that can be learned from the entire concept of evolution and the survival of the fittest—meaning the most adaptable, those who are most willing to transcend the old matrix.

And so, look at the life of Jesus. Born in humble circumstances, born like any other man—despite the myths that were added later about a star appearing. I was there as Saint Joseph – or rather, as Joseph the carpenter – when Jesus was born. You have seen the images of a manger with a star appearing above it. Well, I was there and I saw no such star, my beloved. This was an entirely metaphorical thing, that could only be deduced by those who had inner sight—not a physically visible star, as the legends would have it.

For what have they done to Christ? He embodied as an "ordinary" human being in order to show the potential that all have. The fallen ones, of course, did not want people to realize their true potential, so what did they do. Well, first the Roman emperors tried to suppress Christianity. And then, when it became clear to one pragmatic emperor – one political animal by the name of Constantine – that it could not be suppressed, what did they do? Well, they said, "Let's use it then—if we can't kill it, let's use it. Let's accept it as the official religion, but of course in doing so, let us add a few subtle conditions that no one will notice—a few conditions that twist and turn Christianity."

Not that this was an invention of the emperor Constantine; it was already started by other fallen beings who had joined Christianity, and who had started to glorify Jesus and set him up as an exception rather than as an example. And so, it was easy for Constantine to magnify this, to put the support of the Roman Empire behind those who had that view of Christianity that most suited his political ends. And so, gradually, you saw the formation of a church which elevated Christ to the status of God, thereby being fundamentally different from other people on this planet, therefore being completely unsuited to serve as an example for them and their potential, for he was so different. He was of the same substance as the father, he was God from the very beginning.

Well, my beloved, you are all God from the very beginning, because without him was not anything made that was made. And thus "ye are gods" as Jesus himself said. And that, of course, is precisely what the fallen ones do not want you to realize. They do not want you to realize your true co-creative potential.

Not that you are gods in the sense of the fallen ones wanting to set themselves up as gods on Earth. You are not God in the fullest sense; you are individualizations of God. That does not mean that anyone of you is superior to any other, for how can one expression of God be superior to another expression of God? You are all individualizations of God, you are all equal in your uniqueness. Yet what the fallen consciousness has done is it has imposed that value judgment, whereby it now becomes possible to say that due to certain characteristics here on Earth, one person is unique, one person is above all others—be it an emperor, or a pope or Christ himself.

The consciousness of elitism must be transcended

This is the very foundation for the consciousness of elitism, the consciousness of exclusivity. And this is the consciousness that humankind has been faced with the challenge of transcending during the past 2,000 years. For by the very embodiment of Jesus himself, the challenge became absolute, in the sense that no human being on Earth has been able to ignore it completely. Yet of course, many human beings have ignored it to a very large extent.

And what you see in the past 2,000 years is indeed the pattern that the majority of the population have wanted strong leaders to rule them, precisely because that meant that they could ignore the challenge of acknowledging and expressing their true creative potential. Look at the teachings we have brought forth about the human ego about dramas, personal and epic [Unmasking the Ego and The Secret Path Beyond Ego]. Look at the teachings and read between the lines, and you will see that what we have given you are the very keys to overcoming this precise consciousness that I am addressing here. Whereby you overcome your own reluctance to acknowledge yourself as a co-creator with God, to acknowledge your co-creative potential.

We have given you the keys to overcoming this consciousness, and I dare say there is no other teaching on Earth that gives you these keys so clearly. Yet the problem here is that this requires a certain effort, as it seems. It is not truly an effort, in the sense that you have to struggle against something. But it is an effort in the sense that you do have to go through a process that will seem like a struggle, because you do have to go through the process of raising yourself beyond the downward pull of the mass consciousness—that simply wants to live an unconscious life, an unawakened life. And thus, you have to follow the process – demonstrated by Jesus, demonstrated by the Buddha and other spiritual examples – of raising, of accelerating, your consciousness, your sense of self beyond the level of the mass consciousness. So that you can accept that you are not simply a human being, you can accept that you are a co-creator with God, you are an individualization of God.

And therefore, you do have the potential to be part of the Golden Age of Aquarius, be part of co-creating and manifesting that age as a physical reality on planet Earth. This is somewhat of an effort. Many of you have been engaged in this effort for decades, but you have not fully engaged it—yet. You have fallen prey to a subtle state of consciousness that we have also exposed in our many discourses and dictations, namely the belief that you can follow an outer path. As we have said before – over and over again, many times by Jesus but also by others – even in ascended master organizations and teachings, there is that consciousness of believing that if we only study the outer teaching, give decrees or prayers or rosaries, do this or do that, then we will one day ascend.

But as we have explained, most recently by Serapis Bey, the ascension is not an automatic or mechanical process. It will never happen by you doing outer things. The outer things may have a beneficial effect of transmuting energy, but they will not raise your consciousness. For raising your consciousness can only happen as the result of a conscious will, a conscious decision, a conscious choice.

You have been given free will by God, and what has enabled the fallen beings to rule the Earth is precisely that they have found ways – clever ways – to subdue free will, to make people give away their free will, to give up their choices, and leave the choices to the rulers, the emperors, the kings and the potentates of this and that system. You have been given an individual free will. It can be exercised only by you, and it can be exercised only consciously. And given the current state of the mass consciousness on Earth, it is indeed a certain effort that is required for you to consciously choose beyond the mass consciousness.

This I freely admit, as it was an effort for me as Columbus to choose to go against the mass consciousness and say, "No, the Earth must be round." We all understand this in the ascended realm, yet we have all raised ourselves above it, and we know you can do the same. We also know that you can do it only by doing it as we did it: by consciously making the effort, making the determination, that you are willing to be conscious, that you are willing to make conscious choices—conscious choices, instead of blindly following the mass consciousness, or the leaders who claim to have superiority, even infallibility.

...

For as the Great Divine Director, and my own guru, has recently explained, divine direction is not a straitjacket; it is not that you have one choice to follow divine direction and then you make no more choices, for now you just do what you are told from above. Instead, the reality is that divine direction has only one purpose: it is to help you make better choices and thereby grow in self-awareness and the use of your co-creative abilities.

Overcome the attachment to outcome and stop judging yourself

You see, an aspect of the fallen consciousness is the attachment to specific outcomes and results on Earth. And therefore, they have set up this entire consciousness, that certain of your choices are wrong according to some standard. And they use this to get you to judge yourself, until you have had so much pain of making these so-called wrong choices that you finally reason, "I've had enough of making these wrong choices—I will no longer make any choices." I will follow an outer leader, I will follow a religion, I will follow a guru or messenger. Or, I will seek for some divine direction from someone who will tell me what to do. Well, my beloved, if you are looking for some nonmaterial entity to tell you what to do, I can assure you that that nonmaterial entity will not be a member of the Ascended Host.

For we do not have the goal to get you to a point, where you never make wrong choices on Earth. Our goal is your overall growth in self-awareness. And as we have said many times, you can grow equally from any choice you make, whether it is "wrong" or "right" according to some earthly standard. Our only concern is to help you learn and grow, and thereby transcend and grow in your co-creative ability and awareness. That is our concern.

Do you, really and truly, my beloved, believe that we sit up here and watch your every move and judge you harshly? Do you believe that for every choice you make, the karmic board is sitting up here with a scorecard, and they put a little check when you make a good choice and they put a minus when you make a bad choice. And they add up all the minuses, until you reach some critical mark and then "Bam" you are going down into that fiery hell that the Christians have portrayed so vividly for so many centuries. Do you seriously believe that this is how the karmic board works? Because if you do, I can tell that you that you have fallen prey to the fallen consciousness and their mind control and their brainwashing, and their projection of these false images into the collective consciousness.

And if you seriously believe that this is how the karmic board and the Ascended Host work, then it is time for you to realize that you have been had by the fallen angels. And it is time to wake up and throw away these preconceived image, based on duality and judgmentalness. It is time to go within and be honest and say, "I am beginning to see how the fallen consciousness has affected my view of God and my view of the ascended masters. And I am hereby determining – by my free will choice – that I am willing to know God and the ascended masters as they really are. I am willing to know reality."

My beloved, ask and you shall receive. Ask with a willingness to look beyond your mental boxes, your preconceived opinions, your epic dramas, and we will reveal our true beings to you. For we are right here with you all the time. It is only in your mind that there has been created the impression, the image of a distance, of an unbreachable gulf between you and us. And that unbreachable gulf was created precisely in the fallen consciousness. For there is an unbreachable gulf between the fallen consciousness and the ascended consciousness. There is no question about this. There is a gulf between the fallen consciousness and the ascended consciousness. But you are an individualization of the Creator's Being, and you have a choice: Do you want to step into the fallen consciousness; do you want to step into the ascended consciousness?"

To which station do you want to attune the radio of your consciousness? Turn that dial of consciousness. It may have been stuck on a certain station for many embodiments. The dial might have gotten a little rusty, my beloved. It might be stuck on that station that it has been tuned in to for so long, thinking perhaps it was the only station—or that it would get you to heaven if you just kept tuning in to it long enough. So make that effort to wrest the dial free from the corrosion, to get it moving again. Turn it back and forth perhaps for a little while, just to clear the rust and the dirt. But then turn it towards the higher stations, until you reach us. For it is not that difficult, but it has become much easier, as the planet has shifted from the piscean to the aquarian mindset.

It requires less of an effort today to tune in to the reality of the Ascended Host than it did yesterday. And, as time progresses, and as the collective consciousness continues to progress, it will require less and less of an effort. But it will still require that choice, that you are willing to question your old mental images, the graven images. Without a willingness to question your graven images, no progress is possible. This is the way it has been always—always. For free will is the essence of growth.

Understanding life, liberty and the pursuit of happiness

Life, liberty and the pursuit of happiness—these are three of the rights defined in that document, the Declaration of Independence. But what is life? It is that which does not stand still, but is constantly transcending itself. If there is no self-transcendence, there is only death, which is why Jesus said, "I have come that all might have life and that more abundantly manifest." Life is Christ, Christ is transcendence—self-transcendence, constant, constant, ever-flowing self-transcendence. Without self-transcendence, there is no life, only a repetition of that which is. And that which is is death—this is the death consciousness.

My beloved, if you are a spiritual student of any kind, then I tell you: the cycles of time have turned. You are now in the Aquarian age. You have an unprecedented opportunity to tune in to the aquarian age consciousness, the golden age consciousness. And thus, it is time to let the dead bury their dead. Let those who will not question their mental boxes—just let them be. Move on. Question your mental box, raise your self-awareness, start making conscious decisions. Go within and find the point of stillness, as I have said. And start acting from that point, as Gautama Buddha explained at New Year's.

Now then, life, liberty and the pursuit of happiness. Life is self-transcendence, then what is liberty? Well, men think that it is some permanent state, where they have a certain form of government that gives them certain laws and rights. But I tell you, again, nothing can stand still, everything must be transcended. So liberty is also self-transcendence. Only in constant self-transcendence will you remain free. For, my beloved, you may think that in the past there was a tyrant who did not give the people certain rights. You may think that you have now created a government, even a constitution, that gives certain rights to its citizens, and that these rights are written into certain laws. And therefore, you may think that you have it made. But I tell you that it is not so, for as you can see, even in the United States today, the constitutional freedoms are constantly being eroded. And in fact, the very laws that yesterday seemed to set you free from some tyrant, will now become a limitation in themselves. They might hold society back from transcending, going to a higher level. And thus, again, only in self-transcendence can there be continued liberty.

Which then leads us on to happiness. And what is happiness? Can there be happiness without self-transcendence? Nay, there cannot. There can be, perhaps, some impression of happiness, and that is what people seek two create on Earth by defining an outer standard for happiness and saying, "When I have this or that, then I must be happy!" And then they seek to spend their entire lives acquiring what will supposedly make them happy. And when they get it, they end up realizing that they are not in a permanent state of happiness, for now the main concern is to defend and maintain that which supposedly makes them happy.

So, while they didn't have it, they were striving to acquire it, and now that they have it, they are striving to maintain it. And either way, this takes them away from happiness. For what is happiness? It is constant self-transcendence, and what is self-transcendence? It is that you are not attached to anything on Earth, for you know you are more than anything on Earth, and whatever you have on Earth only serves as a vehicle for your self-expression. And any day, your self-expression might go in a different direction, spontaneously, without you knowing ahead of time, as Jesus so recently explained in Rome. And therefore, if you are surrendered to the flow of the River of Life, you are not attached to any outer possessions. You are willing to flow and to take your self-transcendence in new directions, in new spheres, that you may not have been able to even dream about before, when you were so focused on a particular form of self expression.

Question your preconceived opinions about the Aquarian age

There is nothing wrong in being focused on a certain sense of self-expression right now. But when you become attached to it and think that it has to be this way for the indefinite future, or even for the rest of your lifetime, well, then that self-expression has become a limit to the expression of your Spirit. And thus, I tell you: if you have any preconceived opinions, any preconceived images, of what the Aquarian age should be – or what your life and your contribution to the Aquarian age should be – then this day marks the start of the cycle, where it would be highly advantageous for you to reconsider those images. If you truly are to make the shift from the Piscean to the Aquarian age consciousness, then I can assure you that all of your preconceived images about the aquarian age and your own self-expression must be questioned.

Many of them must simply be transcended, for they are obsolete. They were based on the old consciousness and what you could see and what humankind could see in that old consciousness. But that consciousness is gone, the old cycle is gone. And therefore, it is time for a new vision, it is time to open your imagination to see the reality of what the Golden Age can be—not what it seemed like seen through the filter of the piscean mindset and the piscean cycle.

This is also what Christ represents to you—the challenge of Christ to always look beyond your mental box, to leave your nets and follow Christ for a time, until you begin to see from within what is the self-expression that you desire to bring forth in the Aquarian age. Whatever you have done up to this point was what you needed to do; you needed to have that experience. I am not asking you to blame yourself or think that you have been wrong in doing what you have been doing. It is not a matter of blame. You have done what you have done because you needed that experience, and it was a necessary step on your path. What I am asking you to consider here is that the cycles of Earth have irrevocably changed, and therefore if you want to unlock your true aquarian potential, you need to rethink everything.

You need to realize that the way you have looked at yourself and the Aquarian age and the teachings of the ascended masters so far has been, in subtle ways, affected by the piscean mindset and by the consciousness of humankind. And if you really want to make this shift, you need to rethink, you need to question, everything. Question everything, be willing to question—not in the sense that you evaluate that something was wrong. I am not asking for a dualistic judgment; I am only asking you to question by saying: "Is there possibly more? Could there be more to understand, could there be more to envision, could there be more to imagine? Is there a higher form of expression that is possible for me in the Aquarian age? Is there a higher expression of some aspect of society that is possible in the Aquarian age? Is there a higher expression of some form of technology that is possible in the Aquarian age?"

Moving away from force-based technology

For I can assure you, that in the Aquarian age you will see the emergence of a new form of technology, based on a new state of consciousness that is not forced-based. Look at so much of the technology you have in the world today, especially in the field of energy. Look at how it is force-based. Take oil; how was oil created? Organic life gathered, died and was put under pressure until it became a liquid, black substance. How is oil extracted? By force, by drilling into the Earth. How is it refined; again by force. How is it used to power your cars? In an internal combustion engine, where the force of an explosion forces the pistons to move. Force, force, force—everywhere force.

Contrast this with the statement made by Jesus at the beginning of the Age of Pisces: "Fear not little flock, for it is your father's good pleasure to give you the kingdom." This is the anti-thesis of force-based technology and a force-based economy and a force-based world. Certainly, there is a potential that humankind will one day reach a level of collective consciousness, where they do not even need technology but can manifest their needs directly through the powers of the mind. Yet that stage is some ways off. It would be a potential towards the end of the Aquarian age, if the Aquarian age unfolds to its highest potential. But until then, there will be a need for technology—a new form of technology, however, that is not based on force but is based on a higher understanding of nature, of the material universe and of the spiritual laws behind it. So that people can work with life, with Spirit, with nature—and therefore develop technology that will truly allow you to produce energy without burning any fuel whatsoever.

This is a real possibility in the not-too-distant future, but it will require a major shift. First of all, it will require humankind to begin to question the fallen consciousness. For I, as the Hierarch of the Aquarian age, am not about to release technology that, at the current level of consciousness, would instantly be monopolized or suppressed by the power elite. I will not release this technology until I can be sure that it will benefit all people equally, and will not be used—not only for profit but even for political control purposes by the power elite.

You may think that they are already certain forms of technology in existence that have been suppressed by the elite—I am not even denying that. But what I am saying here is that there is technology in my etheric retreat that is far more advanced than anything that is even dreamt of, save by a very few individuals who have attuned their consciousness to the potential for the Aquarian age. And that technology will enable you to produce unlimited amounts of energy without having a centralized production facility or even requiring a centralized distribution network. And therefore, it cannot be monopolized by any corporation or any country.

It is truly liberating technology, for you realize, do you not, that the reason why humankind has been limited to force-based technology is that humankind has been under the fallen consciousness. The fallen consciousness, off course, cannot conceive of a non-force-based technology. But even if they could, they would not want it, for force-based technology is precisely what allows them to monopolize technology. For those who can conquer the force, or the right to use force, can also gain a monopoly.

And surely, you recognize that no ordinary family can build a nuclear power plant in their backyard. And this is another example of the complexity of force-based technology, that requires such huge and complicated plants that they can only be built by governments or huge corporations—and therefore, by their very nature, are open to being controlled by the power elite. The technology I am talking about is so simple that it can be built by anyone and that you can have a generating plant, a small plant, right in your own home that can meet all of your energy needs, without you requiring to ever pay the oil companies, or the electric companies, or the gas companies ever again. This is the kind of technology I desire to release. It is in existence in the etheric realm, but until the consciousness shifts, it will not be released.

Shifting into the Aquarian age consciousness

And how is the consciousness going to shift? Well, only by those who see themselves as the forerunners of Aquarius being willing to question the way they look at everything, to question what limits their imagination. Be willing to question what limits your imagination. This is, right now, possibly the greatest service you could render to the Ascended Host and to humankind. Question what limits your imagination, including questioning what already limits your perception. For if you will not question your current perception, how could you ever free your imagination to soar beyond what you perceive as the limits for life? How then, will you question your perception? Let me suggest two areas, where you might begin: church and state, religion and politics. These two are like two sides of the coin of life. They truly represent the Alpha and the Omega, the masculine and the feminine.

Politics may be a too limited word, for truly what it involves is everything that is the feminine aspect of life, the practical, outer expression of life in your personal life, in society, in politics, in technology, in education, in the family—in every practical aspect of life; this is the Omega aspect, the Divine Mother. The Alpha aspect, the Divine Father aspect, is not simply religion – as it has traditionally been conceived – but every aspect of how you imagine your potential. As we have recently said, the masculine is "what can be done," the feminine is "how it can be done." And this is the highest potential of church and state, where church, religion, is meant to represent the masculine that gives you a vision of what to do. And then, state, or the feminine, gives you the practical vision of how it can be done, how you desire to express it.

What, then, is the primary preconceived idea that you might question? Well, it is another aspect of the fallen consciousness, namely that there is only one right way to do it. This is, again, tied in to what I have explained about the judgmental consciousness, that wants to set up a standard for what is right and wrong, and evaluate everything based on that standard. Take that consciousness, make an effort to see it as an expression of the fallen consciousness, and then realize that I am not here talking about going into the opposite extreme of saying that anything goes. For, when you reach for the Alpha of the vision of the Spirit, you know what can be done, what should be done and what is not right because it will not provide growth for yourself or for other aspects of life. But even when you see what can be done, and what is right from a higher perspective, there are still many ways that it can be done.

And so many times we see our spiritual students have a correct vision of what should be done, but they cannot agree on how it should be done. And then, what do they do? Well, they fall prey to the belief that there can only be one right way to do it, and that even we of the ascended masters have only one right way to run an organization, for example. And thus, what happens? There is the inevitable division into factions, where one faction will say, "Our way is the way the masters want." And the other faction will say, "No, our way is the way the masters want." And so, they are locked in a battle, they are divided amongst themselves, and therefore the house cannot stand, their organization cannot reach its full potential.

And so, realize that there will be many different ways to do the same thing, that can all be valid and all be a contribution. For we realize that in the fallen consciousness there is this underlying mentality, that there is only one right way to do it, and that all should conform to it. Is this not, my beloved, what we have exposed recently in Rome, in the Roman Catholic Church, of the suppression of individuality by the structure? The submission to the structure, thereby the individual suppressing its individual creativity in order to conform to the structure.

Well, my beloved, if you are ascended master students, question the idea that in the Aquarian age there will be only one valid religion. Question the idea that we of the ascended masters want to see the emergence of one religion. Question the idea that we of the ascended masters want to see all people recognize the ascended masters and one particular teaching of the ascended masters as the superior religion of the Aquarian age.

In the Golden Age, diversity will be seen as the greatest potential

Do you see the fallacy of the fallen consciousness? What is the essence of the fallen beings and their desire for control? They must suppress not only free will, but individual creativity. Each one of you is an individualized extension of the Creator's Being. What makes up your individuality? Certain characteristics, a certain crystalline structure, as the Great Divine Director explained recently. Your individuality is the crystalline structure, and when the light of God shines through it, your individual crystalline structure can bring forth an expression that is unique, that is not in competition with others, that does not exclude or destroy or obscure the expression of others. But they all compliment each other, forming a beautiful facet of life.

This concept cannot be fathomed by the fallen consciousness, for to the fallen consciousness diversity can be seen only as a threat—whereas in the ascended consciousness, diversity is seen as the ultimate expression of God. Why did the Creator choose to individualize its own being? Because the Creator wanted to express itself as many individual facets, having them all form, each, a facet of the diamond mind of God. The Creator has given you free will, because the Creator desires to see variety, individuality, diversity.

This is the Creator's desire; that is why the Creator has expressed itself as many individual co-creators. The Creator could have sat there, as the Creator, and created an entire world – it could even have populated it with robots – where everything was perfect. But the Creator did not desire to do this, partly because the Creator realizes that such a mechanical creation gets awfully boring after a while. Nevertheless, the Creator decided to express itself through diversity. And so, we of the Ascended Host are committed to seeing that expression.

And what is it that is the essential challenge of humankind? You look back at history, and you see that what has brought about progress is diversity. The Egyptian civilization may seem to have built great structures, but it did so by suppressing individuality, except for a very few. And the Egyptian civilization collapsed, as did the Roman civilization and other civilizations of antiquity. What have you seen in Western civilization of today: a greater and greater expression of individuality, of diversity.

This is the vision that I hold for the Aquarian age. This is the age of the Holy Spirit. The Holy Spirit bloweth where it listed, the Holy Spirit does not like to be confined by these monolithic structures. It wants to express itself through individuals, yet an expression where the individual does not see itself as a separate being – which is the product of the ego and the duality consciousness – but sees itself as an expression of the whole. And therefore, the individual expressions on Earth will see their expressions as facets of a whole. And that is how the Age of Aquarius also becomes the age of community.

Come ye into unity by knowing that you are expressions of the same source. It is not "come into unity by being the same," that is what the fallen ones have attempted to achieve on this Earth for eons. That is precisely what Christ embodied in order to challenge—to show that you as an individual have a right to go against the power elite, to go against the mass consciousness, to go against everything that wants to suppress individual creativity. You have a right to do as Jesus did, to express your individuality, even if it flies the face of all conventions of your society. You have a right to go into the most holy temple and overturn the tables of the money changers who have set themselves up in that temple, where they have no right to be.

This is the promise of individual creativity, this is the potential. Christ demonstrated it 2,000 years ago, you – who call yourselves spiritual people, or ascended master students, or whatever you call yourselves, but you who consider yourselves to be the more aware of people here in this age – you are meant to demonstrate today what Christ demonstrated 2,000 years ago. You are not meant to demonstrate that you can do what people have been doing for 2,000 years, namely submit yourself to a Pope or a structure. You are meant to demonstrate individual creativity and your willingness to express it.

Become an expert in one area as a foundation for expressing your individual creativity

How, then, will you express it? Well, we have given you so many keys in these last couple of years, where we have been talking about the duality consciousness and non-duality, that I see no reason to give you more, but I will make one suggestion. If you look back hundreds of years, you will see that people back then lived a very simple life. The majority of the population had accepted a certain station in life. They were peasants, or whatever they were, but that was their station in life. They were content to follow the power elite that ruled their society, they were content to go to war and sacrifice their lives if the king told them so. They were content to live on the lands appointed to them by their overlords, and that was the way they saw life.

Why had they submitted to this? Because they did not want to be awake and make conscious decisions. Therefore, they wanted some overlord to make decisions for them. What has happened in society since then? Look at your society today—what is it characterized by?

The one word is information. There has never been more information available at any time in recorded history. Why did the medieval people not revolt against their overlords? They did not have the information, but why did they not have the information? Because they did not want it, they did not want to take responsibility and educate themselves and open their minds. They wanted to remain where they were comfortable, even if they were not truly comfortable.

Yet, they were still comfortable in feeling that there was nothing more they could do about life. Therefore, they were content to whine and complain about things instead of doing something about them. This is precisely what needs to change today. If you will be part of the change to the Aquarian age, stop whining about conditions in society and start being part of the solution, instead of being part of the problem. Stop whining, thinking that there is nothing you can do and that other people must do something. Start looking at yourself as a part of the change—that you can do something.

What can you do? Begin by educating yourself, begin by making an effort. This has two aspects, again an Alpha and an Omega. The Alpha is, of course: raise your own consciousness, overcome your own psychological limitations, free your imagination. But then educate yourself about some aspect of society that is close to your heart. Become an expert. Study what there is to know. I am not saying you need to get a formal education and some position, but study the information that is available in such abundance. Filter it, sort it out, become an expert, so that you know what you are talking about—and then talk about it. Start talking, start speaking out. There has never been better opportunities, through the Internet, through forums and chat rooms and so many other avenues that are available to you today. Start talking, but know what you are talking about.

Realize that democracy is the most demanding form of government

For this you must overcome the fallen consciousness that only the elite have something valuable to say. What has happened in your society? Look back a few hundred years and you will see that 99.9% of the people were ruled by a very small group of persons. Sometimes just one man and a few dozen people around that leader would rule an entire nation. What do you have today: democracies. Again, there is a tendency to think that the government should rule, the government should make decisions, and so people in America or in other democracies are constantly whining and complaining about their government. But it is, after all, their government.

Where, my beloved, can you show me a contract that says that when you have a democratic government, all you need to do is go into a little booth every four years and put an X in some predefined box? And then you have fulfilled your responsibility as a citizen in a democratic nation. Do you have such a contract? I am not aware that anyone has such a contract. But then why do 99% of the people in democratic nations act as if they have such a contract?

Democracy is an extremely demanding form of government, for it is not a form of government where the people can remain asleep. If they do, then their democracies will not be democracies, for they will very quickly be ruled by a power elite. Yet take note of an essential difference. A democracy is still a democracy, which means that the people have a far better opportunity of taking back their government than they had under a totalitarian form of government, where it often required bloodshed.

There are so many people in today's world who are beginning to awaken to the fact, that there is something wrong in their democracies, that there are hidden forces that are ruling their democracies, and it is not truly ruled in the open or ruled by the people. This is true. I applaud these people for being in the beginning stages, but when are they going to move from the beginning stages to the more advanced stages? For you see, in the beginning stages you realize that something is wrong, but you still think you can do nothing about it. And therefore, all you can do is whine and complain and hope that someday somebody else will do something about it.

Well, let me ask you for a little bit of logical reasoning here. Let us say you are a citizen in a democratic nation, and you come to the realization that not everything is as it should be in your government. There is a hidden conspiracy, there is a small elite, who is doing things behind the scenes that is not honest and not straightforward and not in accordance with what is in the best interest of the people. You become aware of his—I am not disputing that this is happening. But now you become aware of it, and so how do you expect that this might change?

Do you think – in your mind, do you envision – that someday one person will come in – as the hero riding on the white horse, riding into one of the old towns in the American West – pulling out his sixgun and shooting all the bad guys, and then they live happily ever after? Is this what you envision? Do you think Barack Obama was that man on the white horse? Or that anyone else could be that man on the white horse?

Do you see that you cannot overcome the problem of elitism if you are envisioning that another elite is going to come in and throw out the bad elite. For whether it is a "good" elite or a "bad" elite, it is still an elite. And you will not overcome elitism even if a "good" elite is running your society. You will overcome elitism only when a critical mass of the people in that society wake up and decide to take responsibility for their own nation, for their own government, for their own lives, for their own destinies.

Christ proved the triumph of individuality over structures

This is the change that has been underway for the past 2,000 years and beyond, but especially initiated by the coming of Christ. For what did Christ do? He proved the ultimate potential of individuality—the triumph of individuality over structures built by the fallen consciousness. The triumph of the individuality of God over the death consciousness that denies individuality and individual creativity. This is the change that has been happening over these past 2,000 years.

If the Aquarian age is to be a golden age, this change must be greatly accelerated. And it will be accelerated only when all of the people who are beginning to wake up – realizing that there is something wrong in their democracies – go beyond complaining about it, go beyond longing for some other elite to take them away from the bad elite – and realize that the man on the white horse, the woman on the white horse, that is going to ride into town and make a difference is YOU. You are the person who must make a difference, by educating yourself, by speaking out, by taking responsibility.

Do you see, as I have hinted at before, that even the concept of conspiracies and conspiracy theories can be used by the fallen consciousness to make you feel that it is so overwhelming for an ordinary person to fight against this worldwide conspiracy, this secret society, that you do nothing? Do you see that throughout the ages, the fallen consciousness has always done this exact thing: put out some idea – depending on the moods of the time – that there is some overwhelming force running your society and that you, as an individual, have no opportunity to make a difference, that you cannot stand up against it? But did not Christ demonstrate that the individual CAN stand up against it? Even if the power elite kills him, then Christ will bring about their judgment and thus society will progress.

But in today's democracies, it is not necessary that you stand out as one individual and is killed—this is not necessary if many people will stand out at once. For you realize, of course, that a power elite can kill off one or a few individuals. But they cannot kill off tens of thousands of people who are all speaking out. Then they will give up their power—they will because they realize it is the only way they are going to survive.

Look at even the Roman emperors, the most megalomaniac leaders you have seen – just about – in history. They thought they were gods on earth, but why did a Roman emperor build the Colosseum? It was to entertain the people, but it was really to divert the attention of the people. And what does this show you, my beloved? It shows you that even a Roman emperor – who thought he was God on Earth – was still afraid of the people. Because if the people had woken up in sufficient numbers, he knew he would have lost his power. This was true 2,000 years ago; it is equally true today. Whatever secret conspiracy you might envision that is running this world behind the scenes, I tell you: they have no power to stand up to the people—when the people wake up in sufficient numbers and decide to take responsibility and demand that their leaders be held responsible for what they do.

If you could see it from my perspective, you would see that the camel's back, the Dragon's back, has already been broken. The control of any power elite group of this planet has already been broken. The people have not realized this, but it would only take a slight shift in consciousness before the people could wake up and once and for all break the stranglehold of any power elite, no matter how powerful you may envision it to be. As a visible example, look at what is happening to the Catholic Church. Look at how people, after decades of silence, are finally speaking out against the abuse by Catholic clergy. One of the most entrenched institutions that this Earth has ever seen can no longer stem the tide of them being held responsible.

Do you see what is happening behind the scenes here? Do you see what we have talked about, how a structure requires the suppression of individuality? But, a structure also offers something for those who are willing to submit part of their individuality to the structure. It offers them that they can hide behind the structure, as you have seen Catholic priests hide for decades while they were abusing children. If these priests had been abusing children out in secular society, they would have been caught and put in jail decades ago. But they managed to hide behind the structure for decades. Yet the fact that they can no longer hide, and that this scandal will spread worldwide, shows you that a shift has happened.

And if you could see what I see at inner levels, you would see that even the worst conspiracy you could possibly imagine cannot survive in the Aquarian age consciousness. The Holy Spirit will blow where it listeth, the Sword of Christ, as Gautama Buddha said at New Year's, will cut the veils that will expose these hidden power elite structures one by one. And they cannot survive once they can no longer hide. The power elite can only thrive in the darkness, they cannot survive when the light of Christ shines upon them. And the light of Christ is shining upon them through those who are willing to raise their consciousness and make the calls through our rosaries and invocations.

Pessimists will not bring the Golden Age into manifestation

Thus, it is a new day. If you cannot sense my joy and my optimism, then I suggest you do some serious rethinking. For it will not be pessimists or fatalists who will build the Golden Age of Saint Germain. It will be the optimists who are willing to question their mental boxes and question every idea that puts a limitation on the creativity of God, expressed through the individualizations of God. That is the final sentence.

The Golden Age will be built by those who are willing to acknowledge that with God all things are possible—when the creativity of God is expressed through the individualizations of God. And with that, my beloved, I bid you adjeu for now. But I look forward to speaking to you many times in the years to come. I have much to unveil about the Golden Age of Aquarius. And I am anxious, I am eager, I am filled with joy at the prospect of unveiling my vision for those who have eyes to see.

Open your eyes, and you shall see Saint Germain's vision for the Golden Age of Aquarius. Oh what a vision it is, oh what a vision it is. Not fashioned exclusively by me, but by the entire spirit of the Ascended Host who work with planet Earth. It starts at the central sun, filters down through cosmic beings, through archangels and Elohim, through ascended masters, holding various offices, through the Lord of the World, Gautama Buddha, through the cosmic Christ, Maitreya, through the individualized Christ, Jesus, through that beloved being, Mother Mary. And then through the office that I hold, that of the Hierarch of the Age of Aquarius.

We are all one. There are no divisions in heaven, there are no divisions in the ascended realm. There are no different lineages, my beloved, that can be in competition with each other. We are all one, we are one in this vision of bringing about God's kingdom in physical manifestation on Earth. And then moving on to numerous other planets that are ready to be awakened to the reality that there is MORE. Be sealed in that Flame of MORE, that flame that will never stand still, for it is always MORE.

Glossary

Akasha

An energy of a higher vibration than anything else in the material realm. It serves as a recording device, recording everything that has ever happened in the material world. People with developed faculties can read the Akashic records. In the future, it will be possible to read them with technological devices.

Alchemy

In popular belief, the process of transforming base metals into gold. The deeper, mystical meaning is the transformation of the base human consciousness into the gold of a more spiritualized awareness, such as Christ consciousness.

Alpha and Omega

Two spiritual beings who reside in the central sun, the highest level of the world of form.

Angel

A self-aware being that is not created to take physical embodiment. Angels serve in a variety of capacities, the most commonly known for us is as messengers who deliver a message from the spiritual realm to human beings. Another important function is angels who protect us against lower energies or dark forces.

Anti-christ

The consciousness of separation and duality. This consciousness forms a filter that distorts perception in such a way, that it seems plausible that we are separate beings, separated from God, from each other and from the material universe. The more firmly beings are trapped in this consciousness, the more real the illusion of separation seems to them. Thus, they will be acting as if they truly are separate beings, meaning they will believe that what they do to others will not affect themselves. This is the origin of man's inhumanity to man and the origin of evil. Human beings can be trapped in this consciousness, but so can non-material beings, forming the dark forces.

Archangel, Archeia

Angels are organized into bands, and each band is led by an archangel. Each archangel has a feminine complement, called an archeia. There is such a pair for each of the seven rays, but there are also other bands of angels.

Ascended Master

Normally refers to a being who was embodied as a human being on earth and who, often after many embodiments, qualified for the process of the ascension. The term can also be used more broadly to refer to all beings in the spiritual realm, even those who have not taken embodiment in the material world.

Ascension

A process whereby a being evolves to the self-awareness represented by the full Christ consciousness. In this state of consciousness, one can see through all of the lies created by the illusion of separation and duality. Thus, one sees the underlying reality that nothing can be separated from the Creator and that all self-aware beings are extensions of the Creator. One therefore seeks to raise all life, instead of seeking to raise oneself as a separate being. After a being ascends, it resides permanently in the spiritual realm and does not have to reembody.

Astral Plane

Everything is made from energy, and energy is a continuum of vibrations. There are certain divisions of this energy continuum, for example the material universe is made from vibrations within a certain spectrum. Yet the material universe has four divisions: the etheric (identity) level, the mental level, the emotional level and the physical level.

The emotional level itself has further divisions, and the lowest of these are created when people engage in negative emotions, such as fear, anger and hatred. The astral plane is a division within the emotional realm, and it resembles the visions of hell that people have had throughout the ages.

Atlantis

A previous civilization that inhabited a continent in the mid Atlantic. This continent disappeared around 10,000 years ago due to the actions of the inhabitants. The atlantean civilization was technologically superior to our time, but due to the lack of spiritual awareness, the inhabitants caused the civilization to self-destruct due to a misqualification of energy, which led to warfare and cataclysm.

Aquarian Age

There is a precession of astrological cycles, lasting approximately 2,150 years each. The previous age was the Age of Pisces, for which Jesus was the spiritual master. For the Aquarian age, the ascended master Saint Germain is the master. According to Saint Germain, the Aquarian age was officially inaugurated on March 22, 2010.

Aura

An energy field surrounding the human body. There are levels of the aura, corresponding to the levels of the material realm. You have an identity body, a mental body and an emotional body beyond the physical body.

Carnal mind

Sometimes used by ascended masters to refer to the entire lower consciousness, including the ego. Can also be used more specifically to refer to that part of the subconscious mind, which is designed to take care of the functions of the physical body. This includes certain basic instincts, such as protection, food and propagation. The carnal mind will seek to satisfy these needs without any regard for long-term interests and thus needs to be under the control of your conscious mind.

Causal Body

An energy "body" surrounding your I AM Presence. It stores all of the attainment gained and the lessons learned from all of your embodiments. When you raise your consciousness sufficiently, you can make use of this attainment for fulfilling your divine plan.

Catch-22

Described by the popular saying "you can't get there from here." It is a seemingly impossible situation that you cannot get out of. The ascended masters use this to refer to the mechanisms created through the illusion of separation and duality. The mind of anti-christ creates innumerable catch-22s in order to stop or slow down our spiritual growth. They are always based on an illusion, which means you can transcend them by changing your perspective. Note that a catch-22 often appears as a problem that you have to solve. Yet the problem has no solution, so the real solution is to walk away from the struggle.

Chakra

A focal point within your aura. There are seven major chakras, corresponding to each of the seven spiritual rays. If your chakras are pure, high-frequency energy from your I AM Presence can stream through them, and this gives you maximum creative powers. If your chakras are polluted, the stream of higher energies is reduced, and instead the chakras can become open doors for lower energies to enter your aura. Severely polluted chakras can open you to energies from the astral plane.

Chela, chelaship

A Sanskrit word that is often translated as "slave." This refers to Indian spiritual tradition, where a person makes him- or herself the virtual slave of a spiritual teacher, or guru, who will thereby expose the student's ego. Used by the ascended masters to refer to a sincere student, who is willing to submit to the disciplines of the spiritual path, designed to expose the ego.

Chohan

For each of the seven spiritual rays, there is an ascended master who serves as the leader or main teacher. This spiritual office is called the "chohan."

Christ

In its broadest sense, this refers to the basic consciousness out of which everything in the world of form is created. The purpose is to maintain the oneness between the Creator and its creation. This is especially relevant for beings with free will, who have the option to descend into the illusion of separation, thereby believing they are separated from their source. The Christ consciousness ensures that no matter how far you descend into separation, you always have the option to return to oneness with the Creator. Because the Christ consciousness is within everything that is created, you can never go to a place where you are unreachable for Christ.

In a more specific sense, Christ refers to a being who has overcome the illusion of separation and has attained the Christ consciousness. There are degrees of Christ consciousness.

Christ Self

A mediator sent by ascended masters to assist beings who have become trapped in separation and duality. Most people know their Christ selves as intuition or the "still, small voice within." The Christ self does not actually tell you what choices to make. It seeks to give you a frame of reference for making better choices. The Christ self will not necessarily give you an ultimate or absolute truth. It will give you an insight that is a bit higher than your present state of consciousness.

Christ discernment

The ability to see through the innumerable illusions created through the consciousness of separation and duality. Also the ability to see the underlying oneness behind all visible phenomena.

Christhood

When a being has attained the Christ consciousness, that being is said to have put on Christhood.

Conscious You

The core of your lower being. It is the Conscious You that descends from the spiritual realm as an extension of your I AM Presence. It is the conscious you that is the seat of your free will. However, you make choices based on the perception you have. It is possible for the Conscious You to have pure perception, which means it serves as an open door for the I AM Presence. However, when beings go into separation the Conscious You projects itself into an outer self or role, and it now perceives everything through the filter of that separate self. Thus, it will often make choices as if it really were a separate being.

The important point is that the Conscious You is and will always remain pure awareness. This means that while the Conscious You can project itself into any role it chooses, it can never lose the ability to extricate itself from that role and attain the Christ consciousness in which it can say with Jesus: "I and my father (my I AM Presence) are one."

Cosmic Being

A spiritual being who holds a specific spiritual office, usually a focus of a certain divine quality. Cosmic beings have never taken embodiment on earth as they ascended in a higher sphere.

Creator

The being who created the particular world of form in which we exist. There are other worlds of forms created by other Creators. A Creator must create a world of form out of its own Being, meaning the Creator experiences everything that happens in a given world.

Dark forces

Beings who have become trapped in the illusion of separation and duality. Many such beings reside in the astral plane. Everything in the material universe is sustained by a stream of energy from a higher realm. Yet when you begin to deliberately harm other self-aware beings, you are cut off from receiving energy from a higher realm. Thus, you can sustain an existence only by stealing energy from beings in the material realm. This means that dark forces can continue to exist only by stealing energy from humans, and they do this by getting us to misqualify energy through lower emotions and selfish acts.

Dark forces can take over the minds of human beings (if people let them), and most of the warfare and crime seen on earth is caused by dark forces. They do this by agitating people to violate others, and the pain caused releases energy that the dark forces can use to sustain themselves.

Decree

A spiritual technique for invoking high-frequency energy from the spiritual realm and directing it into specific conditions on the personal or planetary level. A decree is a worded expression, usually in rhyme, that is spoken aloud with great power and authority.

Dharma

In Buddhist tradition, the sacred work that you came here to do. Also refers to your divine plan, which is the positive qualities you wanted to bring to earth before deciding to take embodiment here.

Divine Mother

A spiritual office that represents the feminine aspect of God to planet earth. Currently, this office is held by the ascended master Mother Mary.

Divine Direction

Guidance that you receive from a higher source through your Christ self. The guidance can be from your I AM Presence, an ascended master or the cosmic being known as the Great Divine Director, who represents divine direction.

Divine Plan

A plan for what you want to accomplish in this embodiment. This includes the spiritual gift you want to bring to earth, experiences you want to have, lessons you want to learn and karma you want to balance. Often, this means there are certain people you want to meet and with whom you want to engage in various types of relationships.

Duality, duality consciousness

When the Conscious You sees with pure perception, it sees the underlying reality that all life is one and came from the same source. The duality consciousness obscures this oneness, and it makes it seem like matter is separated from spirit, humans are separated from God and people are separated from each other.

Duality also implies a negative polarity between two opposites that work against each other, one seeking to annihilate the other. Thus, duality always involves two opposing sides, and there is usually a value judgment attached to them, making one good and the other evil.

Duality is always an illusion, because nothing can change or destroy the oneness of all life. Thus, duality can exist only as an illusion in the minds of self-aware beings. As long as you are blinded by duality, you cannot attain Christ consciousness and thus cannot ascend.

Eightfold path of the Buddha

Traditionally, the path prescribed by Gautama Buddha for overcoming suffering. However, a deeper mystical understanding is that it represents the path of mastering the first seven spiritual rays and the eighth ray of integration.

Elementals

The world of form is created through a hierarchy of beings that extend from the Creator. For example, planet earth was created by seven beings in the spiritual realm, called the Elohim. They envisioned the blueprint for the earth and projected it into the four levels of the material realm.

However, the blueprint is brought into physical manifestation by four classes of elemental beings. These are beings that have a lower self-awareness than humans, but who can grow by serving to help build the material world. The elementals in the four realms are named as follows:

- Etheric realm, fire elementals or salamanders

- Mental realm, air elementals or sylphs

- Emotional realm, water elementals or undines

- Physical realm, earth elementals or gnomes.

Elohim

Ascended beings with such a high level of consciousness that they have complete mastery over the creation of matter. There is a masculine/feminine polarity of Elohim for each of the seven rays.

Emotional body

An aspect of your aura/mind that houses your emotional energies.

Etheric body

An aspect of your aura/mind that houses your sense of identity.

Evil, the veil of Maya

In Buddhist tradition, the veil of Maya is what obscures reality to beings in embodiment. This reality is that everything is the Buddha nature, in other words that all life is one. This veil is actually created because the matter universe is made from energy of a certain density, which makes it impossible for the physical senses to detect that even matter is made from spiritual light. Thus, this **energy veil** is abbreviated as evil.

Fall

In its broadest sense, the term refers to the process whereby a self-aware being descends into the consciousness of separation. Before the fall, you will see yourself as a being who is not isolated but is connected to something greater than yourself. After the fall, you will be convinced that you are a separate being, who has been abandoned or punished by God.

The important distinction is that after the fall, you will find it difficult to take responsibility for your own growth. Because the fall was caused by your own choices, it can only be undone through your own choices. Yet when you think you are a separate being, you think you can do whatever you want without considering the consequences for others. This causes you to engage in an ongoing struggle against other people, which can lead to a state of mind where you think you have to fight against other people, the matter universe or even God.

This state of mind becomes a catch-22, because as long as you will not accept that you have created your own situation as a result of your own choices, you cannot change those choices. Instead, you are seeking to create a change in your situation by forcing other people, the matter world or even God to come under your control. You are seeking to change the splinter in the eyes of others while ignoring the beam in your own eye.

Fallen beings or fallen angels

In its broadest sense, refers to all beings who are blinded by the duality consciousness. Yet the masters often use this more specifically to refer to a group of beings who fell in a previous sphere. The important distinction is that these beings had attained considerable attainment before they fell, which means they are often superior to the beings who started their existence in this world.

In world history, fallen beings have often become powerful but abusive leaders, and obvious examples are Hitler, Stalin and Mao. Yet many fallen beings hold important positions without visibly abusing their power and thus have a huge influence in society. Their main characteristic is that they are absolutely sure that they are right because they feel they are superior to most people on earth. There are also fallen beings who are not in physical embodiment, but who reside in the astral plane or the mental realm.

Fallen consciousness

The consciousness of the fallen beings. In its broadest sense, the illusion of separation and duality. It can also refer more specifically to the consciousness of feeling superior to others, wanting to have special privileges or wanting others to follow you.

The main characteristic of the fallen consciousness is the belief that the ends can justify the means. This often causes people to believe they are engaged in an epic struggle and that it is their duty to use all means available to eradicate what they have defined as evil. Thus, the underlying belief is that you have the right to define what is good and evil, because you have a godlike status.

Four levels of the material realm

Everything is made from energy, so the entire world of form is made from energies of various vibrational qualities. There is a continuum of vibrations, ranging from the highest level, the level of the Creator, to the lowest. In between one can define several divisions, compartments or octaves of vibrations. For example, one major division is between the spiritual realm and the material realm.

There are several divisions in the spiritual realm, whereas in the material realm there are four divisions. They are, from higher to lower vibrations:

- the etheric or identity level

- the mental level

- the emotional level

- the physical level

Fohat

Refers to written or spoken word that is inspired from a higher source and endowed with spiritual light. Words become cups or chalices that carry spiritual light.

Four lower bodies, four levels of the mind

Corresponding to the four levels of the material universe, the masters sometimes say that we humans have four lower bodies, the identity body, the mental body, the emotional body and the physical body.

The masters also talk about four levels of the mind, where the identity mind houses our deepest sense of identity (who we are and what we can do), the mental mind houses our thoughts (how we can do things), the emotional mind houses our feelings (why we want to/have to do something) and the physical mind relates to the needs of the body.

Free will

The masters teach that it is extremely important to understand free will, especially in relation to the duality consciousness. Free will is the basic law that guides the function of the material realm. For example, the earth was created by the Elohim in a much higher state than what we see today. There was originally no lack of resources, no imbalances in nature and no diseases.

These limiting conditions have been created because a majority of human beings used their free will to descend into duality. Nature – meaning the elemental beings – had no choice but to outpicture as material conditions what was in the consciousness of a majority of the people. Human beings were created to have dominion over the earth, and the elemental beings can only take on the images we hold in our identity, mental, emotional and physical minds.

Yet the important point about free will is that we have the right to, at any time, transcend our previous choices. God and the ascended masters will never seek to stop us from transcending previous choices. It is only the ego and the dark forces who will seek to make us believe we are bound by past choices.

Guru

A Sanskrit word for teacher or master.

Garden of Eden

The deeper symbolism behind the Biblical concept of the Garden of Eden is that it represents a schoolroom in which self-aware beings are being prepared to take embodiment on earth. The "God" mentioned in the Bible was the ascended master Lord Maitreya, who was the "headmaster" of the mystery school.

Students were given graded lessons, and only more advanced students were meant to take the lesson represented by the duality consciousness. However, there was a number of beings in the mystery school, who had fallen in a previous sphere. These beings are symbolized by the Serpent, and they deceived some students into taking the initiation of duality before they were prepared by the teacher. This initiation is symbolized by the "fruit of the knowledge of good and evil," which makes beings think they are like gods and can define what is good and evil without the Christ consciousness.

The symbolism is that the fallen beings have deceived most people on earth into believing in the dualistic lies. This is what causes all conflict and struggle on earth. The only solution is that a critical mass of people follow the true path of initiation and attain Christ consciousness. The real purpose of the ascended masters is to help us do this.

God, four aspects of God

In mystical teachings, the world is seen as being made from one underlying element, called ether, which manifests as the four elements of fire, air, water and earth. One can likewise look at five aspects of God. The ether element corresponds to the original or undifferentiated Creator, which has not yet expressed itself in the world of form. As the Creator begins to express itself, it manifests itself as four aspects:

- Father, meaning the outgoing force, the will to create. For us, the ascended masters represent the father element, yet we also represent the father element on earth.

- Mother, meaning the contracting or balancing force. Compared to the Creator, everything in the world of form is the Mother. So we humans are part of the Divine Mother. Yet when we co-create by superimposing mental images upon the Ma-ter light, then this mother light represents mother for us.

- Son or Christ, meaning the consciousness that unifies the Creator (who is beyond form) with everything that has form. It is also the element that separates the real from the unreal by seeing through all dualistic illusions.

- Holy Spirit, means the force that drives all self-aware beings to return to their source. Since the beginning of the world of form, innumerable beings have gone through the process of the ascension and this has created a force or momentum that makes up the Holy Spirit.

God Flame

Your true individuality is not what we normally call your personality; it is anchored in your I AM Presence. Because your I AM Presence is made from energies of a higher vibration than anything in the material universe, it appears as a flame. Thus, your true individuality is sometimes referred to as your God flame.

Golden Age

At present, the earth is in a lower state than originally intended. This is caused by a majority of people being deceived by the duality consciousness, which inevitably leads to various conflicts and limitations. Yet the goal of the ascended masters, especially Saint Germain as the leader of the coming 2,000 year cycle, is to inspire a critical mass of people to walk the path of individual Christhood. As enough people raise their consciousness, society will begin to outpicture a much higher state than today, and this is commonly referred to as a Golden Age.

Great White Brotherhood

Another name for all ascended beings. The term "white" does not refer to race, but to the fact that ascended masters radiate a white light.

Hatred of the Mother

The Ma-ter light forms the feminine polarity to the Creator. It allows us to project any mental image upon it we want, and then it faithfully reflects back to us physical circumstances that reflect the images in our consciousness. When people enter the fallen consciousness, they cannot take responsibility for themselves, meaning they will not recognize that the Mother can only reflect back what we project upon it and is not seeking to punish us. Instead, such beings feel like victims, and they do feel like matter, the Mother element, is seeking to punish them or prevent them from doing what they want. Thus, they can develop hatred of the mother. Yet since we are all part of the mother aspect of God, hatred of the Mother is a form of self-hatred.

Human ego

An element in the psyche that is created when the Conscious You descends into the illusion of separation and duality. The Conscious You is pure awareness, so it simply cannot act as a separate being. Yet it can step into a separate sense of self, and when it perceives the world through the perception filter of that self, it can believe that it really is a separate being. What makes this distorted perception seem real is the ego.

Human consciousness

In a general way, this refers to the consciousness that is currently considered normal for human beings. It can also be used more specifically to refer to the ego and the carnal mind.

I AM Presence

Your higher or spiritual self. The Conscious You is an extension of your I AM Presence, and your highest potential is to achieve complete identification with the Presence, so you serve as an open door for it to express itself in the material world. Your spiritual identity and individuality is anchored in your I AM Presence, which means it could never be destroyed no matter what happens to you on earth.

Identity body

An aspect of your aura/mind that houses your sense of identity.

Immaculate concept or vision

This refers to the vision of the highest potential or a pure vision that is not polluted by duality. For example, Mother Mary held the immaculate vision that Jesus would fulfill his mission.

Jesus

The ascended master Jesus was the hierarch or leader for the Age of Pisces. He holds the office of planetary Christ, and we cannot ascend without going through this office. This means that all people need to make peace with Jesus – by transcending the distorted images of Christ created on earth – in order to ascend.

Judgment

There is a group of ascended masters, called the Great Karmic Board, who oversee the overall planetary growth. One of their tasks is to determine which lifestreams are allowed to embody on earth and for how long. When a being falls into duality, it is assigned a certain time to turn around and start the path back to God. However, if a being violates the free will of other beings, this time can be shortened. The being is then judged by its own actions. However, the ascended masters also teach that it is lawful for people in embodiment to call forth the judgment of fallen beings. If such beings will not change, then the Karmic Board can authorize their removal from embodiment.

Take note that the concept of judgment is not the same as the kind of value-laden judgment exercised by beings trapped in the duality consciousness. Such beings judge based on their own state of consciousness, often labeling as evil anything they do not understand or agree with. This is what Jesus called judging after appearances.

Initiation

A gradual process whereby you raise your consciousness towards the Christ consciousness. This can be an individual process, where you are guided from within, but it usually involves you following an outer teaching or even a guru or organization.

Karma

Everything is energy, so whatever we do – even what we think and feel – is done by using energy. We receive this energy as a gift from the I AM Presence. The energy we receive is pure, but we will qualify it according to the contents of the four levels of our minds. We are responsible for our use of energy, and misqualified energy becomes stored in both our auras and in the Akashic records as karma. In order for us to ascend, we must balance all energy by raising it to its original vibration.

The masters have also given a deeper understanding of karma, where karma is the images we hold in the four levels of our minds. Because we see everything through the filter of these energies, we are constantly qualifying energy. Yet we have the option to, at any time, examine our mental images and transcend limiting images—which is truly the path to Christhood, where we accept our divine identity.

This gives us two ways to balance karma. We can invoke spiritual energy through decrees and invocations and requalify the energy from our present level of consciousness. This is possible, but it is a slow process because we are constantly making more karma. The faster way is to work on transcending the mental images, so we stop making new karma. Once we achieve this, we can then balance all remaining karma much faster, because our higher state of consciousness allows us to invoke more energy.

Lemuria

A continent in the Pacific Ocean that had a high civilization but was destroyed about 12,000 years ago. It is often called the Mother land because it is said to have had a very high spiritual focus for the Divine Mother. The decline of Lemuria started when a group of fallen beings murdered the embodied representative of the Divine Mother.

Lifestream

A term used for an individual self-aware being. It is often used instead of "soul," as a lifestream refers to parts of our beings that are beyond the soul, including the I AM Presence and the lineage of spiritual beings leading all the way to the Creator.

Light

Usually refers to spiritual light, meaning energy that vibrates at higher levels than the energy that makes up the material realm.

Living Christ

A person who has attained some level of Christ consciousness while still in embodiment.

Living Word

Refers to written or spoken word that is inspired from a higher source and endowed with spiritual light. Words can become cups or chalices that carry spiritual light. This is also called fohat.

Lucifer

A being who rebelled against God in a previous sphere. Thus, it is considered that Lucifer was the first being to fall into the duality consciousness.

Maitreya

The ascended master who was the leader of the mystery school called the Garden of Eden. He is considered the Great Initiator, because his initiations are not obvious, and we often do not see that we are being tested. Lord Maitreya holds the office of Cosmic Christ.

God the Mother

Another word for the Divine Mother, but can also refer to the feminine aspect of God, which is the entire world of form. We are part of God the Mother.

Mass consciousness

Every human being has an aura, a personal energy field. Yet the entire planet also has an aura, and within it we find a combination of the individual energy fields of all people embodying on earth. There are certain divisions within this collective or mass consciousness, but all people are affected by the greater whole to some degree. There is a stage on the spiritual path, where our main task is to pull ourselves above the magnetic pull of the mass consciousness, so we can express our individuality.

Matter, Material Universe

Everything is made from energy, so the entire world of form is made from energies of various vibrational qualities. One can create a continuum of vibrations, ranging from the highest level, the level of the Creator, to the lowest. In between one can define several divisions, compartments or octaves of vibrations. For example, one major division is between the spiritual realm and the material realm.

There are several divisions in the spiritual realm, whereas in the material realm there are four divisions. They are, from higher to lower vibrations:

- the etheric or identity level

- the mental level

- the emotional level

- the physical level

Ma-ter Light,

The cosmic base energy out of which everything that has form is created. It has no form in itself, but has the capacity to take on any form. It also has a certain basic form of consciousness, which among other characteristics has a built-in striving for its source, the Creator.

The Ma-ter light has been stepped down in vibration to create succeeding spheres. We live in the seventh of these spheres, and the six previous ones have all ascended, becoming part of the spiritual realm.

Mental body
An aspect of your aura/mind that houses your thoughts and mental energies.

Messenger
A person who has been trained to receive teachings and dictations from the ascended realm through the agency of the Holy Spirit.

Misqualification
Everything we do, feel or think is done with energy We receive this energy from the I AM Presence and then qualify it with a certain vibration. Anything below the vibration of love is a misqualification and creates karma.

Mother, hatred of
The Ma-ter light forms the feminine polarity to the Creator. It allows us to project any mental image upon it we want, and then it faithfully reflects back to us physical circumstances that reflect the images in our consciousness. When people enter the fallen consciousness, they cannot take responsibility for themselves, meaning they will not recognize that the Mother can only reflect back what we project upon it and is not seeking to punish us. Instead, such beings feel like victims, and they do feel like matter, the Mother element, is seeking to punish them or prevent them from doing what they want. Thus, they can develop hatred of the mother. Yet since we are all part of the mother aspect of God, hatred of the Mother is a form of self-hatred.

Mother Mary
The ascended Master who was embodied as the mother of Jesus. She holds the Office of the Divine Mother for earth.

Mystery School
An environment designed to present self-aware beings with initiations aimed at raising their consciousness. It is usually overseen by an ascended master of high attainment.

Oneness

Before the Creator had created any form, there was only the Creator. Thus, a Creator cannot create anything that is separated from itself; it must create everything out of its own being. It does this by manifesting its being as the Ma-ter light and thus taking on whatever form is projected upon it by self-aware beings with free will. Thus, beneath any form, any appearance, there is still the oneness of the Creator. Separation from God is always an illusion, and it is this final illusion we must overcome before we can ascend.

Path

The masters teach that the ultimate goal of life on earth is to manifest the Christ consciousness, which allows us to permanently ascend to the spiritual realm and become ascended masters. Yet we are originally created at a much lower state of consciousness, and thus we follow a gradual path that raises our consciousness to the ultimate level. The masters say there are 144 different levels of consciousness that are possible for people on earth. You can ascend only after reaching the 144th level.

Physical body, physical mind

Obviously, this refers to the body. The physical mind is that part of the brain and nervous system that is designed to regulate the functions of the body, even prompting us to take care of the needs of the body. This is what gives us certain instinctual cravings for protection, food, sex and other physical needs.

There is nothing inherently wrong with taking care of the needs of the body, but the physical mind is not capable up limiting these needs. Thus, if we do not take command over the physical mind, all of our attention and energy can be spent on fulfilling the needs of the body, leaving nothing left over for spiritual growth.

Rays, or spiritual rays

Everything is made from energy. Even Einstein's famous equation, $E=mc^2$, says that matter is created from a very high form of energy that is reduced in vibration by a factor (the speed of light squared). The masters teach that while Einstein's theory is basically correct, there are seven of these reduction factors. In other words, the material universe is made from seven types of spiritual energy that are combined to form all phenomena in the material realm. These types of energy are called rays or spiritual rays. There is a total of 15 rays used to build the entire world of form.

Retreats

Many ascended masters have a spiritual retreat that exists in the etheric or identity realm. We can make a call to go to such retreats in our finer bodies while our physical bodies sleep at night. A retreat is usually located over a physical location on earth, yet because the retreat is in the etheric realm, it cannot be detected through physical means. A retreat focuses certain spiritual energies that are released to earth. It can also be a focus for giving specific teachings to people who are ready.

Sangha of the Buddha

The community of people dedicated to walking the path towards Christhood and Buddhahood. Not limited to a single organization.

Satan

In its most specific meaning, Satan was one of the beings who fell with Lucifer in a previous sphere. However, in a more general meaning, Satan is a state of consciousness that prompts, forces or tempts us to adapt to current conditions in the material realm.

We were created to be co-creators with God and have dominion over the earth. As Jesus said, "with God all things are possible." Satan is a consciousness that wants to prevent us from exercising our highest potential by causing us to voluntarily limit our creative powers and accepting that current conditions cannot or should not be changed.

The role of the Living Christ is to demonstrate to people that we can transcend the consciousness of Satan. That is why Jesus rebuked Peter when Peter wanted Jesus to conform to his expectations. Jesus said: "Get thee behind me, Satan."

Sanat Kumara

An ascended master of high attainment. In a previous age, so many people on earth had descended so far into the duality consciousness, that the Karmic Board and other cosmic councils had determined that the earth was no longer a viable platform for growth and thus would be allowed to self-destruct. Sanat Kumara then came with 144,000 lifestreams from Venus in order to hold the spiritual balance until enough people on earth had been raised in consciousness, to where they could hold the balance for the planet.

Many of the 144,000 lifestreams that came with Sanat Kumara are still in embodiment and they are often very spiritual people with a great desire to help other people or improve the world. Yet there can come a point, where such people will hold back their own ascensions unless they let go of the desire to help or change others.

Serpent

A symbol for a certain state of consciousness that induces doubt into our minds. The specific purpose is to create a division in our beings, so we start to distrust our divine direction, our intuition, our own inner knowing and our spiritual teachers. Can also refer to a specific group of fallen beings.

Serpentine lie, plot

The primary serpentine lie is that the Christ consciousness either does not exist or is not attainable for us. Instead, the ultimate reality is the duality consciousness, in which we set ourselves up as gods, who believe we have the right and the capacity to define good and evil by ourselves. This inevitably causes a relative definition of good and evil, because good is seen as that which confirms our existing beliefs and desires, whereas anything that challenges them is labeled as evil.

The serpentine plot is to either get us so paralyzed by doubt that we blindly follow the fallen beings, or to get us so blinded by spiritual pride that we really do believe we are always right. In the latter case, we are also following the leadership of the fallen consciousness, which is in complete opposition to the Christ. We now seek to raise the ego to a godlike status, instead of seeking the Christ consciousness as a means to raising all life.

One aspect of the serpentine plot is to get us to believe that even God can be fit into a dualistic world view. God is portrayed as the opposite of evil or the devil. Thus, we are tempted to believe that in order to further God's cause, it is acceptable to do evil, including killing other people. History has many examples of how people have been deceived into fighting these epic battles against a self-defined evil. In order to win this final victory for good, it is necessary and justified to commit this ultimate act of destroying the enemy. In reality, such struggles only serve to misqualify more energy, that feeds the dark forces and thus give them power to deceive people into continuing the endless struggle. The only way out is the Christ consciousness that sees the oneness of all life.

Shiva

Traditionally a part of the Hindu trinity. However, the deeper meaning is that Shiva is a cosmic being who is especially helpful for cutting us free from dark forces and the astral plane. We can make a very effective call to Shiva by simply repeating his name 9, 33 or 144 times.

Sin

In ascended master terminology the same as karma, meaning misqualified energy that we need to balance before we can ascend.

Spiritual Rays

Everything is made from energy. Even Einstein's famous equation, $E=mc^2$, says that matter is created from a very high form of energy that is reduced in vibration by a factor (the speed of light squared). The masters teach that while Einstein's theory is basically correct, there are seven of these reduction factors. In other words, the material universe is made from seven types of spiritual energy that are combined to form all phenomena in the material realm. These types of energy are called rays or spiritual rays. There is a total of 15 rays used to build the entire world of form.

Soul

The ascended masters sometimes use this word as it is commonly used, namely as that part of our beings that reincarnates. However, the masters also give a deeper understanding, namely that it is the Conscious You that originally descended into embodiment. The soul is a vehicle that the Conscious You has created in order to express itself in this world, and it is often highly affected by the duality consciousness.

Jesus' crucifixion is a symbol for the fact that the Conscious You is crucified (paralyzed) by its own creation. Thus, the soul cannot be raised up or perfected. The soul is made from limiting beliefs and misqualified energies. As the energies are requalified and as the Conscious You transcends the limiting beliefs, the soul gradually dies, until the Conscious You gives up the Ghost of the final illusion of separation. The Conscious You can then claim its true identity as an extension of the I AM Presence and can ascend.

Spheres

The world of form was created by the Creator defining a spherical bound-ary and withdrawing its being into a singularity in the center of a void. The Creator then created a sphere in the void by using the Ma-ter light. The Creator defined structures in that sphere and projected self-aware extensions of itself into it. As these extensions grew in awareness, they raised the vibration of their sphere until it ascended and formed the first sphere in the spiritual realm. The Creator then created a second sphere, and the ascended masters from the first sphere then defined structures and sent extensions of their own beings into the second sphere.

This process of one sphere ascending and a new sphere being cre-ated has continued, so that we now exist in the seventh such sphere. In the first three spheres, all beings ascended without going into the consciousness of separation and duality. Yet in the fourth sphere, some beings refused to ascend, and they became the first fallen beings. As the fourth sphere ascended, these fallen beings could not ascend, and thus they "fell" into the sixth sphere. Because the newly created sphere had a generally lower vibration, the fallen beings could still exist there. This fact is the basic explanation for the existence of evil in our world.

Spoken word, Sacred word

The spoken word is a technique whereby we use the human voice to invoke spiritual light or energy.

Saint Germain

An ascended master who is the leader for the coming Age of Aquarius. He also represents the seventh spiritual ray, the ray of freedom. Thus, he is sometimes referred to as the "God of Freedom for the earth." Saint Germain will play an important role for the coming 2,000 years and he has a plan for taking the earth into a Golden Age.

Threefold Flame, sevenfold flame.

Everything is energy, meaning your physical body and conscious mind can survive only because you are receiving spiritual light from your I AM Presence. This light descends into your aura, into a chakra that is behind the heart chakra and called the secret chamber of the heart. The light is first manifest as a tiny white sphere, but then splits into a "flame" with three plumes, a blue representing will and power, a yellow, repre-senting wisdom and a pink, representing love.

These three flames correspond to the first of the spiritual rays, with the white sphere corresponding to the fourth ray. When you go into duality, you begin to express the basic creative powers in an unbalanced manner, which causes your threefold flame to become unbalanced. This limits your creative powers, and you cannot grow beyond a certain level on the path to Christhood until you have balanced the threefold flame and attained the purity of motive of the fourth ray. At that point, you can begin to work on the initiations of the 5th, 6th and 7th rays, whereby you gradually develop a sevenfold flame.

Transfiguration
A spiritual initiation on the path to Christhood. It signifies that you transcend identification with the physical body and its limitations.

Twin flame
The Creator is beyond form. Yet as the first act of creation, the Creator expressed itself as two polarities, masculine or expansive and feminine or contracting. These two basic polarities are represented by two cosmic beings, called Alpha and Omega. In the spiritual realm, we find many beings, who form a polarity of masculine and feminine. For example, Elohim and Archangels all have a masculine-feminine polarity.

There is a popular belief that our souls were created in such a polarity, and thus each of us has a twin flame, who would supposedly be the perfect companion and complete us. Unfortunately, this has led to many romantic notions of finding the perfect love. It is necessary to balance this with the fact that you ascend as an individual being, not with your twin flame. Thus, the path of the ascension is a path whereby you become spiritually complete and self-sufficient, being able to ascend completely with your internal power.

Unascended being
A being that has not yet qualified for the ascension, and thus cannot abide in the spiritual realm. This does not only refer to human beings in embodiment. There are unascended beings in all four realms of the material world. For example, many souls who have ties to the astral plane can descend there between embodiments or can become permanently stuck there, not being able to reembody. We human beings can make calls for the cutting free of all unascended beings, so they can move on to the next station on their path.

Unconditionality, unconditional love

The duality consciousness operates by creating two opposites. Note that the original divine polarity of expanding and contracting are not opposite but complementary forces. Yet when these concepts are colored by the duality consciousness, they will seem like opposites. This is then coupled with a value judgment, labeling one opposite as good and the other as evil. This is what gives rise to all judgmentalness and discrimination found on earth.

When you attain Christ consciousness, you see that all this is an illusion, because the underlying reality is that all life is one and came from the same source. Thus, you see that God's reality is beyond any of the conditions and value judgments defined by the duality consciousness. It is difficult to describe the non-dual reality with words, but the most commonly used word is to say that God's qualities are unconditional, meaning beyond dualistic conditions.

For example, human love is always conditional. People have to do something right and avoid doing something wrong in order to be worthy to receive love. In God's eyes, you are worthy to receive God's love by the mere fact that you were created as an extension of the Creator's Being. Thus, you do not have to do anything to receive God's love, and nothing you do can make you unworthy of it. God's love is unconditional; beyond conditions.

Violet flame

A spiritual energy that is especially efficient for transmuting karma or misqualified energy. Saint Germain received a cosmic dispensation to reveal the violet flame in the 1930s. Since then, ascended master students have been invoking it through decrees, invocations and affirmations.

However, it is important to realize that the violet flame can be misused. Misqualified energy is caused by a limiting belief. The energy gradually accumulates in your aura, making you feel burdened. You can invoke the violet flame without changing the limiting belief, which will make you feel better in the short run. However, if you do not change the belief, you will continue to misqualify energy. And if you continue to use the violet flame to transmute the energy, you are misusing Saint Germain's dispensation, because you are not attaining long-term spiritual growth.

Word

From the Gospel of John: "In the beginning was the Word, and the Word was with God and the Word was God." This is actually a mistranslation of the Greek word Logos, which refers to an undivided whole. This is a symbol for the Christ consciousness, which is designed to maintain the oneness of all life. Thus, the Word is that which helps us see through the illusions of duality.

World teacher

An ascended being who serves the office of teaching humankind. Currently, this office is held by the ascended masters Jesus and Kuthumi. Unascended beings can also serve as world teachers in a lower capacity.

About the author

Kim Michaels was born in Horsens, Denmark in 1957. He has a degree as an architect. He started writing professionally at the age of 19. Over the next 12 years, he wrote articles for Danish magazines and newspapers plus three books in Danish.

In 1987, he moved to the United States in order to pursue his spiritual goals. He worked for several years as a technical writer, until in 2002 he made the quantum leap and became a self-employed writer.

In 2002, he founded the website *www.askrealjesus.com,* which contains a huge amount of material on universal spirituality. He also runs the website *www.transcendencetoolbox.com,* which contains many tools that can empower you to accelerate your spiritual growth.

More to Life Publishing (*www.morepublish.com*) has published all of his 19 books about self-help and universal spirituality.

His personal spiritual journey has taken Kim through many corners of the spiritual supermarket, including levitating meditators in Switzerland, gun-toting New Agers building bomb shelters in Montana, and Mormons in Utah. He has given a funny, profound and disarmingly honest account of his exploits in the book *Question Every Thing.*

During his 22 years in the United States, Kim lived in Montana, Utah, New York, Washington DC and Virginia. In 2009, he moved back to Europe and for a time lived in Sweden. He is currently living with his wife in Estonia, where he is learning about the spiritual effects of Communism, whereas the United States taught him about the spiritual effects of Capitalism.

Kim Michaels' books have been translated into eight languages: Spanish, Italian, Dutch, Danish, Polish, Russian, Estonian, Lithuanian and Korean.

www.ingramcontent.com/pod-product-compliance
Lightning Source LLC
Chambersburg PA
CBHW070707100726
47907CB00001B/83